HERE'S WHAT THE CRITICS SAY ABOUT BLOOD MOON:

D1317789

Erotic and emotional fire! Not since Medea has there been such a saga of deceit and betrayal.

Inferno, Buenos Aires

How far will a man go to satisfy his darkest desires? FAR.

La Trova Roma, Rome

It feels like a gut-punch to the psyche. One poignant vignette after another.

Hinnerk, Hamburg

A torrential new novel like the flooding of a riverbank. An encyclopaedic saga of a university class that went on to fabulous wealth, fame, and glory, except for those who took tragic detours into violence, depravity, and death.

La Movida, Madrid

A first-rate work and a non-stop read disguised as a page-turning psycho-sexual thriller. Blood Moon has kinetic force and the kind of razor-sharp images that mark you for life.

Weintraub Reviews

Highly suspenseful, written in cinematic style...spellbinding...a poignant thriller...quietly breathtaking.

Books Today

BLOOD MOON

A Novel by
Darwin Porter

The Georgia Literary Association
New York & Washington, Georgia

Also by Darwin Porter

BUTTERFLIES IN HEAT
MARIKA
VENUS
RAZZLE-DAZZLE

First Edition Published in the U.S. in February 1999
Library of Congress Card Catalogue No.98-75660
ISBN No. 0-9668030-0-0

Publication made possible by a grant from
The Georgia Literary Association

Cover design by Scott Sosebee
Cover photos by Russell Maynor

FOR DANFORTH PRINCE

Prologue

1977

The wail of an emergency vehicle sounded in Buck's ears, reminding him that it had been a night of sirens. "What a pack of bastards," he groaned in disgust as he fought his way through a milling throng of protesters.

At the edge of People's Park, the glow of a bonfire—a mock funeral for porn—roared like a furnace. Cheering the flames of burning books, high-stepping, short-skirted majorettes, the "Collins Girls," led a school band through its brassy sounds.

He wasn't part of the burst of ecstasy that surged through the crowds. Even in the midst of such strong moral crusaders, he could smell the air, heavy with the fumes of marijuana.

Some of the characters who'd answered Sister Rose's call to arms had made him recoil. By far, though, most of the demonstrators were the evangelist's "normal majority," good church-going people who felt betrayed by the moral drift of much of the country. But the rally also drew the fanatics of the far right, the Ku Klux Klan and the American Nazi Party.

A shouting, occasionally chanting group, some singing gospel hymns, formed a tight circle around a mountain of burning books and magazines. Guarding the print-fed flames, a dozen uniformed men carried a blood-red banner with black letters. Firefighters For Christ.

The police had cordoned off the bonfire but, as the crowds surged closer, the cops desperately fought to hold them back. The heat intensified, making Buck's face sting. Smoldering white-hot sparks shot out, sending streaks into the night. As flaming liquid rain showered down, several women screamed.

Appalled by the spectacle, he broke through the phalanx in time to watch the shapely legs of a Playboy centerfold catch flame and disintegrate.

The implication of the book-burning filled him with an ominous dread. He hadn't heard of a bonfire like this since the Nazis condemned books to the flames in 1933. Then, as it did now, it evoked the superstitions of the Middle Ages.

I

Before the pile of print could burn down, firemen tossed more books into the flaming mass. Turning from it, he stared defiantly into the enraptured faces of the spectators, their gleeful eyes paying no attention to him, as they reflected a spellbound joy. He felt trapped, a reluctant participant in some ancient tribal rite of exorcism.

Deep in its third hour, Sister Rose's moral crusade through the city of Okeechobee's "Combat Zone" of pornography and prostitution had erupted in violence. He was anxious to be at the core of the action.

Cutting a path through the crowds, he raced back to the main drag, The Strip, as a police helicopter hovered over his head. At a shop only twenty yards away, a gang of protesters tossed bricks into a plate-glass window of a store advertising its wares as adult material. Once the glass was smashed, they skirted over the jagged edges, climbing through the display window, seizing pornography from the shelves, and tossing it into baskets to feed the flames of the bonfire in the park.

All along the ten-block Strip, protesters confronting counter-protesters were locked in a macabre embrace. A squad of policemen charged at combatants fighting in the middle of the street. The cops threw tear gas into the crowds, but some young men lobbed the canisters back. Choking on their own gas, the police, facing a barrage of raining rocks, fell back for cover.

Buck stood far out of the way, yet near enough to watch the police regroup to charge again. Their faces protected by plexiglass shields, they'd become more aggressive. Both protesters and counter-protesters were clubbed, as nightsticks flailed wildly. Rocks and bottles sailed through the air. Advocates of non-violence reverted to self-defense. Middle-aged women ran screaming, some of them falling back against broken shards of glass. More tear-gas canisters came crashing down. Mace burned unprotected skin.

Gangs roamed the streets, setting random fires in trash cans. Sirens wailed. Smoke billowed from a movie theater as fire engines pulled in.

For no reason at all, a burly woman in a Salvation Army uniform came up behind Buck, getting a stranglehold on his neck and shouting incoherently in his ear. His eyes smarting from the gas, he broke her hold, escaping her noose. The coins in her collection bucket scattered on the pavement below. Her eyes were crazed.

He ducked out of the way, just as rebellious prostitutes in a "hot bed" hotel overhead dropped water-filled balloons into the crowd who would deny them a living.

In saffron robes, a bedraggled crew of shaven-headed Hare Krishna disciples stood forlornly on the sidewalk, stoically facing the

II

taunts of punks. When one of the punks spat in the young man's face, he didn't resist.

Imitating the Nazis, the punks were clad in brown shirts. Cheering them on in their attack was a band of determined-looking National Socialist League members, both men and women, carrying swastikas and a large metal eagle which wavered precariously over the heads of the Hare Krishna.

Buck slipped through the crowd forming around them for a closer look, the better to write an eye-witness account for tomorrow's Examiner.

Out of the same hotel from which the balloons were tossed, a skinny, sleazily dressed prostitute—a girl no more than fifteen—fled onto the street. Spotting her, the brown shirts broke from the Hare Krishna and chased after the teenager. She ran screaming into an alleyway off The Strip.

In mob frenzy, the National Socialist League members rushed to see what their own punks would do to the girl. Buck headed for the alley, too, just in time to see one of the brown shirts deliver several chopping strokes to the girl's head. Small rivulets of blood cascaded down her temple. Squirming hysterically, the girl cried out in pain and fear, as more blows rained down.

With no regard for his own safety, Buck—outnumbered in a dark alley and surrounded by a pack of Nazis—lunged forward, grabbing one of the punks by his brown shirt, yanking him back and slugging him in the face. As he ducked the man's retaliatory blow, a huge black blur descended upon him. Out of the corner of his eye, he had a glimmer of the big bronze eagle.

The blow to his skull resounded like a sickening, dull thud. In moments, piercing shock waves electrified his body.

As the world grew faint, fainter, a whirlwind of images spun in his mind. On The Strip, the sounds of bullets fired into the air ricocheted in his head. He welcomed the all-encompassing blackness, the spinning, staggering fall into oblivion.

He found himself wandering in a state, almost dreamlike, where the mind travels in the astral world, floating between semi-consciousness and reality.

Everything was viewed like a startling confrontation with a distorting mirror—shattering, overwhelming.

In the mirror, he confronted Medusa's face—intense, savage. Then the image became his own, only to revert to Medusa again, her serpentine headdress coiled to strike him at any moment.

III

Would he, as in mythology, turn to stone, or would he live to slay her as Perseus had done?

As he asked that question, he struggled for control of his mind. It was still foggy, and he found himself drifting back to where all this had begun.

There were no shadows then, no blur.

The way he remembered it, the sun was shining.

IV

Chapter One

The old news tower dominated the southern skyline of Okeechobee. When thirty-year-old Buck Brooke I, already a millionaire, had arrived here in the 1920s and saw spread before him a town of flat one- and two-story buildings on the edge of a mangrove swamp, he'd conceived of the idea of a news tower rising majestically over the emerging city like an exclamation point.

Coral colored, it soared like a Romanesque campanile, modeled after the Leaning Tower of Pisa. The news tower didn't lean, except in its arch conservative view of the day's events. In fact, Buck I came to be known as a symbolic bedfellow of President Coolidge.

When Buck I ran out of white marble, he'd ordered his architect to substitute inexpensive ceramic tiles from Cuba and, in years to come, he would view that choice as one of the wrong decisions of his life. "It was the beginning of compromise," he would tell his son, Buck II. "If you begin by one compromise, the second one is waiting at the door."

Local residents had predicted the belfry would collapse when hit by its first hurricane. They were wrong. It rode out the storm of 1927 and went on to withstand more assaults, both from nature and the public.

Before 1937, three men had leaped to their deaths from its oyster-shell balcony before it was closed to the public.

In time, other skyscrapers would rise to pierce the landscape but, in spite of that competition, the tower defiantly stood—still the tallest building in the city, still the symbol of Okeechobee, at least with tourists buying picture postcards.

Its worst attack came in September of 1969 when Hurricane Rose swept over Okeechobee, a disaster unprecedented since Donna unleashed her fury way back in 1960. The blast from Rose claimed thirteen lives and left hundreds more homeless among those who lived in trailer camps and poorly constructed little frame houses on the marshy swamplands of the city.

The tower bravely stood, but hundreds of its Cuban tiles were sent hurtling into the devastating winds, becoming deadly missiles. When the storm had passed and city building inspectors surveyed the tower, they warned that it was structurally weak and might not withstand another blow like Rose.

To the press the following day, Sister Rose, the evangelist, protested furiously, claiming the hurricane bearing her name was an attempt on the part of the U.S. government to embarrass her and discredit her charismatic Christian movement. The Weather Bureau responded by saying the name, Rose, was selected at random from a list prepared years ago. It had been time to name a hurricane after a woman, since the last big blow was called Quentin and had been even more destructive.

Sister Rose had not been convinced and, in her fury, she'd set about to stir up an even greater storm than nature's death-dealing blow.

*****

The soggy heat came right through his T-shirt as Buck Brooke III, the third in line of the Brooke newspaper dynasty, eased his six-foot frame into the back seat of his Fleetwood sedan. He was fresh from jogging. No window separated the rear and front seats. He'd had it removed. Such a separation didn't strike him as very democratic, and he was also too news-oriented to keep many secrets. He would prefer to ride up in the front seat with the driver, except for one reason. He always read his morning rival, The Okeechobee News, along with The Miami Herald and The New York Times. For that, he needed all the room in the back seat available to him.

He leaned back, finding the most comfortable spot. At twenty-seven, nearly the same age as old Buck I was when he'd first arrived in town in the 1920s, Buck No. Three was already one of America's youngest and most dynamic publishers. His critics labeled him a 1970s breed of muckraker. He preferred to call his relentless, diligent digging for truth honest reporting. The day he'd taken control of the failing, ultra-conservative Examiner from his octogenarian grandfather, Buck I, he'd told his editors, "We're gonna raise some hell!"

At first, few took him seriously, perhaps because of his youth, inexperience, and his reputation as a sexual athlete. In the past few months, he'd managed to raise the ire of the conservative community, as a dramatic shift in his newspaper's readership had come about.

Passing the causeway-linked islands that lay in the blue-green bay, he pressed a button, lowering the window to let the fresh sea breeze blow through his light sand-colored hair.

Sucking the clean air deep into his gut, he leaned forward to reach for his phone. Between work and play, he hadn't been getting much sleep lately. Yet he was still exceptionally handsome, lean, muscular and, as an ex-Marine, still able to pose for a poster advertising the purity of the all-American boy, an image that had plagued him through his college days.

A stubble of blond-red beard appeared like golden flecks on his strong jaws, the only feature about his appearance that made him look solid and reliable. Certainly not his eyes. Flecked with white, his piercing blue eyes always seemed to be searching. It was a fierce, hungry look he had as he stalked the city like a hunter, seeking a story, excitement, a partner for the night—but mostly a story, and the subject didn't matter. He was a "scoop artist," often accused of journalistic excess. He preferred to think he "outreported" his rivals. He didn't believe in secrets, particularly if those closeted facts had to do with the public's business and right to know. He'd read All the President's Men three times.

Hurriedly, he made two calls, one to postpone a karate lesson scheduled for that afternoon, another to delay an interview and photography session with a national magazine that was flirting with the idea of naming him, "The Sexiest Man in America," maybe even "The Sexiest Man Alive!" He didn't exactly picture himself a pin-up poster boy, and he wanted to be taken more seriously, maybe even winning a Pulitzer Prize one day. But his public relations department had convinced him that inviting this kind of publicity would only increase circulation of the Examiner.

He wasn't so sure, but he finally gave in. What the hell! It was the 70s after all. If dropping trou before a photographer would make his paper stronger, he'd do it. After all, it was a national family magazine, and they surely didn't plan to photograph his dick. No doubt he'd be asked to wear the skimpiest and most revealing of swimwear but not show "the full monty," as the British say. Here in Florida and certainly on his private island he went nude or practically nude half the time anyway.

The reason he had to postpone these sessions was that he'd received a sudden and unexpected dinner invitation.

The meeting had been long overdue, and he dreaded it. But the time had come to meet Okeechobee's most famous, controversial, and glamorous resident. The celebrated evangelist herself, Rose Phillips, had invited him "for a little bread and wine in the name of Jesus" at her bayfront mansion.

With pride, he took in the news tower rising on the horizon, glistening in the bright early morning sun. Stripped of many of its tiles, it was still a mighty fine sight, and he felt honored to occupy a penthouse office in it. But that pride was also mixed with fear and apprehension. He wasn't nearly as cocky as he appeared. Many times he wasn't sure if he were right or wrong, and often when he exposed public officials, he agonized over the pain he'd caused them and their families. But he quickly justified that: The wrong-doers shouldn't have had their hands in the public till.

Even now, after more than eighteen months as publisher of the Examiner, he still couldn't believe at times that he was in charge, and only so recently after leaving the Marine Corps. He was always reminded that he got that post by an accident. If his father, Buck II, along with his wife, Margaret, hadn't died in the crash of a private plane near Tampa in 1967, Buck III might still be a copyboy.

When Buck I's doctors had insisted that he—America's last Citizen Kane, as they called him—step down, the old man had done so reluctantly. With no enthusiasm, he turned over the Examiner to his grandson and, within weeks, had accused his heir of "destroying my life's work." That accusation stung Buck III. He wanted his grandfather to like him. He loved the old man, and it was with great pain that he watched him advance rapidly toward senility. He felt protective of his grandfather and would do everything he could to see that he was taken care of and felt loved.

Their differences were political.

Buck III's driver pulled into the no-parking zone at the main entrance to the Examiner, and in a moment Buck had leaped from the sedan, disappearing behind the wrought-iron grillwork. He knew his grandfather would age another year if he could see his heir going to work in shorts. Buck III cared little for formalities. He'd have plenty of time later to shower and dress in a suit.

He relished his new-found freedom and it was only to himself, and then late at night, that he'd admit he often didn't know what to do with it.

Stepping into the precincts of the Examiner always brought back memories, many of them painful. As a kid, he'd often heard his own dad discuss his eventual plans for the day he'd take charge. And then, ironically, his life had been snuffed out fast in that plane crash. That accident, which had blackened young Buck's life, had always served to remind him of how easily one can plunge from power.

He took nothing for granted. He was nestled in the womblike tower, the very symbol of Okeechobee, and he knew that if he made one big mistake, he might lose that post in a second. He was sure his downfall would delight Sister Rose, who had become an adversary of the Examiner.

Although the son of one of the wealthiest families in Florida, Buck III was not spoiled as a child. In fact, he had to deliver copies of the Examiner door to door, and he'd done so willingly. He liked meeting people on his paper route, and had won friends. His granddad had told him, "I want you to learn the newspaper business from the ground up."

On summer vacations, young Buck had taken photographs and was occasionally permitted to write news. He'd told friends, "The only thing the old man hasn't made me do yet is latrine duty."

From copy boy to telephone dictationist to ad salesman, he'd run the gamut. When he'd gotten serious as a reporter and had started to write about slum housing and the problem of guns and their connection to random violence, he'd watched in dismay as those stories were killed.

In frustration, he'd quit the Examiner and joined the Marine Corps. Old Buck had approved of that, as he'd found containing young Buck too difficult. "The corps will make a man out of you," he told young Buck at the time. Not an original idea, certainly, but then old Buck was never accused of having a great imagination.

Now, after being away for several years, he was back and in total charge. He knew he'd been placed at the helm only because of old Buck's declining health, and not because of any great faith in him as a publisher. The thought saddened him. He wanted approval from old Buck, but knew that because of their widespread political differences, he'd never get that.

Sighing, he stepped into the elevator. Brushing aside thoughts of old Buck, he headed for the publisher's suite. He had a gut feeling. This was not to be a typical news day. Some big, hot story was about to break. He just knew it.

*****

Going up in a baroque birdcage elevator, he stepped out in time to encounter one of his city reporters, Susan Howard, both of them refugees from the University of Okeechobee's class of '71. As the daughter of Jim Howard, one of the country's best known criminal lawyers, and Ingrid, one of America's leading female columnists, Susan's news sources ranged from a retired Secretary of State, whom she'd once dated in spite of the age difference, to a feminist *cause celebre* who'd killed a man to avenge her rape.

On seeing Buck in shorts, her vivacious green eyes flashed and she let out a soft whistle. She tossed back her long auburn hair, which revealed her aristocratically pale complexion and the white expanse of her throat. She'd been named after the late actress Susan Hayward, to which, amazingly, she bore a striking resemblance. Half of her mail was still addressed "Hayward" instead of "Howard." She had once told Buck her goal was to become as famous as a reporter as her namesake was as an actress.

"My, what a fine pair of legs!" she said.

"Tacky, tacky," he said. "But if you like looking at them so much, why won't you go out with me?"

She placed her hand on the waist of her beautifully toned and well-shaped body. "What? So I'd be accused of using you to advance my career! No way!"

He smiled and stood for a long moment, watching her as she made her way across the city room. As she did, he remembered when, as editor of the university newspaper, The Okeechobee Hurricane, he'd presented her at the football stadium with an orchid and a kiss when her classmates had voted her "Hurricane Honey of the Year."

He'd always liked her and was agonizingly sorry about the breakup of her marriage to Gene Robinson, who'd been the university's champion tennis player. Buck had wanted to approach her and get to know her, but, damn it, he was her boss. His own reputation in playing the field, plus other rumors, didn't help him, either.

Right now he didn't much care. After that time logged in the Marine Corps, he wasn't interested in restrictions placed on him. He wanted to be free to sample the world. His best friend, Robert Dante, preferred to keep him on a tight leash instead. He often resented Robert's hawkeying his every move but to keep a best friend as devoted as Robert you had to make compromises, and he was prepared to make them. He'd been lonely too long and too many times to turn down love, particularly love as devoted as Robert's love for him. No one else had ever offered love like this. Maybe it wasn't the type of love he'd truly wanted and desired, but, what the hell, he wasn't saying no.

The truth was, he'd never had many friends except for Robert. A lot of people, both men and women, were attracted to him but nothing lasting ever came of it. Before his marriage to Susan, Gene Robinson had been his closest friend. Or at least one of his two closest friends. Robert and Gene used to compete for that best friend label. Buck agonized a lot back then over how to spend his evenings. Would he go out with Gene for a night on the town, or else stay home with Robert?

Robert didn't like to go out much. When Gene started dating Susan, the problem was solved for him. He happily spent more time with Robert, even though he missed Gene something awful.

After Gene's scandal, his fall from grace in the eyes of the community, and his subsequent divorce from Susan, Buck never saw Gene again. He suspected Gene might have called him, but he couldn't be sure. Robert screened all calls and steadfastly claimed that Gene had never called. Buck felt sorry about how he'd left Gene to fend for himself and hadn't stood by him. He'd deserted Gene, and that's what Robert wanted. In fact, Robert had demanded it. If he had it to do over again, he would not have listened to Robert and would have helped Gene through his ordeal. He vowed if Gene ever got into trouble in the future, he'd come to his aid. He owed that much to this longtime companion he'd treated so shabbily. God, Gene must hate him. Somehow he'd overcome Robert's objections if his chance to renew his friendship with Gene came again.

Even before his first year back, Buck had really wanted to ask Susan out on a date. But two problems stood in his way. First, she'd been Gene's wife, even though now divorced. It didn't seem quite right dating your best friend's wife, even if the word "former" should be placed in front of best friend and in front of wife.

The second problem was Robert. He intensely disliked Susan ever since they'd first met in their freshman year at the University of Okeechobee in 1967. Both Susan and Robert had competed furiously, often for the same honors and for the same school offices. Since Susan was more popular on campus, she usually won. Even when named "Hurricane Honey of the Year," she'd told Buck at the stadium, "I bet Robert would like to be here right now getting the kiss from you, the orchid, and the title." He hadn't responded.

The remark wasn't as far off target as it first appeared. Like Susan herself, Robert was a stunning beauty. Many people didn't say he was handsome, actually using the word "beautiful" instead. Even old Buck I had taken notice, and he wasn't known for looking at men too much. He especially didn't like Robert, always referring to him contemptuously as "your sissy secretary." One night old Buck had said, "That little sissy. What's his name again?"

"Robert Dante," Buck had answered so sharply it had sounded like a reprimand. "And he's not a sissy."

"Bullshit!" old Buck had responded. "In my day, we used to beat up boys like that. Any boy who looks like that Robert Dante should have been born a girl."

He didn't try to explain to old Buck his relationship with Robert—not that he could. Even he didn't understand his relationship, particularly the way their friendship had recently been developing. One of the guys at his gym had once asked about Robert. "We're just friends," Buck had said, perhaps too defensively. "There are all sorts of friends," the jock had said enigmatically before heading to the shower.

Buck had attempted to explain the relationship to a few casual acquaintances but no one really understood, or else didn't want to understand. He used to say, "Come on, guys, this is the 70s. A straight guy and a gay dude can be buddies. It's a new world out there. Get with it. What are you going to do? Go around asking people if they're straight or gay before becoming their friend?"

Long ago, he'd quit giving such explanations, figuring ultimately it was no one's business but his own...and Robert's. What he and Robert did in private—or didn't do—was strictly between the two of them, and that's how he planned to keep it.

Sweating and feeling he smelled like a football locker room, he headed quickly for the private quarters of the tower, where in the 1930s old Buck had been known for auditioning some of the editors who worked on the women's page.

Robert would be there waiting for him and their morning ritual of a good hot bath before getting on with the day.

*****

Even when Susan was writing seriously about a subject, one not related to sex such as her University of Okeechobee series, much of her mail still brought up that marriage to Gene Robinson. It was an image that had stuck in the public mind. Their marriage had even made the frontpage of the Examiner. Every now and then she still went to the morgue to gaze at her wedding pictures snapped by the paparazzi. Back then they had been Florida's golden couple. The luminously handsome tennis star "with the great legs" marrying the university beauty queen "with the great legs." Even though it was the 70s, their whole romance had the aura of the 50s about it, evoking prom nights and pink carnations.

After Gene's arrest, and while she was still his wife, she'd been left alone at home to receive the offers pouring in. They were lurid. The most modest proposal came from Playgirl who wanted him to pose nude for the centerfold. At the bottom of the offer, an editor/photographer had written this notation: "We can even go for a shot fully erect, although I hear in his case we'll have to extend it to a three-page spread. Is this true? Or just a rumor?"

The first thing Susan spotted was a pile of mail on her desk. A lot of people objected to her three-part series on her former alma mater. Many readers—former classmates—chastised her for being so cruel to the school that had received her with open arms and honored her with so many awards, even acknowledging her beauty.

Some of the letters she'd read in yesterday's pile were embarrassing. "If you'd been a proper wife to Gene Robinson and hadn't spent all your time in beauty parlors, he wouldn't have exposed himself to that little girl. A good wife could have prevented that."

One gay male reader, having nothing to do with her article, wrote in: "Gene Robinson can expose himself to me any day. The spin is, he's hung like a horse. That's one stud you should have held on to."

Even her female classmates back in college had been open in expressing their jealousy over her snaring Gene. He was the most desirable "catch" on campus with the exception of Buck himself. The gay men at the university and the horny young women were about evenly divided in the debate over who was hotter: Gene or Buck. They were definitely the pin-up boys of the class of '71. Buck was constantly photographed without his shirt jogging around the campus in too tight shorts that showed an endowment larger than that of the university's. Gene was equally pursued, especially by the almost all-gay staff of the university's picture magazine Tempo. One student photographer, Leroy Fitzgerald, finally got the "shot" he wanted: a frontal nude view of Gene snapped while he was showering after winning a tennis match. She'd heard that copies of that picture lined the walls of some gay fraternity houses.

Curiously enough, Gene didn't seem embarrassed about this exposure of his privates at all. If anything, he took perverse delight in his notoriety. Perhaps that should have been her first clue about the streak of exhibitionism in him. But she'd been too blind to see.

That exhibitionism didn't extend into their private lives. If anything, after her marriage he was extremely modest around their apartment. Once when it had been too long between sexual encounters, she'd gone into the bathroom where she'd heard him showering. Hoping to entice him, she'd pulled off her clothes and stepped into the stall with him. He'd been horrified at her action. "You fucking whore!" he'd screamed at her. "Get the hell out of here. There are some things men like to do in private."

She'd been brutally rejected and had fled to her mother's house, until Ingrid had finally counseled her to go back and make the marriage work. "It's just a period of adjustment."

That period of adjustment seemed to stretch on forever until she felt at times she'd never adjust to him. Deep into the third month of her marriage, she came to fully realize that he regarded women either as sluts or madonnas. He clearly wanted her to play the role of madonna. As long as she was the dutiful wife, the perfectly groomed playmate, the meal preparation artist, the toilet scrubber, the grocery shopper, he adored her and often brought her fresh flowers. The moment she wanted sex, she was the "whore of Babylon." He often compared her unfavorably to Sister Rose, demanding she use the evangelist as her role model instead of some "whorish Hollywood trash like Jane Fonda."

"When I married you," he had told her, "I didn't want Marilyn Monroe. I wanted someone like Donna Reed."

"But even she played a whore in From Here to Eternity," Susan had protested.

He'd slapped her face real hard that afternoon and stormed out of the house. Never before had he struck her. She feared this was the beginning of a violent streak in their marriage and she wasn't going to tolerate it. She wanted to rush home again to Ingrid, who had a long background in writing about domestic violence, but she decided to stick it out, learning to solve her problems by herself.

But the marriage hadn't gotten better—if anything, it had worsened. The night before what turned out to be the last big game of his career had been the worst. When he'd stormed out of the house that night, he hadn't come back at all. She didn't know where he'd spent the night. She suspected he'd gone off with Buck that evening, although she could never be sure and figured she could never ask. Gene didn't come home the next morning, the day of the big game.

By five o'clock on the same day, after he'd lost one of the big matches of his career, a call had come in from Jim, her father. Gene had been arrested for exposing himself to that little girl. Jim was willing to take on Gene's case, but Susan had talked him out of it. She greatly regretted her decision today. If only she could find some way to make it up to Gene. Back then she'd wanted revenge. Even though she didn't have the perfect marriage, she had the image of the perfect marriage. The subsequent humiliation of Gene and the public exposure of her imperfect marriage caused her even today to feel a sense of shame and disgrace. She'd never recovered from that day. It'd been not only the end of her marriage, but the end of a lot of things in her life, signaling a downward drift.

Gene's case had never come to trial. After all the publicity, the girl's mother dropped the charges. The mother, it seemed, was not a paragon of virtue herself. As the case gained more attention, the mother didn't want her own background investigated. The evidence was that the little girl had seen men exposed before, often making love to her mother. The mother still had a strong case against Gene, but her lawyers finally told her to drop it.

Susan later learned that Gene had turned over to her all the money he'd inherited from his parents, except his home. Like Buck, Gene was an orphan, his parents dying of cancer within three years of each other. Susan had been equally amazed that Biff, the Police Chief of Okeechobee, in spite of the bad publicity, gave Gene a position as a police officer, but the chief always liked grand plays like that. He appeared understanding and generous to a fallen hero, and, although criticized in some quarters, he won renewed respect from voters for his act of kindness.

After the awful hot smelly afternoon of Gene's arrest, nothing was ever the same again for Susan—not that it'd been that good before. She'd known other men after her divorce from Gene. But with none of them had she been able to capture the excitement she felt when she'd first gotten to know Gene and his best friend Buck. They were both golden boys who had thrilled her. Like the rest of the university, she couldn't decide which one to go for, as she found both men immensely appealing and very sexy. She'd finally settled for Gene because Buck seemed to have a guardian at the palace door, Robert Dante.

She'd heard the usual rumors about Robert and Buck, but she'd known Buck was also dating her rival beauty queen, Pamela Collins, who was Pamela Harrison back then before her subsequent marriage to the present mayoral candidate, Barry. One day Pamela confided to her, "There's no way in hell that Buck can be gay. No way in hell. I'm walking bow-legged."

Susan wasn't sure. She'd even heard rumors about Buck and Gene, although she felt that this was just gay gossip. The gays wanted Buck and Gene to be one of them whether they actually were or not. But who knew what went on behind closed doors with Buck and Gene, or with Buck and Robert. She might never know.

In time she'd turned her sights from both men and had hooked up with an aspiring young attorney. They'd lived together during most of

Buck's time in the Marine Corps. His name was Ron Metzger, and life with him had evoked an interview she'd once had with that oldtime 30s movie star, Joan Blondell.

In describing her marriage to fellow actor Dick Powell, Blondell had confided: "Before having sex he always spent an hour in the bathroom soaping and cleaning every crevice. Then he gargled with Listerine for about five minutes before rushing to bed to do his duty. In five minutes he was back in the bathroom, showering and gargling après sex."

The same had been true with Ron. She'd never known such hygiene.

When Buck had returned to the Examiner after a long absence, he'd been surprised to find her working for the paper. She'd been hired by his grandfather. If anything, Buck had adopted a flirty air with her, but nothing ever came of it. He was always talking about why she never went out with him, but then he'd never called and asked her out on a date.

In eighteen months, she'd called him three times asking him to different events. She never got him on the phone, but always spoke to Robert instead. At the sound of her voice, Robert became the wind of an Arctic night. She never really knew for sure if he gave Buck her messages or not. She was going to ask him to go somewhere in person, but decided against it. She'd gotten mixed up in Gene's murky sexuality. If something were going on between Buck and Robert, she didn't want to interfere. She'd just play along and make light of it. For all she knew, she and Buck would "threaten" to go out with each other for the next thirty years.

A call came in for her. She reluctantly picked up the receiver, fearing it was another irate reader offended by her series on the university.

The caller was anonymous. His voice was petulant and belligerent. "What in the fuck are you wasting your time trying to embarrass the university? We need some culture in this hellhole."

"It's fair game," she said.

"Listen, bitch, and listen good. I'll tip you off to a real story."

"What might that be?" she asked with growing impatience. At least he'd called her "bitch" instead of the usual "cunt." She got about three calls like this per day.

"What would you say to this? There's a house right here in our fair city where teenage boys are being auctioned off every night to older men. Some of the buyers are the biggest names in town. They call the boys Lolitos."

"Wha..." she said into a dying phone. He'd hung up.

"Probably a crackpot," she said to herself, turning to that mountain of mail. She nervously looked into her in basket. She wondered what new assignment Buck would give her, following her series on the university. The basket was empty.

After she'd opened her first three letters, all of them attacking her, the voice of that petulant man came back to haunt her. Unlike the usual crank call, his voice had a certain conviction to it. A teenage boy auction. The idea was so bizarre that she had to consider that it just might be true. After all, it was the 70s.

*****

In his office, Buck III ignored the stern, foreboding portrait of old Buck I staring down at him and turned instead to face the smiling, beaming face of Robert. Regardless of how condemned he might be in other quarters, there was one sure thing in life: Robert was always glad to see him even though he'd just kissed him goodbye at his house only an hour before.

Everybody called Robert his "male secretary." But Robert was hardly that. He was like a co-partner in life. There was nothing Robert wouldn't do for him. He was not only Buck's right-hand man, but also his best friend, and had been ever since they'd first met in their freshman year at the university. Robert was more than best friend: he was the primary moral support of Buck's life. "I couldn't get through life without you, kid," Buck always told Robert, as he did again this morning.

Once the door to the suite was closed, Robert wrapped his arms around him and gave him a kiss, perhaps lingering at his mouth longer than he usually did in the office. "I've missed you something terrible," Robert said.

"I was away only an hour."

"It seemed like an eternity to me." Buck raised his arms as Robert slipped his soggy T-shirt over his head. "But, then, anything's better than your stint in the marines."

"You were always there waiting when I got leave. If I recall, you missed me so much I couldn't even take a crap without you hovering over me."

"You got it, big guy. I didn't want you out of my sight for a moment. I nearly died when you joined the corps. I haven't gotten over it yet. There I was, like Lili Marleen waiting outside the barracks gate."

"I'm back. I'm here. And you're my best buddy, and that's how it'll always be."

As he trailed Robert into the shower room in back of the office, he was struck by his friend's seemingly ageless quality. He and Robert were the same age, and both had been graduated from the university in '71 along with Gene Robinson and Susan Howard. But Robert looked much younger than Buck, or even Susan, for that matter. He could easily pass for twenty-one. Buck could no longer do that. If anything, his years in the corps had made him more ruggedly handsome than that pretty boy look he'd had when he'd first enrolled at the university. He and Robert looked much more alike back then. Through all his workouts and military training, Buck had put on more beef whereas Robert still could wear the same blue jeans he'd bought in his freshman year.

Many people thought Buck and Robert were brothers because of their incredible resemblance to each other. With Robert's tall, lean physique, and with his deep blue eyes and dark blond hair, he could easily have been Buck's twin. The two were often mistaken for each other. But that was happening less and less, and Robert's features seemingly remained locked in some time capsule whereas Buck's look was moving ever so steadily toward the ripe old age of thirty. On two occasions before joining the marines, Buck had had Robert impersonate him at two social functions, and the masquerade had come off. He doubted if they could get away with that today.

Robert had lived in Buck's house ever since he'd been a struggling university student. After Buck had learned that his newly found friend didn't really have enough money to pay for adequate living space after his tuition bill had been settled, he'd insisted that Robert move in with him. After all, Buck owned a big house left to him by his dead parents.

Ever since that day, thanks to Buck's generosity, Robert hadn't gone hungry or without money. In fact, he was the only one left in that house when Buck had gone into the service.

Robert didn't just accept handouts. He'd earned his keep, becoming virtually indispensable in Buck's life from the first day he moved in. Buck wasn't great at details and, as a Virgo, Robert ran his life, handling all the little horrors that came along. Over the years, Buck had come to rely on him completely.

Robert always arrived at the office an hour earlier than Buck to have his desk ready for him and to lay out emergency communications. He was also here to help him through his morning shower, a ritual Robert always insisted on participating in.

Kneeling before Buck, he pulled down his jogging shorts. Taking both hands he caressed Buck's butt and in one sudden move pulled down his jock strap with such force Buck's cock sprang out and hit Robert in the face. Availing himself of the opportunity, Robert flicked his tongue across it.

"C'mon, I'm all sweaty and smelly," Buck said in way of feeble protest.

"That's the sweetest aroma I've ever smelled. You can put your shoes under my bed any time."

"I think I already do that." He pulled Robert to his feet, gave him a quick kiss, and stepped into the shower which Robert already had running for him at the right temperature.

He turned his face up to the showerjet, and it seemed to wash away everything that was troubling him this morning. As much as he tried to make Robert his equal, his best friend always insisted upon the servant role. "It's my life, and I can do what I want with it," Robert had once told him. Buck finally caved in and gave up, fully recognizing that Robert wanted to wait on him.

Their relationship had always been about compromise, ever since that first day he'd discovered that Robert was gay. "A straight man and a gay man can be friends, even best friends," he'd told Robert after their first month together. "Hell, dude, it's 1968."

As he put his face up under the waterjets, Buck wondered how straight he still was, after lying night after night in bed with a hot gay male who did the most tantalizingly delicious things to him without ever demanding that he reciprocate. "It's not fair to you," Buck had said. "This is a master-slave relationship. You service me. I do nothing for you. You deserve better."

"It's okay, it's okay," Robert had always assured him. "I could never settle for anyone but you. In time, you'll grow to love me as I love you."

Even though Robert had been endlessly patient with him, their love had never blossomed like Robert wanted. It still wasn't a full relationship, and Buck felt troubled by this. He knew they were moving closer and closer together as the months went by, but even so there was a part of Buck that wanted to experiment and have other relationships— yes, even affairs with women. He thought a lot about Susan but hadn't done anything about it. Hurting Robert wasn't exactly a turn-on for him. He hated himself for not totally sharing in Robert's love for him and of his vision for their life together. Even though he secretly experimented on the side, he always came home to Robert. He felt this is how it would always be. He could not conceive of doing anything else but coming home to Robert.

He made a little vow to the running water and himself. He was going to begin, regardless of how awkwardly, to give more of himself to Robert. If he could do that, if he could give more, it would ease his guilty conscious about his little experimentations on the side. Or so he thought as he rinsed the last of the shampoo out of his hair.

Stepping out of the shower, he found his ever-faithful Robert waiting to rub him vigorously with a towel. He hummed a low tune as Robert dried off every inch of his body, paying particular attention to his genitals and pubic hair. Robert always kissed both cheeks of his butt to signal he was dry enough to get dressed.

Wrapping a towel around his waist, Buck headed for the dressing room where Robert had laid out a suit and a tie for the business day. The white shirt was starched very lightly, just like Buck preferred it. Robert always knew.

"What's it going to be today?" Buck asked. Robert was a nut about selecting his underpants. He always came up with a new pair every day he wanted Buck to wear.

The underwear was always different, but it was always white. Robert couldn't stand the sight of him in underwear with colors.

He took the latest offering and held it up in the air. "How in the fuck am I going to fit all I've got into such a small pouch?"

"It'll work." Robert helped him into the underpants which seemed designed to show off genitalia more than conceal it. Reaching into the pouch, Robert artfully arranged Buck's cock.

"Stop it!" Buck said. "You're giving me a hard-on."

"Wouldn't be the first time." He stood up and looked Buck in the face with a fierce determination. "Or the last!" He gave him a quick kiss and headed back to the office.

Buck turned from him and slipped on his suit. After a final inspection in the mirror, he pronounced himself okay to enter his office and take up the day's work.

*****

Buck smiled as he walked in and saw Robert at his desk. His friend filled him with a warm glow. God, he appreciated this guy who made his life so easy, and he was damn grateful.

Casting one glance at his grandfather's portrait, Buck asked facetiously, "Can't we liven this place up with a de Kooning?"

Robert laughed softly, as if agreeing the place could sure use one. A frown crossed his brow. "You can't afford one. Not with the salary your granddad's got you on. Those girls who want to go out with you think you're so rich. You're not. You're poor. I should know. I try to balance your personal account."

Buck smiled sardonically at the truth of that. "And you do a great job. But do you have to keep me on an allowance? Like some kid?"

"Yeah," Robert said, smiling to soften his words but meaning them. "Until you stop acting like one."

"Christ," Buck said. "I'm afraid I'll never grow up. Despite your attempts to drag me kicking and screaming into adulthood."

"You're doing just fine. I'm always proud of you." Robert looked up at Buck with so much admiration and approval it made him a little uncomfortable.

"Thanks a lot. You always make me feel good even when the rest of the world's against me." Buck meant what he said. But a lot of emotions and feelings between Robert and him remained unspoken. It was as if each would go just so far, then pull back abruptly at the brink of something.

In his inner sanctum. Buck glared at the tight confines of his tower office. Even though his granddad had given him complete editorial control, the old man severely limited how much money he could draw from the corporation. He didn't even have an expense account.

He glanced up suddenly, feeling Robert's eyes. Sometimes when Buck wasn't looking, he'd sense Robert staring at him in a hard, strong way. Good, dependable Robert knew all his secrets. Buck wished he didn't have to hire Robert as a secretary, but Robert insisted on keeping the job. Three times he'd turned down promotions to more important managerial posts on the paper.

Buck's fingers tightened on a news release. "Stick around," he told Robert, as a determined look crossed his brow. "One day I'll have eight de Koonings in this office. Paid for with money *I've* earned.

Robert faced him squarely. "Maybe more. Even a Matisse."

Buck glanced briefly at the rest of the papers Robert had marked "urgent" and left on his desk.

"I got a call from Sister Rose early this morning," Robert said. "About tonight's dinner."

"What about it? She cancelled, I hope."

"No such luck. You'd better get ready to slip through the womb again."

"Is that a reference to being born again?"

"You got it." Robert's face had an inexplicable look of despair and disgust. It was obvious what he thought of Sister Rose, and Buck was certain that Robert was against his going over to her place.

"I think she'll want to convert me tonight. Might make a headline. Like Jerry Falwell winning over Bob Guccione and having him turn Penthouse into a religious periodical."

The buzzer from the receptionist's office alerted him that his granddad was on the phone with his ritualistic morning call. Muffling the receiver, he turned to Robert and, with a sigh, whispered, "He's just checking up on how I'm doing in potty-training."

Thirty minutes later, Buck stood alone on the balcony of his tower suite overlooking the city below. Old Buck always claimed that standing here gave him a sense of power over Okeechobee. But Buck didn't feel that way this morning. If anything, he felt impotent. Old Buck gave him power, then threatened to take it away.

He tried to forget the argument he'd had on the phone with his granddad, who'd objected to his column on capital punishment, published only yesterday. In it, he'd called the governor "Bloody Bob," placing the Examiner as a firm opponent of the death penalty his granddad had always staunchly advocated. Much to Buck's deep regret, it seemed they couldn't agree on anything. Robert, when he was being extremely critical, said that most of Buck I's ideas were formed before 1914. In some sad way, that seemed true.

Back at his desk, Robert told him that an anonymous caller had given the city desk "a hot tip." Some corporations were buying up those seedy hotels on South Beach, moving out—or trying to—retired elderly Jews, leaving them homeless. A few men working for those companies had boasted to about-to-be-evicted tenants. "We're gonna get rid of every Jew on the beach."

"My God," Buck said to Robert. "That sounds like Hitler and the Warsaw Ghetto."

"It also sounds far-fetched," Robert cautioned. "We get a lot of crank calls."

"I've got a hunch there's some truth to this one. Let's at least put a reporter on it. I liked Susan's series on the university. This might be her kind of thing. She's also a close friend of Rose's sister and nemesis, our darling Hazel. If anybody knows what's going on at the beach, Hazel Phillips does, especially now that she's running for mayor."

"Are you going to vote for Hazel over your old buddy, Barry?" The subject of Barry for some reason caused great apprehension in Robert.

"Of course, I am. Barry Collins and I, even when we were friends, never agreed politically on anything."

"Have you forgiven him for marrying Pamela?"

"You're being bitchy now. You know I never loved Pamela."

"What do you call it then? Making love to her?"

"That was a long time ago. A long time ago. I hear she's drinking a lot these days."

"She's a complete alcoholic. Never got over the loss of you."

"I'm sure there are other reasons."

"Bullshit! Once anybody goes to bed with Buck Brooke, he ruins them for all other sex partners."

"That's very flattering."

"In my case, it's the fucking truth. If you want Roland to assign Susan, I'll convey the message." He turned and walked away, obviously disapproving of Buck's choice as a reporter.

Later, behind the glass enclosures in his office, Buck stood silently after Robert left to give his message to Roland Hunter, the city editor.

Minutes later, the shuffling, bedslipper-shod feet of the city editor headed toward the desk of Susan. Roland placed nicotine-stained fingers on her shoulder as he apparently told her about the tip Buck had received.

Tall, reserved Roland Hunter never liked Buck, and Buck wondered why he kept him in that post.

Hired by Buck I, Roland was good at his work—thorough, competent, efficient, always demanding that a reporter "dig a little deeper."

All his life he'd been plagued by "my afflictions," to hear him tell it, and he gobbled pain-killing pills for his ailments, many of which Buck considered hypochondriacal. Roland tried to control his belly-aching with what sometimes turned out to be two or three extra gin martinis at his long lunches.

Through the glass partition, Buck met Roland's eyes. The city editor turned from the sight of him without acknowledgment.

*****

Tired, sluggish, Buck felt he needed a long-distance run today so he'd be alert for a night that had every prospect of stretching out late. On a paved road for cyclists that encircled the half-moon bay, he could see the skyline of Okeechobee in the background. Skyscrapers, tourist hotels, and modern blocks of steel-and-glass office buildings had replaced rambling, two-story structures built before World War II. But as he ran along at a moderate pace, he felt the city still resisted sophistication in spite of its luxurious bayfront mansions, palm-shaded boulevards, Riviera-inspired architecture, and glittering beachfront strip that drew mono-bikinis and minks in winter, in search of glamour and romance.

Sweat ran down his skin, and he liked the feel, enjoying the smell of his own body. Around a turn he encountered two other joggers, a man and a woman, who easily passed him by. He let them as they aroused no competition in him, After all, he wasn't in a race to the finish line. Pacing—that's what he'd tried to learn, for he knew he wanted to bring about change faster than his readers could accept it.

His muscles, cramped from sitting too long at his desk or at luncheons, loosened the more he ran. For his final lap, he got a second wind. The closing minutes were the liberating part of jogging. No longer earthbound, his buoyant body floated through the air.

As he neared the finish, his trick knee—the result of a college football injury—bothered him. He raced on, forgetting the pain. With renewed confidence, his heart pounding, he picked up speed, as a delirious feeling came over him.

Panting for breath, he collapsed on his own grounds behind his Mediterranean-styled villa. He rolled over on the lawn, enjoying the smell of freshly cut grass until an urgent erection pressed against his gym shorts.

That sent signals to him he had to get home to Robert. After all, he couldn't arrive at Sister Rose's mansion with a full erection. He'd never had an erection yet that Robert couldn't deflate.

*****

On the way to Sister Rose's bayfront-bordering Paradise Shores, Buck suspected she was going to make trouble for the Examiner. Before he took over the paper, his granddad had devoted a lot of space to praising the Rose Phillips Charismatic Association, of which she was the founder and director. It was said to be the nation's largest anti-Communist movement. But, in spite of his granddad's policy, when young Buck took over the paper he'd told Roland, "If Sister Rose wants publicity, let her take out an ad, and pay for it!"

He didn't like the taste of her heady stew of far-right politics with old-time fundamentalism. He didn't know why she needed his paper anyway. She knew how to get her message across, as she'd become the consummate TV and radio reverend—America's most controversial and flamboyant preacher.

Sister Rose's thirty-two room bayfront mansion occupied an entire island, Paradise Shores, with a short coral runway connecting it to the mainland.

"So this is where Miss Flower Petals lives," he said to his driver. "I'm jealous already. Religion sure pays better than the newspaper business."

Once the retirement home of a Detroit car manufacturer, the 1920s winter mansion had been changed and wrenched apart to meet Rose's needs. His limousine entered a tall wrought-iron gate, with a rose petal motif intricately worked into each crossbar. The car came to a stop in the driveway, and he got out and headed for the door. Along the way he passed a heart-shaped pool, each of its two voluptuous curves extending toward the bay. Parked right in front of her entrance stood a Rolls-Royce in dusty rose.

Even though he'd heard stories, he was still awed by the opulence of her mansion and statuary-filled grounds. As he rang the doorbell, he was greeted by the chimes and recorded voice of Rose singing a chorus of "Amazing Grace." The sound beamed not only through the house, but into the courtyard. With a slight smirk, he mumbled to himself, "This pussy's not to be believed."

A black maid led him into the parlor where he waited for Rose to appear. The room itself was a mass of white—not only the carpet, draperies, sofas and chairs, but even the heart-shaped pillows, all fringed and ruffled. In the center was an overscaled coffee table, also heart-shaped. Even the stained-glass windows were heart-shaped. White roses, her symbol, filled every white vase.

Striding into the room in a low-cut, form-fitting white gown that did little to conceal her breasts, the tall, statuesque Rose exuded euphoria. All smiles, she made a striking presence, giving off joyful radiation, the way Loretta Young used to make entrances on her long-ago TV series.

She was one hell of a sexy woman. Without the need to appear sanctimonious in public, in her private life she could be gutsy, even in the presence of a critical young newspaper publisher.

As he took her slender, delicately soft hand, he could see a flirtatious challenge dancing in her eyes. She wore her hair long, and it was almost the exact color of Susan's, a deep auburn that evoked some autumnal scene in a Vermont forest. Around her alabaster throat hung a gold necklace, holding a heart-shaped white locket.

He knew she had to be fifteen years older than he was, and he was surprised at her youthfulness. The woman smiling before him didn't look thirty. He searched for telltale clues of a massive face-lift, finding none.

She moved through the room like a whirlwind, giving instructions to her maid, telling her butler she couldn't come to the phone. In every action, she emerged as a distinct, definite personality—strong-willed, aggressive, yet possessing a *savoir faire* that diffused those qualities.

When she did stop in front of him, he looked into the depths of her almond-shaped eyes, finding a turbulence he hadn't noticed before. Beyond the self-assurance he detected a fear, like that seen in the face of a terrorized girl. As if sensing he wanted to see behind her mask, she said, "I summoned you here tonight to give you hell. Now that I see how good looking you are, I'd rather make eyes at you."

The naïveté of that old-fashioned expression put him at ease, suggesting she had more innocence than he'd initially felt. Up close to him, she smiled again. He noted how big and strong her teeth were, like the Chiclets he used to chew as a child.

Her voice was that of an American radio announcer, showing no regional influence. "What would you like to drink?"

"A Bloody Mary." He gave his request no thought until he noted the shock on her face.

"What about a Virgin Mary? This is a Christian house. I'm sorry I don't serve hard liquor."

"Very well, I like virgins." Even as he said such a crass remark, he regretted it, feeling it made him sound like an ass. He'd slip out later and sneak a drink from the bar in the back of the limousine. By then he'd need one. Virgin Mary in hand, he followed her on a trail that led across her patio into floodlit gardens.

"I didn't want to live in Okeechobee at first," she confessed, walking close to him and reaching out to take his arm. "I came here originally to visit my sister, Hazel. That was back in the days when she still spoke to me and didn't follow a line directly from the Kremlin. Do you know her?"

"Yes, quite well. Our next mayor."

Her face froze with hostility, but she softened it, smiling again. "I was just a smalltown girl, and the way I see it, this wicked place is no spot to bring up kids. I have a wonderful son, Shelley. You know, Shelley was originally a man's name. I adopted him even though I've never been married. Except, of course, as a bride of Christ. We launched our foundation in Tulsa. That is, until every acre of Oklahoma got overrun with evangelists. You know, with Oral Roberts and everybody else who could throw up a tent moving in, I felt I'd better stake out the sinners along the Gold Coast."

"We have quite a few of them here." He'd come here to challenge this woman, but her charm and grace made that difficult. She made him want to protect her from any imaginary ghouls wandering around in her garden.

"If it wasn't for my work, I'd move back to some small town. You know, where a kid could wander barefoot in the woods, build a treehouse, play with tadpoles, things like that. A place where they've never heard of child porn. I could just see Shelley rushing off fishing in the old hole, even skinny-dipping if nobody was around."

As she spoke, he looked over at a luxurious cabin cruiser, Rose II, docked at the evangelist's private pier. "Down here you can take the kid fishing." Noting the size of the cruiser, he added, "Deep-sea fishing."

The sarcasm struck her. "I know," she snapped. "That's not what I'm talking about. My kid will never know the simple life, the simple values, the way I was raised. Even though I send him to a private school, I have to hire a full-time bodyguard to protect him from all the kidnappers and child molesters..." She paused awkwardly, as if forgetting something. Her reflective eyes took in her night garden, and in those eyes a sadness prevailed. She turned to him and reached out affectionately, a little desperately for his arm. "I bet you're starved."

On her back patio, ready for dinner, he'd been the polite guest long enough. After all, he was no candy-ass, but the crusading liberal publisher; Sister Rose, the enemy from the far right. "I read the file we keep on you at the Examiner." Adrenalin flowing, he felt fired up. He paused a moment, letting her think he possessed more information about her past than he did.

He smiled and edged back in his chair, examining her closely. The wind blew through her hair and he was struck by the loveliness of it, how freely it flowed and how gracefully it moved when she turned her head. As she edged closer to him, a lock of it fell over her forehead. She brushed it back with carefree abandon, the way a model might do in a TV commercial advertising hair conditioner. He kept repeating one thought, that she was like no preacher he'd ever known. "Why did you invite me here?" he asked, deliberately abrupt.

She shuddered as if chilled. "You've made me a victim of the press." The words, soft and gentle, failed to conceal the bitter charge.

"I've never written anything about you."

"That's exactly what I mean," she said rising. Nervously, coming to a stop near him, she reached for his hand to plead her case. "An attack is better than silence. You're trying to freeze me and my work out of existence. Old Buck ran our ads free."

He looked away from her eyes and at the white statues of the gods and goddesses standing against her wall. "I'm not that generous."

She moved away slightly, but remained close, as if aware of the mesmerizing influence of her body. In a more conciliatory voice she added, "You're not the only one. I can't get on a talk show. They tell me that most guests don't want to be taped sitting next to Sister Rose. Rod McKuen's allowed to come on and propagandize. Not me! It's a media conspiracy."

"Like hell!" he said, showing anger. "You're constantly on TV and radio. Always in the papers. More so than any other woman in America. Few people, even the president, get so much media attention every time they open their mouths. You don't need our support over at the Examiner. You'll start the war without us."

"What does that mean?" she asked, her eyes widening.

"I don't know," he said, surprised at his words. "Sometimes I just blurt out these things, and then—real eerie-like—they come true."

Feverishly excited, she seemed in some triumphant possession of the truth, as if she'd acquired positive proof of her charge. Returning to her seat, she became less tense. "Old Buck warned me I'd have trouble with you. He thinks of you as a rebel."

She faced him squarely, wetting her lips with her tongue and with a calculated effect, as if searching for the right camera angle, said, "I think you're the anti-Christ. That doesn't scare me off. I'm used to confronting children of the devil and winning them for Jesus."

She exasperated him. He knew she was serious, yet she left open the possibility her remark was a joke. Charm was used like a weapon.

In imitation, he leaned over the table and caressingly took her delicate hand, letting a lock of his hair fall over his eyes. That always turned women on. In a voice used for whispering words of love, he said,

"I don't run stories about you because I consider you the bigot of the year!"

With a gasp, she slipped her hand from his hold and sat back in stunned silence.

Growing stronger now, the wind burst open the door to the utility room and a harsh flow of exposed electric light flooded the patio, altering the romantic setting she had so artfully cultivated. He detected the smell of gardenias in the air, a heady tropical blend of intoxicating odors. She rose quickly and went to the door, slamming it with a ferocity, taking out her aggressions on the door instead of him.

Further diversions were on the way. The black maid arrived with dinner.

Without mentioning the charge, she faced him again with a brave smile. "We're having my favorite food—a juicy hamburger with lots of raw onions and an RC Cola."

Although he considered himself the gourmet of Okeechobee, he entered the spirit of the occasion. "Pass the catsup."

Over dinner, fake pleasantries returned, but when he'd finished his hamburger and had refused another one, he turned to her again. "The B'nai B'rith Anti-Defamation League has for years considered you one of its most dangerous critics. Your foundation has even lobbied secretly to prevent America from selling military equipment to Israel."

She slammed down her fork, no longer able to conceal her emotions behind her facade of grace and charm. "Just a minute, I've had enough of this. I mean, someone told me Gore Vidal in the forties disliked the Negroid people. Now he's a flaming liberal and civil rights advocate." She slowed down for a moment to regain control. "People change, you see. I had never seen a Jew until I was seven years old. In my early days as a preacher, I made some remarks I'm not proud of. But I've grown. I've changed."

Her candid admission came as a surprise. "I'm not convinced." He stared for a moment at the remains of the hamburger. Feeling leaden, he excused himself and followed the maid in the direction of the toilet. More than wanting to go, he needed to escape her overweening presence.

When he came out, he was shown to her petite salon, with its wallpaper of white roses. She had arranged herself invitingly on the white sofa, her feet curled up under her gown. A collection of foreign dolls—gifts from admirers—lined the walls of her study. All were dressed in frilly white.

"You know," she said, "defending yourself against anti-Semitism is so difficult."

With swan-like grace, her hand directed him to a comfortable winged armchair. Her face reflected a kind of martyrdom, making him feel she masochistically liked to listen to accusations from the infidel.

Surrounded by mirrors and splashy white flowers, he was encased in a powder box of her images. He fancifully, with secret pleasure, pictured himself as the invading Hun, storming the citadel of a Renaissance madonna.

She got up serenely, seeking a chocolate-covered mint to give him. Was it a peace offering?

Upstairs, he could hear recorded music playing. It sounded like a children's choir singing. "I don't think we'll ever know your final position on Jews. Lady, it looks to me like you're thirsty for some real power."

"Aren't you?"

"*Touché*. The Examiner isn't going to help you one step of the way. We'll be in very different camps in the months ahead." He got up. "I do apologize for the news blackout on you. Starting tomorrow, I'll assign a reporter to investigate your background. We may even do a profile series on you. From reading our file on you, I found a lot of missing gaps in your life."

"I see I haven't won you over, sinner?" Close to her again, he felt her nearness, the subtlety of her expensive perfume. "Come back and see me real soon. I don't give up easy."

In the hallway she presented him with an autographed copy of her autobiography, Hallelujah! "In this little book is the entire story of my life. Stay up and read it tonight. I think you'll find it inspiring."

"No little volume like this contains the entire story of anybody's life. Maybe the Examiner will fill in some of those gaps."

"I hope that's not a threat. I've been threatened before. Besides, we've all got closets we wouldn't like to open."

At the door she surprised him by kissing him on the cheek. No mere brush, it was a full, sensual caress. Did he detect a flicker of her tongue?

On the way to his limousine, he passed a teenage, blond-haired boy crossing the lawn. The smell of marijuana permeated the air.

"Hi, kid," he called out, wondering if this could be Shelley. "Turning on before burger time?"

The boy appeared startled. "Fuck off!" He disappeared inside the big white door, as a chorus of "Amazing Grace" echoed across the lawn.

*****

It was after midnight when Gene Robinson turned his Volkswagen at the corner and headed down the street where he lived in spite of the Cuban invasion. His yellow stucco house, with its unkempt garden, lay in the sprawling Hispanic ghetto south of the river. Hastily erected after World War II, many of these bungalows had been haphazardly enlarged over the years.

He'd grown up on this street when it was filled with low-income Protestant families—white ones. After the past ten years, he was the only Protestant still left. The Catholic "beaners" had taken over. God, he hated beans, and that was all they seemed to eat. Even the grocery store on the corner carried every variety.

On the way to his house, he heard the sounds of TV sets blaring through open windows. The "beaners" had their own Spanish language TV station. He couldn't understand it. The way he saw it, they lived in America now, parasitically drawing their lifeblood from this country, but stubbornly clinging to their native Spanish—demanding that signs, government documents, and classroom studies be taught in both Spanish and English. "These creeps never go to bed," he mumbled, remembering how quiet the street used to be after ten p.m.

His own modest home had been built by his now-dead parents who'd settled here in 1947. He was determined to stay on in the house they'd left him. The "beaners" wouldn't force him out, in spite of the high crime rate. The first Cuban who ever broke in to rob him would get a bullet through his head.

Some of his new Cuban neighbors had tried to make friends with him. Only the other morning a middle-aged, stringy-haired housewife from across the way had knocked at his door. When he'd opened it, she'd smiled seductively at him, introducing herself as Clara. "I can't find Maria," she lied. "I thought she might be playing over in your yard." She'd breathed in deeply, sucking the air to make her breasts stick out more prominently, thinking in her foolish way that she might lure him. "My husband works days," she'd volunteered, craning her neck to get a look inside his kitchen. When he glared at her, not saying a word, she hadn't been intimidated. "Your curtains are always drawn. I never know when you're home, except when I see you pull into your garage. You rarely turn on your lights. Saving on energy, huh?" She'd smiled

Darwin Porter / 27

flirtatiously again, holding up her pudgy little hand to shield her eyes from the sun. "Say, do you have some coffee? I'm fresh out, and I could sure use a cup."

He'd slammed the door in her gaping face, knowing the bitch wasn't after her stinking little kid or coffee, either. That had just been an excuse to talk to him. She'd hoped to insinuate herself inside.

Driving the Volkswagen into the garage, he padlocked the door behind him. Once inside his bungalow, he surveyed his spotlessly clean, spartan kitchen before heading to the refrigerator where he poured himself a glass of milk, his favorite drink.

Then he headed down a long corridor to the rear of the bungalow to his own little stuffy bedroom, where he'd long ago boarded up all three windows. For his retreat from the world, he wanted complete privacy.

Entering the pitch-black room, he turned on the lamp. He was tired, but he still looked good, he thought, as he ran his comb through thick, wavy, black hair.

Only his large eyes had lost their once lustrous life. A deep black, they now reflected anguish and suffering, as friends and relatives had dropped away. His wife, Susan, had deserted him when he'd been disgraced. Arrested for exposing himself to that little girl. That's why he wore sunglasses now, both day and night. They were mirrored glasses. He wanted nobody looking into his eyes. His mother said his eyes were sensitive, just like the black Irish from which he was descended. "I can always tell what you're thinking just by looking into those black eyes."

On his bed, he removed his black, shiny boots, then rubbed those eyes which rested under brows full and heavy. He pressed his hand against his square-jawed face, fingering the bottom of his deeply molded lip, full and red, fearing he might be getting a fever blister. He winced at the thought, just as he did at the idea of any imperfection. He didn't want the slightest blemish spoiling his good looks. Down at police headquarters, he was known as Tyrone Power, and he liked that—at least he did until he read some unfavorable newspaper publicity and a book about his former screen idol, suggesting that Power wasn't a real man like Gene had imagined him to be. Gene still shared one thing in common with Susan. Both of them were constantly compared to movie stars. Tyrone Power and Susan Hayward, who'd once made a movie together. Dead movie stars, it was regrettable, but movie stars, nevertheless.

No wonder the Cuban woman calling herself Clara was attracted to him. Nearly everybody was. He could tell by the hungry look in their eyes.

That had been more evident than ever tonight in that smelly latrine at the far end of the park. Three of the "beaners," all mariposas, one even with a mouth painted lipstick red, had knelt on the piss-stained floor to swallow him whole, each with gaping mouths eagerly waiting to have their turn with him. He'd been particularly rough on the last kid, who didn't look as if he were out of high school. At his climax, he'd grabbed the faggot and shoved it all the way down his throat and held it there until the Cuban boy nearly choked. Filth like these mariposas deserved no better treatment. Once his climax had occurred, he'd zipped up and made it out of that park as fast as he could. He couldn't stand to look at those sex-hungry faces any more. At least they got to see and feel what a real man was like.

What they didn't know when they'd tried to lure him back to their apartment, what he didn't reveal to anyone, was that he was saving his real self for *her*. He'd never met her, yet he knew she'd want him to be pure. That's the kind of lady she was.

Like an angel.

*****

Robert was waiting in the foyer of Buck's house as he turned the key and entered the all white marbled hallway, with a sweeping Tara-like staircase in the background. In jeans and a white T-shirt, Robert appeared warm and relaxed, and it was obvious he'd had a few drinks. Buck walked over to him and kissed him on the mouth, a little harder and firmer than he usually did.

Robert responded with equal pressure. "I've missed you something awful," he said.

"I wasn't gone that long, and Rose didn't convert me." He pulled at his necktie and took off his jacket with a certain force, tossing it over a sofa as he made his way into their larger parlor furnished exactly as his mother had left it on the day she'd died. "I need a real drink."

Robert appeared in seconds with the drink. "I heard your car coming up the driveway. I rushed to make it."

"As you rush to do everything for me day and night," Buck said. "God, I feel guilty. You do everything for me, and I give you so little." He belted down a hefty dosage of the Scotch offered.

"You give me reason to live. Isn't that enough?"

"It's a good reason. But it's not enough. I've got to give you more. I'm not sure how to go about it. You're giving me too much and you're not being equally rewarded."

"You're all the reward I want."

"That's damn nice to hear." He downed another drink of that Scotch as if he were preparing for something and he wasn't quite sure what. "I want to turn in early tonight. And I hope you'll join me."

"Haven't I always joined you any time of the day or night you wanted to turn in? Turn on is more like it."

"Right from the first." He reached over, taking Robert by his blond hair and pulling him over for a kiss. "What pleasure it's been for me. I didn't know how good it can get until you came here. If I recall, I invited you to live out in the cottage, but from the first night you would have none of that."

"Why in the hell would I want to be in a lonely cottage out back with the dogs when the hottest man in the state of Florida was lying upstairs alone in his bedroom?"

"Why indeed?"

"I won you over on the first night. Your liberal philosophy dictated that a straight man and a gay man could be friends. You admitted you'd slept with your straight men friends many times. Bare-ass on camping trips, dormitories, or at school conventions. I just asked for equal treatment."

"You got it."

"It took a little push and shove. That first night you were going to get into bed with your briefs on. Such awful briefs they were. Blue. You know I insist on white."

"Have I ever worn anything but white since?"

"Always white—that's true. I wouldn't have you in anything else."

"You were right. I wouldn't hesitate pulling off my briefs in front of a straight man. But with you I was holding back. A little afraid of what might happen. But off came the briefs."

"And such a sight it was. And is. Unlike anything I'd ever seen. I think I was already in love at that point. Of course, I had already seen you in the shower at the unviersity."

"Stop it! You're giving me a hard-on, like you always do." He downed more of his drink. "I'll be up in a minute." He got up abruptly and adjusted his suit pants. Crossing the living room, he opened the French doors leading to the terrace overlooking the garden.

Alone in the night air, he felt he was coming unglued a bit. All sorts of contradictory feelings were racing through his blood. There was no place he wanted to be right now more than with Robert, no place more enticing than going up to that bed and sleeping in it with his friend.

It wasn't a perfect picture, though. There was something missing, and he always knew what it was. He didn't love Robert with the same intensity that his friend loved him. In sex, Robert was always the giver and he was the object of affection. He knew this wasn't right. Every night Robert explored every crevice of his body with his talented tongue, bringing Buck to moments of such ecstasy he didn't think he could bear another second of such exquisite torture. That's when he usually begged for more. But he should be exploring Robert's body with the same ferocity, and he wasn't. The truth was, Robert, after bringing him to climax, masturbated with Buck's deflated cock in his mouth. Several times he'd come close to penetrating Robert and still held back as if that were some final frontier to cross. Ever since he was fourteen, he was always willing to receive blow-jobs from almost any source, and he'd had a lot of offers, particularly among his fellow marines. In his mind real fucking was something you did with women. He knew in his soul that the moment he fucked Robert he would be a card-carrying gay male, and he wasn't quite ready for that yet.

He still felt he was straight, and somehow Robert, the skilled seducer, had come along and diverted him from his natural inclinations. Without Robert finding out, he wanted to experiment on the side and find out how straight he really was. He couldn't let Robert learn about this, and he wasn't thrilled at the idea of cheating on him. But he had to see if he could find some fulfillment with a woman he hadn't found with Robert. Even if he found it, he didn't know if he would commit to a relationship outside this house. He was determined that this house where he lived with Robert was their fortress. He wasn't going to damage that, but he wanted to test his limits more. In some ways, he felt he was living only half a life. Other than his being with Robert, no one ever inspired him to great passion. He desperately wanted to give as much love as he received but he always held back somehow.

"I'm fucked up in the head," he whispered aloud. At that moment a flashing memory of Gene came back to haunt him. That night, that awful night five years ago, he had never been able to erase from his memory. Sometimes at the most awkward times, just when he felt he'd forgotten all about it, the memory came back. He sucked in the night air. He wouldn't think of it. He'd tell his brain to stop thinking about it, and he knew his brain wouldn't betray him. He cracked his knuckles in despair.

That night could never be erased. But it was over and he was living in the present. The here and now demanded that he go upstairs to that bedroom and give more of himself than he'd ever given. Even though Robert accepted their arrangement, Buck couldn't continue to treat Robert like some sex slave while he, the Arab sheik, lay back and demanded to be serviced.

"I can't go on doing this," he said out loud. "There's got to be more in it for Robert." Starting tonight, he was going to try to bring about a shift in their relationship. He'd make love to Robert instead of having love made to him. The world's greatest seducer and most talented sexual artist would no doubt view Buck's attempts at certain forms of love amateurish. But if he knew his friend, Robert would be only too willing to accept what was offered, unskilled or not.

Even as he mounted the steps to his bedroom, he was filled with a haunting feeling. On the one hand, he genuinely believed he was doing the right thing by trying to love Robert as Robert loved him. But another gnawing thought troubled him. Was he giving more of himself to Robert to make up in some way for his upcoming betrayal of his friend? There were impulses growing stronger and stronger in him, and he had to act on them. These impulses were so powerful they were almost like the devils he feared controlled his former friend Gene.

At the door to his bedroom, he unbuttoned his white shirt and unzipped his trousers. As he turned the knob, he knew Robert would do the rest.

*****

It was early morning. The first streaks of light were creeping into the bedroom. Buck turned over gently, not wanting to disturb Robert. Then he realized he was in bed alone. From the sounds, Robert was in the bathroom showering.

Stark nude, he made his way across the darkened bedroom and opened the doors leading to his balcony. Here he plopped down in a dew-moistened chair to watch the dawn split the sky. The morning sky was reason enough to live in Florida. Watching the horizon light up was like a ritual for him.

He didn't want to recall every detail of last night, and he especially didn't want to have pictures going through his mind of all the sexual plumbing involved. But he couldn't think of anything but that. The night had been different from all the hundreds of others he'd spent with Robert. It had set a new pattern for them and a new relationship between them.

He knew he wasn't there yet in the sense he hadn't arrived at the perfect man-to-man sexual relationship he realized he was heading toward. But he was on his way, and last night had made a significant change.

From the first, he suspected Robert had sensed it was a different man crawling in bed with him. If Robert didn't know that, he certainly must have been aware of it when Buck had reached out and pulled him so close to him it was as if they were one. He'd kissed Robert, but the kiss was different from before. He'd kissed Robert firmly before, even wet before, but last night he'd plunged his tongue in his friend's mouth, and he'd never done that.

The moment he'd inserted his tongue in Robert's mouth, he realized what a fool he'd been all along in not giving his friend something he wanted. Robert literally sucked his tongue, giving it the bath of its life. It was such exquisite pleasure for Buck he cursed himself and his own inhibitions for waiting this long. It seemed like an hour before they broke contact with each other. It was as if he were fucking Robert in the mouth with his tongue, and Robert was the eager receiver.

As he'd engaged in his longest kiss ever with Robert, his friend used both hands to explore every inch of Buck's body he could reach. It was a gentle, loving caress, only adding to Buck's excitement. Robert's touch was always extremely delicate and almost feather-like but it could arouse such passion.

Tentatively, very tentatively, Buck ran one of his hands down Robert's back, settling on his buttocks. With his index finger, he ever so slowly inserted it inside Robert who'd opened up and accepted it ever so willingly. If anything, it made Robert suck on his tongue even harder.

Impulsively, he'd thrown Robert on his back and lay on top of him pressing down hard. With one hand, he ran his fingers through Robert's hair pulling at the strands slightly. He nibbled at Robert's right ear before inserting his tongue in that ear for a bath. Then he'd done the same thing to his friend's other ear. This action had made Robert squirm, and for the first time ever Buck took pleasure in giving Robert pleasure, instead of the other way around.

Ever so gently he'd bathed Robert's chest with his tongue, almost imitating what Robert did to him night after night. When he reached the left nipple, he'd circled it with his tongue. Robert was moaning and pulling at Buck's hair at the same time, as if goading him on.

He seemed to know what Robert wanted. He'd bitten hard into the nipple and Robert had screamed in ecstasy. It wasn't a scream to tell Buck to stop but to go on to give him even greater pleasure. When he'd had his fill, he'd moved to the other nipple and repeated his action. Robert's chest had been heaving at this point, and Buck had traveled even lower with his lips and tongue, going where he'd never gone before.

The moment of truth had come. It had become time to take the plunge. Why had he dreaded it and resisted it for so long? Robert's hips had been rearing up from the bed signaling what he wanted Buck to do. He'd leaned over Robert and in one gulp had consumed the man. Buck had overestimated his ability in that area. He immediately gagged but didn't back off. Filled with determination, he'd plunged up and down on that prick which had swelled to an even greater thickness. Even as he did, he was glad it wasn't a whopper. He didn't know how Robert managed. Robert was all he could handle and he wasn't doing a very good job of it, or so he'd thought. To judge by Robert's moaning, he was doing a fine job of it. The salty-sweet taste of it had been good in his mouth, and again he didn't know why he'd feared it for so long.

Such white heat couldn't continue, and it didn't. In a rapid, shuddering spasm, Robert filled his mouth with a milky, musky substance. Buck had gagged and didn't feel he'd be able to swallow it. Summoning all his steely reserve, he did manage to swallow it and not only that but had stayed on until he'd drained the last drop from his friend.

Only then after a few departing kisses and licks, had he fallen back on the bed totally exhausted.

Ever so gently Robert's mouth had found his, and parted his lips so Robert's tongue could clean his mouth of Robert's own taste. When Robert's mouth reached his right ear, he whispered softly, "Thank you. Thank you, my lover."

Buck closed his eyes and breathed deeply, but said nothing. From that point on, he knew how the evening would end. Like it always did. From his ears to his neck, from his fingers to his arm pits, from his chest and nipples, from his thighs to his feet and toes and back along his calves, Robert began his nightly ritual of virtually devouring every inch of Buck. He always turned him over and licked his back before caressing each buttock. Then the real good part came when he'd opened Buck up and plunged his tongue as deeply as he could inside him. Robert always stayed there a very long time, and last night it had been more than an hour until Buck was moaning and squirming for relief.

The journey from there to all the hidden crevices of his body, including a thorough wetting down of his testicles, always ended in the same place, with Robert climbing the pole beginning at the base. Last night Buck had been ready to blast off before Robert had even plunged down on him. When his relief finally came, it was shattering. His entire body had seemed to explode, and long after the spasms had died, he'd held Robert down on him. His friend had shown no inclination ever to leave the spot, but Buck had held him there as if the idea of his pulling away at that moment was unthinkable. With Robert still buried there, with him still in his friend's mouth, he'd gradually fallen asleep and he guessed that Robert had too.

As if to erase last night's memory, Buck abruptly got up from the cool terrace and stretched himself in the dawn light, noticing how the sky had reddened. It almost seemed on fire.

Some impulse was stirring in him and he didn't know what it was. He headed toward the bathroom. There was no sound of a shower. As he threw open the door, he spotted Robert standing in front of the mirror shaving, a towel draped around his still wet body. He always shaved and then showered but Robert preferred to shower then shave.

He stood looking at Robert for a long time, wanting and desiring him as never before. Robert looked over to him with more love and devotion than he'd ever seen in his friend's eyes, and he'd seen a lot.

He walked right over to Robert and grabbed him and pulled him close, inserting his tongue in Robert's mouth. He hadn't brushed his teeth or shaved, but Robert never turned him away whatever condition he was in.

Robert clung to him, digging his fingers into Buck's back. He pushed Robert away slightly and knelt before him, ripping the towel from his nude body. Robert's sex looked tasty, tender, and ever so succulent to him. He reached out and started licking and kissing everywhere until he got what he wanted. A full, raging erection. He plunged down on Robert, and this time he didn't gag.

As he worked over his friend, Robert ran his finger through Buck's hair encouraging him to plunge deeper. Minutes went by, and he wasn't keeping time, but Robert's quivering body told him what to expect and very soon. He got his reward as spasm after spasm jerked Robert's body. He swallowed every drop and didn't gag, and that made him proud. When he was certain there would be no more reward for him, he stood up and faced Robert squarely eye to eye. Then he pulled him close and plunged his tongue in his mouth.

Breaking away, Buck headed for the shower with one glance back at Robert who stood by the mirror, still half shaven and looking stunned as if he weren't sure what had happened and even if sure couldn't quite believe it.

"Listen, motherfucker," Buck said to him, "don't you ever call me a cocksucking faggot or I'll beat the shit out of you."

In the shower, he turned on the water full blast and held his face up to the jet sprays, and for one brief moment forgot about Robert, himself, and the day that was rapidly rushing toward them.

Chapter Two

The call came in at 4:31am, and Susan turned over on her side, as if that would shut out the noise. The ringing was persistent. At first she was tempted not to answer it, but feared it might be Roland calling from the office with an assignment, as he often did at this hour. That city editor never seemed to sleep.

"Hello," she said with sleepy hesitation into the phone.

"Listen, bitch, and listen good," came a petulant voice. She immediately recognized it as her crackpot caller from yesterday. She was tempted to hang up on him but decided to hear him out.

"What have you done about that tip I gave you yesterday? About that auction of boy Lolitos."

"I've done nothing about it," she said. "I doubt if it's true."

"You doubt it, bitch? Who in the fuck are you to doubt my word? I tell the truth. I call a spade a spade."

"I'm sure you do, but you offer no proof. A wild accusation. I need some strong, hard evidence."

"I'll give you something hard, bitch. Real hard."

"I'm hanging up."

"I've got proof."

"Yeah, right."

"Don't get smart with me, bitch. I've even got photographs. Documents I stole. I can even provide the address."

"How do I know you're not bullshitting?"

"Come over to this cheap motel room I rented last night, and I'll show you my proof."

"There's no way in hell I'm coming to your motel room."

"If you're worried that this is all a trick to rape you, guess again. I don't go that route."

"Okay, I'll meet you somewhere this morning in a public place. Bring your proof with you."

"Not so fast. I'm broke. I can't even pay the bill here at this motel. I need one-thousand dollars before I let you in on this scoop."

"I don't pay for news. I never did."

"What would you say if I told you I had a photograph secretly snapped of our mayoral candidate?"

"I don't believe it. Surely you don't mean Hazel. You must mean Barry Collins."

"The one and only. The one running as Sister Rose's hand-picked crusader to clean up Okeechobee."

"If what you say is true, that's news. But I'm still not going to pay for it."

"Listen, bitch, I'm desperate. I've got no food, no money, no place to live. The operator of the Lolito house kicked me out. I was the custodian. He didn't even give me ten dollars before showing me to the door."

"I'll tell you what I'll do. I have only five-hundred dollars in the house. If you have some genuine proof, I'll give you the money. But it's a gift to help you out. Call it a charity donation."

"Shitty little charity it is. My information is worth much more."

"Take it or leave it."

"I'll take it because I'm caught between a rock and a hard place. What a cunt you are. There's a place next door to this fleabag, Vista Linda Motel, that serves breakfast to truckers. It's called Crazy Mabel's. Out on Indian Creek Trail."

"I know the dump. I'll meet you there in thirty minutes."

"I want you to buy me breakfast, and we're talking a five-egg breakfast."

"It's a deal. How will I recognize you? I don't even know your name."

"I know what you look like. You're always getting your damn picture in the paper. I'll find you." He slammed down the phone.

At first she was tempted not to show up. He could be a true crackpot or else it might be some sort of trap. But through all his hostility and aggressiveness, there was a ring of truth and conviction in his charges. If he told the truth, this was major news, and she didn't want anybody else on the Examiner, much less the competition, getting such a big story.

Jumping out of bed, she headed for the shower. She'd quickly apply her warpaint later and set out on the trail. Under the jet streams pouring from her shower, she pondered over possible headlines Roland might put on her exclusive. "Boy Lolitos" sounded catchy. It was definitely the kind of story wire services would pick up. The potential of a news story like this was why she became a news reporter in the first place. Ingrid always warned her not to pay for news, but in this one case maybe mother didn't know best.

*****

Pulling into the oil-stained parking lot at Crazy Mabel's, Susan got out of her car and was immediately confronted with a tall, lean man who was unshaven and in his late twenties or early thirties. "I'm Terry Drummond, bitch. Did you bring the money?"

"The *cunt* brought the money," she said, slamming the car door behind her.

"Let's go eat. I'm starved."

Early morning truckers, many of them Hispanic and eating omelets with hot sauce, filled the crowded diner. Susan managed to find a small table for them in the back. She ordered only black coffee and orange juice, but he went for a massive plate of bacon, ham, sausage, and five eggs along with grits and fried potatoes.

He looked over at her while waiting for his order to be cooked. "I had a job as a custodian at the boy brothel. I also had to perform stud duty for the house's owner. Get this, the owner doesn't like young boys. He likes fully grown men. In fact, his alltime fantasy male is Gene Robinson."

She winced at the mention of her former husband.

"I know you were married to him. Leroy's had a crush on him ever since they were in school together. Collects every picture he can find of him, including *that* one. He's got the original negative and has had hundreds of copies made. In fact, he was the one who originally snapped that picture of Gene. The coach later barred him from the locker rooms. He worked for the campus Tempo magazine, the one that always used to run you on its cover as hurricane beauty."

"I know Tempo very well, but I never knew who took that picture of Gene. Anyway we're not here to discuss Gene. Who is this Leroy? Not who I think it is, I hope."

"You got the money, bitch?"

"I've got the money."

"Leroy Fitzgerald."

"I know him if it's the same Leroy who was in the class of '71."

"One and the same."

"I remember he campaigned for and eventually won recognition for a gay rights group on campus."

"That's our Leroy. Now he's a bordello owner. He gives twenty-five dollars to each of the boys every night. Sometimes the men give the boys big tips when they go to private rooms together. But that's only after the show."

"Show? What show?"

"Leroy calls it the flower-petal show. The johns come in and are seated. A spotlight is turned on. The young boys are paraded in naked. They form a ring in the middle of the floor and lie down with their heads touching. Then the customers get up from their chairs and go down on them, moving from one to the other until each john has sampled each boy. Then Leroy auctions off each boy to the highest bidder. Sometimes when a boy is particularly desirable the bidding can go real high. Steve almost always goes for a thousand a night."

"Are these boys underage?"

"All of them except one guy, Angelo. He's eighteen. But to look at him you'd think he was only fourteen. I mean, he looks real young."

"This is going to be a hard story to nail down, particularly for me as a woman. If I were a young boy, I could become one of Leroy's troupe and write an eye-witness account. But it's not going to be easy for me to prove this. You mentioned pictures."

"I've got lots of pictures. You see, Leroy secretly tapes the action. He always claims these pictures—snapped without the john's knowledge—would not only be an insurance policy for him but something he might possibly use as blackmail."

"What a guy! Are you really sure Barry Collins is one of the patrons? He looks like such a straight shooter. In fact, he systematically denounces gays. He worked to defeat a gay rights bill in this county."

"Haven't you heard of hypocrisy? And don't you know that some of the most anti-gay bastards in this country are closeted gays?"

"So I've heard."

"I've got lots of pictures, but the one I wanted to tantalize you with was one of Miss Barry herself. She was so busy sucking boy cock she didn't know we were capturing all the action for posterity." He reached into a soiled envelope and pulled out an eight by ten glossy. As he handed it to her, the waitress arrived with his breakfast.

Susan concealed the photograph until the waitress had left, then studied it carefully as Terry slurped down his breakfast. The man was really hungry.

The photograph was quite clear. It appeared to be Barry, whom she knew well. Although she realized it could be a fake, it didn't seem to be. The right-wing mayoral candidate was performing fellatio on a boy who appeared to be no more than fourteen, if that. "May I take this?"

"Yeah," he said, his mouth full, "if you've got the five-hundred dollars. But before you get any more pictures I'm going to want a lot more money. Leroy's very fickle. I knew he might kick me out when he got tired of me. So I stole as much incriminating evidence as I could get on him. I've got pictures of some of the most important people in this state. Leroy's johns are strictly from the A-list. I even got a picture of a bigtime movie star."

"What's the address of this place?"

"I'll tell you. But that's all I'm going to tell you until I get more money. It's 230 Bayshore Drive."

Susan scribbled that down on a piece of paper.

"It's owned by Leroy. He wanted to be a photographer originally. He's tried for years to get a job on the paper. But old Buck I would never hire him. He was just too sleazy. Maybe the new Buck III would hire him—he's so fucking liberal. But Leroy's taking in so much money today he doesn't need a job. He's shot two centerfolds for Playgirl, however."

"How can I get in touch with you?"

"You can't. I'll call you. That's the deal. Frankly, I don't know where I'll be from night to night."

"I wish we could set up some permanent contact."

"Wish again, bitch. I want that five-hundred, and I want it now. I've spilled enough beans for one morning."

"Here it is." She handed him the money which he grabbed from her hand so eagerly he scratched her skin.

"I'll see you around, bitch, when I run out of money." He took one final sip of his coffee, wiped the bacon grease from his lips, got up, and quickly left the restaurant.

As she watched him go, she suddenly had an idea. This was not just a story for the Examiner. It was a case the police should be working on too. She wanted to do Gene a favor even though it had been years since she'd seen him. At the Examiner that morning she was going to send him an anonymous tip, informing him of what Terry Drummond had told her. This could be a big case for Gene, and it might in some small way redeem his tarnished reputation if he could break it.

*****

After his morning jog, a cold shower, and a long, lingering kiss from Robert, Buck walked to his office from his dressing room.

"Not so fast, big boy," Robert said, taking his hand. "You've made me the happiest man in the world. I'm in heaven."

"I should have put you there long ago," Buck said. "I'm just a slow learner."

"It was worth waiting for."

"Expect a repeat performance tonight."

"I can't wait."

"We'll have to," Buck said, opening the door and entering his office where Robert had neatly arranged his messages and mail.

Through his large windows he spotted Susan crossing through the newsroom. She spoke briefly to Roland at the city desk, then headed for her own desk in the far corner.

On an impulse, he dialed her on his intercom. "Morning," he said, deliberately making his voice sound huskier than it was.

Before he could identify himself, she said, "Buck, good morning. I bet you're calling to find out how I'm doing on that South Beach thing. Today's the day to get into it—really hard."

"Susan," he said, pretending to be shocked. "If you don't stop talking like that, I'll sue you for sexual harassment."

"Men! That's not what I meant."

"It's okay. Come on up to the office. Let's go over a game plan."

"Thanks," she said, "I'll be right up. That is, after I pay a quick visit to the ladies' room. No former beauty queen meets Buck Brooke III without a quick check of her make-up. Besides, I got up much too early this morning. I didn't get my full beauty sleep because of a mysterious phone call I want to tell you about."

"See you later." The moment he put down the phone he feared her reception in the office would be a bit chilly from Robert. He didn't really want to subject her to his friend's jealousy so he came up with an idea. He pressed a button summoning Robert to his office.

He rushed in right away. "I'd kiss you but I just washed my hair."

"It's a slow morning and you've got everything under control here. I want you to do something for us. I'm tired of seeing you in the same white T-shirt and jeans all the time. I want you to get more of a 70s look. Buy some new outfits. Since I suspect you'll wear them only in the privacy of our home, I don't mind if they're a bit provocative and very revealing."

"That's what you want?" he asked, looking astonished.

"Men like to see women in lingerie, don't they?"

"I suppose. God only knows why."

"Why can't I enjoy looking at my boyfriend in some fun night wear?"

"I understand. Wait till you see what I come up with." At the door, he hesitated. "You never called me your boyfriend before."

"Everybody else calls you my boyfriend. Why can't I?"

"I'm honored." He looked at Buck and smiled. "Honored, shit. I'm thrilled out of my god damn skin." He turned and left.

Within the next few minutes, after Robert had gone shopping, he went to the door and ushered Susan into his office. Although she could see most of his office through his glass windows, she surveyed the interior carefully. "I don't get many invitations here. Robert keeps you under heavy guard."

"He's a great guy. You just don't know him."

"I don't think I ever will."

He was embarrassed by this talk of Robert and wanted to change the subject. "You know Hazel better than I do. I mean, I know her and all but you know her much better."

"Hazel and I have always been good friends."

"Would you see if you could make a date for both of us to see her in her apartment on South Beach? By now, she must have a good idea of what is going on there."

"She probably does. But apparently she doesn't know everything or even a lot yet."

"How can you be sure?"

"If she did, she'd be blasting the hell out of everybody and making frontpage copy."

"I suppose you're right. But let's meet with her."

"It's a deal. I'll set it up if she's free."

Without further talk, she walked into Robert's office and dialed Hazel's number. She was back in Buck's office within minutes. "It's on. She can see us. But only at nine o'clock."

"That's fine with me. What say we meet at seven-thirty for drinks at The Rusty Pelican?"

"I know it well."

"If you haven't had anything to eat we can always grab a burger there, even though the food is lousy. But their burgers are good."

"It's a date."

"You've always been promising me one. We'll try to keep this one strictly business."

"We'll try," she said enigmatically. A frown crossed her brow. "I've come across some real disturbing information."

From the main office, he could spot Roland staring through the large windows at Susan and himself. The city editor always became furious when Buck met privately with one of his reporters.

Susan quickly outlined to him all the data she'd learned from Terry about the boy Lolitos and the male auction.

"This is fantastic, but I don't really know how to proceed with it." He looked at Roland again. On an impulse he was tempted to call Roland in on their conference, but decided against it.

"There's this picture. Apparently they have a lot of incriminating evidence on some of the johns who patronize the place."

"Let me see it," he said, reaching across and taking the photograph which she'd concealed in a manila envelope in her purse.

He studied the photograph carefully. "If I didn't know better I'd say that was Barry Collins. It's not a picture he can run in his campaign."

"It sure isn't. It'd be the end of his political career. That's why this is one hot issue. I understand some of the town's leading figures—judges, bank executives, a college president—are involved in this club."

"Who's behind it?"

"Leroy Fitzgerald is the front man."

"I know him. The same Leroy we went to school with. The one who was always trying to take frontal pictures of the school jocks."

"The same Leroy, although in this case I suspect he has backers."

"This is a hot one. The boys are underage, right?" he asked.

"Sometimes only fourteen, or so I think."

"Grown men, pillars of the community, having sex with minors. Wait till Sister Rose hears about this."

"But her own hand-picked candidate is involved."

"We're sitting on a time-bomb and I don't know how to go about it. If I knew some boy who was of the age of consent, a hustler really, but very young looking, we might pay him to infiltrate the club and get all the dirt for us. I don't know anybody like that. Perhaps Robert a few years ago. Maybe there's someone out there who would do it for us. Or maybe we could fly someone in."

"I know, but the whole idea disgusts me."

"It does me too. I've got to think about it. I don't know what to do right now, but the story's too hot not to touch."

"I must tell you I've gone ahead and sent anonymous word to Gene about this sex ring. I figured we'd better get the police involved. He needs a big case. Besides, these kids are minors, and Leroy must be stopped."

"I think that's fine. If the police start to move in on the place, we can report the news. It would remove us from the awkward position of trying to be criminal investigators ourselves."

"That's true but I still want the scoop."

"All that is possible. We'll keep in constant touch. I swear by tomorrow or the next day at the latest I'll come up with some idea. Old Buck will probably call it idiotic but it will be at least some plan of attack."

"Why don't you keep the picture?" she asked. "In a safe."

"I will." He stood up. "Barry? I never would have thought it. I wonder if Pamela knows."

"I doubt it but she might. If she knows, she's a very understanding wife."

"She's very understanding," he said.

"You'd know that better than I would. Still carrying a torch?"

"Pamela and I once talked about getting married, but as you know that was a long time ago. Could I let you in on a secret?"

"Fire away."

"Pamela got drunk one night..."

"Pamela is always getting drunk one night."

"I know, but this night was different. It was the end of our relationship. She told me she didn't love me at all but was carrying a torch for Gene."

"Gene!" she said with astonishment. "Pamela in love with Gene? Maybe that's why she's always hated me so."

"I couldn't believe it but she claimed she'd always had this thing for Gene until you snared the prize. She once told me she'd married Barry on the rebound, even though she wasn't in love with him."

"I not only didn't know this, I find it incredible. Any more secrets?"

"Maybe. But I'm not telling them now."

"It's amazing," she said. "All of us went to college together. All of us were involved in some way with each other. But I wonder how well any of our classmates knew each other."

"I don't think we did at all. We're a complicated class of '71."

"Except now we're playing adult games," she said. "Look at the lives that this story alone will destroy—that is, if it's printed on the frontpage."

"I don't feel too happy about that. I don't want to destroy Barry."

"But then Barry shouldn't be sucking little boy cock," she said.

"Not while running for mayor and not while campaigning to clean up the filth and smut in Okeechobee. We've got to be careful. Plot our next move cautiously."

An urgent call came in for him and he picked up the receiver, putting the caller on hold.

She got up with a promise to see him tonight. "This is a little scary," she said. "I'm going to depend on you to lead me through it."

"I'll do my best." As she neared the door, he asked the caller to hold a little longer. He walked rapidly to the door and softly asked, "Do you mind if I call Gene and meet with him? It's been a long time. I mean involve the Examiner in the investigation."

"That might be a great idea if Gene will cooperate. He's very bitter, you know. About you. About me. He really feels we let him down."

He paused briefly, looking into her eyes. "We did. At least I did. In some small way, I want to make it right with him."

"Good luck."

*****

As he drove across the causeway to The Rusty Pelican, Buck reflected on the transient, ephemeral, and sometimes tawdry nature of Okeechobee Beach, where even as a teenager he went seeking amusement after dark. Linked by umbilical causeways to the mainland of Florida, the beach was like a valuable nugget that reduced miles of sandy coastline into a teeming caravansary of human desires and frailties. A condensed version of Las Vegas, minus the casinos, but with the whiff of Atlantic salt air, it was associated with images of champagne-drinking dolphins, fleshpots and discos, resorts and debauchery, and flashy but expensive boutiques hawking non-essential merchandise at inflated prices. The only exception to the overall glitter was South Beach, which remained, very definitely, a decaying slum.

The city of Okeechobee, on the other hand, lacked such glitter, its major character formed in the sixties by refugees pouring in from Havana and giving the staid place a distinct Latin flavor, its smaller side streets now evoking back alleys of capitals in Central America.

Sucking in the night air deeper than before, he headed north, going to that glittering strip created almost solely for tourists, who outnumbered the local residents in winter by a ratio of ten to one. The ocean-bordering sandbar seemed to exist purely for pleasure, but he was not coming here tonight for that.

He'd already known pleasure that night even before leaving home, and he didn't expect any more for the rest of the evening. He'd only reluctantly left Robert's arms, before driving toward the beach, and his companion didn't want him to go, but Buck had assured him that it was vitally important that he talk to Hazel tonight. He'd deliberately left out the fact that Susan would be with him.

Robert hadn't told him all that he'd acquired during his shopping expedition that morning. "I want you to discover something new every day."

While Buck had fixed himself a drink at the downstairs bar, Robert had gone up to their bedroom to change. Within minutes he was back again wearing yellow tennis shorts and a red tank top. If anything, he'd looked just like he did on the day Buck had first encountered him in their freshman year at college. He'd stood modeling for Buck.

Buck had liked what he'd seen and he'd felt a definite stirring in his trousers.

He'd stood looking at Robert for a long time, appreciating him in a different light from before. For one brief second, he'd almost agreed with old Buck. Robert looked prettier than any woman he'd ever seen. Whether gay or straight, you couldn't help but notice Robert's beauty. He wasn't effeminate—far from it—but he'd had a luminous, melancholy blond loveliness to him that made you want to draw him close to taste him.

Only an hour ago, Buck hadn't wanted merely to taste Robert: he'd almost wanted to eat him. Slugging down the rest of his Scotch, he'd taken Robert by his right arm and gently glided him to the sofa in their living room. He'd taken off his jacket and had lain on top of his friend. He'd begun by pressing his full weight down on the young man and then had virtually attacked his face.

It hadn't been just kissing: it was devouring. His tongue had explored every hidden crevice in Robert's mouth. He'd kissed his lips before biting them gently and then going on to lick every surface of Robert's face including his eyes and nose. With his tongue, he'd fucked each of Robert's nostrils before bathing his ears to lubricate them for a tongue assault on each lobe.

Robert was moaning in ecstasy and writhing on the sofa at this unprecedented assault. His nails had dug into Buck's back as if that would somehow allow him to control his joy at being attacked this way.

Buck had continued his assault on Robert's neck, tasting, licking, and nibbling every inch of it before applying equal treatment to his throat. Robert had actually started screaming at this point. Never had Buck's kisses aroused someone like this before—never. As if to confirm his suspicion, he reached into Robert's yellow shorts and found him not only fully erect but ready to explode. The moment Buck had touched Robert's penis, it'd erupted. Buck held him tightly through the throes of orgasm until he lay in Buck's arms gasping. Buck had scooped up most of Robert's semen in his left hand and had then rubbed it across his mouth before his lips had again descended upon Robert who licked them clean.

Noticing what time it was getting to be, Buck had given Robert a final deep kiss before getting up off the sofa and straightening his hair in the mirror.

"Don't go!" Robert had suddenly called out. "Call Hazel and cancel. Tomorrow night, maybe. I don't want you to go."

"I'll see you later," Buck had said. "I've got to go. It's important to the paper."

"Go if you have to then, but when you get home you're going to be attacked."

"I can't wait." Buck put on his jacket. "I'll tell you what I'll do. I'm not going to brush my teeth until I get home. I want the taste of you in my mouth all night till I can get back home and get some more flavor from you."

Robert had stood before him at the door. "I don't know what's come over you. At times I can't believe it's really you. Maybe a twin. I madly loved you before, but now I'm half out of my mind."

"You're in for a lot more surprises," Buck had promised before kissing him good night and heading out the door.

The taste of Robert still on his lips, Buck drove faster than he should, passing entire blocks of hotels, some in the flamboyant seventies rococo style, others so denuded of architectural details they looked like office complexes. Plushly, iridescent, the beach was a honky-tonk growing out of a former mangrove swamp.

In the remote northern section, he steered his car into the parking lot of The Rusty Pelican which increasingly was becoming a singles bar.

As he got out of his car, he noticed two male punks distributing some bumper stickers. Always curious as to what was going on, he walked over to them.

"Here, put this on your bumper," one of the young men told him, handing him a sign. "Honk every time you see someone with the same sign."

He read the neat lettering: CONVERT A JEW TO CHRIST.

He confronted the young man whose face was a mask of hostility. "Who's paying you to hand out these signs?"

"Fuck you," the man said, grabbing the sign back from Buck. "You one of those faggot liberals, or something?"

His friend shoved Buck. "In case you haven't heard, faggot, this is a free country!" With their bumper stickers in hand, both men turned and left, heading toward a pick-up truck.

Buck watched them go, not really believing that these punks were politically minded enough to be distributing the stickers. He suspected someone was paying them.

Just over the causeway in the redneck section of bars and honky-tonks, or even in the black ghettos, he suspected the men would find people more willing to accept their bumper stickers. That part of Okeechobee had always been anti-Semitic, talking about "dirty Jews who lived on the beach." He'd have to investigate this for the Examiner. It had an ugly ring to it. He knew if someone were blatantly printing and distributing bumper stickers like this, other amusements would be along the way.

"The town's heating up," he said to himself, as he headed for the entrance to The Rusty Pelican.

Glancing at his watch, he saw that he'd arrived about twenty minutes early. Inside that bar, he passed waitresses in rakish wide-brimmed hats with red scarves and pink feathers. He headed for the pulsing red lights flashing in the rear under a mirrored ceiling. Paintings of voluptuous nude women covered the walls and upper-level balconies which overlooked the dancing couples below. Foxy ladies and handsome guys, all suntanned and scantily clad, danced inside this ripe maraschino cherry, making every one look redskinned—perhaps the revenge of the Tequesta Indians, the original settlers, on the descendants of the people who'd chased them from their homeland.

In the rear room, where the actual food was served, he confronted the maitre d', a dime-store Liberace dressed in a jacket of shiny pink sequins.

"I'll get you a table," he lisped.

"Great!" Buck said, then paused suddenly. "Just a minute. I have to say hello to someone first."

"All right," the manager said as if annoyed. "Make up your mind." He turned and swished away.

In the far corner of the dark bar sat Pamela Collins, his long-ago love.

*****

It was obvious to Buck that Pamela was already deep into a Tom Collins lineup. He stood looking at her for a long moment, capturing some of his old feeling for her. Although he'd always claimed, often to himself, that she was only a passing flirtation, he had at one time been deeply in love with her. So had half the rest of Sigma Chi, his fraternity. Only Susan herself had been more eagerly pursued when they'd attended the university together.

Unlike Susan, Pamela hadn't aged as well, and she'd put on several unflattering pounds. Her face looked ashen and puffy, but still retained enough of its beauty to evoke her former look when she'd represented Miss Florida at the Miss America Pageant at Atlantic City. Traces of that youthful beauty and natural grace remained. Her long blonde hair was still lustrous, but in the blue of her eyes he sensed a great sadness, like a promise someone made to her and never fulfilled.

He'd always admired her independence. Take tonight. Here she was, sitting alone in a singles bar with a proud defiance, although her politically conservative husband was running for the mayor's job. She'd never followed the rules, and didn't seem to give a damn what people thought about her. The word he kept wanting to use for her was "ballsy," though that seemed too inappropriate and he didn't know the female equivalent. "Breasty" just didn't sound right.

He went over to her table, and she didn't seem in the least embarrassed that he'd discovered her cruising.

"Have you come back into my life again?" she asked provocatively, "after I foolishly let you go." He found her as serenely cool and confident as ever, with a cheerful sad smile and a soft southern accent. With her slightly upturned nose and expressive wide lips, she was still sexy.

"Do you mind if I have a seat at the table of the woman who got away?"

"I'd be honored," she said in a honey-coated voice. "Your god damn newspaper makes me sound like a southern magnolia. At least in your write-ups, can't you say my blossoms are made of steel?"

He looked into her eyes with a calculated expression of patience. "I don't think Barry would like being known as the husband of a steel magnolia. It doesn't sound right on his family values ticket." He hastily ordered a Scotch from the waiter and turned his attention again to Pamela.

She slammed down her Tom Collins, as a simmering dissatisfaction, perhaps deeply rooted, came over her features. "I want my freedom," she said, her voice slurring. "I'm tired of being abused and threatened. Barry and I just aren't compatible—that's all."

He feigned surprise, although he'd heard plenty of rumors.

The muscles in her face tightened. "I'm tired of being the one who's always smeared by every gossip in town."

He slowly sipped his drink when it arrived quickly, feeling it best not to interrupt the revelations.

"Barry's forever getting written up as Mr. Goodie Two-Shoes," she said sarcastically. "I'm the threat to his career, the one with the drinking problem. And..." She paused for a long moment, her eyes staring deep into his. "You know what they say? That I've fucked half the state troopers in Florida."

He hadn't heard that one, but only nodded.

With a challenging look, she moved closer to him. "Why don't you ask Barry why I'm so promiscuous? Neglected women fill up their time the best way they can."

"Any other women involved?" he asked pointedly. "I'm asking this as an old friend, not as a reporter. Our little meeting is strictly off the record."

"I trust you completely. I know you'll protect me." She asked the waiter for another Tom Collins before settling back into her chair. "Women?" she asked as if belatedly hearing his question. A smirk crossed her face.

A vision of that fellatio picture of Barry flashed through his mind. "If not women, then what?"

Intense red lights flashing in from the dance floor revealed her bloodshot eyes. "Barry spends more time with the Boy Scouts than he does with the League of Women Voters."

"You're leaving a very clear impression," he said, leaning forward, hoping she'd confide more.

She smiled petulantly. "That's all I'm saying for the moment. And nothing on the record. You can read whatever you want into whatever might come out of my pretty little mouth." A rage seemed to surge through her. She was about to say something and kept censoring herself. She was, after all, known as the Martha Mitchell of Okeechobee. "I don't want to leave a completely wrong impression. Although he seems to prefer to work the ball fields at junior high, he is more versatile than that."

"What does that mean?"

"He's been known to throw a mercy fuck every now and then to the town's most famous woman."

"You couldn't possibly mean our dear Sister Rose?"

"You didn't hear it from me."

"That's surprising. All day I've been met with surprises."

"I'll throw one more at you. Maybe two. Sister Rose and Calder Martin—you know her henchman, don't you?—have Barry by the balls. Maybe they're blackmailing him, I don't know. I know he's borrowed heavily from them to finance his get-rich schemes. None of them came to anything. Barry's so heavily in debt he can't get out. Those vultures can command him to do their bidding. He'll make a shitty mayor, just like he's made a shitty husband. Personally, I'm not voting for him. I'm supporting Hazel."

"Now that's news."

"It would be if we were on the record, which we're not. I've always trusted you. I should never have turned down your offer of marriage."

"You loved Gene."

"I thought I did. How in hell did I know Gene was some kind of a nut? You were his best friend. Did you ever think he was so crazy?"

"Sometimes he did strange things. But he concealed it better then. After the university, he seems to have gotten worse."

"Oh, shit!" she said, looking up. Two handsome young men had entered the bar and were eying their table. One of them looked darkly Italian, the other a sun-streaked blond surfer. "Believe it or not, those guys are my jailers."

"I don't understand."

"Calder Martin has hired them to look after me until the campaign is over," she said. "Calder thinks if they take care of me I'll stay out of trouble. Maybe he's right. But every now and then I try to escape from even them."

"If they're threatening you, do you want me to call the police?

"Hell, no. It's part of the deal."

"What deal?"

"I've agreed to stay married to Barry until after the election. I'll divorce him later. He's getting custody of our daughters. My big payoff won't come until after he wins the election. Otherwise, they'll cut me off without a penny. I don't have any money to live on unless I play Barry's dutiful wife."

"Is this what you want?"

"With some money I can go away and make a new life for myself. I'll miss my daughters something awful, but I don't have much choice."

"Let's meet for a drink again some time soon," he said, not really planning to go. "For old time's sake." He raised a toast to her as she downed the rest of her Tom Collins.

She stood up on wobbly legs. "Who knows?" she said. "That new life might be with you. Haven't you heard of people starting over again?"

"I've heard but I think it's too late for that."

"Robert Dante?"

"Something like that." He nodded a good night as she walked over to the bar and the two young men. Casting a final look toward his table, she headed for the door with her "jailers."

Although he hadn't officially invited her for a drink, he ended up paying her bar tab, which had been climbing all night. He'd sit here quietly and wait for Susan.

*****

Within ten minutes the image of Pamela at his table had been replaced by that of Susan who didn't look drunk, overweight, or wobblylegged. "If I'm not terribly mistaken, that was your old girl friend Pamela I saw in the parking lot. Being helped into the car by two very handsome young men. In other words, up to her old tricks. I don't think she saw me."

"It's not as simple as that," he said, signaling the waiter to take their order. "Barry and Calder Martin have got her on a tight leash. Those men work for Calder. Pamela, they feel, needs to be escorted around until after the election. Then it's splitsville for Barry and her."

"I'm not at all surprised, particularly after that picture we saw today. Any ideas about how to go about uncovering this?"

"Not a clue yet. As I told you, I definitely plan to meet with Gene. If he'll see me again."

"I'm almost certain he will. You were an important part of his life. He'll be driven by curiosity if for no other reason."

"It'll be interesting to see how he's going to move forward with this case. If I know him, he's on it right now."

After she'd ordered a burger and Buck had too, she glanced around the bar. "Where's Robert?"

He slammed down his drink. "What are you suggesting? That I can't go out the door without Robert?"

"I didn't mean to make you angry, but it seems that way to me. Okay, since the subject has come up, I might as well come out with it. Are you gay?"

Anger flashed across his face. "Hell, no!"

"I'm glad to hear that because I was thinking of asking you out tonight after we see Hazel."

Finishing off his drink, he ordered another one. "Robert is a great friend. He helps make my life work. I don't even know how to write a check anymore. He takes care of everything."

"Everything?" She raised her eyebrows.

"Don't be provocative. It's possible, you know, for a gay man and a straight man to work together and be friends without being bedmates?"

"I know that. But from the day Robert met you in our freshman year, he's had this obsession about you. It's obvious to everyone."

"Considering all the people who hate me, it's nice to be loved."

"I suppose you're right, but I needed to know. You do admit that you come on to me. I don't know if that's for show or if you mean it."

"Whatever I've done, I've meant. It's not Robert who's held me back. It's Gene. If I ever started dating you, and Gene found out, I think he would go ballistic. We not only desert him when he gets into trouble, but we abandon him and take up with each other."

"I didn't know you felt that way."

"I do."

"What was between Gene and me is dead and gone. It seems like a long time ago. Actually what was between Gene and me never was. We were hardly man and wife. He wanted a madonna. As you might find out later tonight, I'm no madonna. Please tell me what happens when you meet with Gene. Not just about the Lolito case. The personal side too. In some funny way, I still care about him."

"I do too. After all, he was my best friend."

"I thought Robert was your best friend."

"He is. But Gene and I were real close for a very long time."

"Which brings up the second big question of the evening."

"My, aren't you the inquiring reporter?"

"I have to know. Were you and Gene ever an item?"

It was at this point the waiter arrived with the burgers. Buck was grateful. He needed time to formulate a response. "Hell, no! I'm appalled that you or anyone else ever thought that. We were good buddies. Before everyone in the 70s starting thinking gay all the time, men used to be buddies, didn't they?"

"That's true. But you and Gene used to go off and spend long weekends together. Robert was left home fuming. I was left home alone. Pamela fumed for a few hours before rushing off to find someone else. All the eligible guys and girls on campus were left fuming when the university's two most desirable studs would run away together without inviting any of the rest of us."

"Gene and I liked to go on fishing trips together. A sort of Bebe and Tricky Dickie thing. Nothing more."

"I'm glad you cleared the record on that. If you felt any hesitancy dating Gene's former wife, I felt a little awkward about dating his former boy friend."

"Rest assured: I was not, nor have I ever been, Gene's boyfriend. The truth is, I've not even been a friend. Even though they didn't know Gene that much, your parents were willing to stand by him. After that little girl thing, I turned and ran. I never saw any clue in Gene that he'd do a thing like that."

"I saw clues about how unglued he was becoming. But I was of no help to him. If anything, I feel guilty for pushing him toward the edge."

"We didn't know. We were very young. I think back then we really believed our images. Gene was the golden tennis champion. The perfect athlete. The world's greatest stud." He smiled to break the tension. "Except for me."

"How you men talk," she said with a smirk before softening her features. "Forgive me for putting you on the spot like this. But I like you a lot. I just don't want to stumble into another mess like I got into with Gene."

"I can relate to that." He glanced at his watch. "We're going to be late if we don't get a move on."

She finished her burger and looked at him soulfully.

He feared another personal question. "What's it going to be now? Barry and me? Roland and me?"

"Nothing like that. But don't you think the burgers here used to be better when we were in college?"

He smiled and rose from his seat, taking her arm. "Everything used to be better when we were in college."

*****

After Susan's sexual challenge to him at The Rusty Pelican, Buck remained subdued and quiet as he drove her to Hazel's apartment, leaving her own car in the parking lot. He'd known Rose's sister for a long time. One didn't publish a newspaper in Okeechobee of any persuasion—right or left—without getting to know a lot about Hazel. She was very vocal. Although mesmerized by Sister Rose, old Buck always referred contemptuously to Hazel as "that fat cow."

Unlike Rose, the poorer sister lived on South Beach in a residential section filled mainly with elderly Jews, mostly women, of which she was a champion. She was even known to lecture their sons visiting from New York. Once in front of newspaper reporters, she'd told one son, a New York lawyer, "There you are. Living like a fat cat in New York while your mother is forced to buy cat food to keep from starving."

Buck parked in front of Hazel's building and assisted Susan out of the car, the way he used to do for Pamela whenever they went to their many dances. In rapid strides, he followed her across a palm-shaded courtyard of broken tiles, with a moonlit surf curling over the litter-strewn beach in the distance. Susan had been here many times before; this was his first visit.

Twice married, the recently widowed Hazel still used her maiden name of Phillips. "Look," she'd once told Buck, "a woman has to give up a lot in marriage, including her virginity if she's marrying for the first time."

He'd looked dumbfounded. "How many women do you know who are still virgins on their wedding night?"

She'd looked back in a quizzical way, as if the idea had never occurred to her. Then she'd gone on. "Let women at least keep their names. They'll need whatever identity they can hold on to to get through a marriage."

Hazel lived in an overcrowded, ratty apartment in a former South Beach hotel which had been converted into a condominium of retired people.

Buck's pulse raced as he made his way along with Susan through the vacant-faced women sitting in rockers in the austere downstairs lobby. Taking the rickety elevator upstairs, he felt he was getting close to the flame: Hazel Phillips, a dreaded Nemesis to her own politically conservative sister, but a champion warhorse fighting for human rights to her legions of fans.

Hazel had arrived in Okeechobee from Abilene twenty years ago when she was only thirty-five. She'd gotten a job as a desk clerk selling dry goods in a South Beach department store owned by Bernie Kahn who'd come here from Brooklyn. From her meager beginning at a salary of sixty-five dollars a week, Hazel had worked her way up to a position of assistant manager, and then had gone one step farther—she'd married the boss, in spite of a twenty-five-year difference in their ages. At first she'd been troubled that he was Jewish. Bernie had convinced her they wouldn't have children anyway—not at his age—so it really wouldn't matter, since neither of them cared much for religion.

At Bernie's death, Hazel had continued to run the department store, earning a modest living which her accountant had assured her would be far better if she'd stop giving away dresses to the women on South Beach living on Social Security.

Later, at the urging of her neighbors, she'd run for a seat on the school board and had won as the South Beach representative. Even though born a Protestant, she'd earned the love and respect of her district.

After three stormy years in the post, the embattled board had breathed a sigh of relief when she'd run for and won a seat on the city council where she'd become a permanent fixture ever since.

At fifty-five, fearing youth and energy running out, she'd thrown her cowgirl hat into the mayoralty race. The hat had become her trademark, and she was often photographed in it, looking like an excessively chubby Annie Oakley—her ample paunch encased in gaucho-style leather pants, held up by an embroidered belt. She always wore her hat rakishly over her left eye, her frazzled hair sticking out in mats.

This was the outfit she wore on her cattle ranch in Central Florida, which had been left to her when her second husband, Bill Monroe, had died. She still retreated there—"But only when the heat's off in Okeechobee," she was fond of saying.

On South Beach, she deserted the cowgirl outfit and looked like everybody's Jewish mama, in a loose-fitting floral-patterned housecoat with wedgies. Her mouth unwiped, Hazel greeted Buck. "Did you eat? We've got plenty."

He declined but shook her hand—her grip was so hard he felt engaged in an endurance contest. The smile—the friendliest in politics—revealed yellowing teeth.

She met Susan with a kiss on both cheeks, her welcome of her warmer and friendlier than her greeting of Buck. But, then, Hazel always welcomed women with more gusto than men, as she felt men had all the advantages any way.

She didn't bother to introduce Buck and Susan to the mélange of guests, mostly campaign workers, sprawled all over the overcrowded living room floor. In the dining room, she found Buck a seat on a bench at a long wooden table. Susan had wandered off to interview some campaign workers, allowing Buck his not-so-private encounter with Hazel. Once more, he declined food from a big pot of chicken dumplings. He settled instead for a cup of black coffee from a girl with long, unwashed hair. Eight other diners, including two elderly women and a large bald fat man, plus five young "strays," as Hazel called them, were seated around the table.

In her booming basso voice, Hazel directed the serving of dinner as if launching a military invasion. "Sarah, bring more sauce. Water or milk? Want a thigh?"

In some way, she reminded Buck of a shadowy weather-beaten version of her more delicately feminine sister. Despite their outward differences, there remained a distinct family resemblance. It was as if Rose had brought out and toned her lovelier features, whereas Hazel had brutalized hers, showing little or no concern for the way she looked. Smelling steam rising from her own plate, she brushed back strands of strawberry blonde hair, now graying, which stuck out in frizzy clumps.

Flashing a mischievous grin at Buck, Hazel said, "Of course, I need to move into that big mayor's house. With the big crowd I've got hanging out here all the time I'm about to suffocate in this tiny apartment."

Later, in her little study, with her desk burdened with unanswered mail, the earth mother settled comfortably on her tattered sofa, placing her stockinged but shoeless feet on her coffee table. She reached for a bowl of peanuts, firing them into her mouth like a machine gun. Then, with a frown, she pushed the bowl aside and shouted into the next room, "Who in hell put these damn peanuts in here? You know I'm dieting."

Around Hazel, Buck felt his senses rejuvenated, his spirit cleansed, after that seductive but morbid meeting with her sister. Hazel had a way of taking Buck outside of himself.

For the first part of the interview, Hazel, as was her way, did all the talking, her monologue taking on extreme urgency. When she slowed down a bit, Buck realized that her face, without intense animation, appeared far older than her years—a complete contrast to the startlingly youthful face of Rose.

"If I didn't know better, I would never guess you were Rose's sister," he said. "How could two sisters be so different?"

Hazel's face took on a constrained and anxious expression. "I never wanted to be like Rose ever. That bitch stands up there in her pulpit, preaching hate and bigotry, using the Bible as her shield."

An aide kept repeatedly interrupting their interview and Buck knew he wouldn't have a monopoly on Hazel's time much longer.

"Rose still thinks we can make this country free for some—and not for others," Hazel claimed.

"What made Rose oppose minorities and you champion them?"

Hazel dropped a peanut in the ample bosom of her housecoat, then quickly retrieved it. "Bernie—you didn't know him—taught me everything I know about human rights, civil rights, whatever. I was a complete redneck when I married him. But as liberal as Bernie was, he would never have accepted women's liberation."

Abruptly changing the subject, Buck asked, "Don't you think Rose is easy to caricature?"

"Hell! I'm easy to caricature as some big overblown cowgirl. Take Sister Rose seriously. She's dedicated. She has said many times, 'the Lord put me on this earth to bring justice.' That means her kind of justice inflicted on people who don't agree with her."

Bouncing off the sofa, she appeared robust, with a lot of unspent energy. "We've got terrible unemployment. Racial conflict. Parts of the beach are decaying slums. Retired widows live on two chicken wings a day, and Rose spends her time preaching hate." She stopped for a moment and confronted Buck, as if challenging him.

The atmosphere made him uneasy, as if there were a peculiar evil to the whole mess he hadn't detected.

A concerned look came over Hazel's face. "We've been getting reports that some of those far right creatures—types you find when you turn over a rock—have been creeping and crawling into town lately. Calder Martin, for instance."

Buck pressed her long and hard, but she could give him no details about the South Beach evictions, other than to say she was fighting them.

"The lid's about to blow off and my people haven't gotten to the bottom of it. I wouldn't be surprised if Rose is connected with it in some way. No, I wouldn't be surprised at all."

He doubted that, feeling Hazel's resentment of Rose seriously discolored her judgment. After all, what possible interest could Sister Rose have in evicting some elderly Jews? Surely the evangelist pursued loftier goals.

An urgent call came in for Hazel and she barked into the receiver before muffling her voice to whisper to Buck. "I think we're heading for big trouble here."

"What kind?" he said with growing agitation, resenting all the intrusions. A group of women came into the study to talk to Hazel.

"You're a publisher," Hazel said as a parting word. "Get one reporter, two, three—as many as it takes—to get out there and dig."

Unknown to her, Buck had done just that.

"Find out what's going on," Hazel demanded. "What they're planning to do. In Kansas, I always knew when to head for the cyclone cellar. I could feel it in my bones."

He smiled, eager to do some snooping on his own. After all, it was too much work for Susan, and there was a sudden sense of urgency.

Going down in the elevator with Susan after leaving Hazel's apartment, he said, "She knows nothing—at least nothing she wants to share with the press. I suspect she knows a lot but just isn't ready to reveal it yet. When she's ready, we can expect a big press conference and a big blast. She hints that her sister's involved in some way but that seems unlikely."

"I know Hazel well. Whenever something rotten's involved, she always suspects Rose."

On this hot, humid night, he headed up the bejeweled strip of beach, wanting—at least temporarily—to forget about politics, although knowing that was impossible. He enjoyed the fresh breeze from the ocean, the glittering lights, and mostly the feel of being behind the wheel and in control of his life.

This night brought back memories of many other happy nights he'd spent driving up the beach with Pamela before all the trouble began. He pondered what Robert was doing right now. Probably missing him something awful. That made him question if he were in control of his life after all.

In a surprise move, Susan moved closer to him in the front seat, taking his free hand as he always drove with only one hand on the wheel, sometimes only a finger. She didn't say anything but held his hand rather tightly. Ever so gently she raised his hand to her mouth and started sucking his thumb.

"Your thumb is really nice and tastes delicious. What I did to your thumb, I could..."

He didn't let her finish her sentence, but came to an abrupt stop in the parking lot of The Rusty Pelican. He grabbed her and kissed her, inserting his tongue in her mouth. He tried to fight the image flooding his brain, but couldn't stop it. All he could think of was not Susan but Gene's penis. That penis had penetrated Susan's mouth the way his tongue was doing now.

As he kissed her longer and harder, Gene's penis became thicker and longer until it exploded in Susan's mouth. He found himself licking her lips after withdrawing his tongue. In his mind it was Gene's semen he was licking from her lips.

*****

In his Volkswagen, Gene pulled into his driveway. Across the street, the stringy-haired Cuban woman, Clara, was out watering her lawn as her little girl, Maria, sat on a tiled portico sucking her thumb. Clara pretended not to notice him, yet he knew she feasted her eyes on him, devouring him, wanting him.

He gripped the steering wheel of his car as tight as he could, almost wanting to back out of the driveway and flee into the night. He wanted to leave this neighborhood behind him, go forward and start somewhere new where he wasn't known, where he didn't have a reputation, where he didn't have to deal with humiliation every day.

Inside the house he stripped down to his briefs and headed right for his bedroom. He didn't have any appetite tonight and wanted to sleep for twelve or fifteen hours. Before going to his chief, Biff, he wanted to get all the evidence he could about this Lolito ring. This could be the big chance to make himself a hero again, and he'd do everything in his power to break the case wide open. It was long overdue that he position himself as a defender of morals, a protector of minors, instead of a corruptor, as he was so often pictured.

Before he turned off the goose-necked lamp, he stared at his small and gloomy bedroom, with its threadbare carpeting and wallpaper of red roses that his mother had applied when he was still in high school. Now stained with age, the roses had turned a faded yellow, almost like urine streaks on the wall. He planned never to change it. Even though his house and its tattered furnishings were decayed, he was determined to keep everything the way it was when his mother died.

His relatives had accused him of killing his mother, giving her cancer, wearing her down and destroying her spirit after his arrest for exposing himself to that little girl. Though the charges had been dropped, he might as well have been found guilty.

He'd agreed to seek psychiatric help, but never had. No one had ever forced him to do that. He'd lost everything after that day, not only the most important tennis match of his career, but Susan, his hero status, and more important than all of those, his best friend Buck.

A light had gone out of his life after that final night with Buck before the game. Buck had revealed his true nature but had run from it, even though Gene was willing to accept Buck for what he really was and move their friendship into a different plateau. He'd been willing to make that sacrifice for Buck who had betrayed him by fleeing. Gene knew Buck wasn't fleeing from him but from himself.

After his arrest, he'd called Buck repeatedly, always getting Robert, who promised that Buck would return his calls. Buck never did, and for all Gene knew Robert never told him he'd called. Gene had a definite score to settle with Robert. That case wasn't closed, at least in his mind.

He tried to erase Buck and that night from his memory. But before going to bed he always thought of Buck and the way their lives should have gone but didn't. That night with Buck had been preceded by a bitter fight with Susan when he'd stormed out of the house. Susan had unknowingly driven him to find solace with Buck who'd offered a warm refuge until he'd so abruptly abandoned him too.

Both Susan and Buck had tossed him aside. Instead of concentrating on his game the next day, he'd thought of them and their betrayals. That's why he'd lost the game. Even in defeat, the crowds had cheered him on, sensing that he was fighting for his life. It wasn't just a game. If he won the match, he could go professional after that. On many a night after that game he would remember the cheers of the crowd. Sometimes the memory of the cheering fans was what kept him alive. He wasn't to hear the cheer of the crowd ever again.

In three months of marriage to Susan, he'd grown bitter and disillusioned. He'd suspected that she was just a whore, even worse than those Cuban sluts his fraternity brothers used to smuggle into the dormitories at night.

His mother had convinced him that a woman endured sex for the sake of a man, but Susan had been completely different. She'd demanded sex for her own pleasure and had increasingly taken the initiative.

Even though she hadn't said anything on their honeymoon, he'd known she wasn't happy with his lovemaking. He'd preferred quick sex, fast relief, and she'd wanted to draw out the act. The night before the game, when he hadn't been aroused by her, she'd said, "I think I know how to bring it to life." His penis had bobbed limply only inches from her face and her fingers had fastened around it, pulling the skin back to expose the head. Then, in a flash, she'd dived for it, her lips slipping over the head, her tongue working frantically to stimulate him. He pushed her away and, losing control, had slapped her face. "You're disgusting," he'd shouted at her.

"It's normal for a woman to want to do that to her husband," she yelled back to him. "You're the one who's not normal."

Her words had stung him like no others, but it was the accusatory look on her face that had done the most damage. Getting dressed hurriedly, he'd stormed out of the house.

She followed him down the stairs, shouting after him. "What does turn you on? Why did you marry me in the first place?"

At the door he'd shoved her back. "Look at yourself," he'd said. "You're like a bitch in heat." He'd slammed the door in her face.

She'd opened the door and ran after him, as if wanting to strike back in some way. Bitterly rejected, she'd stood on the sidewalk looking hurt and humiliated, her torn housecoat half hanging on her body. In her anguish, she'd cried out dangerously loud enough for all the neighbors on the block to hear. "I thought I was getting a *real* man. You're not a man at all!"

He trembled, even now, just thinking about that confrontation. After the tennis match the next day, he hadn't gone to the showers. Still sweating profusely and dressed in white shorts, he'd driven to a slumlike neighborhood in the northern part of the city. Driving blindly, he hadn't remembered how he got there. Actually, he'd disliked that part of town and resented the people who lived there in their crumbling cottages.

From a block away, he'd seen her coming up the street where his car had been parked at an intersection. She'd been like a strange girl-child, and he'd known at once she held the key to unlock some door that had been closed to him. In that inner padlocked cell—like the retreat where he now lived, boarded up from the world—lay the answer to his own manhood.

As she'd drawn closer, he'd taken in her features while at the same time, he'd felt a rising excitement in his tennis shorts. Her petulant mouth had been a deep red, her pale liquid eyes resting behind long lashes. She couldn't have been more than eight years old. Blonde ringlets had fallen casually about her head and the skin of her slim bare arms was the whitest he'd ever seen.

What had attracted him to her was a look of such openness that he'd felt it could reassure him when confronted with the challenge he was about to present to her. Her face had been like a blank piece of paper, waiting for him to make his mark on it.

How could he have known then that in the next fleeting act, his life would be changed for all time? Maybe hers, too. His blood running even hotter than in the heat of the game, he'd called her over and she'd come willingly, innocently, toward him. In vivid detail, he could still recall how eagerly she'd approached the car, as if she'd known and responded to the deep need he had for her.

At the window she'd looked down for the surprise he'd promised her. A chill of delight had come over him. Reaching in, he'd taken out his penis, and she'd watched in stunned fascination as he'd pulled the foreskin back, letting the thick, vermilion head assert itself—blossoming toward her, the blood pulsing through the rope-like veins of his penis. Her piercing scream had made it stiffen all the more. Susan had been a bitch and a liar, accusing him of not being a man. He had his evidence. His manhood was so fierce and powerful that its exposure had filled the girl with fear, and had sent her screaming up the street. The motor of his car still running, he'd stepped on the accelerator and had driven away. It could have been the end of that, if only a neighbor, spotting the running, screaming girl, hadn't taken down his license plate.

With all the willpower he had, he tried to blot out that scream that sounded as real now as it had back then. Kneeling beside his bed, he yearningly clasped his hands, his face still in shadows. He prayed that God would see him through the night.

After his prayer, he got back in his bed and slowly drifted off to sleep. He didn't know how long he'd slept or what time it was, but he was awakened by the ringing of the phone which he kept in the kitchen. Slowly he made his way through the darkened house to the phone. The only people who called any more were those at the station. It was probably some emergency duty that had come up. He didn't really want to go back to work, and only with great hesitation picked up the phone. "Yeah," he said in a gruff manner.

"Hi!" came the voice on the other end. "Hope I'm not calling too late."

The caller quite rightly didn't have to identify himself. He knew at once who it was. "Old buddy." That's what he called Buck. "It's been a long time. Five years to be exact."

"Right you are. Five years, seventy-nine days, thirteen hours, and eight minutes."

"At least you're better at keeping time than being a friend."

"I'm ashamed. I was fucked up in the head. I want you to forgive me."

"I do. I want my old buddy back. I don't want him to go away this time."

"I want to come back. We have a lot of things to talk over. I want to talk to you about this Lolito case that's about to break. I know you've been tipped off."

"How in the fuck do you know that?"

"We heard about it at the Examiner too."

"That makes things a bit more complicated."

"I know. That's why I thought we should talk."

"Is this call about the case or is it about us?" Gene sounded angry, feeling almost betrayed again, and he'd talked to Buck only a few seconds.

"Fuck the case," Buck said. "It's got to be about us first. You don't think I could meet with you again and talk about anything else but us—at least at first—do you?"

"That's more like it. You know the address. Haul ass."

"I'll be there in one hour, old buddy." He put down the phone.

Gene stood alone in the darkness of the kitchen. He couldn't believe what had just happened. With Buck coming over, with him about to break a big high-profile case, his second chance at life had come again.

*****

Buck put down the phone after having just talked to Gene. He found himself trembling a bit at the prospect of a reunion, almost within the hour. He stood in Susan's apartment, surveying her bleak living room, while she'd gone into the bathroom where from the sound she was running bath water. In his car, he'd trailed her here from the parking lot of The Rusty Pelican when she'd invited him back for a night cap. He could hardly take her to his mansion, imagining what the chilly or even hostile reception from Robert would be.

Her apartment was sparsely furnished, the smell of stale beer and cigarette butts. Nothing suggested her delicate beauty or feminine nature. This was the apartment of two fraternity brothers living off campus.

"What do you think?" she said, coming out of the bathroom and wearing only a robe and a smile.

"A little too macho for me," he said. "Haven't you heard of curtains?"

"Back here in the bushes we're not overlooked by anybody. Now if I lived in the house up front, that would be different."

"But someone could easily slip back through the bushes and peer in the windows."

"I hate to disappoint you, but I don't think I'm that popular these days. Maybe back in my beauty queen days."

"Still it's a little scary." He looked her up and down, suspecting she was nude under that robe. Was this a sexual invitation? Uncertain of his next move, he felt himself saying something stupid but his brain seemed programmed to utter the words he couldn't stop. "All these ashtrays filled with cigarette butts. I didn't know you smoked that much."

"I do. But not in public too much. It's a secret vice. The maid comes in only once a week to empty them. There's not much cleaning to do here since I don't own much furniture."

"I see." He surveyed the unkempt room, then picked up a copy of Penthouse, breezily checking some of its more daring photography before letting the magazine cascade down to its resting place on an armchair.

"You thought I read Playgirl? I do sometimes. But I also read Penthouse. I want to know what you men are into."

"I don't know you at all. I expected you'd live in lusher surroundings."

"Not me," she said, her lips forming a mock-pout. "Not on what my boss pays me."

"*Touché*. You're due for a raise first thing tomorrow morning."

"What about a drink?"

"I'd like some Scotch if you have it."

"That I do have. Scotch and vodka—the only two poisons people drink any more. Would you get an ice tray from the refrigerator?" She motioned toward a door in the rear.

In her small, shabby kitchen, he opened the refrigerator finding only a bottle of fizzled out Perrier and a dried-up lime. He removed an ice tray and headed back to the living room. "You don't keep much of a larder either. I'll have to send care packages."

"That's why I stay so slim. Actually I'm a career girl. Not much of a cook. If I'm eating in, I just pick up something at the deli. It's not much fun living alone. If I'd known you were coming over, I would have stocked the refrigerator just to impress you." She poured some Scotch on the rocks and handed him a chipped glass.

"Cheers," he said, clinking glasses with her. He looked deeply into her eyes which seemed to be dancing.

She'd become suddenly playful. "I've run a tub for you. Real hot. Care to join me for a bath?"

He was amazed at her frankness and challenge as well. After denying he was gay, it was an invitation he couldn't refuse. He'd always been intrigued by her and now was his chance for intimacy, a chance that both of them had postponed for years in spite of opportunities. Blocking off thoughts of Robert and Gene, he followed her to the bathroom.

"You can take off your clothes and put them on the chair over there," she said, dropping her robe. Suspicion confirmed. She was completely nude under that robe. Her beauty matched or even surpassed that of Pamela in her prime. Her breasts were extremely rounded and full, although not grotesquely large. He glanced briefly at her nudity and her auburn bush. She eased herself swanlike into the tub. "Come and join me."

He unbuckled his trousers and stepped out of them before removing his white shirt and undershirt. He slipped off his socks leaving him standing before her in only his white briefs. He reached for the elastic band.

"Don't! The moment of unveiling I like to reserve for myself." With deft hands she reached and pulled down his briefs, his big cock bouncing up toward her face where she gave it two quick kisses.

In the hot bath water, they kissed for a long time, stroking each other's bodies. His whole body tingled with excitement as she played with his fully extended erection. The water was scented with something sweet smelling. With a fluffy sponge, she bathed his chest.

A red silk ribbon held her auburn hair in position above her head. Around her white neck a few stray strands dangled. With his fingers, he made curls of them. His hand sliding across her skin, he gently traced his fingers along her neck and shoulders, cupping her breasts and toying with the nipples. His hand glided through the curve of her narrow waist and then went below to explore further.

He gently lowered himself over her and kissed her. The taste and touch of her lips excited him. His hands continued to feel every inch of her body, and he pressed toward her in complete naturalness. They didn't seem like a man and a woman discovering each other for the first time, but familiar lovers who knew secret spots to touch. His hand moved up and around to her shoulders and neck and then, gently, back down to her stomach and hips—sensual, stimulating, making her an object of worship.

She was different from other women he'd known. He found himself doing things he usually didn't—kissing her hand and holding the palm of it against his hot, uneven breath.

She made him feel like something special, that he'd been hiding a part of himself to give only to her.

Her soft, caressing hands moved gently, yet hungrily, over his body. Just as he cupped her breasts again, she reached below to feel his jewels.

He pulled her to him, lifting her from the waist and seating her on his lap, impaling her. He bobbed back and forth, the way a cork rises and falls in water, the scented suds swirling around them, waves churning against soap-polished skins. He surged against her, plunging deeper and deeper, lunging faster and faster to make up for the lonely, lost time he hadn't discovered her before.

Arms locked around his neck, she kissed him with passion, holding him tighter and tighter, sucking his tongue. He could tell by the frenzied look on her face that he was filling some void deep within her. He imagined that no man had filled her like this since Gene had left. Gene and he were alike in only one way. Although their look was different, their genitalia equally matched each other's.

At the memory of Gene's full erection, his own urgency increased. He made her gasp for breath like Gene must have done at one time. Wrapping her long legs around his waist, she clutched him to her.

The water spilled and splattered, and no one cared. Spasm upon spasm overwhelmed him, as her own body gyrated with the force of their flow. Even at the moment of climax, he wondered if it had been like this with Gene. He wasn't seeing and experiencing the glow of her body any more but recalling his plunge into the tight confines of Gene. Images of his friend exploded in his brain, and he couldn't blot them out. He was plunging into Gene and not Susan—buried inside a woman who'd known Gene's powerful strokes.

He looked into her face fearing in some miraculous way she knew what his secret thoughts and desires were.

Her eyes tightly closed, she gave no clue that she knew a third person had intruded into their love-making. She uttered low, soft moans—strange gurgling noises, as she covered his face with wet kisses, tiny bites. Her hair had come undone and fell like a tangle of spaghetti along her neck. She looked like a little girl.

As they lay in the tub together, he gently withdrew from her. The water was turning cold, and he had a reunion to attend. He didn't dare leave her so abruptly. He still stroked her smooth skin, and his hands continued restlessly across her, as if there were new parts of her yet to be explored. But he was not going to be the explorer of this new geography. Not tonight anyway. Gene was waiting for him and even beyond there was Robert in an empty bed.

As he got out of the tub, he felt dirtier than when he'd entered it. He was confused and uncertain of himself.

"You can spend the night, natch?" she asked.

"I'd love to but I can't." He dried himself vigorously with a towel. "Old Buck is sick tonight and he's demanding that I come over. Each time he gets sick, he thinks it's the last time. He always summons me over for last-minute instructions about the future of the Examiner."

"If that's who you're going to see, I can forgive your leaving like this. You'll miss out on a lot of fun and games. Sure it's not Pamela you're secretly meeting later tonight?"

"I'm sure," he said as he hastily dressed. He suddenly felt embarrassed at being nude in front of her.

"There's one thing I'm certain of," she said.

"What's that?" he asked, slipping into his trousers and zipping up.

"There's no way in hell you can be gay."

"That's for damn sure," he said, giving her a long, lingering kiss. "Gotta go."

*****

Buck hadn't been to Gene's house in five years, and he was mildly shocked at how the neighborhood had deteriorated. The streets were once quiet and deserted in the late evening, but now were filled with bodegas and taverns playing loud music. The whole area reminded him of certain streets in Santo Domingo, and he was amazed that Gene had tenaciously held onto his home here and hadn't sold out and gone to another area.

If his old friend were still the same, Buck knew Gene didn't like Hispanics. Buck had been attracted to Gene for many reasons, including some strange chemistry between them, but they'd never agreed on politics. In politics, Gene was much more on the side of Sister Rose and even old Buck himself than he was in Buck's camp.

As he pulled up in front of Gene's house, Buck at first thought he was at the wrong address. The dilapidated house with the yard unmowed looked uninhabited, with no light coming from it. But he'd visited the house far too many times to be mistaken. He strode rapidly up the walkway and rang the doorbell. A long time went by and he rang again.

This time the door opened slightly as someone from behind peered out. "Old buddy, get your ass inside." It was unmistakably Gene.

Buck stepped inside the dark foyer, there to encounter Gene. He was nude except for a pair of skimpy briefs.

"God, it's good to see you again," Buck said, standing only inches from Gene who smelled like he'd just showered.

"It's good to see you too," Gene said. "Strike that good. I'm fucking overjoyed!"

"What are we supposed to do in a situation like this?" Buck asked. "Shake hands."

"How about a hug?" Gene asked. "Just like we used to."

Buck put his arms around Gene and pulled him close. Gene pressed his body hard against Buck as if one embrace could make up for an absence of five long years.

Neither man wanted to break away, and Buck was severely tempted to let his hands start traveling on a journey of exploration across Gene's body. But that was one temptation he wasn't going to give in to.

Gene held on tighter and began to cry. Buck ran fingers through Gene's hair and pulled back to look into his face. His eyes were watering. He kissed Gene firmly on the mouth, taking his hand as he led Gene into his own living room.

"I could offer you a beer—shit like that," Gene said, "but I know you didn't come here for that."

"I came to see you—and to apologize. I'm ashamed." Even as they sat down on the tattered sofa, he held Gene's hand firmly. He looked into his eyes. "I want you to forgive me."

"And I want you to promise never to leave me again."

"I'll always stand by you—no matter what. That is, if you'll have me back as your best buddy. I don't deserve it but I want to be reinstated."

"You've come home again. Welcome back."

He leaned over and kissed Buck hard on the mouth.

Buck kissed him back even harder. It was a fairly large sofa but they occupied only a small part of it. "Remember when we'd known each other for years and were afraid to kiss?"

"All too well," Gene said.

"Then one night on that fishing trip I just leaned over and kissed you."

"It felt good," Gene said.

"When you didn't beat the shit out of me, I kissed you again. And again."

"I didn't want you to stop. But you did."

"I held back," Buck said. "Back then we thought it was okay for men to kiss. But not to go beyond that."

"I know. Missed out on a lot of fun by holding back."

"Today I wouldn't hold back. God, how we fooled ourselves. There were clues. We both got big hard-ons every time we showered together. We'd get erections every time we wrestled."

"There were plenty of clues we had the hots for each other."

"What do you mean had?" Buck asked. Breaking his hold on Gene, he got up from the sofa. "I came here to talk business with you, and we do have some things to talk about, but that's not why I'm really here. I wanted to see you. To touch you. To feel you again."

Suddenly, Gene was behind him, standing real close, rubbing up against him. "No one's stopping you, good buddy. Certainly not me. You've been looking down at the mound in my briefs ever since you came in the door. If you want to rip them off me, feel free. That's what buddies are for."

Feeling nervous and agitated in front of Gene, and thoroughly confused, he moved away, going over to the far corner of the room and sitting down in an armchair. "I have taken your briefs off before and I never thought I would."

"I remember it well," Gene said, coming over to Buck and sitting down at his feet, wrapping an arm around Buck's legs. "It was the night before the big match. I'd stormed out on Susan and called you. We met at that cheap motel near Crazy Mabel's. God, we had a lot to drink that night. I was coming unglued. The most important match of my life and I was drinking heavily. Blowing my big chance."

"I tried to get you to stop but then I had too much to drink, and one thing led to another."

"A lot of that night is fuzzy for me," Gene said. "I remember standing at the latrine. I couldn't unzip my pants."

"If I recall, and I recall very well, I volunteered to assist. A little too willingly if I remember it right."

"Your reaching in and taking me out was something that almost sobered me up."

"Good buddies often have to help each other at the urinal—that's understood," Buck said. But did I really have to reach in and take out your big balls too? You only wanted to piss."

"Maybe you wanted to feel them."

"Maybe I did."

Gene looked up at Buck. "Maybe I wanted you to feel them. Maybe I could have pissed fine by myself. Maybe it was just a trick to make you reach into my pants."

"The whole night seems unreal," Buck said. "We checked into that motel. You asked me to take your clothes off, and I undressed you like an expert. Everything except the briefs. I left them on."

"But not for long."

"Not for long. I had to take them off because I was determined to suck your cock, and I'd never sucked a cock in my life."

"Shit, old buddy," Gene said, getting up abruptly. "You're giving me a fucking hard-on."

He walked across the room, not certain of where to go. Only his rear faced Buck. He seemed embarrassed to turn around.

Buck got up and stood behind him. "I've got to go on. I've denied it to myself too long. I've got to actually say what I'm about to say. I tasted every damn drop. But that wasn't all. When you turned over to go to sleep, I attacked your ass. First with my tongue, then with my dick. I'd never fucked a man before that night—and, believe it or not—I haven't since. But I fucked you. Fuck, Hell! It was rape. I raped you!"

Gene turned around, his erection sticking out of his skimpy briefs. "I met you thrust for thrust, and when you came, I came again."

"I know. I was the guy who then spun you around and licked up every drop."

"We both fell asleep. I was drunk and I don't remember your leaving. But when I woke up the next morning you were gone. No note, nothing. Gone. That was the last time I ever saw you—until tonight."

"I know. God damn it, I know!"

"I've got a bedroom back there, all boarded up from the world. I owe you one, old buddy, for that night." He gently moved Buck toward the rear of the house.

Buck protested. "Aren't we going a little fast here?" He came to a stop near the bathroom, resisting taking any more steps. "I've got to tell you something: I've never been fucked before. I don't think I can take it."

"Your dick's as big as mine. I'd never been fucked before that night either—or ever again. If I could take it like a man back then, I guess you can do the same tonight." Gene leaned Buck against the wall, kissing him real hard and inserting his tongue which Buck eagerly sucked on.

Buck reached for Gene's briefs and pulled them down. Very gently but firmly Gene pressed Buck's head lower. Buck dropped down to his knees as Gene's erect penis bobbed in front of his face. He planted tiny kisses on it before venturing lower to lick Gene's balls. He pulled Gene's foreskin back, took a deep breath, then plunged down on his old buddy.

*****

On the drive back home, Buck could not believe the sudden change that had occurred in his life. His involvement with both Gene and Susan had come about so quickly and without plan that even now it seemed like a film spinning inside his head. That he'd made love to both of them on the same night was unreal.

Yet he knew it was painfully real. In fact, his ass ached from Gene's assault. At last he'd been fucked and by an expert. The searing pain of Gene's entry had been followed by the most exquisite pleasure he'd ever known. Gene literally had him sobbing with pleasure and begging for more. Once Gene got him to his darkened bedroom, Gene had attacked him with a ferocity in love-making unlike Buck had ever known.

Gene had almost eaten him before the penetration. There was a hunger in Gene that both attracted him and repelled him at the same time. He sensed that if flood gates were opened deep within Gene there would be no way to put a stop to them ever again.

Buck agreed to meet Gene tomorrow afternoon and talk about the Lolito ring, and other matters. Their reunion tonight had hardly been the occasion for such talk.

As he pulled into his driveway, Buck was certain of only one thing, and that was his determination to be uncertain. Tomorrow didn't exist. He knew that each of these involvements would unfold. He wasn't in total control. He'd spend a large part of his time responding to the needs of others and their wishes.

Had he now become Susan's lover overnight? Was his involvement with Gene a night of passion that neither would mention and refer to ever again? As he headed for the door and Robert, he knew where his heart lay. It was with Robert. Regardless of what he'd done only hours before, his love was only for Robert. That man was the only constant in his life, and he knew he'd better not fuck it up even though his newly found needs, as realized through Gene and Susan, threatened the only security he'd ever known with anybody.

In a robe, Robert was at the door waiting for him. He kissed Buck hard on the mouth but said nothing.

"I know it's late, and I'm sorry," Buck said. "I should have called. I'm real sorry. You must have been worried."

"Half out of my mind."

"Let's go stand on the terrace," Buck said, taking Robert's hand and leading him across the living room. "Let's breathe the night air together."

Out on the terrace he reached for Robert and pulled him close, inserting his tongue in Robert's mouth which the young man eagerly sucked.

Robert pulled away slightly. "If I didn't know better I'd swear you just had a shower."

"I always smell as sweet as the ocean breeze," Buck said, pulling him close again. "That's what you always tell me, even when I'm back from a fishing trip and haven't had a real bath in two days."

"I think that's when I like to give you a tongue bath the most."

"Stop it," he said, biting and licking Robert's ear. "You're giving me a hard-on."

"I can feel it."

"I stayed later than I thought at Hazel's."

"No, you didn't. You left early and with Susan."

"She's assigned to the story, you know."

"Just so long as she's not assigned to anything else."

"She's not. I don't have sex with my employees. After I dropped her off at The Rusty Pelican parking lot, I went for a long drive and an endless walk along the beach."

"I might not believe that most nights, but strangely tonight I do. You've been loving me like you've never loved me before, and I know this sudden turn of events—after all these years—has been playing on your mind."

He took Robert's hands and held each palm up to his lips, planting gentle kisses. "Thanks for understanding and being here for me. I don't know what's happening to me these days. Like that attack on you before I left."

"I loved it."

"But I'm left feeling I'm coming unglued. In my mind. Everything. It's all mixed up."

"I understand exactly. You're falling in love with me. Really in love with me. The way I've been with you for years. Now you're feeling what I have always felt. You didn't think it would happen to you."

"No, I didn't and I certainly waited long enough."

"You sure did." He took his hand and unbuttoned Buck's shirt and reached inside to feel his chest. "I fully expect you'll do something really crazy over the next few months. I mean, really far out. But I know it's what's expected before you make a final commitment to me. You'll do some things to really piss me off. I just know it. But what I also know is that in the end you'll be mine. You'll never belong to anybody else."

"I never will, old buddy. I never will."

"Old buddy?" Robert looked at him strangely. "You've never called me old buddy before. That's what you used to call Gene."

"Now I called you that." He pulled Robert close to him and kissed him. "Why don't we go to our bed and exchange some body fluids?"

He followed Robert as his friend headed up the steps, after closing the terrace doors. At midway along the stairs, he slapped Robert playfully on the butt. "Don't be surprised if I get a little kinky tonight. Go just a bit farther than before."

"For me, but only with you, there are no limits."

At the door of their bedroom, he removed Robert's robe. He was nude. "God, you're beautiful. The most beautiful man I've ever seen. And you're mine."

"Your exclusive property."

He bent down and kissed each of Robert's nipples. "Tonight my tongue's going to go where it has never gone before. If you can get so much pleasure out of licking every crevice of my body, the same pleasure can be mine."

"That promise is worth waiting for half the night."

He picked up Robert in his arms and carried him toward their bed. He didn't have to worry about getting undressed himself. Robert was an expert at doing that for him.

*****

Susan placed her receiver back on its hook and returned to her bed. She'd just called old Buck's estate and had spoken to his black butler. Buck had left some important-looking documents at her place when he'd hurriedly left, and she felt he might need them early in the morning. She was going to volunteer to run them over to old Buck's estate.

"I'm sorry Mr. Brooke is ill," she'd told the butler.

"He's not ill. He walked for about a mile along the beach today. One of his longest walks. After dinner, he went to bed at eight thirty."

"You mean he's not sick and his grandson isn't coming over tonight?"

"That old man's not sick. We haven't seen that grandson around here in more than a week."

"I see. Thanks anyway. I'll take the papers into his office in the morning."

"That would be very nice of you. Even as a kid, that child always forgot something."

"Good night." She returned to her bed but couldn't go to sleep. Why had Buck lied to her? He didn't have to lie under the circumstances, but he had. Where could Buck have gone that he didn't want her to know?

This was a troubling beginning to what had the promising ring of an exciting new relationship in her life. She turned over in bed but her mind wouldn't go to rest. A thought occurred to her. He didn't go off to have a reunion with Gene, or did he? He'd already told her he was going to do that, so that was hardly a secret.

Brushing it from her mind, she shut her eyes and went to sleep remembering that scene in the bathroom with Buck. That's what she'd thought life with Gene would be like but it wasn't.

With Buck, she'd found a new reason to be alive.

Chapter Three

After the sexual marathon of last night, Buck was tired and instead of sitting at his desk, he lay on the office sofa on his back, dictating some urgent letters into a machine. He flip-flopped to his stomach and reached for another cigarette, though his present one still wasn't burned down. Sticking it in the corner of his mouth, he continued talking into the tape recorder. The telephone rang but he didn't bother to answer it. Robert had stepped out of the office briefly to deliver a contract to the legal department.

Finishing the letters, he proof-read his Sunday column which Robert had left for him. He decided it was crap. He wanted to tear it into pieces, tossing the bits of paper around the room like confetti. But he decided to run with it anyway. With everything that was happening in Okeechobee, he didn't need to be writing about why plans were stalled for a new city hall. The town was more interesting than that. A hell of a lot going on, and he was not reporting any of the action so far.

A rap at his door, and Roland—shod in his bedroom slippers— came into his office in his usual lurching gait. "You're here early, boss," he said, wandering over to open the draperies and plop himself in Buck's favorite armchair.

"Yeah," Buck said, blinking in the glaring morning light. "My column for tomorrow is shit." He rubbed his dazed and glassy eyes. "Proof it for me if you will. Throw in a few better lines if you can think of any."

"I'll do that." Roland spoke in a dull, hoarse monotone, almost a whisper. "I've been cleaning up your copy for years."

"Don't rub it in."

"You look like you've had a bad night."

"You got that right. Hell, man, with half the beauty queens in town clamoring for my bod, what's a guy to do?"

"You're lucky. With my ailments and afflictions, I have only my memories."

Buck glanced at his disappointing column again. "I thought I'd do something about the mayoralty race. Speculating on Hazel's chances against Barry. And to tantalize the reader, the prospect of Rose coming out against her own sister to support Barry." He waited for Roland's reaction.

When none was forthcoming, Buck went to the bathroom, pulled off his shirt and started to shave. He'd showered earlier, but had completely forgotten about his beard. He left the door open so he could talk to his city editor.

"Did Rose convert you the other night?" Roland asked, an amused look in his eyes.

Buck twisted his head and glanced at Roland and then at his own face in the mirror. "Not quite." He turned to Roland, his eyes imploring, "Do you think she's just a hypocrite?"

Roland took out his handkerchief and mopped his brow, as the faucet was creating a lot of steam. "In many ways she reminds me of an old-time Los Angeles faith-healer, Aimee Semple McPherson. Before your time, I know. She once stunned her congregation by roaring out on a shiny black police motorcycle—dressed completely in black leather, even thick black leather boots. A traffic cop for Christ. That beat all I've ever seen."

"Yeah," Buck said, almost kicking himself. "I remember that story. Something about a fake kidnapping when she'd run off with her lover."

"Aimee *really* lived a double life—believe you me. I was almost one of her converts."

Buck smiled and rinsed the lather from his face. "I didn't know you had a past," he said jokingly. He reached for his shirt and headed back to the office. "I'm suspicious of Rose. I just don't buy her act. She comes on real pious in public, so I've heard. I think there's a very sensual woman there."

"I'm convinced of it," Roland said. "There have been many, many stories. In my day, I've seen enough of these self-styled messiahs who blend theater with salvation. I've seen them create their fantastic temples and their big bank accounts. We used to call them the 'P.T. Barnums of religion.' Nowadays, they don't need a circus tent. They have TV. I think we've got another one on our hands. Sister Rose herself."

"Someone told me she finds the wages of sin just great if it leads to a big collection plate."

"Exactly."

Buck sat down at his desk, a strong, determined look coming onto his face. Looking up, he said to Roland, "I think we'd better start looking at her pretty closely. Grandpa thinks she's a saint, so he did nothing but puff her. But I think she's not that at all. She's very mysterious. There's a lot going on we don't know a damn thing about. Do you think she's got a lover? Lovers?"

"More than one. I'm sure just one man could never satisfy Rose Phillips." Roland settled wearily into his armchair. "Sex and religion among the big-name evangelists have mixed in this country for a long time. If you remember your mythology, many of the ancient gods and goddesses had greater sexual appetites than you and me put together."

"Speak for yourself," Buck said facetiously. "I know something about mythology, but mainly I remember psychology at the university. My professor said that many Freudians felt religious feelings were libidinous."

"If behind this preacher against sin, we find a sinner herself," Roland said, "I wouldn't be surprised. It'd be following in the footsteps of tradition. Many—maybe most—religious cult figures in America enjoyed voracious sex appetites."

Buck fell silent, his mind preoccupied. His phone rang again and he motioned to Roland not to answer it. He closed his eyes briefly, remembering the smell of Rose and how her auburn hair had brushed across his cheek as she'd kissed him good night.

"Are you willing to expose her without mercy?" Roland asked pointedly.

Buck didn't want to be committed like that. "I don't know...maybe," he said. "I've heard a lot of reports about her. Megalomaniac. Outright psychotic. She's a strong and powerful woman, with a big following that's growing fast with this charismatic movement. Any attack the Examiner might run could just increase her contributions. Of course, we'll be branded as part of the 'godless Commie lunatic fringe.'"

Roland rubbed his back and seemed to suffer some intense pain. "You're used to that."

"I suspect Rose is giving a new twist to a long tradition of religious fakery and fanaticism in this country." He placed a bottle of aspirin in front of Roland and handed him a glass of water. "I think she's going to become better known than Billy Graham."

"What is she after?"

"I can't figure her out yet. Money. Power. Her foundation is already one of the most heavily bank-rolled in America. The country's changing real rapidly, too rapidly for a lot of good people out there. Rose provides a lot of easy answers to complex riddles. In her vocabulary, good is good and evil is evil, and she doesn't want to talk about the graduations in between the way her sister does."

"You seem really..." Roland paused, then added, "troubled by her."

"I know," Buck said nervously, "Rose seems aggressive, ruthless. I mean, she could acquire a lot of power. She's got a lot of power now, but..."

"You mean, big power?"

"Yeah. She could be *real* big. I guess that's what scares me. She was quoted as saying, 'You can't fight the devil with just a gospel song.' I'd like to find out what she means by that."

"Sounds ominous."

Buck raised the shade to the window overlooking the news rooms. Just as he did, he spotted Susan heading for her desk, after handing over some documents to Buck's receptionist. He realized he'd left important papers behind at Susan's apartment.

"I suspect Rose wants to lead a moral crusade—you know, clean up America," Buck said. "I've heard rumors to that effect. I think she can pull it off, too. She's already a cult figure. She's got a glib tongue. Like your friend, Aimee, she has real showmanship. She knows enough about people to play on their deep-rooted fears." He looked toward Susan again. "Rose also has that chief prerequisite. A real ego bordering on the narcissistic."

Roland got up, after making a few notations on a pad. "If she's going to launch a moral crusade, let's find out something about its leader."

Buck turned and faced Roland squarely. "I plan to do just that. Her so-called autobiography is a lot of braying brass. Lines like 'my recorded gospel songs have provided inspiration for millions of lost souls.' I want to find out what that voice of sunshine and sweetness is like when it warbles off-key."

"It's just a hunch," Roland said. "You know, an old news hound's hunch. But I wonder if Rose and the South Beach thing are part of the same story."

Just then, Robert came into the office, looking toward Buck. "God's anointed is on the phone."

Bolting to attention, Buck signaled to Roland that he'd like to take this call in private. When the city editor had gone, he picked up the receiver. "I was going to call you," he said, "and thank you for dinner the other night."

Like a cooing, billing lovebird, she said, "I called you last night. I got your unlisted home phone. No answer...I bet you were out dating some very pretty young girl. I've heard tales about you."

Buck recalled last night, but said nothing.

After a slight, awkward pause, she said, "I want to extend another invitation. I'm known, you see, for my southern hospitality. This time, I want you to attend services at my temple. Tomorrow morning at ten." Her soft laughter was almost like a girlish giggle. "*Sinner*."

"I'm not much for church going." In blurred vision, he remembered her face telling him good night. For some reason, he hadn't dared look into her eyes as she'd kissed him good-bye. The kiss, weirdly distinct, lingered on his cheek.

"No, seriously," she said in a more businesslike tone, "this is going to be totally different from my usual gospel hour. It's going to be..." She paused, as if to hold him in suspense. "Newsworthy. I'm not telling you any more. Bye, handsome." She hung up.

Robert stood staring at Buck. "If I heard right, I assume she invited you to her temple. You're not going, are you?"

At first Buck wasn't certain. "Hell, yes, I'm going. I'm starting a series on her, and I've never seen the bitch in action. Want to come with me?"

"Do I ever want to come with you! After last night, more than ever. If you step into our little private room in back, I'll prove it."

"Come on, now. Don't think about sex all the time. You know what I mean. Will you get me out of bed Sunday morning in time?"

"Perhaps. I'm not too good at kicking you out of bed."

"This one time. Promise."

"I promise. But on one condition."

"Conditional love. What are the terms?"

"That you do to me tonight what you did to me last night."

"You got a date, hot stuff." His thoughts turned to Rose again. "Sure you don't want to go with me Sunday morning?"

"I'll get out of bed, I'll bathe you, I'll dress you, but I need the rest of Sunday morning for my beauty sleep. With all the competition I have for you, I've got to look my best."

"As you wish, but this Rose is no ordinary woman. She's carefully packaged herself and is hell-bent on cashing in while she's in her prime. I have a funny feeling she's planning some special entertainment for me Sunday morning at her temple."

*****

As much as Gene tried to concentrate on his work, images of Buck flashed through his mind. He felt he was coming unglued. One part of him wanted to run in one direction, whereas another part of him told him everything was wrong and urged him to take a different path. There were times, and he didn't want anybody to know this, that he felt he was two different people. With Buck, the bad Gene had taken over, doing everything the good Gene told him not to. He'd need to seek redemption for that, yet at the same time he was eagerly awaiting his late afternoon meeting with Buck. In fact, he could hardly get his work done for thinking of his old buddy and seeing him again.

In the past few months, except for those dark furtive times when he ventured into the cesspools of the city, the good Gene had taken over. He'd tried to do what was right, but he'd never been able to prevent himself from giving in to the world's temptations.

In spite of himself, he couldn't deny the pleasures he'd experienced alone with Buck. He'd never known such exquisite joy could be possible with another human being. He'd have to be careful. His meetings with Buck had to be conducted in secret. Even though he loved his old buddy and wanted to be with him every minute of every day, he knew that wasn't possible. What they were doing was evil and wrong. Their private business had to be just that—private. He'd find places to meet with Buck alone and away from the eyes of the world. He couldn't face the judgment of the world condemning him again.

Even now he understood so little about anything. Although he'd been condemned and nearly ruined by his exposing himself to that little girl, he knew that in some pockets of the city lived people who welcomed his exhibitionism. Wherever he went there were places, ranging from latrines to bathhouses, where people wanted him to display himself before them. They were not condemning but worshipful. They wanted to see him in all his male glory, fully exposed and fully aroused. He was treated like a God. In some way, they made up for all the rejection. And after last night he'd won Buck over too. The way Buck had bitten his ear, licked his neck, and moaned in passion had told Gene all he needed to know: no one had penetrated Buck Brooke before. No one had reached the deep inner recesses of his body, certainly not Robert Dante. Of that, he was certain. Gene had been sailing in virgin waters. He just knew that. He eagerly awaited a repeat performance this afternoon.

Even if the devil himself had returned Buck to his life, he couldn't resist the allure of the man. The chemistry between them had been like nothing else he'd ever known. Certainly not with Susan. He'd married Susan, wanting Buck, and look what had happened to that sham of a marriage. He had every intention of seeing Buck on the tennis grounds later in the day. He'd deal with his sin and seek forgiveness, but not now. A need within him was so great he could not turn it off. He cursed himself for his weakness, although having every intention of giving in to it.

His face tightened in a fierce grip as he tossed some papers in a pile on his desk, creating a cloud of dust. As he looked around his tiny cubbyhole of an office, he dreaded the morning's interviews, the new revelations. As a sudden chill swept across him, he slapped his arms across his body and rubbed his hands across his broad chest.

He was deep into an investigation of the Lolito ring but had a long way to go. The address at 230 Bayshore Drive appeared to be the center of an underage boy sex ring. In an hour or so he'd learn the name of the owner of that building. That owner, from all he could gather, arranged for older men, so-called pillars of the community, to meet young boys at little parties. The oldest boys were probably no more than sixteen. He had to find some way to penetrate that ring. He'd told none of this to his chief yet. He wanted a good, strong case before presenting his evidence. It was his big chance and he couldn't fuck it up.

He wanted to see what was actually going on in that house before any arrests were made. Although Buck and the Examiner knew about the case already, he could count on his old buddy to cooperate with him.

The call came in from City Hall earlier than he'd expected. The owner of the house at 230 Bayshore Drive was Leroy Fitzgerald. Gene slowly put down the phone and got up and walked over to the lone window in his office. He looked out at the morning sunshine through the dirty streaks in the glass. The window hadn't been washed in years. He felt a sense of suffocation. Leroy had to be the same photographer who'd snapped the frontal nude of him in the locker room back at college. He knew that Leroy had always lusted for him, and had printed copies of that photograph of Gene to distribute among his gay brethren.

He also knew that Leroy had photographed two centerfolds in Florida for Playgirl. He'd begged Gene to pose for one, and Gene had almost hit him in the face. He was lucky to have this police job. All he needed now was to expose himself in a national magazine. That would be the end of his career for sure. How he wished the owner of that house had been somebody he didn't know, not someone he'd gone to the university with, not someone who had a connection with him, regardless of how remote. He wanted this case to be something new and different for him, and already he was getting sucked back into the past. He sighed and didn't know how to proceed from here.

What he'd heard from everybody, and what he secretly suspected himself, was that Leroy was in love with him. At first it'd started out as a crush, but had developed into an obsession. He'd always spurned

Leroy's advances, and could have prevented him from snapping that frontal nude. But he hadn't. When he spotted Leroy taking pictures back in that locker room, he'd turned his back to Leroy and had soaped himself, making himself even larger than he already was. When he turned around, Leroy had snapped away. Pretending not to notice, Gene had closed his eyes and turned his face up to the jet spray of water. He'd both welcomed yet shunned Leroy's attentions. The only way Gene could define himself was through his contradictions.

He reached for his jacket. Leroy or not, he had to get on this case. To do that, he was headed for the Combat Zone. At least some of the boy prostitutes who worked there had to know about Leroy's Lolito ring.

*****

Heat wiggles wavered over white sand as Buck pulled off his clothes on his own private beach located on a secluded cay about three miles from the Okeechobee coastline. After getting out the Examiner, he'd come to his island with Robert. His parents had acquired the small cay when he was just a kid, and Buck felt he'd virtually grown up here, retreating to the island whenever he could get away from his duties.

Although he had to return to the city in the afternoon, Buck wanted to be photographed on the island for the magazine that very likely would name him "The Sexiest Man of the Year." He felt silly about the whole thing, but was determined to see it through. His own public relations department had set it up in the belief that such massive publicity would forever erase the image of the old ultra-conservative Examiner as led by his grandfather and would ignite a fire in the circulation department when the paper's dynamic new leadership under the third Buck Brooke was widely revealed across the nation.

Robert had insisted on coming along for the shoot. "There's no way I'm going to let you be photographed on a deserted island without me there hawkeying every shot."

Robert had been relieved when he learned that the reporter from the magazine was a well-known dyke. "We'll have no trouble from her," he said. Britt Smithey from their own paper was hired as the photographer. "That guy's so straight he'd make Richard Nixon look like a faggot," Robert had said. "So I think you're going to be okay, but I'll be here anyway seeing that you don't expose too much. Those goodies of yours belong to me."

A blinding orange ball, the sun rose high in the sky over Buck's own mangrove swamps. From the beachfront house, Robert emerged, walking down the sandy path with a white terrycloth robe.

His back in the sand, Buck flexed his muscles, kicking his legs in the air as if riding a bicycle.

"So that's how Arnold Schwarzenegger does it," Robert said with a mischievous grin, as he handed Buck his robe.

"Listen," he said, rising up from the sand and squinting his eyes in the sun. "I want to look as good at fifty as I do now."

"You mean, like Rose Phillips?"

He didn't answer, closing his eyes and turning his face to the blazing sun. He wanted to look good and tanned for the photographer.

Enjoying the last of the morning, he remembered the tropical fish he'd seen swimming in their natural habitat and the rusty wreck he'd photographed earlier. Opening his eyes again, he took in the bright, brilliant glow the sun cast over the pure white beach, the reflections made on iridescent seashells. Somehow that erased the memory of Rose from his mind. But it didn't erase the memory of Gene. Even now he was looking forward to their meeting back in town that afternoon. He was nervous and even a bit shaky at the prospect.

At the beach bar, Robert splashed a Bloody Mary with another drop of Tabasco and handed it to him.

"You make the best Bloody Marys in the world, and you know I couldn't get through a Saturday morning without one. Or a Sunday morning."

"I'll make you a stiff one before you leave the house tomorrow morning to listen to that bitch preach."

Not wanting to talk about Rose, Buck opened his robe and grabbed his balls. "I may give you a stiff one right now."

"Promises, promises. We'll have to put it on hold. But I'm going to have you tonight. Every bit of you. But just as soon as you finish that Bloody Mary, I'm going to give you a bath. You've got sand all over you."

Nude with Robert in the shower, Buck liked the way he was being soaped down by his friend, every part of his body washed. It was a time to relax and let Robert do the work. Robert even washed his ears for him.

On signal from Robert, Buck bent over, making himself an easy target for what Robert was going to do to him. Buck braced himself against the tiles, and Robert knelt down and firmly massaged Buck's ass before opening his cheeks. Within moments, Robert was tonguing him, making him moan in passion. Nothing in his life ever felt this good, and Robert was clearly a master. Robert couldn't seem to get enough of this very, very private part of him. One Saturday afternoon, alone in their bedroom on the island, Robert had stayed glued to his target for almost two hours. Even then he'd seemed willing to continue until Buck had pulled him up to his face to kiss his lips and taste his own scent.

A loud knock on the bathroom door ended Buck's pleasure far too abruptly for him. "Mister Robert, Mister Robert," came the voice of Henry, Buck's tall black servant. It was an emergency call. Robert stood up and kissed Buck on the mouth before stepping out of the shower and covering himself with a terrycloth robe, as he opened the door and headed for the phone.

A little later Buck walked nude into their bedroom, toweling himself dry.

Robert was just hanging up the phone. "Oh, shit! Britt was riding in Bayfront Park on his motorcycle. He slid, fell off, and broke his arm."

"There goes my best photographer. I'm sorry. We'll call him and wish him a speedy recover. Does that mean today's shoot is off?"

"Not at all. At least from the magazine's point of view. From my point of view, I want to cancel the whole thing."

"What do you mean? They can get another photographer."

"They have. Leroy Fitzgerald."

Buck was startled. "Our little sleaze Leroy. Happy school days. Happy golden rule days."

"There's no way that I'd want Leroy photographing you. I saw that frontal nude he took of Gene. He's also a centerfold photographer on occasion for Playgirl. There's no way I'm going to let you do that. Expose yourself in that way."

"Fuck, it's a family magazine. I'm not posing nude, and they don't run nude photographs anyway."

"I guess it'll be okay if I'm around to watch that Leroy's every move."

"Actually, I want some time alone with him."

"What's that supposed to mean?"

"This is my perfect opportunity. He's the leader of that Lolito ring. I can't let him know I know that. I need to figure out some way to entrap him into giving me information. After the shoot, I'll go for a walk along the beach with him. I may learn nothing. But then I might. It's a chance to take."

"Okay, if that's the way it is. I'll entertain the dyke. We'll talk about pussy, I guess, although that's one subject I don't know anything about—and I mean anything."

At the table Henry had set up for them on the patio, Buck tasted the raw conch marinated in garlic and key lime juice.

"What's the matter?" Robert asked. "You look real troubled."

"I am, and it's about us."

"You and I are doing fine. Damn fine. The last two days alone have been the most terrific of my life."

"You're still working too hard to please. You're always doing things for me, and I feel guilty about it. I do so little for you."

"You do everything for me. You always have. Ever since we first met. You even provide a home for me."

"Hell, you could have bought your own home years ago if you'd ever wanted to. I know you've saved the first dollar you've ever made."

"It's yours if you ever need it. I've saved every dollar because I've never spent any money. You provide for everything. You, the same man who claims he's never done anything for me. You even support my mother and pay the rent on her condo."

"It's not that. I want you to take more time off. At least when you come to this island with me. You're my friend, not just the hired help. Henry can take care of us. You're always getting my robe, fixing my drinks. Even giving me a bath. Maybe I should be the one giving you a bath. I want you to stop all this. Rest. Read a book. Go boating. Stop fretting about me all the time."

Robert looked into Buck's eyes, and he knew at once how much he'd hurt his friend.

Robert dropped his fork and stood up. "Did it ever occur to you that my whole life is based on doing things for you? You're everything to me. Without you, there would be nothing." He turned and left the table, heading alone down the stretch of white sandy beach.

Shoving his plate of conch aside, Buck ran after him, easily catching up. He reached for Robert's arm, detaining him. "I was a shit. Forgive me. Everything you do for me is just great. It really is. If you say I don't have to feel guilty, then..." He paused awkwardly. "It's just great."

Robert's look was open and trusting, almost like a child's. "You mean that?"

"I do." Buck put his arm firmly around Robert and directed him back toward the patio. "Hey, kid," he said. "Finish your lunch. You're going to need all your strength when I attack you tonight."

Robert reached over and firmly gripped his hand. "Don't ever tell me to stop doing what I do."

"I won't. Ever again. I promise." Sensing some deep need within his friend, he said, "After lunch, and only if Leroy and the dyke are late, would you massage and lick my balls like you always do? I'm tense today. Nothing makes me more relaxed than that." Remembering the shower, he quickly added, "That and the other thing you do."

Predictably, Leroy and the reporter were late. Buck got his massage and licking while he enjoyed a cigar, leaning back on the soft sofa to enjoy both Robert's mouth on him and the smoke. What he hadn't really told Robert was how much he liked it this way, with him in charge and Robert doing his bidding. How different it was with Gene, when the roles were reversed, when Gene was the aggressor demanding and taking pleasure from Buck's body like no one else had ever done before. He couldn't understand how both men brought out a completely different side of his personality, each fulfilling him as no other had before. His only wish was that Gene and Robert could be found in one man.

When Robert had completely satisfied him, he ran his tongue along the length of Buck's penis, raised up and kissed him long and passionately on the mouth. Robert then got up. "I wish those guys would hurry up so we could get this shoot over with."

"I do too," Buck said. "You know I have to return to the city this afternoon. A little investigative reporting around Rose's charismatic foundation before tomorrow morning. Want to go with me?"

"I'd better stay here. Get things ready for our romantic Saturday night dinner."

Buck was delighted when Robert turned down the invitation. He deliberately concealed from him that he was meeting with Gene.

While Robert went to answer the latest calls that had come in, Buck returned to the white beach. Once here, he let the hushed, muted beauty of the cay fill his system. He didn't want to think—at least not now, fearing his thoughts would betray him. Fists clenched, he was filled with a raging passion but it seemed so misdirected. All the various loves and needs he was feeling weren't going according to standard guidelines. Why couldn't he love just one person and settle down? Why did he need to turn to so many people for fulfillment?

On the beach, his body was taut. He soaked up every ray of the sun and braced himself for the coming afternoon which stretched out before him as long as the white sandy beach. The beach appeared nonthreatening but at any moment danger could wash up along its shoreline.

When he got back to the house, Robert was there. "They're here," he said rather nervously. "I told them to wait in the living room. I got this pair of jeans and a T-shirt for you. Buck Brooke III, young publishing executive, at rest on his private island."

"Thanks a lot." He took Robert's hand and held it up to his lips, kissing the inner palm.

Robert kissed him lightly on the lips. "I've got to go." At the door he paused. "Oh, Susan called. She wants you to call her right away."

"It's about that story I've got her on."

"I hope that's what it is," Robert said before turning and heading down toward the living room.

He walked over to the phone and started to dial Susan's number. He dialed only three digits before he put down the phone. Talking to Susan was a little more than he could handle right now. His most immediate agenda was dealing with Leroy after all these years. Rather tense and nervous, he headed for the living room following Robert's trail.

*****

At the Combat Zone, Gene cruised by in his unmarked police car, hoping to appear as a prospective john. He noticed two young Cuban mariposas, looking no more than sixteen, eying him. At the sight of him, one of the young boys licked his lips lasciviously but Gene ignored them, driving around, circling the square.

As he neared one teenage boy on the street corner, memories of exposing himself to that young girl came back racing through his mind, causing him to break out in a cold sweat.

The young boy with red hair appeared no more than thirteen. Beautifully featured and lithe, he looked like the type of boy Leroy would recruit to work his Lolito ring. Gene reached over and unlocked the door on the right side of his car. Without hesitation and with perfect ease, the teenage boy opened the door and eased into the front seat. He was sipping coke from a Dixie cup. "God, you look like one handsome stud," the boy said. "Hi, I'm Sandy. What's your name?"

"Ralph," Gene said, inventing a name. "Care to go for a drive with me?"

"I'd love to. But I get twenty bucks if you want to fuck my tight ass."

"There will be a twenty in it for you."

"I hope you're not a cop," Sandy said. "The other night two cops grabbed me. I thought they wanted to make it with me. Nearly all the cops I meet want sex. I dig uniforms. I've had at least a dozen cops in the past year. When I get older, I'm gonna join the force, too."

Gene didn't like the smirk on the boy's face as he turned his car and headed away from the twilight zone. The boy looked as if he knew too much, far beyond his years. Gene found himself perspiring heavily, and the young boy seemingly sensed his discomfort. He slouched down in the front seat provocatively, cupping his crotch and beginning to rub it for Gene's benefit.

"Stop that!" Gene shouted louder than he'd intended. "Sit up and behave yourself."

At first Sandy looked as if he hadn't heard right. "Isn't playing with my crotch what it's all about?"

"Maybe. But not here. Later, perhaps."

"Oh, I get it. This is your first time with some boy ass. You're married, right? You're a little embarrassed about the whole thing. That right?"

"Something like that," Gene said, steering the car down by the old water reserve. This was always a nearly deserted park except for some sex-hunters.

As they neared the park, Sandy looked disappointed. "Don't you have a place to go? I was hoping to get worked over by you in a nice comfortable bed. With a guy who looks as good as you, I wouldn't even charge to let you fuck me." He reached over and felt Gene's crotch. "God damn, I don't know if I can handle one that big."

Gene firmly removed Sandy's hand from his crotch.

"You're one uptight mother-fucker."

"Yeah," was all Gene said.

Parking near some deserted picnic tables, Gene got out of the car and signaled Sandy to follow him along the embankment with a stone wall marked by graffiti.

"You're not much of a talker," Sandy said. "What are you into?"

"I'll tell you. Instead of that twenty, how about a hundred instead?"

"A hundred dollars!" The boy looked astonished, then a frown crossed his brow. "Oh, shit. You're a sadist. You're going to torture me for that, aren't you?"

"I'm not going to touch you."

Sandy continued to stare at him in disbelief. "I don't get it. I can't believe you're going to give me a hundred dollars just to have me jack off in front of you."

"You don't have to do anything like that. In fact, keep your fly zipped—and I mean that. What I want is information."

"What kind of information could I have that you'd be willing to pay one-hundred dollars for?"

"You figured, I'm in the closet. I've got to really watch my step. But I hear there's a house in town. A place where men like me can go and meet young boys like yourself. Where it's all private and confidential."

"You want to get included in one of those little parties, right?"

"Yeah."

"That's information I can supply. I work there every Friday night. I pick up quite a few bucks that way. One night I had seven different guys. God, did I have a sore ass the next morning."

Gene reached out to touch the boy but instinct made him withdraw quickly. He looked up ahead along the path that led by a stone wall. Not another person in sight. "Kid, if you want to earn that hundred bucks, as we walk along I want you to describe one of those parties for me. Go into as much detail as you can. I like a lot of detail."

Sandy smiled. "This is gonna be the easiest hundred dollars I've ever earned. I'll give you the juicy scoop. A blow-by-blow description."

Sandy kept his promise. As they walked along, he related to Gene in vivid detail one of Leroy's parties where underage boys danced with older men to booming sounds as in a disco. The boys then stripped and formed a circle in the middle of the room under a chandelier, creating a giant flower of flesh, their adolescent limbs fanning out to evoke petals. The older men—doctors, educators, lawyers, bankers, even politicians—formed a choo-choo train, crawling around on their knees to taste each "flesh petal." Later, each of the older men bid for their favorites at an auction and took them to one of the private bedrooms upstairs.

At the end of his walk and after an hour's description from Sandy, Gene came to a stop at the clearing where the water drained into tanks. He reached for a cigarette.

"Could I have one, mister?" Sandy asked. "You don't have a joint, do you? I mean, a joint different from that obvious mound between your legs?"

"Here, take a cigarette," Gene said, handing him one and lighting it for him. "Considering what you do for a living, giving you a cigarette seems relatively harmless."

"Did I tell you enough to earn my bread?"

"You surely did." Gene sucked in the smoke as images of that sex ring flooded his brain. Sandy had actually been very articulate. At least

Gene knew the mechanics of how the place worked and even some of the club members. Leroy was definitely the master of the bordello. There was no doubt about that, and the address was indeed 230 Bayshore Drive. But what troubled Gene was his awareness that for such an operation to function smoothly, it had to have protection high up. Someone big and important had to be profiting from this operation. He turned to the boy again. "How can I get included one evening?"

"That I can't help you with. Not just anybody can join. It's very secretive. Leroy has to approve of it in some way. Occasionally bigshots from out of town get invited by a member. But it's hard for a local guy to get membership—or so I've heard. It's all very hush-hush. Leroy likes to keep it quiet."

"I can see that he would."

Sandy reached for Gene's crotch again. "There's a men's room over there," he said, pointing to a little concrete structure a few hundred yards away."

Gene removed the boy's hands from his crotch. "I'm fine."

"C'mon," Sandy said. "At least let me blow you. You're the best looking man I've ever seen. If you can get an invite to one of Leroy's parties, please go up to one of the rooms with me. I need a real man to shove it up my ass. Not those two-inch dicks I usually end up with. Did you know that a two-inch dick hurts more than a ten-incher?"

"No, I didn't, and I don't think I'm into finding out."

"I figured you for the fucker—not the fuckee."

"You got that right." Gene reached into his wallet and handed the boy five twenty dollar bills.

"That's great, mister, even if you won't plug my ass."

"I'm taking you back to the Combat Zone. How do I get in touch with you if I need to speak with you again?"

"I'm homeless, but you can always reach me in the zone."

Before returning him to the square, Gene stopped at a roadside diner where Sandy wolfed down three fried eggs and six pork sausages. "I've got an idea how you might get invited to one of Leroy's parties. But you've got to put out."

"Forget it. There's going to be no sex between us." Gene looked around nervously, hoping no one recognized him at this place dining with a teenage boy.

"I didn't mean sex with me. I mean sex with Leroy. Although he recruits young boys, he actually likes older studs like you."

"How's that going to get me an invitation to one of the boy parties?"

"Every morning around ten o'clock Leroy heads for the Vulcan Baths. You know where they are, don't you?"

"What do you think?"

"I thought so. You flash all that meat you've got—and we're talking meat for the poor here—and Leroy will be slurping away. He'll fall for you and big. He's always complaining he can't find enough guys with big meat at the baths. Wait until he gets a glimpse of you."

"Thanks for the tip. I might take you up on that."

Back at the Combat Zone, Gene turned to Sandy and thanked him. He liked the boy and felt a pang of regret at turning him loose into that square again, not knowing what weirdo he was likely to meet next.

Sandy looked briefly in Gene's eyes and seemed reluctant to get out of the car. "I'd really like to make it with you, mister. With you, I'd do anything. You could fist me if you really wanted to, although I don't like that. I'd even lick your asshole clean after you've taken a big crap."

"Stop it!" Gene said with an anger coming into his voice. "I wouldn't ask you to do anything like that, and I'm sorry that others have."

"That's not all..."

"I don't want to hear it."

Sandy grabbed Gene's hand, his eyes tearing. "Why don't you take me home with you? Let me live with you. I'd treat you really nice. I make a great chili. My scrambled eggs are the best."

"I can't."

"That's right. You're married. Probably have a kid of your own."

"I'm not married. I sometimes tell people I am. I'm not married now. I used to be."

"I could be a wife to you. I'd be a better wife to you than your first wife, I bet."

"I'm not ready for that yet."

"Hey, I have an idea."

"What?"

"Tomorrow's Sunday. You don't work on Sunday, do you?"

"No, but I go to church in the morning."

"Tomorrow afternoon around two o'clock I'm going to be walking along by that reservoir. I'd sure like some company."

"I can't. I just can't."

"Hey, mister, I'm going to be there." He held Gene's hand in such a firm grip that it almost hurt.

He sensed Sandy's desperation but decided to brush it aside. After all, he faced teenage desperation daily. "You'd better go, kid. I've got to get back to work. You helped me a lot."

"Glad to oblige." Out on the sidewalk again, Sandy held the car door open as he glanced around and surveyed the square. "This may all end soon."

"What do you mean?"

"It looks like Barry Collins is going to be mayor. He's threatened to clean up this zone of prostitution."

"You may be right. He's a man of his word. I know him. Even Sister Rose is backing him as a candidate."

"I know him too. He's one of those two-inch dicks I've been talking about."

"I don't get it. What do you mean?"

"He's a regular at Leroy's parties. Likes them real young."

Gene didn't believe Sandy. "You must have gotten him mixed up with somebody else. I can assure you Barry Collins isn't into young boys. I'm a pretty good judge of character."

"And Barry Collins is a lousy fuck. See you tomorrow at two."

"That's not definite. I might not be able to make it."

"You'll make it all right. Know why? Because you're not going to find anyone else in this whole fucking city who loves you and understands you the way I do. Hell, I've just met you and I want to move in with you."

"How many guys do you use that line on?"

"One. You, Ralph. Maybe tomorrow you'll tell me your real name. With all the other creeps, I can't wait to escape from them. I don't want you to leave me and turn me out on this God damn square to hustle a buck. Please, don't do that to me."

"I can't. I just can't." Perspiration had coated Gene's body, and he felt he was smothering. "I've got to go."

Sandy wiped his eyes. "You'd better be there tomorrow, you God damn good-looking son-of-a-bitch. You're the nicest guy I ever met."

"It's Gene. I'm Gene." With that, he reached over and shut the car door on the passenger's side. He couldn't bear to look back at Sandy. Without a glance, he drove away from the square, turning down a side street. His whole body was shaking.

Only then did the full revelation of what Sandy had confided in him settle into his mind. Barry Collins? There was no way. It couldn't be. Not Barry Collins! Any man who could satisfy a sex maniac like Pamela and get her to marry him couldn't be gay. No way. Not only gay but a child molester as well. He'd never heard stories like that about Barry. He'd dated all the most gorgeous girls at the university and now had two of the most beautiful daughters in town. He didn't think Sandy was a liar, but the boy could be wrong. He could have made a mistake. Maybe the John was someone who looked like Barry.

A sudden chilling thought came over Gene. Barry was Rose's hand-picked candidate. If this story about the Lolito ring broke, and if Barry were implicated, he would not only be finished in politics, he might be arrested. Worse than that, at least in Gene's eyes, was that such a revelation and exposure could become a cancer growing on Rose herself. Surely she was unaware of Barry's activities. But it was information she'd have to be exposed to at some point. Gene himself might save her if she found out in time.

As he drove along, he realized he'd have to move very, very carefully. Nothing was ever easy for him. This Lolito ring was like an octopus reaching out, ensnaring people with its tentacles. It was frightening yet gave Gene a sense of power. He'd been destroyed by others, and even though he didn't want to hurt Rose, this might be his chance to strike back at all the people who'd considered him sleaze. His whole body was drenched in sweat.

"Keep cool!" he kept reminding himself. "Keep cool." He was breathing heavily. The day was so bright it blinded him but he kept driving even though he'd long ago passed his turn. He didn't really know where he was going and for one brief moment seemed to have forgotten who he was. It was as if he'd temporarily occupied another body but had returned to his own skin. This thought frightened him. "Mustn't come unglued," he said to himself as he turned the car around and headed back in the right direction this time.

*****

Leroy was far from the sleazeball Buck had remembered. Unlike Pamela, time had been kind to him. He'd developed into a rather handsome young man with a swimmer's build. He wore his raven-black hair fashionably long and well coiffed, and his sparkling green eyes and relaxed smile made him look more like a tall model in a male fashion magazine than the master of a boy bordello.

Immaculately groomed and attired in a tasteful elephant-gray outfit, Leroy resembled the kind of a dream date a daughter might bring home to her conservative father. He made a slight concession to the style of 1977, but did not overdo anything. There was nothing flamboyant about him in spite of Buck's memory of him being rather outrageous at the university. Back then he'd been a bit of a campus rebel. But the man reaching out to shake his hand looked like he could run for mayor in a few years. If anything, Leroy appeared smoother and more publicly acceptable than Barry Collins who always had a five o'clock shadow and a slightly disheveled look, in spite of his handsome features.

"Buck," Leroy said, shaking his hand firmly, "it's been years."

"Good to see you, Leroy," Buck said. "You're looking good."

"Thanks and so are you. I can easily see why they want you for the sexiest man of the year. Remember I tried to get handsome hunk contests going at the university. But you guys gave the beauty queens all the publicity."

"You were before your time. Somehow the idea back then was that women weren't interested in seeing men with their shirts off."

"And fools they were." As Robert prepared drinks, Leroy turned around to introduce Isabella de Nicola, a rather statuesque beauty who wore no makeup and had closely cropped her brown hair. "Glad to meet you," she said, shaking his hand even more firmly than Leroy did. "If you look as good on film as you do in person, you've made our job real easy."

"Thanks."

"I must say you, Leroy, and Robert are three good-looking men. But you don't do anything for me at all so I can be completely objective."

"Sorry, we don't turn you on," Buck said.

"Don't you have any beautiful women on this island?" Isabella asked, taking a Bloody Mary from Robert.

"As a matter of fact we do," Buck said, thanking Robert for his drink.

"Where might she be?" she asked.

"I'm looking at her."

"Very flattering but I wish a woman had said that."

"I'm sure they do. Plenty of times." Buck turned from her to guide Leroy over to his sunken living room where the first shots were to be made.

Isabella joined Robert on the sofa in the foyer to work out details.

"This is a beautiful home," Leroy said, taking a hefty sip of his Bloody Mary. "I always wanted to get invited here but I think Robert Dante got to the goodies before I did."

Buck smiled enigmatically. With Leroy, he planned to clearly suggest he was completely gay. That would serve his purpose later.

Leroy smiled back. "Would you have given me a tumble back then if I had pursued it?"

"If I recall, and I do recall, your eyes were always fluttering on Gene Robinson."

Leroy sat down in a wicker chair and leaned into its white muslin cushion. "That's true. I look at that nude frontal of him every night and dream. That's one sexy man. But so are you."

"That's nice. But just how sexy do you want to make these photographs today?"

"Very. I even brought a red bikini for you to wear when I go out to shoot you on the beach. Most men couldn't wear it but I hear you can fill the strap. My gay brethren who showered with you in college gave me a full report. You were the only man on campus who could match Gene."

"Hold it here. I'm a publishing executive with a reputation to uphold. I'm not going to be one of your centerfolds. This assignment is not for that kind of magazine."

"Will you at least try it on?"

"Sure, I'll give it a try."

"Can I go with you to try it on?"

Buck motioned to Robert in the next room.

"I see. I hear that girl is real jealous."

"He is." Buck glanced at his watch. "I've got to go back to the city this afternoon. When do we begin?"

"Right now. Right in your living room. You look plenty hot in those jeans and T-shirt. Let's do some shit of the young publisher relaxing in his living room, no doubt fretting over his Sunday column."

Buck looked up at him and smiled. "No doubt."

The first hour of the shoot went reasonably well, even though Buck felt Isabella was directing a military campaign instead of a photographic layout. At one point over a camera angle, Leroy lost his cool and called her a bitch, although she seemed to pay no attention to that and certainly didn't take offense. Robert remained in the background, interfering in no way.

When time came for the beach shots, Buck disappeared into his bathroom to try on the red bikini Leroy had brought to the island. As he slipped off his jeans and white briefs, he flexed his muscles before a full-length mirror. With all his exercise and jogging, he felt he was prime meat for the shots on the beach. But when he slipped into the bikini, he knew there was no way he could allow himself to be photographed in that skimpy wear. The bikini clearly showed the length of his cock and the size of his balls. He didn't think the magazine would print it anyway, even if he agreed to pose for it.

As if anticipating this, Robert opened the door and walked into the bathroom, bringing him a pair of red swim trunks that would reveal nothing to the camera. "You're looking good, stud," Robert said, "but there's no way I'm going to let my boyfriend pose in that. If you want to pose in it, save it for later when we're alone. Slip these on over it." He handed the trunks to Buck.

"You're right. Leroy's bikini isn't swimwear. It's a posing strap."

"One that leaves nothing to the imagination."

Buck slipped into the swim trunks, without taking off the sheer bikini. "I'll keep the bikini. A gift from Leroy. It might come in handy some time when I'm trying to turn you on."

"You don't even have to wake up in the morning to turn me on." Robert gave him a quick kiss and headed out the door.

Leroy was disappointed Buck hadn't worn the bikini, but Isabella was delighted. In the trunks, or so she claimed, Buck had just the right look they want to convey in their family magazine.

Out on the beach and after a few shots of Buck jogging along the sands and rushing to take a dip in the water, Buck signaled to Robert he wanted to be alone with Leroy as they had already agreed.

As Robert kept Isabella distracted, Buck walked down the beach with Leroy to a lonely strip.

"Sure you won't let me photograph the goodies?" Leroy asked.

"I'm sure," Buck said. He paused briefly for effect, looking out toward the sea. "I'm sorry we never connected at college. I like the way you handled the shoot today. I feel we might become friends after all."

"There are all kinds of friends. How do you mean?"

"I mean friend friends."

"Don't you find me attractive?"

"Very. But I've got to confess something. What really turns me on is someone really young. Someone who looks like Robert did when he first enrolled in our college."

"I see." Leroy appeared as if ready to say something but thought better of it. "Not me, man. I like my men fully grown and mature. Gene, for example. And most definitely Buck Brooke III."

"I can't help it. It's what turns me on."

"I get it. Robert's getting a little long in the tooth for you."

"Something like that." Buck steered him to a hidden cove clearly out of eyesight from Robert and Isabella.

"What would you say if I could get you an invitation to a very private party Friday night?" Leroy asked.

"What do you mean?"

"A place where a lot of important men in this town with your same proclivities can meet guys. Real young."

"You mean...like real young."

"As young as you want."

"I would say I'd died and gone to boy heaven," Buck said, feeling he was a convincing liar.

"Say I could do that, what would you do for me?"

"For openers, I'd take off these trunks and pose in that red bikini. I'm wearing it now."

"Shit, you would?"

"Yes, I'd even fluff it a bit if you want."

"Hot damn, I'm into it. No one can see us. Take off those baggy swim shorts."

Buck took off the trunks and stood in front of Leroy's trained eye.

"Grade A stud meat."

"The agreement is, I'll let you photograph me only from the waist down. I can't have my face showing."

"Honey, when guys get a look at that meat, they won't care about your face. With the ugliest face in the world and with meat like this, you could still score and score big."

As Buck posed for Leroy's camera, he said, "You're serious about inviting me to this party?"

"Very serious. I'll call you Tuesday and tell you the details. Will you let me watch?"

"I like to keep it private."

"Too bad. That's one show I would have enjoyed. I never knew you liked them young. Like Gene himself. Exposing himself in front of that little girl. But nothing surprises me any more."

"So it's a deal?"

"It's a deal, stud. But any time you want a grown man's love, call on me. What a good time I can show you."

"I'll think about it."

"I hope you will. Thanks for letting me shoot you. Both the public photographs and for my private collection."

"Glad to help out."

"You know something, sport," Leroy said. "I think today marks the beginning of a beautiful friendship."

Later that afternoon, Buck returned in his boat to the mainland. He'd decided to check out a few bars in the seedy midtown to see if any were displaying that bumper sticker, CONVERT A JEW TO CHRIST. He figured that any group of Jew-haters willing to invest that much money to launch bumper-stickers throughout certain pockets of the town must have a lot more prejudice and even bigger plans. It seemed too costly a gesture for a bad practical joke.

At the third bar and into his third Budweiser, he was about to give up, but as he drove along he spotted Captain Bogey's on Front Street. This bar catered to an increasing number of rednecks flocking to Okeechobee from North Florida or South Georgia. In this bar he ordered a Coors instead of a Budweiser. Because of the ultra-conservative management of that company, it sounded more right wing. He saw no evidence of any bumper sticker displayed until he went back to the men's room to get rid of some of that Bud. Over the toilet was the sticker he'd been seeking: CONVERT A JEW TO CHRIST.

As he came out of the toilet, he noticed young men in undershirts playing pool or backgammon in the back. An occasional retiree in Bermuda shorts drifted over to the bar for packaged liquor in very small bottles. At the grease-smeared front tables, out-of-work veterans in army fatigues exchanged war stories or fish tales. A really macho WASP place, Buck thought, and just the type of establishment to display such a bumper sticker. Even the open air pissoir in the rear confirmed the masculinity of the place, and the odor was overwhelming.

Sensing what he was smelling, the bartender said, "Sometimes we put ice on it to cool it down a bit. Haven't seen you in here before. I guess you're new in town."

"I've been here a few weeks," Buck said.

"Drop around Saturday night. That's when the local cowboys do some mighty fine picking and singing."

"Sure," he said, smiling, then looking back at the men's room. "My uncle's got a bar way out on the trail. He could sure use one of them bumper stickers you've got in the toilet."

The bartender nodded as he finished washing a glass under cold water and then slowly went over to the cash register, returning with a card on which a telephone number had been printed. "They're giving 'em out free. Will even deliver."

"Do you know who's printing them?" Buck asked, appearing as innocent as possible.

"How in hell do I know? But I'll tell you what I do know. A lot of big money guys have the dough to develop that little Jew haven over there on South Beach. The Jews there are paying cheap rent. But the place could be big. Big new construction projects. All these men you see hanging around here could get real high-paying construction jobs. But the Jews are blocking it." Someone up front called the bartender. He nodded only briefly at Buck.

Slipping the card into his pocket, he paid for his Coors without finishing it.

Later, at the Tin Palace—a hamburger joint by day, a jazz tavern in the evening—he enjoyed a plain burger at a private booth with checkered café curtains. A frequent lunchtime visitor, he went over to the graying owner, Harry Foresman, and asked him if he'd join him for a beer. In the booth again, he explained he was on a story but couldn't discuss it, and asked him if he'd call the number on the card and order some bumper stickers.

He reluctantly agreed, but explained he couldn't display one. "We cater to all types here," he said. "Anybody who can pay the freight."

"Harry," he said in exasperation. "I'm not asking you to put it on the wall—only order some."

About ten minutes later, Harry returned to the table. "That line sure was busy. Maybe everybody in town's ordering one. The guy on the other end told me he'd deliver mine at four o'clock. About an hour from now."

At the appointed time, Buck was waiting outside in his car.

At four-fifteen p.m., a pea-green truck arrived and double-parked at the entrance to the Tin Palace. Package in hand, a driver hastily went inside and came out a few minutes later. When he pulled out into traffic, Buck followed in his car and, five bar stops later, he sensed the driver was ready to return to the distribution source. It was nearly six o'clock, quitting time.

On the south side of the river, in a decaying section of warehouses which originally had been used to store freight, he slowed down but kept close enough to have a clear view of the truck up ahead.

The driver parked in back of the biggest warehouse, got out, and entered through a rear door. Leaving his own car two blocks away, Buck headed toward the large red-brick building to the front entrance and there, to his surprise, found the big bold letters of The Rose Phillips Charismatic Association emblazoned like zebra stripes across the center of the facade. Then he remembered that this was the printing headquarters of Rose's propaganda machine, where her monthly magazine, Charismatic, was set in type, reaching a circulation of four million readers.

He walked into the foyer and met a receptionist who immediately asked his business. He claimed he wanted to pick up some copies of Charismatic to distribute to his Sunday school class tomorrow. With a slight shrug, the receptionist disappeared into the back as he turned and quietly slipped through a side door, going down a long, musty corridor to the men's room. Once here, he concealed himself in one of the enclosed toilets as he heard the printing press grind to a halt for the day.

There was much banging of doors and, from a slightly opened window, he heard motors of cars starting in the parking lot out back. No one, however, had come into the men's room.

As a long, dreary hour passed, he had been seriously tempted to smoke a cigarette, but instead waited patiently in the foul-smelling toilet until he thought the building was completely clear of people. Going out, he peered through a dirty window at the vast printing plant. Once in it, he could find only fresh copies of next month's edition of Charismatic.

Climbing the rickety wooden stairs in the rear, he reached the second floor—a large ramp with an open pit looking down into the plant below. Small rooms opened off the ramp. In the first he found neatly stacked copies of Rose's autobiography, Hallelujah!, ready for shipment across the nation. A large, naturalistic-looking poster of Rose stared back at him, giving him a sensation of having the evangelist in the room with him. All the books he examined had been personally autographed.

Back on the ramp, he took in the rest of the building in the fading glow of the day. Through the large skylights overhead, the sun cast a yellow-orange glow over the plant. In some way, the warehouse was like a nostalgic reminder of the twenties, when this section of town had been part of the thriving port activity before the river became too shallow for large freighters.

The warehouse itself was fairly nondescript, and hardly fitted his conception of the printing headquarters of one of the world's most powerful gospel organizations. Somehow he'd expected steel and chrome. Rose apparently had invested her money where it counted—in her flashy, multi-million-dollar temple.

In other rooms opening off the ramp, he inspected enough merchandise for a blitzkrieg. All of it seemed newly manufactured and he'd never seen any of it on the streets before—everything from charismatic T-shirts with a long-stemmed rose printed on them, to rose petal buttons, to rose bumper stickers and, of course, plenty of glossy movie-star type photographs of that Doctor of Divinity herself, autographed, "Your fellow servant in Christ—love, Sister Rose."

"A hell of a lot of secretaries must have been busy," he thought to himself, "signing all those personal autographs."

He searched eight rooms before opening the final door. "Pay dirt!" he said out loud. Piles of anti-Semitic bumper stickers—awaiting distribution—had been neatly stacked along the walls on wooden shelves.

Triumphantly holding up one of the stickers, hoping to use it as a prop for an Examiner photograph, he edged his way out of the storage room, heading for what he thought would be an exit toward the back. The first two doors he tried were bolted, but in the fading light the handle to the third door turned. Stepping inside, he was aware of the pitch darkness of the room, unlike the twilight visibility along the ramp. The room had no windows.

He searched for the light, finding it to be an exposed electric bulb overhead which he turned on with a dangling chain. The bulb cast a cruel patina over the room.

The powerful eyes of Sister Rose, as seen in that poster seemed to follow him here to this forbidden territory. The poster face of Rose remained like the image on a retina after exposure to a blinding flashbulb.

Here, stacked from floor to ceiling, were crates, boxes, even trash bins filled to overflowing with tabloid-type newspapers, printed on what he knew was the cheapest paper available. He grabbed the first paper, TORCHLIGHT, holding it up to the light. Quickly he scanned the contents, finding it to be an eight-page tabloid billed as "the Revolutionary Newspaper of White Christianity."

On the front page was splashed a hideous caricature photograph of Hazel, caught stuffing a dill pickle in her mouth at a Jewish delicatessen on the beach. The caption read, "This grotesque horror of womanhood, a defender of child-molesters and a Jew-lover, a champion of Communist spies and the lesbian-dominated women's movement, has polluted the city commission for years with her moral stench. Now she dares run for mayor. A card-carrying Communist, she has turned her back on her own Christian heritage, ignoring the rights of white America, and has exploited the Jewish human garbage to gain political power. She has gone far enough. SHE WILL NOT RULE OKEECHOBEE."

He grabbed a sheaf of the racist papers which, along with the bumper sticker, would be his evidence. At what sounded like a noise from the plant below, he switched off the light and stood silently. Sneaking back to the ramp, he noted a night watchman making the rounds. He waited for him to go through the plant, fearing he might come upstairs. When he didn't, Buck tiptoed back down the ramp and the rickety stairs, heading for the front of the building. Once here, he found the doors locked from the outside. Down the musty corridor, he entered the men's room again, forcing open the window. He tossed the papers outside.

Sliding through, he fell five feet to the ground, bruising his knee on a rock. Picking himself up, he half ran, half limped to his car with his loot. He got in quickly and drove back to the heart of the city. He'd attend Rose's services tomorrow morning, but only after he'd filed a story for the front page. He'd still have just enough time to make the last edition.

*****

The young police recruit, an attractive Cuban woman with dark brown eyes and matching shoulder-length hair, liked to tell the men in the department she was "just as ferocious, just as tough as a wildcat." As part of a training program, Gene had been anxious to wrestle with her in one-to-one combat. Along with his chief, Biff, he'd resented it when the department had been required to hire women for jobs Gene felt should have been handled only by men.

Before Sofia entered the gym, Gene had decided he wasn't going to give her any breaks. He intended to be just as rough with her as he'd be in training a male police recruit. The whole setup wasn't fair in his opinion. On the mat, he was forced to stick to traditional wrestling holds, yet the women were allowed to try any tactic, except a kick in the groin.

As the women recruits lined up to face their male opponents, the coach blew the whistle. Sofia slammed into Gene's chest, kicking his legs. Like her reputation, she struck like a wildcat, catching him off guard. Lunging for his throat, she captured his neck in a stranglehold.

Although she'd had the advantage of a surprise attack, he came back in fighting force moments later. With manic cruelty, he broke her stranglehold, savagely grabbing her neck, hurling her across his head, her body landing on the mat. Recovering quickly, Sofia rose to her feet and kicked him again, gouging his eyes.

Losing control, he grabbed her wrists and tossed her on the mat again. Against the rules, he slammed his fist into her breasts. Pinned down, the writhing woman tried to break away and, also against the rules, brought her knee up, stabbing him. He slapped her face—once, twice, harder each time—and in lightning rage socked her in the mouth, then in the nose, her head flopping from side to side like a rag doll. As blood spurted out, she screamed. He seemed blind, his features contorted in rage. Dizzy with pain, he reached for his testicles and gently rubbed them, the sharp hurt searing deep within his gut.

The coach frantically blew the whistle, as two policemen rushed to pull Gene away from the battered Cuban. Fighting to hold back her tears, Sofia was led toward the showers by two other women recruits.

Getting up, Gene felt lost, not remembering clearly what had happened. It was as if a pin had been removed from a grenade inside him. Worn out by the ordeal, he now felt humiliated and strangely vulnerable, standing in the presence of his colleagues, facing the stern, beet-red face of the coach, the veins in his neck popping out just like Gene's father's had done.

"Better get a grip on yourself, man," the coach said in a strong-willed attempt to control his own fury. "These things happen sometimes. No man likes to get kicked down there. She won't pass my program. I'll see to that. But you've busted out of control five times in the past three months. We don't want you volunteering for training any more." He turned and looked at Gene, his face filled with despair. "I'm sorry to tell you this, but I've got to recommend you for a psychiatric evaluation next week. It's just routine. Several guys have been forced to go. You're not alone." The coach turned and with barely concealed anger made his way across the gym to his office.

Frustrated, swept by an overwhelming sense of defeat, Gene staggered toward the locker room. What he feared most was a psychiatric examination. He didn't want some shrink probing inside his head. His thoughts were his own, and that's the way he wanted to keep them. He knew a cadet who'd recently been evaluated. If he got in touch with him, Gene felt he'd at least have a good idea of what to expect before being examined.

Since he was going to meet Buck later on at the tennis court, he kept on his gym shorts but gathered up his street clothes and headed out back toward his car without bothering to take a shower since he was certain to be hot and sweaty after playing tennis in this heat.

Out on the street again, he breathed in the fresh air. Increasingly, violent rages had consumed him. He resented being singled out like that by the coach, lectured in front of the other policemen. He wasn't the only one in the department who'd lost control. Only the other day an officer he knew had answered a routine call and, in the course of the investigation, with no apparent motivation, had pulled out his pistol and fatally shot a fifteen-year-old boy.

He'd seen other members of the department breaking down, too—drifting into alcoholism, wife-beating, divorce, suicide. In the face of such weakness, he had prided himself in keeping himself together, as he felt superior to the others, especially the Cubans and the blacks.

Policemen were constantly faced with sexual temptation and he'd known many who had succumbed to it. But not him. He'd held firm, steadfast, regardless of the offers received—and, as the handsomest, most virile-looking member of the force, those invitations had been frequent and persuasive.

Now he feared word might get out about him that he, too, was breaking down, giving in to stress—the unrelenting stress—with which all members of the department lived.

Psychiatrists had studied several of the men he worked with. Despite denials, it'd been rumored that the aim of the study was to eliminate those men and women whom the psychiatrists judged emotionally unsuited for police work.

Today had been worse than all the others. He'd hated that Leroy had been linked to that case. Now he wished it had been some anonymous person he could arrest without guilt. But he had some strange link with Leroy although he'd always spurned the man's advances. He feared if he broke the Lolito case, his link, regardless of how tenuous, with Leroy might be revealed, even that frontal nude photograph. Then he'd be on display again and connected with exhibitionism. At times—even with a big case like this one—he felt he couldn't win. Everything seemed stacked against him in life.

"God damn it," he said out loud and in rage and, for the first time, realized he was still in the parking lot, speaking to himself. One woman police recruit looked at him strangely, then hurried to her own car.

If he fucked up this Lolito case, he could kiss his big dream goodbye. Here was a chance to win the praise and shouts of the crowds who had once cheered him as a tennis champ. Almost hourly he kept reminding himself of that. Even more important, he wanted to call Rose's attention to him. Even though he'd never met her, she'd surely hear of this. She'd understand and be proud of him. For all he knew, she'd praise him from the pulpit at her Sunday services which he faithfully attended.

He'd made so many arrests, only to have judges turn the men out to rob, loot, and kill the next day. Facing that dilemma year after year, he'd so easily understood Rose's rallying cry to clean up the town. If the police were so ineffective, then somebody—the decent people—had to step in to restore order.

But he could not think of that right now. He was on the street again behind the wheel of his car, driving and taking charge. He knew his meeting with Buck was a descent into evil, but Buck was like a drug to him. He couldn't resist. He was too weak.

Buck was going to take advantage of his weakness, and he knew he couldn't stop his old buddy from doing that, but had to give in to his friend's unnatural desires. He wanted Buck's friendship and needed it desperately even if it meant he had to submit to acts that were unspeakable. But he also knew that God would understand. It was just hours from Sunday morning when he'd be at her temple, hearing her clear, crystal voice. Her voice alone would cleanse him of the evil and the dirt into which he was about to plunge.

*****

After inserting a sidebar in the Sunday's Examiner about what he'd found at Rose's charismatic center, Buck drove to the old Ada Merritt tennis courts where Gene still played every night. Gene and he had gone to junior high here together. He parked his car in the overgrown lot, remembering this place as having been better maintained. Now litter filled the grounds and all the surfaces had been marked by graffiti. He found a seat on the empty bleachers.

On the court, Gene played against a younger man who was clearly not the tennis expert that this former champion was. Behind Buck, the sound of youthful Hispanic voices mingled with the traffic noises, and in a park across the street a few people strolled with dogs. It was a friendly neighborhood setting, even if the setting wasn't as pristine as it used to be. A seedy decay hung heavily in the air.

After Gene easily won the game, he ran across the court and slapped an arm around his opponent's shoulder, just the way Buck used to watch him do. The defeated younger man seemed bitter at the loss and resentful of Gene. They were replaced on the court by two young women, and the first ball that one of them served went low, thudding into the net.

As Buck watched Gene head across the court, he appeared the same as Buck had remembered him in his days of athletic competition at the university. The same athletic build, the graceful body movement, the thick black hair.

As Gene spotted Buck, he ran to him quickly and slapped his arm around him. "Looking good, old buddy."

Buck looked into Gene's once-sparkling eyes, and it was in those eyes he noticed the first major change in Gene. His eyes had grown dim with pain. "You're the one looking good. Still a champ after all these years."

"I just get better with age," Gene said. "Want a sample?"

"I've sampled the merchandise, and it's pure gold." He extended a mock punch to Gene in the stomach. "I wouldn't mind a repeat performance."

"You got yourself a date." Gene turned and looked at a graffiti-marked concrete building at the far corner of the courts. "The showers don't work here. I'll have to shower at home. But I'm dying of thirst. Would you join me for a beer across the street?"

"I'm game."

At a neighborhood tavern, Sloppy Louis, there were only three customers. Buck selected a table covered with a dirty red cloth and an ashtray filled with cigarette butts.

As they waited for their beer to be served, Gene tossed salted peanuts in his mouth and relaxed on a tufted red leather banquette that had two big tears in it. The barmaid was clearly flirting with Gene, and he pretended to admire her legs as she walked away. "I expected you a little earlier. Got held up?"

"Usually in this neighborhood that means held up with a gun. But I was delayed. I had to insert a last minute story. A sidebar about that charismatic center of Rose Phillips."

Gene looked at him intently just as the waitress came back with their beer. A blousy woman with bad stringy hair, she sized Gene up. "There's more where that came from," she said.

"I bet." Ignoring the waitress for the moment, Gene turned to Buck. "What kind of story?"

"That charismatic center is being used to distribute anti-Semitic propaganda."

"I can't believe that."

"I was there. I saw it."

Gene deeply sucked in the air and forced a nervous smile. But this hardly concealed his rage. A bitterness and hatred came into his eyes.

Buck wondered what possible reason Gene could have in wanting to protect Rose.

"Is it too late to kill the story?" Gene asked.

"It's running now."

"That's too God damn bad then." He reached across the table and gripped Buck's wrist so hard it hurt. "You're not fair to her at all. She's really trying to clean up this cesspool of a town, and all you do is attack her."

"Maybe she isn't the evangelical angel she pretends."

Gene tightened his grip on Buck's wrist. "You can't go running bad stories about her. You've been fed lies by her enemies. Especially by that fat pig, Hazel."

Buck pulled his hand away. Gene looked half-crazed. "You and I could never talk politics and religion. Remember how we once agreed to never bring up those subjects with each other?"

"I guess you're right." His facial muscles relaxed for the first time.

"We were friends in spite of our differences," Buck said. "It's important to remember that."

"C'mon," Gene said, pushing his beer away. "Let's get out of this dump. I've got to shower. With all the sweat I've worked up, I smell like a Havana whore in heat."

Buck left the money for the beers on the table and followed Gene out the door.

"Let's take my car to my place," Gene said. "I'll drive you back to the parking lot later. On the way home I'll tell you what I've learned so far about the Lolito ring."

Even as he got into Gene's car, Buck was tempted to tell him about his session that morning with Leroy and how he planned to gain admission to one of the Lolito parties. But he decided against it. Gene might rule that out, and Buck was determined to go through with it, with or without Gene's consent. He was eager, however, for any information Gene had to tell him about what he'd learned about Leroy's parties.

Once safely inside Gene's stuffy house, there was no more talk of Rose, the Examiner, politics, or even the Lolito ring. Buck knew why they were here, and he could feel that Gene did too. There was tremendous tension and nervousness between them, because it was still so new. Buck knew what he wanted from Gene, and his friend seemed perfectly willing to fulfill that need.

No sooner was Buck inside Gene's living room, with the front door shut, than Gene grabbed him and pulled him tight against his sweaty body, inserting his tongue in Buck's mouth. Buck eagerly sucked that tongue as if it contained some life force he desperately needed to survive.

Gene was the first to break the hold. "You smell fresh and clean like you always do. But I'm a little ripe, I fear. Get yourself a beer while I take a shower."

As Gene headed to the bathroom in the rear of his house, Buck called out to him. "There's nothing wrong with the smell of a natural man. If I'm going to get into this man-to-man sex stuff, maybe I like a dude who doesn't smell like a bottle of deodorant."

"You mean that?" Gene raised an eyebrow as if he hadn't heard right.

"Try me."

Gene came and stood before Buck again, not doing anything at first, even though he was only six inches from his face. Buck wrapped his arms around his friend, and this time inserted his tongue in Gene's mouth where it was expertly sucked. Buck ran his hands across Gene's chest before his fingers traveled lower, unfastening the gym shorts. Buck reached inside and tightened his fingers around Gene's prick. It was rock-hard and throbbed at the touch of Buck's fingers. "God, you're big."

"Like you, good buddy. Are you man enough to take it?"

"I've had it before."

"You're going to get it again." Gene led him toward the bedroom where he removed his own T-shirt and let his shorts fall to the floor. Buck knelt in front of him, pulling down Gene's jockstrap. As he did he reached to pull back Gene's foreskin before planting tiny kisses on the tip of his prick.

Gene forced Buck to his feet and slowly helped him out of his clothes until Buck was as nude as he was. Suddenly, Gene reached forward and grabbed a handful of Buck's hair, shoving his face so hard against Buck's it hurt. He began kissing and biting Buck's face, ears, and neck. "God, you taste good."

Gene rather forcibly lowered Buck onto his bed and in seconds he was smearing pre-coital fluid across Buck's lips. This foreplay seemed more than Gene could handle. He slid the knob of his penis between Buck's lips. It scraped against the roof of Buck's mouth but Gene continued to push into the tight confines of Buck's throat. Buck choked but Gene did not give up until Buck could feel the dense, tight curls of his black pubic hair grinding against his nose. Gene's large balls banged against Buck's chin.

As Gene was clearly approaching orgasm, he pulled out suddenly. His mouth traced a wet trail across Buck's chest and navel before reaching the blond pubic hair. Gene pulled at the hair with his teeth, causing Buck to squirm. It was painful but also highly erotic. Without gagging, Gene lowered his mouth on Buck's prick, swallowing it slowly but unrelentingly until it was down his throat. His throat seemed to open up without a struggle and to adjust immediately to this enormous penetration. He held Buck in his throat so long Buck feared his friend would suffocate. Then he pulled back roughly gasping for air. He stayed on Buck until he felt his friend approaching a climax, and then he raised up after giving the knob a final lick.

"Not that way today, good buddy," he said. "I'm going to fuck the juice out of you." Gene's face went lower as his tongue darted out, bathing Buck's testicles. He licked both clean and tried unsuccessfully to put one orb into his mouth. His tongue and lips traveled even lower on their journey to Buck's rosebud. When Gene parted Buck's cheeks and forced his tongue up inside Buck, Buck was squirming and moaning uncontrollably on the bed, enough so that Gene had to restrain him, holding him down. Gene delivered a final wet kiss before pulling away, raising himself up over Buck and forcing his tongue deep into Buck's mouth. He pulled back slightly to whisper into Buck's ear. "It tastes so good I want to share it with you."

He raised Buck's legs in the air, and Buck braced himself for a rough penetration. When it came he screamed and pulled at Gene's hair as if that would force him to pull back. It didn't, only serving to goad him on. Gene didn't allow Buck to adjust to the thick hardness of his cock. He plunged deep inside Buck. Buck screamed again. He was in great pain. But Gene had no intention of withdrawing, and secretly Buck wouldn't have it any other way.

After a minute of searing pain, he began to adjust to this invasion until he welcomed it. Gene slammed more and more forcefully into him. Buck felt like his entire body had been invaded. Wave after wave of the most tantalizing pleasure shot through Buck. In one final lunge, Gene plunged into him almost as if crashing. Staccato bursts of hot juicy fluid were suddenly released like an explosion. Buck could hold back no longer. He erupted too.

His pulsation-racked body collapsed on the bed, and the next thing he remembered was the feel of Gene's tongue and lips, devouring his last orgasmic spasms, licking him clean all over. Gene's lips milked Buck's softening cock with a caressing tongue.

Buck ran his fingers through Gene's raven-black hair, caressing and loving him, fondling his ears and running his hand gently across the back of his neck. He couldn't bear the idea that Gene would ever pull away from him. But he already had. There was a great void in another part of his body which Gene had filled but from which he had now withdrawn.

It was only when Gene was lovingly giving him his final caresses that Buck remembered he had another rendezvous. Robert was preparing a late night dinner back on their private island and Buck knew he must rush home to him. He would leave his friend as he also knew that was what Gene really wanted. Gene was always the loner. If he took love, it was only in secret, guarded moments. Buck could never imagine his old buddy asking him to spend the night. Gene didn't do that. Buck wondered how Gene spent his nights but didn't dare ask.

"How about that shower now?" Gene asked raising up and licking his lips.

"Mind if I join you?" Buck asked, sitting up.

"You're welcome. But I'm not going to turn my back to you for one moment. Guys like you aren't to be trusted."

*****

After the violent passion with Gene, Buck was happy to return to the safety of Robert and his own private island. What he needed most tonight was tender love, not throbbing passion, and he knew he could find that in the arms of his own Robert who seemed to exist for no one in the world but him.

As he steered his boat close to the pier, he could see Robert standing by and waiting for him. Good, faithful Robert. Even as he neared the dock, he was rewarded with Robert's trusting smile. That Buck didn't deserve. That trust and love was something he knew he'd have to deal with at another time—but not tonight. He wanted to escape with Robert into a romantic fantasy and not confront the harsh reality he knew he'd face at tomorrow's temple when he came together with Rose again.

The moment he landed, he sensed something was wrong. Robert raced to greet him and planted several kisses on his mouth, but it was different somehow. Buck returned the kisses and grabbed Robert, crushing his body against his friend's, his tongue exploring Robert's mouth. But he felt a tension there he'd not known before. Had Robert found out about his rendezvous with Gene?

He parted slightly from Robert but still held him near. "I know you too well. Something's wrong."

"I have to go to Miami," Robert said. "I got a call from the hospital. My mother's dying."

"But you haven't spoken to her in years."

"I know." Robert looked grim-faced as he took Buck's hand and guided him toward the living room. He said nothing but poured Buck a Scotch and came and sat with him on the sofa where they'd so recently entertained Isabella and Leroy.

"Do you want me to go with you to Miami?"

"I want you to go with me everywhere I go, but I sense there is going to be a lot of news breaking, starting with your visit to Rose's temple. Mother wouldn't speak to you anyway even if you showed up. I don't know if she'll even speak to me."

"Over the years she hasn't struck me as the most thankful person in the world. After all, we've paid for her to live in a condo and we've sent her a monthly check. I don't recall ever seeing a thank you note. Not even a Christmas card."

"She's a bitter old woman and mean as hell. But I've been so grateful for all your help over the years. I don't know what she would have done without help from us."

"I'm amazed she could accept our charity and still hate us so," Buck said. "She feels I corrupted you."

"If anything, it was the other way around. I was the one who corrupted you."

"Nobody corrupted anybody. We love each other. There's nothing corrupt about it."

"I know that," Robert said. "But she doesn't understand that kind of love. She'll go to her grave hating gay people and especially her gay son."

"I'm sorry, I truly am. Are you sure you want to go see her before she dies? She'll not repent. She'll never forgive you for being gay. For loving me."

"I know she won't." He snuggled his face into Buck's chest. "She'll never make peace with me—even on her death bed."

"Then why are you going?"

"I'm going to sit by her bed and tell her I love her. She is my mother, after all. I'm going to thank her for the gift of life. I'm going to tell her if she hadn't given me life, I wouldn't have been able to grow into a man and to love another man. For that, I'm going to tell her how grateful I am."

"That will kill her for sure."

Robert got up from the sofa. "I think I'll join you in a Scotch tonight. I need a drink."

Buck got up, too, and headed for the bar. "I'll make it for you. You've made me three thousand drinks. Let me make just one for you."

"I'd like that."

Buck poured his drink and as Robert came to the bar he reached out and pulled him in close, kissing him hard on the lips.

Robert returned the kiss with equal force. He lifted the drink to his lips.

Buck held his wrist. "Take the first drink but don't swallow it. Feed it back into my mouth."

Robert took a hefty swig of the Scotch and held his mouth up for Buck. Buck drank from his friend's mouth, then licked Robert's lips in gratitude. "I just knew it."

Robert looked puzzled as he took another sip of his drink, swallowing it this time. "Knew what?" he asked, puzzled.

"Scotch tastes better when it's been filtered through your mouth."

"That's flattering. I liked that a lot. You are certainly getting kinky lately, and I'm loving it. All this from a man who wouldn't let me kiss him when I first met him. I could suck his cock, lick his balls, and tongue his asshole, but kisses were off-limits."

"I know. I was real dumb back then. I felt it was okay for a gay dude to suck your cock, but you weren't supposed to kiss him. How did we break that barrier?"

"I remember it well." Robert walked over and put on some soft, romantic music. "You came home so drunk one night you couldn't get it up. That's unusual for you. Drunk or sober you can get it up. If I recall, it was the night Gene Robinson was arrested for exposing himself to that little girl."

Buck winced at the mention of it.

"At any rate, you passed out on the bed after I'd stripped off your clothes. After I'd tongued you to my heart's content, you just lay there sound asleep with your mouth open. Ever so quietly I pressed my face down against yours and inserted my tongue in your mouth. You at first pushed me away but I was stronger than you that night. I kept returning and pressing my lips against yours and inserting my tongue down your throat. Believe it or not, you finally started responding. You started kissing me back. With some real passion. I reached down and—

surprise—you were rock hard. From that day forth, you never denied me your mouth and you returned my kisses."

"As I'm about to do right now." Buck reached over, pulled him close, and kissed him hard, exploring Robert's gums with his tongue. Then he pulled back and kissed Robert's nose, inserting his tongue, or at least attempting to, in his friend's nostrils before kissing his closed eyelids, tonguing his forehead, and bathing each of his ears followed by gentle nibbles. With the same relentless tongue, he bathed all of Robert's neck both back and front. "Let's strip. I want to try something with you I've never tried before."

"What's that?"

"Sixty-nine."

"I thought you'd never ask."

Buck took his arm and placed it around Robert's shoulder, pulling him in close. Dying mothers, charismatic preachers, even Gene and Susan—all that could be dealt with tomorrow. Right now he wanted more than anything to taste Robert's semen and while doing so deposit a wad in his friend's mouth as well. More so than with anybody in the world, he had this desire to literally drink from Robert's body. He sensually peeled off Robert's clothing and let Robert undress him, as he planted tiny kisses across Buck's body.

As Buck snuggled close in bed, he ran his hand across Robert's ass and with his index finger explored the rosebud. Robert squirmed at Buck's touch and welcomed the probe of his finger. Robert pressed hard against him as Buck's finger entered him. From the way Robert was moving his body, Buck knew what his friend wanted but wasn't quite ready for that yet. Buck didn't know why he was holding back. He'd already crossed that barrier with Gene.

He felt fucked up in the head. "God damn it," he said out loud. Robert didn't seem to understand this sudden rage coming over Buck. Buck abruptly removed his finger and moved toward the area with his tongue out. He attacked Robert's ass with a vengeance, kissing and licking it and probing inside Robert as deeply as he could with his tongue. Robert squealed with delight at this sudden assault. Buck lost all sense of time. He didn't know how long he remained in that spot, probing Robert with his tongue. It was a glorious taste to him.

Robert was plunging down rapidly on Buck's cock, swallowing him deep into his throat, his muscles constricting to cause Buck the most exquisite pleasure. His own orgasm rapidly approaching, he could feel Robert's body almost going into a convulsion. He let his tongue trace a trail to Robert's nutsac and then travel up his cock which Buck encased in his mouth just in time to enjoy and taste his friend's eruption. He returned the favor by shooting deep into Robert's throat. He lay there holding and cuddling Robert and determined to swallow every last drop.

When they reluctantly pulled away from each other, Robert reached out and took Buck's hand, walking with him toward the shower. "Dinner's surely ready by now."

As he stood with Robert under the jet spray, Robert kissed him and whispered into his ear, "I want you to marry me."

Buck broke away. "You mean like married married or symbolically married?"

"The real thing. I know of a minister in Miami who performs such ceremonies. I want you to literally marry me. In front of a pastor."

Buck took a bar of soap and rubbed it across Robert's chest, and as Robert lifted his armpits, Buck bathed each of them lovingly before Robert returned the favor.

"Well, what do you say?"

"I love you, Robert, and I'll never leave you. But would you let me think about this marriage thing a bit? It's all so new for me. I just need some time to think."

"I can live with that. But a week from now, a month from now, regardless of how long it takes, I'm going to want that wedding band on my finger."

"You little devil," was all Buck said. He took Robert's finger, the same one where Robert wanted a wedding band placed, and raised that finger to his lips, then sucked it deep within his mouth.

Chapter Four

At the airport the next morning, Buck embraced Robert before he boarded the flight for Miami. Their hug went relatively unnoticed. Passengers had long grown accustomed to Hispanic men embracing at this airport. As Robert started to walk away, Buck ran after him and embraced him again.

"I can't wait until I get back to your arms," Robert whispered in his ear.

"I love you. I'll think about marriage, I really will. Just give me a little time to find myself."

"I love you." Robert turned and headed toward the gateway to the plane.

Buck stood watching him go and almost impulsively wanted to run after him, but thought better of it. He glanced at his watch. If he didn't leave right this minute, he'd be late for morning services at Rose's temple.

Until that Sunday morning, Buck had never visited the temple of evangelism that Rose built in the northeastern sector of Okeechobee. Many charismatics, fundamentalists, and Pentecostals traveled from all over the country, as well as Canada and Europe, to worship at the multi-million-dollar shrine.

Built of reinforced concrete, the temple had raised funds by selling little bags of cement mixed with crushed seashells at fifty dollars apiece. All the temple's art work, including two stained-glass windows by Chagall, had been contributed by "fat cat" supporters, and was estimated to have a value in excess of eight million dollars.

In the flower gardens that led to the entrance, Buck rubbed his sunburned hands, then looked up at the gleaming white building, dazzling in the morning sun—a gaudy extravaganza created in the shape of a cross and crowned by an overscaled dome, which was pierced with lunette windows. He was reminded of reading of Rose's humble beginnings, a pigsty over which she'd preached early in her career.

Inside the church, painted a sky blue, he had a hard time finding an empty seat, but eventually located a cozy perch down front near the white-robed choir. Under the dome stood a golden pulpit with thousands of luxuriously upholstered pale rose armchairs fanning off from it. All the large, roomy ramps and aisles converged at this metallic point, where it seemed that every square foot of floor space was devoted to whomever stood at its golden focal point.

The symbols were so impressive to him that even now, knowing what he did, he still couldn't believe that such an altar could be used as a forum of hatred.

He wondered how many people had read the Examiner before coming to church. On Sunday, the Examiner appeared in the morning like its rival the News. He had run his story on the front page, claiming that the printing headquarters of Rose's association was used as a distribution center for racist literature. It'd been impossible to reach Rose for comment last night, and he eagerly waited to confront her this morning, as she'd invited him to come backstage to meet her after the sermon.

Looking out upon the sea of worshippers, he estimated the crowd at more than five thousand. Frankly, he'd expected to meet a host of geriatric Southern rednecks, survivors of Grant Wood's American Gothic types. Instead, he gazed upon rows of young faces, both men and women, handsomely dressed and outwardly intelligent, much like a representative group you'd encounter at a large southern university.

Planting his feet firmly on the rose-colored carpeting, he stared straight at the pulpit, waiting for the services. He didn't have to wait long. In blazing sound, a Jesus rock band rose from the orchestra pit, the blasts warming up the crowd. It reminded him of the opening of a splashy Broadway musical. For sheer hoopla, he thought, Rose certainly knew how to exalt the Lord in surroundings worthy of an imperial coronation, and with musical accompaniment, too.

Hidden microphones waited to capture her voice for her syndicated radio gospel programs over eighty stations, and cameras were ready to record her appearance for thirty-eight television stations, from Florida to Louisiana to Texas, all the way to Portland, Oregon.

Rose appeared—a real star's entrance—and to him, she possessed instant appeal. He had a hard time associating this image with the woman who'd passed the catsup at her patio dinner. Her arrival was greeted by a standing ovation, the congregation raising outstretched hands toward her. He fought against the far-fetched comparisons racing through his brain, though he was reminded of Hitler's entrance to the cries of "Sieg Heil." Yet, he kept telling himself, these weren't fanatics—just ordinary middle-class people who believed in Jesus Christ and had probably found some inner peace by turning to her temple. It wasn't the people he distrusted, but the angelic-appearing creature on the platform.

Clad only in a sheer white, flowing Grecian gown, and holding a long-stemmed white rose, she had let her auburn hair cascade down the sides of her face. Shouting: "Joy! Joy! Joy!" she cut a striking figure, tall and slender, as she moved gracefully to the center of the stage to the thunderous applause of her fans.

After the demonstration had gone on for an embarrassingly long time, she extended her hands toward the dome to summon the faithful to quiet down. However, shouts of "Hallelujah!" and "Praise the Lord!" still echoed through the cavernous temple. Unlike anything he might have expected, this jubilant Christian assembly seemed gathered to have a good time, even though he noticed some of the faces around him were vacant-eyed, as if fixed on some star in their own firmament.

The sleeves of her Grecian gown billowing after her, Rose turned her full face to the audience—with her spectacular eyes and mouth, beautifully shaped nose, and a fine high forehead. To him, it was an exquisite profile, a vital and sparkling woman who made an instant impact on her audience.

She waited until the audience had completely quieted down, giving her a sense of control and mastery. "I can do all things through Christ," she quoted Philippians 4:13. "Like Paul, I've gone through many trials in my public and private life, but I've triumphed...and I will again!" One of her arms shot out toward the congregation, her fist tightening in an iron-willed determination. "Jesus has summoned me to carry on his battle here on earth against the worshippers of the devil."

Her melodramatic way of speaking made him squirm as one does at overstatements from public speakers, but her audience wasn't disturbed. In spite of the enthusiastic reception she'd received, he sensed a nervousness in her manner, reflected by the way she kept fidgeting with a large diamond ring and clutching at a camellia positioned around her neck. The pink spotlight shining on her and the bright semi-tropical sun pouring in through the dome seemed to bathe her in a cosmic light and, for a moment, she did appear to him like some Amazon goddess leading Christian warriors into battle.

Somehow Rose transferred the feel of her own metallically tense body to him, and he sensed the change in her mood and voice, depending on the point she wanted to emphasize. At one moment, she appeared almost belligerent, whereas in the moment directly following, she became folksy—a down-to-earth woman in spite of the classy surroundings.

Suddenly Buck, along with the audience, gasped as she tripped over a cord on the platform. She seemed to have broken the heel to one of her pumps. Kicking off both shoes, she tossed them aside and walked back to the podium in her stocking feet. This act of bravado endeared her to her fans, who loved it, breaking into spontaneous clapping. "I never had a pair of real shoes 'till I was eight years old anyway." Again, loud applause, even shouts of "Right on!" Now he suspected she'd deliberately tripped, using the shoes as a piece of stage business.

The comic relief out of the way, she changed her mood, her face tightening, her voice becoming strained. An uneasy mood settled over him, and the seriousness permeated the atmosphere. As if in silent prayer, she bowed her head, then faced her audience, reminding him of an actress who knew how to combine charm with physical beauty and dramatic appeal. A hush descended over the audience, making him feel they'd come to the real point of the gathering.

"I have called you here today to launch a moral crusade," she shouted in clear tones, her voice reverberating through the temple. With one lightning-swift glance to the dome, she tossed her head back, her hair moving rhythmically as she spoke. "If every sex pervert, bomb-thrower, abortionist baby-murderer and radical revolutionary intent on destroying this country through violent means can come out of the closet and assert his rights, then so help me, with Jesus backing me up, I can say that the *normal majority* had better get out of our attics and shout them down before they grab our country right from under our noses."

This stinging call to arms burned right through his skin. He was aware of the shuffling of feet and the sounds, at first a murmur, and then a roar of "Amen, Sister!" She was getting her response—and fast.

The evangelist held up her hands as if blessing the audience, but perhaps to calm them. Even now, with her vilification of liberals and the far left, she seemed to him the personification of purity, a woman whose dictates had to be obeyed without question. Not that he would obey any of them. He was strong enough to resist whatever pressure she might apply to him. He wondered about the rest of the audience.

At first her voice had been halting. The more she launched her attack, the mellower and more vibrant it became—an odd tone for so powerful an assault. Even her face looked younger—effervescent innocence itself. Charging into her subject, she said, "I think there's a lesson to be learned from the movement of the far left. They have taken to the streets to demand their rights, while the rest of us have sat at home watching the action on TV."

He looked in astonishment as in the next moment, she seemed to reach up in mid-air, take a bolt of fire from Jesus himself, and hurl it into the audience. "When one of us stands up—a normal American, like you or me—and says, 'Hey, just a minute. What about us? We've got rights too. The rights to raise our children in a God-fearing country.' What happens then? We're labeled racists."

She paused, and even before she spoke, he knew her next words would be directed at him personally.

"Racists," she went on. "The way I was so painfully characterized by that muckraking newspaper, the Examiner, this morning."

Reddening, he was at the same time prepared to face the assault, knowing it would be the first of many.

"I might as well say it," she added. "In polite circles, they call us the fanatical right. But, to card-carrying Communists, we're always..." She paused, leaning closer.

He knew the word she was searching for, but didn't think she'd have the guts to use it. He misjudged her.

In a throaty sob, she shouted, "We're called Nazis!" She stopped short, as if catching her breath. Near tears, she cried out. "Lies! Lies! All lies to discredit us. Let them accuse." He felt she'd momentarily lost control and was improvising now, but she recovered quickly and came back with a qualification. "I'm not advocating violence. No way. Not like the violence our enemies have inflicted on us. I'm calling for massive demonstrations of normal Americans who want to put an end to the wave of filth and perversion destroying our landscape. If the judges and the police are powerless to fight the rising tide, then we have the strength and the stamina."

The audience rose to its feet, extending its raised hands to show its support for her. Despite the contemptuous stares of those who sat near him, he remained in his seat, knowing he was so opposed to her methods and even her moral purpose that he expected any day to rise to the top of the enemy list.

"Call it revolution if you want," she shouted over the murmur of the crowd. "I call it confrontational politics. Go out...find the sinner. Stare him down—eyeball to eyeball."

He tried to imagine such encounters and wasn't at all certain what she advocated. He definitely felt she had the support of her followers, wherever she wanted to lead them.

Restoring calm by the magnetism of her presence, she said, "Tonight, I'm leading a march into the Combat Zone, a parade by Christian warriors that heads directly into the dirty heart of Sodom and Gomorrah itself. I want you to join me and my family in this candlelight parade. We'll not carry bombs, we'll not break windows. But we'll let the merchants of filth along the way know what we think of their wares which they peddle to corrupt our youth. Our march will be a signal to the prostitutes along the street that they'd better ship out to places like San Francisco that encourage such ilk."

Her voice changed again and, to him, it seemed even more stirring than ever. "If we succeed tonight," she said, "our cause will set an example for the rest of this great country to follow. I promise you, my friends, we'll clean up America, and we'll start right here, right tonight in Okeechobee."

At the end of her battle cry, she broke into her theme song, "The Battle Hymn of the Republic," accompanied by a thirty-six member choral group and the Jesus rock band. She'd had a lot of practice with that song and Buck, as reluctant as he was to do so, had to admit she was good at it. Her voice soared, capturing emotions the words themselves could not express. Everybody in the audience, except Buck, seemed transposed to another plateau.

As she sang, tears streamed down her cheeks. The ominous challenge of her words still echoed within his head. The song itself took on a different meaning as interpreted by her. She made it sound bullish, a symbol of triumphant America embracing the moral fervor of the past century.

He shuddered at what her "terrible swift sword" would do to those who stood in her way—not only minority groups, but other Christians who differed from her biblical interpretations. He felt he already knew which hearts of men she'd sift out before God, in his judgment seat, had a chance to look them over.

*****

In the far corner of the temple, Gene sat silently, totally mesmerized by Rose's rallying cry. In her virginal-appearing state, she sucked in the air, expanding her already full bosom, and sent her gracious voice rolling like an ocean wave over him. He allowed it to envelop him, bathe him, almost drown him.

His spirit, too, wanted to cry out with her the same agony of outrage. For years in the police department, he'd been forced to languish in bitter stagnation, though his idealism burned within him, setting him at times on fire. In Rose's large, feverishly intense eyes that seemed to penetrate to the very core of his body, he felt her command in a hypnotic way. Her determined power held him in domination.

After the devastation of his marriage, he had every intention—and still had—to save himself from the evil that surrounded him daily, from the murk that lurked in his own soul, luring him into one temptation after another. He was a thrill seeker, and couldn't help himself. It was all he could do to resist when Sandy had invited him to that men's room. He liked having sex in public places, as if he wanted to get caught. Again. Although he told himself he couldn't face more public humiliation, he did everything he could to invite it. Forces seemed to take over his body and drive him in strange new pathways, the way his friendship with Buck had gone in the past hours.

He always thought his sexual involvement with Buck would be confined to the dark recesses of his brain, but it had suddenly become a reality he could hardly deal with, much less think about. In this temple this morning, he wanted the better side of his nature to come out—the good Gene. In a way, he felt it had. He felt cleansed and pure in this temple.

He'd wanted to do something to better mankind but didn't know how to go about that, other than joining the police force, the only work for which he felt qualified.

The chief, Biff, had been impressed with Gene's athletic record. "I'd rather have a real man on the force, even if he's had a problem or two in the past, than one of those Cuban punks we're forced to hire these days. After all, that girl's mama never filed charges. You're clean as a hound's tooth as far as I'm concerned. An arrest. But no conviction."

His work in the department had only saddened Gene more, bringing him into intimate contact with the most sordid part of life—teenage prostitution, sex hunters, children mutilated by their parents, old ladies beaten up by rampaging teenagers.

As each long month drifted by, he'd grown more embittered, listening to the scum he arrested complain about their civil rights. Often victims weren't around to claim rights.

On Sunday morning, in total despair, near suicide, he'd wandered into Rose's temple, taking a back seat. Arriving with a sorrowful, forlorn face, he'd had his prayers answered that day. Jesus did care for him after all!

The moment Sister Rose walked out onto the stage, he'd known at once that his search had come to an end. She was the woman he'd been looking for and in his wildest fantasies he hadn't dared conjure up *her*. There she'd stood towering over her enraptured audience, shimmering in a golden light—his idol—everything his doomed mother had never attained, in spite of her prayers, and everything his whorish former wife opposed. Transfixed, he'd moved closer to the source of the heat, finding a front seat so he could be near Rose.

Today, as back then, her words still rang in his ears, only they'd acquired an urgency. "I need each and every one of you," she called out from the pulpit, "to be a soldier in my Army, to help me carry on the crusade of Jesus."

He'd felt that she'd been talking to him directly and he'd wanted to go up after the sermon to tell her that. He was willing to fight for her in her cause. It was his cause, too.

But how could he, a lowly cop, approach an angel?

Yet, after this morning's sermon, a clearer blueprint had emerged. He wasn't certain as to the specifics, but he felt there were deeds he could accomplish for her. Eventually, she'd want him to stand by her side in her Christian battle against the morally sick and diseased of the world.

He'd waited for some specific signal from her, hoping she would spell out what she wanted him to do to help her in her crusade. That signal had come today.

He tingled with the realization that the war had been launched, with Rose the guiding beacon and he the unseen warrior—for the moment—in the field.

On his way home he felt feverish, knowing an excitement unlike any he'd experienced in years. Making his way down to the altar along with other milling bodies, he'd reached out to almost touch her gown. Under the brilliant light coming in from the dome, she'd looked into his trusting face, her eyes like a blast of sunlight, the radiance blinding him. In the midst of a crowd, her eyes had made contact with his, creating a great sense of intimacy and, for a moment, though surrounded by thousands, they stood alone in the temple.

Back on his own street an hour later, he was filled with a tremendously pressing need to begin the battle she'd talked of. He'd be there in the Combat Zone, marching by her side tonight.

Pulling into his garage, he found his flagging spirits revived. As if to remind him of all the evil still lurking, he spotted Maria playing in his backyard. As he yelled at her, the little Cuban girl stood glaring at him—contemptuous, defiant, as if asserting her right to use his own private property.

When he moved menacingly toward her, she screamed and ran across the street to the outstretched arms of her stringy-haired mother, who grabbed her up and took her inside their house.

Back in his own kitchen, he poured himself a glass of natural apple juice. He found the air heavy and hot, yet he refused to raise a window. Still, it didn't matter. At least with the windows shut, he could keep out the pollution from the Cuban neighborhood.

In his back bedroom, he pulled off his clothes and collapsed. He wanted to remember every detail of what Rose had looked like at the temple that morning. He'd never seen her more beautiful. With no thought other than of her, he could lie in his bed peacefully, anticipating the rapidly approaching night and the candlelight parade through the Combat Zone.

But that was a long time from now. The rest of the day was rapidly filling up, however. He eagerly looked forward to renewing his contact with Sandy at two o'clock down by the reservoir, and Buck had left a message that he wanted to meet him for a Jacuzzi bath, a cigar, and some vintage brandy at his cottage on the estate of Buck Brooke I.

Gene turned over in bed, lost in his dreams. After years of loneliness, he felt popular again. Sandy wanted to be with him, his old buddy Buck was back in his life, and he knew it would be only hours—maybe even tonight—before Rose too acknowledged him and wanted to be with him.

*****

An hour had gone by since a well-groomed attendant, in a maroon and gray uniform, handed a card to Buck. It was from Rose. On the back she'd written, "See me backstage. Love in Christ. Rose."

He'd waited impatiently in an anteroom decorated with large blow-ups of Sister Rose attending various rallies. He kept being told by attendants that Rose was still wishing good-bye to her followers, all of whom planned to march in tonight's parade through the Combat Zone.

Finally, the same attendant who'd initially given him the card told him that Rose had asked for him to meet her in her dressing room. She promised to be there shortly but had been overwhelmed by the massive outpouring of support for her crusade, as she greeted followers after the service.

In the corridor leading to the dressing rooms buried underground at the temple, Buck collided with Calder Martin, the stench of whiskey and Clorets powerful on his breath. The leading hatchetman of the far right, Calder, at fifty-five years of age, stood in the shadows of American politics. The original Mr. Dirty Tricks, he was considered far too controversial a personality for even the pre-Watergate Nixon White House to hire, though Calder had repeatedly applied for a post "behind the scenes." Nixon had turned him down three times, claiming, "We want an open administration."

Buck knew all the rumors. Reportedly, Calder's overall strategy was to form a coalition of the "new majority." Up to now, it'd been assumed that he planned to organize his caucus from a variety of right-wing hate groups. His appearance at Rose's temple caused Buck to wonder if he were trying to enlist the support of the more militant right-wing church people as well.

Calder had never made a foray into religion before, preferring to devote his considerable talents as a fund raiser to the "grass roots majority, common sense Americans."

Known by his enemies as "liver lips," he stood only five feet, five inches tall, a pudgy person whose thick neck seemed to bulge out in all directions from his stiff white collar. With a bulbous nose, a puffy face and sunken eyes behind horn-rimmed glasses, he reminded Buck of his former biology teacher at the university. He had met Calder once before when he'd covered a Republican political convention.

"Don't tell me," Buck said sarcastically, "that America's most confirmed atheist is about to be born again."

Calder gave him a wide, insincere smile and then in a booming voice said, "Religion's bullshit and we both know it. But when you're trying to save this country from a Communist takeover, you've got to sleep with some strange political bedfellows."

"You mean Rose Phillips?"

Calder ignored the question. "Take the Examiner. With your granddad, it was on our side—until you took over with your high school Marxist ideas."

"I see you read our story."

Calder leaned closer to him and, like an amoeba finding its prey, seemed to surround him. He steeled himself against the onslaught. The feel of the sterile windowless corridor was depressing enough without getting assimilated into the protoplasm of Calder Martin.

"When I was thirteen, I used to be an ice-shaver for snow cones." Calder confided. "I learned to shave pretty close in those days. Make real thin ice. And that's exactly what you're walking on, boy, if you publish another crock of shit like you did this morning."

"May I quote you?" Buck asked facetiously. "MARTIN THREATENS EXAMINER." His eyes tightened and he moved menacingly toward Calder, just as the hatchetman threatened him.

"You can't quote me at all," Calder said. "I don't want my name ever mentioned in your rag. You got that? If you fuck with me, the old ice-shaver, you might end up with your balls cut off."

"Is that tantamount of Kate Graham getting her tit caught in the wringer?"

"Far more dangerous—and painful!"

"I know you types would like to fondle my balls, but exactly how do you plan to cut them off?"

"What if I told you you're in danger of losing the Examiner?"

"I'd tell you you're full of shit. The Examiner, the last I heard, is owned by my granddad. I haven't heard he's turning it over to you."

"There's a lot a stupid liberal punk like you doesn't know. And I'm not going to be the one to enlighten you."

"I'm having lunch today with my granddad. Perhaps I'll ask him if I'm in any danger of losing the Examiner."

"Go ahead and ask that old whore-hopper. I defy you to ask him."

"Your challenge is accepted." Buck stood tall, towering over Calder. "While I have you on the phone, let me ask you a question. Strictly on the record. Just what are you doing in our fair town?"

"I don't talk to assholes from the Examiner!"

"Your being here doesn't have anything to do with big development planned on South Beach, does it?"

Calder looked up menacingly at him. "Listen, faggot, don't you connect me with that. I'll sue you for more money than you've got if you print one word of crap like that."

"I'm printing nothing for the moment, but know that we're definitely going to check you out. You see, we want to know why you're here. You're not in town for your health—that's for damn sure."

"I'm warning you. I have the power to shut down your slimy rag tomorrow. If you don't think I have that kind of power, just put me to the test."

"I suspect I will."

"Now get out of my way, scumbag." Calder pushed past him, then turned and looked back, glaring at Buck who had obviously touched a nerve and filled him with fury.

"You might be having us investigated. But we're having you checked out too. The moment I arrived in town I've had you investigated. You wouldn't believe some of the shit we've come up with so far. It might get you run out of town, boy."

As Calder faded in the distance, Buck stood watching him go. He was right about one thing: Calder was definitely an amoeba, flowing down the corridor, trickling into every dark corner, every deep crevice, absorbing, filling, then oozing on. He braced himself. Calder had left him feeling high and dry, but he hadn't engulfed him. The question was, had he already seduced Rose Phillips?

*****

Buck stepped up to the door of Rose's dressing room and rapped lightly, even though he suspected the evangelist was still up front, shaking hands and accepting contributions or pledges—including a lot of personal checks. A boy's voice called to him to come in.

At a backstage mirror, lined by a row of electric bulbs, sat one of the world's most beautiful boys. He was wiping makeup from his face with cream. "Fucking pimple," he said into the mirror, dabbing at his cheek with Kleenex.

Buck could not recall seeing a boy who possessed such physical perfection. It would have taken the most skilled of Renaissance painters to capture his essence. He looked androgynous as he pursed his cupid mouth. Ringlets of honey-colored curls covered his head. His blue eyes with long lashes were luminous, and in spite of his protestations about some alleged pimple, his skin was unblemished and peach colored. His features were flawless—his nose, his ears, his forehead appearing as if carved by a sculptor.

At first Buck couldn't say anything. He just stood staring, and then he was struck by an overwhelming feeling that this is what Robert must have looked like when he was fourteen. Buck didn't know Robert when he was fourteen, but he could just imagine Robert looking like this heavenly creature who sat before him. The boy wore a rose-colored suit, a red bow tie with white polka dots, and red leather cowboy boots, an outfit obviously selected by Rose. This boy appeared too hip for such garb.

His eyes darted to Buck, returned to the mirror, and then reverted to Buck again. No whore in any sleazy bar when he was in the service ever evaluated him as carefully as this angelic looking child. Buck felt that the boy possessed x-ray vision and was completely undressing him as he stood for inspection.

"You must be my new driver," he said, his eyes lingering below Buck's belt. "God, you're one sexy hunk. I can't believe it. Rose always hires such old men to haul my ass around. I can't believe she'd trust me alone in a car with the likes of you."

"I'm not your driver. I'm Buck Brooke."

"Holy shit!" The boy rose to his feet. "Forgive me. Fuck! Mistaking you for a chauffeur. On closer examination, I see you're definitely the type to be hauled around with your own chauffeur. I'm Shelley Phillips. Rose's adopted son, as she keeps reminding me."

"I saw you in the garden the night I came to Rose's house for dinner."

"I sorta remember that. If I had known what you looked like, I would have invited you to my bedroom. What an arrogant little prick I was that night."

"Forget it."

"I didn't shake your hand. Rose always insists I shake hands." He reached for Buck's hand and held it firmly in his grasp. "If you're like me and you're not much into hand-shaking, you can slip your tongue down my throat."

"That's a very tempting offer. Mind if I take a rain check?"

"Honey, you can take anything of mine you want." He took Buck's hand and placed it across his left breast. "You think licking women's saggy tits is a turn-on. Wait till your mouth devours my sweet little nipples."

Buck pulled his hand away. "You know, he said, "the penalty for child molestation is severe in this state."

"I'm no God damn child," Shelley said, looking disappointed at the loss of Buck's hand. "I'm eighteen and legal if you'd like to consummate this meeting."

"Hell, I thought you were fourteen. You look fourteen going on forty."

"It's this fucking drag Rose makes we wear. I was supposed to go on today. But she dominated the whole service."

"What do you mean, go on?"

"I was supposed to do my bit as a child preacher."

"Of all the fields open to you, evangelism isn't what I would have picked."

He stared at Buck, then burst into laughter. "It was God's decision. God, I said. Surely you know who *she* is."

Buck smiled. "I still can't see you preaching."

Shelley sat back down at the dressing table and continued to eradicate his makeup. "I should have been a fucking movie star, and I would have been if Rose had listened to me. There were roles I could have done. Children possessed by the devil, shit like that. You know, spin-offs from The Exorcist. One of them was really great. I would have been brilliant in the role. About a kid who had a fourteen-inch cock by the age of four. The character's name was Damon."

"Sounds like a big part."

"It was!" A cold fury came over Shelley's features, his face blanching under the golden curls. "If they actually showed the cock, I bet they could have done a close-up of your dick instead."

"I think I'm about three inches short."

"I just knew it! I just knew it!"

"Knew what?" Buck asked, flabbergasted.

"That you have a big dick. I have this inner radar. Just by touching a man's hand, I can tell the size of his dick. The most I've been meeting up with lately is five and a half inches, or even less. I haven't been plowed by a real man so long I've forgotten what it feels like."

"Maybe your luck will change."

"Maybe it already has, handsome."

Strange as it seemed, Buck enjoyed Shelley's company. With smug satisfaction, he was glad Rose had adopted such a far-out son with whom to cope.

Shelley turned once more to the mirror. "Rose wanted me to try out for all that Disney crap. Let's face it: Great pictures don't carry G ratings. She tried to turn me into a boy Shirley Temple. But the world wasn't ready for that crap." He smiled and looked up at Buck, rubbing off the rest of his make-up. "Who in the fuck is?"

Buck couldn't help staring at the boy. Shelley looked like some seductive pubescent, a true Lolito.

Shelley smiled with a knowledge far beyond his years. He seemed to know what effect he was having on Buck. "Don't be ashamed," Shelley said. "Most men, even the straight ones." He paused. "Especially the straight ones want to plow me when they meet me. Even when I'm shaking their hands, I look into their eyes, and I know what they want. But not everyone gets to plow into the hottest, sexiest, tightest boy ass in Florida. I don't know who you've fucked before. But you've never had a rosebud like mine. It's ready to suck you in any time. You just name the night."

In spite of himself, Buck felt a hardening in his pants, a fact that Shelley noticed too. "Again, you've got to give me a rain check on that. I'm here to see your mother."

"Fuck that cunt! She's always getting the men I want. That's at first. Before it's over I win them over in the end. Get it? The end."

"I get it!"

"I don't think that bitch will be glad to see you. Not after what you wrote in the Examiner about her this morning. Of course, in spite of her denunciation from the pulpit, everything you wrote is true."

"I know it is."

"All this stuff is off the record, stud. Rose doesn't allow me to grant interviews, unless she's around. In fact, I'm hardly allowed out of the house—and never alone!"

"I can see why," Buck said, thinking as he did that if Shelley ever met up with a child molester, it'd be the molester who got seduced. It was easy to see why Rose kept Shelley under careful control.

Shelley wheeled around and stared up at Buck. "You're about thirty, aren't you?"

"I'm getting there. Give me some more time."

"I didn't mean that in a bad way. Normally I don't go to bed with a man until he's thirty. I'm not into skinny boys. I like real men. There are so few of them left. You're a real man."

"Thanks."

"I mean that. I'll also let you in on a secret."

"About Rose? Something I can print in the Examiner? An exposé?"

"Cut the crap! The secret's about us. I'm psychic. I've always been psychic. For example, I'm getting vibes about something in your past right now."

"What in fuck are you talking about?"

"It's awful." He wheeled around and put his hands over his eyes. "I don't want to see it." He burst into tears. "It's awful."

Buck walked over to him and placed his hand on Shelley's shoulders. "It's okay. It'll be okay."

Shelley looked up at him with a certain trust, then wrapped his arms around Buck's waist, holding him tightly. His sobs diminished and still he held onto Buck.

When he felt Shelley was all right, Buck gently broke the hold on his waist and backed away. "Can you tell me what you saw?"

Shelley looked up at him through tear-streaked eyes. "I saw the agonized look and screams of your parents as they crashed to their deaths. It was ghastly."

Buck turned from the sight of Shelley and gasped for air in the stale dressing room. He really believed the boy. It was a scene he had imagined a thousand times in his nightmares, and he felt—really felt—that Shelley had actually witnessed the event in his head. The whole idea made him shudder.

"It's okay, it's okay," Shelley said in a soothing voice. "My head is clear now. But it's not something I can forget easily."

"Me, too." Buck choked back the tears. "I really miss them."

Shelley came up close to Buck and stood before him. He reached for his hand and held Buck's palm to his lips, gently kissing the inner skin. "I lost both my parents too. We have that in common. It's a bond between us. I ended up with this world-class bitch for a mom. What a trip!" He sighed. "I've got to take a shower and then I'll be escorted home, the gates to Paradise Shores shut behind me. It's a fucking prison."

"Excuse me, I'll leave."

"No, stay. Rose will join us soon." Shelley reached to hold his arm and detain him. "I haven't told you my psychic vision about us, and I'm never wrong about these things. Just ask Rose."

"What about us?"

"You're going to take me as your lover. We're going to spend the rest of our lives together. But there's a lot of hell we've got to live through before that happens. A lot of bad things are going to happen."

Buck didn't say anything. At first he wanted to dismiss the boy as crazed, yet he believed he did have that vision about his parents. "Can you tell me what's going to happen?"

"I can't. We can't change it. We've got to live it."

"You sure?"

"I'm sure." Right in front of Buck, Shelley began to undress. At first Buck was tempted to turn away. But it was obvious Shelley wanted an audience. One by one, each piece of clothing was removed. When Shelley took off his undershirt, Buck almost gasped at the pure male beauty of his body. His skin was golden, his chest perfectly formed but not overly developed. His breasts were tantalizing. Buck couldn't keep from staring.

Shelley stood before him in a pair of rose-colored briefs which matched the color of his cowboy outfit. Very carefully, he reached for the waistband of those briefs and slowly removed them before Buck's eager eyes. A nest of blond pubic hair trailed to a long uncut cock which seemed out of proportion to the rest of his frame. Shelley was no fourteen years old but was clearly a man with a man's genitals. Reaching for his robe, he turned around slowly. Buck knew what he was doing. He wanted Buck to admire his ass, which Buck did. It was probably the most alluring ass Buck had seen on anybody, even challenging Robert in that department.

"End of show." Shelley said. "For now. But you're going to have years and years to enjoy every bit of it." He slipped his bathrobe on and headed for the showers in back, slamming a door behind him. Then he stuck his head out again. "If you write something about me in your paper, for Christ's sake, say I'm pretty. The last story the Examiner ever ran on me made me sound like a sick little faggot." He slammed the door shut again and in moments had opened it again. "I'll be seeing you soon. And the next time I see you, you'd better not be wearing that damn suit. I want to feast on everything you've got, every inch of you." He shut the door more gently this time.

As Buck turned around, another door from the corridor was thrown open.

There stood Rose herself.

*****

"I didn't think you'd show up." Rose stood in the doorway, her soft lips parted. She quietly shut the door behind her and moved toward him, her face reflecting an infinite variety of moods, from sad to exuberant.

The changing moods of her face fitted his own conflicting feelings toward her. She appeared so delightfully feminine, so vulnerable, that he felt once more that he wanted to protect her. Yet, he reminded himself, that would be like committing treason. Behind the fabulous flesh, he suspected, lay a soul blacker than the sins she ranted about from her pulpit.

"I wanted to catch your act." He'd already decided to relate to her sermon as a show business performance. "But you didn't convert me. If anything, you stiffened my resistance."

She sat down in front of the dressing table just occupied by Shelley and checked her makeup. Then, in her most tantalizing way, she caught his eye in the mirror. "It's good to know I can stiffen something in you."

Holding that glance for a long moment, he laughed, her remark having broken the tension between them.

Excusing herself, she disappeared behind a screen to remove her gown.

He could still hear the shower running in the bathroom. Frankly, he'd expected her to launch into an immediate attack on the Examiner's story about her headquarters. "You asked about your sermon. I'll ask about our story."

Her head appeared around the screen. "My headquarters doesn't distribute racist literature. I called in reporters from the News. They inspected every storage room. Found nothing. Just my autobiography."

No longer respectful, he moved closer to the screen and then, in a perfectly controlled voice, said, "Babe, you're not fooling me for one moment. That creep, Calder Martin, probably had trucks remove the goodies in the middle of the night."

For a while he didn't hear a sound from her, and even her body stood motionless behind the thin screen. "Listen, I'm not stupid enough to have stuff like that around."

That actually made sense to him. "I know you're not. But your field marshals are."

From behind the screen, he could see her sticking out a leg, removing her sheer white hosiery. As she emerged, wearing a thin rose-colored robe that did little to conceal her slim figure, he felt it wasn't only the gorgeous legs, but the subtle and expressive way she moved her body, that made her such a turn-on.

"Why don't you write about my moral crusade? Not fantasies."

His back arched, he faced her squarely. "I'll write what I God damn please. And you're not going to like it. We're natural enemies."

She sat before him, her hair carrying a subdued jasmine scent, and the fragrance lingered in his nostrils ever so lightly.

"What are you up to?" he asked. "Is Calder taking over your operation?"

"Certainly not!" she said, smiling provocatively. "You know yourself Calder would cut off his grandma's breast if some rich Texas oilman offered him just five grand."

In exasperation, he said, "Then what? Do you want to become the duenna of the far right?"

With confident eyes and an impudent chin, she asked. "And why not? That prize is up for grabs. My appeal isn't just to rednecks any more. That old Bible Belt won't hold up a pair of pants. We're bursting at the seams, going national."

"I don't believe for one moment you're trying to offer spiritual help! And Calder's appearance here confirmed my suspicion. You want to bring church and state together. If somebody's not a born-again charismatic, how is he going to fit into your new America?"

She stood up defensively, her face tightening with her strength and determination. "I believe in the Bible. I adhere to orthodox Christian doctrine. I am personally committed to Christ. Given that belief, what makes you think I have any obligation to advance the cause of Jews, much less Communists?"

"But you must not trample on the rights of others, sweetheart, in advancing your own cause."

"Jews make up only three percent of the population, yet their influence extends insidiously far beyond that. They dominate publishing, the media, you name it. They have powerful groups working night and day to protect Jewish interests. Don't you think, in all fairness, the true Americans who live by the real Bible need just as tightly knit an organization working for our rights, too?"

"The normal majority," he said sarcastically. "For one thing, I don't know who in hell's going to decide who's normal. For another, what frightens me is the tyranny of the majority." Without a good-bye, he turned and left her dressing room, slamming the door in her face. Even before he'd gone far, he knew he'd behaved in a childish, petulant way and wasn't proud of that.

If she were ugly, like Calder Martin, then she'd be easy to hate. But she wasn't. She was beautiful. For him, that made her potentially dangerous.

It wasn't that she was an attractive older woman. He could have all those he wanted. From the age of fourteen, when he'd visited his mother between school terms, good-looking older women had always been after him.

It was more than that. He certainly wasn't a male Unity Mitford swooning after a Lorelei Hitler either.

Frankly, if Rose didn't have power, he would have met her and probably ignored her. It was her possession of power that intrigued him, making him in some way fantasize about taming her.

Her control of a vast and powerful right-wing propaganda machine had an effect like an aphrodisiac on him. If he could win her, have her groveling at his feet, he felt in some way he would be capturing and vanquishing that machine. It didn't make sense, and he could never consider such an unattractive motive, but it was the way he felt.

Even as he tried to concentrate on Rose, his thoughts drifted to Shelley's nudity. It should be against the law to look like that. Other thoughts about Shelley fought for control of his mind, but in the glaring heat of a particularly ferocious noon-day sun he blotted them out.

*****

In the early part of the afternoon and before lunch was served, old Buck Brooke I was in a rare confessional mood.

Secretly, the younger Buck felt the old newspaper czar was nearing the end of his life. Up to now he'd never explained anything, especially one of the actions he'd taken in the past. "Never justify," he'd warned his grandson, although ever since Buck had arrived at the Brooke estate, he felt that's what the oldtime tycoon was doing.

"I'm not as clean as a hound's tooth," he told Buck III, coughing even as he talked. He could still walk, but preferred to spend most of the day in a wheelchair with a small day quilt offering him protection, from the excessively cold air conditioning. "I've done a lot of things in my life I'm ashamed of."

"All of us can say that," Buck said, hoping to dismiss his grandfather's revelations which strangely embarrassed him.

Old Buck seemed determined to continue. "Believe you me, the sins of mine play like a movie in my head every night. I've got a lot of guilt I can't get rid of. A lot." He looked over at his grandson through tired, gray eyes. Although born in the late 19th century, he'd always had a robust physique and a handsome profile until the 1970s. If anything, he appeared to be slowly withering away, losing more and more weight every time Buck saw him. "If I could go back and relive my life, I would, knowing what I know now. I was a man of great passion. I had a great love of life. You're not looking at a saint. My passion for life got out of control at times. I went too far. I would get caught up in something, and there was no way I could control my impulses."

"Why are you telling me all this?" Buck asked. "You've never confessed anything before."

"Listen, fucker, I'm not telling you this for my obit. I sense you're the same man I used to be. A man who can't keep his passions under control. Your father was different from us. He met your mother in the tenth grade of high school, went to the same college with her, and married her on graduation. You're more like me. I don't think you could be true to one person for more than six weeks. You've always got to find out what the pussy is like on the other side of the river." He looked long and hard into his grandson's eyes. "Or, in your case, whatever."

"I don't know what in hell you mean by that."

"Later, we'll go into it later." He started to cough again.

Young Buck got up to assist him and get him some water, but old Buck brushed him aside. "A glass of water won't help me much now. Maybe a brandy."

"Coming up." Buck got up and went of the bar and poured his grandfather a stiff brandy, his favorite, an unmarked brand he'd always imported from some remote province of France.

Old Buck sniffed the brandy and drank a heavy swig. He closed his eyes briefly and then opened them. He looked as if he wanted to say something and didn't know how to say it, or even if he should say it. Finally, the brandy seemed to ease his mind. "One little vixen turned out to be too much for me. I guess she didn't like what I was making her do to me. The God damn bitch just up and bit off part of my dick. Only my doctor knows how much. I don't care to go into any more graphic details. But the stud of Okeechobee could never quite function properly again, and it ruined my life. I even considered suicide. My plumbing was permanently damaged. I continued to have sex with young girls, but I could never satisfy them the way I used to. I had to find another way, and I did. I still carried on a sex life until about four years ago. After that sex didn't seem to matter any more."

"Did grandmother know about this?" I mean, all your affairs."

"I think Nellie always knew. But she never said anything. Once she caught me under the most suspicious of circumstances in that cottage out back. I had my pants down. I told your grandmother the maid was removing an ingrown hair from my inner thigh. She just turned and walked away. She never brought up the subject ever again, but she fired the maid the very next day."

"I always loved Nellie. She was wonderful to me."

"She was a good woman. As good as I was bad. Some of my worst excesses came much later in life. Your grandmother, bless her heart, had the good grace to die in 1960 before I'd made some of my really big mistakes."

"Care to tell me about them? I think in some way what you're doing here is not confessing but warning me somehow."

"You're right about that." He took another hefty swig of brandy. "I want to go to my grave with the dirtiest of my secrets. I can't stand having you or anybody else learn too much about me. I know a biography is being written about me right now by Susan Howard's mother, Ingrid. I don't want you to cooperate in any way. I was a dirty old man. Let's leave it at that. Dirty old men are often subjected to blackmail."

"What does someone have on you? Are you being threatened? Is the Examiner in trouble?"

"So many questions but you'll get so few answers from me."

"Calder Martin threatened me this morning. Do Calder and Rose have something on you?"

"Let's leave it at what I've told you. I will make no death bed confession. Don't even try to get one out of me. In my day men went to their graves with their secrets. Today the fuckers go on God damn talk shows. I'll never do that."

"You're trying to tell me something, and I think I know what it is."

Buck I finished the last of his brandy and held up his empty glass to Buck III. Buck got up from his chair and went to refill it. "The bottom line is, you can't expose Rose," the old man said. "I know you're planning a series on her. It will never run in the Examiner, at least while I'm alive."

"Like hell it won't! I'm going ahead with my investigation. That little bit of news about Rose and her anti-Semitic propaganda that you surely read this morning—that's only the beginning."

"If you expose Rose, she'll go public with what she knows about me. That's no idle threat, not with Calder Martin in town. I'll be publicly humiliated. I'm a dying man." He reached out his withered hand to grasp Buck's fingers. "I want to die in peace. You owe me that much. I've lost nearly all the papers, except two or three minor ones. I used to have twenty big ones. Now, only the Examiner."

"And even that is in danger," Buck said, taking hold of his grandfather's hand and squeezing it. "Are you saying it could be taken away from us?"

"Anything in life can be taken away. Even life itself."

"Won't you give me some more details? My life is tied up with the Examiner. I need to know. Fuck, I'm the publisher."

"You are the publisher, but not with as much power as I gave you at first. In fact, just this morning I've empowered Roland to have a publisher's say. From now on, he can overrule you on any story or series."

"He's only the city editor."

"He's more than that now."

Buck dropped his grandfather's hand.

"He's a city editor with the power to overrule his publisher."

"I've never heard of such an arrangement," Buck III said, edging closer to the end of his seat. "You can't stop me from exposing Rose. It's a free country."

"You're right. I can only stop you from exposing her in the Examiner, and only for as long as I live."

"I'll sell my story to a national magazine. You can't stop me from doing that."

"If you expose Rose, and if you expose what Calder and Rose are up to, your career at the Examiner is over. I'll see to that."

Buck got up and headed for the bar. He poured himself a strong Scotch. "I think my career at the Examiner just ended today. You've given me no choice. I'm too proud to stay on. It'll take several weeks, and I'll continue to operate the paper in a more limited capacity. But not for long. I won't stand for the limitations you're placing on me. Find yourself another boy. I won't leave you short-handed at the moment, but I'll eventually resign."

"You're a fool. A God damn fool. An honest and idealistic fool who knows nothing of compromise."

"You've made plenty of mistakes. You said so yourself. Why can't I make mine?"

"You can and will—that's obvious. I'm sure there is nothing I could say or do to talk some sense in you. You're just as hot-headed and stubborn as your father. He could never make compromises either. He didn't know the meaning of the word." The old man looked at Buck imploringly. "Play ball with me. Play ball with Rose and Calder. If you do, you could become one of the biggest publishers in this country. If you don't, you're staring oblivion in the face."

"I'm only twenty-seven years old. How can you suggest that without you or without the Examiner that would be the end of Buck Brooke III? I have your name and I'm carrying on with the legend. I've got talent. I'm still young. For all you know, twenty years from now, I might be living in the biggest mansion in Okeechobee." He looked at the sprawling grounds in back of old Buck's mansion. "Even bigger than this one."

"The honor of the biggest mansion goes to Sister Rose. I doubt if you'll ever get a bigger mansion than hers."

"You can't predict that. You don't know how far I might climb in my life."

"Listen to me, fucker. Mark my words. You'll never live in a mansion bigger than Rose's, in spite of your talent. You'll never climb as far up the mountain as she's climbed."

"I'll try to go as far as I can in life. If I don't get help from one source, I'll get it from another. There are some people loyal to me."

"There's only one person loyal to you—and that's Robert Dante." Old Buck's words stabbed the afternoon air like a knife wound. "You forget, I'm an old newspaperman. I know what's going on. The only reason that little faggot is loyal to you is because you let him suck your dick. Your dick—not you—buys his loyalty."

"You don't know what you're talking about."

"I know plenty. If you weren't the publisher of the Examiner, you'd be surprised how all your so-called friends would desert you. Not Dante, of course. As long as he can swing on that cock of yours, he'll stay with you forever."

Buck jumped up from his chair. "I'm out of here."

"Sit down, fucker." The old man said that so harshly it brought on a coughing spasm. He reached for the new glass of brandy. After he'd swallowed some, the coughing subsided. "I've got something to tell you. Even if I'm facing a bit of trouble holding onto the Examiner, you are hardly going to be out on the street."

"I know. I have my own home. It's a mansion too. Not as big as this one."

"I know all about it, fucker. I was the guy who gave it to your father. He never earned one penny of money that went into that house."

"I'm really upset. What else have you got to tell me?"

"Cool it! Don't be so impatient. Even though there's much about you I don't admire, I'm leaving everything I have to you, including this estate and all its outbuildings. Even the cottage in back. The fuck cottage."

"Why do you call it that?"

"Because that's what I had it built for, and because that's what you used it for all during your university years when you didn't want your parents to know who you were fucking, man or woman. The Examiner might be a dubious gift. I'm not in complete control there."

"If not you, then who?"

"It doesn't matter."

"It matters a hell of a lot to me. I'm the publisher. I have a right to know who I'm working for."

"What do you care about the Examiner any way? You just told me: you're resigning."

"I can't be publisher under your restrictions."

"Bullshit, fucker, you could if you weren't so damn stubborn. Forget the Examiner for the moment. I have other things to leave you. A lot."

"You've never really told me what you own. To judge from the salary you pay me, you're poor."

"I pay you a small salary to teach you character. I'm leaving this mansion to you."

"The taxes on it will be more than I can afford."

"Don't get smart-assed with me. There are other assets. Those assets will help you pay the taxes. I've got a villa in Palm Beach that I own outright. I've even leased it to the Kennedys from time to time when they overflowed their compound. I've got a triplex on Fifth Avenue in New York. I've got five-million dollars in cold cash lying around in various banks. I've also got about eight hundred thousand dollars worth of jewelry that belonged to your grandmother. I also own a big hunk of land in Central Florida that I bought in 1934 for peanuts. It's worth about eight million dollars, and by the time you're fifty will probably be worth fifty million dollars. That's not all. I own half a block on South Beach, including the very apartment Hazel Phillips lives in. But I'm selling that particular asset for maybe upwards of five million."

"Who would pay that? It's not worth anywhere near that amount of money."

"The buyer's a secret."

"Is Calder Martin behind this? Rose?"

"That's for me to know and you to find out. Until you inherit everything, I'm saying nothing more. When you go over my papers when I'm dead, a lot of things will become clear to you. I also own a lot of land in other states. Even though I have a shaky hold on the Examiner, I am certainly providing for you. Just in case those big ambitious plans of yours don't work out. But even with all I've got, it's just a fraction of the millions Rose will leave to that adopted nelly son of hers, Shelley. Some mind-fucking name like that, although I once had an uncle named Shelley."

"I didn't know you had this kind of money. I knew you were loaded but I didn't know how much. I don't think even my father knew."

"He didn't know. I never told him, and I'm only telling you now because I'm dying, leaving you one of the richest men in the State of Florida. But all those millions come with a price tag."

"Oh, shit. What's the price I have to pay?"

"I want you to marry Susan Howard."

"You can't tell me who to marry."

"I not only can, I am. You'll give up that faggot Dante and marry a good woman and become a real man, or I'll disinherit you. Give every penny to charity."

Buck III looked confused and bewildered. He wanted to strike back, to blast out at the old man, but did nothing but sink back into his chair, his stomach feeling like it'd been kicked in. At that moment, the butler came into the room. "Miss Howard has just arrived."

"Wha...?" Buck III sat up in his chair. He turned to his grandfather. "You've invited her here for lunch?"

"Time is running out for me. Everything must be speeded up. My last public appearance will be at your wedding."

*****

When Susan walked into the room with all its potted greenery to greet Buck I and Buck III, she sensed a bitter argument had just ensued. Young Buck seemed startled to see her. Hadn't he been told that she was a guest for lunch?

Recovering quickly, he walked rapidly toward her, giving her a quick kiss on the mouth. "I've been meaning to call."

"I know," she said demurely. "All of us have been so busy."

Buck I didn't get up from his wheelchair but appraised her from afar. "Susan, it's been a long time."

"Only four years," she said walking toward him to give him a kiss on his withered cheek.

"How time flies," he said. "But you're still one mighty fine looking heifer."

"Grandpa," Buck III said. "They don't call them heifers any more."

Buck I looked up at Susan in surprise. "What do men call women these days? You young people keep changing the terms all the time."

"As I was getting in my car, two Cuban men yelled at me, 'That's one hot puta.'"

"I think I'll stick to heifer." He called to his butler. "Get Susan here a drink."

"A martini," she said. "Make it with gin. I'm an old-fashioned..." She paused, looking down at Buck I, "...gal."

Over drinks, Buck I continued to down his brandy, brushing off the doctor's warnings as conveyed by his butler. "I'm going to die. I probably won't even make it to Christmas. For all I know, this brandy will keep me alive for another year or so."

"You'll live another quarter of a century," Susan said with a kind of breezy optimism. "I hear all the Brooke men are big and strong." She looked enigmatically at Buck III.

"We've all been studs to be proud of," Buck I said. "But even the biggest bull in the pasture has to give up one day."

"It will be a loss for the women of the world." She smiled faintly at Buck III. "But thank God you've left an heir to carry on the tradition."

Buck III smiled back at her, looking acutely embarrassed.

To Susan, this was obviously not the lunch of his dreams.

"I want to get some unpleasant business out of the way before we move on to the festivities of the day." Buck I managed to sound just as forceful as he did in his board room heyday. This exertion of his lungs brought on another coughing spasm. The butler kept giving him fresh handkerchiefs, as he always refused to use tissue paper. "I've been coughing and spitting in handkerchiefs ever since I was a little boy. No need to change that habit at this late hour."

"Exactly what unpleasant business do you want to throw at us?" Buck III asked, appearing in great distress. He looked as if he wanted to flee.

Susan noticed that when Buck I spoke, he looked only at her, completely ignoring his grandson. "Roland told me that young Buck here assigned you a new series: The investigation of this South Beach thing."

"That's right," she said, "and I think we're on to somebody big here."

"Forget it!" he looked harshly at her, like a military commander issuing an order to a lowly recruit. "This is one story the Examiner is not going to break. Let the Okeechobee News drown in it. The Examiner will do no investigative reporting on the subject. If something breaks on the TV channels, we can pick it up from there. But only pronouncements from public officials, providing those pronouncements aren't coming from Hazel Phillips."

Susan felt as if all the air had left the room and there was nothing left to breathe. She looked at Buck III for confirmation of this incredible order, but his face remained blank and passive. It was obvious he had plenty to say about what his grandfather was doing, but chose to remain silent.

In lieu of no protest coming from her superior, Susan turned and confronted the old man himself. "I think this is a big mistake. You've been one of the great newspapermen of this century. You would never have said this fifty years ago. Why today?"

"Because, bitch, I'm an old and dying man. I know more about life than the two of you young farts will ever know. You've got to trust me on this one. I'm doing what's right to protect the Examiner."

"I don't know who you are protecting," she said harshly. "It's obviously not the Examiner."

Buck I glared at her. He bitterly drank the rest of his brandy.

"For the moment," Buck III finally said. "I'm still the publisher of the Examiner. But Roland has been given authority to kill every story or series. In essence, I've had my balls cut off."

"You'll find them again," Susan said.

"I hope so." He glanced disdainfully at his grandfather. "Perhaps not as publisher of the Examiner."

"Now, now," Buck I said in the way of consolation. "Time will tell. God knows what will happen when I'm gone and a young upstart like you is in full control."

An awkward silence fell over the room. Something seemed to disturb the three birds of prey Buck I kept. Susan didn't know one bird from another, but knew that they were considered extremely dangerous if unleashed from their cage. She felt right this minute that Buck I wanted to cage Buck III.

Finally, it was Buck III who spoke. "There are just so many things that we can control from the grave."

"Tell me something I don't already know," Buck I said like a reprimand. He screamed for his manservant. "Why don't you people go for a brief little walk in the garden? I need a little help getting to the table. Come back in about ten minutes when I'll be artfully arranged to preside over my last company luncheon."

Neither Susan nor Buck III said anything, as he took her hand and guided her to the garden.

"What does all this mean?" she asked, once they were out of hearing distance from the house.

"It means he's dying. It means he's deeply mixed up in this Rose mess. Even this Calder Martin mess. It's my worst nightmare."

"But what are you going to do? You can't let him dictate terms like this."

He turned her around and looked deeply into her eyes. "I've just spoken with his doctor. Grandfather has days, or at most, only a few weeks, to live. I'm just going to play along. Take his orders. Put up with his shit. He'll be dead soon and I'll do what I want to do after that. Even if it means taking on Rose herself in battle."

"You mean that? You really mean that? You won't give in to Rose the way old Buck has so obviously fallen to her?"

"Hell no, you know me. I won't do that. That's a promise."

"All of this is happening so fast, I don't know what to think."

"Think about this," he said, pulling her to him and kissing her long and deep, inserting his tongue which she efficiently sucked for him. He broke away slightly, as if gasping for air. "Will you marry me?"

*****

Even as he sat down at the luncheon table, Buck couldn't believe that Susan had accepted his proposal of marriage. If he were her, he pondered what his decision would have been. Even more surprising to himself, was the fact he'd made the proposal at all. But old Buck knew him well. The temptation was too great. He decided he'd be a fool not to accept the agreement. Under the circumstances, he reasoned, the marriage might be a bit of a sham, as he had no intention of ever leaving Robert and might indeed accept Robert's proposal of marriage. But he knew all this mess could be straightened out later, right after Buck died. Once he inherited old Buck's millions, he would be free to do what he wanted, both as a husband and a publisher. The world, at least according to the way he saw it this afternoon, would be his. He was convinced he could win Robert over to his point of view. What he didn't want to contemplate, at least not now, was Gene's reaction. That he feared most of all.

"I had my cook fix me corned beef and cabbage, my alltime favorite," Buck I was telling both of them, although he aimed most of his talk at Susan. "Always did make me fart, though. So you've been duly warned."

Susan pretended to laugh, but it was merely the mock. Obviously she didn't find that remark funny and looked uncomfortable at table.

The butler served Buck I first. "Forgive this breach of etiquette," Buck I said to Susan. "But my good man here knows I'm likely to die at any moment, so he always serves me first."

"It's okay," she said.

"Grandfather," Buck said, "I have to tell you something. During that brief time when we went for a walk in the garden, Susan agreed to marry me."

Buck I dropped his fork, as if his hearing aid were malfunctioning. "My God. I wanted you to speed this thing up, but you were faster than I could imagine. I was going to goad you into asking her hand in marriage after we've chowed down on this corned beef here."

"You didn't have to goad me. I've been thinking about it for a long time."

"It came as a surprise to me, too," Susan said. She smiled demurely at Buck III. "Imagine? After only one date."

Buck I stopped chewing the grainy meat for a minute. He looked proudly at his grandson. "That must have been a hell of a date."

"It was," she said.

"Sounds to me young Buck here takes after his grandfather. Not his own dad. That was one goodie-two-shoes."

"My father loved only one woman in his life," Buck III said. "His wife. And in each other they found total fulfillment."

"That's the case with my own parents, Jim and Ingrid. They love each other very much. After they met there was no one else—there could be no one else—for either of them."

Buck I looked sternly at young Buck. "I fear, and this is a warning to you, gal, this young stallion here takes more after me than he does his own father."

"Exactly what is that supposed to mean?" Buck III asked, slightly embarrassed at his own question, as he feared Buck I's answer.

"What I mean, to be precise, is that there is a deviant streak in this young man here. A streak so deviant that only marriage to a good woman can cure him of it."

A long silence came to the table, relieved only when the butler came in to ask if they wanted more wine. No one accepted his offer.

Finally, Susan broke the silence. "I'm the last gal." She paused slightly to emphasize the word gal. "I'm the last gal a man should marry to cure himself of a deviant streak." She looked at Buck III with a kind of challenge in her eyes before focusing her attention on Buck I. "My record is clear on that point. You forget, I was married to Gene Robinson."

Buck III felt the air conditioner should be turned off. The room was unbearably cold. "Let's forget all this talk and celebrate the joy of the occasion."

Buck I looked first at Buck III and then at Susan. "He's got a point there." He looked around for his manservant who sensed he was needed. Buck I looked into the servant's eyes with a certain weary resignation. "Bring me that box."

In moments the servant returned to the room where he handed Buck I the box he'd requested. Buck I brushed it away, motioning for him to give it to Buck III.

"What's this?" Buck III asked, opening the box.

"It's your God damn engagement ring, considering that you don't have the money—or the time—to buy this pretty gal here a proper one."

Buck III opened the package slowly and stared at one of the most beautiful gems he'd ever seen. "It's a sapphire," he said to Susan.

"Sapphire, hell!" Buck I said. "This is a rare blue diamond. One of the finest you will ever see. It's worth a fortune."

"How did you get it?" Susan asked.

"Back in the 20s. I was going to foreclose on a mortgage of a guy who lost everything in the stock market crash. He offered me this blue diamond. After I had it appraised, I accepted his offer. I tried to give it to my wife, but she was a simple woman. Locked it in our safe where it's been ever since."

Buck III took the ring out of the box and walked around the table. In front of Susan, he got down on his knees and looked up into her eyes. "Will you marry me?"

She smiled. "The answer, handsome, is the same as in the garden. A definite yes."

He placed the ring on her finger and kissed her lightly on the lips. Then he got up and returned to his seat.

Buck I beamed with a certain pride. "Something tells me about nine months from now there's going to be a Buck Brooke IV to carry on the family name."

Susan laughed teasingly. "Does it have to be Buck Brooke IV? Can't we name him James after my own father?"

"Your father is a fine man, Susan, but I just know you'll want to name him after me. After all, some time in the next century it will be my millions he'll be living on. He'll want to remember the old man who set him up so well in life. Too bad I won't be around for the birth."

"You'll be around for the birth," Susan said.

Buck III said nothing. He wasn't even certain if his grandfather would be around for the wedding, and he doubted very seriously if there ever would be a Buck Brooke IV.

"I'm flying to Switzerland sometime soon," Buck I said. "I'm entering this clinic in Geneva. It's my last straw. They have ways there of prolonging life, or so I've been told."

"I didn't know that." Buck III said.

"You know it now, boy."

"I hope you'll be all right," Susan said.

"I'll never be all right ever again," he said in way of dismissal. "But I'm going to hang on to what life is left in me. We Brookes don't commit suicide too easily. Which brings up my final wish. I fully don't expect to return to America again. I have one last event I want to attend before flying out of here."

"What are you talking about?" Buck III said. "We'll take you anywhere you want to go."

"I've had your wedding speeded up. It's to take place at six o'clock in the garden here."

"But we've got to get a license," Buck III said. "A minister. Blood tests."

"Not when you're the grandson of Buck I. I've arranged everything."

"My God," Susan said. "This is a little sudden. I've got to go home and get dressed. Find something to wear."

"No problem about that," Buck I said. "I still have a rare lace dress worn by my wife at our wedding. It's stunning and in perfect shape. You and she were the same size. Right now that dress is being put in the back of your car."

"This is pretty fast going here," Buck III. "I don't even have time to think."

"You can think about it later," Buck I said. "I even have the marriage ring to go with that blue diamond."

"What about it, Susan?" Buck III asked. "You game?"

"Yes," she said. She turned to Buck I. "If this is what you want."

"It's what I want all right."

"I've got to warn everybody," she said. "I have a plane to catch at eight o'clock tonight. Ingrid is being honored at a large banquet in New York. Jim feels too ill to go. I've been asked to present an award around midnight. I can just make it. The following day I'm supposed to deliver a speech at this writer's conference."

"There will be plenty of time for a honeymoon later," Buck I said.

"I would go with you, honey," Buck III said. "But I've got to be in town tonight for Rose's moral crusade. That event, I fear, is going to be a big news story."

"You're right," Buck I. "Your first duty is to the Examiner. "A wife always comes second."

"I'm glad we've gotten that priority straightened out," Susan said, getting up from the table and excusing herself. "If I'm getting married in just a few hours, I've got to go home and get ready, and also get packed for New York."

"I'll walk you to the door," Buck III said, getting up and heading around the table to her.

Susan was kissing old Buck on the cheek again. "Very soon, sooner than I ever imagined, I'm going to be part of this family."

"Welcome aboard," the old man said.

Just as Buck III was escorting her out, the butler appeared. "Young Buck," he called. "Telephone for you. It's Robert Dante calling from Miami."

Susan looked imploringly into Buck's eyes before taking his hand and kissing him lightly on the lips. "I know the way out. See you at six." She hurried from the house.

Buck I said nothing but looked glaringly at Buck III, almost defying him to take that phone call.

Without looking back, Buck III headed for the front hall and Robert's call.

*****

Gene didn't mean to and even at the last minute he swore he wasn't going to show up, but at a quarter to two he found himself getting in his car and heading to the reservoir where he'd talked with Sandy.

It was shortly after two as he walked along the wall where Sandy had shared secrets about Leroy's Lolito ring. There was no one in sight. Did he really expect the boy to show up? Even if he did, what would it mean?

As he turned the corner he spotted the red-haired boy tossing rocks into the water. For one brief moment, and if life had gone differently, he felt that he could have been Sandy's father taking his son for a long walk after a family Sunday dinner. That's the way Sister Rose said was the only right and decent way to live. But life always wrote different scripts for you from what was supposed to be.

Spotting him, Sandy called out, "Gene, Gene." He raced toward Gene and threw himself into his arms. "I missed you. Thank God you showed up. I didn't think you would."

Gene felt awkward holding the boy in his arms, so he gently broke Sandy's hold on him.

"How are you doing, kid?"

"It was awful."

"What happened?"

"After leaving you, I was really confused. I tried to go back to work but I just couldn't. I met this old guy who wanted me to piss on him. I found everything so disgusting. In some strange way, I felt I belonged to you. I couldn't mess myself up with anybody, because from the very first I felt I had to keep myself pure for you from now on."

"You're not talking sense," Gene said, fearing this sudden intimacy. "What did you do?"

"With the money you gave me, I went and rented myself a cheap motel room. They had a little restaurant next to it. I went in there last night and ordered myself a steak. I hadn't had a steak in a long time, and I was really hungry. Then I went back to my room, lay in bed, watched TV. But mostly I dreamed about being your boy. About you taking care of me and about my loving you. You're everything I would ever want in life."

"You're talking shit. Cut it out!" Gene turned from the sight of the boy and walked rapidly along the wall as if trying to escape his presence and that kind of talk.

Sandy raced to catch up. "I didn't mean to say anything wrong. I was just telling you what's in my heart. Is that bad?"

"I appreciate your being honest with me," Gene said, coming to a stop and looking into the boy's trusting eyes. "But this talk of love. You hardly know me."

"You're god damn right. I hardly know you. That's what this is all about. I'm trying like hell to get to know you. You won't let me."

"You're just a kid."

"Hell, yes, I'm just a kid. I've got no one. No parents. I'm homeless. I need someone to help me out, mister. Take care of me. The only thing I've got to offer is my body. But with you I've got something else to give."

"What are you talking about?"

He reached for Gene's hand and held it, squeezing it hard. "That something else is love. For you, it's love. I want to love you, and you won't even give me a chance."

"It's not that..."

"It's what? Tell me. What is preventing you from loving me and taking care of me? Why don't you let me love you? Are you trying to bullshit me and tell me you don't need love?"

Gene turned away from the boy's intensity. The day wasn't going at all according to plan. But then he realized that was the wrong concept. He had no plan, and he didn't know what he was even doing here, even though he felt compelled to stay. He couldn't even think of turning Sandy loose to wander the Combat Zone again. Gene walked over to a park bench and sat down.

In moments, Sandy had joined him on the bench. He reached to hold Gene's hand but Gene pulled away.

"I know a lot about you," Sandy said. "More than you think I know." A defiant look came over his face.

"What do you know?" he asked, his mouth dry. He didn't really want Sandy to answer.

"My friend Jill remembers you very well."

"I don't know anyone named that." Gene felt his anger rise.

"Jill Henson. You remember?"

The mention of that name sent shivers through Gene. That was the name of the little girl he'd exposed himself to. She'd be about Sandy's age today, maybe two or three years older. No, no, he kept telling himself. It couldn't be the same Jill. How would she know a boy prostitute like Sandy from the Combat Zone?

"I know you're Gene Robinson. You've had your picture in the papers a lot. Jill told me what happened."

"Oh, God damn! It's the same girl. I'll never escape the day I exposed myself like that. God, I was sick. Desperate. I needed help. That's when I needed love, and that's the one thing I not only didn't get, but lost forever."

"Jill understands, believe it or not. She's a hooker now. She told me that you caused her no harm. No harm at all."

"She's forgiven me?"

"There is nothing to forgive. You couldn't help yourself. You paid a terrible price."

"I wish I could go back and relive that day. I'm ashamed. It's haunted me the rest of my life. Do you think my doing that to her made her a hooker?"

"It was her damn mama who made Jill a hooker. It was my own God damn mama who made me become a whore. When you kick a twelve-year-old out onto the street with no money and no clothes because you think he's gay, how's the kid supposed to live?"

"I know. I see it every day in my business. I'm a cop."

"I know that. I knew that from the first moment I got in the car with you. Even though I feared you might arrest me, I still got in your car. I felt I wanted to be with you, even though it was risky."

"You're not making sense," Gene said. "It doesn't happen that way." Eager to change the subject, he asked, "How is she?"

"Jill knows how to take care of herself. She's tough and into karate in case some john tries to get really kinky with her. I've seen her once or twice in the Combat Zone deliver some really chopping blows."

"I don't want to talk about her any more," Gene said, getting up abruptly and continuing the walk.

Sandy jumped up and trailed him, falling in with his rapid strides. "I don't want to talk about Jill either. I want to talk about us."

"There is no us to talk about. You're just an underage kid. I shouldn't be seen with you. Probably subjecting myself to another arrest."

"Let me come home with you. Give me a place to stay. I'll work hard for you until I'm old enough to get a regular job. Then I'll pay you rent. I promise."

"It just can't be."

"What can be then? Me going back into that Combat Zone? Trying to find some old creep who wants me to piss on him. Or, even worse, have him piss on me. Someone who's gonna torture me? Is that what you want for me? I'm someone who loves you. The only person in this whole stinking world who loves you."

"You don't love me."

"Try me." Sandy reached for his arm and with a surprising strength held it firmly and looked into Gene's face. Tears were streaming from Sandy's eyes. "Give me a chance, mister."

Gene felt he'd lost his mind but he put his arm around Sandy. "I'm taking you home with me."

"Oh, God, thank you," Sandy said.

He looked into the young boy's face, which was filled with gratitude. "It's not about sex, okay? We have to have that agreement. It's about love. It's about caring for someone. Maybe I could take care of you, and you could take care of me."

"You'll never regret this," Sandy said. "You've probably regretted most things in your life, but not this one. You'll see."

"I can only hope so." Gene looked up as a flock of birds flew low over their heads. "You told me you make a great chili. Let's stop by a grocery store and pick up some ingredients. I love chili. I've got an appointment later in the afternoon, but when I get home I want to smell that chili pot."

"You've got yourself a deal, mister."

He reached for Gene's hand, and this time Gene freely offered it. "And you've got yourself a boy. From this day forth, I'm Gene Robinson's boy, and I'm mighty proud of it."

Gene swallowed hard, enjoying the first strong breeze of the day. As he took the boy's hand and walked along, he realized how incriminating this appeared. He felt he was walking into madness, but could not turn back. He had to follow through on this strange new friendship, regardless of what it led to.

*****

In the cottage in back of the Buck Brooke I estate, Buck III eagerly awaited Gene's arrival. He'd already stripped in anticipation of their Jacuzzi bath, and he'd acquired some illegal Cuban cigars and a choice bottle of Armagnac from his grandfather's cellar for the occasion.

The cottage had always been his retreat from the world, even from his own parents. Buck I had given it to him and the old man had never visited him here ever since, recognizing that it was forbidden territory. "I never wanted to walk in the door and discover something," old Buck had once told him.

Buck III had never even invited Robert here before, although Gene had visited several times during their university years. Once when they'd taken two campus beauties here for sex, they had made love to the women in the same king-sized bed. Buck had become more excited than ever, not by his woman, but by watching his old buddy in action. He'd caught Gene looking at him at the time, and was left with the odd sensation that they were not making love to the women, but to each other.

Buck plopped down on a chaise longue on his back veranda overlooking a ravine, knowing that Gene would arrive in minutes. If nothing else, his old buddy was punctual.

He had a lot to think about, but somehow tried to blot out his upcoming marriage to Susan at six o'clock. He knew he should be thinking about that, but couldn't bring himself to deal with it—not now.

"This is my bachelor party," he told the birds perching ever so briefly on the wooden veranda railing. He looked over at the Jacuzzi. It was ready to receive not only his nude body but Gene's too.

He closed his eyes and listened to the music coming from his living room. His conversation with Robert was fresh in his mind. Robert's mother was holding onto life but her doctors didn't give her much time. Robert said he wanted to return, but was advised to stay on for another day or so because the end appeared close at hand. Buck had promised to fly to Miami for the funeral. Robert claimed he was going out of his mind missing Buck so very much and would call him later tonight.

Frankly, Buck was glad Robert wasn't in Okeechobee to face all the upcoming events. Robert had warned Buck to take extra caution and not put himself in harm's way when he covered Rose's moral crusade through the Combat Zone later that night.

What Buck couldn't tell him was that he was marrying Susan at six o'clock on his grandfather's estate. That would have to be explained to Robert in person, and it would take all of Buck's persuasive powers to overcome Robert's objections. He fully expected the marriage to end in a quickie divorce, as soon as the old man died.

He was hardly proud of himself for putting Susan through this and was completely prepared to make it up to her, assuming you could make up a betrayal like this. He was determined, and he wasn't sure how at this point, but he was prepared to greatly advance Susan's career for agreeing to this hasty marriage. At least the way he reasoned, her career would improve, even though it would surely represent another domestic disaster to her like her marriage to Gene had been. He shuddered to think what her reaction would be if she learned that her former husband was about to have a rendezvous with her future husband. Even he couldn't bear to think of the implications of that one.

As soon as he'd entered the cottage, and before stripping down, he placed a call to Milton Green, his attorney who also represented many of his grandfather's affairs as well. Very quickly Buck told "Uncle Milty" of Buck I's demands and threats of disinheritance.

"He absolutely means what he says," Milty had said. "He'll do it too. You'd be a fool not to agree to it, providing Susan will cooperate. We're told that he has maybe weeks left to live. His will contains no provisions beyond the grave. What the hell, you could get a divorce the day your grandfather dies."

"It doesn't seem right somehow," Buck had said.

"A lot of things don't seem right. In fact, about everything I do every day of my life isn't right. But I go ahead. When you're your own man, you can do whatever you want. I'm sure you'll make it up to Susan somehow. I could propose some sort of settlement for her that would be fair to all parties."

"Maybe."

"There's no fucking maybe about it," Milty had said. "It's an open and shut case. Buck I might have quoted you figures about his worth, but he's completely out of touch with reality. I'm sure he's quoting valuations from the fifties. Hell, this is 1977. His estate is worth millions more than he thinks it is. If all of us live to see the New Year ten years from now when you're only thirty seven years old, can you imagine what it's going to be worth then?"

"I'm sure acting cold-blooded about this whole mess."

"Don't worry about it. It's time you grew up and quit thinking with your liberal heart and soul. One of your former girl friends told me you've got a big pair of balls on you. About time you started clanking them before you turned thirty."

"I don't know."

"Cut the hesitation crap! Go through with the marriage. If it turns out to be a mess, old Uncle Milty is here for you. I've got you out of messes before, and we don't even have to go into what they were."

"No, we don't. Best left forgotten."

"Trust me on this one. Listen to me. Your grandfather bought land in central Florida and several other places during the Depression. He actually made money during the Depression when most of us here didn't have a pot to piss in. I remember as a kid I had to steal oranges and avocados from the fields to stay alive. I even stole chickens for my family so we'd have some meat on the table. When I was a little boy doing that, old Buck was acquiring land for peanuts. My God, I thought he was going to buy up the whole country. Even though much of that land is wilderness now, I predict that in your lifetime entire towns are going to be built on land he owns. Or, as the case may be, land that you will own. You'll be one of the richest men in this country.

"As rich as Sister Rose?"

"Maybe not that rich. But then she's got a staff of twenty-five just counting her contributions. Every time she appears on television, contributions start flowing in. A lot from Social Security checks."

"I don't want to think about that."

"Listen, do what the old man says. If you don't, you'll spend the rest of your life regretting it."

"It really scares the shit out of me."

"If you're dumb enough not to do it for yourself, think of Robert. You guys could have a future of diamonds, champagne, and roses. What a life. A big yacht to sail the world with your own crew. If you can't do this for yourself, do it for him."

"It's all but certain it's a done deal. But I've got a lot of explaining to do. Not only to Robert but to someone else."

"Who is this someone else? I thought you kept me informed of all your nocturnal adventures. After all, I'm your lawyer."

"Uncle Milty, as much as I love and trust you, I can't bring myself to tell you about this involvement."

"Shit, man, I know who it is. After all, I'm the smartest lawyer in Florida. That's why you love me. You're talking Gene here."

"You guessed it."

"Better talk yourself out of it pretty damn quick. You're dealing with a nut case. I learned privately that he's up for a very serious psychiatric examination in a day or so. I hear he's going to get thrown off the police force. Trust me, there's more than one screw missing. Also, what's he going to think when he learns you're marrying his former wife?"

"That I shudder even thinking about, much less telling him."

"Drop him—and I mean that. Drop him!"

"I've got to sort things out in my own way. Everything has happened so suddenly. My involvement with Susan. Back with Gene again. Just when I'm getting ready to commit to Robert in my most serious way."

"Take my advice. You pay enough for it. Marry Susan at six. Dump her later with a settlement. Drop Gene. Other than Shelley Phillips, Robert is the most beautiful boy in Okeechobee. Maybe in all of Florida. Even when you're an old man, Robert will be going down on that big eighty-five year old cock of yours, and you'll love it. Robert is marriage material. A companion for life. Go with Robert. That's my advice. I'll send my bill tomorrow."

"We'll keep in touch, Uncle Milty. I need you."

"I need you, too, you handsome hunk. If I were twenty years younger, and didn't have my own darling Patrick, I'd go after you myself, even though I hear you stretch assholes out of shape."

"Rumors, flattering rumors."

"As soon as Robert gets back from that Miami shit he's going through, I want you two over to our place. You know you like Patrick's cooking better than anybody else's."

"It's a date. I'll call you later."

"I love you, baby. Not just as your attorney. I really love you. You're like my son. God, I love you Gentile boys with your foreskin intact. I'm crazy about each and every one of you. You and Robert, Patrick and me will be sailing the world one day. Having a gay old time."

"We'll see about that, Milty. I love you too. Give Patrick a kiss for me."

"Hey, I hear a decision has been made. You're going to be named sexiest man of the year. The only thing wrong with that, you should be named sexiest man of the decade."

"Is that for sure?"

"It is indeed. I heartily concur. They were late in discovering you. I've always known how hot you are."

"Sounds like you've still got a crush."

"I'll always have a crush on you. I've got Patrick now. But I still think of you."

"That's really nice, Milty. While I've got you on the phone, I've got to ask one big favor."

"For you, anything."

"Has your tux come back from the cleaners?"

"All twenty five of them in all colors. Kept ready and waiting for any occasion."

"Fine, then get your fat ass over here at six o'clock. You're my best man." At that, Buck had hung up the phone.

Closing his eyes, he let the breeze blow across his body. He opened his eyes again, enjoying the way the sun broke through the shade trees. Suddenly, he heard footsteps coming up from the ravine. By the sound of those booted feet, it could only be Gene.

*****

In T-shirts and jeans, Gene stood before a naked Buck on his veranda, as the sun headed down over the trees in the ravine. "Thanks for stripping down," he said. "Saves me the trouble of having to remove all your clothing. I want you naked as a jay-bird for this romp in the Jacuzzi."

"You're looking good, old buddy," Buck said. "Why are you being so modest wearing all those clothes? Got something you're ashamed for me to see?"

"Just for that, old buddy, I'm going to have you screaming very soon, 'Take it out. It's hurting me. I can't handle anything so big.'"

"Promises, promises."

Gene lowered his body over Buck on the chaise longue and inserted his tongue deep within Buck's mouth where it was expertly sucked.

When Buck broke away for air, he said, "Why don't all good buddies like you and me greet each other this way? They're missing out on such fun."

Gene ran his tongue across Buck's eyelids before washing each ear. He raised up slightly as Buck helped him remove his T-shirt. He enjoyed Buck's hands as they traveled over his chest and arms. Buck's fingers were caressing him. Gene reached below to find Buck fully aroused. "Christ, I just walk in the door and you get a hard-on."

"I wish I could arouse you as well."

"You have, good buddy." Gene stood up and removed his jeans, all except his jockey shorts. Buck preferred to do that himself. When Buck slipped down the jockeys, Gene's full erection rose in Buck's face. He gasped for breath as Buck took it in his mouth and expertly with his tongue pushed the foreskin back so he could savor the taste of the head.

Gene lowered himself over Buck again, kissing and licking his lips, enjoying his own taste on Buck's mouth. "I'm hungry today," he said. "Real hungry. There's not one inch of your body that's going to be missed by my tongue."

Buck was breathing heavily and saying nothing. Gene looked into his eyes. Buck excited him as no one ever had. The thrill was even greater knowing he could bring his friend such joy. Buck was completely mesmerized by him. Gene loved having Buck under such total control.

Later, Buck took the plunge into the hot, bubbling waters of the Jacuzzi. Gene followed right behind and spun Buck around, kissing his mouth and biting his neck.

"You're a fucking cannibal," Buck said, breaking away. "I think there's vampire blood in you."

"But you don't want me to stop, do you?" Gene asked.

"Never that."

Gene resumed biting into Buck. He pulled back slightly when he sensed Buck was experiencing acute pain. Gene was overcome with a sudden desire to taste Buck's blood. Maybe it was that talk of a vampire that did it for him. He didn't know how he was going to go about this, but was determined to taste Buck's blood before he emerged from the Jacuzzi. Drinking his saliva or even his semen weren't enough. He actually wanted to taste blood.

Instead of that, Buck reached over to the ledge and poured him an Armagnac that was followed by a Cuban cigar which Buck lit for him before lighting his own and lifting his own drink.

"I don't know what this is, and I'm no fucking food and drink connoisseur like you are, but this is just about the best stuff I've ever drunk. The second best drink. That stuff you make for me in your balls is pure nectar from the gods."

Buck moved closer to Gene and put his arm around him, resting his drink at the edge of the Jacuzzi. He blew cigar smoke in Gene's face, and Gene returned the favor. The aroma of Buck himself, the brandy, and the cigar was a total aphrodisiac to Gene. He found himself growing harder.

"Remember when we weren't so open with each other?" Buck asked.

"Do I ever! Showering together pretending we weren't checking out each other's merchandise. Skinny dipping together. Wrestling in the water so we could make body contact in an acceptable way. Looking at each other fucking a woman so we could see what each other's tool looked like fully hard and all the time wishing it was each other we were fucking. Standing together at the latrine, not really needing to piss, but wanting an excuse to show our dicks to each other."

"Don't remind me," Buck said. "We've wasted so much time."

"I'm here today to make up for lost time." He pulled Buck closer and inserted his tongue in his mouth. Buck's mouth tasted of brandy and cigar smoke, and Gene thrilled to that flavor. He ran his hand down Buck's back and inserted his index finger in Buck's hole. "After I eat that, I'm going to fuck it. But only after I've finished this cigar."

Gene said nothing for a long while, enjoying Buck so close at hand, the cigar, and the Armagnac. He didn't need words right now. His mind was clearing. For weeks it had been in a haze. That haze grew thicker when his old buddy had come back into his life. His thoughts grew even more distorted when he heard Rose's call to arms. He planned to be at her call to arms tonight—in fact, he'd been assigned duty there.

Maybe it was this lethal brandy, but one side of his brain seemed to be winning out completely over the other side. He didn't want the austere life he'd contemplated. A life dedicated to a Jesus he couldn't touch, feel, or love. What he wanted—now more than ever—was a hot body next to him. Someone he could reach out and touch and someone who would love him back. That someone could only be Buck himself. The brandy, the Jacuzzi, and Buck himself had clarified it for him. Right this moment was what he wanted, perhaps had always wanted, but was far too confused to seek it out.

It appeared that it was only an hour ago that he had come to a major decision in his life. He wanted to spend the rest of his life with Buck. No more sneaking around. No dark shadows. Nothing like that. He wanted to walk open and free with Buck, even hold his hand in public if it came to that. He was tired of running and hiding all his life. He desperately wanted openness. Buck could offer him the protection he'd always secretly wanted. What did his stupid job matter any more at the police department? He hated the work anyway. With Buck by his side, he didn't have to grovel for a dollar. Buck was rich and powerful, and when his old grandfather died Buck III would be one of the richest and most powerful men in the state. If someone ever tried to make trouble for Gene again, he knew that Buck would be there to destroy the enemy for him. Gene was a poor and powerless man, but his good buddy would make a safe harbor for him. At first he'd been confused, thinking Sister Rose could provide that for him. Now he knew differently. Buck was that safe refuge.

Hell, they might even adopt Sandy and give him the good life too. He just knew Buck would like Sandy, and might become a surrogate father for him. Not bad, Gene thought. Here was Sandy wandering homeless on the streets one day selling his body to every creep who came along. The next minute he had two surrogate dads waiting to take care of him.

He crushed out his cigar in an ashtray at the edge of the Jacuzzi. Seeing him do that, Buck did the same. Noticing a hefty swig of brandy left in his glass, Gene raised it in a toast to Buck. "Here's to us."

Buck smiled and looked deeply in his eyes. "Here's to us, good buddy." He finished his drink and placed it near the ashtray.

Gene did the same. He turned and faced Buck in the bubbling water. Gene knew what was going to happen next and so did Buck. But both men hesitated for a few seconds before the action began. For Gene, this moment of anticipation of what was about to happen was almost as good as the event itself. No, not quite that good.

He pulled Buck to him and stuck his tongue in his mouth to savor the rest of the brandy. He licked Buck's lips and found himself biting harder and harder, and Buck involuntarily tried to back away but he held him closer, chewing on his lower lip. When the first blood came, he sucked it into his mouth and exerted such a powerful suction that he tasted more and more blood. Instead of Buck pulling away, he moved in closer to Gene. It was as if he knew what Gene wanted and was determined to let him drink from him, in spite of the pain. Gene felt Buck was experiencing great pain but also great pleasure. Finally, he pulled away and gently tongued Buck's neck and ears. He whispered in his ear. "I got carried away. I'm sorry."

"It's okay. I understand."

"I've never wanted to taste anybody as much as I've wanted to taste you. I don't want to miss any flavor from you. Yes, even your blood."

"I understand," Buck said, pushing in closer to Gene. "I really do."

With a surprising strength Gene didn't know he had, he lifted Buck from the water and spread him along the edge of the Jacuzzi, face down.

He kissed each check of his ass, biting gently, before opening Buck up to fully explore his secret spot. But as much as he savored the taste and smell, it was not enough. He wanted to explore more of this secret region. Slowly and gently he lowered Buck into the water, pressing Buck's back up against his body. It wasn't gentleness that prevailed when he abruptly entered Buck. There was no gradual easing in but a violent thrust.

Buck screamed out in pain but Gene held him closer and tighter. The more Buck struggled to free himself from this impalement, the greater the pleasure for Gene. The squirming and attempted flight brought thrills racing through Gene's body. Buck fought back but Gene held him onto the penetration.

The struggle between two evenly matched men seemed to go on forever. Eventually Buck stopped squirming and trying to free himself. He moved his body up against Gene which Gene accepted as total surrender. Even as Gene began he knew it was going to be the fuck of a lifetime, one he would remember always. He'd never experienced such sensual pleasure before. He'd found his mate. This is where he wanted to be. From this night and forever, he'd bury himself inside Buck. He bit his friend's neck and reached around and fondled Buck's cock, before weighing his heavy balls. Gene's hand returned to Buck and it was then he felt his friend's orgasm. Buck couldn't restrain himself. It was obvious to Gene that he was reaching areas inside Buck never explored. Even as Gene was feeling Buck's body going through the throes of orgasm, he continued unrelentingly. For all he knew hours could have gone by as he found himself thrusting even harder into his friend. Only when he felt Buck going through his second orgasm did Gene release himself inside Buck. Buck backed against him as tight as he could, as if not wanting to miss one bit of the penetration.

Long after both bodies had stopped spewing, they clung to each other until Gene gradually pulled out. Even then, Buck's muscles clenched around him, as if resenting and trying to block the withdrawal.

In the shower they were tender with each other, soaping and rubbing each other's bodies. Gene tenderly and ever so gently kissed Buck's bruised lips. "I'm sorry," he whispered in Buck's ear under the running water. "But it tasted good. Before this love affair ends forty years from now, I'm going to taste everything you've got to offer."

"My God, that doesn't mean what I think it means."

"Gene turned him around and looked deeply into his blue eyes. "It means exactly what you think it means. The front part will be easy. I'll have to have a lot more of that brandy, a whole bottle, before I sample the rear offerings."

"You're kinky," Buck said, breaking away and stepping out of the shower. As he was drying himself off, he threw a towel to Gene as he emerged from the shower. The phone rang. Buck answered it. "Okay," he said, "send it on down." He turned to get dressed. "You'd better find your jeans too. Someone's coming down from the house."

Without questioning it, Gene went out to the veranda and picked up his discarded jeans and T-shirt and put them on. He stared into the distance, noticing how much lower the sun had gone down since he'd first raced up the ravine. Stepping into his boots, he wondered if Sandy were indeed at home making tonight's chili. He was going to invite Buck over to join them. As soon as some apparent delivery was made from the main house, he'd ask Buck one very important question, the most important question he would ever ask anyone in his entire life.

He was going to ask Buck to marry him. To live with him as husband and husband. They wouldn't have to go to any church to have any ceremony performed. A total commitment from Buck was all that was needed.

He watched as Buck headed for the front door to answer the buzzer. As Buck walked across that room, Gene realized he loved him as he had no other person on earth. Yet at the same time he was filled with this awful feeling that something horrible was about to happen. It should be the happiest moment of his life yet there was something ominous in the air.

Buck opened the door. It was old Buck's manservant, carrying a dark suit or perhaps a tux for Buck. As Buck shut the door, Gene walked into the living room.

A look on Buck's face told him that something was dreadfully wrong.

"There's something going on here," Gene said. "Something I don't know about but should know about."

"It's all happened so fast," Buck said apologetically. "I'm going to tell you something and you're not going to like it. But once I explain things, I think you'll come to accept it. But you've got to promise to hear me out."

"What is it?" Gene asked, a growing apprehension crossing his mind. He felt he was breaking out in a cold sweat. He didn't like the sound of things.

"I'm going to marry Susan at six o'clock."

Gene wasn't sure he'd really heard the words right. All he knew was he found himself running down the ravine. Vaguely he remembered Buck calling after him. But he was on his motorcycle and long gone before Buck could ever catch up.

As he drove into the oncoming evening, he heard Buck's voice more clearly now calling him. It was as if Buck were right behind him. But when Gene looked back from his speeding cycle, there was no one.

*****

As Buck rushed Susan to the airport, she turned to look at this man she'd just married. As long as she'd known him, he was and remained a stranger to her. His lower lip was bandaged. He told her that in his nervousness about their imminent wedding, he'd cut himself with a razor. That could or could not be true.

When he'd arrived at the ceremony, she was left with the distinct feeling that he'd been in some sort of fight or at least a violent argument. At first she assumed it was Robert objecting to their upcoming marriage, but then she realized Robert was in Miami.

She remained absolutely convinced that Buck had only recently confronted someone in his life, someone who didn't want him to marry her. Was it his other woman? She already knew that Buck was a highly sexual animal. He was getting sex from somebody or many people over the years. Possibly Robert. She felt he might have a mistress or two stashed somewhere, and she even fantasized that Pamela and Buck had agreed to get back together after their accidental meeting at the Rusty Pelican.

A troubling thought crossed her mind. Buck had claimed he was going to meet with Gene about the Lolito ring. But he'd never told her anything else about the meeting. Had Gene come back into his life? Surely Gene would object to the marriage even though his reasoning might be irrational. She was still left with a lingering suspicion that Buck had gone off to see Gene after making love to her in her apartment and lying to her that he was leaving to offer aid and comfort to a sick and dying grandfather.

She searched for some emotion in his steel jaw face but he kept his eyes on the road, as he was driving very fast in a rush to get her to her plane on time.

"Why did you marry me?" she asked abruptly.

"Because I'm madly in love with you," he said, turning to smile at her with the bandage on his lip.

"The real reason. I'm a tough hard-nosed reporter, remember?"

"Because my granddad threatened to disinherit me if I didn't. He'd arranged for everything. It was an ultimatum."

"Not very flattering," she said, "but at least I feel you're telling the truth."

"He may have only days to live," he said, his eyes still firmly on the road in front of him. "You and I will have the rest of our lives to sort this out. It was an old man's dying wish. I felt if I defied him, I would only hasten his death."

"Where does that leave us?"

"I don't know. Fly north, do your thing, and come back here. We'll work on it."

"Does Robert know?"

"I haven't told him yet."

"You're planning to soon, I hope, before he reads it in the paper."

"We're not announcing it to the press yet," he said. "At least not now. Everyone's sworn to secrecy at the moment."

"Are you going to tell Gene?" she asked, looking at his face for some sudden display of emotion.

He remained stone-faced. "When I see him, of course."

"You haven't met with him yet?"

"I haven't seen Gene in years. Have you?"

"Not since the day he walked out the door. I don't plan to either."

"You're divorced from him. What does it matter what Gene thinks?"

"I am his former wife. You are his former best friend. He's bound to have some reaction."

"Let's face that when we have to." He drove for a half a mile or so without saying anything.

Knowing she was treading on dangerous territory, she continued to ask questions, questions he obviously didn't want to answer. But she felt compelled to ask them anyway. After all, he was now her husband.

"How do you think Robert is going to take this?"

"He's going to hate it. He doesn't like us being publisher and reporter. If he resents that relationship, he'll go ballistic over this man and wife shit."

"Shit? Is that what you think of our marriage?"

"Come on, Susan. Get off my case. You're asking me for imagined reactions from everybody. I can't even sort out my own reactions to the marriage—much less anybody else's."

"You've got a point there. I'm not sure of my own reaction. On the plane north, I'll think about what I've gotten myself into. When I get back, we'll see where this marriage is going to go, if anywhere."

"Let's be rather blunt," he said in a rather harsh tone. "Let's face it: it's a marriage of convenience. If it's to become something more, time will tell."

"Where do you want me to live when I get back? At your home?"

"No, Robert lives there and has for many years. It's his home. It will always be his home if he wants it. For the time being, why don't you continue to live in your apartment?"

"Thanks," she said sarcastically.

"I didn't mean forever. I have three beautiful condos on the upper beach. My parents gave them to me. They're all luxurious. You can take your pick. Move into the one you like best."

"That's a generous offer. After all, I have married up in the world."

"You'll have a new car waiting when you get back. A charge card. Whatever you want."

"That's very generous. You make me sound like the mistress of a very rich man."

"Forgive me."

"There's nothing to forgive. I'm going into this marriage with my eyes wide open. I'm no longer some idealistic school girl. I was that when I married Gene Robinson. That was a long time ago."

"It's only fair that you get something out of this marriage. You're doing me a God damn big favor. You'll be rewarded."

"I know you're a man of your word. It looks to me like I'll get a lot out of this marriage. The only thing I won't get is a husband. But what the hell."

"One can't have everything, can one?" he asked, turning to her with a smile. It was a vacant smile as if his mind were somewhere else.

"Before our wedding, you told someone goodbye, didn't you?"

"If you must know, yes."

"Care to tell me who she was?"

"No."

"Do you love her?"

"I think I will always love this person. But I know that a deep and meaningful relationship is not possible. It can't be. But I'll never stop loving."

"Great!" she said. As he pulled his car into the airport she laughed but it sounded so forced her throat constricted. "If we can be this frank the first hour of our marriage, I think our liaison will last for at least another forty years."

"I think that too."

He didn't say anything else, and neither did she until they arrived at the loading ramp.

His kiss good-bye was perfunctory but then he had a cut lip.

*****

The moment he came in through his back door, entering his once dark kitchen, Gene could tell a transformation had occurred. The place was brightly lit, and the open windows let in the dying sun. The smell of chili bubbling on the stove permeated the air. The floor had been scrubbed, the surfaces brightly polished. The place looked like it did when his mother was still alive. But Sandy wasn't there.

Gene searched for him, going first up front to the living room before checking the dining room and even the bathroom. Thinking Sandy might have fallen asleep, he checked the guest bedroom. No one. There was only one room left: his bedroom. He walked back to his bedroom to find Sandy making up his bed with fresh sheets.

"Don't you ever clean up this joint?" Sandy asked, rushing to give him a hug. The boy wore only a pair of cut-off denims, and Gene hugged him briefly, fearing the intimate contact of skin.

"I wasn't gone that long," Gene said. "How did you get so much done so soon? I thought all you teenage kids like to live in a pig sty."

"Not me, handsome. I like things sparkling clean, and this house looks like it'll take me weeks to get it in shape. I'm a good gardener too. That yard really needs work."

"I'm glad you're here. Thanks for everything. I needed someone here when I came home tonight. I really did." He turned and headed for the kitchen for a beer.

"Your eyes are sad," Sandy said following him. "I hope things didn't go wrong at your appointment."

"It didn't go the way I planned. I can't talk about it now. I'm a little blue."

Sandy washed off the beer can for him and opened it for him. "I'm here if you want to talk about it."

"I can't right now. You understand?"

"Sure, I do. There are lot of things I can't talk about either." Sandy went over to stir the chili pot. "The phone has been ringing off the wall. Buck Brooke has been calling. He sounded really desperate. I know the name. He's the publisher of the Examiner. I feel some major story is breaking."

"If he calls again, tell him I'm not home. He sometimes calls me about breaking news. Probably about Sister Rose's march through the Combat Zone tonight. Christ." He slammed down his beer.

"What's up?"

"You don't think he's heard that I'm investigating the Lolito ring, do you?"

"Shit, he might have. Don't worry. If he calls again, I'll get rid of him."

"Maybe we'll have the phone number changed tomorrow. Make it unlisted."

"Not a bad idea."

"I'm starved, man. Let's have some of that chili you're stirring up. I like mine fiery hot."

"Sandy rubbed his fingers across Gene's cheek. "I bet you do."

"I'd like to stay here with you tonight but I can't. I'm on duty. That march through the Combat Zone. There could be violence."

"I'm coming with you."

"You're staying here. This march could really heat up. Marches like this bring out all the hotheads."

"Promise me, you'll take care. You're all I've got in the world."

Gene smelled the bowl of chili set before him before reaching for some crackers. "I'll take care of you, kid. I will."

"I trust you," Sandy said, reaching for his hand.

Gene tasted the chili. "That's the best I've ever had. It's really good. Do you know how to cook anything else?"

"I can make a great western omelette. I can fry a mean steak, and I know how to stuff a chicken and roast it. I noticed a cookbook on that shelf."

"It belonged to my mother. The Joy of Cooking."

"I bet if I read it, I'll learn to cook a lot more dishes."

Gene smiled at him before devouring the chili. "I bet you can." His gargantuan hunger surprised him. He didn't think he'd be hungry at a time like this, but he was ravenous.

Sandy sat across from him, enjoying a coke with his chili. "Thanks for giving me a place to stay. I don't remember when I've been so happy. I'll have our bed waiting tonight."

"No, you'd better fix up the guest room. I'm not wanting sex from you. But I do need to have you here. Every man who's brought you home with him wanted sex. But I just need your company. You understand that, don't you?"

"I'll do whatever you want me to do. If you want me to sleep up in the guest room, I'll be there. But if you want some company, please come up front and get me. Just pick me up in your arms and carry me to your bedroom. I'll make the sweetest love to you that's ever been made. Even if you just want me to hold you, I can do that too."

Gene put down his fork. "I'm going to take you up on that last offer. I need a hug right now."

Sandy got up from the table and walked across to Gene. He grabbed the boy and held him as tightly as he'd ever held anybody before. Then he burst into uncontrollable sobbing, and he was a man who never cried.

*****

Ever since three o'clock that afternoon, protest marchers, heading Rose's call to arms, had been assembling at the entrance to the Combat Zone. Through Roland, Buck had assigned every reporter the Examiner could spare, and he planned to write an eyewitness account himself, hoping it would perk up his column.

He put through a final hasty call to Gene. A young man—or perhaps a boy—answered the phone. He was unaware that Gene lived with someone. It could be one of his distant nephews. The boy told him that Gene wasn't expected home until very late, as he was on duty tonight.

After putting down the phone, he dialed Robert from their home before heading for the zone. "How's your mom?"

"Hanging on but it's hopeless. Now she's in a coma."

"I wish I could be there with you tonight, but I'm covering Rose's march. It's going to be a free for all.

"I'm going to watch it on TV," Robert said. "In the safety of the hospital." Fear came into his voice. "You'll be real careful, won't you? I don't want anything to happen to my future husband."

"He'll be there for you and I'll be safe. You know me. I can look after myself."

"You can't even take a bath without me, good looking, and I'll be returning to my duties soon."

"So, I'm a duty now?"

"Only in the most pleasant sense."

"Thanks."

"You'll be out with every lunatic from the far right and the far left tonight. I bet there will be violence."

"The Examiner will get some good stuff."

"Just don't become part of the violence—and don't play hero," Robert cautioned. "Like trying to rescue somebody. Let the police do that."

"I love you, baby," Buck said. "There will be a lot to catch up on when you get back."

"A lot," Robert said. "I miss my man."

"I miss you too. More than you'll ever know. I love you."

"I love you too. Call me the moment you get back from that shit."

"I will. Love you. Gotta go." He put down the phone before Robert could say any more. He just couldn't bring himself to tell Robert about his marriage to Susan. Time for that later.

*****

As night fell over the city, Rose's parade had begun. Buck, trapped in a parking lot of buses and cars, missed her first appearance. He noted a lot of pickup trucks driven in from the central part of the state. So far, his prediction of violence hadn't come true.

At the completely disorganized tail of the candlelit march, he finally set foot on The Strip. By then, Rose was at least ten blocks ahead, moving toward People's Park at the end.

As he made his way through the crowd, many members of whom were holding candles, he tried to stay on the sidewalk so he could observe the action better. He kept getting pushed and shoved to the center of the street, lost in a milling sea. Drawing a few Yoga breaths, he tried to calm himself and estimate the number of marchers.

They seemed to be in the thousands, and he refused to believe that the march had been spontaneously called only that morning at the temple. He'd learned that the demonstration, at least in the vanguard, had been carefully staged. All afternoon, buses had fanned out to the suburbs, not only hauling in protesters, but recruiting them as well. The Examiner had discovered that all the cultist churches in the city and neighboring suburbs had been notified, with appeals to the various congregations to turn out en masse.

In a shirt and jeans, he found himself swimming in a sea of brightly colored polyester leisure suits. He wondered if all this synthetic fabric were inflammable, because many people were pushed dangerously close to burning candles.

The police had long ago cordoned off the entire Combat Zone so that marchers could parade down the center of the street, the fiery glow of their candles competing against the glaring marquees of the porno movie houses, advertising such X-rated pictures as Jack Wrangler in "Heavy Equipment" at the Adonis and a "luscious new Italian star" at the Pussycat Cinema.

To him, some of the protest demonstrators—spiritual descendants of Cotton Mather—seemed rigid-faced and frightened to be in such hostile, unfamiliar terrain. Many held Bibles and waved American flags. One woman, whose face reflected her firm belief in God and patriotism, carried a placard on which she'd mounted a stern, foreboding photograph of John Foster Dulles, as if she'd been forced to search in America's attic for a man she could really trust.

From the lobbies of the seedy, "hot bed" hotels lining The Strip, television sets blared with fresh reports of the marching taking place right outside their doors. Not since the anti-war protests of the sixties had Okeechobee witnessed such a massive street demonstration.

Most of the "johns" who frequented the zone at night had disappeared from the street, probably going home to their wives. He suspected that some of those sex hunters had joined their wives in the protest march in a neat piece of hypocrisy.

It was one of the hottest nights he had suffered through in the city, a bubbling ninety-six degrees Fahrenheit—just the type of weather to make tempers flare, enough heat to touch off a riot when two groups, violently opposed to each other's beliefs, came clashing together. He needed a drink in the worst way. At a singles bar on The Strip, he fended off at least two women who wanted to relieve him of his solitude.

At first his drinking had been cautious, but the longer he sat at the bar, the more he drank, and soon the liquor fueled a growing anger in him. As whirls of dizziness swam through his head, he realized he was quite drunk and outraged, not so much at Rose, but at his own unwillingness to come to some sort of conclusion about her. Part of him wanted to label her the enemy and treat her as such—a fanatic, devouring harpie using every person who came within her path, exploiting every event.

Surely considering who she was, what she stood for, he should be repelled by her. Yet he knew he wasn't. If anything, just the opposite. He was fascinated by her power, even her power over him. He'd been warned both by Calder and by his grandfather that she held some power over the Examiner, which meant she held power over him. By tomorrow, or perhaps within a few weeks, she might be planning to sacrifice him as a victim. When she spoke of the blood of the lamb, did she mean his blood?

He couldn't answer that. He didn't know the answers to many things. But in the back cells of his brain, he felt that if he could overpower her and conquer her in some way he could force her to become his captive. He felt in some way that might stave off her onslaught of the Examiner.

But this was all too vague for him to sort out. It seemed like only minutes ago that he'd gotten married. Here he was in this bar spending his honeymoon night when he should be out covering the march like one of his reporters. He had to be very careful how he explained his marriage to Robert. Very careful. Obviously he hadn't done a good job of explaining it to Gene, but Gene hadn't let him. He thought Gene might understand if only he would listen to him.

Everything seemed to be coming unglued inside his head, just like the march that paraded outside the door to the bar. Getting up from the bar, he paid the bill and headed back into the street.

"Don't you think you'd better stay in here and sit this one out?" the barmaid asked.

He probably should, but that crazy march outside made as much sense as the thoughts spinning inside his head.

*****

To Rose, the march lived up to her expectations and, at the beginning of her crusade, she knew she'd struck a responsive chord in the public's mind.

The spell of the crowds was almost hypnotic to her. With such mass support of her stand, she believed she could light bonfires across America. Everything depended on Okeechobee. She'd selected it as her test city, knowing she had to win here, and win big, before storming the continent.

That afternoon she'd suffered almost a seizure, as a kind of madness whirled around her. For two hours her staff feared she might have to cancel her appearance and, with that, the protest demonstration, of course. Without her presence, she realized the entire plan she'd worked on for so many years would fail.

Toward sunset, she'd regained control of herself and that horrible shaking feeling that had come over her had left her. She'd felt serene and her mirror had confirmed she'd never looked better. She was ready to face the cameras, and she knew that before midnight in California, her image would be beamed into millions of American homes.

"Look at me," she wanted to say, in an impulsive moment that swept over her right in the middle of the parade. "I'm a witch, able to cast spells over a mob."

When she faced the biggest glare of the TV news cameras, she'd deliberately moved away from some of the older and more overweight followers and toward the direction of a tall, young, and handsome man who kept getting closer to her, looking up at her like a love-sick puppy. He bore an amazing resemblance to Tyrone Power.

With him at her side, she hoped to hit the front pages across the nation tomorrow. She wanted her crusade to appear to be a spontaneous demonstration of the young and vigorous. At no point did she want to connect herself with caricatured members of her own generation. That's why she'd tutored Shelley so carefully for his appearance tonight.

She held her hand to her chest, as if embracing herself. The delusion and panic gone now, she knew she was on the verge of fulfilling some of the wildest dreams that had grown out of her dark moments. There, she'd heard voices that could direct her, compelling her to march.

*****

Caught unaware, a few ultra-left groups had tried to mount a hasty counterprotest, but they appeared weak, vastly outnumbered. Some lesbian mothers wheeled empty baby carriages, and a few shirtless bartenders from the topless singles bar paraded, along with a scattering of black militants. One young minister carried a placard asking, "IF JESUS HAD HIS PETER, THEN WHY CAN'T I?"

Buck was astonished to find a group of male high school students in Ku Klux Klan hoods. Accepting one of their tabloids, he learned at a glance that it was the same newspaper he'd discovered stored at Rose's printing headquarters. He stepped up to one of the hooded boys. "Who prints this shit?" The boy yanked the paper from Buck's hand and ran in the other direction.

Buck was distracted by a wide-eyed, almost crazed-looking girl who ran right into the sea of marchers, flaunting a large blowup of Anne Frank at them, with a provocative question hand-lettered on it. HAVE YOU FORGOTTEN HITLER? Her boyfriend, dressed as an American Indian, carried another placard with the bold claim, DISCIPLES OF HATE ARE NOT CHRISTIAN.

Not only were the two trying to block the marchers, they seemed to tantalize them, as if goading them to strike back. Buck immediately feared for the couple's safety. A burly man knocked the young woman down, and her boyfriend slugged her attacker in the jaw. This seemed to anger the marchers even more. A few people kicked the young man as he lay screaming on the sidewalk, his nose bleeding, his placard crushed under marching feet. A group of counter-protesters, sensing the brutality of the marchers, rushed into the melee, even though policemen tried to cordon them off. The police flailed the air with their night sticks, sparing no victim.

Buck watched in horror as a TV camera recorded a scene that, to him, was reminiscent of so many other movements. Suddenly, the acrid smell of tear gas permeated the street, as hundreds fled with running eyes, raw throats. Covering his mouth with a handkerchief, he stumbled back into an alleyway, hoping for a breath of air to cleanse his lungs.

*****

In plain clothes, Gene had been assigned to the parade to spot potential trouble. To do that, he'd joined with the other protest marchers, pretending to be one of them. He felt he was. At one point he had come intimately close to Rose.

Before he left police headquarters, Biff, his chief, had made it clear to him what was *real* trouble and what was merely "just honest dissent from God-fearing people."

Biff didn't need to tell him not to interfere with Rose's supporters.

Up front with Rose, Gene experienced no disorder, no clashes of opposing forces, no violence.

The presence of the evangelist herself seemed to mesmerize the crowd—not only her followers, but the spectators who'd lined both sides of the street, perhaps to jeer and hurl insults. Even they appeared subdued, their gawking faces aware they were witnesses to a spiritual phenomenon.

When Rose passed in front of a massage parlor, Jupiter's Retreat, she stopped and mounted the steps. All the patrons had fled. Only the maintenance crew flocked to the entrance to see what was happening.

At first she didn't speak, standing there regally, waiting for the marchers to quiet down. Someone gave her a hand microphone. Her violet eyes glanced neither left nor right. She stared straight ahead, as if fixed on some star unseen by the rest of her followers. In her radiant face, with its wet sensuality, Gene detected an irresistible combination of the angel and the devil, and in that moment he knew Rose had struggled with the same demons he had. It was obvious to him that she'd conquered hers. The intensity of her face shattered him.

In her soft, well-modulated voice that seemed to grow in power and tempo as she talked, she told her audience, "God drew a ring of fire and invited me to step into it." As she spoke, and Gene moved closer to the steps, her voice took on a curious erotic quality to him.

"In tomorrow's newspapers," she said, "I'll be attacked, abused and libeled, as I always am. My own life will be threatened by forces working to undermine and ultimately topple the government of this great country. One way to weaken us is to encourage degeneracy, destroy the nuclear family."

As she looked up at Jupiter's Retreat, the windows overhead appeared as dark as the lust they hid within. The evangelist's face became pallid with bitterness, the more she stared at the fortress-like windows. The candlelight caused her silver earrings to shimmer and, more than that, it made her face suddenly luminous as she turned from the windows and into the soft glow again. Shadows streaked her cheeks, making her infinitely desirable to Gene, a feeling he'd had for no other woman, not even Susan. Yet at the same time, she seemed to pull him into a sphere of terrible temptation, as one might be drawn to death.

"They call this a pleasure palace," she said. "We call it a cesspool of human depravity. Join our crusade in wiping it out!" Loud cheers went up from the protesters. She raised her hands to acknowledge the support and to quiet the marchers.

"We feel sorry for the poor, mentally disturbed individuals on this street who have lost their way. Not knowing life's real blessings, its true joy, they have turned instead to the artificial and the tawdry, the sinful and evil. For that, we pity them. What we can't do is to allow them to pull us along with them in their leap to suicide." Again, more shouts of approval, none louder than from Gene himself.

When she resumed her leadership of the vanguard of the march, she'd picked up a lightness of step, almost a waltz. Gaily triumphant, she headed for People's Park, where she knew a police squad car waited to take her away before any trouble began.

No longer fearing his flesh would betray him, Gene joined her in a kind of liberation. Never before had he felt so confident of conquering the demons within himself, and also those who lurked outside, waiting not only to destroy him, but to harm Rose. Even though Rose might not know it, he'd be out there, protecting and defending her, following her wherever she appeared in public. After all, she'd warned tonight that there were those waiting to take her life. Before that happened, those forces would have to kill him first—and he didn't destruct easily.

*****

Buck fought his way to the bandstand in the center of the park where, to his disappointment, he learned Rose wasn't going to appear. Policemen in gas masks holding shotguns stood ominously by as children ran through beds, trampling over the flowers that someone had worked so hard to plant. Seeing the well-armored policemen, one girl near him said, "Somebody could get killed."

On the bandstand, a group of Tennessee "Possum Hunters" were soothing the crowd with the sound of—

"Gimme that ol' time religion,
Gimme that ol' time religion,
Gimme that ol' time religion,
It's good enough for me..."

One fiddle player in pink sequins seemed straight from the stage of the Grand Ole Opry. A dumpy, over-the-hill blonde deep-throated the microphone.

Uncle Skeeter Hay, the chief "Possum Hunter," stepped up in front of the microphone in his ten-gallon hat and pot belly that bulged over his buttercup yellow, double-knit trousers. His chartreuse jacket had a covered wagon imprinted on its back. He announced, "We've got some spontaneous words from a little preacher, a child of God."

Buck braced himself, knowing, but still not wanting to believe, that that could only mean Shelley himself.

And it was. Shelley at first seemed nervous, terrified of his audience, and Buck feared he could never make it as the Billy Graham of the pubescents.

"I will not be recruited into sin by one of my teachers," Shelley promised his audience. "No law in the land is going to force me to look upon moral lepers as role models."

Buck winced at this blatant slander and gross vulgarization, as he realized what kind of tone Rose's moral crusade was ready to sound.

As Shelley moved deeper into his speech, Buck felt he was warming to his task, showing greater ease and stage presence in front of the audience. The boy switched gears, becoming more emotional, his voice filled with a mounting hysteria as he beseeched his audience to, "Join me and my Christian family in a nation-wide campaign against the offensive on God and his moral laws. Though the deviates in all walks of life will try to sabotage our moral crusade, with God's help we'll fight them every step of the way."

The air seemed heavy and hot to Buck. He found himself arching his body, as if poised for a fight.

"The moral lepers of this world are going to hell where they'll burn for eternity," Shelley predicted. "The anti-Christs. The job before us tonight is to save the children—young boys like me—from such a road of sin. Keep us out of the jailhouse of the damned!"

Buck was fascinated at Shelley's blue eyes as they were cast upward to the spots lighting the stage, making him appear almost cherubic, although Buck, with wry amusement, felt that Shelley was probably—at least potentially—the biggest moral leper in the park.

"Even though I'm very young," Shelley said, "my mother has taught me what it means to be lost to Jesus. Because I believe in my mother's holy war against the worshipers of the devil, I'm going to set aside my school lessons, all my personal dreams, in fact, to devote my little self to the cause of saving our children from the clutches of the godless moral lepers. I'm giving up everything to help my mother, Sister Rose."

The mention of her name brought an almost overwhelming roar of approval from the crowd, followed by a few catcalls at the far end of the park.

As Buck turned and made a hasty retreat through the crowds, he heard Shelley's final words. "We need your help, your contributions."

Still trapped in the middle of the spectators, he believed that both Shelley and Rose would get that help, and certainly those contributions which he imagined would pour in from all over the country once this story hit the wire services and the late night news across America.

*****

Back on The Strip, the crowd had started to scatter. Many of the protest marchers had been in the Combat Zone since mid-afternoon, responding to Rose's rallying cry. Tired and hungry, they headed now for the security of home, having stood up, they felt, for decency.

Maneuvering through a throng of spectators, Buck came to a stop near a small contingent of mounted policemen on sleek horses whose hooves made fiery sparks when they hit the pavement.

The band's rendition of "When the Saints Come Marching In" was interrupted by an explosion that sounded as if someone had tossed a small bomb into the crowd. Buck jumped back before realizing it was only the popping sound of a giant balloon. Others, not knowing that, ran screaming in fear. Not wanting to be swept into the mass of milling bodies, he darted into the entrance of a building and just stood there, taking in the scene for a long minute before he realized he'd come to a stop at the doorstep to Jupiter's Retreat.

At the sound of another explosion, a large chestnut horse whimpered in fright, then jolted into the air, his forelegs poised menacingly over a group of running people. The patrolman mounting him pulled the reins, but was thrown onto the street. His helmet jarred loose to roll down the side walk. Two other patrolmen rushed to their fallen comrade's aid. As they did, the horse broke away, galloping toward the crowd which was pouring out of the park.

An old man slipped and fell down on the street. The runaway horse—his head tossing frantically from side to side—galloped over the victim, an iron-shod hoof pounding the old man's head into the pavement.

To the squawk of bullhorns and the rasp of police radios, the old man, only ten feet from Buck, lay dying. Cops crouched over his body and a helicopter circled overhead. Even now, the man looked rigid-faced, his yellowing teeth clenched in a bitter determination that fell like a pallor over his death mask.

Buck swallowed hard, knowing this was the first of what could be many casualties in Rose's moral re-armament.

The riderless horse raced toward the terrified crowd. A small child broke free from his mother's hand and ran toward the horse. Misdirected and confused, the child—perhaps a little boy—stumbled and fell. Caught in the frantic, darting horse's path, the child was crushed under the hoofs of the powerful animal. One man suddenly whipped a gun out of his pocket holster and shot the horse in the head. It whimpered in fright and, with its last gasp, tried to hurdle a fence bordering People's Park. The horse's body was too weak to make the fence. The animal impaled itself on one of the sharp spikes and hung suspended there, blood running from its eyes. With one weak whine, the animal collapsed in death.

Running up the street, Buck recognized Gene as the man who'd fired the shot.

Two other patrolmen came up to Gene to talk to him, and in seconds he was gone, racing away with the men to confront some other emergency.

A great animal lover, Buck was sorry that Gene had to shoot that horse, even though he recognized the need for it. The wild animal might have killed someone else. The whole spectacle of tonight's parade disgusted Buck. It all seemed so unnecessary.

His head low, Buck turned and headed back to People's Park. Since his was an afternoon paper, he didn't have to rush back to the office to supervise coverage. The round-up of tonight's events wouldn't come out in the Examiner until noon tomorrow.

*****

Fear, rage, humiliation—all these emotions combined to make Buck come to. He found himself slumped over in the alleyway, where the Nazis had attacked him. An aching lump reminded him of the descent of the bronze eagle on his skull. The teenage girl had disappeared.

He licked his lips, his throat feeling sore and parched. Vividly he recalled the agonizing pain that had shot through his body. His side hurt, as if someone had kicked him in the gut when he'd fallen over.

Every muscle in his body winced in sharp agony as he forced himself to stand up, his head spinning. Dizzy and nauseous, he stumbled toward The Strip.

Once there, he noticed that a heavy rain had fallen, just what was needed to thin the crowd and cool the excessive heat. The steamy street was nearly deserted, except for a few patrolmen and late-night stragglers. Broken glass and debris littered the sidewalks.

The cold white light of night was reflected by the puddles of the wet car roofs of the patrol cars. He headed back to People's Park, where the gingerbread bandstand had been washed clean by the pelting rain.

At the opposite end, the bonfire had turned into a pile of flaky ashes, with only a few dying embers remaining from the most defiant of books.

A policemen in a rain jacket shouted for him to move on and, as he started to, he noticed some books, not quite burned, near the edge of the bonfire. He scooped four of them up and, in the night light, looked for their titles.

Though charred around the edges, the jackets were clearly visible. He'd assumed that sleazy porno books had fueled the bonfire. These were hard-cover editions. The first title page revealed to him the book was the property of the Okeechobee Public Library. It was an English translation of Proust's Remembrance of Things Past. Quickly he looked at one of the other books, Whitman's Leaves of Grass. The third, Oscar Wilde's The Picture of Dorian Gray. The final one was a more recent edition, Tennessee Williams' Moise and the World of Reason.

He scooped up the books, planning to take them back to his office to be photographed for tomorrow's edition. Evidence in hand, he still found it hard to believe that someone in self-appointed judgment had actually removed these titles from a public library shelf for book-burning. The hate literature circulating had been bad enough, but the burning of respectable literature by world-famed authors was intolerable.

Trudging along in the light rain, he felt his shirt and jeans were sopping wet. The moisture ran down his shins into his boots, leaving a cold, trickling sensation. His whole body felt clammy, but maybe it was his troubled thoughts, not the rain, that caused that.

Earlier in the evening, he'd been drunk. The knock-out had sobered him. In this sea of fear, hate-peddling, censors, and destroyers in which he swam, he'd need a clear head to keep from drowning.

With a determination to get a good grip on himself, he walked with a fast step along the Combat Zone.

*****

From the darkest alley she'd emerged, standing before Gene in the light cast from the street lamppost. The girl was oddly familiar to him, but different from some vague memory in his head. Her face was badly bruised, still showing traces of blood, and her blonde hair looked as if she'd just showered, or else had been caught in the rain.

She looked up and down the street before returning her attention to him. The crowd was gone, the violence over. She appraised Gene suggestively. "Hi, good looking," she said. "As soon as I fix my lipstick, we can get on with the business of the night."

"You okay?" he asked.

"I'm fine. Johns, even Nazi johns—especially those—have roughed me up before."

"Aren't you a little young to be working the Combat Zone?"

"Sugar, men like 'em young. I'm old enough. Name's Jill."

That name always made him shudder. It was the same name of the little girl he'd exposed himself to.

"I need to make some money something awful tonight," she said. "But when a john looks as hot as you, I'm almost tempted to throw a free one."

"I'm not here for that. I'm here to help you."

"Don't kid me. They're all here for that."

"Not me. I think you'd better get checked at a hospital. I'll drive you there."

"Yeah, right. Once in that car with you, it's no telling where you'd haul my ass."

"I'm not going to harm you."

He stumbled over some debris left by the march. Bracing himself, he stood up, his face fully lit by the streetlamp.

"I know you. You're Gene Robinson."

"How could you know me?"

"You're famous. You and me—how shall I put it?—were once linked romantically."

"What in hell are you talking about?"

"I'm that girl—grown up now—that you showed your hard-on to. What a grand sight it was. Been looking ever since for its mate." He stepped back, feeling he was lost in darkness. This couldn't be happening. It was a dream from which he'd soon awake.

"Don't worry about it. It didn't do any permanent damage. Not at all. It also didn't turn me into a whore. My mama had something to do with that."

"I'm sorry," he stammered awkwardly. "I've been sorry about that every day of my life since then."

"Don't carry around such a guilt trip. It's wasted on me. All is forgiven."

"Thank you. That means a lot."

"In fact, I wouldn't mind a repeat performance. This time you can do more than just show it to me."

"I'm not going to touch you. But let me help. I will take you to the hospital."

"I'm not going."

"Wait a minute. I have a young friend who knows you. His name is Sandy and he works the Combat Zone. Or used to."

"I know Sandy. He's practically my best friend."

"He's living at my place now."

"Lucky boy. It's just my luck that you'd turn out gay. All the good-looking ones go that route."

"It's not what you think."

"Sugar, it's always what I think."

"If you won't let me take you to the hospital, come home with me and hang out with Sandy. At least you can get a bath, and Sandy will put something on your bruises. He also makes a mean bowl of chili."

"I know," she said. "We've often shared motel rooms together. You know, the type with kitchenettes."

"Then you'll come?"

"If it's with you, Gene, just say the word."

He glanced apprehensively around him, as he helped Jill into his car. He had a feeling he could be arrested at any minute, in spite of the innocence in his heart. Once in the car, Jill was strangely silent. He knew he was reliving that day he'd exposed himself to her, and he suspected she was recalling it too.

He pulled into his driveway, hoping none of the neighbors was observing him. Braking his car in back of his house, he helped Jill from the seat.

"I think I'm a little more bruised than I thought at first," she said. "It's beginning to hurt a lot."

"We'll fix you up," he promised. At the back door and before he had a chance to turn the key, Sandy threw open the door.

"My God, you're safe. I called everywhere. Even down at the station."

"I'm okay," he said. "A couple of bruises—that's all." He ushered Jill inside. "This is the one who's beat up."

"Jill," Sandy said. "What happened to you?"

"A pack of Nazis roughed me up, but I'm gonna be okay. Handsome here rescued me."

"I did nothing like that," Gene said. "I think some other guy tried to help you, but he got hit over the head."

"Come on in," Sandy said. "My new home. If you'll come with me to the bathroom, I'll tend to those bruises."

Gene sat at the kitchen table having a beer and listening to the sounds coming from the bathroom. He didn't want to think tonight, especially not about Buck and Susan getting married.

Sandy was the first to come back into the kitchen. "She's more beat up than you. I've put a couple of bandages on her, and now I'm going to heat up the chili."

"Thanks for helping out. When I spotted her, I offered to take her to the hospital but she wouldn't go. Since she knew you, I thought of bringing her here. I hope this won't get me into trouble."

"Jill's a good woman. She won't make trouble for you."

"That's good to know."

In minutes Jill was back in the room. "I may look a little roughed up, but I can take on both of you guys in a three-way."

"That won't be needed," Sandy said, pulling up a chair for her. "Have some of my chili instead."

"That's hotter than a three-way," she said, sitting down and reaching for the crackers.

"You okay?" Gene asked. "I hope you can stay the night."

"Sure I can. As many nights as you want." She dug into her chili bowl with a spoon.

"You can take the guest room up front," Sandy said. "I get the back room with Gene." He eyed Gene provocatively. "I have to warn you in advance."

"What's that?" Gene asked, sipping his beer.

"I don't sleep with my underwear on."

"I'll get you some pajamas." Gene pretended to ignore him, turning to Jill. "You got a home?"

"Any hotel will do. Whatever john's got the room rent."

"I see. You can stay the night. Tomorrow, I'll start trying to find a home for you."

She looked about the kitchen. "Good chili," she said to Sandy before turning to Gene. "This place will be just fine. It definitely needs a woman's touch."

"You still got any parents?"

"None that seems to know me," she said.

After dinner, Gene helped Sandy wash the dishes, and he checked the front bedroom to see that it was right for Jill. As he was telling her goodnight, she reached to kiss him in gratitude but he backed away, her lips only brushing his cheek. "Thanks for the bed, mister. I'm grateful and all."

"We'll take care of you." He turned to Sandy. "Let's hit the hay, sport. I've got an early call."

In the bedroom he felt embarrassed taking off his clothes in front of Sandy. He could see the boy eying him appreciatively. He stripped but retained his briefs. He slipped quickly under the covers.

In the glow cast by the lamp, Sandy stood in front of him and removed all his clothes. His body was young and thin as if he'd missed many meals.

Gene turned over, his back to Sandy. "Get in. We both could use some sleep."

Sandy crawled in and reached to hug Gene but Gene pushed him away gently. "No stuff like that. I mean that."

"You can at least kiss me good night. I'm your boy now."

Gene reached over and planted a light kiss on Sandy's cheek but the boy clasped his face and kissed him hard on the mouth. "I can kiss a lot more places than that too."

"I'm sure you can. But I'm not going to use you for that. Enough men have used you."

"All except one—and that's the only one I've ever wanted."

"What do you mean?"

"You."

Gene turned over, lying flat on his belly. He didn't trust Sandy's roving hands. "Good night. Jill and you will be safe with me."

Chapter Five

The next morning found Buck again on the beach of his private cay. He'd had a troubled sleep and only minutes ago had called Robert in Miami to see how his mother was. It didn't look good. Mrs. Dante's doctor had warned Robert that he didn't think she would last another day.

"Are you coming back before the funeral, or will you stay in Miami until it's all over?" Buck had asked.

"I don't know yet, but we'll be in touch. I'll let you know everything that's happening."

Buck cringed at Robert's openness and wished he could be the same way with him. But he had too many secrets. "I'll fly down for the funeral. I want to be with you."

"I want you by my side too—in fact, I don't think I can face it without you."

"I'll be there."

"I love you, you handsome hunk."

"I love you too, pretty boy, and do I ever miss my man and his loving."

"You're turning me on."

"You always turned me on. Which reminds me. I've got something to tell you."

"Sounds ominous. Have you gotten into trouble? I mean, last night you sounded okay even after the attack by those God damn Nazis."

"It's not ominous. I'm popping the big question."

"Does that mean what I think it means?" Robert asked.

"It means I want to marry you."

"Hot damn!"

"Make the arrangements down in Miami. We'll get married when I fly down."

"I can't believe you're actually saying that."

"I'm not only saying it, I'm meaning it. Let's go for it."

"Don't worry: I will."

"There's only one thing I regret."

"What's that?"

"That you asked me first. I'm the man. I should have made the proposal."

"Better late than never."

"I love you, pretty boy, but I've got a call coming in. You've got plenty of time down there. Go buy our wedding rings. Make sure they match."

"I can't wait to put one on your finger. I love you."

"I love you too. Bye, my pet." He put down the phone only to take a call from Roland at the city desk.

Buck had left the office early today because he'd resented Roland's taking charge. The staff seemed to have sensed there had been a shift of power. Key issues and major assignments were funneled toward Roland, not to Buck's office. When he'd realized what was happening, he'd stormed out of the tower and gotten into his boat at the marina and headed for his private cay.

On the phone, Roland told him that he'd had to tone down his column about Rose's march through the Combat Zone. "You were pretty rough on her," the city editor said. "We can't offend much of our readership. A lot of good people marched in that parade. It wasn't exactly a Nazi rally."

"I'll tell you what," Buck said. "You've got plenty of stories about last night's march, right?"

"Tremendous coverage."

"Then kill my piece," Buck said before slamming down the phone.

Impulsively he had dialed Gene's house only to hear the same voice, that of a young boy. He'd left urgent messages for Gene to call him after the boy had told him that Gene was already at work. When he'd dialed Gene's office at police headquarters, he'd suspected that Gene was there but was refusing to take his call. An assistant had claimed that Gene was out on assignment but would get back to him later. Buck was left with the feeling that it was an empty promise. He suspected that Gene would never return any of his calls, and he had to figure out some way to approach him and explain things. Right now he didn't have a clue about how to do that.

After that phone call he put on those bikini briefs Leroy had given him but decided to slip his trunks on over them—not that he was expecting company but somehow it seemed more discreet. Later, alone on the beach, he'd removed the trunks and strutted around in those briefs. He liked the way he looked in them. They certainly flattered his assets.

Before going to the beach, he'd put through a call to Susan only to find she was not in her hotel room. She'd left a message at the newspaper office that morning that she and Ingrid were going to spend two days in New York shopping and seeing some theater. She'd also alerted Buck that she'd told Ingrid about their marriage but hadn't informed Jim yet.

Finally, all those phone calls behind him, he was alone on the beach.

Raising his head, he gazed out over the shifting whitecaps of the water. One wave rising higher than all the rest caught his attention. It was big and brave enough to trespass far upon the white sand. On its way to shore it seemed to drown, getting mixed up with another wave which diminished its force. By the time it crashed against the beach, the wave had become part of the general tide, no longer distinctive.

As the tide reached its flow, he lay back, gazing at the sky, letting the warm water wash over his feet. For a moment, he felt it could carry him out to sea, the way it caused the sand to erode gently. The waves washed over him, caressing his legs. He seemed to drift off until awakened by gentle fingers on his shoulder. "Mr. Brooke, you have a visitor," Henry said. "I don't know who."

Slipping on the jeans Henry held out for him, a puzzled Buck strode bare-chested and barefoot down to his pier where another yacht had anchored beside his own. Ever since his late mother had given him the cay, no one before had intruded upon his retreat without an invitation.

There, all glistening shell pink in the morning sun, stood the luxury cruiser, Rose II. Running up the gangplank, he called out, "What the fuck's going on here?"

From the cabin below, Rose emerged in a flowing white robe, her auburn hair wrapped in a turban, her violet eyes concealed behind large sunglasses. "Is that any way to talk to a lady?"

He stood staring at her, his emotions churning. Two of her crew sat at the far edge of the deck. Though excitement surged through him, he at the same time resented the intrusion. "What do you think Jesus would say of your coming unannounced to Buck Brooke's erotic paradise?"

"From what I know of Jesus, he would definitely approve." She removed her sunglasses, her eyes dancing. "It'd be a race between me and Him to see who got you first." In the sun, her face was exuberant, as he'd remembered it—excitingly flamboyant, daringly provocative, deliberately flirtatious.

"Then you, Jesus and me could have a *menage à trois*?" Buck asked.

She kissed the tips of her fingers, then released the caress to the wind. "That would be the thrill of my life."

As she moved across the deck of her yacht, he had the same feeling he'd had about her at the temple—total confusion. It was a relief to know that a woman who seemed to take Christ so seriously could also be flip about him. He couldn't connect the public Rose with the private woman, for, in a schizophrenic way, those two Roses spoke a different language.

The quiet, reserved Henry had set up a breakfast table right on the wooden pier, with its peppermint-striped awning. On the linen-draped table stood a freshly brewed pot of coffee and a platter holding slices of papaya.

"Seeing you're here, I might as well invite you to breakfast."

"Thanks." She reached for his arm. "Shelley's still asleep."

He frowned. "How great for me you brought him along. I heard his speech last night. That boy has such a winning way."

Active distress came over her face. "If I knew how Shelley would turn out, I would never have adopted him. But enough about him. Did you read my book?"

Feeling the curve of her back under his hand, he guided her into a director's chair, then sat down near her. "I'm not too much into fantasies."

She leaned over to him and shaded her eyes with her free hand. "Cruel, but I still love you." With graciousness, she focused on Henry, showering him with her charm. Henry didn't seem too concerned with her as he poured coffee.

A light breeze blew in, enough to chill Buck. The coffee felt good and warm going down. As he ate the papaya, he smelled the fresh salt odor of the sea, which was a deep cobalt blue today.

Whatever she was doing—drinking coffee or adjusting her turban— she never took her eyes off him. "You have a magnificent physique. Your face, too. So strong. And I love the way that forelock dangles over your brow. Like a fallen cockscomb. In some way, you're a child-man. I can't believe there isn't a Mrs. Brooke." Her look was suggestive. "There's nothing wrong with you?"

"I'm put together for whatever you've got in mind. Wanna climb the mountain? Then give me a certificate or something?"

"What a fabulous invitation." For a while she sat there in silence, gazing at him, a slight tremble on her lips. "I found out you'd come here by yourself. After the horror of that march, I needed a place to retreat to, too. More than that, I realized that I needed to be with you."

A quick shiver of apprehension went down his back. "I don't know why. You've got the racists, the anti-Semites, the crypto-Nazis, and the patriotic simpletons marching for you. What do you need me for?"

She reached out tentatively for him, never actually touching. "Don't talk like that. You know I can't help but attract some far-out types. I just try to do what I think is right. What God tells me."

She seemed to cling to his hand, and her face turned pale in the orange glow of the sun as she stared at a slight mist that hadn't burnt off the horizon yet. She pressed her head against his nude shoulder and he noticed her rapid breathing. Her soft hair rubbed against his unshaven face and it, too, felt as fresh as the morning.

With a will of its own, his broad palm cupped the back of her neck. His free hand traced her delicate bones, beginning at the curve of her brow and descending along her cheekbones to her chin.

It was hard to imagine what was going on in Rose's mind, and he didn't really care to find out, at least not now. All he wanted was to see the image the mirror saw when she looked into it. Not the mystery of her past or the highly questionable maneuvers of her present.

He sought the woman. His hand traveled to her thin waist and he crushed his mouth over hers and tasted her lips—soft, moist, yielding.

He felt extraordinarily alive, unthinking, wanting to love her, burying his doubts for the moment.

*****

Although Buck had been pissed when Shelley, awakened from sleep in his cabin on the yacht, had walked up, catching him kissing Rose, he'd forgiven the boy later in the day when he'd taken him for a stroll along the beach. It was hard to be miffed at Shelley for long. He was so incredibly beautiful you almost had to forgive him. If anything, he was the type of boy you wanted to grab and shower with kisses. Today he appeared more luminous than ever.

Rose had gone to the house to make some very private telephone calls, which gave Buck time alone with Shelley before Henry prepared lunch later in the day for Buck's two uninvited guests.

As Shelley played in the water, Buck had a chance to observe him closely. He looked fourteen, not his true age. The boy, bathed in a golden glow, belonged nowhere and to nobody. Yet at the same time he seemed to be crying out for someone to come and possess him, as if belonging to somebody was more important than being his own man.

At the breakfast table, Shelley had been filled with self-mocking humor, his commentary on Rose's moral crusade and his own role in it so crackling, his mother had asked him to leave the table. Delicate and fair-skinned, Shelley had a thin face that seemed masked, like one of those ghostly countenances one glimpses briefly behind a curtained window.

At first Buck had been tempted to teach him to swim, but he'd resisted that impulse. At People's Park, Shelley had preached about what he couldn't accept in a role model. It seemed ironic to Buck how much the boy did need someone to look up to. Rose herself, Buck felt, was the worst choice, forcing Shelley into the hardsell evangelical movement which he obviously hated. Shelley was too cynical, too worldly wise to succumb to the line Rose so successfully fed to the more fundamentalist mind. Shelley seemed locked in, his own jailer, caged with his own fears.

He was lying on a blanket on the white sands with Shelley when he was overcome with an impulse. He got up and peeled off his jeans standing only in the see-through red bikini Leroy had purchased for him. Shelley was treated only to his rear view as Buck rushed toward the water, hoping that the boy would follow. He didn't. Shelley still lay on the blanket staring in the distance at him.

When he emerged from the water, he didn't look down but felt that in this now wet bikini he might as well be nude. It left nothing to the imagination, hugging every line and contour of his genitals.

Back at the blanket he stood with his hands on his hips, his long legs widespread. He stood tense and silent, his toes dug into the sand. Shelley did not look into his face but seemed mesmerized by the attraction below his navel. It was all Buck could do to admit to himself that he liked displaying himself in front of the boy.

The day was hot and getting hotter, and the heat made Buck's mind bubble. The sun seared the beach, turning the white sand whiter, creating an overwhelming glare. In such a setting he tried to leave one question that had been troubling him unanswered. Just why was he being host to Rose and Shelley? They were the two most unlikely candidates he'd ever select to visit his cay.

Ever since breakfast, he'd felt Rose's kiss lingering on his lips. He'd pressed his nude chest tightly against hers, their mouths seeking a communion. As he'd driven his tongue inside the velvety smoothness of her mouth, he'd heard a gasp from deep within her throat, the sound betraying her need for him. The urgency inside her had communicated itself to him and, for a moment, he'd been lost, as if immersed in the rushing fluids of his own body floating into hers. She'd covered his face with wet kisses, tiny bites. Then, like hot, molten lava raining down,

Shelley had interrupted. It had the same limp effect on his hard-on that had occurred once when his mother had walked in on him at the age of nine, catching him masturbating.

Eyes tightly closed, he still thought of that moment with Rose before Shelley's interruption, and then he became uncomfortably aware of the boy's deep, penetrating eyes.

"Looks like you've got quite a pair of balls on you," Shelley said when Buck caught him looking.

"I need them," he said, sitting down on the sand and crossing his legs to avoid inspection.

"Wish I had a pair worth talking about. Maybe that's why I admire everybody else's so much."

"Maybe," he said in some vague, non-committal way, hoping to put an end to such talk.

"I knew you had a big dick—suspicion now confirmed—when I first met you," Shelley said. "I didn't know you had big balls too. Even on that rare occasion when you can meet up with a man with a big dick, the balls are often small. Lucky you. You've got both pieces of equipment. Or lucky the person who gets to drain those balls every night."

"How you talk for a sweet little evangelist being rescued from all the moral lepers in the world."

"Don't bring up religion when I'm talking about the big dick of Buck Brooke III. My eye is like a tape measure. You've got five and half inches soft. Maybe even six. That's soft. I bet a dick like that expands to twice its flaccid size when hard. With my sweet ruby red lips sucking it like a lollipop, I bet I could get it to rise a bit more."

Buck was glad he was crossing his legs because Shelley's talk was giving him a hard-on.

"You know you want it," the boy said, running his tongue around his lips. "Why don't we just take this blanket behind the bushes and give you some relief right now? A big juicy blow job. I'll let you fuck me later. Before I let you dismount, you're going to come twice inside me. Not only that, when you pull out and are lying panting on our bed, I'm going down on you for a final taste."

Buck was definitely getting hard and was hoping to distract Shelley with some other subject.

Shelley reached out and took his hand and pulled it toward his mouth. One by one he began to suck Buck's fingers in the most lascivious way. "I'm going to drain your balls. I've got to have that big dick in me. I can't stand it any more. You can make this real easy for me or else I'll have to revert to other means."

"What do you mean? Other means?"

"I'm determined to have you. If you don't pull off that bikini, I'll get it off you one way or another. *I've got to have you.*" He continued sucking Buck's fingers with more determination than ever.

Buck was fully aroused now. The red bikini could hardly contain him. Jerking his fingers from Shelley's devouring mouth, he flipped over on his stomach, his hard cock rubbing into the hot beach blanket.

Embarrassed at his own arousal, he quickly changed the subject. "Would you tell me something? I thought Rose disliked minority groups. Yet she went out of her way to be friendly with Henry. I've never seen her so nice. And Henry's not just black. He's blue-black."

"Rose loathes Jews. She considers them dangerous saboteurs, working to undermine America and taking their orders directly from Israel. But in some parts of the country, blacks make up about three-quarters of her audience. A lot of them believe in Jesus the way she does, and with no outside interference from rabbis. Besides, in Rose's new social order, she's going to need servants and I'm sure her faithful 'Negroids' will fit the bill."

"I bet they also contribute heavily."

"They sure do!" Shelley looked out over the water, "Even if they can't afford it. One woman on welfare with eight kids saved up a hundred dollars and sent it to Rose."

"I'm sure Rose needed it." Buck sounded sarcastic.

"Like hell! That bitch has green bambinos she hasn't even counted yet."

Looking intently at Shelley, Buck asked sharply, "Do you hate Rose?"

"I don't want to say hate," Shelley said, a smirk on his face. "It's just that I have dreams at night. You know, torches all around me lighting bonfires. White-robed choirs singing Hallelujah. Then Rose, with these great big white wings, swooping down. In the dream she's got a face like a falcon. She grabs me and swings me in mid-air. Then tosses me into hell's fire. Some dream, huh?"

"Powerful stuff!" For a fading instant he sensed a recognition in Shelley's face, a suggestion that the same nightmare could happen to him.

"Listen," Shelley said in a soft, confidential voice. "I know it's smart-ass for a kid like me to tell a super-honcho like you anything, but I'm stuck with the bitch. You aren't. Rose will snip off those big balls of yours the first chance she gets. She's already got a trophy room of testicles. Don't you be the latest catch."

He got up quickly, wondering as he did if Rose possessed such ruthlessness, or if Shelley was exaggerating in his usual overstatement. "Thanks for the tip. I intend to hang onto my jewels." He quickly slipped into his jeans.

There was little motion on the beach, not even a slight breeze. The waves seemed lethargic. The blinding sun had momentarily robbed Buck of energy. Sand flies droned in the air, circling him, then landed on his neck. He slapped them away.

As he strolled the beach, he noticed Shelley following along behind. Whipping the towel from around his neck, he snapped it at Shelley, tanning his buttocks.

"I love it!" Shelley shouted playfully. "More, more."

At the crest of a hill, Rose, still clad in her sheer white robe, stood regally, gazing down at them.

As Buck headed across the sand dunes toward her, he found his pace quickening.

As he did, he remembered Shelley and reached back and took his hand. He didn't know why he did that, but he did. He'd established some bond with the boy and deliberately wanted Rose to know that.

He sucked in air from a giant breeze that seemed to have come down from some snow-clad mountain to wake up the deadness on this blistering hot cay. With Shelley's hand firmly encased in his own much larger hand, he headed toward Rose. His confusion about his own feelings were more disturbed than ever. With all the emotional complications in his life, he needed these two new strange bedfellows. It was more of a statement of fact than a question.

*****

After a lunch of conch salad prepared by Henry, Rose was summoned to the phone on her yacht. In minutes she'd returned to join Buck at table with Shelley. A look of great distress was on her face.

"Is something wrong?" Buck asked.

She hesitated. "There have been some complications. I have to meet with Calder Martin this afternoon."

"Oh, shit!" was Shelley's only comment.

"I understand," Buck said.

"I must go back to the city at once."

"Enjoyed your visit," Buck said.

There was a hint of desperation in her voice. "I didn't come all the way over here just for lunch. It's urgent that I talk to you. If you don't mind, I'll return at six. I have some vital things to tell you, and I'll know a lot more at six than I do now. Am I invited back?"

"By all means, come back for dinner. I'd like to hear what you have to say."

"Rose, I'm loving it here," Shelley said. "Can't I stay on until you get back?"

Rose looked first at Shelley, then imploringly at Buck. "That depends on your host."

"Sure, kid, you're welcome to hang out." He reached for the salad bowl. "Have some more conch."

At the pier he told Rose good-bye, then returned to table with Shelley.

"I hear raw conch makes a man out of you," Shelley told Buck. "As soon as we get this luncheon out of the way, I'm ready for action. Prepare yourself for the fuck of a lifetime. I don't know how many holes you've plugged, but with me you're going to face your ultimate turn-on. By three-thirty this afternoon, I will have answered the ultimate question troubling me: in its full glory does it rise to ten inches, ten and a half, or even eleven?"

"That's one thing you'll never find out."

Shelley reached across the table taking Buck's hand as he'd started to lift a cup of coffee. "As Rose's friend, Nixon, might say: let me make something perfectly clear. I've got to have you and I mean *now*. I can't wait. I've never wanted anybody as much as I've wanted you. When I want something, I've got to have it."

"Forget it," Buck said, removing his hand from Shelley's grasp. "It's not going to happen. The answer is no and that's that."

"Bullshit! I'm determined to have your semen deposited in this beautiful boy's body before sunset. Shelley gets what Shelley wants, and, big boy, Shelley wants you."

Buck sipped his coffee and eyed Shelley as if for the first time. There was such a determination on the boy's face and such a conviction in his voice that for a moment he convinced even himself that his own seduction was near at hand.

Shelley tasted a Bloody Mary Henry had prepared for him and frowned at its flavor. "I think I'm the only one in the world who knows how to make a real Bloody Mary. Someday I'll tell you my secret, because I heard it's one of your favorite drinks. Do you also like margaritas?"

"Even more than Bloody Marys, I love margaritas. I could drink them all day and night."

"I've also make the world's greatest margarita."

"I've had some pretty good ones."

"You haven't tasted mine." Shelley's eyes traveled Buck's body provocatively and suggestively.

"So I haven't."

"What do you say to this? Let me go into Henry's kitchen and return shortly with a pomegranate margarita. I saw some of that tasty fruit in there."

"A pomegranate margarita. That sounds like heaven. I'm game."

"I won't be long. Why don't you go out and rest in that Florida room? I'll join you there."

"It's a date," Buck said.

Shelley stood up but looked back at him. "More so than you can ever imagine."

*****

Gene put down the phone. It was nearly three o'clock, and he knew he was due at the office for a psychiatric evaluation in just thirty minutes. He'd learned what he wanted from a cadet acquaintance of his who'd only last week gone through the same evaluation.

"That guy spent more time evaluating what's in my pants instead of what's in my head," the cadet, Phil Graham, had told him. "He couldn't take his eyes off the outline of my meat. What a cocksucker! I had him so flustered he couldn't hold his pen steady."

"Did he put the make on you!" Gene had asked. "You could report him."

"He wasn't that much of a fool. But I'm sure if I'd whipped it out for the faggot, he would have gone down on me right in his office. After all, he locks his doors."

"Thanks, pal," Gene had said before hanging up the phone.

An idea had quickly occurred to him. Instead of appearing in a suit, he had another plan. Back in his bedroom, he pulled off his clothes and headed for his closet. He was glad Jill and Sandy were out shopping, as he didn't want them to see his transformation.

In the back of his closet he pulled out a pair of faded jeans he hadn't worn since he was in college. Stepping out of his briefs, he slipped into the jeans, having a hard time buttoning them. Even though his waist was still trim and his stomach hard, the jeans were clearly a size or two too small. Over the years the jeans had been laundered so many times they were now a very pale blue. These pants clearly served their purpose: they outlined the full length and thickness of his cock and formed a perfect basket to capture his low-hanging balls. He was so exposed in them that he felt almost nude.

Thinking fast, he put on a plain white T-shirt but decided he looked too indecent to appear in any office. Quickly he slipped on an old army shirt, leaving its tails hanging out to conceal his package of goodies. That way, he could partially conceal himself until he was actually in the psychiatrist's office.

He waited for what seemed like an hour before he was finally ushered in. A bald, short man with a tendency to put on weight looked up as he came in. Seeing Gene, his dead eyes seemed to come alive.

"I'm Dr. Valibus," he said, reaching for Gene's hand and perhaps holding it for too long.

"I'm Gene Robinson."

"Sit down," Dr. Valibus said, motioning to a chair to the side of his desk.

Gene eased his frame into the chair letting the army shirt slip open. If anything, the chair seemed to make his jeans ride higher up his waist, revealing more of his genitals.

Dr. Valibus gave him a long, steady appraisal. It seemed hard for him to ask questions. "You work out a lot?"

"Yeah."

Dr. Valibus stammered, checking out Gene's basket. "I've been going over your file. An interesting record."

"You mean, that I was once accused of exposing myself?"

Before he could say anything, Gene became more forceful. He decided he had to be the aggressor because he didn't think the psychiatrist would dare initiate any moves himself without strong encouragement. "I've got a lot to exhibit."

"I can see that."

"I don't mind flashing every now and then. That little girl was one thing, but the rest of the world seems mighty interested in what's hanging."

"What do you mean?"

"I noticed when I go into a men's room, guys often follow me in. Even if there are ten urinals there, two guys always stand on each side of me waiting for me to reveal myself."

"Do you?"

"I've got to take a leak, don't I? I can't help it if the world is fascinated."

"Does it ever get hard?"

"Sometimes I shake it a few extra times and stand there at the urinal for a few extra moments. Often I drop my hands or light a cigarette while standing there. That gives them extra viewing time."

"Do they reach for it?"

"Nothing wrong with touching."

Beads of perspiration were forming on Dr. Valibus's forehead. "This is not the usual procedure. Most of my exams are here at the desk. But in some unusual cases I also conduct a physical exam." He motioned to an adjoining room. "Why don't you go into the other room and remove your clothes? Even your briefs."

"I'm not wearing any today," Gene said.

"Fine." The doctor put through a call to his front desk before following Gene into the examining room.

In the examining room and in front of Dr. Valibus, Gene removed his army shirt and slipped his T-shirt over his head. Sitting down, he removed his black boots and socks, then stood up and unbuttoned his jeans, sliding them down slowly until his penis burst free of its tight confinement. Dr. Valibus's obvious excitement was causing Gene to harden. Totally nude, he placed his hands on his hips and stood with his legs widespread.

Dr. Valibus moved closer to him and reached for his low-hanging testicles. He gently encased one of them in his sweaty small hand. "Cough," he said.

Gene didn't even attempt to cough, and Dr. Valibus didn't seem to notice. The doctor began to play with Gene's testicles, as Gene's cock expanded to its full size. The psychiatrist seemed fascinated by the length and thickness of it. He pulled the skin back and began to plant tiny kisses on the head of Gene's cock, nibbling on the sides. He turned his head from side to side, giving the cock a circular, caressing movement. Then he took the cock into his mouth, pushing down on it, taking as much as he could swallow. And he could swallow a lot. He was extremely skilled. The head of Gene's cock pressed against the doctor's throat which miraculously opened for him. Gene enjoyed the tight confines and kept his cock in as long as he dared before withdrawing so Dr. Valibus could breathe. A slurping, gurgling noise filled the room.

Gene seized both sides of the doctor's head, raising himself on tiptoe. "Eat me!" he commanded, increasing the speed of his pumping. "Your tonsils are going to get a bath."

Dr. Valibus cupped a free hand under Gene's balls, squeezing and tickling them, pulling at them as he prepared his throat for another deep penetration. Gene continued to pump furiously. "Damn it," he said. "Oh, damn it." Almost without warning, he filled the doctor's mouth to overflowing. Although he found the doctor personally detestable, he'd been one of the most skilled cocksuckers Gene had ever discovered.

Even when he was spent, the doctor's mouth remained glued to Gene's cock, milking the urethral canal empty of its last sweet drops. Long after Gene had gone limp, the doctor continued to tongue and kiss him. Finally, Gene slowly pulled himself from the man's eagerly devouring mouth.

"What a swell blowjob," Gene said, rising to his feet, although the doctor remained on the floor, staring up at him. "Where did you learn all those tricks?"

"I have been a psychiatrist for the men in blue for twenty years," he said, slowly getting up. "You learn a lot in twenty years."

Gene quickly slipped on his clothes.

"You were the best ever. I imagined your come was blue like a police uniform. That it was sprinkled with sapphires and diamonds."

"In that case, you've got a lot of jewelry in that fat belly of yours."

Dr. Valibus didn't seem in the least offended at this insult.

"Going to give me a good evaluation?" Gene asked, buttoning up his jeans.

"I definitely am going to report what a healthy specimen you are, both mentally and physically."

"Thanks, doc."

As Gene was heading for the outer office, Dr. Valibus called him back.

"There's a catch, though."

"What do you mean?"

"You've got to report to me every week at the same time."

*****

Buck felt he'd been on a long journey somewhere but was slowly returning to earth. It was somewhat like the same feeling he'd experienced when he'd been knocked over the head by those Nazis. But this time, although his mind had been sent on a long drift, he felt intense pleasure—not pain.

He gradually began to come to, but his body still didn't seem connected with his brain. In some way, he felt he'd just smoked six powerful marijuana cigarettes and was a bit giggly from the experience. His head was swimming a bit but in a most delightful way.

His cock was fully hard and was being serviced by an expert. He was coming back to earth but didn't want to arrive yet. This sex dream was too real and vivid. He didn't want it to end and hoped it would go on forever, satisfying him in this deep way.

He was dreaming about Robert. Only his friend could satisfy him so expertly. He was certain that Robert had returned from Miami and was going down on him, causing his entire body to experience the most incredible sensations. This was Robert's welcome home present to him. Only Robert, not Gene, could swallow all of him this way. Only Robert had the power to open his throat and receive his full penetration.

Keeping his eyes fully closed, Buck pumped harder, raising his hips from the bed, wanting to receive more and more of this suctioning mouth and throat. He reached down and placed his broad hand on his seducer's neck, the other hand on the back of his head. Almost unconsciously he wanted to force his seducer down on him for the final blast-off. He was going to hold the face down on him by force if he felt for one moment his seducer was not going to take his load and swallow every drop of it. He wanted this homage from the suctioning mouth.

When his release came, it was violent and overpowering, almost like none he'd ever experienced before. It seemed to go on forever, and his seducer showed no signs of letting up. There was no need to use force here. If anything, he felt he'd have to use force to withdraw from the mouth which seemed to want to hold him in bondage until it was certain it'd drained him to the last drop.

Buck fell back on his bed, panting. He seemed to still be in the throes of orgasm. His recovery was slow. Gradually he opened his eyes, finding himself in his bedroom. He could tell by the light coming in that the afternoon had faded. All he remembered now was standing in his Florida room, tasting the pomegranate margarita. Shelley had fulfilled his promise: it was the best Buck had ever tasted. The only sensation that disturbed him was a slight almond taste. It was only a hint. The power of the pomegranate quickly overpowered that flavor. He'd taken another long sip, savoring the taste. But that was all he'd remembered. The drink must have gone suddenly to his head. He'd felt an overpowering need to sleep. It wasn't unpleasant. In fact, he'd welcomed the all encompassing drift into oblivion, like crawling into a safe, warm nest on a cold winter's night.

He was emerging from that nest now. The long nap was over. He opened his eyes, recognizing his bedroom ceiling. The devouring mouth was still on him, but was now gently licking his cock and planting tantalizing little kisses on it as it gradually returned to its flaccid state.

Raising up on his elbows, he looked down at his seducer. It was not Robert.

"Shelley!" he said harshly. "What in hell are you doing?"

The boy raised his head and looked up at Buck with a kind of wonder and awe. "Hi," he said.

"What in the fuck do you mean, Hi? What have you done?"

"I've just had the most thrilling experience of my young life. I've just found the cock of my dreams. What I've been waiting for all my life. I've found my mate. I'm going to spend the rest of my life servicing this fabulous cock." He ran his fingers along the length of it.

Buck pulled away but made no effort to cover his nudity. There seemed little need to prevent exposure now. "Don't I have something to say about this? Or do you plan to spend the rest of your life drugging me and seducing me?"

"The next time I won't have to drug you. You'll be begging for it."

Buck eased himself from Shelley and headed for his closet and a fresh pair of jeans.

"That's some bubble-butt ass you've got on you," Shelley called after him. "I should know. I've been an hour licking it and tasting the sweetest rosebud God ever gave to a white man."

"You got to that too?" Buck said, slipping into a pair of jeans, although remaining shirtless. "Is there any part of me you're not intimately familiar with?"

"There isn't. My tongue has been over every inch of your body so many times I know it better than my own."

"It'll never happen again. I can assure you of that."

"It'll happen thousands of times. This is only the beginning of a lifelong affair. But I've told you that already."

"You may be the world's most beautiful boy—there's little doubt about that—but beautiful boy might be a little touched in the head."

"Not at all," a fully dressed Shelley said, getting up from the bed and licking off the last flavor of Buck on his lips. "I'm not going to brush my teeth for the rest of the night."

"Don't you ever do that again, and I mean it."

"You also sound very unconvincing. I warned you. I was going to have you. You didn't believe me. Surely by now you believe me."

"By now I believe you're capable of anything."

"Keep that thought."

A light rap at the door and Buck was in front of it, opening it to discover Henry.

"Mrs. Phillips has returned from the mainland," Henry said. "She's asking you and Mr. Shelley here to come down to the dock for a drink on her yacht."

"We'll be right there," Buck said, looking for a shirt.

"Great," Shelley said with a smile. "I'll whip up some pomegranate margaritas."

*****

At New York's Waldorf-Astoria, Susan eyed her mother with great approval. Ingrid always wore Chanel dresses, some of them twenty years old. "Good clothes never go out of style," she always proclaimed, often in her national column. Immaculately groomed and perfectly made up, Ingrid never appeared disheveled. Even in a windstorm, she seemed to keep every hair in place. Refusing to dye, she'd let her hair turn a lovely salt-and-pepper which softened her features as she moved deeper into her fifties. With a bit of aggression, Ingrid pushed aside her plate of eggs Benedict.

"You look like you've got something very serious to tell me," Susan said, downing the last of her coffee. A waiter rushed to refill her cup.

"That will come later," she said, eying the lobby. "Actually I was thinking of an old movie I once saw. Weekend at the Waldorf, or some such silliness. I think it starred Lana Turner, but who can remember at this point?"

"Thanks for agreeing to go shopping with me. Somehow clothes always look better on me when I buy them in New York than in Okeechobee."

"You'll be able to buy any outfit you want now," Ingrid said. "Now that you're married to Buck Brooke III."

"I didn't marry Buck for his money."

"But he married you to hold onto his money, his inheritance which is going to come sooner than later."

"Are you absolutely sure?"

"I'm not called the smartest woman columnist in America for nothing. Robert Dante has his claws in your man and will never let go. I noted with interest that Buck is moving you out of your tacky apartment and into a luxurious condo—not his home."

"I could hardly live under the same roof with Robert. He hates me."

"Where will your husband spend his nights? With Robert or with you?"

Susan frowned, feeling a slight irritation at Ingrid's questions. "I'm prepared to share him if necessary."

"Is Robert?"

"I don't think so." She frowned again. "In fact, I don't know if Buck has even told Robert of the marriage. I fully expect a confrontation, although Buck denies there's anything between them."

"You didn't expect him to admit to anything, did you?"

"Until I know differently, I'm taking the position of believing my man. Facts could change, but right now I'm taking him at his word."

Ingrid leaned back, reaching for her coffee, wincing as she tasted it. She liked her coffee scalding hot, and obviously this cup didn't meet her standards. She signaled the waiter. "I suspected for a long time there was something between Gene and Buck."

"That I doubt. You're far too suspicious."

"I have an unfailing instinct about these matters. But I'm also very understanding. I'm not a homophobe even when one of those guys marries my only child. You know how many of my friends are gay. I just don't want unhappiness for you."

"I managed to find plenty of that before I married Buck."

"So you did. I don't want you to set yourself up for heartbreak again."

"That thing with Gene was then. This thing with Buck is now. Even though it was spur of the moment, I entered into this marriage with my eyes wide open. I was thrilled that he asked me."

"Well," Ingrid said, smiling. "It was a smart career move. You certainly married up in the world. I'm very proud of you. Mrs. Buck Brooke III. Your husband is going to be one of the richest men in Florida. Maybe the richest. That's not bad. So what if he doesn't come to the marriage bed. Are you prepared to live with that?"

"I told you, he's a great lay. Hung like a horse too, and does he ever know how to handle it."

"In that case, we can assume he's at least bisexual."

"From personal experience, I would say that's a smart conclusion."

Ingrid smiled again. "It just occurred to me this marriage might work. If you're completely realistic, completely accepting, you might have it made. I anticipate tremendous career advancement for you. If Buck is cynically using you, use him back. Take full advantage. It's very hard getting ahead in the world. I suffered greatly to get where I am. You just advanced up the ladder to a dizzy height only hours ago. Congratulations!"

"Thank you. I wish it could be a full marriage. But if it's not, I'm prepared to live with that too."

"You can always have something on the side. I'm sure Buck would be very understanding. If he's fucking Robert and maybe Gene too, he would hardly be in a position to challenge any conquest of yours, now would he?"

"Not at all. I just can't believe he's going to settle down and play house only with me. I'll be lucky if I see him one night a week. He's got a busy schedule. I'll probably have to make an appointment with Robert just to see him."

"What do you care? You don't love him, do you?"

"I don't. I think of him as a great date—not a husband. When his grandfather dies, he can always divorce me. By then, he will have gotten his inheritance."

"I don't think he's going to divorce you at all."

"What do you mean?"

"If he's really gay and wants lovers on the side, I think he's going to need a cover like you. He's going to want that understanding wife for public consumption, romantic pictures in the news. You're perfect. Lovely, intelligent. You'll be the most charming and romantic couple in Florida. The Examiner's circulation will climb. Except you may not have a sex life—that is, with each other. But I'll tell you this, you're going to be one rich and powerful woman."

"There is no doubt that when the news breaks that I've married Buck Brooke III, the world will be impressed."

"It will indeed. I've always been in awe of power and money. Why not? I've spent most of my life writing about that very subject."

"At least you and Jim have been devoted to each other."

The waiter finally arrived with coffee hot enough to satisfy even Ingrid. "Oh, my darling daughter, now that you're married for the second time, I must tell you the truth. Jim and I have created our own fantasy for not only your consumption but the world's. We're viewed as a perfect loving couple. Each one devoted to each other. That is hardly the case."

A lump formed in Susan's throat. "What are you telling me?"

"It was always understood: Jim would have his life and I would have mine. When we are together, we are fine and have always stood by each other. But what I did away from him and what he did away from me remains our own private business."

"You mean you've had affairs? I know all men do. But you?"

"Just as many or maybe even more than he has. My lovers have ranged from John Kennedy to a certain general who used to live in this very hotel."

"Not that one."

"Yes, that one!"

Susan sighed and looked at her mother as never before. Never a beauty, with somewhat harsh features, Ingrid was a compelling personality, a kind of latter day Barbara Stanwyck in appearance. Many men must have found her appealing.

"Pillow talk gave me some of my most sensational columns," Ingrid said.

"Mother," Susan said sternly. She usually called her Ingrid but somehow said "mother" like she was feeling the need to chastise her. "I know you told me this to help me in my own marriage and with all the problems you know so well I will have. But it's also destroyed a dream of mine. You took away one of my final fantasies—that of you and Dad as a couple devoted to each other since their university days."

"You're confusing me with Buck's parents. Buck Brooke II and his wife—bless them—were the only people I knew who could claim that kind of fidelity to each other. Jim and I never demanded fidelity. We demanded loyalty from each other. He's always been there for me, and I for him. It's been a great marriage. I wouldn't change a thing."

"You certainly got the world to believe in your myth."

"And as such Jim and I can be the perfect role models for you and Buck."

Susan's voice was hesitant, her mind cloudy.

"I have one more revelation, and then I promise I'll quit blowing your mind for the rest of the day," Ingrid said.

"Let me have it. I'm sitting down."

"One of my longtime lovers was Buck Brook I. The original one. Not one of the two clones."

Susan stared at her mother in amazement. "I think we could have gone through the day without my knowing that. Why did you want to tell me?"

"Not to shock. I want to throw out a challenge to you. For years, I've been writing a biography of Buck Brooke I. I've discovered some amazing things—not only what I know but what I've learned from others. However, in the last few years, I've lost interest. I want you to take over where I left off. You can have all my data and even some of my early already written chapters. I'll give you full credit. The byline is yours. You might even win the Pulitizer Prize, and you'll have a lot to keep your mind occupied during those nights Buck is in his own home with Robert, or perhaps in the estate of Buck Brooke I, which he'll inherit. Or in some real estate somewhere. God knows he's going to own enough of it."

Susan stood up from the table, as if to signal Ingrid she didn't want any more secrets revealed. She reached for her mother's hand. "Now that I'm Mrs. Buck Brooke III, I think I'm going to change my image. Become a 1977 version of Ingrid Howard herself."

"What do you think I am?"

"A little bit too conservative Eisenhower era for me with those old Chanels. I'm going to be a 70s type of woman. A late 70s woman. I still have clothing I wore in the university. Out it goes. When I land in Okeechobee, I'll have a new wardrobe, a new look, and even a new husband. Guess where I'm sending the bills?"

*****

At sunset, Buck's cay turned golden until shadows fell across the hill. Out on the patio, Rose's cheeks glowed with color, and his imagination was filled with possibilities.

He eyed her, hoping to turn on the sexual current that had flowed between them when he'd kissed her at breakfast that morning.

He was confused by his own emotions. With all the sexual liaisons in his life, why did he need a new conquest? With Rose, it wasn't just sex. Sex was just a weapon he could use against her. He feared her, sensing she might be behind some unknown force trying to take over the Examiner. Although he wasn't sure how rational the thought was, he felt in some far corner of his brain that if he sexually overpowered her, he'd have her groveling at his feet and her threat against him—and possibly the Examiner—would evaporate.

Even if he knew this was an unlikely proposition, he continued to move forward with his plan, as if spinning a web and inviting her to enter to become his captive.

Barely speaking, uncertain as to what to say, he poured her a dry sherry which, to his surprise, she accepted. As he offered her the glass, he detected a tremor in her hand. She reached out and gently caressed his fingers.

The twilight air was clear and he felt proud of himself for getting Shelley to take a nap. Finally!

At first Rose had wanted to talk business, but he clearly wasn't interested. As if compelled, she persisted in discussing what an important force religion was in TV programming and station ownership.

Slim and elegant in her clinging white gown, she braced her shoulders as a triumphant glee came across her face. "Since launching my moral crusade, I've picked up ten new stations just for myself."

In a way, he was shocked that she'd appear so unveiled before him, exposing her fiercely ambitious dreams.

"What I'm really going to do is go national with a 60 Minutes type of program to take up where the religious broadcasts leave off. After all, it's my responsibility to keep the American public informed on issues other than religion."

He closed his eyes, letting the fresh breeze bathe him. As he enjoyed that, the implication of her mass media assault on the public disturbed him. What terrifying, special dark vision had she planned to spring on America?

As if asking herself that same question, she said, "In my own 60 Minutes, I'll see to it that the grievances of the silent sufferers will be heard and the unjust exposed without mercy." Her pronouncement carried ominous overtones, as if she personally had been wronged and was anxious to seek her revenge.

"I get it," he said with weary resignation. "The overburdened taxpayer against the welfare cheat; the God-fearing Christian against the deviate, godless Commie, the puritan WASP against the child-molesting Jew pornographer. That program should run forever. The possibilities, as you say, are endless."

Her eyes still filled with the vision of her goals, she seemed not to notice the sarcasm in his voice, and went on spinning her dream.

"That Arab-Israeli war ten years ago regrettably has resulted in a wave of Arab stereotypes. The Jews have objected violently to their own stereotypes, but the Arabs have never found a voice in America to champion their rights. If an Arab speaks, no one listens. On the other hand, if I with all my Christian influence spoke, the whole country might listen."

"You'd like to become the spokesperson for Arab America?" The prospect left him dumbfounded.

"In this land of immigrants, national and ethnic societies are all over the place. But there has been no really effective Arab-American society to stand up and defend the rights of Arab-Americans. Such a society could counter the demonizing stereotypes. It could lobby in Washington for policies favorable to the embattled homelands of the Middle East that live in fear of aerial bombardment by Israel."

"I'm sure if you set up such an organization, contributions would pour in by the billions from Arab states. As spokesperson, you'd be richer than you already are. You might even be given vast oil wells to call your own."

"You may sound sarcastic, but what you just said is absolutely true. My organization would dwarf that National Association of Arab-Americans set up in 1972. I don't think they've been very effective. I could stand at the forefront of the movement."

"Why? Because of your love of Arabs? Why would a little Christian Oakie like you love Arabs and want to advance their cause in any way? If not for financial gain."

"There's nothing wrong with financial gain," she said defensively. "The last time I checked this was still a capitalist country, although Hazel and such ilk would like us to take our orders directly from the Kremlin. My job would be public relations. Is it illegal to take a public relations job in this country?"

"Nothing that you're proposing is illegal. But do you want to do it?"

"Coming from such a Christian leader like me would give the movement a validity it has never had."

"I'm sure that's true. Everything you're saying is true."

"Then why do you seem so shocked?"

"It just seems so unnatural coming from you."

"There are at least three million Arab-Americans in this country. Probably a lot more than that. Most of them are Lebanese. But there are many other Americans here who came from Iraq, Syria, Palestine, Egypt, wherever. They need a leader."

"I'm sure they do. But you?"

"Who else? I could serve as a bridge between them and the Christian world. Calder Martin has enormous political contacts. He could make the voice of Arab America heard in Washington."

"I totally agree. If you want to pursue this, I have no doubt you could become the mother of the Arab-American organizations in the United States. A daunting prospect."

He could take this talk no more. He felt he was wandering into a potential nightmare. He got up and headed for the liquor cabinet and a vodka. "You certainly have shown you can whip up Christian America. Why not Arab America too? You've got your act together, and I'll give you credit for that. At your parade, one of your supporters held up a sign. WIPE OUT VIOLENCE AND IMMORALITY ON TV. Yet your damn crusade brought more violence into the home than a gangster movie."

"Darling," she said, her face flashing anger which she quickly and artfully concealed. "We've agreed before, I'll eventually have to be more picky in my choice of followers. All in good time." She came up real close to him. "Right now I need all the help I can get."

"From any quarter?"

"I welcome support. When I get contributions for my foundation, I don't ask where the money comes from. A devout follower of mine—a prostitute, really—firmly believes in our work and regularly sends me a check."

"How quaint!" he said bitterly. "Ten percent of her earnings."

As he looked into her eyes, he knew—and she did too—that talk about religion and politics would only keep them apart. That obviously wasn't her desire. Or his. He looked straight in her eyes, as if sending out a signal to keep quiet.

Through her own kind of radar, she picked up his message. From that moment on, she became seductively compelling—as if deliberately moving, walking, talking in ways that would attract him.

Later, as Henry served dinner, she wondered why Shelley was still asleep. "I usually can't get him to go to bed."

He didn't want to tell her he'd placed a sleeping capsule in the boy's soda.

Out on the patio after dinner, he was no longer confused. He planned to take her. The boy in him enjoyed manipulating the buttons that controlled the lights in the house and, in a second, everything went dark. Only the sound of a fountain could be heard, and then a frantic gasp from inside the living room where she was caught unaware.

He rushed to her side, finding her trembling, her brow feverish. He reached to turn on a lamp and she stopped him. "I'm terrified of the dark," she said, "unless someone holds me. Ever since I was a little girl, I've been afraid of the dark."

"There are no demons here," he said calmly, pressing his body close to hers.

Her long fingers reached inside his shirt, feeling his chest as if it were a flawless piece of sculpture. He quickly yanked off his T-shirt, knowing she wanted that. He wanted it, too.

Creating a slow-moving choreography of their own, he danced with her around the center of the room, no longer listening to the rhythm of the background music, but to their inner melody. Their bodies moved together, tighter and tighter, and she gracefully let him slip off her gown. She was completely nude.

Her skin felt terrific to him. She seemed as strong and energetic as he was.

Reaching, exploring, he put his hand on her thigh, and the quiver of her body was a compelling clue she wanted him to go farther. He groaned as she rubbed against him, and though her features were indistinct, he knew she had a funny little smile of accomplishment on her face. She had him, that was true.

The lines of her body were lovely, sensual and ripe, the breasts large with prominent nipples. With both hands, she tugged at his jeans, and he was ready for any consummation, no matter what.

He eased her onto the sofa, mesmerized at how her shapely arms and legs glistened in the soft, natural light. His chest pressed harder against her breasts. As she lay her head back on the cushions, he gently kissed her neck and, reaching to pull him closer, she laughed softly, her tongue flickering in his ear.

Under his deft fingers, he felt her heart beating fast and in this moment of love-making, he was still aware that this was a famous evangelist, a self-professed moralist, but also a passionate woman whose skin was just as smooth and fragrant as any he'd known. This paradox amazed and scared him. He slid his tongue over her mouth and then put it deep inside her, as if trying to reach the voice that had preached to millions over the radio and TV about sin, adultery, and fornication.

His penis thickened in anticipation as her fingers slid over him. He writhed in pleasure as she continued to stroke and tease.

As her hand reached lower, he uttered a low moan, only to find her slipping beneath him, licking and biting his chest like a lioness lusting after warm meat. Her mouth encircled his penis and, once inside her, he finally reached the throat from which sprang the voice that brought reassurance of heavenly rewards to the devout. Now that throat existed only for his pleasure, and he'd silenced that voice except for a deep gurgle. Pounding with excitement, no longer wanting to delay, he lubricated her throat.

Later when they were in his bedroom, he took her, her writhing hips creating a frenzy of joy within him. She seemed to swallow him whole, and the more deeply he penetrated, the greater her rocking thrill. The irresistible force of orgasm gathered within him. She hard-gripped him, and he never wanted to break free. Arching his back, he tried to gain more momentum. She held him down with a masterful light touch, as if she were taking control, directing his movements, telling him as if by some inner radar where to move and how to bring her even more excitement. Soon, actual movement wasn't needed, and he collapsed on top of her. She grabbed him tightly, her climax surging through her.

At this point he was overcome with a sense of dread, as if he'd desecrated a national monument. In some ways he felt his sex act with her could produce repercussions as violent as his climax. Yet, even as he recovered from his exhaustion, he planned his next assault on her.

She flickered her tongue across his eyes, nose, and lips, then let it form a wet trail down his spine until she'd reached his rosebud. She attacked it violently, savoring the taste and eagerly swallowing her own now scented saliva. When she'd licked him clean, she planted a wet kiss on each cheek followed by a gentle nibble. Getting up from the bed, she strolled through the open doors that led to the pool and dived in.

Nude, he ran after her, plunging in with her. The sudden coldness of the water startled him. He caught up with her and pulled her close, kissing her face and inserting his tongue in her mouth. He could taste his own odor on her, and for some reason that thrilled him all the more.

Her left hand travelled and fondled his jewels. He was soon fully erect in the water and wanting more relief. He decided to take her right in the pool. Her back was against the tiles of the pool, and she could not see the lone figure who'd emerged out of the shadows.

It was Shelley. The sleeping powder had obviously worn off. He was wearing only a pair of briefs.

The pool lights were on but Shelley remained in a dark corner of the unlit patio. Rose's eyes were closed as she moaned and gripped Buck tighter.

Buck knew Shelley was watching their every move. Strangely, instead of deflating his hard-on, Shelley's presence seemed to thicken and lengthen his penis as he plunged deeper into Rose, who was now digging into his back with her fingers and nibbling at his ear.

Shelley pulled down his briefs and began to masturbate. As if he were having sex with Buck—not his mother—he beat himself furiously. Even though Buck couldn't clearly see, he knew that his orgasm and that of Shelley's was perfectly timed.

*****

When Gene drove into his driveway, he thought at first he was at the wrong house. The windows were open and the place looked bright, cheery, and inviting. The house had been boarded up for so long, it was always dusty and mildewed. Not today. Jill and Sandy had aired out the place. As he entered the kitchen, he could tell the difference at once. Everything was freshly cleaned and polished. Someone, possibly Jill, had taken down the curtains at the kitchen sink and washed them. Not only that but a stew was cooking on the stove. Not since his mother's death had this place been a home. It was now.

Coming from the bedroom with a stack of old newspapers, Sandy broke into a smile when he spotted Gene standing over the stove inspecting what was in the pot. "My man," Sandy said, putting down the papers and rushing toward Gene. Almost before he knew what was happening, Sandy kissed him on the mouth.

"Cut that shit!" Gene said but not in a harsh way. "We'll have none of that."

"Since when can't a boy kiss his old man? It's done all the time."

So as not to reject the boy totally, Gene ran his hand across Sandy's smooth face, the soft skin momentarily offering him comfort. "What's going on here? I don't know the place."

"You may be the best looking man who's ever walked the planet, and the sexiest, but you are the world's worst housekeeper. Jill and I have killed ourselves around here, and we're far from through. When was the last time this place got dusted? Five years ago?"

Gene smiled and squeezed Sandy's arm. This time it was he who reached over and kissed the boy on the cheek. "Thanks a lot. I'm dying to see the front of the house."

Sandy took his hand and led him up the corridor. "The living room actually looks like someone might live here."

"Where's Jill?"

"You won't believe this, but she's out back planting some flower seeds she bought with her ill-gotten gains. She said she's always wanted to have a garden, and here's her chance."

"I find this hard to believe, but almost overnight we've become a family."

"It's an odd one, but it's a family."

At this moment, Jill, dirty from the garden, came into the living room. "Welcome home, big man. We've missed you." She walked over and with perfect naturalness kissed Gene on the cheek. "Do you like our little transformation?"

"I love it," Gene said. "Thanks for all the hard work. I guess I'm not much of a housekeeper."

"I'll agree with that." She sat down across from Gene. "In a few weeks we're going to have some flowers growing in our secret garden."

"No one's planted flowers around here since my mother died."

"You've got them now."

Sandy reached for Gene's hand and held it like a caress. "Jill wants to ask you something."

"Fire away," Gene said.

"I knew your invitation for me to stay here wasn't forever, but could I stay on a few more days? I don't have any place to go and I love it here with you and Sandy. Please, let me stay a few more days until I can figure out what I'm going to do. I don't want to go back out there on the street."

Gene tightened his grip on Sandy's hand. "You can stay here as long as you want. That goes for both of you. Suddenly, I can't imagine life without you."

No one said anything for a long moment. Jill got up and kissed Gene again on the cheek. "That's damn good news to a girl who'd never had much good news in her life. You two studs can excuse me now. I've got to wash off some of this dirt before dinner."

When she was off in her bedroom and presumably showering, Gene turned to Sandy. "I still can't get over having Jill here." A frown crossed his brow. "Especially considering how we met. Having her here and letting me help her and take care of her in some way helps me get over the guilt of what I did to her."

"You did nothing to her. It's all gone and forgotten."

"I wish that were true. This town has a long memory. There are a lot of people here who haven't forgotten it. They won't let me forget it either."

Sandy took Gene's hand and raised it to his lips, planting a long, lingering kiss on his inner palm. "I love you, daddy."

With some awkwardness, Gene pulled his hand away.

Sandy got up from the sofa and looked down at him. "You liked my chili last night but you're going to love my beef stew."

"Thanks for cooking it."

"And thank you for leaving some money on the kitchen table so we could buy some groceries. I felt like a real homebody going to the market to shop with Jill. Sorta like man and wife. I never felt that before."

"I'm sorry you were kicked out of your own home."

"Hell with my parents. If they don't want me, fuck 'em. I got by on my own. Now I've met you. Things have changed for me." He reached for Gene's hand pulling him up from the sofa. "Come on back into the bedroom. I want to show you something."

"Now, none of that."

"C'mon, that's not what I'm going to show you. You've already seen that, although you haven't reciprocated by showing me your jewels yet."

"I'm not going to either."

"Oh, yes you will. We're living in the same small bedroom. I'm bound to see them sooner or later."

In their bedroom, Gene noticed the transformation at once. It was never so brightly cleaned and polished. The pillow cases looked fresh. Inside their bathroom Gene noticed that all the mold had been miraculously washed away.

Back in the bedroom, he noticed Sandy standing in front of his dresser drawer. The boy pulled open the drawer. "What do you think?"

Gene looked inside. All his briefs had been neatly washed and stacked up in three piles.

"You sure wear sexy briefs. Before I put them back in the drawer, I kissed inside each pouch knowing what goodies it will contain."

"Thanks for arranging everything so neatly. But those kisses weren't really necessary."

"It was for me. I have to do that until I can get the real thing down my throat."

Gene reached out and touched the boy's arm. "You're just a boy. You don't need some grown man using you for sex. Haven't you had enough of that?"

"I've had enough of that. But I haven't had enough of you. I could never get enough of you."

"C'mon, don't make this rough on me. You're a very desirable boy, and I've got to admit I've had thoughts. But you're too young. I can't give in to my temptations."

"Like hell you can't. I'm very patient. I'm going to have you sooner or later. By holding out on me like this, you're just delaying the inevitable. It's gonna happen. We both know that."

Gene reached over and kissed Sandy's cheek again. "Right now we're going to go into that kitchen and have an old-fashioned family dinner."

*****

After a good dinner, and after Sandy and Jill retired to the living room to watch some television programs, Gene excused himself and headed for the back bedroom. Tomorrow might be one of the most important days of his life, and he needed sleep to prepare for it.

Relieved that Sandy didn't follow him to the bedroom, he stripped off his clothes and headed for the shower. Instead of the important business he had to handle in the morning, his mind was preoccupied with Buck and Susan. Were they together right this very moment making love? He turned his face up to the spray, and, even though the water was a bit too hot, he let it wash over his eyes, lips, nose, and throat, as if that act alone would blot out the memory of Buck. Just when they'd gotten back together and their relationship looked more promising than before, Buck had betrayed him. He still couldn't believe his old friend would turn on him like this. The act of marrying Susan was unforgivable.

His face still under the jet spray, he was aware of a movement in the shower. He jerked his face away from the water to discover that a nude Sandy had entered the shower with him. The boy was fondling Gene's genitals. Gently but forcefully Gene removed Sandy's hand, although as he did he could feel himself hardening.

He turned his back to Sandy to avoid contact with him but the boy sank to his knees and began planting tiny kisses on Gene's buttocks. Within moments the kisses became licks. In one lunge, the boy's tongue was slurping at Gene's most private part. He moved to force the boy's head to break the contact but Sandy clung to him tenaciously as if he were not going to be denied this pleasure he had so long anticipated.

With one hand he slipped his fingers from Gene's buttocks to his genitals where with expertise and skill he massaged Gene to a full hard-on. The boy seemed to be lovingly measuring the length and thickness of Gene's penis with his fingers as he continued with his tongue to explore as deeply into Gene as he could. Gene was gasping for breath. The blood was pounding inside his head and his words were undecipherable even to himself.

Sandy abruptly stopped his assault on Gene's buttocks and moved his head between Gene's legs. His lips slid tightly along Gene's throbbing cock, encasing a good part of it, a feat that amazed Gene. Gene felt he couldn't endure another minute of this exquisite pain. One part of his brain told him to push Sandy's devouring mouth from him. But his actions were completely different. Instead of pushing Sandy's head away, he held the boy even more firmly to his body. In minutes rapid-fire swellings in his spasm-wracked prick told him the inevitable was happening. Erupting with a loud, gasping cry, he shot hot bursts into the boy's eager mouth, coating far back into his throat. Sandy devoured the offering and held on until he'd milked every last sweetness from Gene.

After this explosion, Gene felt awkward in the boy's presence. He let Sandy make the next move. The boy took the soap from Gene and began to lather and clean Gene's body. Even when Gene had stepped from the shower, Sandy was still at his side, wiping him dry with a thick towel.

Neither had said a word to each other. In bed with Sandy, Gene turned over on his stomach. Sandy seized on this opportunity, running his fingers along Gene's back and planting tiny kisses there.

"You're so tense," Sandy said. "I'm going to massage and relax you."

Gene closed his eyes and said nothing even when Sandy's caressing fingers were replaced by Sandy's tongue. Even though he'd just bathed, Sandy was bathing him again with his tongue. He wetted each of Gene's legs and sucked and washed each of Gene's toes in his mouth before returning to Gene's buttocks, his favorite field of exploration.

Still without speaking, Gene drifted toward the sleep he so desperately needed. He was vaguely aware that Sandy was masturbating as he tongued Gene's rosebud, but he felt he was incapable of calling a halt to this. He hadn't intended for this to happen. But given Sandy's strong needs and desires for him, and this tiny room, he knew that Sandy's prediction was true. It was inevitable. It had happened a lot sooner than Gene had fantasized. Even when he tried to do what he thought was right, he always stumbled into some temptation.

Was he the instigator of this? he wondered. He didn't initiate sex with others. Sex was demanded from him by others. It had always been that way and his experience with Sandy was so typical of so many others, except he felt loving and protective of Sandy. Sex with so many other faceless ones was often an act of aggression on his part.

Long after he'd drifted into sleep, Gene woke up suddenly. When he came to, he felt drenched in his own sweat. Sandy was sleeping peacefully at his side. Gene had been dreaming, or at least it seemed like a dream. Increasingly, it was difficult to tell these days, as reality often took the form of a nightmare. His eyelids moved over and over, as if trapped by a mechanical rhythm like a stuck record. He tried to make the blinking stop but couldn't.

In the dream he'd been in some warm, moist, sensual place with Rose. He was just a boy in the dream. Rose his mother. At first she'd held his hand and guided him through the vastness of a tunnel and, as long as she'd been with him, he'd felt secure. Then she'd run away from him, and his legs had been too short to keep up with her long, graceful strides.

The wind blew through her long auburn hair and though he reached to clutch it, it was beyond his grasp.

As darkness closed in, he stumbled, falling several times. Yet he kept picking himself up and running faster. The air that had been as protective as the womb suddenly grew harsher. From out of nowhere a strong wind blew in, so cold it made the liquid in his eyes turn to ice.

He called out to her and she answered, her voice a faint, distant echo, urging him to run faster. Then no sound at all.

He was trapped in the cave, buffeted by the wind, encased in total darkness.

Blindly he ran on, banging into rocky walls. Up ahead her face appeared, illuminated by purplish spotlights on the wall of the tunnel. As he rushed to catch up with her, the image faded, only to reappear shortly at some more distant point.

She taunted him and he begged her to stop. "I love you!" he shouted. She didn't seem to hear him and her melodic voice changed, becoming cruel in tone, harsh like the cry of a great wild animal in the forest.

He fell down a ravine and when he pulled himself up from the jagged rocks, he became aware he was touching the tip of a white diaphanous gown.

Slowly he hugged the woman's body close to his. Then he discovered that the body wasn't Rose at all, but a hissing snake disguised as a woman. Shrieking in horror, he stepped back, the ground giving way under him. Falling into space, he woke up with a start.

He got up and stumbled to his bathroom, slapping cold water on his face. When he came back, the sheets on his bed seemed on fire. Even though he needed sleep, he dared not return to bed. In sleep, the demons came out and took possession.

As Sandy slept, Gene dressed silently in the bedroom and tiptoed out. He feared his long overdue confrontation with his chief, Biff, which was scheduled for two o'clock that afternoon. Biff had left word to be in his office at that time. Gene wondered what the meeting was all about. Had the psychiatrist cooperated or had he filed a bad report on Gene?

At three a.m. he'd left his house, buying a bottle of Scotch and driving the causeway that led to the beach. He'd heard over the radio that Sister Rose, after the trauma of the march, had retreated to a quiet place on the beach where she could meditate and decide what the next step was in her crusade. How he wished he could be with her.

As he drove, the memory of the man who'd sold him the Scotch came back to him. That man had hated Gene on sight. He could tell. No one liked him. Gene knew if he died right tonight, he'd leave no mourners. All the Cubans on the block hated him, too. That woman across the street seemed to watch his house all the time, just waiting for him to come home so her face could show her contempt for him. He suspected that the Cubans would like to storm his house—the one holdout against their invasion—breaking his windows with bricks.

Jill and Sandy remained in his life, but each evoked sexual implications too murky for him to want to explore this morning.

At a marina he got out and stood under a streetlamp, taking another drink before heading for the pier. Streaks of early dawn appeared in the sky and the screech of unseen birds could be heard.

The yachts of the rich lined the harbor, and he resented the affluence of the owners. Here he was, earning wages so small they destroyed self-respect, protecting the lives and property of these idle people who contributed nothing to society—only extravagantly burned up its vital energy. Without him, and others like him, he knew that the police were the only force preventing the blacks and Cubans from moving to confiscate all the wealth in the country.

Back in his car, he swung onto the causeway as the sun broke through, casting bright reflections on the green-blue bay. On one of the uninhabited islands in the bay, split by the causeway, he pulled off to the side of the road, got out and, bottle in had, walked across the sand to stand motionless as the sun rose, the orange ball making him squint.

Back in his car once more, bright shafts of sunlight poured through his windshield as he reached for his mirrored sunglasses. The car made a sickening noise as it hit the causeway.

The radio announced another record-breaking heat wave, with the temperature expected to climb to ninety-eight degrees. He knew he could stand the heat. Picking up the bottle of Scotch, he tossed it out the window, the glass rolling and breaking on the pavement.

Chapter Six

A sliver of light cut through the drawn shade of Buck's bedroom. It fell over the curved, naked thigh of Rose. Not the world's most youthful thigh, it was still creamy, well-preserved and smooth enough to elicit lust in him, making him want to touch and feel her as he had last night. His passion was made all the sweeter the more the sun progressed and sparkled on her body. Relaxed now, innocent in veil of sleep, she had driven him into a whirlpool of excitement last night until somewhere in the half-dreamy hours of morning he'd fallen asleep, her arm resting casually across the expanse of his broad shoulders.

Her face was covered with an eyeless scarlet-colored satin domino to protect her from the morning glare. He was more exposed, vulnerable to the piercing light that crept through.

Outside his window he heard the shrieks of birds and the sound of the wings of sea gulls descending for their prey. Immediately, he was overcome with a sense of cannibalism. He wanted a cigarette but was hesitant to light one.

The island was bathed in silence, yet within his head he heard the toll of church bells, a choir singing "The Alleluia Chorus." He'd been to bed with an angel, except, in truth, she wasn't *that* any more than he was.

Filled with bitterness, hatred, she could also deliver wild, passionate love. After their thirsts were satisfied last night, they'd seemed to huddle together like two lost children, and it wasn't sentimental. She held him with a kind of dignity he imagined two brave people might summon when they were about to face a firing squad.

She was lonely, tender and also fearful, and she'd clung to him with a tenacity he'd found in no other woman. He brought her a joy, comfort and fulfillment he suspected she'd known in few men. What troubled him was his reluctance to continue to provide it. He'd never entered into any relationship that had all the earmarks of a catastrophe right from the beginning.

He kept his eyes tightly closed, enjoying the languid heat of the room. They'd agreed to turn off the air conditioner and to leave the doors to the patio and pool open all night.

His memory traveled through the feelings and emotions she'd evoked in him, and he rested on a hypnotic moment there before going on to some fleeting, distant caress only vaguely remembered like a sea breeze. The day moved in on him, regardless of how silently he lay there trying to hold it back.

He was fully awake now, no longer dreaming. He'd become uncomfortably aware of the invasion of some foreign presence. He opened his eyes and looked down near his feet where Shelley slept peacefully, clinging to his leg. He'd thought Rose's feet had become intertwined with his.

Gently removing his leg from Shelley's embrace, he also eased out from under Rose's arm and slipped out of the room, dressing quickly in the bathroom. Touched deeply by Shelley's apparent devotion, he still knew he would never become his daddy.

In the kitchen, he told Henry he wouldn't be joining Rose and Shelley for breakfast.

On his yacht, he spoke to one of his crew, telling him he wanted to return to Okeechobee at once. As the yacht pulled out, he paced the deck in his bare feet, watching the cruiser, Rose II, fade. A pain in his chest came unexpectedly.

He sat down to compose a note to her, telling her he couldn't see her any more. His words were too empty for the message, so he tore up the paper and tossed it to the wind.

He wanted to push past her and close the door.

Last night her offer had been stunning and had taken him by surprise. Although she'd made it clear there was a "cancer" growing on the Examiner, and she might not be able to save the newspaper for him, she promised far greater rewards if he'd join her in her crusade. She'd promised him a position with a massive salary as her media director—television stations, newspapers, whatever. It could all be his if he came aboard her staff and worked for "Jesus instead of for the Devil."

A gnawing restless energy, an itch to get back to the office, filled him. Even if he were no longer in charge as before, even if he had to give in to Roland's expanded command, he wanted to make himself a presence there, to remind Roland and the staff that he hadn't abandoned his responsibility. He was still the publisher, if in name only.

For a moment he stood looking at the restless ocean in silence. The sudden rise of a wave somehow reminded him that two major items loomed on his agenda: Susan returned from New York today and he was going to pick her up at the airport. He couldn't believe that she'd become his wife. He also had a date to fly to Miami to join Robert. Another marriage loomed for him, even if the second one were only the mock. He couldn't sort all this out this morning, so he went below to get dressed for a day that appeared ominous.

Off-tune, Shelley's singing must have wakened her. Before she figured out what he was doing in Buck's bathroom, Rose turned over in bed after adjusting her satin domino.

The memory of last night stirred her flesh. Buck had loved her with a fervor she hadn't known in a man in years. He'd worshipped every part of her body separately and at his touch, she'd felt like a work of art. Cheeks, thighs, nose, hair, feet—each part of her had been fondled and adored.

His love-making had left her half-drugged and, as she lay here quiet and languid, she desired him again.

Once, while he was still asleep, she'd removed her domino just to stare at his body, sprawled on the bed next to hers. In the rosy, pre-dawn light, everything had looked beautiful—especially him. His hand had lain gently across her stomach. Completely relaxed, the hand an hour before had been a feverish tool of lust, probing every inch of her nudity. She'd gently fondled his hand, circling his fingers until he'd started to stir. His handsome face had nestled almost innocently against the curve of her breast where her nipple had looked slightly puffy and bruised from his all-night attack. Her whole body had tingled as she'd traced the light feathering of blond hair on his chest, across his washboard stomach until she'd stopped to fondle the source of so much pleasure.

Still remembering that scene, she reached out and searched for his body in bed, coming up empty-handed. Sitting up, she jerked off her domino and stared at the empty room in fright, as a sense of loss came over her.

A towel draped around his shoulders, Shelley paraded nude into her bedroom, a beaming smile on his radiant face. She resented his youth and beauty. It made her feel old somehow. Would Buck one day desire Shelley more than he wanted her? Why hadn't she adopted someone ugly or even deformed? Why had she adopted the world's most beautiful boy?

Ever since puberty, he'd been her sexual competitor. The first time she'd caught him with a lover, the All-America football player, Don Bossdum, had come as a shock and had led to a screaming fight over who was to have the six-foot-two-inch blond hunk. Even now, she recalled Shelley screaming to her, "He's practically signed an affidavit that he prefers my tight rosebud to your overripe pussy." She'd cringed at those words and feared her son might be right. Don had, in fact, ended up spending more evenings with Shelley than with her.

"Buck's gone," Shelley said. "Maybe we wore him out yesterday."

"We?" she asked, sitting up in bed. "Don't tell me you tried to move in on him."

"My lips are sealed."

"Get out!" she shouted. "You're disgusting."

Tossing the towel at her, he stood completely nude in front of her, then headed for Buck's pool and an early morning swim.

Rising reluctantly from her bed of lust, she headed for the same bathroom from which Shelley had emerged.

In front of the full-length bathroom mirror, she examined herself critically, hoping Buck would not apply so keen an eye. Even if he did, he'd find a slender, youthful-appearing body, in spite of her years. Perhaps not as young nor as firm as his own, but one possessing immense physical appeal all the same.

Through an open window a sudden ray of light stabbed the room, one of such brilliant intensity it momentarily blinded her. When her eyes adjusted to the light, her body appeared more vulnerable, indecently nude. Instead of a perfect curvature of figure, she detected telltale clues as to future and ominous sags of flesh. Just signs, but still evidence to alarm her. She retreated into the shower to avoid seeing her own body.

As she showered, her troubled mind realized she'd have to leave the cay at once to place her one important phone call of the day. Buck's line might be tapped, and this ritualized international call demanded total secrecy.

As she dried herself, she found herself trembling in dread at having to face her problems back on the mainland. All the violence, horror, the bloodshed. It seemed impossible to her that she'd surrendered so much of her own life to others. She felt trapped, forced to do what she did. How wonderful if instead she could have spent the day in Buck's arms, making love again. She'd sold out long ago, and now her bosses were insistently demanding the return of that loan in ways she'd never imagined.

Buck remained her one grand hope. If only he'd accept her deal to become her media director. She knew that Calder wanted the job and felt he had the post in his pocket. There was a great struggle for supremacy with Calder within her own organization. She felt she couldn't fight him alone. But with Buck firmly allied with her, she could slay Calder.

To her, he belonged to the old-fashioned school of politics. His tactics were too brutal for her. She wanted to present a gentler image to the world. If Buck truly loved her, and after last night he more or less confessed that he did, he could help her fight Calder. But she had to make it so enticing to Buck that he would forever stand with her.

She might not be able to save the Examiner from a hostile takeover by Calder, but there would be other newspapers to conquer, new television and radio stations. The salary would be fantastic. As proof of her generosity, she was this very moment having a treasured gift sent to Buck's office. This gift would remind him that there was plenty more where that came from, if only he'd cooperate with her and write glowing praise of her image instead of his attacks.

Coming back into the bedroom, she wrapped a robe around herself and headed for the patio where Shelley was completing several laps in the pool. When he pulled himself from the water, he looked like an Adonis. He was so compellingly beautiful that even she would have desired him physically if he weren't that way.

She realized she had to be very clever about her son. Instead of viewing Shelley as a competitor for Buck's sexual favors, maybe she should look upon him as part of the package. Buck would not only get her, but Shelley too. Surely the two of them would be more than adequate to satisfy Buck's sexual needs and keep him in permanent residence at Paradise Shores.

She knew Buck was involved with his secretary, Robert Dante. Calder had presented her with all the evidence, including secretly taped messages between them. That's how Calder played the game. But she also knew that Buck liked women and had made many conquests. It would serve her purpose if Buck developed an interest in Shelley. She feared the boy's philandering would eventually lead to a sexual scandal that would threaten her own image and her charismatic foundation. At least with Buck fucking him, he might stay home at night and out of trouble and harm's way. Judging from last night's performance, Buck was certainly man enough to satisfy both of them.

She might even invite both of them into her bed at the same time. She'd always been curious about why men turned to each other for sex and rejected women. Maybe she should learn this lesson up close.

When Shelley came up to her and stood tantalizingly looking down at her from her position on a chaise longue, she tossed him a towel. "It's quite generous in size, darling," she said. "But Buck's got you beat by several inches."

"You should know after he lubricated your tonsils last night," he said. "Not to mention what else."

"You sound jealous. You want him just for yourself." She sat up as Henry appeared on the patio with morning coffee and juice. "This time I might let you share some of the goodies, but not possess him totally. I think I'm falling in love with him."

"He really must have been good for you. You don't usually fall in love so easily."

"I know. I don't fall in love at all. I've never been in love, and I'm not sure I am now. But I'm thinking about it. Don Bossdum had the physical endowments of Buck, but he didn't have the brain power. I think we both got tired of a man who sat around in his jockey shorts all day watching sports programs."

"Don had his charms. It was he who left us, remember?"

"I don't exactly recall. There have been so many. They come and go. Buck is special. He could become part of my dream."

"You mean your nightmare."

"Drink your coffee, faggot," she said harshly. "We've got to get back to the mainland. I've got God's work to do!"

*****

Robert had mysteriously disappeared. Back in Okeechobee, Buck had placed several calls to his friend but could not locate him. A call to the hospital revealed that Robert's mother had died only hours before. Buck was amazed that Robert hadn't called right away. Buck would be there for him. Why wasn't Robert sharing his life with him? Had Robert secretly learned about his marriage to Susan? Perhaps he had and in a fit of anger had run off somewhere, not even planning his mother's funeral. This seemed so unlike Robert. He was always responsible, always in touch with Buck no matter what the circumstances.

Before the end of the day he'd know more about that and other issues, even Gene. Okeechobee wasn't that big. He knew where Gene went. Even if his old friend wouldn't return his calls or pick up the phone, Buck knew he'd encounter him somewhere. He had to explain to Gene about his marriage. Fuck! He had to explain to Robert about the marriage. He hadn't told Rose either. Eventually the word would leak out. He couldn't keep it a secret forever.

In the park this morning he needed his morning jog more than ever before facing whatever it was back at the office. For all he knew he would return to the news tower and find Roland occupying his main office instead of sitting at his usual place at the city desk.

A faint breeze was stirring but even so the day was muggy. He felt his clothes soaked in perspiration only five minutes into his jog. A red headband was catching his sweat that otherwise would pour down into his eyes, clouding his vision. His vision was clouded enough as it was.

Only vaguely he became aware of a white limousine moving slowly along the street, seemingly following his trail as he jogged. Fearing trouble, he decided to veer inward through the park instead of running along its border. As he cut deeper into the park, the limousine stopped abruptly. The back door was thrown open, and a portly man with some difficulty emerged.

"Brooke! Wait up!" The voice was that of Calder Martin.

Seeing it was Calder, Buck ran toward the limousine. What possible reason could Calder have in wanting to talk to him? Nearing Calder, Buck stopped abruptly. One didn't want to get too close to pit vipers. "The last time we accidentally met," Buck said, "you told me you didn't talk to assholes from the Examiner. Why the sudden shift in policy?"

"Get in!" Calder commanded.

At first the thought of a kidnapping flashed through Buck's mind. But even Calder wouldn't dare that. Buck decided to get in. He knew Calder wasn't in this park to breathe the fresh air. Surely he had something interesting to say.

In the air-conditioned back seat of Calder's limousine, the hatchet man of the far right offered him a whisky.

"No thanks."

"Too early in the morning for you, sissy boy? Real men can drink at any hour."

"Help yourself, macho man."

Calder poured himself a generous drink from the limousine bar, then settled back against the plush upholstery. "Rose, so I've heard, has been making you all sorts of tempting offers. But you can forget it."

"Exactly what do you mean?"

"I'm the only media director that cunt will ever need."

"But what if she wants me for the job?"

"Listen, and listen good, you little faggot slime. Rose and I are jockeying for position within our organization. She thinks she can run things. She's wrong. She'd got no power to offer you anything. I'm the only one who can make offers."

"I'm not convinced of that."

"Rose is not convinced of it either."

Without responding, Buck called to the driver. "Take me to the Examiner news tower." He looked over at Calder. "Don't worry. I'll pay him the regular taxi fare."

"Cut the bullshit! This is a serious talk. I don't think you realize how easy it is for me to ruin somebody. I think you need a demonstration."

"What in hell are you foaming at the mouth about, liver lips?"

"Don't you ever call me that name. I can't stand to be called that."

"Get used to it. It's so apt."

"Fuck you! Okay, faggot, I'll prove something to you. I know how—what can I say?—fond you are of Gene Robinson. Let me demonstrate to you how easily I can destroy him. When you see how I do that, you'll get just a tiny preview of what I'm going to do to you if you don't cooperate."

"You leave Gene out of this," Buck said, perhaps a little too defensively for his own comfort. A look into Calder's steely eyes revealed a determination that frightened Buck. "What are your demands?"

"I want you never to see Rose again. Stop any plans you have to expose her in the Examiner. In other words, back off!"

"I can't do that. She's too hot a news item for a publisher to ignore. And on a personal side far too alluring."

As the limousine neared the news tower, Calder looked over at Buck too intensely for his comfort. "You've got to be taught some lessons. A little too cocky for me. This old ice shaver has warned you about my ability to cut off balls. You apparently need a demonstration of my power."

"You fucker! Don't you do anything to Gene. Your fight's not with him. It's with me. If you want to threaten and attack somebody, make it me. Let him alone."

"Too late now. Get the hell out of my car. Somebody might see us together and think I'm a faggot like you."

"Go to hell, you slimebag bastard."

"Let's lunch," Calder called mockingly after him, as the limousine pulled away from the curb.

Buck landed on the sidewalk. But he could still smell the stench of Calder. It was odor he feared wouldn't go away.

*****

His stay on the island had stretched out far too long and, as Buck arrived at the news tower entrance, he dreaded facing the accusatory eyes of Roland. The new arrangement of power was a bit unclear. Had Roland become his boss instead of the other way around? Buck was still the publisher, but was he publisher in name only? He intended to test his power against that of Roland's this morning.

He didn't like anyone thinking he was doing a bad job as publisher, deserting his post as Okeechobee became a hot news beat. He hoped Roland didn't know he'd just slept with one of the prime news figures herself.

Rose was so baffling to him that all he could do was grab at every clue, hoping one day to fit all the pieces together.

Frankly, he had a hunch that she personally did not direct the shadowy, octopus-like far right movement involved in various black and gray deeds and, instead, that she was being used and manipulated by characters and corporations whose purposes were far more insidious than hers.

Calder Martin had obviously been assigned to direct her political maneuvers. Who paid Calder's salary?

One thing he did know. Rose Phillips was a woman of almost unbounded ambition. She had a devout following of at least four million believers and, perhaps, after the media coverage of her moral crusade, that figure had increased by at least another million. If such support could be turned into a voting bloc, then she stood as a powerful figure and symbol to those hoping to make political gains. Five million voters following a strict mandate from her charismatic foundation could be such a formidable concentration of power that, if properly organized, it could determine the outcome of a national election.

At the news tower, a lone protester paraded around in a circle at the Examiner's main door, carrying a placard proclaiming: HITLER WAS RIGHT—PERISH JUDAH.

He came up to confront the man—a short, thick-necked, extremely pale and middle-aged protester with a bulbous nose. He handed Buck one of his tabloids with a smile.

On the elevator to his executive suite, he scanned the paper quickly. Called The Free American, it billed itself as "The Battle Organ of Racial Fascism." "No subtlety there," he said to himself, crumpling the paper as the elevator came to a stop.

When he came into his office, a temporary secretary had been hired in Robert's absence. An older and overweight woman with a bad hair style of flaming red greeted him and told him her name was Blanche Scott.

"Any messages for me?" Buck asked, anxious to hear from Robert.

"Nothing," she said rather curtly as if she disliked him intensely. "There is a memo on your desk from Roland."

In the rear quarters, Buck showered—this time without Robert's assistance—and dressed hurriedly and headed for his desk. As he eased into his seat, he could see Roland in the news room. He looked more like a traffic director than a city editor.

The memo from Roland was waiting on his desk. "I know you've had Susan Howard on special assignment. She is now being relieved of that assignment. When she returns from New York, I'm putting her back on the university coverage with instructions to go easy on those guys. We don't intend for the Examiner to become a thorn in the university's side. Please abandon any long-range investigative reporting you may be doing, especially about Sister Rose and her religious foundation. In the future, I will direct coverage of her foundation."

He crushed the note in his hand and glared at Roland through his window. The city editor did not look up but concentrated on the papers before him. Buck was determined to test his power anyway. In a high-pitched state of nervous tension, he managed to write an editorial he was fairly pleased with, although he suspected it would ignite rage in Rose. He'd penciled in the headline himself—HEAVEN IS ON HER SIDE, SO SHE SAYS. In the piece, he'd attacked Rose and labeled her a "pious bigot."

As he copyedited it, he still tried to sort out the puzzle of having enjoyed the woman's body as much as he did—every part of it, except her mind. It continued to amaze him how she could satisfy him so much physically, while at the same time he stood opposed to every idea that seemed to pour forth from her head.

For a respite, he sat in his swivel chair looking out at the sky shining like a polished copper gong. Blanche knocked briefly on his door and entered. Seeing her, he handed her his editorial and asked her to deliver it to Roland.

"I will," she said curtly as if this would be a major imposition. "But that's not why I'm here. You've got a surprise." Turning again to the door, she ushered in two security guards from Rose's temple, carrying a carefully boxed frame. Buck identified the men quickly from the emblems worn on their uniforms.

"What's this?" he demanded to know.

As if Buck had surrendered his soul, Blanche announced. "Would you believe a de Kooning? While you were out on the island, Rose's secretary called. She said she wanted to give you a gift. To pay you back." Blanche paused, "For your hospitality."

The implication was clear enough. "You told her I wanted a de Kooning?"

"I told her nothing. I had no idea what kind of gift you wanted."

A frown crossed Buck's face as a dreadful uneasiness settled over him. The only person he'd ever confided in that he desired a de Kooning was Robert. Robert hardly had conveyed that request to Rose. That meant one of two things: either his office was bugged or else his line had been tapped.

"Maybe the gift was actually made to her temple from a wealthy contributor," Blanche said. "Maybe she personally dislikes de Kooning."

"Why don't you tear off the casing?" Buck asked.

One of the security guards removed the casing.

Blanche picked up a tag attached to the painting. "It's called East Hampton II, 1977. Painted only this year. A review attached says it's in shocking magentas, blushing Neapolitan yellows."

Buck took in the painting and found it thrilling. It was one of the best de Koonings he had ever seen.

"Are you going to accept it?" Blanche asked.

"Rest it on the sofa," Buck ordered the guard. "I'll talk to Ms. Phillips later about it. If this is a bribe to the Examiner, the painting is unacceptable. This paper can't be bribed, as long as I'm publisher."

The guards gently rested the painting on the sofa as directed.

When the men had gone, Buck turned to Blanche. "After Ms. Phillips reads what I have to say to her in tomorrow's Examiner, I think she'll want the painting back. I'm sure she'll send those guards with machine guns this time to get it."

Staring rather wistfully at the painting once more, Buck headed for the bathroom. He'd forgotten to shave.

When he came back into his office, Blanche reappeared. "Ms. Phillips is on the phone. She said to tell you she's back in town and wants you to come to Paradise Shores for lunch."

"Tell her I have to meet someone at the airport and can't make it."

"Are you sure?" Blanche asked. "I mean, she did give you this valuable painting."

"I'm sure," he said, looking down at the paper on his desk. It was another memo from Roland.

"We can't publish your editorial," Roland had written. "I'm sorry. But that's the way it is. If you want to challenge my judgment, take it to your grandfather. If he calls me and grants permission to run it, I will. Otherwise, I must say no."

After reading the memo, Buck looked through his office window at Roland. Again, his look wasn't returned.

In the foyer he paused and turned to Blanche. "Are you certain Robert Dante didn't call?"

"Yes," she said rather matter-of-factly. "But someone did call while you were in the bathroom."

"Who?"

"Leroy Fitzgerald."

"Tell him I'll call him back this afternoon. If he calls again, tell him I definitely want a meeting with him. He'll know what that means."

In spite of Roland cancelling any special investigations, Buck was seriously going to pursue his work even if he had to run the series in the arch rival of the Examiner, the Okeechobee News. He was certain the editors over there would be only too willing to publish his reports. It seemed terribly disloyal to the Examiner, but he wasn't going to let old Buck and certainly not Roland completely stifle his voice.

At the elevator, he paused. He felt he should walk over and say something to Roland who had avoided him all morning, except by memo. But instead he found himself returning to his inner office. There he stood and looked briefly at the de Kooning. It was a stunning work. He loved all de Koonings, this one especially. A sigh escaped from his throat. Then he turned and left, glancing briefly at the office clock. He'd have to hurry to meet his new wife.

*****

The Vulcan Baths at the Twenty-Third Street Beach had been built at the turn of the century, but now were deep in decay. The four-story building was painted a pea-green and many of its outsized windows had been broken and never repaired.

Gene walked up the steps to the second floor and registered at the desk. After checking his watch and wallet, he was given a locker in a dormitory room with plain iron cots covered with sheets. Opening off these were a few private cubicles with a single cot in each. The attendant told him the steam baths, massage room and swimming pool were in the basement.

After signing in, he wondered if he'd been wise in giving his real name. He stripped, placing his jeans and T-shirt in the locker assigned to him. He put on a robe of white sheeting similar to a hospital nightgown. It reached mid-thigh. On the way to the steam room, he noticed that the private cubicles were divided by wooden partitions reaching up about nine feet, but not touching the tall ceiling. "Cages for animals," he thought in disgust. He spotted holes drilled or crudely cut in the walls by voyeurs.

At the entrance to the steam room, he left his robe on a numbered hook outside and entered nude, his sudden appearance attracting much attention from the shoppers.

He hoped he'd be able to spot Leroy in the dim light. He'd been told the leader of the Lolito ring hung out here at this time of day.

Brushing caressing hands from his body, he perched on a shelf, lined with Cuban tiles. The other bathers paraded around just to look at him. After fifteen minutes, he could hardly breathe and decided to go outside. Maybe Sandy had been wrong. Perhaps Leroy didn't spend his mornings in the steam room.

Just at the point he'd given up hope, he spotted Leroy joining the shopping circuit. At least he thought it was Leroy. He couldn't be sure. On closer inspection, he definitely recognized his old schoolmate, the photographer who'd snapped the frontal nude of him and then distributed it all over town to his gay friends.

Leroy cruised him making eye contact, but showing no flash of recognition. Leroy was the only man in the room who hadn't been rejected by Gene. One elderly man warned him to stay away from Gene, though Leroy didn't take the man's advice. He sat down beside Gene and groped him. "Let's go upstairs," Gene whispered in his ear. "I don't want to put on a show."

Almost feverish with excitement, Leroy gladly acquiesced. As Leroy turned to leave with the prize catch, he faced hostile stares from the other men.

In the shower stall outside, Gene kept his back turned to Leroy as he rinsed off his sweat. "Got a room?" he asked.

"Yeah," Leroy said, as he dried himself and reached for his robe. "Twenty-one."

"I'll meet you there," Gene promised, turning his face up to the water jet.

"Don't forget," Leroy called over his shoulder, moving toward the stairs. "I'll be waiting."

After Gene finished showering, he dried himself off and reached for his robe. He smiled. So far, his plan was working.

After a quick rap on cubicle twenty-one, he was ushered inside by Leroy. "The bastard," Gene thought to himself. "He still hasn't really looked at my face." Not that Leroy could see anybody's face very well in the near blackness of the room. Without saying a word, Leroy removed Gene's robe and dropped to his knees.

"God, you've got a big one," Leroy said, fondling him. "And the balls to match."

At that point Gene informed him he was under arrest. "You son of a bitch. You still don't even know who I am. The next time, look at his face when you proposition a guy." He grabbed the string of an exposed bulb overhead and turned it on.

There, to his horror, Leroy saw who it was. "Oh, my God," he said, his eyes wide with terror. "Please, let me off, just this one time."

"You creep. Do you want to leave peacefully, or do I have to handcuff you?"

"No," Leroy said, trembling. "Don't make a fuss." He sighed in a resigned weariness. "I'll go."

Gene left the cubicle and went to his locker on the same floor. He rapped on the cubicle's door again and when he opened it, Leroy was dressed too, in jeans and a T-shirt just like Gene. He'd put on his sunglasses this time, and so had Gene. Leroy's face was reflected in Gene's mirrored lens. "I thought you guys had stopped all this entrapment shit."

"Biff's decided to crack down all over again," Gene said. It was a lie. He grabbed Leroy's arm. "You should have kept your brownnose clean, cocksucker!"

Gene had no intention of arresting Leroy, at least not at this point. He wanted to scare him into giving him information so he'd be better prepared for his meeting with his chief, Biff, later that day.

At the squad car, he shoved Leroy in and got in himself, taking the wheel. According to the car radio he turned on, the temperature would exceed ninety degrees Fahrenheit by noon, and the present humidity seemed to match.

He wanted to go to the beach today, and instead found himself in this hot car with an air-conditioning system that gave off nothing but hot fumes.

His neck stiffening, he felt an uneasiness that had settled first in the pit of his stomach. "Do you want to go to police headquarters?" Gene asked. "Or do you want to take me to that Lolito house where we can talk first? I'm giving you a choice. You can also call your lawyer."

"Let's go to my condo instead," Leroy said with surprising confidence. "Unless you're afraid to be alone with me, handsome. Afraid of what it might lead to."

"Shut up, faggot!" Gene answered harshly. "I'm not afraid of you."

"I think before hauling me into the police station, you'd better learn some things and see some things I've got to show you. I'm saying this for your own good."

As Gene took his eyes off the road to observe Leroy closely, he felt he had touched only the tip of an iceberg. Today it felt more like a red hot poker. This was no simple boy prostitution ring, he feared, but something bigger.

"Your taking me in could cause more harm for you than for me," Leroy threatened.

"Cut the shit man!" Even as he harshly rebuked Leroy, Gene feared the photographer might be telling the truth.

Leroy stared vacantly out the window, waiting for Gene to decide. The relaxed look on his face indicated to Gene that Leroy didn't expect to be taken to police headquarters and booked. Gene knew he didn't have enough evidence for a booking anyway, and he suspected Leroy was only too aware of that.

For one brief moment this morning, Gene felt his investigation had started to move. He'd hoped to get the praise from his department so long denied him, but now he wasn't sure. He squirmed in his seat. "You're in big trouble," he warned Leroy.

For some reason, Leroy seemed to have the upper hand. "Take me to my apartment. It's at 400 West View Street."

Without saying another word, Gene drove in that direction, wondering as he did how many times Leroy had seduced Sandy. The idea of Leroy's hands and mouth crawling all over Sandy disgusted him. He felt contaminated sitting in the same car with such a pervert. His nausea seemed to have settled permanently in his stomach.

"This whole thing is messier and bigger than you think," Leroy said finally, as the squad car neared his apartment. "I'm their victim too. They make me do what I do. I'm not taking this rap alone—not by a lone shot."

Gene said nothing but strangely believed Leroy. He felt his old schoolmate was telling the truth. There was much more going on here than a boy ring.

Even going up on the elevator, Gene said nothing. When Leroy stood in front of the door to his apartment and inserted the key, Gene entered quickly, glancing down the hallway as he did. He didn't want anyone seeing him enter alone with Leroy.

Once inside, Leroy said, "You can relax now. I'll get you a drink. You can take off anything you want. I've seen it all. Years ago I even photographed it, and what an impressive sight!"

"We didn't come here for a seduction," Gene said.

"Too bad. You're missing out on the thrill of a lifetime. I'm an expert sword swallower."

"I'm sure you're very talented at your work."

"You don't know what you're missing."

"I'll take a raincheck."

"I can't believe you're here in my apartment. That we're alone together. Do you know how many nights I've dreamed about this? I've known many men, but you're my all-time fantasy. If you don't believe me, take a look at my bathroom."

"What are you talking about?"

"Go on, take a look. It's just down the hallway. The light switch is on the right."

Out of curiosity and feeling no longer in charge, Gene walked down the corridor and flipped on the light switch in the luxurious bathroom. To his shock and amazement, the walls were covered with seemingly endless reproductions of that frontal nude photograph Leroy had snapped of him in the shower room at the university. It was a gallery of eroticism. He felt a sudden thrill at this mass exposure of his private parts. He wondered how many men Leroy had invited here to view the show.

As if anticipating his question, Leroy stood behind him. "All my gay friends have seen it. They all have a crush on you. You don't need to exhibit it to that little girl. You can exhibit it to my friends any day. We'll even pay you and I mean a lot."

Gene turned around and grabbed Leroy, shoving him up against the wall. "You little shit. I need to beat the hell out of you right now."

"That's okay with me providing it ends with a brutal rape. I love that! From you, it would be divine. Any physical contact with you, even a beating, would be welcome. You're the man of my dreams. I'd do anything for you."

"Even help me with this investigation?"

Leroy sighed. "Come back to the living room. I'm not going to be the fall guy on this one. I've protected myself this time. If I go down, I'm taking a lot of the movers and shakers in this town with me." He looked into Gene's eyes with a fierce determination.

Back in the living room, Gene turned to confront Leroy. "You don't really run the show, do you?"

"You got that right."

"Who's the big enchilada behind it?"

"I'll make a deal with you. If you fuck me with that big cock of yours, I'll nibble on your ear while you're doing it. As you blast off in me, I'll whisper the name in your ear. Is it a deal?"

Gene stood in the bright sunlight of the apartment, with its views of a nearby park. There was a sudden stillness in the room. He moved closer to Leroy's picture windows. All he was thinking now was about that long ago day when Leroy had photographed him. He'd known what Leroy was doing. It was hard to admit it but he was thrilled to be photographed totally exposed that way. He'd wanted to be desired by the worshipful eyes and lens of Leroy. In spite of himself, he felt his penis lengthening.

*****

In a black modern Chanel suit, Susan felt she'd never looked better than when she'd entered a terminal at the Miami International Airport. Before disembarking, she'd gone to the airplane bathroom to apply the final touches to her makeup. She'd even indulged herself in a final inspection in the same bathroom, just before getting off. Getting her hair styled in New York had helped too.

As she raced toward a waiting Buck, she felt confident, secure in this marriage, although knowing that was only a fleeting impression. As he ran to hug and kiss her, he evoked an image of his university days when she used to spot him jogging on campus in a pair of shorts that revealed an endowment greater than that of the university.

After kissing her on the lips a second time, he lifted her off her feet and whirled her in the air. He seemed delighted to see her, but perhaps he was putting on a show for the other passengers milling about.

"I send you off to New York a country girl and you come back a fashion star."

"Wait till you get the bill."

"I'll survive."

"Glad to be back," she said. "We haven't even gone on a honeymoon."

A frown crossed his brow.

She wondered if it were an indication there would be no honeymoon. He obviously had a full agenda without a marriage to cope with.

"Come on," he said. "I'm driving you to your condo. I hired someone to get it ready for you. I think you'll like it."

She noted that he said "ready for you"—not ready for us.

In his car on the way to the beach, she kept the talk light with tales of her experiences in the north. She confessed she'd like to go there at least once a month, preferably with him.

He didn't immediately accept such an invitation. "I'm such a Florida boy. I always feel out of place in New York. Anywhere for that matter. Except Okeechobee."

"Don't tell me you're as provincial as all that. I just can't believe it."

"I'm a simple man with simple tastes. All I want is a mansion, my own newspaper, a private island, a luxurious yacht, and the most beautiful woman in Florida."

"You've got those, except perhaps the most beautiful woman in Florida. Some of my worst enemies say I'm only the second most beautiful." She smiled to indicate she was teasing.

He laughed and didn't say anything for a long while, as if thinking about something he didn't want to tell her. She wanted to ask him about Robert. Had he been told of their marriage? But somehow she didn't dare.

"It's been very rough at the Examiner. Roland's clanking his balls. I gave you all the details on the phone. Old Buck went ahead and told him to take you off the South Beach thing. I don't think Roland even knows about the Lolito story."

"The son of a bitch." Her heart seemed to sink.

"He's got you back covering university news. Figures you can't get in too much trouble there."

"Are you going to take this? Aren't you going to fight back? Did I marry a man or a mouse?"

"Please," he said. "Give me a break." A flash of anger crossed his face. "As long as grandfather is alive, he calls the shots."

"And when he goes?" she asked.

"I don't really know what's going on at the Examiner. There's some mysterious transfer of stock going on. Who will own it or run it, especially after old Buck is gone, I don't know. I wish I did. I've got to be really honest with you. I may not be the big cheese there any more."

"But I always thought you owned twelve percent."

"I do. That was left to me by my parents. But that's hardly a big enough percentage to control the paper."

"Buck is going to will you his share, won't he? Especially now that we're married?"

"I assume he will. He owns twenty-five percent. That would give me thirty-seven percent—still not enough to control the paper."

"You'd at least be the biggest shareholder. The other stocks are diversified. No one has complete control."

"What if someone acquired the majority stock? I mean, secretly bought it up. They could do that."

"I can't imagine that happening." She looked out the window as he sped along the causeway. After the grayness of New York, the brightness of Okeechobee momentarily blinded her. She reached into her purse for her sunglasses, more to hide herself from the world than from the glare of the sun.

"I can imagine anything happening," he said. "Our lives are going to be completely different in the weeks ahead. Not just because of our marriage, but because of everything. I can just feel it."

She reached for his hand on the wheel and delicately ran caressing fingers across it. "I'm a little bit afraid. I truly don't want you to be in harm's way."

"But deep down I feel I am. I feel there are forces out there working against me that I don't even know about." He turned and flashed a smile at her. "God, I must sound paranoid."

"I don't think it's paranoia. It sounds like a real feeling to me. I don't trust this bitch, Rose Phillips. She may want to do you in."

At the mention of her name, she noticed a strange look come across Buck's face. Was it a concern about what Rose might possibly do against him in the future, or something else?

As Buck's car neared a condo complex, so much more luxurious than the one Hazel occupied, she realized she didn't know this man riding in the car with her. Of course, she'd known him for years. But now she felt it was only an acquaintance. She had married a complete stranger. There seemed to be a wall between them, and she was determined to crack through it, or at least make a gateway in it. Once inside the privacy of that condo, she hoped to get to know this man of mystery she'd married such a short time ago.

*****

With his back on the living room carpet, Leroy eagerly received Gene's pounding thrusts, sighing deeply each time Gene plunged into him. It was obvious that Leroy's longtime fantasy was at last coming true. Instead of thinking about the present penetration, Gene's mind had drifted to a point only minutes before when he had strained Leroy's jaws wide and exerted pressure against the lining of his throat. Although filled almost beyond capacity, Leroy's devouring mouth had welcomed this discomfort. It was obvious heaven to him to be licking and sucking the prize for which he had waited for so long.

A burning desire kept Gene at fever pitch. He suspected he hated Leroy but this in no way decreased his heat and pressure, as he moved deeper into the photographer. He had yet to achieve full penetration. He wanted those final two inches in Leroy. With all his strength, he lunged forward. Leroy screamed in pain but his hands reached to clutch and claw at Gene's back, signaling Gene how eagerly Leroy wanted his aggressive plunges. Gene knew that Leroy's insides were turned into a boiling pit. Even though he realized he was hurting Leroy, Leroy did nothing to resist the invasion but opened himself completely to Gene.

A feeling of triumph came over Gene as he neared his climax. He liked having Leroy under his control and power. Nothing was going to hold Gene back now, as he pressed his body brutally against Leroy's. Gene began his final full thrusts. Deeper and harshly he drove into Leroy. He would pull back rapidly until only the lip of the head was showing, then he would drive into Leroy with greater force than he'd ever used with anybody.

Leroy was not only yelling loudly but crying as well. Gene's pulsating, hammering cock spewed forth within Leroy which triggered his own spectacular climax, bathing Gene's chest. Collapsing on top of Leroy, he lay here for several minutes. Leroy was still moaning softly and running his hands caressingly over Gene's body, feeling every part within his reach.

Leroy put his lips against Gene's left ear. "Calder Martin."

Gene pulled out abruptly and headed for the shower. Glancing only briefly at the nudes of himself lining the bathroom walls, Gene welcomed the cleansing effect of the hot water spray jets from the shower. He not only wanted to wash off all traces of Leroy, but almost the revelation itself. Leroy had kept his promise, telling him the real leader of the Lolito ring.

Gene thought not of the Lolito investigation but of Rose. Little did she know that two key figures in her moral crusade, Calder Martin and Barry Collins, were part of the filth she rallied against. If only he could get to her and warn her before these men formed a cancer on her body that she might never get rid of. Both Calder and Barry, at least potentially, had the power to bring Rose down, if only by association.

If Calder were behind this, Gene had to be extra careful. Even though he was only hours from his meeting with his chief, Biff, he could not reveal what he'd learned without knowing and being able to prove more than he could now. Of course, there remained the possibility that Leroy could be lying but for some reason he believed him. Naturally, Calder Martin didn't operate a sex ring for gratification. Gene knew enough about this shadowy figure to realize that if Calder were behind the ring, blackmail would be the motive. But who was he blackmailing? Obviously Barry Collins, for openers. But there could be others.

As he held his face up to the water jet, Gene feared this case was too much for him. He was too vulnerable. The very forces he might be investigating had the power to move in on him at any moment. They could destroy him.

For a few brief hours, he felt protected and secure once again when he'd resumed his friendship with Buck. Buck had power in the town. Gene didn't. If something went wrong, Buck would be there for him, but that too had turned into a fake promise. At this very minute, and for all Gene knew, Buck could be lying in the arms of Susan. Both of them could be plotting against him. He now knew he could never trust either of them.

He'd opened himself, at least to Buck. Buck was privileged to his most secret desires. He feared his old friend would use what he knew against him, although he didn't know just how.

Before stepping out of that shower, he vowed never to trust anybody ever again, not even Sandy. Maybe even Sandy was a plant. Maybe he'd been sent by Calder Martin to trap Gene and send him plunging once again into the murky world of child molestation. Today everyone and everything seemed a trick to him. He wasn't making it up. He wasn't paranoid. The world was out to get him. To save himself, he had to strike back. Even as he realized that, he didn't know how he could. There must be a way.

After drying himself and wrapping a towel around his nude body, he came back into the living room. In his bathrobe, Leroy was putting down the phone.

Gene stopped and looked intently at Leroy who only smiled.

"That was the most thrilling seduction of my whole life. I've never experienced anything like that. It was worth the wait all these years. It was better than the stuff of my dreams."

Gene heard not the sexual flattery but was left with the distinct suspicion that Leroy had just hung up the phone on Calder Martin.

*****

"It's severe and masculine—that's why I like it," Susan said, surveying her new home, a nine-room condo overlooking the ocean. Her own possessions, she noted, had been moved here, and they appeared shabby in contrast to the luxurious furnishings. The decorator obviously liked shades of black and brown.

"It's certainly not pink and girlish, now is it?" Buck asked, beaming like a little boy asking approval from his mother.

The sunlight streamed into the apartment, making his blond hair blonder. She had never seen him look this handsome before, and found it hard to believe that she was actually married to him.

"I'm glad you moved my stuff over. That took a bit of phallic thrust. Weren't you afraid I'd object?"

"I wanted it to be a surprise for you. I thought if we took all your stuff and mixed it in with the new stuff, you'd feel more at home."

"Something old, something new. And you...are you what is borrowed?"

He looked awkwardly around the room. "I don't exactly know what that means."

"Am I borrowing you from someone else?"

"I'm a free agent."

"I wonder." She walked toward the kitchen to pour herself a drink. "Want one?"

"No, thank you. It's a bit early, isn't it?"

"Perhaps, but I thought I needed a bit of fortification before I pursued this conversation."

"You don't have to pursue it—you know that. A lot of things are better left unspoken."

"Have you told Robert Dante about our marriage?"

"No." His voice became aggressive and a bit hostile. "Robert's in Miami. His mother died. I can't get in touch with him. I don't even know where he is right now."

"That's unusual, isn't it?"

"What's this? The third degree?"

"Call it what you like, but I want to know. Don't you usually know where Robert is every minute of every day?"

"Yes!" he virtually shouted, turning his back to her and walking toward the picture windows overlooking the ocean. "Every minute of every hour of every day of every week of every month of every year." He turned and glared at her with a certain hostility. "Is that what you wanted to hear?"

"It was at least a suspicion confirmed. I want to understand things. I'm your new wife. I'm to live here. Robert is to live in your real home. I'm not to go there, is that right?"

"That's exactly right. That home belonged to my parents. It's where Robert lives now. If I have anything to do with it, he will always live there. It's as much his place as it is mine."

"Forgive me for bearing down on this so. But it's a new marriage. My second, your first. I want to understand the ground rules."

"That's fine with me. You live here. Robert lives there."

"I can accept that. It was all too clear to me that this was a marriage of convenience. Such marriages must have rules. Understandings. Are you in love with Robert?"

"I don't know about the in love part. But I've loved him from the very first moment I ever saw him. He and I share a bond that's unbreakable. As long as I live, I'll be with him on some level."

"Do I interpret this correctly? You'll be spending your nights with Robert?"

"Robert would have it no other way." We may be married, but Robert has rights too."

"You mean rights to you?"

"Any time—day or night—that he calls for me, I'm there for him." Through the picture windows, he kept his eyes on the ocean—not on her—as if that were easier for him.

Drink in hand, she stood only a few feet from him, facing his back. "I'm not opposed to anything you told me. I went into my marriage with Gene like a blind fool. I'm not going into a marriage with you with the same innocence. It wouldn't work otherwise."

"Thanks," he said, turning around to face her and staring deeply into her eyes. "Can we be friends? Sometimes lovers?"

"Yes," she said. "We can be fantastic friends and occasional lovers. If I play by the rules, this can be a great marriage for me. You're the most desirable bachelor in the state. Former bachelor. You have much to offer a woman. I was going nowhere at the Examiner. Now with Roland in charge, I'll be writing obits. You and I can go anywhere together. Our marriage may be unconventional, but it can work if we both want that."

"I'm prepared to make it work," he said.

She downed the rest of her drink, bracing herself for the final tough question. "Since you're being honest with me and not deceiving me like you did that night at the Pelican, I have one final question. You only love Robert. You're not in love with him. Who are you in love with? I really need to know. It'll make it easier for me."

At first he looked as if he wouldn't answer the question. He breathed in deeply. "Gene Robinson."

A gasp escaped from her throat. Before she could recover, the phone rang. She went over and picked up the receiver.

It was old Buck's butler. "You and Mr. Buck have got to come over right away. He's demanding to see both of you right away. He's leaving town. Flying to a clinic in Switzerland. Maybe for good."

"We'll be right there." She put down the phone. "We've got to take this man and wife act of ours on the road."

"What do you mean?"

"Old Buck wants to see us right away. And why not? That's what this marriage was all about anyway, wasn't it? A show for a dying man about to leave you a vast fortune."

"I wouldn't put it that way," he said hesitantly. "Sounds a bit harsh."

"Let's go!" she said, looking for her purse. "Something major is about to happen."

*****

Thoughts and sensations gushed through Gene. He felt Leroy should be caged in some cell like the rat he was, not living in luxury. The more he studied Leroy's tremulous face, his jerky, nervous movements, the more he did seem trapped in a cage.

Leroy did what he could to delay getting dressed, including offering Gene a drink three times and presenting him with cigarettes. Gene found himself enjoying the control he still had over another person.

"I don't think Biff is going to like your running me in like this," Leroy said hesitantly. "That is, if you plan to run me in at all. I don't think you ever had any intention of taking me to police headquarters. Especially now. Especially after the fuck of my life."

"Biff, is it?" Gene walked to Leroy's terrace, pulling back the draperies and looking out at the sea beyond. The water seemed to be asleep in the sun. Perhaps that was what Gene had been doing, too, not really knowing much about the very case he was investigating.

Still half dressed, Leroy followed him out onto the terrace. "It's pretty out here, isn't it?"

"Yeah, yeah," Gene said, his eyes still fixed on the sea. He knew he must pretend to possess more information than he did. It was as if they were reviewing what both of them knew all along. From the terrace he spotted two motorcycle policemen weaving through heavy traffic. The sight chilled him. For a moment he imagined they were looking for him.

Leroy, drink in hand, trailed him. "Even though he's paying for this beautiful condo, Calder Martin is so damn mad at me he nearly popped a blood vessel. Naturally he blamed me for being indiscreet. He's known for some time that you've been investigating the Lolito ring. There's nothing in this town that escapes him. I think he bugs everything and everybody."

"Gene shot a quick, distorted glance at Leroy, then stared vacantly at the sea again. The mention of Calder Martin's name had sent a shock wave through him. He could only hope that Leroy didn't sense Gene's own vulnerability. "Does Biff, as you call him, already know of this sex ring?"

Leroy smiled enigmatically. "What do you think?"

Gene could feel his own heart pounding. The investigation for which he'd anticipated receiving the praise of the department had begun to crumble. "Do you think Biff and Calder know the Examiner knows about it, too?"

"They know all about it. They even know that a guy named Terry Drummond met with Susan Howard. I'm sure you remember her well."

"Cut the shit, man! You know I was married to her."

"Of course, I do." He walked over to Gene and reached for his arm. Gene pulled away.

"C'mon," Leroy said. "You know how much I like you. Hell, I love you! I'm giving you some hot advice: drop this thing. Pretend it doesn't exist. These men can destroy you. And if you don't believe me, read an item on page two of this morning's Examiner. It's right over there on the sofa."

Gene scanned the page quickly. All the news was international except one local item. A vagrant, Terry Drummond, had been found dead this morning along Indian Creek Trail near the Vista Linda Motel. Apparently while wandering drunk along the side of the highway, he'd been struck down by a hit-and-run driver. "Who is this Drummond?" Gene demanded to know.

"He used to be my lover," Leroy said. "We had a fight. I replaced him. A big mistake on my part. Unknown to me, he'd accumulated hardcore evidence about the boy ring. He even sold some of it to the Examiner. He had a lot more evidence. Enough to bring us all down. But he doesn't have it now. At the time Terry was struck down by this mysterious hit-and-run driver, the evidence was removed from the Vista Linda. Terry wasn't terribly smart about protecting documents. But Susan now owns some incriminating photographs of Barry Collins."

All this was too much for Gene. The world was truly conspiring against him.

Still close by his side, Leroy took the Examiner from Gene's hands. He seemed to have no regret about the loss of his former lover, or even his own role in Drummond's death. "Of course, the brothel has already served its purpose. Even before you began to investigate it, Calder has gotten all the blackmail evidence he needs. He's really got some of the top men in this town by the short hairs."

"Like Barry Collins?"

Leroy looked puzzled. "Of course. When Barry beats that dyke Hazel for mayor," Leroy predicted, "Calder will really have him then." He sipped his drink and nervously ran fingers through his hair. "It's your call. Knowing what I do, do you think Biff is going to let you charge me with anything? No way, sweetheart!"

Gene felt he was the one trapped in a cage now. "I think what you told me is rather obvious. I'd better drop this Lolito thing. Like right now."

"I think you should if you know what's good for you. You don't have to be some stupid policeman. Not with what you've got. I could market you. That's like as in meat market. Within a year you could be rich. Hell, you could make a fortune in porn. I've got connections. My friends in this town will pay—and pay plenty—for exhibitions...or whatever. You can always come and live here with me in luxury. Why not opt for the good life with plenty of money? No one at that crooked police department gives a damn about you or your moral crusade." Leroy raised his eyebrows provocatively. "Here in my little nest, you could be loved, and do I mean loved!"

"Thanks for the offer. Perhaps you're right. I'll consider it. But aren't you worried for your own safety? You do know a hell of a lot."

"I've protected myself. I'm not some dumb turd like Terry."

Gene was overcome with a strong suspicion that Leroy would be dead within weeks.

Leroy went into a small library off his living room, as Gene trailed him. In the room Leroy opened a safe and handed a small book—bound in black leather—to Gene.

Slowly Gene read the names in that book. It was a list of Leroy's most preferred customers, stating their preferences in young boys and detailing the sex scenes they were into. In stunned disbelief, Gene sounded each name on his lips, substituting the position of the man in the community—the vice president of the Okeechobee First National Bank, the dean of students at Okeechobee High School, a Catholic priest from the neighboring town of Cypress, the director of the Okeechobee Memorial Hospital.

Then his eyes focused on one name. It stood out from all the rest. "Barry Collins," he said out loud. Thoughts of Barry and their life together in the university flashed before Gene's eyes. He'd even dated Pamela. After his arrest for indecent exposure, Barry had bitterly rejected him and refused to associate with him. "What a hypocrite!" Gene said to himself and not really for Leroy's benefit.

Trembling, Gene continued to turn the pages. A local Boy Scout executive. A circuit judge, William F. Gamble. "My God, the chief's best friend."

He closed the book quickly, knowing that exposure of such a dynamite list could bring disruption and scandal to the entire city. A dread anxiety came over him. Not one name in that book was on Biff's enemy list. He handed the secret file back to Leroy. It was too hot for him to handle.

Leroy placed the book back in his safe. "That's not all. I have pictures too." He reached into his safe and removed a manila envelope. "This is just one envelope. There are many others. Of course, Calder has the first ones I developed. After all, it was his idea to open the brothel— just as a means of blackmailing its clients. He deserves the originals. He paid enough for them. But this one fox had copies made, plenty of copies. I believe in protecting my own interests, just in case someone tries to get rough with me. I'm not going to end up like Terry

Drummond. Dead and drunk along the side of some dark road." He presented the envelope to Gene. "See for yourself. If anything happens to me, I have the negatives locked in a bank vault. They're going to go to the Okeechobee News, the only honest paper in town."

"You mean the Examiner?"

"No, they can't be trusted. In a matter of weeks or even days the Examiner may be taken over by Calder Martin."

"I didn't know that."

"Apparently, you didn't know a lot of things. So, baby, don't you think you'd better have that drink now?"

"Yeah," Gene said, fingering the envelope. "Think I will after all. You're right. About the last thing Biff wants is for me to haul you into the station." He smiled at Leroy. "Looks like you've got it made in this town."

As Leroy went to pour a drink, Gene opened the envelope. There were pornographic pictures of the men whose names he'd seen in the black book—glossy eight-by-tens of the so-called pillars of the community, photographed secretly in various sexual positions with teenage boys.

He swallowed hard when he came to the picture of Barry. The face of the mayoral candidate was clearly obvious. In one picture he was sodomizing a teenage boy. Another photograph showed his fully nude body, as two young boys, really children, made love to him. Secretly he slipped three of the most revealing pictures of Collins under his shirt.

He returned the manila envelope to the safe as Leroy came back into the room. "I don't think I'll have that drink after all. I have a meeting with Biff later in the day, and I don't want to show up drunk."

"Suit yourself."

"One thing you said really bothered me. You said Calder might be taking over the Examiner. I happen to know that Buck Brooke—the young one—hates Calder. What do you think about that?"

"Don't be naive," Leroy said, heading for the safe and removing another manila envelope. "Buck's one of them."

"I don't get it."

"He's all part of the sorry mess." He reached into the envelope and pulled out a picture of Buck snapped on his private island.

Gene took the picture from him. Buck was wearing a bikini so transparent he might as well be nude.

"I shot that of him recently. He agreed to pose because he wanted a favor from me. I'm fixing him up with my most delectable boy. Buck is a child molester too. Just like Barry Collins."

Gene thrust the photograph into Leroy's hand. "I'm out of here. It's been fun," he said to Leroy, heading quickly for the door.

"You come back any time," Leroy said, racing after him. "Any time of the day or night. You can make big money."

"Thanks for the invite." Gene felt his blood bubbling.

At the door, Leroy said. "You know what I think. I think you made up that story about arresting me. I probably caught you at the Vulcan, and you had to say something. Frankly, dear, you weren't very convincing. I just played along."

"You're right. Let's keep the Vulcan and my little visit there a secret. I know you're good at keeping a secret."

When he'd sought out Leroy in his familiar turf at the Vulcan, Gene had been on a fishing expedition. The catch he turned up was far larger than his most imaginative expectations.

Out on the street again, the rich stench of frying grease and onions from a Cuban hamburger stand made him remember he hadn't eaten all day. He couldn't take time for that now. Another hunger gnawed at him.

*****

Later that day, with his head partially buried in a newspaper, Okeechobee's police chief called Gene into his office, peppering him with questions that were occasionally barbed with recriminations and abuse. Today, Biff was more than usually dismissive of Gene, pretending to be partially absorbed in his copy of the paper as a means of concealing the true depth of his fury. The motivation, Gene soon realized, involved Biff's strong objections to his off-duty investigation of the Lolito ring. Far from winning praise for his dedication, Gene once again faced condemnation for his good intentions and idealism. Each time Gene was in the presence of Biff, he was amazed at how small and scrawny-looking the mustachioed chief was, as he always appeared taller and more commanding on television than here, within the drab confines of police headquarters.

Gene returned Biff's glare. It was all he could do to conceal the depth of his hatred and contempt for his chief. No more than five feet tall, Biff was belligerent and slightly hunchbacked, with prominent veins on his temples that bulged alarmingly beneath a thick mop of russet-colored hair. His desk was prominently positioned on a platform, giving him an immediate advantage over persons he interviewed who were forced to look up at him.

Feeling he had made his point, Biff eventually focused more and more on the newspaper, eventually ignoring Gene completely, burying his head in the rustling pages as Gene fidgeted uncomfortably. Gene eventually broke the silence. "I'm onto something big. This is a scandal that will blow Okeechobee sky-high."

His face still buried in the paper, Biff muttered, "You're history, boy. I'm going to take over this case personally. Stick to your usual duties, and butt out."

"You old son of a bitch," Gene raged to himself. He was disgusted by the sickening cologne his boss splashed on so lavishly before putting on his plaid suit and vest. No longer able to sit in a lower position in front of Biff, Gene got up and stood before a window, looking out over the Okeechobee skyline. He straightened his broad shoulders and tightened his stomach muscles, as if that gave him superior power over the anemic-looking chief.

"Is there something wrong with me?" Gene asked. "I was the one who heard about this ring. I really want you to let me continue."

Biff slammed down his paper and turned intense eyes of hatred on Gene. "You believe in the scorched earth policy. I don't! That's why I'm directing this investigation. That is, if there is going to be an investigation."

"What do you mean? You're going to allow underage children to be exploited?"

"Sometimes you have to overlook certain infringements of the law if you're pursuing a greater goal."

"What's that goal?"

"Allowing Barry Collins to win the mayor's race. He's a great friend of this department."

"Barry Collins is a fucking child molester." In barely concealed rage, Gene said, "The law's the law. I thought you'd be real pleased when I first uncovered the Lolito sex ring."

In a more consoling voice, the way a patient parent might deal with an unruly child, Biff said, "Of course. But certain information has come to my attention. Instead of exposing that ring, it's in the best interest of this department to keep it quiet."

"A cover up!" Gene's words stabbed the air.

Biff appeared unconcerned at such an emotional outburst. His eyes focused on a paragraph of copy in the News. "God damn paper!" he ranted. "It's getting worse than the Examiner, and that rag's the last stop before the sewer." The telephone rang and he answered it, his conversation about some bureaucratic snag seemingly going on forever.

Gene was stunned to get the same old crap from Biff he'd gotten from judges. Did Biff mean to let the guilty go free? He'd always been proud of the chief's defense of law and order. Now Gene suspected "they" had bought Biff, too. Was Calder Martin really in charge of the police department?

Slamming down the phone, Biff glared at Gene. "We don't need to punish the patrons of that boy whore house. Their only crime was in getting a little virgin boy ass." He smiled lewdly. "Even I've indulged in a bit of that myself when I was in the university and had this fag roommate. When I'd come home at night, and my pussy of the moment wouldn't give me any, I'd ram it up the fag and make him squeal with delight. I understand such things. Some boy asses can be much tighter than a pussy. You should try it some time." He smiled lewdly again. "From what I hear tell, you're shacked up with a piece of boy ass right now. Word gets out. I know what's going on in this town. Don't get so God damn righteous with me."

Gene's heart just seemed to sink. It was as if Biff had thrown him in a cell and tossed the key away. It was all Gene could do to conceal his disgust as he confronted Biff. The chief was no better than the filthy-minded officers with whom he was forced to share a locker room. "I'm not a perfect man," Gene said. "I've tried to do what's right. I've fallen along the way some times. I know that. You don't have to remind me. I'm a man. Sometimes strong. Sometimes weak. Like all of us."

"Now you're talking," Biff said, pleased at a remark of Gene's for the first time during the interview. "That's the kind of tolerance and understanding I can live with. Recognizing that all men are weak. All men have temptations. Even me who likes to drink too much sometimes." Biff went over to his liquor cabinet and removed a bottle of Chivas Regal, offering Gene a drink which was refused. From a bucket filled with ice, he extracted two cubes and poured himself a generous one. "Deciding which law breakers to pursue and which to leave alone is tough for me. But that's why they made me head of the department. You can't lock up the whole fucking town. There's probably a million people in Okeechobee right this minute breaking some God damn law. Selective enforcement—that's what the law is all about. Every day an honest citizen breaks some law, maybe a law he doesn't even know he's breaking. There are so many damn laws on the books, we can't enforce them all."

Gene knew at this point that a protest to Biff would fall on deaf ears. It was just as well. He didn't have his heart in the Lolito case any more. If anything he felt a sudden warmth and compassion toward Leroy. He didn't want to make trouble for his old schoolmate. Hell! For all he knew, Leroy might be the only person in the world who loved him. He didn't love Leroy, but it made him feel good to be the object of someone's desire instead of the object of someone's hatred.

Biff slowly sipped his drink and eyed Gene cautiously. "Some of our best supporters participated in that sex ring. Destroying the careers of some of our most diehard friends isn't too smart. Harming Barry would allow that cunt, Hazel Phillips, to get at our soft underbelly. Could you imagine what the police force would be like with Hazel as mayor?"

"Would you be proud to serve under Barry?" Gene blurted out, shocked at the rage in his voice. As he asked that question, he feared he'd regret Biff's response. You didn't put questions like that to Biff.

The chief moved menacingly toward him, the way Gene had seen him do with criminal suspects. "Barry Collins might have pumped it to a little boy with that boy's consent, with that boy getting paid and with that boy being nothing but a cheap hooker who loves to get plowed anyway." He came to a stop only inches before Gene and was forced to look up to him. "Gene Robinson, on the other hand, exposed himself to a little girl and, as you damn well know, probably destroyed that poor child's life."

As Biff returned to his desk, Gene had a sinking feeling. Dreading what was coming next, he feared he'd throw up.

"Do you know what the guys call you around the department?" Biff asked sarcastically.

Gene cringed, not answering.

"The flasher! Yeah, you heard me. The flasher!"

The word cut into Gene and he headed for the door.

Determined to go on, Biff called after him. "Just the other day, one of my men washed off a little ditty someone had written about you in the men's room. I had him make a copy before erasing it." The chief reached into his desk and pulled out a piece of paper which he held up for Gene to inspect. Gene made no attempt to retrieve the paper. "I'll read it," Biff said threateningly.

A lover of tennis, 'tis said, called Gene
Could piss away with a golden stream
And though we hear his penis is thick

We regret to say that something is sick
Because when, well seasoned, it came into sight,
A little blonde girl would quickly take flight
A pity, you say, that matrons do lack
So often for dick in the depths of the sack
When sickies like Gene, a tad adolescent
Jerk off in the face of females pubescent.

Gene closed his eyes, then opened them to the blazing light streaming in through the large picture window. He stood very still and, though the office was air conditioned, he felt intense heat.

"You don't look well. Frankly, I've been hearing reports that you're coming unglued. Acting real irrational. I thought you might be fucked up in the head. But then I've just received this psychiatric evaluation of you. The psychiatrist we hire to observe you men thinks you're in great mental and physical condition. Still, I have my doubts. Those shrinks don't know everything. I want you to take the day off. Hell! Take the whole week off. It will do you good."

At the door, Gene looked back. "Thanks." He felt defeated. "When I come back on the job, you tell me what you want me to work on."

"Good. That's the way it should be." The look on Biff's face revealed his pride in knowing he'd won this round. A smirk came over him. "You're lucky I hired you in the first place. You should have been thrown in jail as a child-molesting flasher. Now get out of here."

Gene closed the door behind him, trying to blot out Biff's words. Biff made him feel weak and had humiliated him to the point he felt he could not tolerate it. But how could he fight back? He went to the phone and dialed the psychiatrist's office, and was granted an appointment right away. Even before going home, he needed to be with that psychiatrist. That shrink made him feel big and important, and he'd even written a report stating that Gene was in good mental and physical condition. Biff had stripped Gene of his dignity and manhood, but he knew the psychiatrist could restore his faith in himself.

The psychiatrist, Gene knew, would worship him and make him feel like a man again, the way Leroy had done only this morning. He desperately needed that restoration of his dignity, perhaps even more than he dared admit to himself.

*****

At Buck I's estate, his luggage was neatly stacked in the hallway waiting for a limousine, and the old man himself was sitting in a wheelchair in his overly air-conditioned living room, wearing a heavy wool coat in spite of the stifling heat outside.

Buck III, his arm linked possessively with Susan's, went over and kissed his grandfather on the forehead. The coldness of the man frightened him. One look into those steely blue eyes told Buck what he always knew and suspected: his grandfather was none too happy turning over his riches and his world to Buck III. He knew that it was only because of their shared blood that his grandfather was giving him everything and not donating his estate to charity.

As he pulled back from the dying man and Susan kissed his forehead, Buck III suspected another reason. His grandfather truly hoped there would be a Buck IV to carry on the family tradition, which he probably feared Buck III would fail at. This mythical Buck IV would be the old man's insurance that his blood would flow through some young buck's veins in the 21st century.

After he'd been dutifully kissed, Buck I glowered at his grandson. "It took you long enough to get here. A dying man doesn't like to be kept waiting. I've got a plane to catch."

"You'll be on it," Buck III assured him. "The plane doesn't leave for three hours, and we've got plenty of time to get there."

"I like to get to the airport real early and watch the people," Buck I said. "You young people today wait until the last minute for everything." He looked toward Susan with more kindness than he showed his grandson. "You even wait too long to get married. Right now you should be holding up Buck IV for me to kiss good-bye, and I fear he's not even in the oven yet."

"We're getting there," Buck III assured him. "Just give us time."

"I know what time it is," Buck I said. "Time..." He paused briefly as this thought seemed to escape him. "Time, that's something I don't have in great supply any more."

"You're going to be fine," Susan said, although her voice didn't sound that reassuring. "If you've got anything that can be cured, the doctors of Switzerland can cure it for you. They're good."

"I've got something that can't be cured," Buck I said. "Old age. I've lived a long time. Considering how I've abused my body, I've lived a very long time."

"You'll live a lot longer," Buck III said, placing firm fingers on his arm. In a display of affection that was real, Buck III lifted his grandfather's withered hand and pressed it against his cheek before kissing the palm.

The old man withdrew his hand. "We Florida swamp studs don't go in for hand-kissing." He called for his butler to bring him a final brandy. He offered one to both Buck III and Susan. Even though it was obvious neither of them wanted a drink, Buck III graciously accepted. So did Susan. Clearly this was their final drink together.

"A toast to your marriage and a toast to the future Buck IV." The man raised his glass but he seemed so weak he could hardly lift it. Rallying and summoning energy from some reservoir he didn't know he possessed, he lifted the glass to his parched lips and downed the brandy in one gulp. This set off a coughing spasm which caused both Buck III and Susan to rush to help him. But the butler was there before they could assist. He was used to these coughing spasms.

"Are you okay?" Buck III asked.

His grandfather looked at him harshly. "No, God damn it!" he said. "I'm not okay, and I'm not going to get okay ever again. Don't you get it?"

"We still have hope for you," Susan said reassuringly. "Buck and I want you to live to see little Buck IV grow up. I bet he'll take after you."

Buck I looked up at her and smiled. She was obviously catering to the dying man and saying what he wanted to hear.

From a slight distance away, Buck III realized she was better at these goodbye scenes than he was. She was playing her role. A vast fortune was at stake. He'd definitely owe her one for this.

"As soon as I arrange some things here in Okeechobee," Buck III said, "I'll fly to Switzerland to join you."

Buck I looked up at him with the first kindness he'd shown him all day. "That would be nice, providing those arrangements you're making here in Okeechobee aren't my funeral."

"Who knows?" Buck III said. "As tough as you are, you might outlive us all."

"That I doubt," Buck I said, coughing again but the sound came out more like a clearing of his throat this time. "There are one or two final requests I have before heading out."

The butler came into the room to announce the limousine had arrived.

"Tell him to wait." He motioned for Buck III to come closer to him. As Buck III neared his chair, Buck I reached out and yanked at his grandson's tie, choking him and pulling his face almost against Buck I's nose. When he spoke, spittle peppered young Buck's face. "I want you to promise me something, and I want you to keep that promise."

Buck III pulled back slightly but instinct told him not to take his hand and wipe the spittle from his face. "What do you want me to do?"

"I don't want Robert Dante to set foot in this house. Ever! Have I made that perfectly clear?"

"He'll not come here. I'll see to it."

"Another thing. I want you to will this house to Buck IV when you're finished with it. I want him to get married and settle down here, and the little fucker had better leave all the portraits of me hanging on the walls. I want him to remember that it was his old grandpa—not you—who fixed him up so grandly in life."

"He'll treasure your memory," Susan said. "His only regret will be that you weren't around to see him grow up. But who knows? Buck and I hope you will be. We'll pray that you will always be with us."

"That's nice," he said. He looked over at Buck III. As if to warn his grandson that he'd hardly become a sentimental old fool, he reached for Buck III's arm and again pulled him close. "Hear this one thing, this one final thing, and hear it good. In case you think you can pull a fast one, and divorce Susan the moment I die, I've had a provision written in my will. It was signed at ten o'clock this morning."

Buck III looked startled. "What is it?"

"The provision reads that if you and Susan divorce, everything I've left you will go to my favorite charity which is dedicated to preserving the wildlife of Florida."

Buck III felt overheated and he knew sweat was about to drip from his brow, but he dared not make the gesture of wiping it away. That would make him appear too uncomfortable with this provision. He walked over to Susan and kissed her lightly on the lips. "We have no intention of ever getting a divorce."

Susan smiled back and then leaned forward and kissed Buck I on the forehead again. "Rest assured: we'll be together when we're old and gray."

"Or until death do you part," the old man said. "That's the way it should be. That's the way it was with my Nellie. I was at her bedside the night she died. We were always together. A man and a woman. That is what God intended." He looked again at Buck III with a disapproval in his eye. "A man and a woman. That was God's intention. No other combination."

These final instructions from his grandfather made Buck more determined than ever to marry Robert. Even though the ceremony wouldn't be legally recognized, it was a commitment that Robert had wanted, and Buck was determined to honor it. His grandfather could dictate the course of his life only so far, using the powerful weapon of money. It was Buck's life and he was going to live it according to his wishes.

"You'll be proud of your grandson," Susan said, "and definitely of your great-grandson. We'll work hard to honor you and make you proud of us."

"I'm sure you will." Buck I looked at both of them.

Did Buck III note a skepticism in his eye? He couldn't be sure. "Can't we go with you to the airport?"

"Hell, no! We can handle that ourselves. Now I want both of you to leave. The garden is beautiful this time of the year. Go walk in the garden. Not that long ago I could walk myself. But now I don't want you seeing the way they lift me into the limousine. I want you to remember me here in this peaceful living room."

"We'll go," Susan said, reaching to kiss him again.

"No more kisses, no more hugs. I hate farewells. Just go." He signaled the butler to come for him.

"Until we meet in Switzerland." Buck III took Susan's hand and headed for the garden as instructed. He stood with her in the garden taking in the flowers, the trees, and the bright day. He didn't want to think any more of Buck I or his dying. "You're beautiful," he told her. "I've never seen you more beautiful." He pulled her to him and kissed her passionately on the lips. "If only we could lead the dream life envisioned for us by the old man."

"If only we could," she said, breaking away to inspect a bush around which a butterfly hovered.

A breeze drifted up from below where the cottage stood. Although the day was peaceful and the scene looked harmless, Buck felt someone was spying on them. He couldn't be sure. He excused himself claiming he had to retrieve something from the cottage. He walked rapidly to the back where he spotted a recently smoked cigarette ground out in the dirt. There were tire marks too. They looked like the marks of a motorcycle. He reached down and picked up the cigarette butt. As he did, he heard the sound of a motorcycle in the distance.

"Oh, God," he said out loud, feeling a sense of impending danger. He had to get to Gene and make it right again. He had to get to Robert and do right by him too. Instead he walked toward the garden and Susan. This tranquil scene was no longer peaceful to him. The day and the garden had grown sinister.

Chapter Seven

The session with the psychiatrist had gone well. Gene could still feel the excitement of the sucking, devouring mouth taking pleasure from his body. He had been worshipped, his manhood had been praised, and he'd literally reduced the doctor who was to evaluate him into a quivering ball of lust. When he'd left the office, the doctor had begged him to stay. "I'm in love with you," he told Gene. "I've had a hundred police officers—maybe a lot more. Married, unmarried, whatever. No one was ever the man you are. No one!"

Those words still echoed in Gene's ears. After his meeting with Biff, he needed that kind of praise.

When he got home, he came in through the kitchen door, wondering where Sandy and Jill were. He thought they might be up front in the living room. As he walked up the hallway, he heard noises coming from Jill's bedroom. He knew the sound well. They were making love. Not just love, but mad, passionate love. Through the young girl, Sandy was discovering another side to his personality. Gene smiled, relieved somehow. Sandy's involvement with Jill took the pressure off of a relationship with the boy, which he found disturbing and potentially dangerous. "It's best this way," Gene thought to himself.

Quietly, so as not to disturb them, he tiptoed back down the hallway and into the kitchen.

The house felt strangely confining. Almost overnight, it'd become a love nest. But he felt excluded. Even though it was his own home, he didn't seem to belong here right now. He retreated to his garden.

The sun had made its full rise in the clear sky and now was beginning a long, slow descent that would last the afternoon. Its rays reflected across Gene's shaded backyard, turning the plants a green-gold. He entered a gate and went behind his garage where he'd built a sundeck. It was completely fenced in and could only be entered through this private gate. It was his retreat from the world. Nervously he ran fingers through his black hair as a shadow fell across his forehead.

Removing his T-shirt, he sucked in the fresh air, enjoying how it inflated his smooth, broad chest. Despite his humiliation earlier that day, he felt power surge through his body, which was in such vivid contrast to Biff's frail frame. How could such a weak-looking man as the chief wield such power? Gene's tight, flat stomach was tense as he dug his fingers into it, hoping that would somehow relieve a sharp pain that had come suddenly.

He slipped off his jeans and jockey shorts. He could still smell the aroma of sex that lingered after the psychiatrist had devoured him. Sitting down on a canvas chair, he shut his eyes firmly, enjoying the velvet flashes of red, orange, and yellow that came through the trees overhead. Drops of sweat lubricated his skin. Opening his eyes, he admired the form of his taut body, tanned to a deep bronze except for the vee which his brief bikini usually protected. Tracing his flesh with his hands, he lay back again, shutting his eyes once more.

Under feathery clouds gathering on the horizon, he eventually dropped off to sleep. He didn't know for how long he'd slept. A burning sensation on his skin caused him to wake up. Maybe it was a mosquito bite. At first he didn't open his eyes, but lay there calmly as he began a slow, stroking movement of his cock. As he massaged it, it started to swell. Buck may have rejected him, and it appeared that even now Sandy had found other interests and no longer worshipped him as a hero as he had done before. But Leroy thought he was a god. After only two sessions, the psychiatrist had fallen in love with him.

Eerily, he became aware of a presence. Slowly, he opened his eyes. No longer blue, the sky was streaked with pink. He cast his head up and, as he did, he saw her standing there, her eyes wide with a child's wonder.

Maybe it was a bad dream. Perhaps he was reliving that awful experience of long ago when he'd exposed himself to that little girl, the same little girl who was grown up now and making a woman's love to Sandy in the front room.

How did she get here? How and why had she invaded his private garden, his retreat from the world?

Maybe it was a blurry dream. It was a flashback from his past. But he wasn't in his car. The little girl didn't look the same. Not blonde and fair as before. No—definitely different, ominously different.

She was one of the "invaders." The little Cuban girl, Maria. Her stringy hair was as black as her eyes—heartless, vaporless. Her grubby fingers were held like a shield at her unwashed face. "You're dirt," she accused. "It looks like a snake."

The muscles in his stomach tightened as he sought to get control over his rage. Before, with the other girl, he'd seen the blush of tender bloom. Now he confronted vulgarity—a coarse, crude little monster who cringed at the sight of him.

Jumping to his feet as if in a state of madness, he lunged toward the trespassing girl, ordering her out of his retreat. She backed off, letting out a scream that pierced the air.

Without taking the time to put back on his clothes, he hurried to his back yard where he wanted to retreat into the privacy of his home.

Hearing her daughter's scream, Maria's mother, Clara, came into his backyard. She shouted something in Spanish at him he didn't understand. At the sight of his nude body, she crossed herself and protectively grabbed her sobbing daughter, who'd rushed into her arms. Once safely cuddled there, Clara shielded her daughter from the sight of Gene.

From the adjoining backyard, two Cuban women crossed into his driveway to see what the disturbance was. Enraged at the spectacle, they stared defiantly at him. He stood menacingly at the head of his steps leading into his home.

Here he was, caught without his clothes. He didn't even have his mirrored sunglasses to protect his eyes from the probing stares.

"*Policia!*" one of the Cuban women shouted.

"Call the emergency number," Clara yelled. Picking up her daughter, she carried her in a run toward the street. The other women followed behind.

Gene darted into his kitchen, slamming the door behind him, locking it, and pulling down the shades. A note was on the kitchen table. It was from Sandy and Jill. They'd gone shopping for fresh vegetables. The flounder they planned for dinner had been left out to defrost. Without a protective wrapper, blue-green flies buzzed around it, descending. He imagined them laying filthy eggs to contaminate their meal.

He rushed into his bedroom, as if approaching an abyss. The hallway itself was actually like a serpentine stream, seeming to move.

Outside came angry shouts, then an enraged man shouting in Spanish at his front door. Was it Maria's father backed up by a posse of other men?

He'd locked the back door tightly as if that would keep out the world. He'd done nothing wrong. He was innocent. But who would believe that?

Angry voices continued to come in from the street outside, resounding inside his own tortured head. In the far distance, he imagined he heard the sound of children playing.

*****

Haunted by the fear that Gene had been secretly spying on Susan and him at Buck I's estate, Buck III jogged in the park, inhaling the fresh breezes from the sea. He'd agreed to meet with Susan on his private island in the early evening, but he needed this time alone.

He'd made several efforts to reach Robert. In his frequent calls to Miami, he'd learned that Robert had made no arrangements for the funeral of his mother and had seemingly disappeared. Since Robert had such a love-hate relationship with his mother, Buck suspected that his friend hadn't disappeared to be alone with his grief. There was some other reason. He feared that Robert had learned of his marriage to Susan. After all, several people were privy to that wedding, and Buck knew from long experience that that many people couldn't keep a secret for long.

As he ran close to the northern tier of the park bordering the boulevard, he spotted a stretch limousine in a bright shade of rose. A memory of a similar encounter with Calder Martin crossed his mind. That luxury car could only belong to one person in Okeechobee. As if to confirm his suspicion, a chauffeur in elephant gray attire opened the driver's door and got out to assist the passenger in the rear. Rose emerged onto the sidewalk. She was clad in a form-fitting white dress with a rose-colored belt which was matched by a scarf in the same color at her neck. White high heels effectively called attention to her shapely legs. Her auburn hair seemed set afire in the afternoon sun and, as she walked toward him, she appeared like a young girl, not a mature woman. Her body was amazing. In spite of her years, Rose's body looked just as young as Susan's. If anything, she seemed to make Susan look out of shape. By comparison, former beauty queen Pamela, his old flame, looked deep into middle age. Slowly his jog came to a dead stop, as he stood and let Rose approach him. Her skin was porcelain, her face vibrant. Her flame-red lipstick gave her the look of a 40s movie star, the make-up of Betty Grable. He didn't know why but that dated look almost always gave him a hard-on, proving to himself he had a straight streak in him in spite of his constant tumbles with Robert and his beloved Gene, whom he still felt more passion for than anybody he'd ever known.

Without saying a word, Rose stood in front of him and kissed him deeply, inserting her tongue in his mouth. It was a kiss that spoke of possession as much as passion. Surely she wasn't naive enough to believe that a night of passion—regardless of how great it had been— would be followed by immediate ownership of him. He didn't want to feel immodest, but he knew there were others who had a claim on him, none more so than Robert Dante, and, at least by legal rights, Susan. Perhaps the time had come to reveal this to Rose, who by now had possessively linked her arm with his, as they strode through the park.

"I won't dare ask," he told her, "how you knew I wanted a de Kooning. But I loved the gift. Too bad I can't accept it. I'm going to return it."

"Don't be a jerk, darling. I paid nothing for it. It was a gift from one of my followers. She left it to my temple in her will. I can't stand de Kooning. But I must admit I kept the Matisse she left for myself. Shelley, that precious dear, took the two Picassos and hung them in his bedroom. He's entitled to them. I don't like Picasso either."

"You're amazing, truly amazing, but as much as I want to I just can't accept it. I feel it's presented like a reward for a great roll in the hay which it was."

"Indeed it was. I think we both owe each other one for that. It was the greatest I've ever had, and I'm not exactly the Virgin Mary. As for the de Kooning, I know how to make you keep it."

"What do you mean?"

"If you return it to Paradise Shores, I'll slash it to ribbons."

"My God," he said looking deeply into her eyes. "I believe you would."

She returned his look with a certain defiance. "You know I would!"

"Then it's settled. The de Kooning is mine."

"So it is. Now let's press on to other matters. But let's get out of this dreary park. Let's get in the back seat of that limousine and head for Paradise Shores at once."

"I can't," he said, breaking away. "I've got another appointment."

"Can't you break it?"

"It's very important."

"Bullshit!" she said. "I have two important dinner guests tonight. Ronald and Nancy. They're flying up from Miami but I'd turn them down if you asked me to."

"I didn't know they were coming to town. We should cover it for the Examiner."

"It's a secret visit. This broken down actor wants to be president of the United States. Can you imagine? He's privately seeking the support of my foundation. Of course, he'd like my support. Millions of voters delivered to him, not to mention how much cash."

"Are you going to sign up? This is strictly off the record."

"In the weeks ahead, Ronnie and Nancy will deny ever having met me."

"Why's that?"

"That's for me to know and you to find out." She smiled enigmatically.

"You're a powerful woman. I suspect some of the biggest men in this country will be trying to win your support."

"Reagan's okay. I once went to bed with him."

"How was it?"

"Just so-so. He likes to shower before the act, then rush to shower at the end. Squeaky clean sex. Not down and dirty like we had last night. Reagan certainly doesn't have your stupendous equipment."

"Thank you."

"It's Nancy. That's the problem. I just don't like her. She and I have competed for the same guys before. You know, she was known as the fellatio queen of Hollywood. But I think I'm better at that than bitch Nancy."

"You're very good. But I haven't sampled Nancy yet."

"I'm sure she'd go for it. I have an idea. Why don't you join us at dinner tonight? While I'm entertaining Ronnie, I can arrange for you and Nancy to go for a walk in the garden. I'm sure you two can duck into my guest bungalow. She can try out her fabled technique on you, then the next morning you announce the victor. Nancy or me."

"That sounds tempting, but I do have an engagement I can't break."

"Very well," she said. "You turned down my invitation to lunch. Surely you can't deny me afternoon tea."

"I'm pretty busy."

"As I was saying, you can't deny me afternoon tea, especially when I tell you I have some top-secret news to report to you about the Examiner."

His eyes came alive, and he truly believed her. He was the publisher of the Examiner, at least in name only, but he just knew she had news about its fate. "You're going to let me in on the secret?"

"Over a cup of tea. My porcelain was once owned by the Queen of England. You'll love the tea but I fear not the news I have to tell you."

"That bad? I've been expecting it."

"But with the bad news, I'll have some stunning good news. Fantastic!"

"A cuppa is sounding more enticing every moment."

"Good. Let's crawl into the back seat of that limo. I like a man who's all hot and sweaty."

"But I need a shower."

"Paradise Shores has the most luxurious showers in Okeechobee. Shelley told me if you'll agree to come over, he'll help bathe you."

"I don't think I need assistance there." A memory of Robert crossed his brain as he headed for the rear of the limousine to disappear into the afternoon with Rose. Where in the hell was Robert?

As he was encased in her car, the chauffeur sped off.

"You can fuck me now," she said, "while you smell like a randy jock or after you take a shower if you want to make Ronald your role model."

*****

It was *déjà vu*. Arrested on much the same charge as before, Gene felt trapped in the back seat of a squad car. Other, more distant memories floated through his mind, as they had haunted his reveries for years after his first arrest for indecent exposure.

His head spinning, Gene sat grim-faced, a cold sweat bathing his body. When the two officers had arrived at his house, he had let them in. He'd expected them and was dressed and ready to go. Routinely, they'd frisked him. That he'd understood. But he did feel he deserved better treatment than having handcuffs placed on him. If he were going to run away, he'd have done so before now.

What had been worse was walking the gauntlet of leering-eyed Cubans who'd lined up along the street to delight in his arrest. Even now, on the way to the police station, the hysterical babble of their Spanish-speaking voices resounded in his ears. One contemptuous woman had spat in his face. He had never been as humiliated and defeated. After all these years of holding out against them, the "invaders" had caught up with him and brought him to defeat.

He'd learned from the officers that the charges involved enticement of the little girl into his garden where he exposed himself and started to masturbate in front of her. All of it one big lie. But a lie so powerful and compelling that it took on greater validity than the truth. Since he'd exposed himself once before to a girl, it was easy to believe he'd done it again. The irony of it was that Jill was now living in his house. What would she make of all of this? Even more daunting was the prospect of how the world would judge him if news broke that Jill was now living with him.

He knew the papers, especially the TV night news, would pick up the story and sensationalize it. Of course, the press would rehash those old charges, even though they'd been officially dropped. Shivering in the heat of the late afternoon, he feared his latest arrest would destroy him. Before he'd managed to save himself. God was punishing him now, even though he was innocent.

He suspected he'd been framed, and that Clara had planned all this. She'd wanted to go to bed with him and when he'd rejected her, she'd plotted against him.

"My God!" he thought, words forming on his lips. It had just occurred to him that Rose might hear about this. Maybe she'd even attack him from the pulpit, citing his case as that of a supposed defender of the law who secretly preyed on innocent young girls. Rose might use him as an example of moral degeneracy. He couldn't allow that. Somehow he had to find a way to get to her and tell her his side of it.

As he was ushered into police headquarters, two reporters and a photographer recognized him. A blinding flash, and the photographer had snapped his picture. A chill came over him as he imagined what that picture would look like on the front page.

After he'd been booked, he was shown to a cell. He was to be held here while bail was raised. Though offered a chance, he'd refused to call a lawyer. He didn't want to go back out in the world, at least not now. All he could remember was a big steel door closing.

He drifted off for a while and when he woke up, his heartbeat had come under control again. Before, it had been beating so fiercely he could hear it. He got up and walked around in his cell. Here, he felt insulated and free of the prying eyes that followed him everywhere. One of the officers had let him keep his mirrored sunglasses.

He promised himself not to think about Maria or her fellow Cubans who'd taken over his neighborhood. He'd think only of *her*.

To him, Rose was blindingly, painfully beautiful. And she was good, a woman fighting the very evil forces that now threatened to ruin him. How he longed to reach out and touch her gown right now, feel her waist-length auburn hair, caress skin white as marble, her body, luscious and breathtaking. It was her face he remembered the most from those Sunday mornings. The face of a patron saint who could protect him from the all-encompassing slime.

*****

The porcelain tea set once used by the Queen, and even the tea itself, were the finest Buck had ever known. Rose poured the tea with such precision that she'd be more than qualified to entertain Elizabeth Windsor and her consort, Philip, instead of Nancy and Ronald, who were, presumably, less demanding in their tea ritual. Rose had even promised that Shelley would be arriving in less than fifteen minutes, although she assured Buck her son was no tea drinker. "Personally, I think he drinks brandy. There's always a faint smell of it on him, although he does many things to disguise the aroma."

Buck looked at her with a certain puzzlement. She'd held out the prospect of Shelley's arrival as a kind of enticement to get Buck to stay. That was only a glimmer of an idea in Buck's head. Surely he was mistaken. Why would she do that?

"Before the darling boy arrives, I must tell you what I know of the Examiner."

"Since I'm the publisher, I seem to have a right to know."

She sighed and slowly sipped her tea. It wasn't as if she were tantalizing him by withholding information. It was more as if she were figuring out the best way to break the news to him. "Before he flew to Switzerland for those tests, old Buck sold his twenty-five percent interest in the Examiner."

Buck slammed down his tea cup. "What the fuck! Without even telling me. The sleazy old fox."

"There's more. The parties who purchased it already own a lot of Examiner stock. In other words and in spite of your holding twelve percent of the stock, these parties or party are now in control of the newspaper. You're out the door, and I don't say that with any glee."

"Do you think they'll allow me to go back into the tower and retrieve the bar of soap I use to take a shower? Not only that but my de Kooning."

"Indeed they will. I'm sure of that."

He bit his lip. "I'm flabbergasted. More than hurt. I'm a little bitter. I feel I've been doublecrossed." He gasped for breath in the hot patio. "I don't know what I feel right now."

She reached out her hand to comfort him. "Please don't blame me. Believe it or not, I'm just a puppet in this whole God damn mess. In a lot deeper than I ever expected to be."

He looked at her closely. In spite of what he perceived as her immense power, she seemed vulnerable somehow. A front. A spokesperson, nothing more. But a spokesperson for what?

"I don't suppose you're going to tell me who is the new power behind the Examiner. Who's in charge? You?"

"No way. I don't expect to have any authority over management and decisions there. Personally, I don't own one bit of the stock."

"But who does?"

"Actually, and this is all I can tell you, that is going to be revealed to you in a few days. I'm to set up the meeting between you and the new owner. I can't give you the details yet. I've told you too much already. But the meeting is to take place in Los Angeles. Or maybe not. I'm lobbying for Palm Springs."

"I won't go. If I'm out, there's no point in my going to such a meeting."

"There's a major reason you should be there." Her face looked dazzling in the light. She had never been more alluring and beautiful. But she appeared to be but a Lorelei leading him into some nightmarish trap. This time he poured his own tea and studied her face closely. She held secrets, that was obvious. But she seemed unwilling at this point to tell him much more. It was as if the door to her face had shut, and he was staring at a gate he could not open. Nevertheless, he planned to press forward, to demand more revelations from her.

"I think we've paused long enough for theatrical effect," he said, not entirely concealing the biting sarcasm in his voice. "What is the major reason I should be there?"

"You're to be presented with a check for eighteen million dollars!"

He gasped. "Did I hear that right?"

"Indeed you did. Eighteen million dollars."

"Why?"

"Old Buck is turning over his entire share of the sale of the Examiner directly to you. All eighteen million dollars of it."

"But his one-fourth interest in the newspaper isn't worth eighteen million dollars. At least according to my attorney."

"Darling, property is worth whatever somebody is willing to pay for it. In this case, eighteen million."

"I can't believe this is happening."

"Welcome to the big time. You're a player now. Right up there with the big boys."

"It's all so sudden. I've got to get a grip on myself."

"There's more."

He frowned, dreading any more revelations. "There's a dreadful catch here somewhere. I just knew it. What are the strings attached to this eighteen million?"

"There are no strings. The eighteen million is yours. Of course, the stock will vastly rise when news of a takeover is announced. Your own twelve percent in the newspaper will go through the ceiling. Maybe another three million over its present worth. Maybe a lot more."

"It sounds unbelievable."

"Of course, since you'll have no more power at the Examiner, you might want to sell all your stock now while the iron's hot. I predict another cool twelve to thirteen million if you're interested in releasing all your stock."

"It's incredible the way millions are being tossed about here. My head is spinning."

"And well it should. I learned that your grandfather was paying you only forty-five thousand a year. I hardly know how you lived on that."

"It wasn't always easy given the way I spend money."

"I've know poverty too in my life. From the patio she surveyed her mansion. "Of course, that is hardly my story today."

"Hardly."

"With your newly acquired wealth, you can lead the good life. You don't have to be a publisher any more. You can be a playboy." She smiled provocatively at him. "Maybe spend more time keeping me entertained than writing those dreary editorials attacking me. Editorials that no one reads or believes in, incidentally."

"You're probably right about that."

"Considering you're out of a job, I can present my offer to you again. I want you to become my media director, although the Examiner is a bit out of our orbit. I can sign you to a three-year contract at a salary of three million a year." She smiled that same provocative smile again. "There will be many fringe benefits. More than you can ever know at this point."

"I suspect you are the devil. Throwing temptation at me left and right. Frankly, my last dream in life is to become your media director. Then you make me an offer I can hardly refuse, especially considering that I am now in the ranks of the unemployed."

"It took a little manipulation to get you that salary. After all, I'm not entirely controlling this operation."

"I imagine it did. I'm not being bought off or something?"

"Not at all." Her arm reached out and she ran her fingers across his hand. "You'll be asked to sing for your supper now and then."

He sat uneasily on the edge of his chair. "I'm sure that's true. You've given me a lot to think about. I've got to go home and make some calls. This is all too much."

"I understand you need to think things over. But I do want you to come to my dinner tonight. You'll get some keen insights into how power works in America. You'll see Ronald and Nancy grovel a bit. An eyewitness view. How can you turn down such a dinner?"

"It's very tempting. I'm a little confused right now. You'll forgive me, won't you, if I need to get centered before any dinner? I've got to call my lawyer. Maybe you're a dangerous fantasist. Maybe none of this is real. Milton will know if this is true or not. He won't know about any media director's job, but he'll know about the transfer of stock. Few things escape his attention in this town."

"Why don't you place the call from my library?" she said, getting up. "I've got to get changed for dinner anyway."

"Thank you. Thank you also for the tea."

"What about those millions?" she asked provocatively.

"Those too," he said.

She moved toward him and kissed him firmly and passionately on the mouth. "God, you smell good," she said, backing away and running her lips across her mouth, savoring the taste of him. "Pure jock sweat."

"I'm glad it turns you on," he said, not really knowing if he meant that. Excusing himself, he headed toward her library where a a rose-colored uniform suddenly appeared at the door to the patio, waiting to direct him down the right corridor.

As he trailed the butler, he inspected the mansion more carefully. It wasn't really like a home, more like a government palace. Cold marble greeted him at every turn. That little girl, Rose Phillips, was far, far from her poverty-stricken background in Oklahoma. She was now a major player on the world stage, and perhaps because of his very limited and very recent association with her, he too had joined the ranks with some of the big boys. He was so seized with his own ambition that he'd momentarily forgotten all the personal liaisons in his life. That would come later. Surely there would be time for that later.

The door to the library was being held open for him by the butler. Buck seemed in a daze. He entered the room, shutting the door behind him, and headed for the phone that rested on an antique desk. He had to call Uncle Milty and see if any of this news was true.

*****

"It's all true," Milton said when Buck finally reached his attorney. "I've been trying to contact you all afternoon. I only leaned of old Buck's latest maneuvers when he'd landed safely in Switzerland and I couldn't confront him directly."

"But the price tag," Buck said in way of protest. "It's incredible. I mean, that someone would pay so much."

"It made no sense to me either. But if that's what someone is willing to pay, the only thing you can do now is take the money and bank it."

"Rose Phillips tells me there is hot interest in buying out my share, too. She's talking another twelve to thirteen million for my stock alone."

"For God's sake, take the fucker's offer. What would you want with twelve percent of a paper you don't control? One that might be run by a lunatic. Some religious fanatic. A Christian, no less. And you know what I think of Christians."

"C'mon, Uncle Milty, don't kid at a time like this. I'm turning to you for some sort of help. I don't think I've ever been this confused in my whole life."

"I'll stop joking. I'll get really serious. Dump your stock, especially at that price. Your whole world's ahead of you. When old Buck goes, and that could be sooner than later, you'll be able to buy the Okeechobee News. Why not that? Why not become the publisher of the Okeechobee News? It's a better paper anyway than the Examiner. Old Buck kept too tight a lid on the Examiner. The News is a more honest rag. Without your grandfather censoring every word, you could make it even better."

"That's not a bad idea. I might buy it for Susan. Make her the publisher."

"Now who's joking?"

"I'm perfectly serious."

"Like Miss Scarlett, we'll think about that tomorrow."

"There's more. Rose wants me to become her media director. Three million a year. A contract guaranteed for three years."

"Hot damn! Another nine million."

"You're not urging me to do it, are you? I don't know what the job entails."

"That nine million sounds very enticing. I'm going to ask you to put more trust in me than you've ever done before."

"In what way?"

"Let me meet with Rose's lawyers. Let me determine if you should or should not take the job. Believe me, I'll protect your cute ass at every turn. Let me make the final decision for you as your attorney."

"Why should I? Don't you think I'm capable of making up my own mind?"

"Frankly, no. Not now anyway. You're on the verge of becoming one of the biggest farts in the southeastern United States. You've always trusted me to handle everything for you, and I've done a good job. Right?"

"You know you have. You've saved my ass one time after another. I don't know when you ever gave me bad advice. There were times I didn't want to follow that advice, but I generally went along."

"You've got to go along with me now. This Rose deal. The selling of your stock. The settlement of old Buck's estate. Even this so-called marriage with Susan."

"You want to handle that for me too? My marriage? You'll fuck her for me?"

"Please, I only got close to a woman like that once in my life, and when I gazed upon all that gaping horror I threw up."

"Oh, Uncle Milty. I don't know what to do. I really need help. This is a time when a guy needs a father."

"Let me be a father to you. I'll guide you through all this pile of shit. I'll protect you."

"Since I don't know what to do, I'll welcome the help. Do what you can for me. I don't trust my own judgment any more. You know, I've always felt grown up. But this afternoon I feel like a kid."

"That's no problem, not when you have your Uncle Milty. After all, you've always told me I was the smartest lawyer in the state of Florida."

"Okay, you make the decisions. You handle all this for me. You're all I have to turn to right now. I don't even have Robert with me. I can't get in touch with him and I fear the worse. I want you to hire a private detective—detectives, whatever—and trace him. His mother's dead and I can't find him anywhere. I've called every possible place I know where he might be."

"I have been holding back on you. I know where Robert is. He's flying back here. He knows about the marriage to Susan."

"I didn't tell him. Who did?"

"You know how close Patrick is to Robert. I mean, Patrick, other than yourself, is not only my lover, but he loves Robert almost as much as he loves me."

"Patrick was at the wedding. He knows everything."

"And he told everything. Those two girls have secrets from the two of us. I warned Patrick not to tell him, but he went ahead and did just that. Although he didn't show it at your wedding, Patrick was completely opposed to your hooking up with Susan. He thinks you should not have caved in to old Buck's demands. I, on the other hand, think you did just right. Patrick and Robert too don't realize that men like us have to pay the bills around here."

"Oh, shit, Robert knows, and before I could explain it to him my way."

"I'll say this for Patrick, and I drilled him thoroughly, he did explain to Robert why you were forced into the marriage. The money. The threat of disinheritance. That it won't be a real marriage."

"Did Robert understand?"

"Not at all. He went ballistic. Threatened to kill himself. Maybe it was because he'd become unglued over the death of his mother. You know gay men and their mothers."

"When can I see him?"

"As soon as I know something, I'll get back to you. I won't let Patrick know we've talked. It seems that Robert is going to stay here with Patrick and me. He said he'll never set foot in your house again."

"He used to call it 'our' house."

"No more. He feels you've betrayed him. He also said you promised to marry him, not Susan."

"I will marry Robert. Tell him that. The thing with Susan is just a business arrangement. Nothing more. He's got to understand that."

"He will in time. But if you'll go through with the plan to marry Robert—right after his mother's funeral—I think this will bring him around. He's just strung out right now."

"Then set up a wedding. You know it has no legal standing. But it might mean something to Robert. I can't believe he's lost all feeling for me."

"He's fanatically in love. I'll arrange for a minister to marry you in Miami. Both Patrick and I will fly down. I'll be your best man, and Patrick will be Robert's maid of honor. After all that's gone down, you've got to cater to Robert like never before. Convince him you love him more than life itself."

"I'll do my best."

"Have you stopped seeing Gene?"

"He's stopped seeing me."

"Good. It's better that way. Promise me you'll never go into another bedroom alone with Gene."

Buck sighed audibly. He gasped for air. "I promise. But I won't lie to you. I want one final meeting with him. Not for sex. To explain my side of things to him. I owe him that."

"One meeting perhaps, but I hope it doesn't lead to anything. You've got enough going on right now. You don't need Gene."

"No one's ever needed Gene. That's the point. He's a human being. He's been stripped of his dignity so many times I feel he can fall apart. He never was wired together too well anyway. A beautiful man but his heart doesn't always beat in the right place."

"Be careful around him. Maybe you can offer him money. Set him up in life somehow. The police force isn't for him."

"I'll see how it goes. But I abandoned him once before when he got into trouble. I can't desert him twice. Not if he needs me."

"You've given me a lot to do, and I suspect I don't have much time to accomplish half of what I've got to do."

"Do it for me, Uncle Milty. I know you love me and you'll look after me. Especially when you meet with Rose's pit vipers. But the most important thing you've got to do is to reach Robert and tell him how much I love him. Tell him I can't live without him. Get him back to me where he belongs. I should never have let him go away without me."

"The old miracle worker himself will accomplish everything you asked me to do. That I can guarantee. Love you, handsome hunk."

"I love you too. Thanks for being there for me. Get Robert back." He put down the phone.

As he did, he became aware of a strange presence in the library. At first he thought it was Rose. Instead of going to dress for her political dinner, she'd decided to eavesdrop on his conversation. As he turned around, he confronted not Rose, but Shelley. He'd entered the library without Buck being aware of it.

"It's pointless to get Robert back," Shelley said. You're mine now—not Robert's."

*****

Ignoring this claim of ownership, at least for the moment, Buck turned to confront Shelley. "I know it's your own home, but don't you think you should at least knock when I'm having a private conversation with my lawyer?"

"Not when two people know each other as intimately as we do," the boy said, moving toward him. "I know every inch of that gorgeous body of yours. More to the point, I even know the sweet taste of your nectar. I can smell the aroma of it right now. It's the most delectable drink I've ever had in my life. I want to drink it forever." He moved even closer to Buck, and almost before he knew what was happening Shelley had kissed him firmly on the lips with a brush of his sweet tongue. Almost as if his body had a will not connected to his brain, Buck wanted to return the kiss.

But he backed away, moving away from Shelley toward the window where views opened onto Rose's well-manicured gardens. It was the panorama of Shelley that clouded his vision, not the cascades of multi-colored roses in Rose's fabled rose gardens, rumored to be the rarest and most spectacular roses in the world.

Fresh from a match, Shelley was wearing a rose-colored tennis outfit, his golden legs never more shapely. Flecked with golden hairs, they weren't legs that belonged on a human, but on some god. Everything about the boy—his lips, his face, his eyes, his long eyelashes, his blond hair, his swimmer's build—was perfection itself. Buck suspected that never had a more rotten core been camouflaged into such an Adonis-like appearance. Buck found it amazing that Shelley could express love for anyone else. If anything, he should be self-enchanted, staring endlessly at his own reflection in a mirror.

"I have some advice to give you," Shelley said.

"Why should I take it?"

"Because it'll leave you laughing all the way to the bank," the boy said, plopping down in a chair and letting one leg droop over the arm.

Buck glanced briefly at how tight his tennis shorts were. With Shelley's leg raised Buck could see upward toward Shelley's crotch. Buck averted his eyes, turning again to Rose's roses. "I assume you mean take the deal Rose is offering."

"I do indeed. Now's the time for you to clean up. How else are you going to support me in my old age?"

"I don't know. I fear there are too many strings attached."

Shelley looked up at Buck with his luminous blue eyes. "The fringe benefits are not to be believed."

"By that, I assume you mean yourself."

Shelley slid deeper into the chair accenting the tightness even more of his tennis shorts. "You've got that right."

Instead of looking at those roses, as beautiful as they were, Buck kept his eyes glued to what was even more enticing to him: Shelley's state-of-the-art boy ass. He truly believed there was nothing more polished and delectable on the earth. He could search continents and turn up with nothing as fine as this.

Shelley with his hawkeye knew where Buck was looking and said nothing, letting the man take in his full glory. "Be honest with yourself," Shelley finally said, breaking the spell.

"What do you mean?"

"I mean tell me exactly what you're thinking right this minute."

"You know exactly what I'm thinking. I'm dreaming about plowing my big dick up that tight rosebud of yours. But only after I've devoured it for an hour or two with my lips and tongue." He slammed his fist into his hand. "Is that what you wanted to hear, God damn it?"

"I did want to hear that more than I've wanted to hear anything in my life. I didn't need to be told but I wanted to hear the actual words coming from those lips of yours that I've tasted, licked, and sucked while you slept. I've even tongue fucked your nostrils, and I never did that with anyone in my life."

"Stop it! This is going nowhere. Everything's driving me crazy."

Shelley jumped up from the chair and stood behind Buck, reaching out and putting his arms around the man. The boy rubbed his chest and traced light fingers over his rock-hard stomach. Suddenly, Buck whirled around, grabbed Shelley in his arms and pressed him close, sticking his tongue down the boy's throat. When he broke free, he traced his tongue along the boy's neck and nibbled his ears before inserting his tongue in each lobe, there to devour and savor the taste. "God damn it, I want to eat you alive, then fuck you all night."

"I'm yours," Shelley said, gasping for breath. He'd seemed to melt under Buck's touch and caresses, as if this was the one moment he'd waited for all his life. "I'll always be yours."

Buck broke away. He couldn't control himself any more. As Shelley could see, Buck's penis was practically trying to break out of his trousers and assert itself. "I can't go on. I belong to Robert. I owe him my loyalty."

Shelley stood defiantly, looking intensely at Buck. "You won't have to be disloyal to him. Not the way it's going to work out."

"What in hell are you talking about? You're making no sense."

"You know."

Buck stared at him intensely. "You mean, you're going to have Robert killed?"

"I have this vision thing. He's going on his way. I don't know how or why. But he's going on his way. Very soon. You and I are going to spend the rest of our lives together."

Buck was gasping for breath. Instead of wanting to denounce Shelley for what he was saying, he believed every word—at least for the moment. The library, in spite of its air conditioning, had grown oppressively hot. He couldn't stand to be here for another second. He had to escape Paradise Shores or he felt he'd die. Life was too intense here. It was so unreal it was very real, and reality all of a sudden was the last thing he wanted. He bolted for the door and vaguely remembered Shelley's pleas for him to come back as he rushed through Rose's garden.

Out on the street he hailed a taxi and ordered the driver to take him home.

"Where's home?" the driver asked.

Buck realized he'd forgotten to give him the address. After he did, he settled back in his seat to sort things out, if only he could.

"You're going home, right?" the driver asked enigmatically.

"I hope so," Buck said. "If you'll take me there."

The driver sped along the streets in silence for a moment. The air was sticky. There was no air conditioning in the cab. The driver's voice broke through the stillness of the late afternoon. "Oh, to go home but where?" he said. "I never yet was there."

*****

In the privacy of his own garden, Buck—clad only in a robe—sucked in the twilight air deeply. Ever since Uncle Milty had called him about Gene's arrest, he'd been tempted to phone Susan to discuss the latest disaster to strike Gene. He'd wanted to tell her the news himself. But Susan was en route to his private island where he'd agreed to meet with her later. He knew this latest arrest would arouse too many painful memories for her. She'd been through it all before. He just hoped she didn't turn on the radio on his boat or flip on the TV news, although he knew she frequently did both.

Near some of his more exotic flowers, he came to an abrupt stop, his face one of grief. He still loved Gene, and the news of this latest arrest struck a blow to his heart. He just couldn't believe it could be happening again.

Uncle Milty had been even more suspicious, fearing a conspiracy here. His attorney was a great believer in conspiracies. Not only did he think Castro ordered the shooting of John Kennedy, but that Robert Kennedy personally murdered Marilyn Monroe. And Milton loved the Kennedy brothers.

Something about Gene's arrest didn't strike Buck as valid. As he understood it, Gene was nude, but nude in the privacy of his own deck in an enclosed area shut off from public view. If someone could be arrested for that, then half of Florida would be in jail. What was that little girl doing in Gene's private space? Was she sent there? Was Gene set up? And if Gene did expose himself to another little girl, perhaps he needed psychiatric treatment more than confinement. Milty had also learned that Gene's chief, Biff, had suspended him from the force. It was more than a suspension. Biff told TV news that he'd never "let this child molester work another day on the police force."

Memories of that dreadful day when Gene had been arrested before on a similar charge flashed through Buck's mind. He hadn't contacted him that time, even though Buck was—in theory at least— Gene's best friend. He hadn't helped him then, but he vowed to himself to help him now. Even though Gene wouldn't see him, he wanted to do what he could. He called Milty back. "I can't let Gene down this time. I just can't."

"What can you do? He won't even talk to you."

"I can do plenty. You know I can do something, God damn it, Uncle Milty. What's his fucking bail?"

"Ten thousand dollars."

"Is he being held in jail? Right this minute?"

"Yeah, he can't raise bail."

"Get the lead out of your fucking ass. You're my lawyer. What is this shit about me not being able to do anything? You're smarter than that."

"Okay, dammit to hell, I just didn't want you to get involved. I'll hustle my fat ass down there and post the ten-thousand dollar bail."

"Immediately."

"I'm out the fucking door, okay?"

"I'm sorry to get so testy with you. But I'm really mad. Gene's been framed. But by whom? What enemies does he have powerful enough to frame him?" Buck breathed in deeply again. "Oh, my God. I was with Calder Martin. He threatened to ruin Gene. It wasn't Gene he was after. But me. He wanted to show me how quickly he could ruin another man's life. It was to be a lesson to me. I can't believe this is real. It's not Gene who Calder is after. It's me. Damn, damn, damn. I'm going crazy."

"Fucking Calder. Right-wing mad dog from hell. Fuck him! But pull yourself together in the meantime. Want me to come over?"

"I don't want to see anybody right now. Maybe Gene. But then I'm afraid to see him. I want Robert Dante. Get Robert for me. I've never fucked his ass before, but tonight I want to fuck Robert."

"I can't believe you've known Robert all these years and never fucked the world's most delectable ass."

"Believe it! We did other things. Get him back here!"

"Honey, with all the money you're about to come into, you can call me day and night and I'll be over there—rain or shine—licking that rosebud of yours. I mean it. You've got power. We're going to have all the money in the world. Money talks."

"Get me Robert. I'm losing my mind. Doesn't that mean anything to you?"

"It means my world. You are my world. I'm dropping all other clients. From this moment on, I'm going to work only for you. You're numero uno in my book. I'll do anything you want. Eat your shit. Anything!"

"Don't get carried away. I won't get that demanding unless you get fucking out of line. I think I'll buy you, Milty."

"I'm for sale. God knows with all your money, you can afford me."

"Get Gene out of jail. Bring me Robert before the night is over. That's all I'm asking." He paused in hesitation. "For the moment." He hesitated again.

"And resolve that Rose deal, whatever the fuck that is," Milty said.

"And resolve that too. Buck breathed deeply into the phone. "You know I love you, Uncle Milty. I confide everything in you. Even the fact that right now I'm so fucking horny I can't stand it. I've got to get my cock sucked."

"You're crazy. With all you've got coming down, you're thinking about getting your cock sucked."

"You know me. In moments of great tension, I need my dick sucked. But that's how I feel. It's always been that way. Faced with danger, I always get a hard-on that requires immediate relief. Lock me up in the ward for lunatics."

"If you didn't have me so busy, I'd rush over there and suck you off myself. But you've got me doing all this other crap."

"Get to it and get back to me." Buck slammed down the phone. "My God," he said out loud. He was acting like a mogul, and he hadn't even bagged the millions yet. It was amazing how even the prospect of all that money enthralled him, even changing his personality. Being a multi-millionaire had seemed to give him a perpetual hard-on. He opened his robe and exposed himself. He decided he had to do something immediately about his massive erection. Robert wasn't here. Susan was headed toward his private island. Shelley was no longer around panting for him. That left only his own trusty right fist which he resorted to only in cases of dire emergency. Just as he was about to bring himself relief, he heard the sound of car wheels pulling into his driveway.

*****

Still clad in his robe, Buck opened the front door, there to confront a stunningly beautiful Rose in a diaphanous white gown and her even more stunningly beautiful son, Shelley, clad in a white dinner jacket. Shelley's only dress code defiance was in wearing a purple polka dot bow tie. In his driveway Buck noted the rose-colored Rolls-Royce limousine with an older driver attired in elephant gray.

"Don't you believe in phoning?" he asked them, standing at the door barring their entrance and certainly not inviting them in. His feelings were so mixed and confused by both of them he didn't seem to know what to do at first, other than to gaze at their beauty. This was one gorgeous pair.

"I tried calling," Rose said, sliding past him and entering his foyer. "But your line was always busy." She turned and smiled provocatively at him. "No doubt talking to one of your other girl friends."

"Who are you, anyway?" Shelley asked, also brushing past. "The love 'em and leave 'em kissing bandit?"

Rose stood serenely in his foyer, eying the decor and looking into the large living room beyond. "We'll have to redecorate. I'll pay for it, of course."

"You always pay, bitch," Shelley said heading for the living room. He looked around vacantly, as if having no reason to be here. "Where's your bedroom? I always like to see where a man sleeps. You always learn so much about a man that way."

"I'm sure Buck is not going to show you to his bedroom, at least not now."

"Or ever!" Buck said, brushing past them and clutching his robe even tighter around him. In the presence of their formal wear, he felt nude somehow. He was nude under the robe.

For what seemed like an interminable time, although it was only thirty seconds, he stood facing her in his foyer.

Her face was startlingly white in contrast to her burning dark eyes. She possessed the profile of a huntress, and he suspected he was the big game she eagerly sought. "I've spoken to Nancy. She said Ronnie and she would be delighted if you could join us for dinner. They know who you are and would welcome the Examiner's support. Of course, they think your politics are the same as old Buck's."

"I might accept. If she truly was known as the fellatio queen of Hollywood, I might be in luck. I'm real horny tonight."

"Why didn't you tell us sooner?" Shelley said, moving closer to him and reaching to caress his cheek. "When a stud like you is horny, you needn't look farther than mommie dearest and me."

A slight laugh escaped from Rose's throat. "Don't worry about messing up our outfits. Both Shelley and I swallow."

He was startled for a moment, not thinking he heard right. He laughed nervously too and invited both of them out to his pool area, leading the way.

On the way there Rose stopped briefly to peer into his private library. "The taste in furnishings are a bit old-fashioned for a young man like you. I'm surprised."

"My mother did everything. She's dead now." A slight defiance came into his voice. "I'm not going to change a thing."

"I understand," Rose said, seeming to back away from her earlier statement. "A sentimental attachment."

"Sentimentality is something Rose and I don't adhere to," Shelley said. "We are strictly 70s people."

"That must be nice for you," Buck said non-committally as he led both of them across a flagstone terrace and quickly poured himself a large splash of Scotch, reaching for the rocks. "May I offer either of you something to drink?"

"You can," Shelley said. "Your own cocktail, big boy. I like it white and creamy."

"Oh, Shelley," she said. "You're always so graphic. I prefer more subtlety in my seductions."

Shelley took the glass from Buck and ran his pink tongue around its rim before handing it back to Buck. Almost without thinking, Buck put the glass to his lips and downed a hefty swig.

Then Shelley turned to his mother, as if deliberately postponing a response to her latest challenge. "Subtlety, did you say? Like the time you got drunk on that yacht and rolled in your cabin screaming for the young and handsome captain to come and fuck you." He turned to Buck and smiled. "That young captain was a bit worn out when he finally got to Rose's suite. You see, he'd visited me earlier and I didn't leave him with much left."

As music murmured in the background, Buck stood before a glass-topped table and lit two candles. White gardenias floated in a large bowl on the table. He invited both of them to sit down. But neither one seemed to pay any attention to his invitation.

Wincing at the sight of Shelley and the story he'd just told, Rose recovered quickly and, smiling with bravado, went over to his kidney-shaped pool. In her white gown, with a lone string of pearls, she stood at the edge of it, the glitter of its shimmering green waters reflected on her face.

"So let's go upstairs," Shelley said, running his delicate fingers lightly and tantalizingly around Buck's left ear lobe. "I'll help you get into your tux and let's head for this dinner. You might as well take off the robe. It's not that Rose and I haven't seen the ample goodies before. No need for shyness around us." Without Buck realizing what he was doing, Shelley slid the robe from Buck's body. He stood completely nude on the patio.

Rose turned to take in the view. "I do believe I am staring at the world's greatest male specimen."

Feeling awkward, especially in view of the fact they were in formal attire, Buck noticed the oncoming night sky had an uncomfortable chill factor. He dived into the water and swam several lengths of the pool as both Rose and Shelley watched him. Lit from underneath, the water was a clear as sapphire.

After his swim, he climbed up the pool ladder where Rose waited with a large white beach towel she'd retrieved from a nearby rack. Water streamed down his neck as he emerged from the pool, making no effort to cover himself. Shelley came up from behind, seemingly out of nowhere. He began to towel the water off Buck's back. Rose moved forward and rubbed the droplets off his chest. He felt the blood beating in his temples. Both Rose and her son had a delicate, sensual touch, as if massaging him. His lower lip caught between his teeth as he started to say something, but then thought better of it.

Their towels and the caresses of their experienced fingers were having its effect. He felt himself rising and hardening. Shelley was now toweling his ass and Rose's fingers moved lower to towel and massage his balls. She knelt before him to wipe his legs of the water from the pool. As she looked up, she saw him fully extended in all his glory. Shelley's hand traveled underneath, fondling and weighing Buck's balls, almost dangling them in front of Rose. Then the boy's hands traveled the full length of Buck's penis, uncapping it for Rose as if inviting her to taste it.

And that is what she did, plunging down with consummate skill. He almost wanted to scream in ecstasy as he felt Shelley's tongue entering him from the rear, delicately kissing and probing his innermost part. With one hand, he sought Rose's head, pressing her face into his body and with his other free hand he reached around for Shelley's neck and pressed his face even closer into his ass. Buck didn't want this moment to end. Not ever. But his body had needs and wants all its own, and it signaled him that such exquisite torture couldn't last forever. The climax when it finally arrived seemed to go on forever. These skilled seducers knew how to extend it until the last possible gasp. They were devouring mouths almost insatiable in their desire.

Even after Rose had had her fill, and had retreated to his downstairs bathroom, Shelley moved around in front of him, there to lick and to polish his penis entirely clean and to drain any last drops.

*****

Buck retrieved his robe and headed for the bar, where he joined Rose who looked so fresh and alluring it was impossible to imagine only moments before she'd been down on her knees with his cock buried deep in her throat. Without asking permission, she poured herself a sherry from a decanter, as she eyed him speculatively. "You're one hell of a man," she said, kissing him on the lips. "I've had them all—the good, the bad, the ugly. But you're the best thing that's ever come along."

"Thank you very much," he said rather formally. "Not only for the compliment, but for the action. I don't think if I traveled through all the bordellos of the ancient Orient would I come across talent such as you and Shelley. Did you teach him all he knows?"

She laughed a bit nervously. "I taught him nothing. But somebody obviously did. No doubt, my many boyfriends."

Shelley came to join them at the bar and reached for a brandy, again without being invited to do so. Buck observed that these two generally took what they wanted.

"Put the fucking liquor down," Rose said harshly to him. "I don't want you showing up drunk to meet Ronald and Nancy. And get in the

God damn bathroom and wash your face. You've still got come on your cheek, you little faggot cocksucker."

"Don't you of all people ever call me cocksucker, you slimy bitch," he said with a rage and hatred Buck had never seen in him. "You're better at it than even I am." He turned to Buck and smiled as he softened his voice. "Today the leading cocksucker of the East Coast, mommie dearest, will sup with the leading cocksucker of the West Coast, Ms. Nancy Davis. At least we know why Reagan married her."

"Get to that bathroom and make yourself even more beautiful than you are," she said to him. "Brush your teeth so that when Nancy kisses you she won't smell her favorite liquid, semen, and get all hot and bothered."

Shelley kissed Buck on the lips. Buck returned the kiss. What the hell! If the world's most beautiful boy kisses you on the mouth after having done you the big service of licking your cock clean, you kiss him back. Who wouldn't?

Breaking away, he said nothing to Buck but reached out and gently ran delicate fingers across Buck's right cheek. He then turned to Rose. "Mama, I want you to buy me this for Christmas. You can afford it." He moved quickly across the patio and into Buck's ground floor bathroom, so recently vacated by Rose herself.

Buck poured himself another Scotch and toasted Rose, who ever so gracefully held her sherry up into the night air.

"What would be your big objection to your becoming my media director?" she asked, abruptly shifting the subject from sex to business.

He downed a stiff drink before speaking. "Okay, bluntly, that big ego of yours. It's so off the wall I think it would constantly interfere in anything I said or did. It's like you've invented a drama in which you can be the star. A false show. The big lie. I don't think there's much future in me hanging out with you."

He'd been avoiding her eyes as he said those words, but she came around and stood before him in the light of the patio. "I only use lies to cover my flaws. Maybe I do overstate my case a bit." She reached out and gently took his hand. "I'm a gambler. Many of the risks I've taken have paid off, miraculously so. But sometimes I've put out my hand to receive a reward, like in your case, and my gift just vanishes."

His temper flaring, he turned and headed for his living room. "I'm no God damn gift." He looked back over his shoulder. "No reward for you. Stop thinking of me that way."

"Forgive me," she said, coming to sit beside him on the sofa. She reached for his hand again which he reluctantly offered.

"I'm sorry to react so strongly. But I think I'm the wrong guy for your organization."

"Why?" she demanded to know. "You could become a media star yourself. With my help. I happen to know a magazine is about to be published naming you the sexiest man alive! Did they ever get that one right."

"To begin with, I'm not even a Christian. Definitely not. I'm not even sure I believe in a God. If I do, it's not any God you believe in."

She laughed and took his hand and pressed it against her lips. "My darling man, do you think I believe in God? I don't! Do you think Shelley believes in God? Don't be ridiculous. The only thing my darling son believes in is what stares back at him when he looks in the mirror. We're not Christians. Do you think Calder Martin believes in God? We use these stupid Christians for their money—nothing else. It's a way to gain power. Surely you realized all that."

"I wasn't certain. You're so convincing up there in that pulpit."

"That's because I'm an actress. Believe me, I'd rather curl up with a hunk with an eleven-inch dick than the Bible."

"I think you've told me the absolute truth. I believe you now."

"It's money, baby. Power. I'll share it with you. We can climb the highest ladder together. Do you think I want to be climbing that ladder with Calder Martin? For one thing, he stinks. That breath of his. Ghastly. But he's strangely effective. Calder should be kept down in the sewers with the rats and the shit doing his dirty work. You, on the other hand, are what I'd like to present to the media."

"I can't deny I'm not tempted. I might dream of escaping from old Buck's shadow, but chances are I never will. I'll always be the grandson of a famous man. But in some way I think you might help me become bigger than old Buck. I really believe that about you. I don't like to think what I'd have to do to get there, but I am fiercely ambitious. You know that already. Even as we speak, I can tell you know that, and you're playing on that so-called flaw in my character."

"It's not a flaw, baby." She rose abruptly and stood before him, almost whirling around in a little dance of glee. He realized that she was more fiercely ambitious than he'd ever be. "Don't leave me," she almost shouted into the living room. "Don't ever leave me. Until I met you, I'd gone from one poor substitute to another. I'd almost face the inevitable decline of hope and joy. Now you've given me faith."

In amazement, he looked up at her. Her statement startled him. How could he give faith to the woman who had inspired it in millions of others?

"I'm in love with you," she said with such authority it almost challenged the night. "Completely, hopelessly in love with you, and I've never loved before."

"Listen," he said, as if to counteract her melodramatic words, "you're no school girl who lets a man fuck her and then falls madly in love with him. There's more to it than that."

She raised a wrist, sparkling with diamonds, and reached down for his arm. He got up from the sofa to stand facing her. "Suspicions. Why can't you trust somebody? Me?"

He grabbed a drink and took another swallow. The tension was too strong between them. He knew it was the tension of two people who strongly desired each other. He went over and pulled back the sliding glass panels that overlooked his floodlit garden. The night air revived him. Looking at her again, he said, "Since that march your power has grown. It's like a force to be reckoned with. You've hit a nerve ending in a lot of people out there. You're developing real clout. Yet who's behind all this? What's your motive? You ask me to trust you. Isn't that dumb?"

"You're smart. You know there's more behind all this than what I'm presenting. Much of it will become clear to you very soon—that is, if you come aboard. I will be completely honest if I tell you I'm a mere player. I don't control everything myself, and I'm not always certain what's going on. I'm like a hired actress given a script to read. I don't actually write the script myself."

"I can believe that. The more I looked into your situation, the more I came to believe other forces were at work here."

"Forget for one moment the business part. Time for that later. I want to talk about us. At one point in my life I was passive. Taking every blow on this chin." She stood in the shadows of the room but had a luminous quality that hovered about her. At such a distance from her, he could still feel the current of life flowing in her. "Then this big change came over me. I decided to fight for what I wanted, what I believed in."

"What do you believe in?"

"Money and power." She paused, her voice softening. "I also believe in love. I have a right to run after love. Would you deny me that?"

"You can chase it all you want. That's your right."

"My chase just came to an end. I've met you. I can stop running."

"No, you can't."

"What does that mean?" she demanded to know.

A long silence followed. Though he couldn't see her eyes clearly, he felt their anguish. "There can be no big romance between us. I don't love you. I was fascinated by you, and I still am. Fascination. Sexual attraction. But nothing more. No love. I can't give you that."

"But I want to marry you. Look at the press we'd get!"

"We'd get press all right," he said. "I'd be indicted for bigamy."

"You are married?"

"Quite recently. Susan Howard."

"That silly little girl reporter who writes articles for the Examiner."

"She's my wife. That's why I can't join you for dinner tonight. I've promised to meet her on my private island. It's our honeymoon night. How can I go to a dinner party and desert my wife on her honeymoon night?"

Staggeringly wounded, she ran toward the foyer and, in moments, he heard her throw open the front door, her high heels hitting the gravel of his driveway. "Tell that faggot son of mine I'll send the limo back for him. I'm out of here." As the chauffeur helped her into the back seat of the limousine, Buck went into the foyer and softly closed the door.

He returned to the garden where the twilight glowed with a rare radiance, breaking through the gray overcast that had hung over the garden most of the evening. If only she were different, he thought wistfully to himself. If her inner qualities matched her physical beauty, then loving her would be like falling asleep in the bower of heaven. He could snuggle against her breasts, yielding to a mysterious protection. That was only myth. To succumb to the real Rose would be like taking a long night's exploration into a glacier. He could not be happy there. No joy. He could lose himself there.

Seemingly emerging from nowhere, a presence appeared in the garden. Startled he turned around to confront Shelley. No longer in his formal wear, the boy was completely nude. The soft lighting in the garden accentuated his beauty, making him look almost ethereal. For as long as he might live, Buck thought he would never see such beauty in a young man. It wasn't a question of giving in to temptation. When Adonis himself is extending his hand, you reach for it.

Shelley's fingers were on his body removing his robe. It fell to the brick patio. Buck was completely nude like the boy himself.

"Welcome to the Garden of Delights," the boy said softly, his voice like a caress.

Buck was breathing deeply. He'd fallen under the spell of the night, a spell cast by this enchanting young man. Forgetting everything else coming down in his life, he reached out for Shelley, crushing the boy in his arms, as his tongue attempted in vain to reach the back of Shelley's throat. He wanted not just to embrace Shelley. Not just to have sex with him. He wanted to devour him.

*****

Consumed with rage, Gene drove home, feeling like a bottled scorpion eating his own tail. It had come as a complete surprise—a shock, really—when Buck had posted bail for him through his attorney, the man Buck called "Uncle Milty." Gene had realized Uncle Milty was just doing Buck's bidding. If given his wish, Uncle Milty would have Gene rot in jail. He knew that lawyer had always hated him and did what he could to persuade Buck not to get involved.

At first, when Buck's offer to post bail had come into the police station, Gene had rejected it. As he'd reconsidered, the help had grown more appealing. Why shouldn't he receive aid and comfort from Buck? He could afford it. Gene couldn't. It was just a small favor from Buck. He could have Uncle Milty write a check and not miss the outflow of cash at all. To Gene, that ten thousand dollars meant freedom or jail. It also meant he could continue to provide a home to Jill and Sandy.

The first time with Jill had been real. For reasons still not clear in his head, he'd exposed himself to her. But with Maria, he had been set up for a fall. In time, he planned his revenge on Clara and her daughter. His most horrible suspicion was that he was paying this price and suffering this humiliation because he turned down Clara's sexual advances. But would she go this far? Even involving her own daughter? He didn't know the answer to that, and suspected he never would find out. There were many questions he didn't know the answers to, but each day things would become clearer to him. He'd find out some of the answers as to why the world was threatening him and moving in on him.

When he knew more, he might take the law in his own hands. He'd have plenty of time to do that. He'd learned that Biff had suspended him from the police department, awaiting the resolution of his latest case. In his heart, he knew the suspension would last forever. There was no way he was going back to that police department. He'd never belonged there anyway.

Before he turned the corner of his block, he heard the clang of a fire alarm, its glaring sound followed by the familiar echoes of police sirens. The street had been cordoned off, and instinctively he knew what had happened. He slammed on his brakes, abandoning his car double-parked in the street, and raced in the direction of his home.

Bumping into chattering Cubans, almost tripping, he reached his home. It was too late. Flames leaped from his windows as firemen turned on their hoses full blast. The house had long ago been built of wooden timbers, which only provided easy fuel for the leaping flames. It was all he owned in the world. Every one of his possessions, even his prized tennis trophies, were being consumed by flames. The water from the hoses seemed to have little effect. To him, the water almost appeared to be gasoline fueling the flames.

"Oh, my God!" he cried out loud, suddenly realizing that Jill and Sandy might be trapped in that house. He shouted their names wildly into the night, but his voice was drowned out. He rushed toward his house to rescue Jill and Sandy.

Two policemen, recognizing him, restrained him, even though he kicked and fought violently, trying to break through. "They're in there," he shouted at one of the policemen. "You're letting them burn to death."

"Okay, it's okay," one of the officers shouted back. "That boy, Sandy, is in the hospital. The girl is with him."

"Is he okay?"

"He's badly burned," the officer said. "He tried to rush in to save you, thinking you were there. The girl is okay but we rescued the boy. He's at Okeechobee Memorial. Being treated for burns. The girl's with him."

Gene gasped for air at the news, but his lungs filled with smoke instead. His eyes smarting, he watched helplessly, as curls of smoke, fed by his possessions, floated into the night sky. The flames rose fan-like toward the beams of the wood-framed house, igniting the roof. Women and children screamed as policemen forced them back behind hastily erected barriers. The flames beat up through the rafters, making him shut his eyes, remembering his childhood toys stored there.

As he opened his eyes, he spotted Clara and Maria on the far side of the street, looking not at the flames engulfing his home but glaring at him triumphantly, as if they'd done something of which they could be proud.

The stink of smoke choked him as he pressed as close to the blaze as the policemen would allow. He'd been born in that very house. His mother didn't believe in hospitals. Black drifts of smoke flowed down the street that was no longer his. As flames mixed with the sky, bands of red turned to orange, creating an eerie silhouette against the darkness.

Before a screen of flames, a policeman he knew spoke to him. "I'm sorry, Gene. It's arson. We found empty gasoline cans out back."

He didn't need to be told that. He could just picture the beaners—angry, outraged Cuban fathers plotting over their cheap wine-drinking to set fire to his home and chase out the one lone WASP who had remained in their neighborhood, the former residents having long since fled to other pastures. He shut his eyes real tight, remembering how the neighborhood used to be when he was a kid. Things were so peaceful then.

For a while he stood still, watching the flames, mesmerized by them, the way he always was by Rose at her temple. Eyes cast hostile stares at him, hands touched him, as he was pushed and shoved among lurking bodies. As in a nightmare, he could almost make out the fat, stubby fingers of Clara, reaching across the flame-lit street to choke him.

When he could no longer stand the strain, he broke through the crowd and cut across a neighbor's driveway until he was safely screened by a thick row of hibiscus bushes at the edge of his own backyard. He could hear his heavy heartbeat as he stood here, watching the firemen extinguish what was now a wreck. His stomach felt like a tangled knot, as he cried, thanking God that no one was here to witness him break down like this. No one—ever—must see him cry.

He also thanked God that Sandy and Jill had not burned in that firetrap. He'd wanted to offer them a safe haven, but it could have led to their deaths. He shuddered at that prospect.

As he stood here trembling in shock, hours seemed to pass but it was a relatively short period of time. He'd lost all track of time. It didn't matter any more. He didn't have a job to report to in the morning. It was amazing how a scene of such intensity would wind down so suddenly. With the flames dead, and after inspecting the damage, the Cubans wandered off. Eventually the policemen and fire trucks departed too. Within the hour, the blaring sounds of Spanish from a hundred TV sets filled the night air.

Gene remained in the bushes, staring vacantly at the charred beams of his home, which very much resembled a skeleton. He would never re-enter what was left of his home. That was foreign territory to him now, belonging to the invaders. They had won.

There was nothing left for him to do now, other than go to the hospital and pick up what remained of his life. He was deeply touched that Sandy had tried to rescue him, but also profoundly shocked that the boy had injured himself in the process.

The moon blazed against one remaining side of his white-painted house, and the effect was like snow-light. As hard as it was to face, he now had to admit that his nest and refuge belonged to "them."

Feverish with memories, he crept toward the ruins of his house, stumbling over his rocking horse that had been stored in the attic but somehow had come to rest forlornly on the ground, its rockers broken.

His picture had been beamed into almost every home in the city on the television news round-up. That made him feel stripped naked, the way he'd felt standing before those Cuban women earlier in the day. He was totally vulnerable.

For many years, the Cubans had been curious about his life and, because of the charred wreck before him, the last vestiges of his privacy lay open before them.

He stood on the back steps looking at the still-smoking ruins in the moonlight. His house was dead. Soon the land itself would be sold, and a new house erected by some Cuban trying to re-create a distant memory of a long-faded Havana. He would have to forget his own feelings and attachments to this house. In just one day, all traces of his former life had been wiped away and, with its going, a part of him had died.

Another part of him wasn't dead at all. In fact, it was just beginning to stir into life. The bottled scorpion wasn't going to bite its tail any more. Instead, it was going to crawl out of the bottle and sting the city. But only when the time was right.

*****

In the corridor of the Okeechobee Memorial Hospital, painted a sickening pea-green, Gene dodged a stretcher carrying a young black male who'd been knifed in the stomach. He was rushed into emergency medical. Gene had seen too many cases like this with all his years on the police force. In spite of all the hysteria going on, he knew the man would be resting peacefully in the morgue in only a matter of hours. But he wasn't here on official duty any more. His official duties were over with the force. His police career had gone up in flames, along with his home.

It was then he spotted her. She was sitting anxiously on a bench as if waiting for some news. The moment he called to her, Jill jumped up and rushed to his side. She gave him a hug, then burst into tears, crushing herself into his chest.

"How is he?" Gene asked.

"He's going to be okay, but in a lot of pain," she said, sobbing. "His left arm and shoulder are badly burned. They're doing what they can, I'm sure. He was burned so badly he screamed in pain in the ambulance taking us here."

Tears welled in Gene's eyes. "God damn them all! I wish I had been there."

"He loves you," Jill said. "He thought you were asleep in the back bedroom. He broke through the police line and tried to rescue you."

"I think he's the only person in the world who would have done that for me. I'll make it up to him somehow. My God, I tried to provide a home for you. Now this."

"I can't believe how everything happened so suddenly. It was all so peaceful. Everything was going just fine. You gave Sandy and me a home. We were so grateful."

"I'll still provide a home somehow." He brought his hands together in desperation, cracking his knuckles. "There's a way out of this. I just know it. I've got two-thousand dollars in the bank. That will hold us over for a little while."

"What are we going to do?"

"I know a place that rents studio efficiencies. I'll make a call later. We can hole in there for a while until I decide what to do next. We don't even have clothes."

"I'm used to being out on the street. I could go back to work. Make some money for us."

"Forget it! You don't have to do that. The main thing now is to nurse Sandy back to health. The poor guy. To think he did that for me."

"You need all the help you can get. I heard what happened to you. That God damn Cuban bitch. You were doing nothing wrong. That girl invaded your private space. She should be the one arrested. For trespassing."

He took her hand and looked deeply into her eyes. "I can't believe you're defending me. After what I did to you. That's when I deserved to be arrested. Not this time. I was set up for this one."

"I know you were. We should have been there to protect you."

A young woman intern appeared in the corridor. "Sandy wants to see both of you. He's calling for you. But would you go in one at a time? It's better that way."

When the attendant had left, Gene turned to Jill. "You go first. That's what I think he would want. You've known him longer."

"I was with him earlier. You go first."

In the dimly lit room Sandy shared the cramped quarters with another patient who was almost entirely bandaged. The man in the other bed seemed to be resting peacefully.

Sandy's eyes were wide open, his brow feverish. He sat up in bed but winced in pain. "Gene," he said. "Come here. Tell me you're okay."

"I'm okay, kid. It's you we're worried about."

"I'm gonna be okay. It hurts like hell. But I'll heal. At least all of us are alive."

"I'm just glad that you and Jill weren't in that house. You shouldn't have gone in after me."

"Yeah, right, just stand outside and watch you burn to death. I couldn't do that, and you know it. Jill agrees. It was the only damn thing I could do. The fucking firemen wouldn't do it."

"I'll always be grateful to you for caring so much." Gene leaned over and kissed Sandy on his brow.

With his good hand, the boy reached out to Gene. "I love you, big guy. I always will. I'd do anything for you—you know that."

"I would never have predicted this, but you've become the best friend I've ever had. I used to think I had a good friend. But he let me down just when I needed him."

"You mean the guy who calls all the time?"

"That's right—that's the one."

Sandy squeezed his hand. "That other thing that happened to you today—I'm so sorry. You're innocent, I know that."

"I was set up by someone. I don't know why or how. But maybe I'll find out."

"I'm with you. All the way." He tried to sit up again but Gene pressed him back against the pillow. "What are we going to do now?"

"I'll think of something," Gene said. "I told Jill I've got two thousand dollars. That will hold us over for a little while. She knows that."

"When I'm well, I'll be able to make money for us. Maybe not a lot. But it will keep some food on the table. Wherever that table is going to be."

"Thanks, kid, we'll manage. Some long-ago friend posted bail for me. Ten thousand dollars. I'll have to get money for a lawyer, though. That will cost. The two thousand dollars won't last long."

The attendant entered the room signaling Gene it was time to leave.

"Will you come to see me in the morning?"

"I'll be here first thing."

"How will I know where you guys are?"

"I'll leave word at the desk. But we'll be here bright and early. Just as soon as visitors are allowed. We'll tell you all about our temporary home."

"I'm also sorry you lost your job. It's gonna be real rough finding another one, huh?"

"It might be easier than you think."

"What do you mean?"

"I'm not without my resources. I might be able to turn up with some money after all."

"That's great. How?"

"I can't tell you. Maybe I'll never tell you. But there is a way."

"Don't do anything dangerous. Don't get into trouble."

"I'll be okay." He kissed Sandy's forehead, then took his hand and pressed it against his cheek. "You'll pull through this."

"We'll pull through this," Sandy corrected him. "Jill, you, and me are in this together. I love both of you. We'll lick it."

"That's the spirit." Not wanting to witness the boy's pain for another second, Gene turned and headed for the door. He paused briefly. "I'll send Jill in now."

In the corridor he hugged Jill. "He can see you now."

"How is he?"

"I just know he's in a lot of pain. But he's covering it up real well."

"Wait for me," she said. "We've got to find ourselves a place to live."

"How well I know."

Jill kissed him on the cheek, then headed for Sandy's hospital room.

Spotting a bank of phones, Gene saw a free one. In the booth next to him, a large, fat black woman was shouting into the receiver. He's dead! They killed him. Stabbed him right in the gut. He didn't have a chance. All for some stupid little container of drugs."

Closing the booth behind him, although he couldn't block out her sobs, Gene reached into his wallet, searching for a slip of paper. Fortunately, he'd managed to write down the private unlisted phone number of Leroy Fitzgerald.

*****

There was still a little trace of light in the early evening sky as Buck, clad only in a white T-shirt and a pair of white shorts, stood at the gangplank of his yacht as it pulled up to his pier.

Susan was here to greet him. "That's one pair of legs you have. Not to mention everything else."

"I'd call that sexual harassment." The banter was similar to some vaguely remembered exchange they'd once had at the Examiner office. He eyed her lovely body. She, too, was clad in a pair of shorts. "You've got legs too." He smiled. "Even better than Pamela's."

She knew he was joking, but looked at him with a pretended offense. "Your old girl friend's lost her looks. I'm getting better looking every day."

He knew that was true. If anything she looked more incredibly beautiful than she had during their days at the university. Her body, slim and exquisitely formed, was like a piece of sculpture. He couldn't believe that this was his wife.

For the moment at least, he'd overcommitted himself emotionally. "My God," he thought to himself as he walked down the gangplank and into Susan's arms. "I'm out of control." Even as he gave her a deep kiss on the pier, he vaguely remembered, that in a moment of intense passion he'd grabbed Shelley and confessed his love for him.

The golden boy had taken this confession in his stride. "Tell me something I don't know," he'd said before plunging his sweet pink tongue deeper into Buck's mouth. Even as he was kissing Susan, he still felt the taste of Shelley on his lips. The boy's mouth had been sweet, perhaps enhanced by the brandy. But Susan's mouth tasted of old cigarette smoke, the way an ashtray smelled after a party. He backed away from her, but carefully so she wouldn't notice. He feared she smoked excessively when alone, no doubt to relieve much of the anxiety of her life, a lot of the anguish caused by himself.

He looked straight in her eyes. "Welcome to my island."

"Its reputation has preceded it." She mockingly poked him in the ribs. Her look was open, warm and inviting. "Forgive me," she said. "I'm just a little nervous. I don't know if this is a real marriage or not. I don't really know how to be."

"Don't worry. You'll be perfectly safe alone with me. I never take advantage of my employees."

"Sorry to hear that!" Her voice was deliberately flirtatious as she preceded him to an outdoor patio where Henry had arranged supper.

"I should say, former employee."

She stopped and looked back at him, as if she hadn't heard him correctly. "I don't get it. What's wrong?"

He spoke with great pain over the loss of the Examiner. "We're both out of a job," he said. "But not for long. I've got other plans. Even an offer for you."

"I'll find another job," she said. "I'm not worried about that. My mother wants me to quit the paper anyway and devote my time to writing a book."

"About what?"

"Buck Brooke I."

"Is she still trying to get that old turkey off the ground? I can't be a lot of help. All the big and private events in his life are still a secret. I think he'll go to his grave with his secrets. Some of them, I suspect, are pretty dark."

"I can imagine. Just like you."

"*Touché.*"

"What's that offer you have for me?"

"Word can't get out. But I'm tentatively considering buying the Okeechobee News. I think I'm going to have the money. Let them take the Examiner. We'll be back in fighting form. Once I'm in control our first story might be the Lolito ring. How would that be? Let the town know that a real kick-ass publisher has taken over."

"That would be sensational, but the investigation of the Lolito ring has broken down. I don't think it's going to get off the ground unless we come up with a strong lead."

"I can't tell you all the details, but I think I can trick Leroy Fitzgerald into letting me in on what I want to know."

"But why would he tell you anything? It doesn't make sense."

"It's a long and complicated story."

"You're wasting your time with Leroy. He'll tell you nothing. He's behind the whole thing. He'll throw you off course. We've got to find another way."

"Trust me."

"That I will never do. You're too devious. What was that offer you have for me? If you become publisher of the Okeechobee News, will you hire me as an obit writer?"

"Something even better than that. If I can secretly buy the paper, and I know they're in deep shit financially, I'll make you the publisher."

"You're kidding?"

"I'm perfectly serious. You're more than qualified. You'll make a lot of mistakes at first. But you'll learn. Quickly. I think you'd be a great publisher."

"But what would you do?"

"I'm considering another job offer. A well paying job, that is. At least I'll be able to afford you. I'm considering writing a book all my own. About Sister Rose. That's why I might become her media director for three years. I'll get not only the insight I need, but I'll probably pick up a Pulitzer Prize for my efforts. Not to mention nine million dollars I've been offered."

"This is too incredible for words. I can't believe you'd consider being the media director of a right-wing Christian movement. So-called Christians. Nazis might be the better term."

"We can't let our liberal sentiments get in the way of a bigger agenda. My book." He pushed the stone crabs away Henry had placed in front of him. He didn't have much of an appetite tonight, at least for food. He craved other things.

"Who could have predicted this?" she asked. "I still can't believe anything you're saying is true. You're going to crack the Lolito ring with the help of Leroy. Right! You're going to buy the Okeechobee News and make me the publisher. You're going to become media director for a pack of Christian fanatics, forgetting for the moment that if you attempt such a thing Calder Martin will surely have you killed."

"I know it sounds bizarre but that's life. We must not be afraid to face the surprises of the future."

"I think there will be quite a few of them," she said, devouring her stone crab. Unlike him, she seemed to have a hearty appetite tonight.

"We've got our whole lives ahead of us. Let's seize every opportunity."

"I'll go for it. That means I don't have to cover any more Kiwanis meetings."

"That's right. Of course, your salary will be a lot more."

"I'm expensive."

"I think I'll be able to afford you."

She reached over the table and ran her fingers along his left hand. "I think you can indeed."

Just then Henry appeared, informing Buck he had three urgent phone calls. All of them had come in at once.

Excusing himself, he went into his private library. He feared each of the calls might be quite confidential. Even though Susan was his wife, he didn't want her to be privy to any of them. This was not to be an open marriage.

As he shut the door behind him, an incredible reality came over him. Not once during dinner had she mentioned Gene's arrest to him. That could only mean one thing: she hadn't turned on a radio or TV since coming to the island. The news was being widely broadcast. He'd have to tell her after he took these calls. At this point he didn't know how she'd react. He was definitely going to let her know he'd posted bail.

The first call was from Uncle Milty. "Patrick went to the airport to meet Robert. But he wasn't on the flight. I've called everywhere. I've even hired a Miami detective agency. But Robert has up and vanished."

"Keep trying, baby. I'm half out of my mind."

Putting down the phone, he picked up the other line. It was Leroy Fitzgerald. "It's on for tomorrow night at eight o'clock. Be on time. Slip in through the back entrance. I don't want anyone to see you. You know the address. Are you still game?"

"I'm game, all right. Hot and horny."

"I've got the most delectable piece of boy ass in the whole fucking eastern seaboard lined up for you."

"Sounds very enticing. Count on me being there."

"By the way, the pictures of you came out just great. Just great. You photograph magnificently."

"Thanks for the compliment." He put down the receiver and switched to the other line. The third caller was Shelley. "She's taking it badly."

"What do you mean?"

"Rose. Your marriage to Susan. I never saw her like this. I think she's really fallen for you. She's drinking heavily and making all sorts of threats. You'd better come over to calm her down. There's got to be a way out of all this. Everyone's trying to get a piece of you. Rose. Susan. Robert. But what nobody knows yet is you belong to me."

"I don't belong to anybody."

"Do you remember what you just told me?"

"I'd rather forget."

"You're not going to forget it. I'm not going to let you forget it. You told me you loved me. You told me I gave you the most exquisite pleasure you've ever known in your whole life. Was that a lie?"

"No, God damn it! It was not a lie. I've got to go now. I have an urgent call coming in."

"I'll talk to you later."

"No, don't call me again."

"I said I'll talk to you later, and that's what I meant."

Shelley had such determination in his voice that Buck recognized, almost for the first time, there was a strong man hiding behind all that cherubic look. "I've really got to go."

"If you're out of my range for two hours—three at the most—expect a call from me. From this moment on, you and I are a thing."

"Okay, we're a thing. Now let me get off this phone."

"I love you, fucker." Shelley finally hung up.

On the other line, a doctor who spoke with a French accent came onto the phone. "The test. I know you've been calling the clinic here a lot. But we've had no information—that is, nothing specific until today. Your grandfather is eaten up with cancer. It was far more advanced than we ever thought. He must have been in great pain at all times but trying to conceal it. It's incredible. There is no hope. He has only days to live."

"I'll catch the next plane."

"He absolutely refuses to see you or anybody. He doesn't want you here. It is useless to fly over. We must respect his wishes. He has, after all, given us a huge donation for our research work. We're very grateful to him and we're going to make his final days as comfortable as possible."

"But I must see him!"

"There is no way. You cannot see him. If you come over, we'll bar the doors to you. I am so very sorry. But this is his wish, and we're going to respect that."

"I understand. What's your name if I need to call you back?"

"Dr. Euler."

"I see. Can I keep calling you? Will you let me know his condition?"

"You are his grandson and heir apparent. That is the least I can do. I'll keep you informed of his condition. That is all. You cannot see him."

"I really want to."

"It's impossible." Dr. Euler hung up.

Coming back onto the patio, he looked over toward Susan who'd finished her dinner without him. Sensing something was wrong, she got up from the table and walked over to comfort him.

"I've got some bad news. Two bulletins. One about old Buck, the other about Gene."

*****

Arriving at Leroy's condo complex, Gene was carefully cleared by reception. Without hesitation, Leroy agreed to let him come upstairs. Gene had already installed Jill in a little two-bedroom efficiency in a slummy part of town down by the East River. It consisted of only two small bedrooms, but it cost just sixty-five dollars a week and had a makeshift kitchen as well. It would have to do. They had no other choice at the moment.

Riding the elevator to the top floor, he blotted out the memory of his house in flames and Sandy's bad burns. There would be time to think of that horror later. Right now he had to divert his mind to more important matters: Making money.

Clad only in a very short silk bathrobe, Leroy opened the door and beamed at the sight of him. "What a thrilling surprise! No doubt here for a repeat performance. I can't believe I had such an effect on you."

Without saying a word, Gene barged into the apartment as if he owned it. "Yeah, I'm back."

"Let me get you a drink," Leroy offered.

"I need one."

At the bar, Leroy eyed him with a shrewd appraisal. "My, oh my, but you've been in the news lately. That story about you and that little girl sounds fishy. More like entrapment."

"It was!" Gene virtually shouted. "I was set up. But who did it?"

"I certainly didn't—not that I could." Handing Gene the drink, Leroy sat with him on the sofa. "My aim is to bring joy into your life. Not trouble." He placed his hand on Gene's knee. Leroy downed his drink and looked speculatively at Gene. "Losing your job on the force. Having those God damn Cuban bastards burn down your house. It seems you need some comfort, and you've come to the right place. After I give you a long, leisurely bath, I'll massage you." He ran his tongue around the rim of his glass. "Not with my hands, but with my tongue."

"Sounds tempting!" Gene said, barely able to conceal his rage at having put himself in Leroy's power. "But I fear I need more than that. I need money."

"I always knew your life would lead you into hustling. Don't worry. I have plenty of money. It depends on how far you're willing to go. There's five-hundred for the usual works."

"What do you mean?"

"If you're strictly rough trade."

"If I'm not?"

"We could easily turn this into a thousand-dollar night."

"What do I have to do?"

"Let me suck your tongue. I want you to kiss me. Really kiss me, then go down on me too."

"I'll think about it. But I'm going to need more than a thousand."

"That's higher than I've ever gone. But in your case, I'll make it one thousand five hundred."

"I was thinking somewhere in the neighborhood of ten thousand. I really need money."

"Wow! You are setting a high price."

"I don't mean just for our night together. You mentioned friends of yours. Friends that really dig me. I bet they're rich fags like you. Right?"

"I see what you mean." He got up and went to the bar and poured himself another drink. "My feverish brain is already going into overdrive. I think I could arrange quite a party. A party with your own private fan club, guys you probably don't know. They paid plenty for those pictures of you. I bet they'd pay a lot for the real thing. At least two-thousand dollars each for a long, all-day session."

"What do I have to do?" Gene asked apprehensively.

"Everything. You'll also have to agree to let us film it."

"A big order. But I'm real desperate. I really need the money. Let me think about it. Get up my courage. I don't know how I can make money so fast anywhere else."

"You can't," Leroy said, coming back over to the sofa. "You'll do it. There's no where else you can make big money like this. You'll agree to everything. I just know it." He reached down and took Gene's hand.

"Let's go have that bath together. I want to bathe every part of you. After I've dried you off and put you to bed, I want to give every inch of your body another bath. From your earlobes to your toes, I don't want to leave one dry spot on you."

Gene got up from the sofa. It wasn't real. It wasn't happening. But he found himself trailing Leroy to his bathroom. As he went down the corridor, he started removing his clothing piece by piece. At the door of the bathroom, he reached down to unbuckle his belt having already discarded his T-shirt and dress shirt.

"No," Leroy said, sitting on the closed lid of the toilet and motioning Gene to him. "That little pleasure I reserve for myself." His hands reached into the air to claim Gene's large metal buckle.

*****

Three o'clock in the morning found Buck alone on his patio where he'd romped with Rose and Shelley. Right now they seemed far removed from his life. He wondered if Rose had pulled herself together in time to greet Ronald and Nancy. He suspected she had. He couldn't really guess what role Shelley had played in that evening.

Still no word from Robert. Buck had placed a call to Uncle Milty at one that morning. Nothing. Robert had seemed to vanish.

Earlier in the evening, Susan had drifted off to his bedroom. He knew it was expected of him that he join her there. But somehow he'd lagged behind, finally drifting off to sleep after watching the two o'clock news with its sad, tragic report about Gene. It seemed he'd slept only an hour before waking up with a start.

He felt his island had been invaded but he wasn't certain. At first he feared Gene was here stalking them again. "Get a grip," he cautioned himself. He felt he was coming unglued.

It was here on this forlorn patio that Susan found him slumped over in a deck chair.

Not saying a word, she reached for his arm and, linked that way, led him down the stone path to the beach.

Clad only in his jockey shorts, he strolled along the white sands with her. Despite what was going on beneath its surface, the ocean appeared at rest. On the far horizon, the distant night lights of Okeechobee could be seen. The city gleamed at them.

"It's so beautiful here," she said in a voice so soft it was like a whisper.

"Mmmm," was all he could manage.

He didn't want to talk. Neither did she. At his little cabana on the beach, he went inside and brought back a big white beach towel, making a blanket for her.

She lay down on it, looking up at his nearly nude body, as he stood against the background of a sky where the first hint of dawn streaked through. Below him, she had a dreamlike quality to her, the kind of woman he used to think he wanted. These days he didn't know what he desired. He usually settled for what was in front of him. But settle was hardly the word. He felt the loveliest and most luminous people in the state were waiting to give themselves to him: Robert, Susan, Gene, Rose, and Shelley. But all except Susan were gone this morning. Here she was waiting for him. It was a honeymoon of sorts.

There was no compelling urgency to his love-making. Nothing was entered only for quick climax. He instinctively wanted to prolong it and he knew she did too.

When he'd finished plunging and darting, hungering and lusting for her body—when his surging blood was still, he lay in her arms, not wanting to move, to break the mood. For an hour or so, they had lain here as the morning sun slowly returned from the other side of the world. He'd watched sandpipers run up the beach as gulls circled overhead.

After drifting off, he'd awakened suddenly to find her still here, his need back again, stronger than ever. She seemed happy to have him wake up in her arms, and he sensed that she also had a strong desire for him. Putting his arms tightly around her, he buried his softly sucking lips in her neck, as she caressed his right ear with her long fingers.

There was a little moan he discovered that came from a deep recess in her throat. In his loving her, he gave and gave of himself until he could hear that little moan. When that sound became a loud gasp for breath, he knew he'd gone over the top with her.

The sun had burned away the dark shadows on the beach. Everything was streaked with red, orange and yellow; in the distance he could see the tall, slim black figure of Henry, slowly making his way down the path from the house with freshly brewed coffee.

"That silver pot belonged to Queen Victoria," he told her.

*****

After breakfast, Buck took Susan back to his bedroom to sleep. He left the doors open leading to the pool, and he drifted off in an apparent feeling of warmth and openness.

To Susan, the house was opulent, yet casual, so unlike her former barren apartment. The lush life of the island invaded every room. For a brief, groggy moment, she tried to lull herself into thinking there could be no death here, only life. Then troubling thoughts descended. She wanted to sleep as easily as he did, but she was concerned for their future. Did they have one? How many women had he taken to the island, seduced, then never invited back again? She resented herself for plaguing her mind with such questions, the answers of which could only cause her pain.

Cradled in his arm, she brushed aside such disturbing intrusions, drifting where he'd drifted—into a deep, deep sleep—her last vision that of the mid-morning sun reflecting its rays off the pool, which caused a brilliant light.

She didn't know how long she slept. Maybe two hours. She woke up, sensing a foreign presence in the house. But there was no one she could see except Buck beside her.

The heat of the day and the intensity of light coming from the pool told her it was around noon.

Her eyes traveled his large bed which was big enough to sleep four comfortably. The oversize pillows—so many of them—added a touch of decadence. He was still deep in sleep, looking like a man-child. His body was strong, well developed and mature, yet, caught in the naturalness of sleep, it had a touch of innocence. His blond hair fell over his forehead and his mouth, which hours before had brought her such pleasures, was half-open. She listened to the sound of his heavy breathing, and it thrilled her.

Knowing it was time for them to get up, she reached over and stroked him, feeling the muscles of his chest beneath the smooth skin. She played with the light brush of golden hair on his chest as she slowly slipped the sheet from his body, revealing his penis which lay curled over one thigh, comfortably at rest.

He twitched slightly as her mouth gently captured one of his brown-red nipples. Her tongue then began a graceful journey down through the hair of his chest to his stomach where her mouth opened to engulf his navel before continuing on its way to the golden tangle at his groin. He was waking up now as her fingertips lightly combed the bush of his pubis.

She felt it as he blew his breath out, then took a deep inhalation. First she went for his jewels, taking each one in her mouth separately, pressuring them between her palate and her tongue. Then her tongue climbed to the bulbous, swollen head of his penis, where it did a little dance on the tip before plunging down on him. She let the organ ease into the arch of her throat. That type of love-making, to which Gene had objected so violently, seemed to please Buck immeasurably. Soon he couldn't take any more, and he bubbled over. The first of several spurts splashed against her tonsils. She could feel his heat and intensity. When she'd drained him completely, his head fell back in the pillow, where he'd slumped in exhaustion.

As she raised her head, she was overcome with a strange feeling. She had the distinct impression that someone had invaded the bedroom during the heat of their love-making, and that Buck had seen who it was. She quickly brushed aside her apprehension, feeling that, if anybody, it would have been Henry.

In the shower, she bathed hurriedly, hardly drying herself before slipping into a white robe and heading for the living room. Before reaching it, she eyed Henry suspiciously. Seemingly oblivious to everything, he poured her a cup of black coffee from Queen Victoria's silver pot. Buck must have gotten up, too, because she heard the shower running in his bathroom.

To her surprise, when she did turn into the living room, Buck was sitting on the sofa, his back turned to her. How could he have showered and dressed so quickly? In fact, she still heard the sound of his shower. Surely he didn't leave it on, considering the water shortage on the island.

She slipped up behind him, covering his eyes with her hands and gently blowing a kiss into his ear.

The head jerked back and confronted her. It wasn't Buck at all.

It was Robert.

Chapter Eight

He looked at her for a long moment. Then he got up and glared at her. Long, lean and muscular, he radiated power, his beard like golden flecks against his tanned skin. He looked as if he hadn't shaved in two days. She found herself strangely drawn to him. His resemblance to Buck was amazing. She always thought he looked like a twin brother. He had the same thick blond hair, the deep blue eyes. At a distance, if she'd approached him on the beach, she'd think he was Buck.

Now a new realization came over her. Ever since their university days, Robert had artfully cultivated that resemblance to Buck until he'd become more and more like him every day.

Robert didn't say anything, but stood looking at her, as if filled with an inner torment. His lip quivered, and she instinctively found herself reaching for his arm, but she checked that impulse.

Then a dreadful feeling came over her. Robert had walked in on Buck and her unannounced. Henry was just too skilled as a servant to have done that. If walking in on that scene had caused such torment with Robert, the conclusion was obvious to her. Robert was in love with Buck.

Staring at his face, and witnessing the hurt and pain there, was the final proof Susan needed. She'd always known Robert loved Buck. But until today she hadn't realized the extent of that love. She feared it went beyond mere love into obsession. She also suspected that Buck did not fully return such intense love. It was almost as if Buck were the victim of Robert's obsession. She feared Buck was caught in a web, with Robert the spider. She knew that a world class beauty like Robert could bring great pleasure to any man or woman, but she feared there was a price to pay for that ecstasy. Buck, she knew, would soon learn what the price of that pleasure he'd enjoyed from Robert entailed.

Robert was the first to break the long silence between them. "Let's go for a walk down by the pier. It's a lovely day."

Without saying anything, she left the room with him and headed out to the pier. She could still hear Buck in the shower.

Out in the bright light of day, she turned to him. He'd put on a pair of extremely dark sunglasses to hide his eyes. He wore a beige linen suit, not removing the jacket even though the day was scorching.

"I was very sorry to hear of your mother passing away," she said. "Buck told me. He's been trying to get in touch with you. We didn't know where you were."

"Thank you. My mother is dead now. She disapproved of me all her life. She warned that a life of great unhappiness lay in store for me. She claimed I would perish in hell's fire because of the way I chose to lead my life."

"I am so very sorry she was intolerant."

He paused and moved closer to her as she too came to a standstill. She searched his eyes but could see nothing behind those dark glasses.

"I'm just as intolerant as my mother."

"I don't understand. Surely not." She really wasn't clear about his meaning or his intent.

"I cannot tolerate your marriage to Buck. You see, he belongs to me. Always has. Always will. For as long as we both shall live, he will always belong to me. There is no hope for you. All you can decently do at this point is to leave the island. From this day forth, your marriage to Buck will be in name only."

"Forgive me," she said, not bothering to conceal the anger in her voice. "I don't see what gives you the right to make such demands. Surely Buck has some say in this matter. It's his life."

"It's not his life. It's our lives. Mine and his. There is no room for you here."

"I can't possibly allow you to set such terms."

"I know the reasons for the marriage. Uncle Milty explained everything to me. Buck was forced to marry you. It is hardly a marriage based on love. Surely you admit that's true. Even you must admit that."

"Yes," she said weakly.

"And while you're at it, why not admit something else? You married Buck to see what you can get. I'm sure you'll drain him for plenty. After all, he's going to be very, very rich."

"I'm not quite the hooker you suggest. Of course, there are tremendous advantages for me in this marriage. I don't love Buck. Certainly not the way you do. I'm just getting to know him. I love his love-making. I'm sure if this continues, I'll be mad about the boy in just a matter of weeks and can't live without him."

"But your love-making with him isn't going to go on. This morning was your last session. He's got to stay married to you for financial reasons. Fuck that old fart, Buck I. He hates me. He's trying to control my Buck from the grave where he will soon be if I've been informed correctly."

"How do you propose to control Buck in such a way? On the one hand, you attack old Buck's control over his grandson, yet at the same time you're demanding complete control over Buck's emotional life."

"That's right," Robert said, resuming his walk, heading in the direction of a second boat anchored near Buck's yacht. The skipper of the craft called down to them, but Robert motioned for him to disappear for a moment while he spoke privately with her.

"Let's go aboard," Robert said.

Very reluctantly she followed him. She didn't really trust him but went aboard anyway, wanting to hear exactly what he had to say. All this banter was leading up to a very serious conclusion, and she couldn't walk away from the encounter without knowing the result. Exactly what was Robert planning for her?

He held the door open for her, and she entered a small stateroom. Pictures on the wall revealed that this was not Buck's boat but a yacht belonging to old Buck I. Somehow Robert had managed to acquire access to old Buck's yacht.

"Have a seat," he said. "Make yourself comfortable for some uncomfortable news."

She nervously sat down. Suddenly, she feared him as never before. She felt she'd been foolish to come aboard. It was a trick somehow. Was he going to kidnap her?

Robert reached inside his linen suit and removed a revolver. She recoiled in fear.

"I'm not going to kill you," he said. "Not now anyway. I'm only showing you this revolver to let you know how determined I am."

"Determined about what?" she said, sitting awkwardly on the edge of her seat.

"Determined that from this day forth, you and Buck will be married in name only. No more rolls in the hay. How can I prevent that? Not through him, but through you. If you ever attempt to be his wife in anything but name I'll kill you."

"You'd never get away with it. You'd be the first suspect. The insanely jealous boyfriend, and you are insane."

"Don't be a fool. Of course, I know I couldn't get away with murder. But I haven't told you the final part. After killing you, I'd put a bullet in my own head."

She stood up, wanting to flee from this stateroom but somehow not daring. "I think you mean everything you said. Every God damn fucking word of it."

"You've got that right, bitch." He moved menacingly toward her. Only one foot from her face, he removed his dark sunglasses. She stared into his blue eyes which were red no doubt from crying.

"Look into these eyes," he commanded.

She stared deeply at him.

"I'll repeat once again. I'll kill you. Then I'll kill myself."

She didn't need any more convincing, feeling he was perfectly capable of carrying out such a threat.

"You win. What do you want me to do?"

"I'm getting off this boat. You stay on. You'll be delivered back to your condo."

"But what will Buck say? What kind of excuse are you going to give him. How much of this are you going to tell him?"

"Don't you worry your pretty little head about this. I'll handle Buck just fine. Buck is, in fact, going to fly to Miami where we'll not only conduct a funeral for my mother, but he'll marry me. Uncle Milty and his friend Patrick are making the arrangements right now. My marriage to Buck will be a real marriage, not the sham yours is."

"I see." She sighed. "I don't want to die. I think I can have a great life. My whole world's about to open up. I'm going to write a book about old Buck I. Our Buck..."

"My Buck," Robert interrupted her.

"Yes, your Buck has virtually promised me the job of publisher of the Okeechobee News which he plans to buy if he can."

"In other words, you've got a lot to live for. You don't want to fuck it up, now do you?"

"No, because deep down I don't really love Buck. I find him sexy and attractive. But I don't love him. You not only love him, he's an insane obsession of yours. I don't think you love him as much as you want to possess him."

"That will be my business. Buck and I will work out our relationship in any way we see fit."

"Good luck to both of you. And congratulations on your upcoming marriage. As for me, I'm taking your suggestion and getting the hell out."

"This is the smartest move you've ever made. We'll keep our conversation private, if you don't mind. If you don't keep it private, you risk the consequences."

"It'll be private."

"Fine," he said, putting his sunglasses back on. As he turned to leave, she heard the motors starting. He looked back at her before going on deck again. "He's made love to you. Now you know what I'm fighting for. As you know from having tasted him, Buck is no mortal man. He's a God. An Adonis from heaven. Even the smell of his socks after he's been jogging in the park is like a divine aroma."

"Fuck that!" she said. "His socks stink when he's hot and sweaty. He's no God. He's just a man. God was kinder to him than he was to most men. But he's still a man."

He shrugged. "I'm joining him now. You may think he's just a man. But I'm going to worship him like a God. That's my role in life."

She said no more, turning from the sight of Robert, sensing madness here. He left the stateroom.

After she'd sailed away, and minutes had gone by, she went back out on the deck. In the distance she could still see him clad in his linen suit, standing on the pier watching her disappear.

She turned from the sight of him and the life that might have been. Determined, she would not return to that island again. Being in Buck's arms had been bliss. But she wouldn't experience that again. It was best that it had ended before it had begun. Her challenge lay in conquering this city, not coming between Buck and Robert in their upcoming predictable tragedy. She sucked in the fresh breezes of the sea. Out here everything was clean and pure. She was not despondent. There was just too much hope in her for that. She suddenly burst into tears but they didn't last long. By the time she landed she would have repaired her face and would be ready to assault what new challenges awaited her.

When she got back to the condo, she decided to call her father and invite herself over to see him. It'd been a long time. Sometimes a girl needed to visit her dad, and this was one of those times.

*****

In the bathroom, Buck finished showering, deliberately dragging out the act. He was confused and uncertain as to how to handle Robert. Of all times for him to have walked in. Yet, he felt, such a confrontation had been inevitable. Buck wished he could have postponed it. But would any time be right?

When he opened the shower curtain, he fully expected Robert to be here waiting for him with a thick towel to dry him off. Or had that wonderful, sensual pleasure become part of their past?

After drying himself off, he covered his nudity with the wet towel and headed into his living room. No one was there. He looked into his bedroom where he found Henry changing the sheets. He pretended to see nothing but Buck secretly knew he was aware of everything going on.

"Where's Susan?" Buck asked.

"Miss Susan returned to the mainland."

"What? But my yacht is still here."

"Miss Susan took old man Buck's yacht. Mister Robert came over on that boat with a crew. He said Uncle Milty let him have it."

"I see." Buck was completely confused. If Uncle Milty knew that Robert was descending on the island, why didn't he call? His attorney/friend usually looked after him better than this. "Where is Robert? Did he go back with Susan?"

"He went for a walk on the beach."

"Thanks." Forgetting to dress and with the towel draped around him, he ran down the beach, increasing his pace when he spotted Robert in the distance. He caught up with him. "Please come here and give me a kiss and don't take your tongue out of my mouth until at least an hour's gone by."

Tears in his eyes, Robert turned to face Buck. Buck had never known such hurt as that showing in his friend's face.

"How could you?" Robert demanded to know.

"You know I had to marry her. Old Buck will cut me off without a penny. I not only had to marry her, but I've got to stay married to her."

"You shouldn't have brought her here. This is our island. It belongs just to us."

"I'll never do it again, I promise you that."

Robert moved closer to him. "That's one promise you're going to keep. At least you didn't bring her to our home."

"I'd never do that, and thank God you're calling it our home. I should have kept the marriage with Susan a marriage in name only. I was wrong. But it's all your God damn fault for leaving me. You know I'm emotionally unstable. I come completely unglued when you're not around to care for me."

"I believe that's true. I'm back now. You belong to me. I've come back from Miami to take what's mine."

Buck put a broad, firm hand on Robert's shoulder. "That's the way to talk. You're my lover. You drove me crazy when I couldn't get in touch with you. It's true: I belong to you. I always will." His grip on

Robert's shoulder tightened. "Do I have to beg you to let me suck your tongue?"

"I should make you beg. I should punish you some way."

"I don't want to be punished. I want to be loved. You're one hell of a good-looking guy."

Through tears, Robert half-smiled, his eyes dancing. "That's because I look so much like you."

"I never thought of it that way."

Robert still didn't let Buck possess his mouth. He held back. At first Buck was tempted to grab his lover and force himself upon Robert. But he decided to let Robert come to him at his own pace. Buck knew he'd betrayed Robert and he couldn't expect him to rush back into his arms immediately.

Robert took Buck's hand in his, signaling that he was taking Buck back. Still dressed in his linen suit, although he'd removed the jacket, Robert walked along the beach.

Buck walked beside him, his hand enclosing Robert's in a tight grip. "Now that you're back, there will be changes."

"What do you mean?" Robert asked.

"I mean, our love-making is going to take on a new dimension. This oral stuff is great. It's the most fantastic love I've ever known. I don't want to give up one bit of that. But from now on, I'm going to spend at least one hour of every day with my tongue buried up that rosebud of yours, licking and slurping until I have you squirming. Then I'm going to give you such a deep penetration you'll be begging me to stay in you forever. I want to totally possess you. I don't need Susan or anyone. I want you, and I'm going to have you. In fact, I don't think you're going to get off this beach without getting raped. I'm stronger and bigger than you are. I can overpower you and take what I want. Right now and forever I want that ass of yours. I don't know why I've denied myself your ass all these years. In the last few days it's all I could think about."

"You really mean that?" Robert turned and looked deeply into Buck's eyes. "I can't tell you how long I've waited for you to stake a claim on that part of me. It's been too long. What were we thinking? It was insane to have denied ourselves this. For whatever reason."

"I'd like to remedy that right now."

"I'll remember this day forever." Robert grabbed hold of Buck, pressing his mouth hard against his. Holding Robert in a tight embrace, Buck plunged his tongue into Robert's mouth, exploring every crevice there, even polishing Robert's teeth. Just as fast as Robert could produce saliva, Buck swallowed it. It was as if he were sucking the life from Robert.

Robert's hands had ripped the towel from Buck, completely exposing him on the beach. Lovingly but with an aura of possession, he fondled Buck's balls as his friend drained all the pleasure he could from his mouth.

When Buck broke away from Robert's lips, he descended on his friend's ears, lovingly kissing and biting each lobe, before plunging his tongue deeper inside for a penetrating bath. Between inserting his tongue in each of Robert's ears, he cupped each of the cheeks of Robert's buttocks, fondling the mounds with a love and devotion he'd never displayed before. With his free hand, he began to unbutton Robert's shirt. He wanted to get to his friend's nipples, to love them, bite them, and suck them as he never had before.

"Your balls feel bigger than ever, if that's possible," Robert said.

Buck kissed Robert really hard, then took his tongue and slurped Robert's lips. "They're yours, baby. To drain for the rest of your life."

"Are you still going to marry me?" Robert asked, tracing his fingers along Buck's fully aroused shaft.

"I can't wait. There's only one problem."

Robert broke away slightly in astonishment. "What?"

"Do you believe in sex before marriage?"

Robert laughed slightly as his hand moved along Buck's thigh, feeling the silky hairs here. "Do I ever believe in sex before marriage!" His face up close to Buck's, he kissed Buck's nose and ran his tongue over Buck's closed eyelids before returning to his nose. Expertly he inserted his tongue inside Buck's nostrils.

Buck was gripping the cheeks of Robert's ass more firmly than ever. Robert had him moaning.

"Let's go to our little secret place off the beach," Robert said. "I want to test you out. See what kind of husband you'd make before I'll agree to marry you."

Buck put his arm around Robert and guided him along the flower-lined path leading to a little gazebo where they often used to go for drinks. "I'm ready for that test. Once I get inside you, you'll beg me never to take it out."

"That's my kind of man."

A huge ocean wave crashed across the beach, but Buck turned his back to it, not really noticing. "Welcome home, my sweet man."

At the gazebo, a nude Buck removed Robert's shirt which he had already unbuttoned. His hands were almost trembling in anticipation as he reached for the buckle on Robert's trousers. On his knees, he hesitated for only a moment before unbuckling the belt and unzipping the pants. He pulled them down, burying his face in Robert's white jockey shorts. With his teeth, he pulled down Robert's shorts, completely exposing him.

Robert was fully aroused, and he became even more so when Buck planted tender wet kisses on the tip of his penis. He gently lowered Robert onto the sofa in the gazebo, as his tongue caressed Robert's balls and began its long wet trail to what was his real target for the day. Robert raised his legs in the air and rested them on Buck's shoulders. Then he reached down and parted the cheeks of his ass, stretching himself as far as he could as he awaited the invasion of Buck's tongue.

*****

On the Florida patio of her father, Jim, Susan enjoyed her first drink of the day, taking off her shoes and propping them up on a chaise longue. Instead of a strong drink, her father preferred to go into the kitchen and prepare himself a pot of fresh coffee. Ingrid wasn't here. She was in Fort Lauderdale giving a speech to an environmental group with an agenda to save the Everglades.

Before he went for his coffee, Susan had informed Jim of the events of the day, including her threat from Robert. She knew he wouldn't say something stupid, such as advising her to go to the police.

"Take his threat very seriously," Jim had cautioned. "Robert may be a bit insane. But understand that he was driven there by love. Or is the word obsession?"

When Jim returned, Susan questioned him again. "I guess I'll never understand men. Robert seems to want to own Buck."

"So he does, but let's not make Buck blameless in this whole thing. Obviously Buck wants this type of devotion or he'd kick Robert out on his ass. After paying him off, of course."

"Do you agree I shouldn't tell Buck what happened between Robert and me? The threats, everything."

"I do indeed," he said, sipping his coffee black the way he liked it. "I don't think it would do any good. It might flatter Buck to think Robert cares that much. Enough to give his own life. That's true devotion."

"I think for me to come between them is dangerous."

"Stay out of it. Maintain the marriage. But at a safe distance. You're lucky this happened right at the very beginning. Before you fell in love with Buck. You're not in love with him, are you?"

"I don't think so." She sighed, finishing off her drink and getting up to pour herself another one. At the canopied outdoor bar, she paused. "I could fall in love with him. It would be so easy. But I'm not in love with him now. I don't think I even know him. I've felt from the first day I met him that I only knew one personality. Buck is hard to figure out. There are many parts of his personality that inhabit strange, dark worlds. I don't think Robert has a clue as to what is going on with Buck."

"What do you mean?"

"His relationship with Gene, for one thing. I think Gene and Buck have a powerful relationship, even more powerful than the link he has with Robert. But I think his relationship with Gene is so strong it's likely to explode at any moment. It's a relationship that seems doomed—and not just because of Robert, but because of Gene. That's one fucked up former husband of mine."

"I know," Jim said wearily. "Arrested again on the same charge. But this time it seems different. As if he were set up somehow."

"I feel that way too." She poured herself a drink, tested it for strength, approved, and came to stand before her father as he rested in his favorite outdoor armchair. "Will you represent Gene? I know he doesn't have much money. I'll pay you myself. After all, I'm married to a multi-millionaire, if in name only."

"I knew you'd ask me, and I've thought it over. Providing you will give me wide berth, I'll do it. I'll definitely take his case, and I'll win."

"I knew I could count on you." She bent down and kissed him on the forehead, noticing how thin his gray hair was. "You've always been here for me."

"And I'll be here again and again. Any time of the day or night you need me."

"Even for my present tragedy?"

He eyed her sternly and continued to sip his coffee. "Your marriage is not a tragedy. It would be a tragedy if you loved Buck. You care for him. You feel a compassion for him. There is, I'm sure, a strong sexual attraction. Hell, if I were thirty years younger, I'd go for the hunk myself."

"Since when did you turn gay?"

"I'm not gay. But I had a couple of affairs with guys in my university days. One of them I really cared about, and then along came Ingrid. She wouldn't want me telling you this."

"I'm not shocked. You were always liberal, always experimental. You've always had gay friends. In fact, I think half of your clients are gay. You have almost as many gay clients as Uncle Milty."

"Well, not that many. Milty is the legal queen of Okeechobee. But with all the millions your husband is going to come into, I suspect Old Milty will have to work full time for Buck. Maybe I'll run around picking up his discarded clients. That should prove interesting."

"You may not know this, but Uncle Milty may be spending a lot of time acquiring the News for Buck."

"That makes sense. Buck's lost the Examiner. He's going to have millions to burn. Right now the News is in deep financial shit. They need a bail-out. New blood. Buck might be their salvation."

"Or I could be their salvation."

"I don't understand," he said.

"Buck said if he can get the News, he'd make me the publisher. What do you think of that?"

"I'm a bit awed. I think that is no idle threat on his part. It might happen. I think you'd make a damn good publisher."

"Of course, if you want to be cynical, you could say he's buying me off. Giving me a paper to put to bed instead of a husband to put to bed."

"Whatever. If you learn the rules, and play by them, you might have a great marriage. You'll be rich. Successful. Your career will soar. Speaking of that, I definitely think you should take up Ingrid's offer to write that book on old Buck Brooke. It might be a bestseller. God knows, there's a lot to report on with that one."

"I might do all those things. The paper. The book. But what about love? Where's the love to come from, or don't you think I need it?"

"All of us need love. I hardly think Buck is going to object to your having an affair or two on the side."

"I don't even seem capable of managing that. Where are the boys? All of them in Okeechobee seem to be sleeping with each other."

"There is one that I would virtually guarantee is straight."

"A straight man in Okeechobee? I don't believe that."

"Don Bossdum's back in town. He called for your phone number. He tried to reach you at the Examiner. No such luck there."

"Don Bossdum. Who could forget him? Other than Gene and Buck, he was the most pursued man at the university. Football captain. Big and blond. Pamela told me he was a terrific lover. In fact, he looks a bit like Buck. Maybe he would be a good substitute for my husband."

"Why don't you call him? After the university, he said he got married to a Cuban girl in Miami. But it didn't last long. There was some minor scandal, I think. I don't know what it was. Nothing important, I would suppose."

"He didn't expose himself to a little girl, nothing like that?"

"Nothing like that. I think his wife caught him cheating. I really don't know."

"Well, if it's nothing more important than that." She inhaled the fresh air as some distant memory came back to her. "I vaguely recall some rumor. Something about Don getting involved for a while with Rose Phillips."

"That I doubt. There are so many rumors spread. But what would a handsome football hunk like Don Bossdum, with every girl in the state of Florida throwing herself at him, want with a vintage tomato like our dear Sister Rose?"

"You've got a point there. She could be his grandmother. So I'll give the stud a ring. Maybe find out what all the excitement is about."

As she moved to gather her things, Jim got up and walked toward her. "Do you really have to go? Why don't you stay here and cook dinner for me?"

"There are few men I cook dinner for. But as soon as I get settled in, I'll invite you and Ingrid over to my new condo. It's spectacular. Another fringe benefit of being Mrs. Buck Brooke III."

"We miss you," he said, kissing her lightly on the lips. "You don't come around very much any more."

"I'll come more often." She paused as if she'd forgotten something. "Did you write down Don's number?"

"I'll get it for you." He exited quickly and returned with a piece of paper. "Here it is. Enjoy."

She lingered for one final moment. Another disturbing memory flashed through her brain. "If I recall, Don was rumored to be involved not only with Rose, but with her son, Shelley. Some disgruntled servant once came to the Examiner. She'd been fired and wanted to sell us an exposé about the whole thing."

"Doesn't something like that happen every day at a newspaper office? She was probably lying. Don and Rose—that's a bit much. Don and Shelley. Get real!"

"It does tax the imagination a bit," she said, "but I've been burned so many times I don't want to walk into another bizarre sexual thing."

"I understand. I think you'll be totally safe with Don. Your biggest problem with him is that he'll probably want to take you to a football game instead of a night club."

"I guess so." After kissing Jim again, she wandered out to her car. A vague apprehension had settled over her. As she got inside her car and started the engine, she headed for the causeway and the beach. At first she was tempted to visit Hazel and see how she was, but decided to spend the night alone, getting used to her new condo. She fully suspected she'd be spending many a night there alone, unless that good-looking and charming Don Bossdum had other plans for her. On second thought, why not spend the night with Don Bossdum?

*****

Totally nude and completely exhausted, Gene lay in Leroy's bed alone. Leroy had to visit a photo lab that secretly developed film for him.

Gene had just placed a call to Jill, who was doing fine in their bleak efficiency, and another to Sandy. Sandy's pain had eased, and there was hope he'd be out of the hospital in a day or two. When Gene got some sleep, he was going to move them into a better apartment right in Leroy's building. Leroy was going to make the rental terms very favorable, providing Gene would continue to "cooperate."

Gene assured him he'd keep putting out as he had today with Leroy's rich friends, only he planned to get a real job too. He knew no one would hire him except one man. That man wouldn't want to give him a job, but Gene planned to insinuate himself into his life whether welcome or not. Somebody out there was playing rough with him, and he was determined to fight back.

He'd had to leave his new address with the police since he was out on bail, with a trial pending. Through that link, Jim Howard had called Jill and left a message. He claimed he wanted to represent Gene and would do so for free. On hearing this offer, Gene at first wanted to turn it down until he realized he'd accepted that bail money from Buck. If he'd done that, why not accept free legal representation?

To defend himself would costs thousands, and the ten thousand dollars he'd recently earned he wanted to use to rebuild his life and to help Jill and Sandy so they wouldn't be forced to go back on the streets.

He'd never gotten along with his former father-in-law, but right now he didn't see that that mattered. Other than Buck's so-called "Uncle Milty," Jim Howard was the best attorney in Okeechobee.

He'd even gotten a black man off on a murder charge in a case that Gene had been involved in. Gene and his fellow officers had all the evidence they needed to convict the defendant who'd killed another black man in a drug deal. But through a series of legal maneuverings, hinging on technicalities, Jim because of a brilliant defense allowed the murderer to go free. The mostly black jury had returned a verdict of not guilty, even though the defendant had clearly killed his fellow drug dealer. Gene figured if Jim could get someone off for murder, he could bail him out of this obviously trumped-up charge.

Before falling into a deep and much-needed sleep, Gene relived the events of the past few hours. All his life he'd been contemptuous of whores, and now he'd become a performing whore himself. It was a decision deliberately made. No one forced him into it. He wasn't even blaming his present troubles. He was a fully mature adult and had made a conscious decision to pick up much needed money in this way. He certainly wasn't proud of what he had done and what he'd agreed to do for Leroy in the next few days.

His life could have turned out real good like Buck's, but those breaks never came to him. Both had parents who'd died relatively early in their lives. Gene used to identify with Buck as "a fellow orphan." Except Buck's parents had been killed in an accident, and Gene's parents had died within a year of each other, both from cancer.

Sometimes late at night Gene feared the same cancer was eating through his body as well. Unlike some people who could imagine themselves growing older, Gene never could. He felt he'd be forever young, and the implication of this was all too clear. He'd die young too. Lately his entire life had taken on a surreal quality. For some reason, he feared the end of his life might be approaching. He felt he'd die by violent means. They would get him yet, and he didn't even know who "they" were.

He would not go down easily. He intended to fight back against them with all the power remaining in him. His most recent arrest, he feared, was only their first assault on him. There would be others. He had to find out who was doing this to him. Who set him up. When he found that out, he'd also figure out a way to strike back.

Lying in this bed with its rumpled sheets, he could still feel the devouring mouths taking pleasure from his body. With a cameraman recording everything, five men—all friends of Leroy's—had descended with sucking mouths and lapping tongues to taste every crevice of his body. He'd never been devoured so hungrily and in such a way before. The men were physically disgusting to him, often overweight and in one case at least seventy years old. But he'd given them what they wanted: his flesh. It was as if they'd wanted to suck the blood from him.

Even when he rose from the bed and had momentarily escaped the camera, the seventy-year-old man had followed him into the bathroom lined with nude photographs of Gene. At first Gene assumed that the man had wanted to watch him urinate but it soon became clear that the pathetic looking creature was begging Gene to use his open, gaping mouth instead of the toilet stool. Closing his eyes, Gene inserted his cock into the man's mouth. The old man eagerly swallowed every drop, continuing to suck and drain even when Gene had fully relieved himself.

"That's the sweetest cocktail I've ever tasted in my life, even sweeter than that of my sixteen-year-old grandson." The man slowly rose from the floor. Standing before Gene, he'd fondled Gene's balls as he licked his lips, savoring the final taste. "I'm going to arrange through Leroy some very private sessions with you. I've got a place up in Jupiter where I go for fun and games. You won't believe what I've got planned for you."

"I can believe it," Gene said, turning away in disgust, although concealing the loathing on his face.

Gene had returned to the bed and the camera. Here more eager, hungry mouths had waited for him. The men had sucked him with great excitement. Their prodigious talents in fellatio brought him to the brink. As his first scalding spurt of jism exploded, a mouth had withdrawn itself suddenly so that all of them could witness his explosion, especially the camera. After he'd delivered his last blast, mouths had fallen on him again to taste the hot sweetness of his sperm.

As he lay gasping for breath on the bed, the men had turned him over, prying open his ass cheeks for their own amusement and to record his most private spot for the benefit of the camera. Even though they'd drained him in front, those same devouring mouths descended on him, licking, tasting, probing with their tongues. The seventy-year-old man firmly clamped his mouth on Gene's anus and inserted his tongue so deeply into Gene he felt he was getting fucked. After five minutes, two of the other younger men pulled him away from Gene. Frustrated and cursing them, the old man then descended to Gene's toes where he proceeded to devour each of them on each foot with a tenacity Gene had never known. There was no slowing of his rhythm. In spite of his age, he'd never stopped. The other men had taken breaks and gotten a drink, but through the five-hour ordeal the old man's mouth never left Gene's body, descending at one point to bathe each of Gene's arm pits with his tongue.

The climax of the long ordeal had arrived when each of the men had lined up on the bed, each demanding to be penetrated by Gene. He'd serviced all of them, never losing his erection. As kneading, stroking hands worked his body, he'd entered each of them, fucking wildly and brutally, not caring whether he hurt of not. He was inflamed and his cock seemed to follow a life of its own, making each cry out at the enormity of his penis. Each of them felt him in the deepest recesses of their bodies, and each had surrendered to him. He was no longer their hired whore. He was their master and they were forced to service him. As he plunged for a final time, the fifth man had screamed when Gene had penetrated him. He begged Gene to take it out. "It's killing me," the man had yelled. But he was helplessly pinned down. His obvious pain seemed to excite the other men who held him down. It was this man that Gene decided was going to get another scalding load from him. His cock had seemed to double in girth and length as it pounded into the screaming man. Gene himself screamed at his final orgasm. All he remembered after that was more devouring mouths descending on him to lick him clean. As he sat up, he noticed that the old man had finally quit sucking on parts of Gene's body and was eagerly exploring the ass of the man he'd raped, trying to suck out Gene's deposit there.

The victim of the rape had been sobbing but his tears had subsided as he looked over at Gene and ran his fingers through Gene's hair. "That was the first time I've ever been fucked. I want many more private sessions with you. I want you to do that again and again—except I want you to wear your police boots, a police cap, and a short sleeved blue police shirt with the emblem of the department sewn on. And nothing else."

"That can be arranged, baby," Gene said huskily. "But it'll cost plenty."

"With me, money is no object," the man said. "There is just one catch."

"Oh, God, here it comes," Gene said.

"Nothing spectacular. You'll have to agree to do it in front of my wife. She loves to watch."

Gene closed his eyes. He felt he'd earned his money and it was time for them to go, as he wanted sleep. He was completely exhausted. Gradually after giving him final licks and tongue lashings, all the men had gone except the seventy-year-old man whose tongue remained glued to Gene's ass.

Long after the others had left Leroy's condo, the man wouldn't leave him alone. It took all of Leroy's strength to pull him away from Gene and to usher him from the apartment. The old man vowed to watch the film of Gene's seduction every night for the rest of his life. "Who would have ever thought that an old geezer like me would get to eat Gene Robinson. If you live long enough, you get to see it all."

*****

Sleep would not come as she tossed in her luxurious satin-padded bed, reaching out and clutching a fluffy pillow several times, imagining it was Buck. But no sofa pillow could be the stand-in for the rock-hard body of her man. Even though she'd run out the door at the news of his marriage, and had reacted hysterically at first, she felt calmer now. The announcement of his marriage was but a temporary setback for her. Like Scarlett O'Hara, one of her role models, she would begin plotting even before morning on ways to get him back.

What could some silly little beauty queen like Susan Howard who covered university news offer him that she couldn't? In her mind, it was tantamount to the horror as depicted in Sunset Boulevard of Joe Gillis deserting Norma Desmond for that weak little piece of liver as portrayed by the forgettable Nancy Olsen. Joe Gillis did walk out on Norma Desmond, but what did it get him? A bullet in the back and a dead swim in a pool with his face in the water.

If Hollywood ever remade that movie, Rose felt she'd be perfect for the part of Norma Desmond. By the time the script was written and the movie shot, Buck would be ripe enough to play Joe Gillis, a man in his early 30s.

Considering his maturity, she still couldn't believe Buck was only twenty-seven years old. She'd known many men that age—in fact, many men who worked for her temple—were that age. They seemed like children to her. Buck was certainly a mature man for his age. She felt he was an adult in every sense of the word and was relieved that he hadn't flatly rejected her offer to become her media director, although Calder Martin felt he had squatter's rights on the post.

That job was but one of many temptations she planned to place in front of Buck. She was in love with the man and was still not aware how it'd happened so suddenly. She'd known many men, even one as well endowed and good looking as Buck. That Don Bossdum. But from the moment Buck had penetrated her, she was in love with him, although not knowing why. It was the feel of him, the way a lock of his blond hair had fallen and kept grazing her forehead as he worked to bring her the deep satisfaction she wanted and demanded in a man.

Many men like Barry Collins had moved over her body and had penetrated her, even bringing her to climax. But they were inadequate. They never reached a spot deep within her body that made her want to belong to them forever. Buck did that for her. Her climax with him was the most spectacular she'd ever known. It literally made her scream, and no man had ever done that for her, except perhaps that one night with Don Bossdum.

He'd been special too. But, unlike Buck, he was so immature. When he wasn't fucking, his first and foremost specialty, he liked to spend endless hours watching sports broadcasts or working out in the gym to fine-tune an already perfect body. His idea of a good night out on the town was to go to a sportsbar and watch reruns of football games on giant videos while drinking beer with his cronies. She couldn't go to places like that. In fact, she didn't dare appear at any event that served alcohol. Don had never understood how limited her choices were because of her overwhelming fame.

Right this moment she wanted sleep more than anything else. She reached for a scarlet satin domino and put it over her eyes, as if it could shut out the world or even blind her mind to her increasingly agitated environment. She felt a noose was about to tighten around her neck. She'd accepted a check for twenty-million dollars, which she'd deposited in a bank in Vienna, and very soon she was going to have to start to sing and dance in public to earn that much money. There was a promise of more money to come, but she had to convince certain interests that she could deliver on her first act before she saw any more millions. With Buck at her side, she felt she could perform and do what was expected of her.

The truth was, she wasn't the powerful personality she conveyed in front of TV cameras. She was a weak and frightened creature who needed a good, strong man behind her who would protect her even from herself, because she feared at times she might be her own most destructive agent. In Buck, she felt she'd found a man strong enough to guard her against harm. She wanted him back, and just knew in her heart she'd win him to her side. She realized he had to be at least fifty percent gay, maybe even seventy-five percent gay, but no man who hated women could fuck like that. She'd tried it with gay men before. Some even managed to reach climax, but it was nothing when compared to Buck. He was truly a man who could bring satisfaction to both men and women.

She smiled with a certain confidence. To lure Buck into her net she had the greatest arsenal of all. Shelley. If all her beauty, wealth, and power weren't enticement enough, surely Shelley was. Although she pretended to hold her son in disdain, she was also in awe of his beauty. The word luminous kept cropping up whenever anyone spoke of her son. It wouldn't take Shelley long to make Buck fall in love with him. He'd seduced some of her former lovers who'd presumably never had sex with a boy before. There was a magic allure about him that was captivating. For all she knew, Buck was already falling under the boy's spell. Shelley was definitely her secret weapon.

As a film of sleep began to drift over her body, she turned over and tried to shut out the world. Already a plan was formulating in her brain to have Buck racing over to Paradise Shores. It was a bit risky—maybe lethal—but she was willing to take the chance. Her mind was deep at work plotting how to make her scheme work. At least it was better for her to think about that than the disastrous dinner she'd had with Ronald and Nancy Reagan.

*****

In the comfort of their island bedroom, Buck lay nude on the bed, enjoying the soft lights of the patio. Also nude, Robert had inserted himself between Buck's legs where he was worshipping Buck's balls with this tongue and lips. It was as if he were rewarding them for having given him such exquisite pleasure.

There was no doubt that Buck's life had changed that afternoon. A new doorway of pleasure with Robert had opened for him. In spite of all the opportunities, he had never penetrated him before. In some murky part of his brain, he'd always felt it was the last frontier with Robert. As long as he was being serviced or even doing a little servicing himself, he somehow secretly believed that didn't make him gay. Fucking a man made him gay, and that's why his experience with Gene had blown his mind. At this point in his life he didn't care about such a distinction since he was preparing to marry the man he'd so recently fucked. He'd crossed the frontier, first with Gene and now with Robert, and was God damn happy he'd done so. It had been a thrilling experience for both Robert and him.

At first he'd had a hard time achieving entry, as Robert had winced at the pain and had even cried out, "It's killing me." Buck attempted to withdraw, but Robert had grabbed him, digging his nails into his back and demanding he continue his assault. Inch by inch, Buck had continued to penetrate his friend who was goading him on in spite of his anguish.

In three, maybe it was five, minutes Robert had seemed to open to him. Instead of pain, the most exquisite ecstasy had come over his face, as he'd opened his mouth and stuck out his tongue for Buck to suck. As Buck had fucked him, Robert's body had come alive as never before. In spite of the initial awkwardness, he had discovered that Robert was a true bottom. At last he'd found the total sexual gratification that had eluded him for so long. Buck could see that in Robert's face. He'd been transported to a world of sexual bliss never known to him before. Buck had nibbled Robert's ear and licked his neck, sometimes descending to devour that very neck even though he knew it would cause a hickey or maybe more than one. He couldn't help himself. Robert was giving him too much pleasure. At one point he even found himself biting Robert's neck really hard. The thrills going through his body were of such intensity he had to relieve the pressure in some way.

After one very deep plunge Robert had screamed. At first Buck thought it was the pain. But it was soon clear Robert was experiencing a shattering orgasm. Without completely removing himself from the young man's body, Buck lowered his lips and mouth over Robert to reward himself with the liquid offering of his friend. Robert's semen had never tasted sweeter. Mounting him again, Buck had continued his deep penetration of Robert. Amazingly, before Buck achieved his own shattering climax, Robert had reached orgasm two more times. He'd seemed thrilled beyond his wildest expectations to have Buck inside him, and to judge by the way he'd held onto Buck he never wanted him to leave his body.

When Buck's own climax finally did explode, and he'd held it back for as long as he could, he'd collapsed onto Robert and didn't want to pull out. Buck had found himself crying at the sheer joy of what he'd just experienced. Robert licked Buck's tears away. When Buck had opened his eyes, he was greeted with Robert's smiling face. There was such gratification here that Buck knew he had fulfilled Robert as his friend had never been satisfied before.

The memory of such pleasure still raced through his body as he reached down and ran his fingers through Robert's beautiful silky blond hair. His friend was back at his side. He knew that Robert was so hopelessly in love with him at this point, and maybe forever, that Robert would never leave him again. Robert's intensity of wanting to possess

Buck used to disturb him. Now he welcomed it. He needed this complete adoration and acceptance from another human being. It made him feel more like a man in charge of his life and in control of his environment. He didn't know if any of those thoughts were true, but Robert's worship of him made him feel powerful. Did he dare say it? Yes, powerful enough to conquer the world.

Buck eased gently into the soft comfort of the bed, enjoying the feel of Robert's beautiful pink tongue as it paid homage to his balls. Buck was proud of their shape and size and had been since he was fourteen years old. He was delighted that Robert recognized their power and potency. But even so powerful an attraction as his balls was not enough to keep Robert buried between Buck's legs forever. His tongue began to travel, and Buck knew where it was heading. Buck groaned in anticipation of the assault that he knew was forthcoming. This was love making as he'd always known it with Robert, and Buck would demand that it remain a part of their life together.

In less than a minute, Robert's tongue had found its target and there it would stay for long after an hour had passed. One sensation after another shot through Buck's body as he surrendered himself completely to Robert's expert lappings. Deep into the hour, Buck was lying moaning on the bed, clutching and grabbing Robert's head and forcing him into even closer contact with that target if that were possible.

Buck knew now that Robert had diverted him into taking a sensual path he might not otherwise have followed. Buck was delighted at the change of course on the trail. Such joy, such pleasure, such exquisite ecstacy awaited him at the end of the trail that he never wanted to turn back to what was but go on to welcome the surprises of the future.

Even in the throes of love-making, Buck remembered the one night that had changed his life and that had forced him to enter his marriage with Susan. The consequences of that once seemingly innocent night would live with them forever. If he remembered correctly, it had been Robert's idea and at first Buck had resisted. But Robert was persistent, and eventually Buck had given in.

The plan was to invite old Buck over to their home for dinner. His grandfather hadn't entered his house since his parents had died. But without making any announcement Robert had wanted old Buck to see how they lived. In some way, Robert felt that if old Buck had seen them functioning as a couple, he would gradually come to accept them as such and remove his opposition to their ongoing relationship. Looking back, Buck knew that he could not have realized the dire consequences of what had set out to be a relatively harmless dinner.

*****

The evening had begun uneventfully. Buck sat alone in his living room, staring at the portrait of his grandfather, posed in 1924, a copy of the original which hung in the reception office of the Examiner. Robert had discreetly placed the portrait here for tonight's dinner. After Buck I had gone, his portrait would be replaced by a Mondrian inherited from young Buck's father.

The old newspaper tycoon could still fill Buck III with fear and dread, and even at the last minute he'd urged Robert to cancel the dinner. But Robert had remained adamant.

At the sound of his granddad's limousine in the driveway, Buck III rose from his chair and headed out to greet the man on his portico. By the time he'd reached the steps leading down to the driveway, Buck I's chauffeur had already helped him from the back seat.

One foot carefully placed in front of the other, old Buck, with the aid of a cane, slowly made his way up the steps and into the foyer. Only then did he stop to acknowledge Buck III's greeting. Buck hugged the old man, but he quickly broke the embrace. Buck III gingerly held onto the elderly man's arm, guiding him into the living room, even though old Buck seemed to resent that assistance. Buck I stood for a moment and looked proudly at his portrait. "Like your taste in art."

"It's Buck's favorite painting," Robert said, coming up behind them.

Buck I turned around and glared at Robert, almost as if he'd been unaware that he'd be in the house tonight. Not greeting Robert, his co-host, Buck I barked at him harshly. "Why don't you get me a drink? I know you don't have a stock of my favorite libation, but bring me some good bourbon with branch water instead."

Crestfallen at being treated like a servant, Robert turned and headed toward the bar behind the foyer.

When he was out of earshot, Buck I turned to his grandson and asked, "Why do you keep that sissy around?"

"He's not a sissy. He's really a decent man." Buck III guided his grandfather toward the most comfortable chair in the room.

But Buck I stood up for a few moments, as if enjoying the feeling. He'd been sitting for too long these past few years. Aged and leathery, he still stood more than six feet tall—a lean, austere person with a full head of hair. To his great regret and embarrassment, he'd often been mistaken for Carl Sandburg over the years, a poet for whom he had no respect. "I don't look folksy at all!" Buck I always protested. Young Buck never saw the resemblance either. Unlike Sandburg's, his grandfather's eyes were ominous.

Those eyes traveled over the frame of his grandson. "You get better looking every day. Just like I used to be." A frown crossed his wrinkled brow. "For the life of me, I can't understand why some good woman hasn't captured you a long time ago. Someone like that Susan Howard." At this point Robert came back into the room with the old man's drink. Buck I turned and cast an accusatory eye toward Robert.

With Buck III's assistance, the old man settled into his chair and took the drink offered by Robert.

"I hope it's all right," Buck said, sipping the drink with distaste. "It's not my usual." He slammed the drink down on the adjoining end table. "Go tell my driver to bring my bottle in. I think I'll have my own drink. I can't stand that rotgut shit you gave me."

"I'm sorry." Robert backed away slightly, standing awkwardly in the room for a moment before heading outside to Buck I's limousine.

"Please don't treat him like a servant," Buck III said when Robert had gone.

"If he's not a servant, what in the hell is it? You always told me he was your secretary. Has anything changed? Is he still your secretary or has he become something else?"

Buck III didn't know what to say. "He's my associate," he finally said.

"Associate," Buck I said with contempt. "I've heard it called everything in my day."

"I'm sure you have," Buck III said, desperately wanting to change the subject. "I'm glad you're here. It's been a long time. When mother and father were alive, you came here often."

The mention of his long dead son seemed to send a painful memory racing through Buck I's brain. He coughed slightly.

In moments Robert was back in the room. "Hope this will hit the spot." He handed old Buck his favorite libation, which appeared to be some form of rare cognac.

"Thanks," was all Buck I could manage to say. He didn't make eye contact with Robert.

"Now that I know what you drink, I'll make sure I keep it in stock for future visits from you—and I hope there will be many," Robert said.

"That's crap!" old Buck said. "In the first place, you can't get this bottle. Only I know how to do that, and I'm not telling. In the second place, this is my last visit here."

Robert looked at Buck III in embarrassment and surprise. "Well," Robert said after a long silence. "I'd better go check on dinner. Buck and I have a Cuban cook, but she'll be leaving us soon. I've got to find a replacement. In the meantime, your grandson here will have to be content with my own specialties."

"Exactly what is your specialty?" Buck I's voice had never been sharper or more piercing. It was as if he'd become a prosecutor in a courtroom.

Buck III decided to rescue the situation. "He does roasts, omelettes, the world's greatest lasagne." He accepted a glass of scotch from Robert, caressing his hand when old Buck wasn't looking. "He does everything well." Buck III's voice had a ring of defiance. "In fact, I couldn't live without him."

Buck I looked first at his grandson, then at Robert. "I see."

"Excuse me," Robert said, leaving the room.

Not seeming to know what to do or say, Buck I looked again at his portrait. "Yes, indeed, I was once considered the best-looking man in Florida." He lifted his cane, pointing at the portrait. "There it is. See for yourself."

"You were a lady-killer," Buck III said.

Some foggy memory of long-ago conquests seemed to stir in Buck I's brain. But then a look of anguish came across his face. "Damn chair's too low. Gotta pee."

Buck III helped him from the chair. "I'll show you where to go."

"Forget it," Buck I said. "I know this house very well. Who in the fuck do you think had it designed? Who do you think paid for it?"

"You did and I thank you."

Without saying anything more, Buck I tottered off to the toilet in the foyer.

When Buck I came back into the room, recently formed urine stains spotted his trousers. "Why did you take out the toilet that used to be there? I had to piss into some God damn gold dolphin."

"That's a ceramic Robert got from this dealer. We thought it was high camp."

"High camp—whatever the fuck that is." He seated himself in the chair again and picked up his drink. Like a stern pilgrim father, he slowly scanned the richly decorated parlor. "You sure spent enough of my money on this place."

"It's just as mother left it when she died," Buck III said. "Besides I entertain advertisers here." He knew his voice was a little too defensive. "It's important to keep up a good image for our paper. The News publisher puts on a real big act."

Buck I slammed down his glass. "Let me worry about the reputation of the Examiner." A cold silence came over the room as Buck III realized his grandfather still bitterly resented his being forced to relinquish editorial control because of failing health.

"If I need any new furniture these days," Buck I said, "I buy it real cheap. I had to have some folding chairs the other day, and I sent my man to Woolworth's. You wouldn't have heard of that store. It's a five and dime. No dolphin ceramic faggot toilet stools to take a crap in."

Buck III sipped his drink slowly, his heart sinking that the evening seemed to be disintegrating fast.

"I want to see the news," Buck I commanded.

His grandson rose quickly and turned on a gigantic colored television screen just as a newsreel film of Rose flashed across the set.

"That woman makes a lot of sense to me," Buck I said. "She calls things by their right names. She says what needs to be said, what most Christians really feel but keep their mouths shut about. I refuse to change words I learned a long time ago. I grew up calling a nigger a nigger. Then someone came up with the bright idea of calling them Negroes. It seems it offends the shiftless bastards less. Now someone told me the other day they object to being called Negroes. Seems they prefer black. What a butt-grabber. To me, a nigger is still a nigger. Still!"

Buck III swallowed his drink, but its taste was bitter. "And a Jew is still a Hebe!"

Anger flashed across old Buck's face. "I'm not a Jew lover either."

Buck III shuddered. "I know that." Before he could say more, Robert came into the room to announce dinner. Buck III turned from the old man, who was reluctantly letting Robert help him out of the armchair.

However, Buck III was waiting to give his grandfather the honored position at the head of the table.

"You'll really like this Cuban woman's cooking," Robert predicted. "The best I've ever had. Buck and I are going to be so sorry to lose her."

Buck I greeted the news contemptuously. When the Cuban cook emerged from the kitchen with a heaping platter of paella, he sat back stiffly in his chair, as if its aroma offended him.

Buck III reached and loaded a big helping onto his grandfather's plate.

Old Buck pushed it away. Turning to Robert, he said, "Make mine a chicken sandwich—hold the mayonnaise. No skin."

"But we used fresh lobster, lots of good things," Robert protested.

The cook was summoned again, and she hastily and angrily carried old Buck's plate of paella toward the kitchen. Under her breath, she cursed in Spanish, her voice drifting back.

Buck III had had enough. He couldn't go through with the dinner either. Instead of paella, he opted for a glass of wine resting on the table. "What is it with you and Sister Rose? You're always so defensive of her. It's like you're afraid of her. Does she have something on you?"

Shocked at his grandson's sudden aggressiveness, Buck I took a moment to come into focus. "We'll talk business after I've had my chicken sandwich."

"We'll talk business now!" Buck III shouted, and he feared it was more to show off in front of Robert than to test the old man's steely resolve.

"Tell my driver I'm ready to go," Buck I barked at Robert. "I'll go home and make my own damn chicken sandwich. I don't eat beaners' food anyway."

At the front door, the old man paused and called to his grandson. "I'm going now."

Momentarily in control of his emotions, Buck III came into the foyer. "You still didn't answer my question."

"I'll be flying to Geneva again soon," Buck I said. "A monkey gland transplant. Each day life grows a little more precious to me, and I plan to prolong it as long as possible. Imagine. A monkey gland transplant. It's supposed to rejuvenate the elderly." He chuckled to himself. "Now what would my old friend, William Jennings Bryan, have thought if he knew I planned to have monkey gland transplants in me?" He looked around the room, not really wanting to stay, but not wanting to go either.

Buck III looked at his grandfather for a long moment. He no longer felt rage. If anything, he felt pity for the trapped look in those tired old eyes.

Saying nothing, a disappointed Robert held the door open for him. "Buck and I are so sorry you have to go."

The old man glared at Robert. "Does every God damn sentence you utter have to begin with Buck and I? Why don't you quit being a parasite on my grandson and get on with your own life? Get married. Have some children. Raise a family on your own and quit smothering young Buck to death day and night."

"Robert's not smothering me," Buck III said. "I really resent that. Robert's my best friend. This is his home. You can't tell him to get married. He'll do what he wants. You can't tell anyone to get married— not even me."

Buck I stared at him with a ferocity his grandson had never known before. "We'll see about that. We'll God damn see about that."

Robert turned and left. It was obvious to Buck III that Robert was on the verge of tears.

Assisting his grandfather toward the limousine, Buck III said nothing.

Buck I stood shakily, his eyes closed tightly. When he opened them, his lips quivered pathetically. Slowly, some control returned to his wobbly legs. "Son, I want you to remember me for what you think I stood for." In a practiced, closed smile, he added, "Not for what I was." Buck I glanced toward the open terrace facing the city with its vista of the news tower of the Examiner. A frail hand shot up, seemingly having no act to perform. It fell by his side again. Some tiny little noise, not quite a sob, escaped from deep within his throat. Bracing himself on his grandson's arm, he slowly walked toward the car.

In stunned silence, Buck III stood here, watching the limousine pull out of his driveway. He didn't really want to know the old man's secrets. Let him take them to the grave. He turned and walked back to the foyer. His only mission now was to go and find Robert and offer him comfort for the humiliation he'd suffered.

*****

She must not have slept more than four hours before she sat up in bed, ripping off her domino. Her troubled mind wouldn't allow her to sleep any more, and she didn't want to become addicted to medication. She was tempted to press the buzzer and order black coffee but decided she needed these moments alone. Until now she'd tried to blot from memory her troubling dinner with Ronnie and Nancy.

Maybe if Buck had accepted her invitation, the evening would have gone better. As it went, there could have been no more incompatible grouping of dinner partners than Ronald Reagan, Nancy Davis, Shelley, and herself. Before the first twenty minutes had gone by, Rose knew she wasn't going to be asked to join the rich and powerful inner circle that was trying to propel this broken down actor into the White House. It was to be no Alfred and Betsy Bloomingdale, Walter and Lee Annenberg, Earl and Marion Jorgensen, *and* Rose Phillips.

Even though always stylishly dressed for the 70s, the Reagans still carried with them a 50s aura—barbecues in the backyard, potluck picnics, and outings at the ranch. That was hardly the evening she had planned for them.

Paradise Shores had never looked more beautiful. She'd filled it with flowers and had personally overseen the soft lighting. She'd wanted to appear stunningly glamorous before the Reagans and had dressed in a low-cut red evening gown that glittered and gave off a gentle rustling sound when she moved. The dress had cost twelve thousand dollars and had been shipped down from New York where it had required extra fittings. She wanted it to be perfect, knowing that Nancy was increasingly becoming a fashion plate.

Before the Reagan limousine arrived, she'd checked all the final arrangements and had even hired an extra staff of ten to service the dinner. Wherever she looked bowls of open roses in all colors had floated, and the candlelight had cast an enchanting glow.

She'd been determined that the dinner would be perfect, beginning with the caviar and smoked salmon. She'd even booked a world class pianist to play softly in the music room, although he'd been warned not to come out and introduce himself as he was a flaming liberal who'd detested Reagan's role as governor of California.

Shelley had remained in his bedroom getting dressed, and she'd feared he wouldn't wear the dark blue suit and white shirt she'd selected for him. He was always rebelling against what she forced him to wear. Even before she had a final chance to go up and check on Shelley's wardrobe, the Reagan limousine was in the driveway.

She'd wondered which one of their fat cat supporters was paying for it, as she'd been informed that the Reagans had been virtually paupers all their lives. They certainly didn't make much money appearing in all those bad films. She'd once seen Nancy Davis on the late show, flipping off the channel after ten minutes. She'd only seen one movie starring Reagan himself. Something about John Loves Mary. She didn't like to waste her time on such dribble.

Nancy's dress was also red but it hadn't been half as stunning as hers. It fell just below her knee, whereas Rose's gown was floor length. Although a permanent smile had been fixed on her face as if sculpted there, Nancy had appeared to examine her critically. It was obvious from the beginning that Nancy had not approved of her, and certainly didn't like the low cut of her gown. It apparently was too revealing for Nancy. But Rose had caught Ronnie taking a peek at the goodies. Perhaps a remembrance of things past, despite the fact that at least to her, their former sexual involvement had not been memorable.

She'd planned to have drinks at the pier down by her yacht. It had been carefully planned, and it was also the best place to see the sun set. But Queen Nancy had intervened. "He's been on his feet all day. Get him off his feet."

Changing plans abruptly, Rose had ushered them into her sunken Florida room filled with roses. You couldn't see the sun set here, but at this point that didn't matter. Shelley still hadn't made an appearance.

"What kind of First Lady will you make?" Rose had said after drinks were served. No sooner had the words escaped than she realized how abrupt that sounded.

As if the cameras were still turning, Nancy had said, "I'll be no Mrs. Roosevelt—that's for sure. That woman had her own agenda. I will devote myself totally to Ronnie's causes."

"What Nancy meant," Ronnie had interjected, "is, of course, that we had the greatest respect for Mrs. Roosevelt, Democrat or not."

"My mother was a southern Democrat," Nancy had interjected.

"And I too was once a Democrat," Ronnie had said. "You see, we all make mistakes and can learn from them. He sipped his drink and leaned forward. "To my knowledge, you don't have a party affiliation."

She had gotten up abruptly from the sofa to stand before the fireplace. She'd felt that her artfully arranged position there had shown off her figure to its best advantage. Unlike these former actors, she at least had a figure to show off.

"I only do a solo," she'd said. "I'm not affiliated with any group but my own."

"What do you mean?" Nancy had asked with a slightly raised eyebrow.

"I run my own show. So far, my charismatic movement hasn't backed political candidates, but all that is about to change."

"We're hoping that our ideas and causes, which I'm sure you've read about, might intrigue you enough to support us," Ronnie had said, smiling with a certain courtly charm.

She'd studied him for a minute, checking the roots of his hair, detecting no gray. "I think in a few days when my true agenda becomes clearer to the American public, that you will not welcome my support."

"That's astonishing," Ronnie had said. "What's going to happen in a few days?"

"That is an absolute secret," she'd said. "But I'm going public with my agenda. No doubt it will be different from your own."

"We assume that you're following an agenda much like that of Pat Robertson and Jerry Falwell," Nancy had said.

"No, nothing like that," Rose had said.

"But Christian...," Ronnie had stammered, not realizing what she was alluding to. He'd seemed acutely uncomfortable, and the evening had only begun.

"Of course, I will always be a spokesperson for the Christian movement in this country," she'd said. "But I will also be representing other misunderstood interests in this country. I will become a lobbyist for another group as well. I fear this new group is too much of a hot potato for you to handle, and because of various affiliations of mine you may want to seek support elsewhere."

"I don't understand," Ronnie had said.

"You will, you will," Rose had countered.

He'd cleared his throat which had seemed to bring on a coughing spasm. Nancy had tried to comfort him, but her steely, disapproving eyes had glared at Rose even though her smile remained permanently fixed on her face. It had been as if she were blaming Rose for bringing on Ronnie's coughing fit.

From this point on, Rose knew that the dinner would be a disaster. She'd also been certain that all of them had suffered through disastrous dinners in the past. Being the consummate professionals they were, she'd known somehow they would manage to get through the evening, even though its whole purpose had vanished at the beginning with her enigmatic statements. She couldn't tell the Reagans exactly what she was planning to do, but she'd also warned them to back off and not come knocking at her temple door again. In the next few days, they'd probably deny this dinner had ever existed.

Ever the diplomat, Nancy had rushed in with something to divert the conversation. "I noticed your rose-colored limousine out in the driveway. It's very impressive. I ride around a lot in limousines these days. But my fondest times are not in these limousines, but in a red Pontiac station wagon I used to drive in the 50s."

Ronnie had sat back, as if relaxing for the first time this evening. "We used to have the best barbecues. No politics then. More show biz friends. Bill Holden came over a lot. George Burns and Gracie Allen.

And long before I became governor of California, Jack Benny used to call me governor. Feature that."

At this point Shelley had entered the room. He hadn't worn anything flamboyant, but had put on that dark suit, a conservative tie, and white shirt she'd laid out for him.

Far from being the menace she'd feared, he'd actually been quite delightful, charming, articulate, and completely gracious. Knowing how dangerous politics was, he'd used his extensive knowledge as a movie buff to entertain and delight them with secrets of Hollywood that even they hadn't known.

Over dinner Shelley had turned to Nancy and said, "Did you know that Olivia de Haviland maintains that Jimmy Stewart was the best lay in Hollywood. Not any more, of course."

Nancy had appeared slightly shocked but had seemed mildly titillated by this bit of information, whether true or not. Ronnie had seemed embarrassed. The evening wasn't going at all as he'd planned.

After the main course had been served, Shelley had put down his wine glass. "Did my mother tell you that I have the gift of prophecy?"

"No, she didn't," Nancy had said, obviously intrigued. "In fact she didn't tell us much about you at all."

"It's true," Rose had said. "He can predict the future. He's never wrong."

"Then that brings up a big question," Ronnie had said.

"Yes," Nancy had echoed, taking a cue from her husband. "We have to ask."

"You're the next occupant of the White House," Shelley had said matter-of-factly and with such conviction that at least for one moment everybody at the table had seemingly believed him.

"That's wonderful," Nancy had said.

"There's only one problem," Shelley had warned. "I hesitate to bring it up."

"I can handle it if Ronnie can," Nancy had said, reaching over and taking the hand of her husband.

"I think Shelley has predicted enough for one evening," Rose said, hoping to steer clear of this trap.

Ronnie had interceded. "I want to know. If I'm going to be president of the United States, I'll have to learn how to handle a lot of bad news."

"I see this assassination problem," Shelley had said.

The table had fallen strangely silent. After that, no topic of conversation could enliven the evening again. There were long periods of silences.

Rose had understood when the Reagans had excused themselves, not taking dessert.

"I can always tell when Ronnie is getting a cold, and he's getting one right now, and I must take him back to our hotel," Nancy had said.

In the foyer Rose had stood under candlelight, bidding them good-bye. Both Ronnie and Nancy had told her what a lovely evening they'd had and how delightful it was to have met her son.

"Shelley's remarkable," Nancy had said as a parting remark. The boy had seemingly disappeared. "He's certainly the world's most beautiful boy. But..." She'd hesitated. "As a prophet, I'm not so sure."

"Let's hope he's wrong," Ronnie had said.

The final good-byes and kisses were staged theatrically, and the Reagans had departed in their limousine, never to grace the grounds of Paradise Shores again.

Shutting the door behind them, Rose had turned and faced the emptiness of her mansion. She'd demanded that the servants find Shelley and bring him to her. After a search of the house, they couldn't find the boy. He would suddenly disappear like this and then turn up hours or even days later with no explanation as to what he was up to. She shuddered to think what he might be doing right this minute.

*****

Buck gave Robert a long, lingering kiss before going above deck to step aboard in Okeechobee. Buck I's yacht was left behind them on the island.

"You certainly caught me by surprise yesterday," Buck said. "I've got a bone to pick with Uncle Milty. He should have warned me you were coming."

"I told him I was taking the yacht over to a hotel on Key Lagoon," Robert said. "That's where I was going to be holed up, waiting for you to come and beg my forgiveness. But I surprised both of you."

"And what a delectable surprise it was after a few preliminary awkward moments," Buck said.

"Those are behind us now. You've made everything right for me again."

Buck pulled him as close as he could possibly get, crushing a willing Robert into his body. "You and I are just starting to get acquainted. I've got to get to the Examiner and move out. I've got a million things to do, but all I can think about is you."

"I'll be waiting at our home. I'm here for you day or night."

"I'm counting on that." He moved toward Robert's mouth, his tongue already out. When he was satisfied that he'd drained all the liquid from Robert's mouth, he turned and left quickly without looking back. He dreaded his agenda for the day.

A very large and glamorous limousine was waiting at the pier for him. After asking the driver to take him to the Examiner's office, Buck instructed him to return for Robert who was still busy on the boat arranging his gear. The funeral of Robert's mother was scheduled for tomorrow morning, and Uncle Milty had assured him he was making all the arrangements. Uncle Milty, along with Patrick, would fly with them to Miami in the morning on a privately chartered craft. The wedding of Robert and Buck had been arranged for that afternoon.

At the Examiner's office, only the early shift had reported for work. As Buck walked into his office, he noticed Robert's empty desk and a feeling of great regret came over him. He was going to remove only his most personal and urgent files. The rest of his papers and possessions would be gathered that afternoon by a bonded moving agency. Buck sighed as he looked at the gift from Sister Rose of the de Kooning. That he was going to take with him.

At his typewriter, he banged out copy about his resignation from the Examiner. Resignation sounded better than being booted. He enigmatically promised his readers to "return" soon, without spelling out exactly what that meant. At this point in his life even he didn't know exactly what that meant.

Roland came into his office, staring straight at him like a spent runner.

"Bad night, again?" Buck asked. "What's it now?"

"My back. Kept me up all night."

He was so used to Roland's afflictions he didn't inquire further. "Well, what do you think?" he asked, handing the copy to Roland. "My resignation. It's not long. I suggest you run it on the front page with a box. Use that picture of me snapped last year by that photographer from Time. The one that makes me look like a fucking movie star. No, better than that. What movie stars want to look like but don't."

Roland quickly read the copy. "I know the one. Your wish is my command."

Buck eagerly sought his face, hoping for some sort of approval, some acknowledgment, but that had never been granted by the city editor. As Buck looked closely into Roland's burning eyes, into the crevices of his face, he knew no approval was forthcoming.

"I'll run it after correcting a couple of typos. After all, we want to make you look good, something I've always tried to do on this paper, especially with those awful columns you used to write."

"You don't think I'm much of a newspaperman, do you?"

"I think you are a playboy born with a silver spoon in your mouth, and I always resented how fast you moved up the ladder. I came up the hard way. Copy boy, obit writer, you name it."

"It doesn't matter now whether you approve of me or not. I'm out of here."

"My advice to you is to take all your millions and get out of town. Move to some other city where you can be a big deal. Where you're not known the way you are here in Okeechobee. With your looks and money, you'll impress the hell out of the people in that new town. Too many people know too much about you here in Okeechobee, and we're anything but impressed. Facile charm has carried you far."

"Thanks for the vote of confidence, but you're not so lucky. You think you're getting rid of me but every day of your life you're going to have to contend with me."

"I doubt that." He paused to search Buck's face. "Exactly what scheme do you have planned?"

"I'll give my scoop to the News."

"I see. Do what you like. I'm going on a long vacation. Then I'm coming back to take up my new post as managing editor of the Examiner. At three times the salary you were paying me."

"Good luck in your new post. I'm sure we'll be seeing a lot of each other." Although tempted, Buck didn't dare tell him that he might become the Examiner's chief rival if Uncle Milty could acquire the vastly weakened News. Not only that, Buck might even become Rose's media director. Roland, in time, would learn these horrible developments, probably when he read about them in the News.

"Hope your back gets better," Buck called out to Roland in the way of parting words. The city editor did not look back or bid him a fond farewell.

*****

As Buck reached to retrieve his de Kooning, the persistent ringing of his desk phone lured him back for one final visit to his office. Almost no one knew that he was leaving the Examiner, so he expected it would be a routine business call. But no routine business caller would ring for so long. He decided to answer it.

"Hello," he said hesitantly into the phone.

"At last I got you. It's Leroy. I've been calling all over town trying to reach you. A deal's a deal, and I'm a man of my word."

"Sorry, I've been busy."

"I'm just reconfirming tonight. I've got it set up. You know the address. Eight o'clock sharp. I've got some real surprises planned for you. You're going to love it."

Anxious to get on with this Lolito investigation, Buck reviewed a few more details with Leroy before agreeing to the ever-so-secret rendezvous. Through the windows of his office, he noticed Roland looking in suspiciously. Obviously he was wondering what Buck was up to. Buck thought Roland might think he was handling some fairly routine business before departing. He imagined that even so toughened a news veteran as Roland would be shocked at the exact nature of the conversation going on between Leroy and him.

No sooner than he'd hung up on Leroy than a receptionist from the front office, a young woman in her early 30s with jet-black hair, came into his office. "A Cuban woman's waiting out in the foyer. Said she met you when you came to visit Rose Phillips. Until very recently she was a maid there."

Surprised and not remembering the woman, Buck directed the receptionist to show her in.

Rather timidly she entered Buck's about to be abandoned office. He recognized her at once. She'd served drinks at Rose's mansion. Her face appeared distraught. "How can I help you?"

Before saying anything, she shut the door behind her. "What I've got to say to you is real private like. The bitch has fired me."

"You mean, Sister Rose?"

"That's right. I've been fired. I spend my weekly salary as soon as I get it. That means I've got no job and no money, and I need both. I was hoping you might give me a job."

"You don't think I'm going to fall for that, do you? Rose has probably paid you to come here to say this. She'd like me to offer you a job, wouldn't she? That way you could report back to her everything going on in my house. No way!"

"Hell, no!" she said, angered by his words. "I was fired and that's the God's truth. I asked too many questions. Questions about little Shelley. I really like that little boy. A mariposa, but I still like him. And I fear for that boy's safety."

Suddenly, this maid had aroused Buck's interest. "Is Shelley in some sort of danger?"

"He's in plenty of danger."

"Tell me what you know," Buck demanded, believing the woman for the first time.

"Let's not go so fast here," she cautioned. "I've told you enough already. As I said, I need money. The information I've got is worth a lot of money."

"Okay," he snapped, growing impatient. "I'll give you a thousand dollars. But it had better be good stuff."

"Make it two thousand and it's a deal."

"All right. What do you know?"

"I overheard Calder Martin and Sister Rose having a big fight. It was over Shelley. Calder's found out a lot of stuff about Shelley. About where he goes and what he does when he leaves Paradise Shores. Shelley's been acting up. Been a real bad boy. Running wild."

"This is not worth two-thousand dollars. Rose is very well aware of Shelley's habits."

"I know that." The woman looked miffed. "Sister Rose lets the boy be. She knows he does bad stuff, and she doesn't try to stop him. But Calder thinks it's going to blow up in Rose's face, that Shelley is going to ruin everything. Calder found out that some big magazine—I don't know which one—has investigated Shelley and come up with some bad stuff. Calder thinks that getting written up in this magazine will fatally wound Sister Rose's movement and his own fat deal."

"Exactly what does Calder want to do about Shelley?"

"He wants to do something that I'm sure Sister Rose would be dead set against. Yes, she wouldn't go for it at all."

"What would she oppose?"

"There's this clinic in Switzerland. I heard him talking on the phone with someone about it."

"What sort of clinic?"

"It's a clinic where bad children are sent. Boys like Shelley. They're given some sort of treatment there as best as I could hear."

"You mean brainwashed."

"I don't know what the treatment is. But after getting this treatment Shelley is supposed to be a good boy again. At this clinic they change his mind around or something."

"To your knowledge does Rose know any of this?"

"I don't think she does. Calder's planning to do all this behind Rose's back."

"That would be kidnapping."

"But like he told somebody on the phone, Rose wouldn't be able to do anything about it. They've got her where they want her. She could not go to the police. They've got too much on her. They'd do something to his brain, and Sister Rose couldn't stop them."

"I assume that all of this happened at her house?"

"I was working in a room right off the library. Calder didn't know I was in there. I remained very still until he'd left the room."

"I would have thought you might have told Sister Rose about this instead of coming to me."

"I guess I might have told her. But something else happened instead. I got caught."

"Doing what?"

"I'd borrowed this diamond necklace of hers. I was invited to this big Cuban dance. I wanted to show off a bit. I figured she wouldn't miss it for one night, and that I could return it the next day. It was just my luck. With all the jewelry that woman has, who would have thought it was that diamond necklace, the very one I took, that she wanted to wear that day. A security guard searched me when I was leaving the house. He found it in my purse. I got fired."

"I can understand why. Maybe I shouldn't, but I believe your story. Shelley may be in some sort of danger."

The phone rang, and this time he picked up the receiver without hesitation. It was Robert claiming he was waiting downstairs with the limousine to take Buck home.

"I've got to go," he told the woman.

"My money. What about the money you promised me."

"I don't have that much on me, but my car's waiting downstairs. I'll stop at the bank and get you your money. You've earned it."

"I'm glad to hear you say that. For another five-hundred dollars, I'll give you another little scoop. You are a newspaperman, aren't you?"

"Your stuff's been good so far. Okay, I'll give you another five-hundred bucks. What is it?"

"When Calder was talking to some strange person on the phone, he seemed mighty proud of himself. He was the one who hired that Cuban woman and her little girl to bring charges against Gene Robinson."

"You mean it was a setup?"

"That's right—a real Calder Martin dirty trick. He told the guy on the phone that what he'd done to Robinson was just a tiny preview of what he was going to do to Buck Brooke. I think he meant you and not your grandfather."

"Did he indicate at all what he was going to do to me?"

"That's all he said. But he was real proud how he could ruin Robinson's life and felt he could do far more damage to you because you've got a lot more to lose than Robinson."

"That's for damn sure."

Without knocking, the same receptionist came back into his office. "There's an urgent call that's come in to the switchboard," she said. "It's a man. He won't give his name. He demands to speak to you personally. Says it's a matter of life or death."

*****

The reporter in him bit at that bait. Hesitantly he picked up the telephone, expecting almost anybody on the other end of the line.

"Mr. Brooke." The man's voice was civil and polite, downright courteous, the way certain headwaiters address clients in deluxe restaurants. "I've been reading what the Examiner has said about Sister Rose."

"Yeah," Buck said, "and you approve?"

There was a long pause. "You don't understand, Mr. Brooke. You can't run any more stories like that on her. I won't allow it!" The voice grew stronger, more ominous and threatening.

"Who in the fuck are you?"

"That's not important." His breathing grew heavier and he became extremely agitated. "In just ten minutes you and the Examiner are going to be blown off the face of the earth." He slammed down the phone.

In astonishment Buck looked at the Cuban maid. She appeared bewildered, although fearing something very bad was about to happen.

The shock of the phone call immobilized him for almost thirty seconds. "Oh, God, oh, God," he repeated to himself.

"What's wrong?" she demanded to know, obviously fearing for her own safety.

Stunned by the threat, he at first started to dial the police. But that would take too long. Right now he had to clear everybody out of the building. The irony of it all, he thought. His final act as publisher. He sighed with relief when he realized it was only a skeletal crew. He pressed the buzzer, calling the Examiner's security guard. "A bomb threat!" he said as calmly as he could. "We've been given ten minutes to clear out."

The Cuban maid screamed and dashed for the door, knocking down the receptionist on her way. Grabbing the de Kooning, Buck headed for the lobby elevator, only after inquiring if the receptionist was all right.

In moments the security guard was on the loud speaker system, demanding that everybody evacuate the building. Buck looked frantically around the city room but didn't see Roland anywhere. Perhaps he'd already left the building. Buck heard the fire alarm go off. A plant manager hustled workers out of the printing room.

On the elevator going down, Buck was struck with the sudden thought that the Examiner might be taken away from him sooner than later.

Barred from entering the building, Robert stood on the sidewalk in front of the limousine. He rushed up to Buck, appearing he wanted to hug and kiss him but in all this crowd he restrained himself. "Thank God you're safe. What's going on in there?"

"A bomb threat," Buck said, reaching for Robert's arm and handing him the de Kooning. Straining his neck he looked up at the news tower from which he'd so recently descended. At any minute he expected it to be blown into pieces, its dust and debris forming a mushroom cloud. Police sirens cut through the air, as crack members of the police chief's bomb squad arrived for a sweep of the building. Buck spotted Biff getting out of a squad car. The chief would probably have plenty of questions for him later.

With the police now firmly in control, holding back the rapidly forming spectators, Buck's fear of a bomb going off vanished. "It's not going to happen," he repeated, not exactly to Robert, but to the air.

"I think it was just a scare."

"Let's hope so," Robert said, clutching the de Kooning.

A policeman ordered the limousine to leave the area. Robert opened the door and told Buck to get in. "We're going home," he said.

To Buck that invitation had a ring of security. The ominous tone of the recent threat—the possibility that a bomb could explode at any moment—hung in the air. Buck could still hear the sound of the strange man's quiet, polite, almost courtly voice. The gentleness of his speech had made the threat seem more deadly.

Breaking through a police flank, Rose's former Cuban maid ran toward the limousine and jumped into the back seat with Buck, practically kicking Robert out of the way.

Robert grabbed her arm and tried to yank her from the seat.

"It's okay," Buck said, tugging Robert and urging him to get into the car. "She's with me."

Buck took the painting from Robert and lifted it into the back seat.

Robert sat on a jump seat, staring defiantly at the maid. "Who is this I might ask?"

"He owes me money," the maid said defiantly.

"You'll get your damn money." Buck ordered the driver to take him to his local bank. After the car sped off, he turned to Robert. "She provided some information I needed. I can't discuss it now."

"I see." Robert looked at the maid skeptically. "If you're applying for a job with Mr. Brooke, it's too late. The position is filled."

"I would like a job." The maid looked hesitantly at Buck.

"Ever since we lost our Cuban cook I've been searching for the right person," Robert said. "When I read what Gene Robinson did to that poor girl and how her mother must be suffering, I went by to see her. I hired her on the spot. She's terrific. Claims to make the best arroz con pollo in the state of Florida."

Buck looked at Robert in complete surprise. He didn't want to reveal what he knew and had always concealed the extent of his deep involvement with Gene. "I don't know if that was a good idea," he said to Robert in a non-committal way. "I mean that case hasn't been solved. It sounds suspicious."

"I know the woman you hired," the Cuban maid said. "Her name is Clara. She's a puta. A lying, thieving, scheming bitch. You'll be sorry the day you ever hired the likes of that one."

Robert was caught by surprise. He obviously didn't expect such a reaction from either Buck or the maid. It appeared that he thought he had done something good and noble. "Well," he said to Buck, "if you think I made a mistake, we can always change it. Up to now, I've always had a free hand to run the house any way I chose." He appeared to be miffed.

"It's okay," Buck said as the limousine neared his bank. "I'm sure it'll be fine."

"Yeah, right," was all the maid said. At the bank, Buck had Robert wait in the car with the maid. He feared if Robert went into the bank with him, the maid might steal the painting like she'd done with Rose's diamond necklace.

Back in the car, Buck handed the maid her money. He offered to have her dropped off some place, but she preferred getting out on the sidewalk instead. As a final good-bye, she turned to Robert, "When you fire that puta, and I know you will, I'll be available providing you pay more than that tight fisted cunt, Sister Rose."

After the limousine turned from the curb, Robert confronted Buck. "You're paying Sister Rose's maid for information?"

Although he planned to conceal much from Robert, Buck preferred a limited hang-out at this point. He wouldn't mention Shelley, but as the driver sped to their home, he felt the time had come to tell Robert about the offer to become Rose's media director. Even before he brought up the subject, he suspected Robert wouldn't understand and would violently oppose such a move. But he'd already decided that if Robert protested too violently, he'd grab his friend, tear his clothes off him, and rape him which is what he wanted to do anyway. From now on he was going to use penetration of Robert not only as a way of silencing his objections, but for his own satisfaction. He reached over and put his hand on Robert's thigh. "When we get home, let's go upstairs."

"You're a man who can't get enough."

"I'll never get enough of you, kid," Buck said, tightening his grip on Robert's thigh. "Even when we're old and gray."

"Am I ever glad to hear that." Robert laced his hand over Buck's and pressed Buck's fingers deeper into his thigh. "Now what do you have to tell me? I know you're up to something."

*****

A manila envelope tucked tightly under his arm, Gene strode into the orchid-colored room of a small convention hall. Defiantly, he marched forward to take a seat in the front row. A woman attendant informed him that the red chairs, sprinkled with silvery dust, were reserved. But he refused to budge. With a slightly embarrassed anguish, the attendant gave in and let him occupy the seat. After all, he figured, no one wanted to alienate one potential voter at this point.

In a wrinkled suit and a white shirt that should have been retired the day before, Gene seemed out of place in this hall of well-groomed fat cats. Unlike them, he'd had his clothes set afire and hadn't bothered to replace his wardrobe. Time for that later. He had other things on his mind. He was engulfed in a bright, gleaming "Star Spangled Banner" atmosphere, as most of Barry's supporters wore stripes of red, white, and blue.

On stage, an all-white Dixieland band played to warm up the crowd of some two hundred supporters. About a dozen "Collins Boys & Girls," juniors from the local high school, moved through the audience, handing out leaflets extolling their candidate's qualifications. The girls wore red dresses with straw hats enclosed in blue-ribbon bands. The boys wore the same hats but white pants and red, white, and blue shirts. The fresh faces and eager eyes of the students, combined with their toothpaste smiles, suggested the youthfulness and vigor of their candidate, although they were not of voting age themselves.

Gene wondered how many of these fresh-faced boys Barry had seduced.

One girl stepped up in front of Gene and tentatively offered him a leaflet, but for some reason withdrew suddenly, flashing her smile instead at a large, heavily perspiring man who had just seated himself next to him. Gene waited in anticipation for the spectacle to get under way. He kept wiping his hands on the legs of his trousers. His palms wouldn't stop sweating. His hope now was that at the very exact moment Barry announced his candidacy, his eyes would meet Gene's, and in that split second Barry would know his doom was sealed.

To the sound of music, Barry bounded onto the stage, running up the platform to kiss the eagerly awaiting lady Republican chairman on the cheek. The lights came on for the TV cameras.

In Gene's opinion, Barry was everything in appearance Hazel wasn't: young, good looking, trim and lean—a mild-mannered man who chose his words carefully. He'd been called the John Lindsay of Okeechobee, but only in physical appearance.

Starting slowly, the applause intensified. Balloons were released, going up in the air, turning the already flamboyantly painted hall into a riot of clashing colors. Some of the spectators touched lit cigarette tips to the balloons, causing Gene to speculate that the hall at that moment would be the perfect setting for an assassination. The exploding balloons sounded just like gunfire.

The clapping grew louder, as did the Dixieland band. To Gene's surprise, the only person missing in this cozy scene was Pamela.

A jam of guests, some uninvited, had filled the back corridor, and more crowded in as Barry launched into his prepared text. A polished performer in front of TV cameras, he explained that Pamela was sick, but would soon join him on the campaign trail.

"We're going to clean up the filth in this town," he promised his supporters, echoing Rose's familiar words at the launch of her moral crusade.

Gene looked with increased loathing at Barry, sick to his heart at how the candidate parroted Rose's challenging battle cry. Right now, Gene had seen enough. He got up from his chair and left.

He decided not to ruin this moment of glory for Barry. There would be plenty of time for that later.

Outside the convention hall, Gene—pushed and shoved by the girls waving "Barry for Mayor" signs—waited for the candidate. He noticed Barry's long, sleek, midnight-blue limousine, with its luxurious, gunmetal-gray upholstery, waiting at the edge of the sidewalk.

After announcing his candidacy and leaving the hall to loud cheers, Barry's face looked ashen as he stepped in front of a waiting microphone to field questions from the press. Gene knew that Rose's moral crusade had heated up the mayoralty race, and he suspected that Barry had been in strategy sessions with his campaign advisers, seeking a way to handle the controversial position of Rose's support.

Gene listened eagerly to see how Barry would go, wondering if he'd embrace Rose or seek more moderate support.

"Are you going to join Sister Rose in her moral crusade?" one reporter asked.

Barry licked the slit-thin corners of his mouth, as if he himself was hesitant about which stand to take. It was so obvious that he didn't want to lose support from any side and resented being forced to take any position at all. On anything.

"Sister Rose," he said hesitantly, "is standing up for decency." We must defend our culture, our religion, and our communities against outside forces. We have a 60 percent divorce rate. We've got kids killing kids in our schools. We've got illegal gambling destroying families. We've seen the appearance of increasingly militant gay rights groups demanding that we not only tolerate them but endorse their so-called lifestyle. The increasing openness of gay life in this city is symbolic of a broader moral decay. Okeechobee may be the last bastion of decency left in America. As mayor, I will work to personally see that it doesn't become another New York or San Francisco."

These were crowd-pleasing remarks, but Barry had delivered them unevenly and with some reluctance as if he didn't believe his own words. Although that was obvious to Gene, it didn't seem to strike a discordant note with his supporters, who loudly applauded his remarks, shouting "Barry for Mayor."

Barry looked warily ahead as he moved toward his waiting limousine. He plunged into the midst of his women admirers, shaking hands, flashing his smile, and nearly losing his necktie to a determined, long-nailed souvenir hunter. Swimming through a sea of wedgies and rhinestone sunglasses, he was the darling of the Republican matrons.

After waving to the crowd and giving a victory sign, he crawled into his limousine. Clutching the damaging photographs, Gene reached for the badge he hadn't yet returned to Biff's department. He showed it briefly to Barry's chauffeur, then trailed the candidate into the rear of the vehicle. "Police," he muttered to Barry, turning his back to the candidate as if checking out some disturbance in the crowd milling around the limousine.

As the vehicle pulled out, Barry paid little notice to Gene. "You guys should do a better job of keeping those animals off my back," Barry protested. "Twice I had my balls pinched."

"Those broads too old for you?" Gene asked provocatively, moving closer and looking Barry intently in the eye.

Barry turned to confront him. "You." He looked astonished. "Gene Robinson."

"Right." Gene smiled but his eyes were concealed behind dark glasses. "It's been a long time. How's Pamela?"

"Get out of this car!"

"I'm along for the ride."

Barry leaned forward to summon the driver to stop the limousine, but Gene held out a restraining hand.

"I have pictures for you. Snapped by Leroy Fitzgerald. You make one move to kick me out, and these pictures will end up with the news services. Remember our old school pal, Buck? That muckraker would love to see the X-rated goodies I'm carrying. He's backing Hazel for mayor."

"You've got pictures?" Barry's eyes looked helpless somehow.

"That's right. Want to see them?"

"Put them away," he said angrily. "What do you want? Money? We can arrange that."

"I want to go somewhere and talk. Real private like."

After Barry told the driver where to take them, he settled back in his seat in a stiff silence. Miles from the beachfront hotels, the limousine sped past scrubby palmettos and decaying stucco buildings with long verandas encircling them, evoking the colonial style of Africa.

At a roadside tavern, far removed from the city limits of Okeechobee, a jukebox blared and the cowgirl waitresses served barbecued spareribs to interstate truckers, hustling the orders across the sawdust-littered wooden floors. Barry ordered a double Scotch, Gene preferring a black coffee instead.

A savagery came across Barry's face, then he settled back with a resigned weariness. "I know these pictures exist. Biff already showed them to me. I didn't count on someone like you getting copies. What's your price?"

"I'm not here for blackmail money. I want a job."

"To work for my campaign?"

"To be your private security guard. You know what's happened to me. Biff has fired me from the department."

"Listen, fucker, as a moral crusader, I can't have some child molester working as my security guard. Even you must know how dumb that is."

"I'll stay out of sight. A private security guard at your home. I'll never leave the grounds. Never be photographed."

"I don't really need someone like that."

"You will as the campaign heats up. My salary will be two-thousand a week."

"Two thousand dollars. You don't come cheap."

"I don't think you have much of a choice."

Barry took a long drink. "I don't think I do. My advisers have set out a long trail for me, ending up in the White House at least by the year 2000. I guess if I'm ever going to make it to the White House, I have to begin compromising right now.

"You started compromising a long time ago."

"It's agreed. It's not my money anyway. Someone will pay you the God damn two thousand dollars. Not me. But you'll get paid."

"That's good to hear. I need a job. Things are a little rough right now."

"I heard your house was set on fire. I guess this means you'll be moving in with Pamela and me." The remark was more a statement of fact than a question. "Pamela was always attracted to you. When you exposed yourself to that little girl—the first one—she said, 'Gene never did that to me. I wish he had.'" Barry raised his glass in a mock toast.

"From one child molester to another. Different scene, different style, but we're still in here together."

At first Gene wanted to punch him, but when he looked again he sensed a desperation in Barry's eyes. That served to remind him of his own hurt and humiliation at being trapped. He felt that Barry felt caged right not. By becoming a candidate, he was also the victim of others.

Sensing none of the other patrons were looking, Barry reached over and fondled Gene's hand. "You know you look as good as you did at the university. God, were you hot then. You still are. You haven't aged at all. In fact, the more I think about it the more I know I'm going to like the idea of you moving in with me. You can share my bedroom. Pamela and I don't sleep together any more. My girls occupy the other bedrooms."

"What you're suggesting isn't part of the two thousand package."

"Don't be unreasonable. Leroy showed me those pictures he took of you in the shower. That's some piece of meat to flash."

"I thought fourteen year olds were your specialty."

"For fun and games. But a man needs to get penetrated now and then. For that, you need a real man. One like you."

"I'm not going to be your boy. That's not part of the deal."

"We'll see." He rose quickly from the booth and plopped money down on the table. He headed for the swinging doors leading to the parking lot. Gene followed behind.

Later in the limousine heading back to town, Gene turned to Barry. "I'm curious about something. Do you ever get to see Sister Rose? I'd like to meet her."

Barry looked at him with total skepticism. "Are you kidding? Pamela's got one of my balls, that bitch Rose the other. If I had a third ball, I bet you'd be squeezing it."

Gene kept his eyes on the road ahead, not saying a word. Barry's reference to Pamela and him he understood. But what could he possibly mean about Sister Rose?"

*****

At the boy bordello, filled with young men known as Lolitos, Buck felt shy and out of place. A relaxed Leroy was completely at ease, however. The role of male madam seemed one he was destined to play. Buck had already warned Leroy that he didn't want to be seen in the public areas of the house whose ground floors were draped in black velvet with music playing like he'd heard at night in Tangier, Morocco. There was something of an Arabian Nights aura about the place. The atmosphere was seductive. Everything suggested forbidden fruit.

"We often entertain important guests here," Leroy spoke softly to Buck. "Many are so well known they can't show their faces. We have private rooms upstairs for them. For others, being out there enjoying the fun in the arena is what it is all about."

"Arena?" Buck asked.

"You'll see what that means in about ten minutes or so when it begins," Leroy said. "I'll arrange an eyewitness viewing post for you." He raised an eyebrow as he looked at Buck. "Are you sure you don't want to join the fun and games in the arena?"

"I'm sure," Buck said, feeling embarrassed. On his private beach, he'd been brash and cocky with Leroy, posing for those photographs. But now he wanted out of this place sooner than later. He didn't belong here. It wasn't his thing. He'd even forgotten the lie he'd told Robert that allowed him to come here in the first place. Uncle Milty and Patrick were having a dinner tonight for Robert and him. It was to be a celebration of their reconciliation, and Buck felt he was betraying Robert bitterly by being here in the first place. He kept reminding himself he was not here seeking some forbidden pleasure but was on site as a working journalist. Somehow he didn't quite convince himself of that, and he also felt that before the evening ended he might not be a completely innocent voyeur reporting what he'd seen. He sensed he was heading for some confrontation but it was just a hunch.

In a small, cramped room in back of the arena, Leroy ushered him into a comfortable seat. "This is where you can sit back and enjoy the fireworks. Can I get you a drink?"

"I'm fine."

"You won't believe the famous men who have sat in that chair before you. Could I ever drop names." Leroy reached and pulled back the curtains to reveal a two-way mirror. Leroy and he could see everything inside the dimly lit arena but the audience saw only their own reflections in the mirror. "Actually the mirror was designed so that when the boy was showing frontal the men in the audience could see his backside. When he showed them his backside, they could see frontal in the mirror."

"I get it," Buck said uncomfortably. Although air conditioned, the little viewing room felt stifling.

"I've got to leave you for a while," Leroy said. "Enjoy the show which is about to begin. I have a very special prize for you later. Wait until you see what I've got lined up for you. The prize of prizes. The real special boys work only the private rooms. The other boys—and they're great too—do the shows. We call it the cattle call. They have to take on all comers. The special boys have a great deal of leeway in who they will bed, especially the one you're getting."

"Thanks for everything," Buck said, eager to get rid of Leroy whose presence made him uncomfortable.

After Leroy had gone, Buck carefully studied the mirror. The lights in the arena were very dim but he could make out the heads of men in the audience. They were waiting expectantly for something to happen. Not to keep them waiting, a spotlight was turned on the stage. Buck expected disco music with a go-go boy arriving on stage doing gyrations as part of some striptease act. But it wasn't to be exactly like that.

A young blond boy dressed in a sailor's uniform far too tight for him came out, his cap resting at a cocky tilt on his head. He was a beauty evocative of Robert as a teenage boy. He stood for long moments in the spotlight but didn't turn. Apparently he was standing on a revolving medallion much like a lazy susan.

The medallion began to spin slowly, allowing the boy to be viewed at all angles. When it had revolved around so that Buck was staring at the boy's frontal part, he saw that his sailor pants were so tight that his genitals were clearly outlined. He appeared overly endowed, as if his crotch had been stuffed. Taking his eyes from the boy's crotch, Buck looked up into his beautiful face with his long blond hair, heavy eyelashes, and penetratingly blue eyes. The boy winked at him.

Buck was taken aback and felt himself flushing. He realized that the boy knew what the rest of the audience presumably didn't: that someone on the other side of the mirror was there watching him.

The boy took his left hand and placed it on his crotch as he pivoted around on the revolving metal. He was working himself to a full erection. When he'd made a full rotation and had faced the audience frontal again, there was raucous applause from the appreciative audience who was allowed to study the changes in the boy's bulging basket.

As the medallion started to spin again, the boy tossed his sailor's cap into the audience where a hand reached up to ensnare it. He then began to slowly remove his top, revealing a stunningly well-defined chest with golden hairs centered between two tantalizingly brown nipples.

Even though he couldn't see their faces, Buck knew that this talented young man was working the audience to a feverish pitch. Part of the excitement, Buck felt, was the knowledge that many of them would get to enjoy this young man in all his glory later in the evening.

As the boy reached Buck for a full frontal view, he winked again and kept turning. He was now nude except for his tight sailor pants. Very slowly he began to unbutton them as the audience shouted for a total revelation. They were more eager for full exposure than the boy was going to allow immediately. Provocatively he continued to unbutton his pants and when he did that he slowly let them slide down, revealing first his blond pubic hair. As he came into Buck's vision again, Buck saw the beginning of what appeared to be a thick and hard penis.

By the time the boy pivoted around completely he dropped his pants and revealed his fully erect cock to the audience which brought loud clapping and cheering. When the medallion had turned so that only his side view was visible, Buck could see the full extent of the boy's penis. Leroy had made a wise selection. The penis not only stood out straight, long, and capped, but it was reinforced by an exceptionally large ballsac. When the boy came full frontal at the window mirror, he smiled, as if a private smile to Buck, then uncapped his penis to reveal a large red knob. This unveiling of its head was met with loud applause once the audience could take it in more fully as the medallion continued to revolve.

The boy's sailor pants were down at his knees. Leroy had been smart in instructing the boy not to step out of his pants entirely, as this was always an awkward moment for a male stripper to perform while on stage. As the medallion revolved three more times, the boy continued to masturbate himself slowly in front of his newly acquired fans.

The faux sailor had done his job. Buck was fully aroused, and he suspected that most of the rest of the audience was too. After this brief show the house lights went totally black and the boy somehow disappeared behind the curtain.

When the spotlight was turned on again, it revealed an empty medallion. But in a program that would ultimately stretch out for two hours, that medallion was occupied 11 more times. Buck was certain that Leroy had selected all the outfits for the stripteases: a construction worker, a cowboy, a pilot, a police officer, a U.S. marine, a football captain, a lifeguard, a Roman gladiator, a boxer, Elvis, and a Canadian mountie.

Each one performed virtually the same routine, although none aroused Buck as much as the first "sailor," no doubt because of his resemblance to a much younger Robert.

A voice came over the loud speaker, announcing, "It's not the finale but the beginning." The voice was that of Leroy.

Each boy, beginning with the sailor, emerged barefoot and fully nude on the stage with a full erection. One by one the boys appeared on stage, each following the sailor's example and each proudly revealing a full extended penis.

As each boy stepped from the stage, he lay down on his back on a gigantic fluffy white mattress in the center of the arena. Each performer continued to masturbate himself to maintain a full erection.

When the final performer emerged, the boxer, he too joined the other eleven on the mattress. Their heads came together at the center, but their bodies extended outward like a giant flower petal of flesh.

The disco music that Buck had anticipated suddenly came on. The first member of the audience came out of the dim glow and lowered himself onto the first boy, the sailor. The rather portly middle-aged man plunged his mouth down on the sailor's penis, devouring it. Other members of this small audience emerged from their seats and lowered their mouths onto each boy.

Buck thought the show would come to its obvious conclusion there, but he was in for another performance. After two minutes, the music stopped, and Leroy's voice came on the speaker again. "Time to move on, little doggie," he said. The music then started to blare up again.

At that signal, each man changed partners, in some cases reluctantly leaving the boy they were enjoying as they moved around in the circle fellating the next boy in line. This would continue until each of the twelve men in the audience had sampled the wares of each boy.

When the full circle had been completed, the music stopped suddenly, and Leroy's voice came over the speaker again. "This time we go over the top." The music, more raucous than ever, then came on again.

Buck noticed that the portly middle-aged man had gone full cycle, returning to the source of his first enjoyment, the young blond sailor.

It didn't take long. The boys had already been worked to a feverish pitch, and each of them, beginning with the blond sailor, began shooting off. The sailor reached for the portly man's head, forcing him down even more onto his penis as if protecting himself from the man pulling away at the crucial explosion. He need not have feared. The man stayed on him until the eruption had long ceased.

With an apparent reluctance each man lifted his satisfied mouth off each performer and retreated into the dim recesses of the arena.

Leroy's voice came over the speaker again. "Gentlemen," he said. "The party's not over. Now that you've sampled the wares of our young men, I presume you're in a position to make your final appraisals from upclose knowledge. It's time to select a boy of your choice and to disappear into our private chambers. Each boy has already agreed to give every part of their bodies to you, including their mouths and lips. There are no limits to what you can do, including penetration. But nothing sadistic. If you cause pain or hurt one of our boys in any way, the party's over for you. House rules. Otherwise enjoy, enjoy!"

Buck remained alone in the cramped room as the lights in the arena eventually dimmed. He found his whole body soaked in sweat from having watched the performers. He was sexually aroused by the show almost more than he'd ever been in his life. He wanted relief at this point so badly he would have given in to Leroy.

At the thought of Leroy, there was a soft tapping on his door which was immediately opened by Leroy. "I wanted to give you a warning I was back in case you were jacking off after watching our show."

"Thanks. Some show!"

"You can say that again. But there's more to happen. I've got a prize for you to top them all. Come with me."

*****

In a little foyer off one of the upstairs bedrooms, Leroy ushered Buck into even more cramped quarters than downstairs. "If you thought the show put on downstairs was something, wait until you see this one."

"You're a real pal, Leroy."

"Thanks. After posing for those pictures, I owe you a favor. You're going to get to see the whole thing. The boy knows you're watching but the john doesn't. Both the boy and the john are known by you. I don't think you've ever met the boy but you know of him. The john you certainly know."

"You make all this sound real intriguing. I can't wait."

"The boy has volunteered to be with you tonight if you're hot for him after watching the performance he's putting on especially for you."

"I'm honored."

"Sorry, I can't be here for the action, but I'm arranging things all over the house. Just Call Me Madam, or Ethel Merman." After a quick kiss on Buck's cheek, Leroy departed from the little room. "Enjoy,

enjoy, enjoy," he whispered. "Pull back the drape at any moment. The show has already begun. Curtains up!"

For some reason Buck was shaking as he pulled back the black velvet curtain on another two-way mirror. A young boy dressed in white had entered the room and was slowly and very tantalizingly removing his clothes. First went the shirt revealing a perfectly formed hairless chest. The look was all too familiar. Buck raised his eyes and looked directly into the face of Shelley.

Although the boy couldn't see Buck, he knew he was there and stared defiantly at the mirror. A slight smile crossed his beautiful face as he unbuckled his white pants and lowered them. He was wearing no underwear. In moments he'd exposed his genitals to Buck.

In the cramped little room, Buck was sweating profusely. Leroy had indeed surprised him. He hadn't expected this at all and was acutely uncomfortable. His mouth was dry, and he kept clenching and unclenching his fist.

Fully nude, Shelley lay down on the bed, raising one leg provocatively.

Fresh from the campaign trail, Barry Collins came into the room. On seeing Shelley, he said something but Buck couldn't hear. Shelley ran his fingers up and down his flawless body, then rolled over, presenting his buttocks to Barry.

Barry quickly removed his coat, shirt, and tie, then slipped off his underwear top. He unbuckled his pants and dropped them to the floor, easing out of them as he slipped off his loafers. Reaching inside the band, he lowered his jockey shorts and stepped out of them. Never taking his eyes off Shelley, Barry was already fully aroused.

On the bed with Shelley he reached for the boy, pulling his buttocks against his genitals and pressing hard into Shelley's flesh. He bit into the back of Shelley's neck as one hand traced patterns on Shelley's chest before settling on one of the boy's brown nipples which he pinched something fierce. Shelley winced with pain but made no protest.

Barry was running his fingers over Shelley's smooth ass, fondling each buttock with gentleness before inserting a finger between the crack. Buck looked into Shelley's face as the finger was inserted in him, and the boy stared right back at him in the mirror.

Suddenly, Barry forced Shelley to rise up on his knees, his buttocks sticking up in the air, his face buried in a fluffy pillow.

Beginning slowly Barry slapped Shelley's buttocks. At first they were gentle slaps but the intensity increased until they became sharp and stinging. Shelley's buttocks were turning red. The boy writhed and arched his back as the blows rained down. The whipping hand finally stopped and Barry leaned down and licked each buttock gently, tonguing all around the area as if that would bring relief from the pain he had so recently inflicted.

He then took Shelley in his arms, turning the boy's face to his as he pressed his body against Shelley. When Shelley's face met his, Barry kissed the lips of the boy, running his tongue around the upper lip before biting down on the lower lip. Before Shelley could protest, Barry had inserted his tongue inside Shelley's mouth. That tongue was sucked expertly.

Very gently Barry started to kiss and lick Shelley's trembling body. He had clearly aroused passion in the boy who now seemed prepared to accept whatever Barry wanted to do with him. Barry raised his body up over Shelley's after a tongue attack on the boy's stomach. Their eyes locked. They were lovers about to make love.

Barry leaned down and kissed the boy long and hard. Breaking from Shelley's mouth, Barry spit in his hand and jerked the boy's legs apart. He inserted two fingers in Shelley's butt as he pinched one of the boys nipples. Barry rubbed his sweaty, hairy chest against Shelley's hairless one. Shelley wrapped his legs around Barry, who supported the boy's thighs on his shoulders. Shelley was about to get fucked, and he appeared eager for the penetration.

Buck had had enough. Even though he was fully erect and had been aroused by this scene as he had by no other in his entire life, he simply couldn't take it any more. Blind rage drove him on at this point. He tried to hold back, to let his sanity take charge. But other forces were driving him now, as he opened the door to his cramped cubicle and headed with anger and determination to Shelley's room. He'd noticed that Barry hadn't locked the door when he came in and spotted Shelley lying there nude.

At the very moment that Barry was pressing his dickhead between Shelley's buttocks, Buck threw open the door and came into the room, slamming it behind him.

Barry looked up and was totally startled. "What the fuck? Buck? What in hell are you doing here? God damn you! Can't you see this is private business."

"Listen, Collins, if you don't want the shit beat out of you, I suggest you get off that boy, get your clothes on as fast as you've ever dressed in your life, and get the fuck out of this house."

"Hi, Buck," Shelley said provocatively as Barry rose from the bed. "God, you're handsome when you're mad."

Without saying another word, Barry rushed to retrieve his clothes, slipping into his trousers and forgetting his jockey shorts. With his trousers still unzipped, he made for the door, retrieving his shoes, jacket and shirt.

Before opening the door, he stood to confront Buck. "It's very clear. You're not going to expose me. No way. You're not going to ruin me and my campaign. I know why you're here. You're jealous. You want the boy for yourself."

"Get the fuck out of my sight, stink ball. I could never stand you, and right now I even hate you."

"Go fuck yourself," Barry said defiantly, opening the door to the hall. "Better yet, fuck the little minister here. He's the best lay in town." With that parting remark, Barry fled down the hallway.

Buck shut the door and turned to confront Shelley.

"I hope you're going to finish the job," Shelley said, raising his eyebrows. "I need to get fucked. I mean, really fucked by a real man. The oral stuff is great with you, but it's time we took our love affair to a different plateau. Besides, your cock is three times the size of Barry's."

Without saying anything, Buck went over to the chair and tossed Shelley his white pants. "Get your clothes on. I'm taking you out of here. Forever."

Reluctantly and with a slight pout on his mouth, Shelley crawled off the bed and began to dress in front of Buck's appreciative eyes.

"Listen, you little whore, if I ever catch you with another man I'll beat the shit out of you. If you want to get fucked so badly I'm the guy to do it. I'll fuck you all night if that's what you want."

As he was slipping into his shirt, Shelley stopped dressing to turn and look at Buck. It was as if he'd heard the words but couldn't believe them. "That's exactly what I want to hear." Putting on his shirt, he moved toward Buck and stood only inches from his face.

Buck was shaking. He was completely out of control. He didn't know what to say or do. Since he couldn't utter words, he decided to let his body speak for him. That body of his reached out and crashed Shelley in his arms, as Buck's tongue made a vain attempt to reach and overpower Shelley's throat. Shelley folded his body into Buck's, pressing hard against the older man's flesh. He sucked Buck's tongue voraciously as if it were the finest meal he'd ever been fed.

Buck ran his hands across Shelley's body, cupping each buttock forcefully, not really wanting to let go of the left one but also eager to possess the right one. Shelley was moaning, and for one brief moment Buck was tempted to rip off the boy's clothes and take him on the spot.

But sanity was beginning to return, and he wanted to flee this house with Shelley.

When Shelley finally released Buck's tongue, he planted little wet kisses on Buck's nose, forehead, cheeks, lips, and chin. Buck felt Shelley's tears on his face. He knew they weren't tears of sorrow but of pure joy. He felt he could almost cry himself.

"I'm yours forever," Shelley said. "I set this whole thing up just to see if you'd come and claim me. I'm yours. I'm your boy. I'll do anything for you. I'll give you pleasure you've never known before. But there's one thing." He moved his face slightly away from Buck's and looked into Buck's eyes with such love and intensity that Buck found it hard to breathe. "You must say it. I must hear it from your lips."

Buck swallowed hard. He started to speak but the words wouldn't come out. As he looked more deeply into Shelley's demanding eyes, he knew he had to say it. He'd deal with the consequences later. He pulled Shelley up close to him and tongued his left ear, biting and nibbling at it. "I'm in love with you," he whispered in the deep recesses of that ear.

*****

At The Rusty Pelican on the beach, the same place where she'd gone on the date with Buck, Susan almost experienced *déjà vu* as she stared into the face of Don Bossdum. Just as she'd been taken back by the similarity of looks between Robert and Buck, now she was intrigued by how much Don resembled Buck as well.

What was obvious to her was that Buck was an American type. Every campus in America had a Buck. Yet her husband wasn't ordinary. Although the classic American blond stud, Buck somehow pulled the package together better than most men. His features were more refined, aristocratic.

Don, on the other hand, appeared a cruder version of Buck. Since she'd last seen him, the lines in his face were more pronounced, and he'd gained a bit of weight. In spite of that, no one—man or woman—in a singles bar would say no to him.

Ever since she'd returned his call, and he'd invited her immediately for dinner, he'd been charming and gracious. Don was most attentive. In spite of all the other beautiful women in the room, he'd never taken his eyes off her all evening, and they were into their fourth drink, Don preferring beer to her chilled white wine.

On the surface, he appeared everything that a woman could dream about: tall, blond, lightly sun tanned, luminous blue eyes, a gracious smile, pearly white teeth, ruggedly handsome but not beautiful, masculine, articulate but not overly educated, and athletic. It was easy to succumb to the charms of such a man, especially if the bleak evening had caught you wandering around your new condo wondering where your husband might be—and with whom—and pondering what an awful trap you might have stumbled into, one of your own making.

Reaching for her hand and cradling it gently, Don said, "I can't believe I finally got you to go out on a date with me. As you know, I tried several times at the university but Gene always beat me out. I could see why you and a lot of other girls went for him—even Pamela Collins. He was one good-looking guy. Sorry things didn't work out for you two. I heard all about it."

"Even in Miami?"

"Even down in Miami." He sighed and leaned back. "I don't know if you know this but I got married too."

"I think I've heard that. I guess your marriage didn't work out either. I'm sorry."

"So am I. I guess we didn't have the love we thought we had. I think it started out based on physical attraction. I thought the love might follow. It didn't."

"Too bad."

"In more ways than one. I lost everything I'd ever worked for. She didn't leave me with a stick of furniture. You may not have known this, but when your call came in, it was to a seedy rooming house. In the morning I'm out looking for a job. Otherwise I won't be able to pay the rent. Talk about getting cleaned out. My savings, everything."

"What a rotten break."

"Do you know where I might find work? I'll take any job."

"Let me think. I've just been fired myself. From the Examiner."

"Sorry to hear that. I always thought you were a damn good reporter."

"I still am. I wasn't fired because of incompetence. It was political."

He leaned back in his padded seat. "The bastards."

"Sounds like you'd better get a job—sooner than later." She sipped her wine. "I'm coming up with an idea. I don't know if you've ever met my father, Jim Howard."

"I've certainly heard of him."

"He's got a lot of clients in real estate. I'm sure there would be something there for you. How are you at showing rental properties to prospective clients?"

"I'd be really great at that. I can be very convincing."

"I bet you can. I'll call him tomorrow and beg him to set up an interview for you right away since your cash is running low."

"Running low," he said. "It practically doesn't exist. This is my first meal of the day, and I've got to admit to you I can't pay for it."

"Don't worry about that. This is the liberated 70s. Besides, I like to pay when I go out on a date. Makes me more in charge somehow."

"Then if you're paying it, I won't hold back when the waitress comes. I'm starving."

"Order anything you want—the lobster, whatever."

"A lobster?" He smiled with a certain charm. "It's been a long time since I've seen one of those."

"Here comes the waitress now."

After Don ordered a heavy meal—the lobster dinner with all the works—and she requested a light one, she settled into the booth with him with a certain comfort. He didn't threaten or intimidate her. In fact, knowing that he was broke gave her a certain power over him. When she was with Buck, the cards were so stacked in his favor that she felt she must at least to some extent, do his bidding. But with Don things could be different. She liked the idea of that. After all, he wasn't a cheap hustler. He wanted to work for a living and she admired that in him.

"You're too big a guy to skip meals." She finished the last of her wine and reached for his hand which he willingly offered. "I could help you out. Tide you over until you get on your feet again."

"But you said you're out of a job yourself."

"I'm out of a job, but I may be set to take over the biggest position of my life. Sorry, I can't tell you what it is now." For one brief moment she feared that Buck's promise to buy out the News and make her the publisher might be an empty one. "I'm not exactly down and out. You'll see that later if you come back to my condo."

He smiled and laughed a bit nervously. "I thought you'd never ask."

"There is something I should tell you. It's going to be officially announced later, and it's a deep, deep secret although many people already know about it."

"I can keep a secret. Trust me."

"I'm a married woman."

"Didn't you get a divorce from Gene? I didn't know you were still married to him."

"Gene and I divorced a long time ago. But I recently got married."

"And you're out dating me?"

"The marriage isn't an ordinary marriage. It was a marriage entered into to save an inheritance." She looked skeptically at him. "I don't really want to tell you, but if you and I are going to get involved, you'd find out sooner than later. I married Buck Brooke quite recently."

"I assume you mean the younger version and not the old crone."

"I do indeed."

He arched his eyebrows. "That surprises me a bit. Of course, you did say it was a marriage of convenience. I always thought that Buck was gay. He even came on to me one afternoon in the locker room while we were showering."

She looked at him suspiciously. For the first time this evening, he had struck a glaring note. In her bone marrow, she didn't believe what he'd said. He was lying. But she decided not to challenge it.

"I thought Robert Dante had his hooks so deep into Buck that he'd never release him for a woman."

"As I said the marriage was to save an inheritance." She was relieved that the waitress was arriving with the food. The conversation had made her nervous, and she feared she'd been very indiscreet to have confided even this much to Don.

As Don attacked his lobster, she felt she'd use her recent confidence to extract some very secret information from him as well. "Since I'm confessing everything, I want us to even the score. I mean, let me ask you a question. A big one. It's personal and you, of course, don't have to answer it."

"Fire away. My life's an open book."

"You've heard rumors about Buck. I'm sure plenty of rumors have been spread about Gene and me. But I've also heard rumors about you."

He stopped eating for a moment and carefully searched her face, seemingly looking for clues as to what she might know. "What kind of rumors?"

"About you and Sister Rose."

His face registered no emotion. In fact, it remained blank as if the name were unfamiliar to him. "I'm not a born again Christian if that's what you mean. I've never even seen Sister Rose, much less had an affair with her. I didn't know the moral crusader slept around."

"Forgive me for asking. It was impertinent. Absolutely none of my business."

"With beauty queens like you running around, what do I need with an old bag like Rose?" Avoiding her eyes, he attacked that lobster with a kind of fury. He was one hungry man.

She believed his story about not eating all day. What she didn't believe was his denial about Sister Rose. Call it a woman's instinct or a reporter's intuition, but she felt he knew Sister Rose very well. She sensed that long before she planned to climb Don Bossdum mountain, Sister Rose had been there before her, carefully scaling every inch.

"Speaking of beauty queens," he said, interrupting her disturbing thought, "unless I'm seeing things I just saw Pamela Collins go into the women's room. My old flame. I sure don't want to run into her tonight."

"You probably don't need your vision checked. She's been known to hang out here. Which reminds me. I too need to powder my nose. Perhaps I'll run into Pamela. I won't tell her I'm with you. Her husband's running for mayor. Barry. You remember him."

He slammed down his fork, a sense of fury and rage consuming his features. "If I ever run into that son of a bitch, I'll bash the asshole's face in."

She was momentarily taken back by this sudden emergence of a violent streak in him. "He must have done something real bad to you."

"He did. But I can't talk about it." He looked down at his plate and resumed eating but not with the same vigor as before. "While you're gone, can I get the waitress to bring you another wine?"

"You can indeed, my good man," she said, getting up. "I think I need all the fortification I can get for tonight."

Brushing his hand softly, she headed for the women's room where she encountered Pamela in front of the mirror. The former Miss Florida was checking her appearance. Her makeup was slightly smeared. She was definitely drunk.

"Susan Howard as I live and breathe. You're looking good."

"So are you. If they were giving away a prize for beauty you won it. Not just Miss Florida. If I recall, you were voted rodeo queen when the cowboys hit town."

She smiled back at Susan. "There was more to it than that. I did some of the boys a certain favor."

"I see," Susan said. She turned from the woman to go into a nearby booth, but Pamela reached to restrain her.

"I need to talk to somebody. Somebody with good connections. Like you. You've got powerful parents. I hear you're dating Buck Brooke. He's got connections.

"Sure, I'll talk to you." She reached for her purse and jotted down her new number on a pad of paper. Fired reporter or not, she always kept a pencil and a pad of paper in her purse.

"I'll call you," Pamela said. "It's urgent." She had a sense of desperation about her that deeply disturbed Susan.

A lot about the way this evening was going disturbed her but she decided to retreat to the toilet instead.

"Oh, Susan," Pamela said, smiling graciously as two older women entered the room. "I may not look exactly like I did when I won the Miss Florida contest, but Santa Claus comes to those who wait even though he's left you empty-handed before."

"I'm sorry but I don't get it."

Speaking in a low voice so as not to be overheard by the women who'd come into the room, Pamela leaned over to Susan and gave her a light kiss on the cheek. "Gene Robinson is moving in with Barry and me tonight. I'm sure it'll be a cozy arrangement." With those parting words, she looked once more into the dressing mirror and turned and left.

Susan was completely bewildered, not really believing she'd heard this right.

"Aren't you Susan Howard?" one of the older women asked, studying her carefully. "And wasn't that Pamela Collins? Isn't she the wife of Barry? We're voting for him for mayor."

"No," Susan said before retreating into a booth. "We're just imposters."

*****

In the back seat of his limousine with its darkened windows, Buck reached out for Shelley and pulled him close. He kissed the boy's lips feverishly before inserting his tongue for Shelley to suck. "Don't you ever let me catch you with another man." He knew the chauffeur could see him kissing Shelley but didn't care at this point.

"I belong to you," Shelley whispered as he nibbled at Buck's ear. "I always will."

"I love you, boy. It was an immediate attraction. The first time I saw you in the dressing room at the temple, I wanted to grab you and rape you."

"Why didn't you?"

"Great self-control."

"You can lose some of that God damn self-control." Shelley's skilled fingers had settled comfortably between Buck's legs. He was handling, fondling, and massaging the basket of goodies here as if he owned the package. "There can be more later—a lot more—but for the moment I've got to drink some of sweetest tasting nectar on earth," Shelley said.

As Shelley unzipped him and removed his already fully aroused cock, Buck settled comfortably into the well-padded upholstery and ran his fingers through Shelley's beautiful blond hair as he was serviced expertly. Soft groans were escaping from Buck's throat, and he wanted to do more than that. He wanted to scream in ecstacy at getting loved with such a talented tongue but tried to control himself considering where he was.

Shelley had removed Buck's balls and when he wasn't deep-throating Buck, he licked and devoured each one. What Buck liked about Shelley's love-making was that he gave almost equal attention to the balls as to the cock. He wanted more from Shelley, but this expert tonguing would have to do for the moment. He ran his hands across Shelley's back, heading for his buttocks which he squeezed and caressed. He slipped his hand inside Shelley's trousers, his finger moving gently down the crack until it found its target. Once there, Buck with ease and care inserted his finger deep as it would go inside Shelley.

The boy moaned in pleasure devouring Buck with even greater ferocity. After Buck had been thoroughly kissed, nibbled, licked, and sucked, Shelley raised himself over Buck, then plunged down on his cock, letting it slowly invade his throat.

Buck didn't know how the boy managed this, but it was the most delectable sexual thrill he'd ever known. He reached for Shelley's throat with his free hand, as if he could feel himself buried there. In moments Shelley backed up and gasped for air, but when his lungs were filled he returned again and again to let Buck penetrate his throat.

Buck couldn't take much more of this without exploding. When his eruption fired, it was directly into Shelley's gasping throat. It was as if Buck's semen was being shot directly into Shelley's stomach avoiding the mouth. But Shelley backed off slightly, obviously wanting to savor the final blast in his mouth. When Buck was long spent, Shelley continued to lick him clean. Only when the tool was mostly deflated, he pulled off, releasing it from between his lips. He crawled up and reached for Buck's mouth. As Buck kissed Shelley, he tongued his mouth, tasting himself. He put his hand to Shelley's throat again, massaging it. "That was a sensation I'll never forget."

"You've got a lot more sensations coming, big boy," Shelley said. "I plan to devote my life to giving you the most exquisite pleasure."

"I'll have it no other way." Suddenly, a reality came over Buck. As long as they were cruising aimlessly within the confines of this big dark limousine, he felt protected as if in a womb. But he had to get on with his life. Uncle Milty and Patrick were throwing a dinner for Robert and him. Buck was already hours late and hadn't called. He instructed the rather blasé driver to take Shelley to Paradise Shores.

"I've got to go to my lawyer's house, and I'm late. I'm dropping you off. He's had his first meeting with Rose's money boys. About the media director thing."

"I demand that you take the job, and the fringe benefit that comes with it."

"You mean yourself?" Buck asked.

"You got it!"

"You sweet, beautiful boy, you are no fringe benefit. You're the pot of gold waiting at the end of the rainbow." He reached between Shelley's legs, fondling his cock and finding it fully erect. "I can't let you get out of this car without handling this. I want to empty those luscious golden balls of yours."

Without saying a word, Shelley unzipped and freed himself, moving over Buck's body as he lay back in the seat. He plunged his cock into Buck's devouring mouth and Buck eagerly sucked and tasted the boy. It was the most delicious taste and aroma he'd ever known in his life. Shelley was able to hold back for at least 10 minutes and never once did Buck release him but continued to tongue, lick and suck until he had the boy moaning. Without warning, Shelley blasted into his mouth and Buck didn't want to swallow it right away. He wanted to keep the load there to taste and savor. But when Shelley kept pushing into his mouth demanding that Buck swallow his offering, Buck did, savoring every drop.

As the limousine sped to Paradise Shores, Buck truly believed he had ensnared Florida's most luscious golden boy. There could be nothing better than Shelley. He was thrilling, almost like a fantasy.

As he licked Shelley's lips and gently kissed them, Buck reached once again to cup Shelley's buttocks and to rub his finger up and down the crack, paying attention to the soft, yielding tissue of the rosebud.

"The next time we meet, and it's going to be soon and constant, I'm going to spend an hour or two with my tongue buried here. After that, I'm going to bury something else in you and I'm not going to take it out until you've come three times and let me taste every drop."

"That's a promise I'm holding you to, big man." Shelley licked Buck's left ear and ran his tongue along Buck's sweaty throat, cleaning it and enjoying the salty sweat.

Buck returned the favor, wetting down and licking Shelley's throat and still marveling at how the boy had managed to open it to his invasion and give him such joy.

"I'm in love with you, and I'm sorry I did what I did tonight," Shelley said. "But I smoked you out of the closet. Like I said, I planned the whole thing with Leroy."

"Forget about it! I don't ever want to think about it again."

"I'll never mention it."

At the gateway to Paradise Shores, Shelley adjusted his clothing before getting out. He gave Buck one long, lingering kiss. He reached for a pad resting on the limousine bar and wrote down a telephone number. "As soon as you have a free moment at your attorney's, slip away and call me. I have to know how I can reach you at all times. Until we start living openly together, we're going to keep this relationship in the closet. But it's active and hot. I need to feel I can call you at all times.

"But you can't identify yourself."

"I've got that all worked out. I'm a man of many voices. I think you're going to take that director's job in spite of Rose being upset at learning about your marriage. She'll learn to deal with it. I'm going to be Arlie Ray Minton, your associate secretary, one authorized to call you day and night regarding developments in Rose's empire."

"That will work. I'll call you later."

"I have a plush condo," Shelley said. "Even Rose doesn't know I own it. We can meet there at any time. Even if both of us have only thirty minutes, that will do until we can spend long, long nights in each other's arms." He kissed Buck once more and got out of the car, pressing a secret code to enter the gates at Paradise Shores. Without looking back, he walked with confidence and a certain swagger into the compound.

Buck instructed the driver to take him to his attorney's home. As he leaned back in the seat and marveled over the past hours, he was relieved that there had been no mention of Robert. It was Robert who now moved into his thoughts, consuming them. He loved Robert as deeply and passionately as he loved Shelley. He loved them both and wanted them both. As of this moment, he couldn't even bear the idea of losing either of them. Tomorrow he would try to figure out what to do. He couldn't think of a solution right now. He closed his eyes, thinking of

Robert loving and kissing him. As soon as Robert's image invaded his mind, it gave way to Shelley's radiance and beauty. Buck shut his eyes and tried to think of anything but his two loves. But he couldn't. They overpowered his mind.

Buck bolted upright in his seat. What about Gene? Gene had revealed a side of Buck that he didn't even know existed. With Robert and Shelley, Buck was in charge, but with Gene he'd become the yielding object of affection, the pliant one, the endless giver, the receiver. It was as if his role with Gene was the same role that Robert and Shelley acted out for him. But there was no time for Gene now, not even to think about him. Gene had rejected him or was it his rejection of Gene that had caused this break in their relationship?

As he peered out the window of the limousine, he realized he'd been delivered to the dimly lit home of Uncle Milty. With trepidation, he entered the gates and walked with fear and dread to face what might be waiting for him on the other side of the door. Only then did he remember the excuse he'd told Robert about why he'd be late for the dinner.

*****

In a tank top and too-tight shorts, Patrick opened the door to welcome Buck. Uncle Milty's former toy boy—picked up on a beach in Fort Lauderdale in 1969—had stayed around ever since. No longer quite as young and beautiful as he once was, Patrick still had a masculine beauty and charm, and Buck always understood his appeal to Robert as a friend. His hair was blond, aided in part by bleach and in part by the sun. He kissed Buck on the mouth...hard.

"Sorry I'm late," Buck said.

"We went ahead and had dinner without you. I'm a great cook. You really missed out, but I'll whip something up for you. Milty can always throw another steak on the grill."

Seeing Robert emerge, Buck rushed toward him and kissed him and held him close. "I've missed you, baby, but I couldn't help it."

Robert backed away slightly. "Chivas Regal, is it?"

Before getting out of the limousine, Buck had rinsed his mouth thoroughly with Scotch and spat the wash on the sidewalk, hoping the liquor would obliterate the taste of Shelley's semen.

"What kept you?" Robert asked.

"They detained me at police headquarters," Buck lied. "Biff thinks he's got the man who called in the bomb threat." Actually Buck had received a call from Biff who'd given him the news. Buck was asked to come down to the station in the morning, not this evening.

"Who was it?"

"Julius Forster, or so they think."

"You mean, our local Nazi?"

"One and the same," Buck said. "Biff called Forster in for questioning. You know, round up the usual suspects."

"Good, they found the bastard. I hope they lock him up." Robert took Buck's hand. "Thank God you're here and safe. When you're away from me, I don't feel like a whole man. I feel that half of me is missing."

"That's great news for a lover to hear." He leaned over and tongued Robert's ear. "You're going to get it tonight."

Robert looked trustingly into Buck's eye. "I love you, big guy. Really love you."

Feeling guilty but hoping it didn't show, Buck returned Robert's look of devotion. "I love you too, Robert. I always will. I'll always be here for you no matter what."

"Now let's get Uncle Milty to hustle up a steak for my hungry man. You'll need the energy for what I have planned for you tonight."

Buck wrapped an arm around Robert's waist. "But aren't we supposed to wait until after we're married?"

"Sex out of wedlock—sounds hot. Of course, sex after marriage sounds even better. I really want this marriage. The wedding's set for late tomorrow morning in Miami. We've made all the arrangements."

"Great!" was all Buck managed to say as he trailed Robert into the patio. He'd tried to say the word with as much enthusiasm as he could muster.

Out on the patio Uncle Milty with a cooking fork waved Buck over to a grill where a steak sizzled. "Come over here, handsome hunk, and give your Uncle Milty a big sloppy wet one."

"Got held up—really sorry." He kissed Uncle Milty on the mouth as he always did. His attorney demanded that, although these kisses between friends were always a little too sloppy for Buck. Attired in a white apron sprinkled with red hearts, Uncle Milty wore baggy shorts and, like Patrick, a tank top. Unlike the other three specimens of male flesh on the patio, each finely tuned to perfection, Uncle Milty let his pot belly grow an inch or two every year. He was a bit bow-legged, his eyes bulged, and he had craters in his face left over from what he always called "the world's worst case of acne as a teenager." But Patrick obviously adored him, even though Buck used to view Patrick as a mere street hustler. In spite of the physical differences between them, there seemed to be a strong bond.

Buck was also grateful that Robert liked Patrick. He wanted Robert to have some friends and not focus exclusively on him all the time.

"Patrick's going to give away the bride tomorrow—and ain't that just great?" Uncle Milty asked.

"Come on, Uncle Milty," Buck said as a way of reprimand. "You know I don't like to hear Robert referred to as a woman."

"But one of you has got to be the bride," Uncle Milty protested. "You look too much like a Roman gladiator to be a bride. The captain of a football team, but no bride."

"I prefer to call it a marriage of husband and husband," Buck said, taking Robert's hand and kissing the inner palm. It tasted so good he began to suck Robert's fingers in devotion. Robert ran his fingers through Buck's hair. Robert had always liked to do that. Buck looked over at Uncle Milty after his finger sucking. "I love this beauty here. Don't let him get away from me again."

"Robert will never leave you," Uncle Milty assured him. "It's going to be one of those until-death-do-you-part kind of marriages."

Patrick came up from behind Buck, offering him his favorite Scotch and soda. "I give you guys at least forty years—maybe even fifty. I'll throw your golden wedding anniversary."

"Fifty would be stretching it for me," Uncle Milty said. "I'm not as young as you beautiful boys. And these God damn varicose veins."

As Buck ate his steak, Uncle Milty related the details of his meeting with Sister Rose's money boys. "Apparently, there is money here from God. At first I thought this media director thing was some press secretary shit which wouldn't have been right for you. But it's big and getting bigger."

"Exactly what would Buck have to do for this kind of money?" Robert demanded to know.

"A little bit of everything. They want to take over newspapers. Buy radio and television stations. Even go into entertainment. Finance films. They're even considering buying up several TV sitcoms from long ago."

"You mean I'd end up negotiating the rights for I Love Lucy?" Buck asked.

"Something like that—it's really big," Uncle Milty said with all seriousness. "As I warned you, I'd quit everything and devote myself full time to my favorite client."

Buck held a fork with a morsel of steak at his mouth. "What did you do, Uncle Milty? You're not telling me everything."

"I more or less accepted for you."

"You did?" Robert's words stabbed the air. "Without really sitting down and talking to us. I'm not happy at having Buck work for this Christian psychotic."

"I'm not either," Uncle Milty said. "I can't stand the holy cow. But wait until you hear the terms."

"You mean three million big ones a year?" Buck asked.

"A little more than that. I'm a greedy Jew bastard when I'm not your loving Uncle Milty. I kick ass. When all those deals are being made, I'm going to see that Buck Brooke III's name comes in for a lot of stock. As far as I'm concerned, the three million is only the down payment. You see I think I'm smarter than Rose's boys. Unless they're real killers at reading the fine print, I'm going to take the fuckers for all I can get."

Buck finished his dinner and didn't say much. It was more than he could handle at any rate. "It's a strange new world I'm heading into."

"We'll just have to play it one step at a time," Uncle Milty said.

"It scares me," Robert said. "I'm afraid for Buck to get mixed up in all this crap."

"Don't you want a rich husband?" Uncle Milty asked. "One who could buy you a mink or sable every week."

"Fuck mink or sable," Robert said, reaching possessively for Buck's hand. "We live in Okeechobee where it's hot most of the time. Who needs fur?"

"A few fur coats are always good to have. After all, Buck's going to own a condo in New York when the old man passes on."

"Any news on that front?" Buck asked apprehensively.

"I'm in secret touch with his doctors," Uncle Milty said. "Three times a day I speak to them. They're not hopeful, monkey gland transplant or not. They think it's a matter of just a few more months to live. Weeks maybe."

"I'll fly to his side at any moment," Buck promised.

"As long as he's coherent, he keeps saying he doesn't want you there," Uncle Milty said. "But that could change. What I think is, he doesn't want you to see how weak and pathetic he's become. Still trying to maintain some macho image with you. But his nurses have even got him on the bed pan now."

Buck shuddered at the images flashing through his mind. "Poor man. I know he's a bastard in many ways, but I still love him."

Uncle Milty signaled Patrick to bring him a piece of paper. "Here's a number for you to call. It's an office in Los Angeles. Rose's boys want to set up a meeting with you sooner than later. They're flying the contracts to Miami. After they're signed, they want to turn over the millions to you personally. I demanded to go but they want to talk privately with you. Of course, all future deals have to be run by me. They understand that."

"What do you think they want?" Buck asked.

"Just to check you out in the flesh. After all they're paying triple for everything. The Examiner isn't worth what they're paying."

"I don't understand. If they want me to be media director, why not let me handle the Examiner too?"

"I know," Uncle Milty said. "That's a mystery to me too. But it seems the Examiner was promised to someone else."

"Who, for God's sake?"

"I'm not sure—it's a real mystery."

"I'd better get used to mysteries if I'm getting involved with these goons," Buck said. "I'll make the call right now from your library." He kissed Robert good-bye for a moment. "I'll be right back to claim those lips."

In the library he dialed Shelley's number.

The boy sounded sleepy. "I was just dreaming about you."

"Wake up and write down these numbers," Buck said. "I'm here at my attorney's home. Here's his private number. Here's my private home number." He gave both numbers to Shelley. "I'll be home around two o'clock this morning. That media director thing's getting hot."

"I knew it would. They're going to make you offers you can't refuse."

"Who is they?"

"That's for you to find out."

"I've got to go, hot stuff," Buck said. He looked over his shoulder, finding that he was alone in the room. "I love you, boy. I truly love you. I can still taste you."

"I need you right now to come and hold me in your arms until I fall asleep. That brings up another point. I might as well confess something. The way I like to fall asleep is to have you gently lick all over my body until I go off to dreamland."

"That's an offer I'll take you up on. I'd better go now. I love you."

"I love you too, Buck, and miss you something awful right now."

"Me too."

He put down the phone and immediately dialed the California number. A heavily accented male voice came on the phone, and he couldn't detect the accent.

"We were expecting your call," the mysterious voice said. "Actually, there's been a change of plans. Our supervisor would like to meet with you. The venue will be Sister Rose's estate in Palm Springs, not our offices here in Los Angeles. You're to make arrangements through her. Thank you for calling, Mr. Brooke." Without saying another word, the man hung up the phone.

Buck walked back into the patio and immediately went over to kiss Robert.

"What did they say?" Uncle Milty asked.

"A meeting is going to be set up in Palm Springs, but it's going to be arranged through Sister Rose. I think they preferred Los Angeles but Rose is holding out for Palm Springs."

"You're going to walk out of that meeting with a lot of money," Uncle Milty said. "I think I'd better start raising my fees."

"Another thing I learned," Buck said, knowing he was going to lie. "For the loot they're paying me, I've got to be at their beck and call 24 hours a day. They've got to know a number they can reach me at all times. They've even hired a guy, Arlie Ray Minton, to keep track of me." He turned to Robert. "So if Arlie Ray calls, whoever that creep is, I'm all ears. Okay?"

"Okay," Robert said, looking disappointed. "I don't like them having such control over you."

"They're entitled," Uncle Milty said. "I mean, we're talking millions."

Patrick came onto the patio carrying some flambé dessert he'd just put the finishing touches to. "This is a pre-marriage celebration," he said gleefully. Robert rushed to help him serve the desserts.

"Incidentally," Buck said, "I didn't come completely clean with those guys in California."

"How so?" Uncle Milty asked.

"I didn't tell them I'm rushing off to get married in the morning." Buck paused and looked over at Robert and smiled. "To a man."

*****

In bed, his body entwined with that of Robert, Buck heard the phone's urgent ring. The sound was coming from a sitting area off his bedroom but it seemed miles away in his foggy brain.

Robert separated himself from Buck and went to answer the phone. Within a minute, he returned. "It's that Arlie Ray Minton guy you mentioned. Sounds like a creep. You haven't even signed the contract and they're calling you at three o'clock in the morning." The nude Robert crawled back into bed.

Suddenly bolting up and awake, Buck walked naked across the bedroom floor to answer the phone.

"What is it?" Buck asked.

At the sound of his voice, Shelley said, "It's Rose. You've got to come over here at once. She cut her throat but she's okay."

"Are you serious? This can't be. I'll be right over." He put down the receiver and returned to the bedroom. "I've got to go to Paradise Shores. The shit's hit the fan. Sister Rose tried to kill herself."

Robert sat up in bed. "She's crazier than I thought she was."

Hurriedly dressing, he kissed Robert good-bye, promising to check in with him later. On the way to Paradise Shores, he drove as fast as he dared. The trip was agonizing, and at one point he feared a motorcycle patrolman might stop him for speeding.

At Paradise Shores, he got out of his car as a distraught Shelley, clad only in a pair of rose-colored jockey shorts, rushed out to meet him. "Thank God you're here." He threw himself into Buck's arms, hugging him tightly and kissing him on the mouth.

"Where is she?" Buck asked.

"The doctor's with her now." The boy appeared on the verge of tears. "A little while ago she called for you."

Entering the grand marble foyer, Buck turned to Shelley. "Just what happened?"

Taking his hand and guiding him into the living room, a nervous, almost nude Shelley tried to piece together the story. Earlier, Rose had pleaded with him to have the chauffeur drive over to her doctor's house to obtain more Seconals. The doctor had refused. "He told me not to let her take any more pills," Shelley said. "She was already on Dexedrine."

Not really knowing what to say, Buck walked to the patio off the living room. To divert his mind, he looked up at the night sky. What was he searching for? The Big Dipper? The Southern Cross? He didn't know one from the other.

"Sometimes she has these wild mood swings," Shelley said, coming up behind Buck and putting his arms around him. "She just bubbles over at times. Tonight she was at her most self-destructive. Instead of turning on someone else, she turned on herself. She kept saying over and over, 'Buck wants a younger woman. I'm too old for him. Too old for anybody. Nobody loves me.'"

Buck turned around to confront Shelley. "Buck doesn't want an older woman. In fact, I think I'll swear off women forever. Buck wants her younger son."

Shelley reached up and kissed Buck's lips tenderly. "I love you, but I'm afraid."

"I'll take care of you." He slipped off his light rain jacket and insisted Shelley put it on. "Your body belongs to me now, and I don't want anybody else viewing it. It's mine. Okay?"

"Every part of me belongs to you."

He followed Shelley into the living room again. "How could I know I'd upset Rose that much after a roll in the hay?" he asked, realizing belatedly that he sounded as if he were pleading his case. "Don't tell me that a woman who has known as many men as Rose and who has the iron will to stand up against massive organized attack will freak out over a little rejection from me."

"Little rejection!" Shelley said with a sneer. "You told her you were married—that's all."

"I didn't know how serious Rose was about me."

"Her mind's all fucked up. With Jesus on her side she's like a tigress—you know that. But sometimes when she leaves the stage, she'll regress. I mean, I once caught her cooing to a rag doll. Stuff like that. She's weird."

The more Shelley talked, the more Buck realized how involved he'd already become with Rose. He feared he'd been cruel to her.

"About two o'clock I heard this crash coming from her bedroom," Shelley said. "I rushed there but her door was locked. I ran around to the terrace and got in through a glass panel. The door to her bathroom was locked. I called out to her. No answer. Finally, I got our driver to bash the door in. We found her sprawled on the floor. At first we could barely see because of all the steam from the hot water. She'd cut her throat."

"God damn!" he said, horrified as he made a fist and slammed it into his own open palm.

"There was blood everywhere. She'd used a razor. The doctor's patching her up now."

"The wound? Was it bad?"

"Just a flesh wound. But she may be disfigured. She'll spend the rest of her life wearing very expensive scarves."

Getting up suddenly, Shelley went across the hall and into the library. He returned in a minute with a joint which he lit and then offered to Buck. Buck settled back on the sofa and shared the smoke with the boy. "Do you think the doctor will let me see her soon?"

"Of course, he will," Shelley said, sucking the smoke into his lungs. "You're a real bastard, you know. Flashing those big balls at the Phillips family and getting each of us to fall madly in love with you."

"That was not my intention," Buck said. "There's only one member of the Phillips family I want to be in love with me, and I'm looking at him right now."

Shelley smiled and offered Buck the next drag on the joint. As Buck inhaled the smoke, Shelley stuck his tongue in Buck's ear. "When I drugged you—and I'm really sorry about that—I tasted every part of you, and I mean every part. Forget the usual parts. I devoured them. I also went for some parts often overlooked."

"What does that mean?"

"I parted your hair so I could tongue your scalp."

"I'm sorry I wasn't awake to enjoy it. Very soon I want you to do that again, and I want to be wide awake—not stoned or drunk—so I can feel every delectable caress of that talented tongue of yours."

"I can't wait. I wish it could be right now. But we've got this medical emergency."

"I bet within two days that throat she tried to cut will be coming out with guillotine words for everybody she hates."

"I fear you're right. But I still bet she'll be disfigured. The fact she went that far really disturbs me. I don't want her feeling that strongly about you. I don't know what I'm going to do."

"Correction. What we're going to do. We're in this together. "I'm going to play along with any game now to hold onto you. I'll even pretend I love her just so I can stay next to you."

"You'd do that for me?"

"At this point I'd do almost anything for you. Do I have to make love to her? I don't want to."

"We'll see. We've got to be real careful. It will all be weird. But we'll work out sleeping arrangements in this household some way. I'm very imaginative. I know the bitch well. I'll be your guide through this murk."

A nurse came into the living room, sniffing the pot-laden air but showing no obvious disapproval. "Mr. Brooke, the doctor said you can go up to her bedroom in an hour. She's okay. She did cut herself. Rather badly. But the wound isn't deep. It's not life threatening. She did lose a lot of blood though and she's going to need an injection."

"I'll be right up as soon as I'm called for."

"Knock on my bedroom door," Shelley said. "I'll let Mr. Brooke rest in my bedroom until he's summoned. He's very tired."

"Indeed," the nurse said, turning to leave. "I'll call for you later."

Shelley led Buck upstairs to his bedroom and ushered him in, locking the door behind him. Without wasting another second, Buck reached for the boy, removing the rain jacket he had put on him. He reached down and kissed him long and hard before inserting his tongue for Shelley to suck. As Shelley sucked, Buck used this chance to run his hands all over the boy's body, or at least as much as he could reach. "Those rose-colored briefs have to go," he whispered to Shelley. "When you and I are alone in a room from now on, I want you completely nude for me."

Shelley slipped off his briefs as Buck cupped each of his buttocks. He searched for the boy's rosebud and gently inserted his finger. "I want to penetrate you right now. But when I do that for the first time, we're going to need all night. Tonight's not that night. But I do want to put you to sleep the way you said you liked."

Shelley's only response was a soft moan. It seemed he couldn't wait for Buck to stop talking so he could suck his tongue some more. Buck gave him what he wanted. But in a minute or so, he picked him up and carried him to the bed where Buck loosened his shirt but didn't get undressed.

With the boy spread out lovingly on the bed, Buck viewed this golden youth as a delectable meal for him to devour. He wanted to taste every part of this offering, and that is exactly what he did. There wasn't an inch of the boy's body that Buck didn't sample and at times devour. He'd never known such tender, responsive flesh. Shelley completely opened himself to Buck, allowing Buck to savor every morsel. Throughout the long ordeal Shelley constantly uttered soft little moans. He appeared to be in some dreamy state. He kept running his fingers through Buck's hair and when Buck brought him such pleasure the boy could not stand it, he pulled at that hair.

Buck noted what turned the boy on more than anything else. Before his exploration of Shelley's body was over, Buck knew his one most sensitive part. When his tongue first entered the boy's most hidden part, and began to penetrate as deeply as Buck could, Shelley had writhed in ecstasy. Even without Buck sucking the boy's penis, Shelley had erupted in a powerful climax. Buck pulled up and hastened to capture the deflating cock and enjoy all its sweet nectar. He licked Shelley clean before returning to his rear target.

He didn't know how much time had passed, but when the nurse knocked on the door to Shelley's bedroom, the boy was exploding again, this time in Buck's suctioning mouth. He held Buck's head down as he called out to the nurse. "He'll be right there."

That turned out to be a lie. Fifteen minutes passed before Buck could pull himself away from Shelley's cock. He'd never tasted anything so good in his life. Finally he pulled himself off, raised up, and pressed his face against Shelley's. "Clean my mouth out." He pressed his mouth against Shelley's, inserting his tongue for the boy to wash clean.

*****

As he slowly entered the softly lit room, shutting the door gently behind him, he saw her lying on pillows in her white satin bed, her throat bandaged. Her hair was combed and her face made up with bright red lipstick, yet her skin looked ghostly pale, perhaps from the loss of blood. Slowly, sensing he was in her bedroom, she opened her eyes.

"You're beautiful," he said. "Why ruin that beauty?"

At the sound of his voice, her eyes seemed to dance alive. "I didn't mean to do it. To take one's own life is wrong. Even now I don't know why I did it. I just don't remember. It was like another side of me took over and did it, and I didn't have anything to do with it."

"I understand." He sat down beside her on the cushiony bed, reaching for her delicate hand. "You're going to be okay. I'm sure the doctors told you that." As he looked into her eyes, he didn't know if she were still on stage in her vast auditorium, creating a drama in which she, the wronged one, could appear as a sympathetic, grief-stricken, aging heroine used and then abandoned by a heartless young man.

"The news of your marriage—it was more than I could take," she said weakly.

"Don't worry about it—it's just a marriage of convenience. Old Buck made me do it. He threatened to disinherit me unless I married Susan Howard and stay married to her. There is no love here. It's just a business arrangement."

"I guess I never really understood."

"I don't understand much of it either. I hate the way he's trying to rule over me. But I'd be a fool to let such an inheritance slip through my fingers."

"Of course, you would." With one hand she reached over and gently rubbed his face, then ran her fingers through his hair. "You're the beautiful one. The most elegantly handsome man I've ever known. It's as if that other beauty, Shelley, were actually our real son. That he got his beauty from the both of us."

"That's a wonderful thought," he said, not meaning it at all.

"Since it's a marriage of convenience, we'll see that the bitch is paid off. I'll pay the cunt off myself just to keep her out of our hair and her slimy paws off you." She reached out and unbuttoned his shirt. "I don't want anyone enjoying these muscles and that incredible dick but me." She paused as a thought seemed to occur to her. "And, of course, Shelley when you like a little change of pace. But with Shelley we're keeping it all in the family, aren't we?"

"I suppose," he said, concealing his astonishment at her words and her openness at sharing him. It was so unexpected he still couldn't get used to it.

"If I were a man, I'd want to fuck Shelley too. Who wouldn't? He's incredibly beautiful. All my boy friends have thought so." She clutched his hand as if regaining some lost strength. Her look became feverish, her eyes pleading. "You won't leave me, will you?"

"I'm not going anywhere, babe. I'm going to stay right here. At least till morning."

She hung onto those words as if he'd delivered a miracle. Her eyes closed lightly, and he realized the doctor must have given her a heavy sedative. She tried to say something, but it was only a faint mutter. Soon she'd drifted into what appeared to be a peaceful sleep.

He got up and pulled back the draperies so he could see the bay through her sliding glass panels. The water below shone like a metal sheet, reflecting the moon. The joint had soothed him.

After he felt assured that she was sound asleep, he slipped into her study and made a call to Robert informing him that this emergency at Paradise Shores would detain him all night.

He yawned as he returned to a Queen Anne armchair beside her bed. No sooner was he comfortably settled in the chair than he fell immediately asleep. He didn't know how long he slept. When he woke up, he could see it was morning. His watch told him it was seven o'clock, and he still had three hours before joining Uncle Milty, Patrick, and Robert on that flight to Miami to get married.

Rubbing sleep from his eyes, he headed toward the bathroom, unzipping his fly.

He met Rose coming out of the bath. Seeing he was unzipped, she reached inside, fondling his cock with its morning hard-on and cuddling his balls. "That's just to reassure myself that it's as big as I remember."

"That's all me, babe, but I've got to seek relief somewhere else for the moment." He walked over and pissed loudly into her rose-colored bowl. He stood at an angle because he knew she wanted to see his cock dangling from his trousers.

As he stared back at her, he took in her beauty for the first time today. She had a luminous glow to her, and it was hard to imagine only hours before, she'd tried to slit her throat. She wore a rosy dressing gown and had beautifully arranged her hair. Even the rose-colored scarf concealing the bandages on her neck looked chic.

She was walking toward him. On her thickly carpeted floor, she kneeled in front of him. She reached for his cock and shook the last drops of urine from it. Then she pulled back the foreskin and slurped it voraciously into her mouth. His penis thickened and hardened at once. The throat that she'd tried to cut was back in full action servicing him. She was a true expert at sucking a man's penis, and could take his full penetration without gagging. She weighed his balls in her delicate hands, fingering and testing their size and fullness as if he were a prize bull. He let her do all the work, not wanting to plunge into her and face fuck her because of her bandaged throat. So skilled was her tongue and lips that he felt his climax building faster than it usually did. When the eruption did explode, she swallowed his offering eagerly and kept his penis in her mouth for the longest time, almost not wanting to relinquish her prize.

Pulling himself away from her, he stripped off his clothes and headed for the shower to wash off Rose and the night before. He stayed in the shower an extra long time, as the water seemed to purify his soul.

When he opened the shower doors, Shelley, clad in a silk robe, was waiting with a thick rose-colored towel. The boy kissed Buck good morning and Buck gave him what he knew he wanted: his tongue to suck. He drew back when he spotted Rose entering the bathroom carrying a morning cup of coffee for him. Shelley made no attempt to move away from Buck's body but licked and kissed each nipple before taking the towel and drying Buck's chest. Kneeling before Buck, he skinned back Buck's penis and dried its thick head before planting soft little kissings and tongue lashings on it.

Rose in the meanwhile took another towel and dried his back, kneeling to wipe the water from his legs before softly drying his ass. She planted little kisses on his buttocks, her tongue occasionally darting inside the crevice to sample and taste.

Breaking from his assailants, Buck went over to a rose-colored sink and reached for a red rosy toothbrush. The toothpaste was white, however. He brushed his teeth and thanked Rose for the coffee. Shelley remained in the room. Seeing a man's white terrycloth robe hanging nearby, Buck reached for the robe and attempted to put it on.

"You won't need that," Shelley said. "Rose and I know what you look like."

"What the hell then?" Buck said, striding naked into the bedroom. Rose was in her alcove talking to someone on the phone. She sounded upset, her voice taking on a certain hysteria.

Buck spread his nude frame on a rose-colored chaise longue and enjoyed his first cup of coffee. Shelley settled between his legs to lick his balls.

Rose appeared in the room looking rather solemn. At no point did she even seem to take notice of what Shelley was doing. If it didn't upset Rose, it certainly didn't bother Buck. Besides it felt real good.

"My great aunt died this morning," Rose announced, but didn't appear shaken by the news.

If Shelley had a reaction, it was concealed by his slurping.

"She was the matriarch of the Phillips family," Rose said. "A real frontier woman. She always said I took after her. The funeral's in Durant. That's in Oklahoma where I come from. Since I'm a little unsteady on my feet, I was hoping you'd go there with me."

"I'd really like to," Buck said, taking his fingers and fondling Shelley's blond hair. "But I've got to fly to Miami this morning. I'm due in court. If I don't show up, a judgment will go against me."

"Oh, I see," she said. "A libel judgment no doubt."

"Something like that. I'm flying down at ten but I'll be back tomorrow morning. I'm going with my attorney."

"That will still fit into my plans. Shelley and I aren't flying out until tomorrow morning for the funeral. I'm also due in Abilene for a big press conference. This one is a surprise, and are you ever going to be surprised."

"You're always full of surprises."

Shelley continued with his licking and kissing, as if he'd never come up for air.

"After Abilene we fly to Oklahoma. But there's more. After that I want you to go with us to Palm Springs. There you're going to meet the boss. He'll be your boss too if you sign on as media director, and I know you will. You'll also get the check owed to your old grandpa. All those millions. You'll also get another check if your damn attorney will ever agree on the exact price being asked for your share of Examiner stock. In other words, you'll fly to Palm Springs a fired $45,000-a-year publisher, and you'll return to Okeechobee with millions."

At the mention of millions, Shelley removed his lips from Buck's balls. "That's not all he's going to get. When Grandfather Time, your old pal, croaks, Buck will have more money than he can count. We've got ourselves one rich stud."

"We've got our own millions," Rose said defensively.

With one hand, Buck finished his coffee and with the other hand he reached for Shelley's neck, returning him to his balls. Shelley expertly went to work again, servicing Buck and bringing him such exquisite pleasure that Buck occasionally moaned in joy.

"I'm misunderstood here in Okeechobee," Rose said. "I'll certainly be misunderstood after that press conference tomorrow in Abilene. But in Durant I'm understood. This will be your chance to see how the real grass roots America responds to me."

"I can't wait," Buck said. "I especially can't wait to fly to Palm Springs. I've already taken to riding around in limousines and leading the good life. That's a private charter I'm taking to Miami. I need to get a check cashed before all those bills start coming in."

Shelley raised his head and stared lovingly into Buck's eyes. "Don't you ever worry about bills any more. You've got bills to pay? Send them over to us." He looked over at Rose with a certain contempt. "We've got more money than God."

Without Buck seeming to realize it, Shelley's kissing and licking of his balls had produced his second roaring hard-on of the morning.

Rose walked over presumably aware for the first time of the sexual foreplay going on between Shelley and Buck. She ran her long tapered fingers up Buck's penis, causing him to moan again at her touch. She reached and gently uncapped his cock, running her fingertips over its engorged head. She was incredibly gentle with Buck, but when she reached for Shelley's hair, she yanked him up roughly and virtually forced him to go down on the long, thick penis. In spite of her pulling his hair, Shelley was only too willing to take the plunge.

When Buck had deeply penetrated Shelley's throat, Rose got up and headed toward the door, moving with a swanlike grace. She looked almost ethereal. But when she turned around to face them again, Buck noted a harshness to her features. She yelled to her son, "Enjoy yourself, cocksucker, but I've already beat you to his first load of the day." Turning on her heels she slammed the door behind her.

Chapter Nine

In his office, Biff had placed his feet on his desk in an arrogant, cocky pose, as he stared long and hard at Buck. "I don't know why you're questioning my judgment," Biff said. "One of my men made a mistake. It was not Julius Forster—and that's that."

"But your headquarters were so certain last night," Buck protested. "His voice was very distinctive when he called in that bomb threat. Don't you at least want me to hear Forster's voice? Maybe I could make an identification."

"Let me tell you something," Biff said. "Something police chiefs know and apparently something newspaper publishers don't know. Voices can be disguised."

"I know that but I at least should hear his voice."

"Don't you think I know how to run this department? Besides, I hear you're no longer with the Examiner. You've been fired. Why are you so concerned at this point with a bomb threat? It's not your building to worry about?"

"I fucking don't like receiving bomb threats on any building I'm in, whether I own it or not. I think this Forster is a menace. We have a long file on him. I bet you do too."

"What we have on Forster is our own God damn business. He's a bit right wing."

"A bit right wing? Is that what you call a card-carrying neo-Nazi?"

"What you liberals don't understand is that we can't go around arresting people for their politics."

"I see," Buck said, getting up. For some mysterious reason, it was all too apparent that Biff didn't want to pursue Forster. Obviously he did last night but somebody had gotten to him. Buck wondered whose payroll Forster was on. Forster's boss, it seemed, was more powerful than Biff. A thought occurred to him. Did Forster work for Calder Martin?

"We'll keep looking into the case." Biff lifted his legs off the desk and reached for a newspaper. It was the Okeechobee News. "I always read the News. But now that you're off the Examiner, I think I'll start reading that rag again. Roland is a good man. A level head in a news room that up to now has been directed by hot heads."

"Thanks a lot," Buck said sarcastically, heading for the door. He had a plane to catch.

In their privately chartered plane, a sleepy Buck buckled up as it took off the runway in Okeechobee heading for the airport in Miami. Robert was beside him, smiling and looking a little sleepy too. No one was getting enough sleep lately.

In a seat across from them, Uncle Milty and Patrick sat looking out the window as the plane went airborne. They were holding hands and apparently were devoted to each other, as always.

A sudden thought occurred to Buck. Uncle Milty and Robert had arranged for the matching wedding bands, but Buck had always planned to give Robert an engagement ring. He'd never gotten around to it. As he'd climbed into his waiting limousine at Paradise Shores, Shelley had raced toward the car to give him a present. "Go on, open it," Shelley had demanded eagerly. When Buck opened Shelley's gift, he'd discovered one of the most beautiful rings he'd ever seen. It was a circle of blue diamonds and rubies. "It was created for some Arab sheik," Shelley said. "Designed in Italy. Do you like it?"

"Shelley, it's spectacular. But I can't accept such a ring. It must be worth a king's ransom."

"More than that. I want you to have it." He'd taken the ring and slipped it on Buck's finger. "God," Shelley had said, "it makes you look more gorgeous than you already are." With that, Shelley had kissed him on the lips in front of the chauffeur, and told the driver to get Buck to the airport, but only after he'd written down the phone number where he could reach Buck in Miami.

Before he'd gotten to the airport, Buck had slipped the ring off his finger and concealed it within his pocket. On a sudden impulse, he reached inside his pants and retrieved the ring. Taking Robert's hand, he put each finger to his mouth and sucked on each one tenderly. then he took the ring he'd been concealing and slipped it on Robert's finger. He pulled Robert close to him and kissed him real hard, inserting his tongue.

Robert eagerly sucked it. Breaking away, he looked down at the ring. "That's the greatest ring I've ever seen in my life. It's gorgeous. I'm stunned." He kissed Buck lightly on the lips. "Thank you. Those are hardly the words. I think I'm going to cry." Diverting himself, he showed the ring to Uncle Milty and then to Patrick.

Each man appeared amazed. "I'm sure I'll be sent the bill since I'm handling all your affairs," Uncle Milty said to Buck. "It'll be some bill." He turned to Robert. "And are you ever worth it."

"This calls for champagne," Robert said, getting up and heading for the rear of the plane.

"I'll help you," Uncle Milty volunteered, trailing Robert to the rear of the craft.

When they got up, Patrick rose from his seat to join Buck on the other side. He reached for Buck's hand, kissing the inner palm. "That was some ring. That's the most drop dead ring I've ever seen. Uncle Milty will have to tell me what you paid for it. I promise I'll never tell Robert."

"You'll never tell Robert because you'll never find out. There will be no bill. My family has always owned that ring. The stones belonged to my mother. I had them reset for a man."

"Oh, I see." Patrick smiled. "It must be nice to have rich parents. I grew up in a trailer in Arkansas. We had nothing. My parents still don't. Uncle Milty sends them a two-hundred dollar check every week. That's the most money they've ever had at one time in their lives. They think they're rich. At first they didn't like my living with Uncle Milty. Mama said I'd burn in hell. But when those 'wages of sin' starting coming in, and she started eating properly for the first time in her life, she shut up. Daddy doesn't care who I sleep with as long as he's got enough money to buy some whiskey every week."

"I didn't know Uncle Milty sent money to your parents, but I'm glad to hear it. We helped out Robert's mother but she never thanked us. In fact, she never said anything one way or another. But I noticed she always cashed the checks."

"I dread the funeral," Patrick said. "I'd much rather attend the wedding instead."

"So would I," Buck said. "But all of us must go. For Robert's sake."

"We should be there for him. I can't believe it. Death and rebirth, a funeral and a wedding, all on the same day." He reached for Buck's hand again, kissing the palm before suddenly licking it.

Buck withdrew his hand. "Come now, Patrick, I'm already spoken for."

"Sigh," was all Patrick said. "When I saw you reach over and grab Robert to kiss him, and I saw your tongue dart out for Robert to suck, I wanted to be the guy to suck that tongue. I had to conceal the instant hard-on I got."

"I'll forget you said that. My life's complicated enough."

"Remember that time on the island when all of us went swimming in the nude. When you pulled off your bikini, I'd never seen the likes of that in my life. I don't know how Robert takes it. You know what Uncle Milty's got. Not much to mess up my mouth with."

"But you love him."

"I guess. He takes care of me. For a kid who spent most of his life out in the cold, it's good to come in to a warm fire. Ever since I was nine years old, I've been servicing men like Uncle Milty, although not as kind as he is. I've never had a partner that I could choose for the sheer sexual thrill of it all. I was hoping that someday, just as a favor to me, you'd take me off for an afternoon or a night. We'd make up some excuse. You could show me what it's like to have a real man make love to me."

"Let's forget we ever had this conversation."

At this point Robert and Uncle Milty came back to the front of the plane, Robert carrying the tray with the poured champagne and Uncle Milty following with an extra bottle.

As each man was handed a glass, Uncle Milty said, "I'd like to make a toast."

"Feel free," Buck said. He looked over at Robert who returned his smile before holding the ring up in the air as if he couldn't believe it was on his finger.

"Back in Okeechobee, there may be a faux Mr. and Mrs. Brooke III," Uncle Milty said. "But here's to the real Mr. and Mrs. Buck Brooke III."

*****

After a bad and restless night, Gene, behind the wheel of his car, felt more in charge today. He was going to the hospital to pick up Sandy who would be released soon. Although in some pain, the terrible ordeal was over, and doctors assured Gene that Sandy would heal from the burns.

Thanks to Leroy, Gene had a beautifully furnished condo waiting for Jill and Sandy. Gene wasn't proud of what he'd done to earn that condo, but it was better than life on the street. At times he really liked Leroy, and having sex with him wasn't so bad. Leroy never humiliated him—in fact, it was getting increasingly hard to dislike someone who loved and worshipped you as Leroy did him. He felt Leroy was becoming very possessive. But he was helping Gene when no one else would, and Gene was grateful for that.

Actually he was proud that he had such a lovely nest in which to deliver Sandy after the sacrifice the boy had made for him, putting his life at risk to rescue him when he believed Gene was in that burning building. Even now Gene could not believe that Sandy had done that for him. No one cared about him like that. Maybe Leroy. In the last few encounters, Leroy seemed to be falling in love with Gene. "This thing of sharing you with my friends," Leroy had said with a certain hesitation. "We're going to have to review that. I'm not sure that is a good idea."

Within fifteen minutes of the hospital, Gene reviewed the events of the past evening as if it were a film being played in his head. He'd moved into the Collins household almost effortlessly. On the first night, he hadn't met Barry's daughters. They'd left hours earlier for Tampa to visit with their grandmother. Gene had found himself alone in the house with Pamela and Barry.

In Barry's bedroom, Gene had spotted a pair of swimming trunks and had stripped and put them on, crossing the carpeted floor of a terrace which overlooked a ball-shaped, Olympic-size swimming pool. Barry had retreated to his library where Gene had heard him shouting hysterically to someone on the phone.

The irony of Gene's new position had struck him. Imagine the mayoral candidate hiring as a bodyguard the one man in Okeechobee who could destroy him.

Pamela hadn't been sick, as Barry had told his supporters at the rally that afternoon. When the chauffeur had delivered Gene and Barry to the Collins home, they'd found Pamela, her blouse unbuttoned, sprawled on a beige-colored sofa in their sunken living room. Barry had gently slapped her to arouse her from a drunken stupor.

At first she hadn't recognized Gene but, after a while, her memory had seemed to return. Looking with contempt at Barry, she'd said, "At least now we'll have a real man around the house."

In the borrowed trunks from Barry, Gene had walked to the edge of the pool and had dived in with a loud splash. In spite of the hot temperatures, the water was cold, as if artificially cooled. But even the cold water couldn't lower Gene's excitement at being in Barry's compound, close to the center of power he'd sought for so long. Going under, he'd emerged at the deep end, pulling himself out by an aluminum ladder, his body covered with water crystals, his skin glistening in the lights around the pool.

As he'd glanced over his shoulder, he'd spotted Pamela standing at the edge of the pool staring at him as if transfixed. In her white bikini, she looked somewhat as she had when she'd entered beauty contests in their university days. Picking up a towel from a nearby stand, she'd headed toward him. He'd stood completely still as she'd dried his back, her hands caressing him. Her laugh had been mischievous, low and husky. "I should think an exhibitionist like you would wear something more revealing when going into the water." She'd stood directly in front of him, staring deeply into his eyes. "Or else nothing at all."

Her words had been like a thousand lashing whips lacerating the inner walls of his brain.

She'd rubbed her body against him as he'd thought what a hussy she was—just like Susan, so different from Rose. It had been all he could do to endure her touch and to smell the sickening stench of her powerful perfume. A chill had gone through his body as her fingers had traced patterns on his chest, encircling a nipple and pinching it. The dying sun had gone beneath the horizon, as the light in the garden grew dimmer.

"Cool it!" he'd said, breaking from her. "Barry might come out here and see us."

She'd stood forlornly on the bricks, as if debating how far to go with this encounter. "Honey, it won't matter none if Barry does see us."

With a force he'd found surprising, she'd kneeled in front of him, pulling down the trunks, completely exposing Gene. She'd pushed him back on an air mattress and had fallen upon him, devouring his cock with a loud suction noise. In spite of himself, he'd found himself hardening and thickening in her experienced mouth. Maybe those rumors about her were true after all, he'd pondered. She was said to have given head to half the state troopers in Florida.

With her free hand, she'd unfastened the top to her bikini, exposing her still ample breasts. He'd closed his eyes and had lain back on the mattress. To his surprise, he'd found himself taking pleasure in her sucking and licking of him. He'd been tense all day, and her love-making was bringing him the relief he'd needed. It wasn't like it was with Buck. The act with Pamela had been more mechanical. An experienced sword swallower and that had been that. He'd used her. Gradually rising up and pumping himself into her mouth, he'd begun to fuck her face. She'd been an equal match for him, meeting his every forward lurch with her devouring mouth which had been not only able to accommodate every inch of him but was somehow sending signals to him that she could take his entire offering and even handle more. She'd been incredible.

But in moments his penis had been left wet and bobbing in the night air. Barry had suddenly come onto the patio wearing only a terrycloth robe. He'd jerked Pamela by her hair and pulled her off Gene. In moments he'd replaced her suctioning mouth with his own equally skilled one.

"You fucking cocksucker," Pamela had shouted at her husband. "That load belonged to me. I worked for it."

Without removing his mouth from Gene's penis, Barry had not even looked up as Pamela had raced from the patio in tears, heading toward the living room.

Even before Barry had claimed his penis, Gene had been near a climax. Barry's sucking, experienced mouth only led to the inevitable. As he'd felt himself in the throes of orgasm, Gene had reached down and captured Barry's head and forced him to go all the way down on his penis which produced a shattering orgasm. Gene hadn't cared whether he'd choked Barry or not. At that moment, Barry had existed for his own pleasure, and nothing else mattered.

The moment Gene had erupted for the final time, he'd pulled Barry off his penis and had headed for the bathroom in the main house where he'd locked himself in. He'd wanted to shut out both Pamela and Barry.

In front of that mirror, his head had slumped in defeat between his shoulders. There had been a loud rap on the door. He'd only vaguely noticed it. Sibilant gasps escaped from his throat, and when he'd looked up again he'd seen a wild thing staring back at him in that mirror. His face was a ghostly white.

But later when he'd entered Barry's bedroom, the candidate hadn't found his behavior out of the ordinary. Completely nude on the bed, Barry was fucking himself with a dildo. Upon seeing Gene, he'd said, "Get your ass over here. I need to get fucked with the real thing."

That was all Gene cared to remember in the morning light. Lately, he'd been able to blot out entire episodes in his life, although they'd occurred only moments before.

After parking his car in an open air lot, he'd raced down the hospital corridor eager to see Sandy.

*****

In a slumlike section of North Miami, Uncle Milty directed the chauffeur to a cement-block structure with a hand-painted sign out front, "Jews for Jesus."

"What's this?" Buck asked, taking Robert's hand and feeling a surge of great insecurity. "You converting to Christianity, Uncle Milty?"

"It's not always easy getting a pastor to perform these ceremonies," Uncle Milty said. "This guy, Doug Potter, will perform any ceremony for anybody. If you wanted to marry your dog, that's okay by Doug. He's not Jewish but he specializes in converting them. They give him gifts for their conversion."

"What fun," Robert said. "But is he legitimate?"

"As legitimate as any of your Christian ministers—and that's not saying a lot," Uncle Milty said.

"Now, now," Patrick cautioned him. "Don't let your prejudice show."

Uncle Milty looked over at Patrick and smiled, stroking his hand. "The only thing you Christians ever gave us that's truly worthwhile is uncut cock."

"Glad we could help out," Buck said, opening the car door and anxious to get on with the ceremony. He wanted this behind him. Standing in the litter-strewn unpaved lot of the ministry, he almost wished he'd withheld permission for such a ceremony to take place.

Robert came up behind him. "I know you're uncomfortable here. But it's important to me. It will be over soon, and we'll get on with our lives."

"I thought your mother's funeral was to come before the wedding."

"That didn't work out. Her church is tied up this morning with a wedding. We won't be able to have the funeral until three o'clock."

"I see," was all Buck said and that was mainly to himself. Actually he didn't see or understand anything about his life. All these rites of passage—a wedding, a funeral—were mixed up with other commitments he'd made: with Shelley, with Rose, with Susan. Not only that, but the ever-present Gene seemed to have occupied a permanent perch in his brain. If it were possible, he felt he should slice himself into little pieces. Maybe there would be enough of him to go around.

The door to the temple was open and Buck led the men inside. The place was empty and two phones were ringing. Papers were scattered everywhere, including unopened mail. In the rear was a small chapel with a makeshift altar and some folding chairs. Presumably this was the venue for the actual wedding ceremony. What saved the ambience were a dozen wreaths of the most gorgeous flowers, some of them exotic.

"I ordered those," Patrick said, catching Buck's eye. "Milty and I had to do something to take the curse off the place."

"Thanks," was all Buck could manage to say.

To thank Patrick, Robert kissed him on the cheek. "You're always there for me. A real friend."

To Buck's surprise, Uncle Milty answered one of the phones, perhaps thinking it was Doug calling that he'd be late. Manning the phone, Uncle Milty spoke to someone and starting writing down the details about a possible contribution. He put his hand over the phone. "It's an old lady and she's living on social security but she wants to give ten dollars."

At this point Doug stuck his head out of a side door. "Welcome guys. I see you're all here. I'm not dressed yet. Hey, you're Buck Brooke. I recognized your picture. You know that magazine has just been published. They call you the sexiest guy alive. Get your ass back here."

Buck cringed, as Robert smiled and took his hand. "Did that magazine ever get that right," Robert said.

Excusing himself, Buck headed for the minister's office.

It turned out to be a bedroom with an unmade bed. Reaching to shake his hand, Doug was clad only in a pair of jockey shorts far too tight to cover the ample load. Although older, he evoked a young Marlon Brando as he appeared in A Streetcar Named Desire.

"Forgive the look of the place," Doug said. "Only an hour ago I was fucking two cunts—one blonde, the other brunette. I always like two at a time. It takes two pussies to handle me anyway."

"I see you're a minister—not a Catholic priest."

"Damn right I am," Doug said, reaching for a white shirt. "I believe if God didn't want us to have sex, he wouldn't have invented it."

"I'm sure you're right on that point," Buck said, growing more uncomfortable by the minute.

"I'm not one of those right-wing religious leaders," he said, buttoning his shirt and reaching for his pants. "I'm not against gay people. In fact, I conduct special services for them. I figure if they contribute to my temple, what the hell. I've never been able to tell a gay dollar from a straight dollar. When you put them together in your bank account, what in the fuck does it matter?"

"I completely agree with you on that."

"Indirectly it was gay men who helped launch me in my temple."

"How so?" Buck asked, not really wanting an answer.

"I saved my bucks. For years I was one of the highest paid male hustlers in Miami. Earned the big ones. In fact, James Herlihy, the writer, used me as a role model for Joe Buck in Midnight Cowboy. That guy could really suck cock. I don't care how many women try it, it takes a man to really suck cock. Don't you agree?"

"So far," Buck said, "I'm agreeing with you on every point. You've converted me already."

"Fine," Doug said, zipping up his pants and searching under the bed for his shoes. "I expect a big contribution for this wedding ceremony. I'm not charging to perform the service. I'm counting on your generosity, and I mean yours and not Uncle Milty's. He's a Jew, and they start out stingy. But when I convert them to Christianity, I find they can be very generous. Two old Jewish ladies who became Christians even willed me their homes when they died. That's the kind of contribution I like."

"Thanks for agreeing to perform the ceremony," Buck said. "I'm gun-shy about the whole thing. But it's important to my friend, Robert, and I want to go through with it for him. I feel really awkward."

"I'll make it easy for you. I've got two assistants from my church to help out. Don't worry. They're both gay. I wanted all gay people here, except for myself of course. You know a lot of straight people still object to gay marriages, and I've been criticized a lot for performing them."

"Keep up the good work." Before Doug could say something, Buck quickly added, "and I'll contribute generously. In fact, I'll contribute very generously if you'll agree to keep this ceremony strictly among the family here."

"Reliable and trustworthy. That's what I am. My lips are sealed, even though it occurred to me that that magazine that named you the sexiest man alive would love to do a follow-up cover with the juicy details of this wedding."

"But we'll deny them the privilege, won't we?"

"For a generous contribution, I'd deny my own mama."

"You're my kind of guy," Buck said, looking anxiously at the door as Doug finished tying his leather shoes.

"You're not a bad looking guy," Doug said. "I'm forty-five now, but twenty years ago when I was in a different business I might have let you swing on my pole. I used to get a hundred dollars a night, and that was in 1957. Do you know what a hundred dollars was back in 1957? Most guys back then were giving it away for ten bucks."

"I bet you were worth every dollar."

"You bet your sweet ass I was. But I've given that up. I occasionally let one of my gay temple members feel me up—but that's about it. Sometimes I go to their private parties and drop trou for a nude swim. Give them a look, providing they contribute. But in the last few years the only thing that turns me on is pussy."

"Whatever you like."

"Not just pussy—sixteen-year-old pussy. I find sixteen-year-old pussy just right. Fifteen is too young, and by the time these little white-trash vixens are seventeen they've already had it banged too much for my tastes."

Buck glanced nervously at his watch. "Don't you think it's about time we got moving with the ceremony?"

In front of a mirror combing his hair, Doug said, "Let's go for it." He paused as he straightened his tie. "Do you mind if you write your check to me before I perform the ceremony? I like to get all contributions out of the way beforehand. At the end, it's kiss the bride and all that shit and the money might be overlooked."

"By all means, we'll write the check first. I know you've spoken with Uncle Milty on the phone before, but come on out and let me introduce you to everybody, especially Robert. That's the blond guy. He's the one I'm marrying."

"You've got good taste. I wouldn't mind plowing his ass myself."

"I thought you liked sixteen-year-old pussy."

Doug smiled and kissed Buck on the mouth.

Buck was taken aback but didn't do anything stupid like wipe traces of the wet kiss from his lips.

Doug winked at him. "I could be converted."

After that, the wedding itself was anticlimactic.

*****

Still bandaged from his burns, Sandy was in awe at the condo. He went from room to room inspecting everything. "Wow," he said, "this is great. I can't believe it. I've lived in dumps all my life. Cockroaches, everything. This is the way real people live."

For the first time in a long while, Gene was proud. He felt like a father, and was surprised that he was even experiencing such emotion. "It's all ours."

Sandy ran his hands over the upholstery and even felt the thick gold draperies. "It looks like a movie set." A sudden frown crossed his brow. "How did you afford all this? I thought we only had two-thousand dollars. This place must have cost millions."

"Not millions. Thousands." Gene went over to the bar to pour himself an orange juice. Without asking, he poured one for Sandy too. The boy eagerly took it, holding his glass up to toast Gene as if it were champagne.

"Sit down," Gene commanded. "I've got to tell you something."

Taken aback, Sandy sat on the sofa and stared at Gene, his face revealing he didn't want to hear what Gene was about to tell him.

"I've become a whore, something I always detested." Gene's eyes averted those of Sandy's. "Just like you were doing, I'm selling my meat to the highest bidder. The whole thing makes me feel real creepy."

"I know the feeling well. I'm real sorry to hear this but I thank you for telling me. I think you're doing it for us. We brought this on you."

"Like hell you did. I brought it on myself. Life brought it on to me. We've had a lot of bad breaks. All of us have. I need a lot of money and quick. I'm in a lot of jams. The opportunity came and I took it. The job I have with Barry and Pamela pays two-thousand a week. That's good money but it won't last. I've got to accumulate a nest egg for us, and get out of all this shit."

"Who's actually paying for this apartment?" Sandy asked.

"Leroy. You know him well."

"I don't know him that well. He doesn't go for young kids like me but guys like you. He's probably falling in love with you."

"Something like that."

"But where does that leave me? Us?"

"You're my friend, my best friend. I feel like a father to you. That's the way I want to keep it."

Sandy sighed as he moved closer on the sofa to Gene. He held Gene's hand in a strong grip.

"Besides, you've got Jill now," Gene said. "I want you and Jill to make it, and I'm going to help you get there if it's the last thing I do."

"My God, you talk like you're about to die. You're only twenty-seven years old and in good health."

"People twenty-seven years old in good health often die."

"You're not going to die. You're going to live for decades. All three of us. We're going to become a family. We don't have any God damn family so let's create one for ourselves. Jill, you, and me."

"That's what we're trying to do, believe it or not. That's what this condo and everything is all about. We are family." He reached over and kissed Sandy on the cheek. "You're my son."

"I may be your son, but this is one son who sure loves his daddy. I'll never stop loving you." This time Sandy reached over and kissed Gene—not on the cheek, but on the lips. "I really love you, big guy."

"You just think you do," Gene said pulling away. "There's Jill to think of."

"Jill understands everything. By the way, where is she?"

"I gave her a thousand dollars and told her to go buy a wardrobe for herself. A real respectable wardrobe. Not some hooker crap!"

"She'll do it. She'll look really good. You'll be proud of her—I just know it."

"I'm proud of her already. But what did you mean she understands everything."

"We've had long talks. She knows there's one side of me she can have but another side of me that belongs only to you. A woman can do it just so far for me. I've got to have you too. It's very important to me. Jill knows she can't deliver all the love I need, and she accepts that. She wants me to turn to you to find that fulfillment that only you can supply. You've got to tell me you understand all this."

Gene rose from the sofa and headed for the bar to pour himself another orange juice. "I think I understand a lot, and then at times I think I understand nothing. I need time to sort all of this out. Everything is happening now like speed motion. I'm lost somehow. Everything has come down on me real hard like. I don't know who I am any more. It's you who has to be understanding with me. I know you won't press anything right now. I've got to get a lot of things straightened out in my mixed-up head, and that's going to take me a little while."

Sandy came over and stood behind Gene at the bar. With his good arm, he wrapped it around Gene and hugged him. "I know what you're going through, and we're going to be here for you. I'm not going to press it, but every day I'm going to be ready, willing, and able to receive your love. I want your love, big guy. It's the single most important need I have in the world. When I thought you might be dying in that house fire, I didn't think about my own safety—unlike those fucking firemen—I thought only about saving you. It was you I wanted. You I can't live without. You I think about day and night. I can still taste you. It was the most glorious taste in my life. There's nothing like you. No one will ever replace you in my life. I'm in love, God damn it!"

Even though troubling to him, Gene thrilled at Sandy's words. To be loved by someone was luxury he thought he would always be denied. He tried to say something but tears welled in his eyes, and he was too big a man to cry. Or was any man too big to cry? He reached over and kissed Sandy on the lips. "I love you too. From the first day we met, I felt this bond with you. It was a bond I've never felt with anybody else."

"Not even that guy who was calling all the time and trying to speak to you?"

Gene winced at the memory of Buck. "Not even him. That thing is not like this thing with you. That thing belonged to my past. It was something that was doomed from the beginning, and something I should never have gotten mixed up in in the first place. It was like my marriage to Susan Howard. Why Susan and I ever got married I don't know. I don't know anyone less suited for each other than Susan and me. It was wrong from the first night, and, of course, it led to disaster as these things always do."

"That shit in your past is dead and gone." He came real close to Gene and looked deeply into his eyes. "What we have is now. It's here. It's real. It's all that matters."

Before Gene knew what he was going to do next, the phone rang. It was like an awful intrusion on their lives and their privacy. Thinking it might be Jill in some sort of trouble, Gene picked up the receiver. "Hello," he said cautiously.

"Thank God you're there," came the voice of Leroy over the wire. "I hope your young friends, Sandy and Jill, like the condo."

"They think it's great. They never had such a great place. They're real thankful to you."

"They shouldn't thank me but you. You earned it, my friend. That Sandy's real cute. I remember him from the Lolito ring. Too young for me but the older guys there really loved him."

"He's not turning tricks any more."

"Too bad. A hot little number. But he's nothing compared to the guy I've got."

"Who's that?"

"You, you handsome stud. Forget Buck Brooke III. You, Gene Robinson, are the sexiest guy alive."

"That's very flattering, but..."

Leroy interrupted him. "I've got to see you right away. There's something I've got to tell you. A complete change of plans. Get on the elevator and come up here right away."

"Sounds real urgent. I'll be right up. Give me a minute or two."

"Hurry," Leroy urged.

After putting down the receiver, he turned to Sandy, kissing him lightly on the lips. "I've got to go upstairs to see Leroy. He says it's urgent."

"Not more trouble, I hope."

"I hope not too. But I'll let you know."

As Gene searched for his keys, Sandy came over to him and reached for his hand. "I was hoping you could spend the day with me here since you don't report to work until six o'clock. This could be our quiet time together."

"I'm sorry but duty calls. Barry is my boss at night. Leroy calls the shots during the day and on weekends."

"I see," Sandy said, disappointed. As Gene turned to leave, Sandy held his arm. "There are only two bedrooms here—not three."

"Sorry, but Leroy wouldn't give us a three-bedroom."

"That's fine with me," Sandy said. "Actually that's the way I want it."

"You and Jill can have the front room," Gene said, "and I'll take the rear one overlooking the courtyard. I prefer that."

"Correction," Sandy said, kissing him again on the lips. "Jill is welcome to the front room. You and I are going to take the bedroom in the rear."

*****

It must have been one o'clock in the afternoon when Susan woke up. But she and Don hadn't really gone to sleep until around six in the morning. What a wonderful, glorious evening it had been for her. She ranked it as the most memorable of her short life. With memories of the night still clogging her brain, she reached over in her bed, seeking to run her fingers across Don's broad chest and feel his velvety skin. Her hand came up empty.

As she gradually awakened, she heard sounds of Don in the shower. At first she was tempted to join him but decided against that. She wanted to linger in bed, still pretending to be asleep, so she could relive the events of the past night after she'd left The Rusty Pelican with Don. She'd call Pamela sometime this afternoon and set up a time for drinks around six o'clock. Now that she was out of a job and her husband was off in Miami doing God knows what, she had all afternoon to spend with Don. Perhaps she'd invite him to go the beach. The sands lay right outside her condo.

Don had made her forget Buck in one night. Unlike Gene and Buck, Don was the straightest man who'd ever lived, at least in her view. During her marriage to Gene, that athlete could hardly stand to touch her, viewing a love-making session as something calling for sterilization of his body parts. Buck's love-making had been competent in every way, even passionate, but in the dark, murky corners of her brain she suspected that he'd been dreaming about Robert, perhaps even Gene, when he'd made love to her. He had the potential to be the greatest lover of all times, but not with her. His body performed magnificently and on cue. He touched all the right places, said all the right things, and even plunged to depths never realized in her before. But she suspected his soul wasn't there for her, that he really wanted to be some place else in somebody's arms other than hers. No doubt he was at this very moment getting the fulfillment he'd sought in Robert's possessive and overpowering embrace. She shuddered as images of them together flashed through her brain. He was, after all, her husband. She knew she'd have to learn to release him, and Don was the man to help her do that.

She'd never known love-making like that which Don could deliver. He'd virtually devoured her, and no man had ever done that to her before. There was no part of her body he hadn't explored with his tongue. More than once he'd made her scream and pull his hair. His tonguing of her had been the most exquisite pleasure she'd ever known. She suspected it was the kind of loving Robert engaged in with Buck. No wonder Buck loved it so much and couldn't stand the idea of breaking with Robert ever. That love-making was irresistible. Chills went across her body even this afternoon as she'd remembered the great pleasure she'd felt at Don's lashings, pleasure at times so great it was almost painful.

When his long, deep penetration had come, it was evocative of Buck's, although he'd ridden her with a fury she'd never felt from Buck. Don had wanted to take her on a journey to where she'd never been before into a world that made sex the adventure it should always be and so seldom is. He'd worn protection and at their first climax when she'd thought he'd gradually withdraw from her, she'd been wrong. Still partially erect, he'd lingered inside her until a second steam had formed in his engine. He'd plowed her again, more forcefully than before.

The second time had taken much longer and in many ways it was more enthralling because the great urgency for climax was no longer important, and she felt she could take her time with him and he with her. There had been no rush for a second explosion. She'd fondled and caressed his balls, and he'd loved that.

In their weight and fullness, they'd felt like Buck's. It'd amazed her how closely Buck's body was like that of Don's. Don perhaps weighed a few more pounds, but both men were the same height, and their genitals were surprisingly similar. Don's penis was just as thick and as long as Buck's, although it curved slightly to the left, an amusement she'd detected when loving him for the first time.

She was thrilled at how much pleasure the male penis could provide a woman, and Don's love-making of last night made her more determined than ever that she wasn't going to deny her sexual side any more. There's been too many nights alone. Married or not, she was going to pursue this man regardless of the consequences. She hardly expected Buck to protest. He, in fact, might be delighted that she'd found a distraction.

She'd not known that many men in her life, but she was convinced that Don, Buck, and Gene were gifts from nature. The other men she'd been sexually involved with were quite ordinary. One temporary lover had a rather small and crooked penis and had always climaxed within less than a minute of entering her, leaving her completely unsatisfied and unfulfilled. Other lovers were just ordinary men into ordinary love-making, not wanting to extend the act too long before getting back to watching a sports program or rushing off to the gym. It was as if they viewed a bed as someplace not to linger. Sex was something these men needed every now and then—one lover only once a week—and then it was on to the business of the day. One stock broker probably wanted to conduct business on the phone while he'd made love to her.

Opening her eyes, she felt fully awake for the first time this day. The noise from the shower had long stopped, and Don seemed to be in the kitchen making some phone calls. No doubt he'd already found the fruit juice. At the rate that man performed, he needed to be in training, the way it was with him back at the university.

Since Don was all fresh and clean, her vanity dictated that she greet him the same way. She'd sneak into their shower and her powder room and look gorgeous when confronting him for the first time this afternoon. Right now she feared she looked like a woman who'd taken on twelve studs in combat.

As she passed by the bedroom door, she detected anger in Don's voice. He was speaking to someone on the phone, and obviously the conversation wasn't going according to his wishes. She didn't mean to eavesdrop but couldn't help herself. After all, she reasoned, she was a reporter and had an instinct for wanting to find out what was going on. Also she'd never really known Don at all in spite of their university days. She'd moved in completely different circles from him. Last night she'd taken a stranger into her life, a man she feared had been involved with Sister Rose and one whose marriage and life in Miami had never been satisfactorily explained to her. She'd pressed him for details on his life down there and his subsequent divorce but he'd been reluctant to talk about it. She suspected it might be to avoid remembered pain, but there could be other reasons too. Perhaps he was hiding some deep, dark secret.

"God damn you, Shelley," Don said into the phone. "You can't drop me like this just because you've captured Buck Brooke. What's he got that I don't have?"

She was already moving away from the door, deciding to grant Don his privacy. But at the sound of those words, she'd stopped short and gasped for breath. That was Shelley Phillips he was talking to on the phone. No one else had a name like Shelley. "My God," she almost said aloud. The rumors are true, she thought. Not only had Don been involved with Sister Rose but with Shelley too. Surely, though, Don was mistaken. Or maybe she hadn't heard right. Shelley wasn't involved with her husband. Buck was in Miami with Robert, not with Shelley.

"I've been with you too long to settle for a lousy fifty-thousand dollars," Don said. "It's not enough. It was always you and me, babe, long after Rose and I broke up. Rose didn't know you kept slipping down to Miami to see me. That you've never stopped seeing me. That is, until my wife found out. Until Buck Brooke entered your life, until you decided you'd rather have a faggot than me."

Shelley obviously had plenty to say on the other end of the phone.

"I told you, it's not enough. I need one-hundred thousand dollars. Fifty just won't do. I could make it real rough on you, cocksucker. I could go to the press. I could tell them plenty. I could sue. It would ruin you, cocksucker."

There was a long pause. It was clear Shelley had plenty of reaction to that.

"I'm glad you're coming around to my way of thinking—that's my boy." "One hundred thousand dollars and in cash. You've got so fucking much money you'll never miss it. But I must warn you: that's not going to be enough. It'll get me by now because I have another gig, but it won't get me through the long haul."

She put her hand at her throat. So she was viewed by Don as a gig, a working commitment. Well, he was certainly good at his job. She'd landed herself the most expensive hustler in the state of Florida.

"It's just not the money," Don said to Shelley over the phone. "I love you. I've always loved you. Sex with you is better than any sex I've ever had in my life. I want to be with you. When you get over this God damn thing with Buck, I want you back. You come back to me, you hear. I'll fuck you like you've never been fucked before, better than Buck could ever fuck you. With me, you know you're getting a real man. That's all that can satisfy you. Not some fucking pansy."

She'd heard enough. She didn't really want to hear Don pleading with Shelley for the boy to come back to him.

Under the shower she'd tried to blot out the words she'd heard. If she'd been twenty-three, she would have burst into the kitchen, grabbed the phone from Don, and denounced Shelley. Then she would have slammed down the receiver and demanded that Don leave her condo, never to darken her door again.

But she was no longer that young. She turned the shower on extra hot, as if that could burn away some of the pain. But then she readjusted the nozzle. To her surprise, there was no pain to burn away. Who in hell was she to cast a moral judgment over Don? Wasn't she a paid courtesan herself? The only difference between them was that she didn't have to fuck on command. Wasn't she secretly hustling Buck Brooke III? Didn't that make her a whore? Because of the terms of her marriage, she couldn't find a regular guy anyway. What was left for her? A married man? A trick on the side? For all appearances, she had to appear Buck's dutiful and loyal wife.

She felt better about things all of a sudden, more realistic somehow. Don was a great lover, and she needed his particular type of love-making. She admired Shelley's taste: Don Bossdum and now Buck Brooke. That little preacher rat knew how to pick them. His taste probably paralleled that of her own. Perhaps they should get together some time and compare notes.

Stepping from the shower, she reached for a thick towel. She was going to call Uncle Milty as soon as he returned from Miami. Without going through Buck, she was going to inform Buck's attorney of her new living arrangements and tell him to send Don a check every week for seven-hundred and fifty dollars. She'd supply the rest of the money for him, including a new wardrobe. Don didn't need a job: he already had a job and that was being with her. Let Buck have his Robert. Let Buck even have his Shelley. She didn't know how long Buck could pull that one off. Robert, she knew, was suspicious and would soon find out about Buck and Shelley. But that was Buck's problem.

Applying the finishing touches to her face, she liked the reflection staring back at her in the mirror. Instead of diminishing her, Don's love-making seemed to have given her a new vitality and glow. She looked radiant.

She paused only briefly at the bedroom door. The only sound coming from the kitchen was the television. Don was watching some sports broadcast, so obviously he'd concluded his phone conversation with Shelley.

She came into the kitchen. He looked up at her at once, reaching quickly to cut off the television. At least he had the grace to turn off that blasted set. She hated sports programs.

"Good morning," she said in a soft, modulated voice which she hoped sounded sexy. "Did anyone ever tell you you're the world's greatest lover?"

*****

Instead of looking at Mrs. Dante being lowered into her final resting place, Buck searched Robert's face for some clue as to how he felt. Behind dark sunglasses, Robert showed no emotion as he looked vacantly at the casket being lowered. He'd been married only hours before, and it should have been a day of joyous celebration but he was now at his mother's funeral. Buck thought that ironic. His mother even managed to sabotage Robert's wedding day.

There were no other mourners except three old women in flowery purple dresses. Buck learned from the pastor, a Florida cracker who'd renamed himself Hesus Saviour, that these bedraggled elderly women tried to attend a funeral in the area every day. It didn't matter if they knew the deceased: they just liked attending funerals and singing gospel songs over corpses. Buck found them ghoulish.

Before the ceremony, Buck and Uncle Milty had met with Mr. Saviour out of earshot of Robert and Patrick who'd brought flowers to Mrs. Dante's grave.

"Do you want to be called Hesus or Jesus?" Uncle Milty had asked.

"Listen, you stupid kyke faggot, I don't have to take no shit from a fucking Christ killer."

"That's getting to the point," Buck had said.

"Fuck you, cocksucker," Hesus had said. "I'm here to bury a Christian woman. She told me all about you and her son, and asked me to pray for you queers every night. I took her money from the collection box on Sunday but I swear I never prayed for you pansies. As far as I'm concerned, faggots will burn in hell, and all the prayers in this world won't save their sodomized asses."

"At least you have strong beliefs," Buck had said sarcastically.

"I'm entitled to my opinion." He'd turned to look with contempt at Uncle Milty, although addressing Buck. "Why don't you have your creepy Jewish lawyer here fork over one-hundred bucks or else there might not be a funeral at all."

Buck had glanced at Uncle Milty. "Give this creep five-hundred dollars and tell the asshole to make the funeral short and sweet." He had spat on the ground in front of the pastor who had turned to walk over to Robert and Patrick. He'd whispered in Robert's ear, "Glad you married me?"

"It's the happiest day of my life," Robert had said. "I'm even burying the one woman who hated me more than anybody else has hated me in my life. There wasn't a day that went by that she didn't tell me she hated me. Every day of my life as a little boy she told me how sorry she was that she allowed me to be born."

"Oh, God," Buck had said, "I don't want to hear it."

"There's more," Robert had said. "She used to say if she'd known how I would have turned out, she would have had me aborted, and she was the world's leader attacker of abortion."

"And your father, whoever in the hell he was, wasn't there to help you."

"I don't even want to know what he was like."

"He must have been a beautiful man," Buck had said to comfort Robert. "You certainly didn't get your looks from your mother."

Buck tried to blot out what had happened before the funeral. He didn't want to think about it. Even though the day was the brightest he'd known, and the heat was more than 95 degrees, and all of them were clad in dark suits, he felt the ghosts in the graveyard were rising to get him. Sweating profusely, he wanted to escape this funeral site sooner than later.

The funeral ended so quickly Buck hadn't realized at first that it was over. Hesus had followed instructions and kept the ceremony simple and short. When the pastor had gone through his "ashes to ashes" speech, he abruptly turned and left, not saying one word to the mourners, even to Robert.

"That's called taking the money and running," Buck whispered into Uncle Milty's ear.

"Good riddance!"

In the air-conditioned comfort of a long black limousine, Robert collapsed in Buck's arms. For the first time today, he sobbed, as Buck sought to comfort him.

"In spite of it all, I loved her," Robert said. "Some part of me loved her even though she did everything she could to make me hate her."

Out on the causeway, speeding away from the scene of this disaster, and heading for a private villa on Key Biscayne, Uncle Milty turned to Buck. "I've asked the driver to drop us off at the villa. You're to proceed to the airport."

Robert stopped sobbing and sat up in panic. "You're not leaving me?" he asked Buck.

"I'll be here for you, babe," Buck said in way of reassurance.

"Buck's not flying anywhere," Uncle Milty said. "But Sister Rose has flown her private jet down to the Miami airport. You're to go aboard and retrieve two contracts from a member of her staff. I'm to read them tonight. Three contracts, actually."

"What?" Buck said. "What's the deal?"

"Her geeks have met all my demands. One contract calls for a payment of eighteen million dollars. Old Buck's share of the Examiner. Another grants a very generous twelve million for your share—and were they suckers on that deal. The final contract calls for a three-year salaried deal for you including three million up front, all expenses paid, and the use of a private jet plane and a limousine twenty-four hours a day among other fringe benefits."

"Christ, you're going to be rich," Patrick said. "I mean, really rich."

"That's not all," Uncle Milty chimed in. "When Old Buck passes on his way, you're going to be a hell of a lot richer than we ever thought. My office is doing a deep down appraisal right now of his assets. That old boy bought a lot of land in Florida. Tomorrow's shopping malls, even Florida cities, will rise on land that guy owns. But it'll all be yours soon."

"Let's don't count on that," Buck cautioned. "He's not dead yet. Anything can happen. Like he could disinherit me. What if he found out about this wedding? That would be the end of that."

"He'll not find out," Uncle Milty assured him.

Buck leaned down and kissed Robert on the lips, brushing away his remaining tears. "I'm going to the airport, an unemployed former publisher making forty-five thousand dollars a year, and I'm coming back a multi-millionaire."

"I just want you," Robert said. "Not your money."

"You still have to fly out to Palm Springs to pick up the checks," Uncle Milty said.

"Sure you don't want me to go along to carry your luggage?" Patrick asked. "Uncle Milty only gives me two-hundred dollars a week allowance."

"You don't need any more money," Uncle Milty said. "I give you an American Express card. You charge everything, and do you ever charge."

"I'm worth it," Patrick said.

"So you are, you little uncut dickhead."

Buck looked out the window at the rows of dreary houses and felt he was suffocating. Actually he was trembling at the prospect of what awaited him. You could not casually anticipate such a windfall of cash without it doing something to you. He wondered if Robert detected that he was trembling.

As the limousine pulled into the driveway of the luxurious Key Biscayne villa, Buck grabbed Robert and pressed his body hard against that of his friend's. He kissed Robert long and hard. "I'm a married man now, and I've got a husband to support, so best I head for that airport and bring home the bacon."

"Bring yourself back to me sooner than later," Robert said, kissing Buck's nose and eyelids. "I'm anxious to begin our honeymoon."

"And I'm anxious to read those contracts," Uncle Milty said. "If they're good enough, I might up Patrick's allowance to three-hundred dollars a week."

"You're too good to me," Patrick said, squeezing Uncle Milty's arm and giving him a peck on the cheek.

"And, you, my little sugartit," Buck said turning to Robert. "You're going to have whatever you've ever wanted."

Robert ran his fingers through Buck's straight blond hair. "I've got him."

On the way to the airport, Buck leaned back and closed his eyes. He didn't want to think about anything. Until he got there, he wanted his mind to go completely blank.

He was suddenly aroused by the chauffeur addressing him. Up to that moment, he hadn't taken notice of the man at all.

"I hope you don't mind my asking you something?" the tall, blond-haired driver said. In some respects he reminded Buck of Gene. Except for the color of the hair, the driver's features and build were very similar to Gene, although the driver had a more rugged look. He was about Buck's age, and had a bright, mischievous grin. "I'm Casey Wilson. Glad to meet you."

"Thanks for driving us around," Buck said non-committally, wondering how closely he'd been observing the action in the rear.

"It's okay. It's what I do. But I can do other things too. Forgive me but we don't have much time, and I don't know when I'll be alone with you again. I couldn't help overhearing that talk about millions and all. Listen, you can see I'm a good-looking guy. I've also got a big dick. A real big one, and I know how to use it. I can suck cock with the best of men. I'm good for four or even five sessions a day."

"You sound mighty impressive," Buck said, his face turning red. He didn't embarrass easily.

"I'm serious, man. You don't need to be hanging out with those faggots I dumped on Key Biscayne. You need a real man, and I'm the one for you."

"I'm sure I do," Buck said, trying to humor the man but also finding him compellingly attractive at the same time. It was a temptation, though, that he had no intention succumbing to. In a way he was amused and flattered at being hustled as a john. Had he matured to the point in life where he could in the future be treated as the hustled? It made him feel grown up.

At the airport and out of the car, he told the driver to stay in his seat and not get out. Buck came up to the open window and leaned in and gave Casey a big hard kiss on his lips. "That's one tempting offer, and I'll think about it," he said. "In the meantime, when I get off that plane, a thousand-dollar tip is waiting."

"A thousand dollars?" Casey questioned in astonishment. "That's a lot of money."

"Maybe the beginning of a lot of thousand-dollar tips in the future," Buck said. "Maybe some day I'll whip out my dick and you can whip out yours, and we'll compare."

"May the best man win," Casey said, his hand reaching out and grabbing Buck by the back of his neck and forcing him inside the window for a long, passionate kiss with tongue this time.

The kiss still lingered on Buck's lips as he raced through the airport where arrangements had been made for clearance for him. As he almost ran up the steps leading into Rose's private plane, he fully expected to encounter Sister Rose herself waiting here for him with the contracts. But as he stepped aboard, it wasn't Rose who greeted him.

*****

In a pair of shorts and a T-shirt, Leroy looked younger and more vibrant today than Gene had ever seen him. As soon as Gene had entered the apartment, Leroy kissed him on the mouth and took his hand, directing him to the terrace. Here he had laid out some hors d'oeuvres including large, fresh shrimp. "It's my own special cocktail sauce," he said. "My mother taught me how to make it."

Gene picked up a shrimp, dipped it in the sauce, and tasted it. "It's real good. I love shrimp."

"And I love you," Leroy said, standing close to him with a paper napkin wiping a dab of cocktail sauce from the corner of Gene's mouth.

"Don't you think love is a rather strong word?" Gene asked. "Don't you think love is different from having the hots for someone?"

"I do indeed, my pet," Leroy said, reaching for one of the shrimp himself.

Gene winced at being called someone's pet. "I don't think anyone who loves me could put me through all that crap I had to go through for your so-called friends. Caught on camera, no less."

Leroy looked crestfallen as he turned and headed toward his living room, no longer interested in the hors d'oeuvres.

Gene followed him. "I didn't mean to insult you. But I felt really nasty doing what I had to do. I'm not proud of it. That's why I tried to get the job with Barry. To tell the truth, I'm ashamed of what I did. I'm ashamed of a lot of things I've done."

"So am I." Leroy plopped down on the sofa, putting his feet up on the coffee table. "I'm ashamed that I put you through that, and I want you to forgive me. Only this morning I was trying to buy back the films. I don't want anybody having that film of you."

"Maybe it's too late for that now."

"Maybe it is, but I'm still going to try. Money talks."

"Why do you want the films back?"

"Because I've decided I'm in love with you. I don't plan to share you ever again with another man—or a woman for that matter. From this day on, you're my own exclusive property."

Gene looked astonished. "Don't I have something to say in this matter? It's my body. Even if I don't seem to own my body these days, at least I own my heart."

"I didn't mean to put it that way. I've never known how to be diplomatic."

"I'm not going to lead you on. You've helped me out of a tight jam. The condo—everything. I owe you a lot, and I'm willing to go along to a certain degree. But I'm no lying whore pretending to be in love with a john when I'm not. I'm here for you—the body that is. But not the heart."

"Do you think I'm just some silly little faggot? I know you don't love me. But you could learn to love me. It would take time. I could show you a different side to myself. I'm not a total shit, you know. I've got a heart too. I don't just use people, although it would seem like that at times."

"I know you're human. It took a bizarre form but you did bail me out. I mean, I was out on the street with nothing and nowhere to go. I had to sing for my supper but at least you let me sing."

"Let's try to put that little episode behind us. Things are changing. When and if I get those films back, I promise not to see those creeps again. I don't want to be reminded. The Lolito house is closing. Calder has ordered it shut down. It was getting too hot. Too many people knew about it. It's too dangerous to run it any more. Besides, he's got what he wants. Mainly enough footage on Barry Collins to make that prick Calder's slave for life."

"I'm glad to hear that. Even Sandy was exploited there."

"I know that, and I'm sorry about that too. But things can change. Listen." He reached for Gene's hand and pulled him down on the sofa to sit beside him. "I'm going to see you through this shit you've gotten yourself into with that little Cuban girl. Through no fault of your own, I might add. Once that's behind us, I'm going to beg you to come to California with me. Leave Okeechobee and all this crap behind us. I've accumulated one and a half million dollars—don't ask me how. That's more than enough for us to live on in California. I'm also the world's best God damn photographer. I can make big bucks out there. We'll live in grand style." He reached over and kissed Gene on the lips. "Say you'll come with me."

As Leroy embraced him, Gene returned the hug. He didn't even resist when Leroy started kissing his neck and unbuttoning his shirt. "I'll think about it, dude. I'll think about it."

He sighed as Leroy began to tongue his nipples, working himself up to a feeding frenzy over Gene's perfectly sculpted body. Pretending to moan and enjoy Leroy's tongue lashings, Gene smiled to himself. He'd lied to Leroy. He had no intention of following him to California or anywhere else for that matter.

As for love, there was only one man he loved—and that was Buck Brooke III. He also hated Buck for betraying him. When Leroy unbuckled his trousers and sought his jewels to fondle, kiss, and suck, Gene closed his eyes and imagined it was Buck down there devouring him. No lips, no mouth, no tongue, no throat ever felt like Buck's. Even as Leroy worked desperately and frantically to bring Gene to climax, Gene retained the image of Buck in his mind.

As his release neared, he felt tears well in his eyes. When his eruption came, he cried out, knowing Leroy would take it for passion and heat. But it was something else. He was crying out for someone—make it Buck—to barge in that door and rescue him.

*****

On the plane, Shelley looked like jail bait. Resting on a sofa at the rear of the private jet, and surrounded by paintings, Buck had never seen him appear younger. It was hard to believe he wasn't fourteen instead of his real age. Clad only in a white T-shirt and a pair of denim cut-off shorts, he was Tadzio—no, more than that, better than that. He was Adonis in the glow of sunlight. Even though Buck knew that Shelley might live for another eighty years, Buck realized that the boy might never again appear this enchanting.

He deliberately restrained himself from rushing toward Shelley and crushing him in his arms, which was his first impulse, and decided to savor the moment instead. Shelley returned his startled look with a mischievous grin. His eyes were of such a clear blue Buck felt Shelley had definitely descended from Vikings. His skin was golden, and Buck felt himself becoming aroused at the sight of the boy's legs. He'd seen beautiful legs on men before, notably Robert's, but he'd never seen legs with quite the sculpted perfection of Shelley's. It wasn't just the beauty of the legs, but the way Shelley had provocatively arranged them to enhance their loveliness. Buck wanted to take his tongue and bathe every inch of those legs, wetting them down and loving them before he explored more hidden areas of the boy's body.

"Surprise!" Shelley finally said. It was as if he'd known that Buck had been mesmerized by his beauty, and he'd wanted Buck to take in the full spectacle before breaking the mood with words.

"You're not only in Miami, but you look like something Botticelli created in heaven and sent down as a gift to me."

"It's all yours, my darling man, every delectable inch of my body. Every orifice. There's no part of me that's off-limits to you—now and forever. You mentioned Botticelli," he said, rising a bit from the sofa. "Actually, we're concentrating on a more modern artist today. De Kooning."

It was only then that Buck became aware that the airplane cabin had been turned into an art show. One by one he took in the glory of each painting, and by the time he'd viewed the final one he was almost salivating.

"A gift from Rose," Shelley said. "Each and every one of them. She feared that the one de Kooning she gave you wasn't enough. You might as well have a whole fucking gallery of them."

"It's too much—I love them, but I can't accept. It doesn't seem right somehow."

"Forget it—they're yours. Actually Rose until a few days ago never heard of de Kooning. As far as art goes, she probably knows the Mona Lisa, although I'm not sure about that, and that's it."

Buck glanced nervously over his shoulder. He seemed alone in the plane with Shelley, and couldn't resist the boy's allure any more. Easing himself gently over Shelley's body on the sofa, he inserted his tongue into the boy's mouth. It was expertly sucked, and Buck's cock swelled immediately to its full glory. He reached down to adjust himself and make more room for his extended state. When both hands were free, he kept his tongue inside the boy's mouth, withdrawing every now and then to taste his delectable lips. It was the sweetest taste he'd ever known in his life. No matter what the time of day or night, Shelley's breath was so sweet it was virtually intoxicating.

With both hands he riffled through Shelley's golden hair, savoring its silky texture. Feeling that hair was actually one of the most sensual pleasures he'd ever known. Shelley was sucking sensually, swallowing the saliva from Buck's mouth. Buck was shaking, his whole body trembling. The boy was giving him pleasure that was so exquisite it was almost painful.

Slowly withdrawing his tongue from Shelley's mouth, he inserted that same tongue in one of the boy's ears, washing it although the taste was as clean, sweet, and pure as every other part of the boy. "I've got to fuck you, boy. I can't control myself. I've got to give you the deepest penetration you've ever had. Reach areas in your body where no man has gone before."

When he looked down at Shelley again, Buck feared he'd fainted. He'd momentarily grown limp, his whole body sagging. In moments, Buck realized what a powerful affect he'd had on the boy. It was as if his love-making had sent Shelley into a dreamy trance. Buck knew at once that Shelley was his now, to do with as he wished. He picked up his body, planting gentle tongue kisses on his neck before returning to lick and taste the boy's lips.

He carried him toward the back, opening a door marked private. The cabin inside was dark but he could tell it was a bedroom on the plane. Still carrying Shelley in his arms, he locked the door behind them with his one free hand and gently laid the boy on the bed. It was Shelley now who was running his fingers through Buck's own golden blond hair. Moving his body and cooperating in every way, Shelley allowed Buck to remove every stitch of his meager clothing. When Buck had pulled down Shelley's briefs, he planted several quick kisses on the boy's fully aroused penis before descending to bathe his balls.

Standing over him, Buck removed every piece of his clothing but slowly. The boy was staring at him and Buck knew that Shelley was as turned on by him as he was by Shelley. It was a striptease Buck was performing. Soon he was out of all his clothes, all except his briefs which were stretched almost beyond their limitations. As he took his hands to remove his briefs, Shelley reached out and stopped him.

"That is a pleasure I reserve for myself," Shelley said, slowly slipping down Buck's white cotton briefs personally selected by Robert. As Shelley pulled the briefs down below Buck's balls, his penis stood hard and rigid in the air. But it wasn't allowed to remain there for long. In seconds it was captured by Shelley's lusting lips, and the impact was so tantalizing Buck moaned and reached to fondle the boy's velvety throat. Both Shelley and Buck knew that an invasion of that throat was imminent, and Shelley responded to Buck's massaging hands as if preparing himself for it. Buck knew it must be hard on the boy to take him but was determined to press forward anyway. The sheer pleasure that awaited him when he'd penetrated that throat was just too great to deny himself.

*****

At The Rusty Pelican, the pub was nearly deserted. It was too early at what was essentially a place that didn't become active until after ten o'clock. Susan sat in a deserted corner, studying closely the anxiety in Pamela's tremulous face.

Don had stayed behind at Susan's condo, wanting to "try out that Olympic pool." He also wanted to avoid seeing Pamela. Susan had noted with wry amusement the bikini he'd selected to wear to that pool. Before leaving the condo, she'd said to him, "Why bother with that bikini? You might as well be nude." He turned to her with a wicked grin, saying, "Them that's got flaunts." After a wet, slurping kiss good-bye, she'd driven over to meet Pamela after arranging a rendezvous. The subject of Don Bossdum and what to do with him would be resolved much later by her. For the moment she focused her entire attention on a distraught Pamela.

"Gene moved in on us in more ways than one," Pamela was saying. "He's become Barry's night bodyguard."

"I would think Barry would be sensitive about being seen with Gene—I mean with his latest case still pending and everything."

"That so-called case is a pile of crap!"

"I couldn't agree with you more. But he's still in deep do-do, and my father is going to defend him."

"Thank God. I hope the judge throws it out of court."

"So do I. Gene's suffered enough."

"No bitterness?"

"Every day I think about Gene and our life together. It was such a big mistake. For the both of us."

"I was a little sad when you made off with him. I've always had this crush on him."

"Still?"

"Still." Pamela sighed. "But someone is always moving in on my turf. Even now."

"I don't exactly understand your meaning." Susan raised an eyebrow. "But you're living with Gene. The night bodyguard, whatever that means."

"That means Barry is not seen in public with Gene."

Even though no longer married to Gene, and certainly no longer in love with him, Susan couldn't help but feel a bit of jealousy over Gene. She didn't want to think too much about Pamela and Gene together. "If Gene's the night bodyguard, I guess you'll have plenty of chances to be alone with him. Maybe something will develop."

"Something has developed. I might still have the hots for Gene, but Barry has senior rank in our marriage. I fear Gene was lost to me before we even got started."

Susan tried to conceal the look of astonishment on her face. "The implication is all too clear. I can't believe it. Barry likes them younger, I thought."

"My husband is very versatile. He has many tastes."

Susan made a decision then and there not to pursue the matter any more. She just didn't want to know. She'd hardly recovered from learning about Don and Shelley. Or was it Buck and Shelley? But Gene and Barry? The coupling was inconceivable to her. She'd always known that Gene intensely disliked Barry, and she didn't think anything had changed in that regard.

"In fact, just this afternoon, Gene flew with Barry in a private jet to Miami. They're staying at this villa in Key Biscayne. I don't know what's going on. No one tells me anything. But Calder Martin has arranged for Barry to meet the big boys in our party. Barry is being groomed for big things, and I mean big. Of course, he's got to win this stupid mayor's race first."

"From what I hear, he's got it made," Susan said. "Hazel is just a little too crude for the average voter, even though I adore her and personally plan to vote for her." She reached to touch Pamela's hand. "Forgive me, but I had to tell the truth."

"What in the fuck do I care who you vote for? I'll probably not vote myself, but if I did I'd vote for Hazel too. I don't exactly owe Barry Collins any favors—certainly not my vote."

"I'm surprised at how candid you are with me."

"We've always talked off-the-record. Besides you're not a reporter any more. You were fired from the Examiner."

"Don't remind me." Susan sighed and sipped her drink. "But I'll go on to bigger and grander things."

An increasing desperation came across Pamela's face. She seemed to be trembling, as she nervously glanced around the room. "I have no doubt that you'll make it real big some day. As much as I loathe to admit it, I think Barry will make it big. He'll do anything to get ahead. Make any deal. Compromise his soul, if necessary. He's definitely got what it takes."

"If he makes it big, you'll be big too. He'll pull you kicking and screaming to the top."

Pamela looked at Susan for a long moment without saying anything. She then belted down her drink, her face tightening into a controlled rage. "I think Calder Martin doesn't want me around for the long haul. He adores Barry because he can control him. But he feels I am a dynamite liability."

"That's no news, and you know that. You've always been considered a liability for Barry. Let's face it, Pam. You're not the ideal politician's wife, especially if you're catering to a rigidly conservative element like Barry's is."

"Tell me something I don't know. That's not why I called you here. I think matters are getting out of hand." She leaned over toward Susan, her voice becoming a whisper. "I think Calder Martin wants to get rid of me."

"Buy you off, you mean?"

"That was the plan originally, and I more or less agreed to the idea of remaining—at least outwardly—an obedient and dutiful wife throughout the campaign. But the only thing everyone in this charade agrees on is that divorce is a liability that Barry can't afford. And what's especially ironic, considering that he's otherwise a complete sleazeball, is the fact that Calder doesn't believe in divorce, and Sister Rose preaches against it."

"So you think that Calder will insist on Barry staying married to you?"

"If I wasn't so goddamn outspoken, and if I wasn't so enraged most of the time, that plan would probably work. But I think they've begun seeing me as a liability that's out of control. It might be more convenient for them if I had an accident."

Susan sighed and, like Pamela, took a much stronger sip of her drink. She studied Pamela's face closely. Was this Pamela's paranoia speaking, or was her companion truly on to something? "I can't believe they'd dare go that far. Buying you off was one thing—risky, but perhaps effective. But the other just seems too risky for them to get away with."

Pamela cracked her knuckles in desperation. "I didn't expect you to believe me. No one believes me. Perhaps after I've had this accident, then people, including you, will believe me. By then, it will be too late for me."

"Even assuming I did believe you, what can I do about it?"

"Not a God damn thing."

"Then why did you want to meet with me? Just to unburden your chest? Share your most awful suspicions with me?"

"I came here for a very definite reason. I want you to make me a promise."

"I'd have to know more about it. I don't make promises easily."

"If I do have that accident, would you and Ingrid investigate it? I mean, she's got the column and everything. She could raise some real strong evidence."

"By all means we'd investigate it. Hell wouldn't stop us from investigating it. You've alerted me. I'd do anything to find out who murdered you. It'd be murder if someone arranged an accident for you."

"I wanted you to promise me that. Even though I'd be dead, I wouldn't want the bastards to get away with it. I'd want them to burn."

"I've promised you. But at the same time I have to tell you that even though I think Barry and Calder Martin are bastards, I don't believe they'd go this far. They could get caught. It'd destroy them. They could end up in jail."

"Believe me, they wouldn't do it themselves."

"Nixon didn't commit the Watergate burglary personally, but it kicked back on him. The same would be the case here."

"I'm not so sure," Pamela said, glancing apprehensively at her watch. "I've got to go. I can't stay here any longer." With a trembling hand, she reached for Susan's arm. "Please, if something ever happens, carry out your promise."

"I will." Susan tried to comfort Pamela. "It's only a mayor's race in a not very important town. I don't think it calls for the tactics you've suggested. Hell, it's a mayor's race that Barry practically won the moment he announced he was a candidate."

On wobbly legs, Pamela stood up and looked down at Susan. "You don't understand. The mayor's race is only one tiny little step on the road to their horizon."

"Exactly what is their horizon?"

"Twenty years from now they want Barry in the White House. Yes, president of the United States. Believe it or not, that's what this secret meeting in Key Biscayne is all about. Barry is only twenty-seven years old, and already he's been singled out for a top strategy meeting. I guess if you want to make it to the White House, you've got to start early."

"You'd be First Lady."

"I'll never live to be First Lady. That's for damn sure. Barry may be known as the widowed president. His hostesses will not be me but my two darling daughters. The press would probably love that. After all, Barry is movie star handsome. My daughters are adorable as you know."

"I don't think this nightmare is going to happen."

"Nightmares often come true," Pamela said in way of a parting greeting. She headed for the door, leaving Susan alone at the table. Susan felt alone in more ways than one until she remembered she'd recently acquired a male hustler—that is, when Shelley Phillips didn't have him occupied which meant the times when the little minister wasn't with her newly acquired husband. A few years ago she viewed Pamela as her major rival on campus. Times had changed. Pamela with her fading beauty was no longer a rival but an ally somehow. In the very sophisticated world of 1977, Shelley Phillips had become the major competition for the men in her life.

*****

In the darkened room of the airplane cabin, Shelley whispered in his ear. "I need you."

The words were like an aphrodisiac to Buck. With one hand he laced his fingers together with Shelley's on the soft fluffy pillow, and with the other he guided himself into the boy. With Robert, it had been new and experimental. Entry had been difficult at first. But with Shelley it was different somehow. Shelley grabbed his penis and guided him to the target, and when he was completely engulfed Shelley began a soft and thrilling massage of Buck's balls.

Once inside the boy he didn't move at first, letting Shelley get used to his invasion but enjoying all the sensations that surged through his body. He had entered paradise, and he didn't want to leave. Ever.

Noting the red flush filling the blond-haired youth's cheeks, Buck leaned down and licked his sweet lips before inserting his tongue for Shelley to suck. He could never get enough of that.

Very gently at first he began to move inside the boy's velvety channel. He had never desired anyone or anything more in his whole life. He felt in total control, in complete possession of the boy. As he moved his cock up and down, he was deliriously happy.

"Fuck me harder," Shelley commanded between moans.

That was all the incentive Buck needed. He'd been afraid to plunge too deep or violently but Shelley was massaging his ballsac all the harder. With his other hand, he dug his fingernails into Buck's neck and gently nibbled on his ear. From the look on Shelley's face, Buck could tell he'd transported Shelley to a plateau of such exquisite joy that the boy could hardly stand it. After each plunge, Shelley moaned and almost cried out in his pleasure. Buck rammed harder into the boy and set his own pace, adjusting his movement at any time when Shelley's face told him he'd hit a particularly sensitive spot. He was thrilled at this seduction but even more thrilled that he had the power to enrapture anybody as much as he did Shelley.

It was Buck's firmness against the softness of Shelley's body that goaded him on to more adventures. Shelley's breathing became ragged. Buck felt the boy's hardness pressing against his belly, and he knew that Shelley was close to orgasm. He wanted to delay it because he was far from finished with his penetration. But Shelley suddenly screamed and exploded.

Fearing he might be sadistic, he kept pumping into Shelley all through his orgasm. The boy was crying now and holding him even tighter. Buck never let up, not even when he felt that Shelley had been completely drained. Buck wasn't drained yet—far from it and he was going to continue to the end until he was completely fulfilled and satisfied by Shelley. The boy belonged to him now, and he wanted his full pleasure.

Shelley seemed to enter a dreamy trance after his orgasm as Buck continued to pump into his depths. In moments the boy was hard again. Buck could feel Shelley's rock hardness rubbing his belly every time he plunged into the boy. He lowered himself over Shelley again with his tongue out. Shelley knew what to do and what Buck wanted. He'd never had his tongue so expertly serviced.

He slammed hard into Shelley. He couldn't keep this up much longer without an explosion, and he didn't want it to end but couldn't help himself. Buck felt his blood boiling as if heated by steamy water. Shelley's insides felt fiery hot to him. Shelley's butt flared wide and eager. Even as he pumped him, he wondered where his cock went. He was amazed that Shelley could take all of him so effortlessly and without any obvious pain. In fact, with almost cruel plunges, Buck rode Shelley's tender tissues, ripping into him, slamming into him, growing incredibly thick as he neared the end of his ride. Shelley's mouth opened and for the first time he seemed to gasp in pain. As he pumped him he stared deeply into Shelley's eyes. Without the boy saying anything, he seemed to convey to Buck that he'd found the man of his dreams.

That was all the spark Buck needed to go over the top. He lifted Shelley's right leg into the air to give him more access. He reamed and twisted inside the boy's body.

Shelley's eyes were wide open now. He clenched his mouth into a tight grimace, and Buck felt the boy was going for his second orgasm. This time Buck wanted to time it so that he went into bliss at the moment Shelley did.

Shelley clamped down around the large, invading penis, welcoming it and holding it. Shelley's buttocks raised and rammed forward to meet Buck's every thrust. Buck's body slammed against Shelley's. Buck grabbed a handful of Shelley's hair and forced his face up to meet Buck's lips. He slurped at Shelley's mouth. As he exploded inside Shelley he screamed a primal triumph inside the boy's mouth. With his guts filled by Buck, his own insides wrapped tightly around Buck's cock, Shelley exploded at the same time. Buck shagged him harder, the impact causing Shelley's head to hit the top of the bed. Shelley reached for the base of Buck's cock and seemed to force it even deeper into himself.

He didn't know how long he stayed inside the boy because time didn't matter. Twisting and struggling to remove himself, he felt Shelley resisting and trying to keep him inside. But there would be so much more of this later, so very much more, the act repeated endlessly over the years. It was time to withdraw.

Buck collapsed on the pillow lying on his back. He placed his hand on Shelley's neck forcing him into a face-to-face confrontation where he licked the boy's entire face and bit his neck several times before nibbling each ear and washing it with his tongue.

With one hand on Shelley's neck, the other grabbing his hair, Buck forced Shelley's head lower and lower on to his body. Shelley's tongue left a wet trail as it glided down Buck's chest, lingering at his bellybutton as if he'd found some special nectar here.

"I don't have time to bathe now," Buck said in a voice that sounded strange even to himself. "Lick me clean."

He encased his head in his hands and enjoyed the comfort of the pillow. He spread his legs to give Shelley total access. Even drained as he was, he felt he was getting an exquisite bath from the world's most talented lips and tongue.

*****

Back at his limousine, and accompanied by two flight attendants from the plane carrying the de Kooning paintings, Buck leaned over into the driver's seat and kissed Casey on the lips. "Miss me?"

"I've had a hard-on all the time thinking about plowing your ass," Casey said, kissing him back. "Other than that, no."

Buck told the chauffeur to stay in the driver's seat while he opened the rear door to allow the attendants to place the paintings carefully inside. Giving each of the attendants a hundred-dollar tip, he slammed the door and walked around to the front of the vehicle, getting in the front seat with Casey. After he told Casey where he wanted to go, Buck settled back in his seat and shut his eyes for the moment. He didn't remove Casey's right hand when it settled between his legs to fondle and feel. "My God," the driver said, "you feel like you've got as much down there as I have."

"As I said, we'll compare sometime, but right now I need your help."

"I'd do anything for you. I know a motel I could take you to."

"I'll hold you to that promise," Buck said. "Give me a raincheck. I had mentioned a thousand dollar tip. Up that to five thousand."

"I'd do anything for that," Casey said, and I do mean anything."

"I'm sure you would, but first, we've got to store these paintings, and never mention to anyone that we've even seen them."

"Agreed."

"How would you like to become my permanent driver in Okeechobee?" Buck asked. "At a real fat salary."

"I'd go for that in a minute. I accept. I'm available to you at any time of the day or night."

"I'm not sure we're going to become lovers," Buck said. "I've got a pretty full date card at the moment. But I need a driver I can trust. One who's very discreet and doesn't report everything that goes on in the back seat of a limousine."

"I'm very discreet," Casey said, as he began to work Buck up to a full erection. "I'll haul you anywhere at any time of the day or night. I'll see nothing but the road ahead of me."

"That's the kind of talk I like to hear," Buck said. "My life's pretty mixed up right now, and I've got a lot of complications. In the future, I'll need to get around from place to place back in Okeechobee. One household is not to know I'm visiting the other household or households as the case may be."

"Now that I've got you fully hard, I can see what the attraction is. No wonder you're busy." He sighed. "By the way, while you were on that plane, doing what to whomever, one of those flight attendants came to my limousine and handed me a box and a document. It's a gift for you. The guy told me to take real good care of it. It's in the glove compartment."

Buck reached into the compartment and removed a small gift package. He unwrapped it to discover one of the most stunning diamond and gold rings he'd ever seen in his life. He placed it on his finger. It fitted perfectly. Noting the rose-colored small envelope, he opened it to read: "My darling, darling man, love of my life. Shelley confessed to me that he gave you a special blue diamond ring. How Shelley got that ring is not something I care to go into right now. But I wanted you to know that if the little cocksucker can give you a ring that you could sell and retire on, I could top him. The ring I'm giving you was made especially for John Jacob Astor. A photograph in color of it often appears in books devoted to jewelry. It is a rare and special gift, and I don't dare tell you how much it's worth. But I want you to know that it and all the other jewels of the world don't equal those jewels dangling between the legs of Buck Brooke III. You are one hell of a man. Please eat plenty of oysters because Shelley and I are going to be spending the rest of our days fighting over squatters' rights to that wonderful package that only God granted you, and which he granted to so few men in this world. You are very precious to me. Our plane is leaving for the west in the morning, with stopovers here and there. Those millions are waiting in Palm Springs, and I'm eager for you to claim them. All God's love. Sister Rose."

"That looks like some ring," Casey said. "What did you do to earn that?"

Buck flashed a mischievous smile. "You wouldn't want to know, my good man. But you and I now have something else to put into that safe you're taking me to."

At a top security building on Miami Beach and only after passing a thorough inspection from the guards, Buck led Casey down a long corridor. Two security guards trailed with the paintings. After Buck's identification was checked for the fifth time, the men were ushered inside a darkened room of large bank vaults.

Turning his back to Casey, Buck worked the combination and the door opened. "This vault belonged to my parents." One by one Buck stacked the paintings in the bank vault. Finishing that task, he then used another combination and opened a small vault within the vault. He raised his hand to his mouth, kissed the ring, and placed it in the smaller vault. "I don't know when I'll see that ring again," Buck said to Casey. "I'm not much into jewelry."

"I am," Casey said," if you ever want to give me some."

"Okay, what do you want?"

Casey leaned over and whispered into Buck's head. "A cock ring studded with diamonds."

"I think that can be arranged," Buck said. "I know a jeweler on the Beach who makes anything for anybody."

"Then let's go and get me fitted."

Buck glanced at his watch. "I'm going to be needing you more and more. You've got yourself a deal."

Back in the limousine, Buck said to Casey, "That place we just left is open twenty-four hours a day. I've used it for years. In a town like Miami, a lot of people need to store things at odd hours. We don't have anything like that in Okeechobee." He ran his fingers through Casey's hair. "Now let's go and get you fitted for that cock ring. I hope you don't mind if I attend the fitting."

"I'm anxious to show you the goodies."

*****

In a pair of shorts, Barry stood at the pool bar in their Key Biscayne villa. "Okay," he said into the phone. "Eight o'clock it is. I'm really looking forward to it." He hung up and poured himself a stiff drink, calling over to Gene, "Want anything?"

In a white bikini, Gene lay by the pool, sunning himself. "I'm fine." He was surprised that Calder Martin had agreed to let him accompany Barry to Miami. He'd been instructed to keep Barry out of trouble. The way Gene figured it, he was to be Barry's distraction and amusement. Actually, he didn't want to be here at all, and felt completely out of place. He'd rather be back with Sandy and Jill. Every time his mind turned to thoughts of Leroy and what he'd told him, Gene tried to blot out the image. He wouldn't have to deal with Leroy until tomorrow.

Barry came over and plopped down on the chaise longue in front of Gene. "God, man, do you ever fill out that bikini."

"Thanks for the compliment," Gene said, hoping this wasn't going to be the beginning of a come-on.

"My greatest disappointment in life was that I wasn't born with a big dick like yours. God made up for it, though. I'm one good-looking mother fucker. But I often wondered if God could have made me less handsome but with a bigger dick."

"There's not a hell of a lot you can do about that now."

Barry sighed and sipped his drink. "You're right. So long ago I decided if I didn't have a big dick I'd spend the rest of my life sucking others who did."

"A noble compromise." Gene didn't want to sound sarcastic, and he didn't want to insult Barry but he was hoping to steer this conversation away from sex.

"I think I first got mixed up with young boys because I figured they were inexperienced and wouldn't judge me too harshly. I mean, they wouldn't know whether I was a good fuck or not. But with adults, men or women, who have had a lot of experience, they might find me lacking something."

"Pamela married you, didn't she? She'd had a lot of guys chasing her."

"I still don't know why Pamela married me. It wasn't the sex—that's for God damn sure. She always thought I was handsome. Maybe that was enough. Not a lot of women turn down a handsome husband who might be rich and powerful one day."

"They marry them every day," Gene said, turning over on his chest to avoid Barry's eyes which seemed glued to his crotch which was all too exposed in that white bikini Barry had insisted he wear to the pool after they'd made love upstairs in Barry's bedroom. Gene had done what was expected but had refused Barry's kiss. Kissing Barry was a bit much for him. The only men he'd ever kissed were Buck and Sandy. Maybe Leroy too, but he didn't want to think about that.

"Sister Rose thought I was handsome," Barry said. "She went for me in a big way until she found out I wasn't a great stud in bed."

Gene raised himself abruptly. "Are you telling me you had sex with Sister Rose?" He felt his heart pounding.

"On more than one occasion," Barry said, coming up to join Gene where he began to gently massage his shoulders. "I not only fucked Sister Rose, but I fucked Shelley too."

"Her son?" Gene lowered his head again and closed his eyes. He was trying unsuccessfully to blot out Barry's words.

Barry ran his fingers up and down Gene's bikini, going lower to fondle and caress Gene's buttocks. "Fucking Shelley was a lot more fun than fucking Sister Rose. She's a bit ripe for me."

Gene breathed slowly and tried to control himself. Barry was a braggart, he'd come to realize. He'd never had sex with Sister Rose, much less Shelley. The future mayor of Okeechobee was a liar. That didn't surprise Gene in the least. Barry was always known as a liar, especially when it came time for him to make a speech.

"I could really go for that Shelley," Barry said. "That's one real hot number. But I've lost even him."

Gene raised himself up and adjusted his position to make himself more comfortable. Barry's lies were beginning to infuriate Gene, but he was determined to show no emotion.

"Shelley belongs to Buck now. Why would Shelley want to get plowed by me when he could have Buck Brooke's legendary inches shoved up his ass?"

Gene rose abruptly from the chaise longue, brushing aside Barry's wandering, feeling hands. He headed for the bar.

"What's the matter?" Barry called after him. "You can't stand for a man to play with your ass or something?"

"I just need a drink—that's all." At the bar Gene found himself trembling. He almost dropped a whisky bottle. "I'm not myself lately," Gene said as way of explanation. "I've been through a lot.

"Of course, you have," Barry said, getting up and heading to the bar to join Gene. At the bar he poured himself another strong drink. "I'll need this to face the assholes I've got to lick tonight."

"What I don't understand," Barry went on, "is why Buck is in Key Biscayne right now marrying Robert Dante. If he's in love with Shelley, why is he marrying Dante?"

"Slow down a little bit," Gene said. "You're going pretty fast here with all these news bulletins. Buck is on Key Biscayne?"

"Yeah, in a house about a mile from here. The real fancy one owned by that faggot movie producer, a friend of Buck's lawyer. That's the one that Bebe originally wanted for love trysts with his friend Tricky Dickie. But he decided not to buy it."

"You're saying Bebe and Nixon were an item?"

Barry laughed nervously. "No one would believe that. At any rate, Bebe and Tricky aren't in the house. Robert Dante, the bride, is there with her newly acquired husband, Buck Brooke III. That Jew, Uncle Milty, is also there with them, presumably enjoying their honeymoon. The bastard lawyer brought along his own hustler boy friend. It must be some cozy household."

"I'm sure," was all Gene could manage to say. "I know the place."

"Tonight after my political caucus is over, should we walk down the beach and visit them? Toast them on their honeymoon?"

"You can if you wish. I don't attend honeymoons when men marry men."

"Smart thinking," Barry said, taking another drink.

The way Barry was drinking, Gene feared the candidate would be drunk before he met with the power-brokers.

"I don't understand what Buck is up to," Barry said. "Calder has him under close observation. He's secretly married to Susan Howard. Did you know that?"

"No," Gene said, lying.

"Your former wife?" I don't know why they want to keep that marriage a secret. You'd think they would want to announce that marriage and keep the marriage to Robert Dante secret."

"You would think, wouldn't you?"

"Aren't you surprised?"

"That he married Susan? Susan and I are long divorced. She's free to marry any guy she pleases. What have I got to say about it? She's better off marrying Buck than me. What could I offer her?"

"You're right. Buck's got the money, the power, the looks, and I hear his dick is as big as yours. In fact, there used to be rumors about you two guys." Barry took another long drink. "Tell me, did you guys ever make it together?"

Gene slammed down his drink. "Hell, no, we never did. Until all your revelations on this patio this afternoon, I never knew Buck was gay. I still don't."

"Trust me, he is. Calder has accumulated massive evidence."

"That Calder seems to have the goods on everybody." He stared harshly at Barry. "Even you."

"Even me." Barry too slammed down his drink as if it bored him. He stripped off his clothes and stood totally naked in front of Gene. Gene averted his eyes. The sight of Barry naked did not entice him.

"I'm going for a swim," Barry said. "Want to join me?"

"No thanks."

"What the hell!" Barry said. "Come on. Drop the bikini and let's go for a little skinny dipping. Maybe in the water we'll compare dick sizes. The one with the biggest dick gets to fuck princess tiny meat."

"I'm not into it," Gene said. "Wasn't that session upstairs enough for you?"

"I can't get enough of big dick—if that's what you mean."

Barry raced toward the pool and jumped in with a big splash. Raising his head above the water, Barry called out to Gene. "Calder's not a total shit. He's done you a big favor."

Gene was heading for the bedroom upstairs, but stopped when he heard that. He looked back at Barry. "Exactly what does that mean?"

"Calder's got all those charges dropped against you. Biff has even promised to give you your job back. Too late for that, though. I told Calder I want you permanently assigned to me."

"You mean that?"

"Calder can get anything done in Okeechobee he wants. He's got Biff by the balls. The little girl and her mother are going to announce to the press that you did nothing wrong. That the girl wandered into your private space. That you didn't entice her there."

In the dying sun, Gene felt dizzy. He'd heard too much. Everything was too much. He wanted to get out of this house. Flee from Key Biscayne. From everything. It seemed that forces were toying with him. Bringing charges. Ruining his life, then dropping those charges as recklessly as they had launched them. He had to get dressed and get out.

From the pool Barry called to him again. "You're on your own tonight—at least until the meeting is over. These blow-shits coming over tonight are going to talk about grooming this girl here to become president of the United States one day."

"You'll make a great president," Gene called to him. "Don't worry: I'm out of here." Hurrying to the bedroom to dress in a T-shirt and jeans, he knew exactly where he was going for the night.

*****

The jeweler and leather master, Ted Albury, ushered Buck and Casey into his backroom after pulling his draperies and putting out a *CLOSED* sign when he'd heard their request.

"I can fix you up real great," Albury said. He was a portly, bald-headed man in his late fifties. The visible presence of Buck and Casey in his shop seemed to make him sweat a lot. "It's not often I get to service two men like you," Albury said.

In the back room Albury showed Casey various pieces of merchandise that could be inserted with diamonds.

"Don't make the diamonds too big, now," Buck cautioned, although laughing slightly to take the edge off. "A modest hang-out."

"Babe, when I hang out it's not modest," Casey said, winking at Buck.

"Oh, my goodness gracious," Albury said. "How you butch numbers carry on."

Casey finally decided on the color, a magenta leather piece.

"Of course," Albury said, looking Casey up and down. "I've got to take measurements to make sure it's an accurate fit. You wouldn't be opposed to dropping trou, would you?"

"Not at all," Casey said looking over at Buck who'd seated himself on a sofa and was enjoying a glass of Albury's brandy. "Showtime," Casey said to Albury but Buck knew the offer was meant for him.

Instead of dropping his trousers, Casey began to slowly remove all his clothes. As the shirt and then the T-shirt came off, Albury was sweating more profusely by the minute. When Casey removed his boots and stepped out of his trousers, he was clad only in the tightest white briefs that left little to be imagined.

"You didn't exaggerate," Buck said, tossing Casey a kiss. "That's some package."

The moment he pulled down the briefs, Albury's fingers were there taking measurements. He tried the cockring on Casey. "A perfect fit," he pronounced as he managed to fondle the low-hanging penis at the same time. When he reached to cup Casey's large ballsac, the driver reminded Albury that he wasn't being fitted for a cockring there.

"Gentlemen," Buck said, standing up abruptly before the party got out of hand. "I think we've found our leather piece. All that remains now is for us to implant it with a few modest diamonds—nothing too showy. We wouldn't want to steal the show from the main attraction," he said, eying Casey's lengthening penis. "My good man," he said to Casey, "you'd better slip your trousers back on before Mr. Albury here has a stroke and I rape you on the spot."

Casey laughed as he spun around, slapping Albury's face with his penis. "I do like to show off," Casey said. "Should have been a stripper."

Within half an hour, the jewelry deal was concluded and Buck was in the front seat with Casey again heading for Key Biscayne. "Oh, I forgot," Casey said. "There was another envelope that Sister Rose's attendant delivered for you. It's in the glove compartment. You opened the gift box but didn't check the document."

Buck reached into the glove compartment and removed a thick envelope addressed to him. He opened it to find a letter and a deed from one of Rose's attorneys. In his new job as media director, he'd been given the old private plane where he'd seduced Shelley only so recently. The attorney advised Buck that Shelley was in Miami to pick up their newly acquired plane painted Rose, both inside and out.

"Shit! Fuck! Damn!" Buck said to Casey. "I've been given ownership of the fucking plane I boarded at the airport. The whole God damn plane." He held up the deed. "I can't believe this. I saw Rose's son, Shelley, on board. He didn't even mention it. He gave me the paintings but didn't even mention the fucking plane was mine. Hot damn! My own private plane."

"Maybe you distracted Shelley while on board, and he just forgot."

Buck winked at Casey who was crossing the causeway heading for Key Biscayne. "Maybe I did. But just as I was blasting into his ass, he could have yelled out, 'The plane is yours.' Something like that." Buck was enjoying this sudden bonding with Casey. It was as if he sensed that Casey was just as much a rogue as he was. Buck had only lately started thinking of himself as a rogue and not as an idealistic young publisher. "Casey, my good man, I think I'm becoming a hustler just like you."

"You seem to be doing better at it than I am, although I'm going to get a diamond-studded cockring."

"I'm sure a man with your obvious talents will go far in the world," Buck assured him. "Especially with my help."

"I'm grateful for that."

"I want you to pack up tonight. Quit your job here and be ready to fly with me on that plane back to Okeechobee in the morning."

"I'm ready, willing, and able to do that," Casey said. "But where will I live?"

"Don't worry. I'll get you a place somewhere. I have a bit of real estate here and there. For the time being, you can occupy a cottage on my grandfather's estate. It's a beautiful place near a ravine. Furnished with antiques. A swimming pool. Jacuzzi, everything. You'll love it there."

"Perhaps you'll come to visit me there one night."

Buck reached over and kissed Casey on the cheek. "Perhaps I will. You are one prize studhoss."

"So are you. Maybe you'll do a striptease for me. I saw that magazine. I'm going to go out tonight and buy up every copy of that magazine naming you the sexiest man alive."

"Why?"

"I'm afraid too many guys will read that magazine and be after you. They'll want you for themselves."

"Don't worry. Your job and our deal is safe. As I said, I need you. Your salary will be paid by Uncle Milty, my lawyer. Patrick, the guy you met, is his boyfriend. Robert is my boyfriend. When we're in the presence of Robert, I want you to be a little chilly, just a bit cold."

"He's one jealous motherfucker, right?"

"You might say that. Robert wants me to be one way. Very loyal and faithful. I have decided I am very loyal. I'll always be loyal to Robert. I'd do anything for him. As for the faithful part, I don't think it's in my nature to be faithful to anyone. I want to be but I just can't. I see an opportunity for sex and I take advantage of it. I was always like that. Why can't I be faithful?"

"You're just like me. I think when we started talking you felt I was a kindred soul. I understand that. I couldn't be faithful to anyone with one exception."

"Who's that? You in love with someone?"

"You got that right," Casey said, pulling into the Key Biscayne honeymoon villa.

"Tell me about it," Buck said, glancing anxiously at his watch and a little nervous about the wedding reception of Robert, Uncle Milty, and Patrick waiting for him inside.

"I can't tell you about my love right now," Casey said. "There isn't time and in a minute I've got to revert to the servant role. But I will tell you who I'm in love with."

"For God's sake, who?"

"You."

*****

The sudden approach of footsteps on the grass had caused Gene to dart across the yard of Buck's borrowed Key Biscayne villa, taking cover in the shrubbery. From that vantage point, he not only had a clear view of the house, but he had a coral rock wall against his back for security. He sensed that the other intruder had been hesitant, afraid to go any farther onto the grounds. Gene had moved so fast he didn't think the stranger had detected the presence of anybody else in the garden. He smiled sardonically at the thought that it was a burglar. If he were, Gene wasn't going to arrest him—not that he had the power to arrest anybody anymore.

It was a beautiful night, a clear one, and a full moon was out, giving the vegetation in the garden an eerie lunar sheen. He felt protected enough to breathe more easily now. He could afford to wait and watch, something he'd done a lot of lately.

Those footsteps again on the grass were clear and unmistakable in the still night. In shadows, the stranger approached slowly, foolishly standing in the middle of the yard where he could easily be spotted by someone in the house. Light from a window shone into the garden and, as the stranger lurched forward, he could see the outline of his face. The unknown man stood tall and rigid, an expression of arrogant defiance on his face. The more he studied the stranger, the more familiar he became. Gene had encountered him once before.

Then he knew. The stranger was Julius Forster, the self-styled Nazi who went around Okeechobee distributing racist literature, just the type of radical to jump on Rose's bandwagon.

Once Gene had arrested Julius for causing a public nuisance, but charges were later dropped by the police chief. Biff considered Julius a lunatic of the far right, but a harmless one, although Gene had heard reports that Julius was the prime suspect in the bomb threat to the Examiner's offices.

The more he stared into the intensity of the intruder's face, the more he wondered how harmless he really was.

Julius fished a cigarette out of his jacket pocket and lit it. "How dumb!" Gene thought. The stupid Nazi was asking to be spotted. Buck, or perhaps Robert, would detect a strange presence in the garden and call the police. Maybe they already had. A squad car might arrive at any minute. Trapped in the walled garden, Gene could be arrested, too.

His heart pounding, he knew he had to get rid of Julius—and fast. He had plans for the occupants of that household. "Who's there?" he said in a clear, commanding voice.

At the sound, Julius dropped his cigarette and ran back across the lawn toward the main gate.

Gene was amazed that Julius knew the location of Buck's Key Biscayne villa and that he'd flown here from Okeechobee. Exactly where did he get this address and what was his motive? It made no sense to Gene. Hazel Phillips once had stormed into police headquarters, accusing Julius of stalking her. Those charges were dismissed. Julius did attend every rally Hazel spoke at, and had been arrested and searched twice. But each time he didn't have a weapon, and his defense lawyer maintained that Julius had as much a right as anybody else to attend a public rally.

If Julius did indeed call in that bomb threat to the Examiner, he must have added Buck to his list of enemies to be watched and perhaps fatally attacked one day. Julius had money from some mysterious source, and seemed on someone's payroll but Gene didn't know who his boss was. Surely Julius was too much of a firecracker for Calder Martin to link himself to. Even the Watergate crew would have stayed clear of this nut.

With Julius fleeing in the night, Gene crossed through the garden again, using the thick shrubbery as a shield. From where he stood in the moonlight, he had a clear view of the patio garden yet was completely concealed.

Buck was seated at a candlelit garden table with Robert by his side. They faced Milton, his attorney, and also a young companion. Another young man, apparently Buck's driver, was bringing champagne for all of them to drink.

"I couldn't believe it," Buck was telling his companions. "She gave me the God damn plane. Her private plane. I own it now. Of course, she's getting another one tomorrow. I'll be on her new plane flying west with her late tomorrow morning. But we'll return to Okeechobee on my own jet plane. I just can't believe this."

"The first fringe benefit of working for Rose Phillips—a private plane," Milton said.

Gene sucked air deep into his lungs, not making a sound, though. Had Buck gone to work for Sister Rose? All this was unbelievable.

"You've not done badly," Robert said. "You may have lost the Examiner, but there are other rewards."

First, Barry was filled with revelations that blew Gene's mind. Now Gene was learning things he'd never known because of his eavesdropping on this private conversation. Had Buck been fired from the Examiner?

"While you and Robert retreat to your honeymoon bed," Milton said, "I'll study those contracts. If the signing goes okay in Palm Springs, you're going to come back with millions to spend on us."

"Uncle Milty loves multi-millionaires," Patrick chimed in.

Although the driver said nothing, Gene noticed him looking at Buck several times throughout the champagne drinking. He appeared a dutiful servant but there was a barely noticeable exchange between them that suggested they shared a secret somehow. Was this chauffeur Buck's new lover? The whole evening was plunging Gene into chaos, and he wished he'd never wandered down the beach to this villa after all. He was seeing too much, learning stuff he didn't want to know. He felt hurt and excluded. This little dinner party dramatized to him more than he ever wanted to know that he was not part of Buck's agenda. Gene felt he didn't belong in this rich league of powerful men—Buck and Milton— with their pretty little boyfriends and mysterious chauffeur who obviously was the boyfriend of one of them, no doubt Buck.

Gene couldn't move from his secret hiding place without a fear of getting detected. Whether he wanted to or not, he felt at this point he had to remain here until the party had left the patio.

"A final toast," Milton said, "to the newlyweds." He raised his glass to toast Buck and Robert. He also offered a glass to the driver who joined in.

After drinking the toast, Buck turned and gave Robert a long, lingering kiss in front of everybody. Gene averted his eyes. He didn't want to be a witness to that kiss. Even as the image flashed through his mind, he remembered and could almost feel Buck's lips on his.

An hour must have passed before the party broke up. There were no more revelations, however. The men were joking and getting drunk, really having fun and enjoying each other's company. Buck appeared so devoted and in love with Robert that Gene doubted if he were also involved with Shelley. But now that Gene knew that Buck had gone to work for Sister Rose, the possibility of an involvement with Shelley was there.

Finally, Milton got up from the table. "Before dawn breaks, I've got to stay up tonight and read every tiny little line, before I can sanction

Buck signing those contracts in Palm Springs. "You'd better sleep in the guest room down the hall tonight, Patrick. I don't want to be too distracted when you pull off those jockey shorts."

"Okay, Uncle Milty," Patrick said, "but I'll miss you something awful."

Milton gave Patrick a big kiss, then kissed both Robert and Buck on the lips as well. He shook the driver's hand. "Welcome aboard. Our boy here is going to need a full-time chauffeur, and I think you'll be great at the job."

"Thank you, sir," the driver said.

Buck got up from the table and took Robert's hand. He kissed Patrick good night on the lips and Robert did too. Both men shook the driver's hand and wished him good night.

After Buck and Robert had disappeared into the master bedroom, Patrick asked the driver to get him another drink. "Make it Scotch," Patrick instructed. "I've been drinking champagne all day."

Gene could clearly see the two men, and he felt more the voyeur than ever.

"Watching sexy Buck kiss that Robert has got me all horny tonight," he said to the driver.

"Me, too. I need relief real bad, and I wished they'd invited me to join them on their honeymoon bed."

Patrick studied the driver very closely. "I've been wanting to ask you something all evening. Do you stuff a great big sock in your crotch or is that prime grade-A meat for real?"

"Why don't you find out for yourself."

"I think I will," Patrick said, getting up and staggering a drunken path to the driver. With his left hand, he reached between the driver's legs and began to massage his genitals. "It's for real, all right. Not only that, it's getting bigger by the minute."

"You do have magic fingers."

"I've got to taste it," Patrick said. "Let's go to the back of the garden where I'll get down on bended nylon while you deep-throat me."

"That's an offer I can't turn down." The driver glanced up the hallway toward the master bedroom. "Since I didn't get any other offers tonight." He followed a drunken Patrick deeper into the garden.

Gene didn't want to witness any more. With the final two men from the party distracted, Gene seized upon the moment to escape. Passing by the window of the master bedroom, he heard no sound. He shuddered in the night breeze from the ocean, and wandered across to a little pier overlooking the house. The meeting might go on at Barry's villa for hours yet, so he decided to take up a position overlooking Buck's temporary villa. He had nothing else to do.

The beach appeared deserted. It was a lovely night. Without meaning to, Gene found himself crying. Since he was sure no one could hear him, he gave himself in to the crying. He had to get it out, all the pain and hurt in his system. The tears turned to soft moans escaping from his throat. He'd never felt so much alone in the world as he did tonight.

*****

A digital clock beside his honeymoon bed told Buck it was three o'clock in the morning. A totally satisfied Robert was asleep beside him. Until just now, Robert had been wrapped in his arms. But in his sleep Robert had moved away slightly so that he was no longer in body contact. Buck was relieved. Without Robert noticing it, he hoped to slip free of the marriage bed and go for a walk on the beach. He needed the early morning air to revive him and, he hoped, clear his head.

He felt he'd done his job well. Robert had told him repeatedly it was the best sex he'd ever had with Buck. Buck hadn't held back. He felt he'd done anything and everything that Robert wanted and needed. But the awful truth—and Buck knew this now more than ever—was that he was performing and not making love from the spontaneous nature of his heart.

He loved Robert, and loved him dearly, but he did not *love* Robert. You couldn't buy loyalty like Robert's, and Buck knew and appreciated that. He desperately wanted to hold onto Robert and his friend's trust, love, and devotion. He would give Robert the good life, even offering his body any time he wanted it. What he could not give Robert ever again was his devotion.

The feeling was gone. It had never been there, he suspected. Through his years of ferocious support and loyalty to Buck, Robert had created whatever love Buck felt for him. But it wasn't the love he felt for Shelley.

With Gene, it was raw passion, an intensity of love-making that could easily have gotten out of hand. Buck knew it was best to have ended the episode with Gene before it intensified. As each day went by, thoughts of Gene began to drift to shadowy corners of his brain. Gene was not his future. Shelley was his future.

The challenge facing him was to keep giving himself to Robert but to find the time to be with Shelley. Shelley was what he wanted and desired. As unlikely a coupling as that had seemed at the beginning, Shelley was now his love. But what had Shelley meant about Robert leaving his life? That sleeping partner next to Buck didn't seem to have any intention of leaving. If anything, Buck felt Robert had grown more demanding and possessive. Buck feared both qualities would make it increasingly difficult for him to have a life with Shelley.

In this honeymoon bed, Buck could admit something to himself for the first time. The only reason he'd accepted the job as media director with Rose was to be near Shelley. It was the perfect excuse. He could pull that off. There would be frequent trips all the time, endless opportunities to be with Shelley, all under the guise of business.

What made it easier was Rose's complete acceptance of the relationship. If anything, she seemed delighted that Buck had shown an interest in Shelley. Shelley was her bait. It would keep him in her life, although she must know in her heart that he didn't love her and loved her son instead. Yet she seemed prepared to live with that.

Shelley and Rose were not two redneck preachers. If anything they were power brokers and ultra-sophisticates, moving in a jaded world where they reached out to obtain what they wanted, regardless of the consequences. But Buck saw trouble even there. Calder Martin obviously wanted Buck out of the way. No doubt he wanted Shelley put under control too. The boy was like a hand grenade thrown into Calder's camp fire. It could explode at any minute.

Rose didn't have the heart to challenge Shelley and, in fact, seemed totally satisfied to let him go on his sexual path. As soon as possible, Buck wanted to talk to Shelley about what threat Calder was for both of them. Buck viewed Calder as a serious demon to be dealt with, especially when Calder learned of his upcoming appointment as media director, a job he coveted for himself.

Buck realized that Calder couldn't be fired from Rose's organization. He knew too much. He'd have to be bought off in some way. Surely as Buck moved deeper and deeper into Rose's organization, he would not only learn more about who was running it, but Calder's role in everything. What did the power behind Rose plan to offer Calder? Whatever it was, Buck knew it wouldn't be enough to satisfy this greedy lunatic from the shadowy far right.

Slipping nude from the bed, Buck reached for some clothing but could find only a pair of jockey briefs. "What the hell," he thought. If anyone happened to be on that beach at night, an unlikely possibility, the stranger could assume in the dark he was wearing a bikini. Besides, he didn't have anything to be ashamed of. The magazine had told the world that, and he got assurances from everybody wherever he went.

Into the briefs, he slowly opened a side door leading into the garden. In the moonlight he headed for the beach enjoying the sand under his bare feet. He always liked beaches in the moonlight more than he preferred the burning sun of midday.

He sucked in the night air and raised his arms for a total stretch and liberation. He enjoyed being alone in the early morning. He might stay on the beach at least until streaks of dawn split the sky. He knew he never could leave Florida, because he found the morning skies here more spectacular than he'd ever seen anywhere in the world.

It was a special time for him. He only wished he could be enjoying these precious moments with Shelley in his arms. He'd kiss the boy, lick him, and demand that Shelley suck his tongue, which he was liking more and more, and then he'd walk with his arm around the boy on the beach, maybe stopping somewhere in the sand to make love to him. He was glad Shelley would be aboard that plane in the morning. He desperately wanted the boy with him. The way he felt right now he resented any intrusion in his life that took him away from Shelley. He had a compulsive need to be with the boy at all times, although that was very unlikely. He had other obligations.

Memories of Susan and Gene came racing back through his brain. He resented having married Susan. His times with her weren't special. As the months or even years passed before them, he planned to involve himself less and less in her life. Perhaps she'd find some secret lover on the side. If she did, he'd encourage that. He'd look after her, and it appeared all but certain that he could acquire the News. Uncle Milty said the prospect looked very good. With Susan installed as publisher, she'd have so many responsibilities maybe she wouldn't even think about him.

He decided to return to the house to get something to smoke. He really wanted a cigarette right now—a cigar would be even better. He thought he could slip into the living room without arousing anyone in the house. He wasn't sure they'd locked the back doors when they'd retired for the night.

He was right. The door was unlocked. He slipped into the living room but at the sound of whispered voices he ducked behind a palm to conceal himself. The door to Patrick's room opened. A nude Casey came out. He stood in the hallway, giving an also nude Patrick a long, lingering kiss. Casey then headed for the little suite in the cottage out back in the garden. Buck knew Casey didn't see him.

He also knew that Patrick was taking an awful chance, and he must have had a real compelling need for Casey's body to be so foolish under the same roof with Uncle Milty. Buck realized that if Uncle Milty had come and knocked on the presumably locked door that Casey could have escaped through a side door leading into the garden. The whole house was designed, or so it seemed, to slip lovers in and out with discretion.

Buck didn't condemn Patrick's new relationship. Patrick was a good-looking, young, and charming man, and Buck had always known that he couldn't possibly be satisfied with Uncle Milty's sagging, overripe flesh. Buck always assumed that Patrick was getting the rock-hard stomachs and bulging baskets on the side without Uncle Milty's approval. Uncle Milty always bragged to Buck about how faithful Patrick was to him. Loyal, perhaps, Buck realized, but hardly faithful.

Buck decided to forget about that smoke anyway. He headed back to the beach, passing the master bedroom with Robert. The screened windows were open, since they didn't like air conditioning all the time. There wasn't a sound coming from the bed with the sleeping Robert, so Buck returned to the beach, wishing he hadn't gone into that house.

He didn't want to learn Patrick's secrets. At least his new driver wouldn't be focusing all his attention on Buck too much any more. Buck knew, and he suspected that Casey knew too, that theirs would be only a harmless flirtation in the future.

Even though he'd been out in the early morning air only a short time, Buck's head was clearing. He was getting his priorities straightened out. He didn't love Susan. Never had.

His troubled relationship with Gene looked like something best left to a murky university past when he was unsure of his sexual nature. He'd found that nature now. He'd known such intense passion with Gene. But it was sex and not love. He wanted sex and love to come together in a winning combination like it was with Shelley.

There would be the mercy fucks in the future, undoubtedly with both Robert and Rose. But the only person that would have all of him, including his love and devotion, was a little preacher boy named Shelley Phillips. Shelley had all the looks and charm that God could bestow on any man, he seemingly possessed untold wealth, and now he had Buck.

"I'm the sexiest man alive!" Buck whispered to the wind, parroting the headline in the magazine.

"That you are, good buddy."

Seemingly coming out of nowhere, the voice was from the past. Startled and a bit frightened, he turned around to stare into the moonlit face of Gene.

*****

He had meant to return to Barry's Key Biscayne villa before midnight, estimating that the power brokers would have left by then. But he couldn't bring himself to leave his stake-out in front of Buck's temporary villa. The hours had gone by, and Gene knew that dawn would break and he'd be forced to go. Still he stayed on, looking and observing any movement or sign of life from that darkened villa. Nothing came from it, not even a light. At one o'clock the lights had gone out in the room where the attorney, Milton, was staying. Gene had already figured out where everybody was sleeping. No light was ever turned on in the room where Robert and Buck were sleeping in their honeymoon bed.

The thought of the two of them there disgusted Gene. At one point he thought he was going to vomit. If Buck liked men, and Gene suspected that was the case, he didn't know why he didn't go for a real man and not someone like Robert. To him, Robert was weak—not masculine at all. He was more like Leroy, and no one would accuse Leroy of being a real man. Leroy worshipped real men but wasn't one himself.

This lonely vigil had given Gene plenty of time to think. He realized now he'd been wrong not to return Buck's calls. He'd fled without giving Buck time to explain his marriage to Susan. There could have been a reason, something Gene didn't know about. He knew Buck still loved him. He'd come forward with the bail money—that alone was proof of his love and loyalty. He hadn't deserted him like he had that time with Jill. This time Buck had been here for him, and Gene was grateful for that. In his hurt and humiliation at learning of the marriage, Gene had fled. He needed to lick his wounds. News of the marriage had devastated him, but he wanted to talk to Buck about it now, to hear his side of it. He had to give Buck a chance to explain himself.

From out of nowhere, a nearly nude Buck had appeared before him. In the moonlight he'd looked like the most golden man Gene had ever known. Buck didn't need to proclaim he was the sexiest man alive, because Gene already knew that.

"What in hell are you doing here?" Buck asked. "How did you know I was here?"

"So many questions so early in the morning," Gene said. "I'm working as a bodyguard for Barry. He told me where you were staying. I thought I'd drop by. Check it out."

"First, I didn't know Barry was here, and, second, I didn't know that Barry knew where I was staying."

"That's not all," Gene said. "You had a stalker earlier in the evening."

"Who, for God's sake?"

"Julius Forster."

"That lunatic. He threatened to blow up the Examiner."

"I thought so. At any rate, I chased him off. I thought I'd stick around in case he came back. It was a return of the favor you did for me when you posted bail."

"I can't imagine how Forster knew I was here. I think he's dangerous. I thought my whereabouts was some deep dark secret. Now I realized I should have taken out an ad on the front page of The Miami Herald."

"You're becoming a big and powerful man in the world," Gene said. "The higher you go up in the world, the more lunatics you'll attract."

"That seems so. I'm sorry you had to spend the night out here. That makes me feel really bad. You don't owe me any favors."

"Good news. You're going to get your bail money back. The case against me has been dropped."

"Thank God. I knew you were innocent all along. The whole thing seemed a set-up."

"It was. I plan to find out who did it. When I find out, it'll be payback time."

"Don't do anything crazy. Don't get yourself into any more trouble. You've suffered enough already."

"That's for God damn sure."

Buck hesitated for a moment. "About the marriage, I can explain."

"The marriage to Susan or Robert Dante?" Gene asked.

"The marriage to Susan. I can't explain the marriage to Robert. I'm surprised you knew that too. It was just something I got caught up in and went along with. It wasn't my idea to marry Susan. It was my grandfather's. He insisted on it. Threatened to disinherit me. It's not a real marriage. I don't love her at all."

"I believe you're telling me the truth. I couldn't imagine you and Susan together. I can't imagine you and Robert together either."

"I'm loyal to Robert. He's always been there for me. I didn't know how to get out of this mock marriage. I just went along with it not knowing what else to do."

"You're in love with someone else. I know you are."

"Yes, I am. But how could you have known that? You seem to know everything about me."

"I'm no fool. I know you're in love with me."

Buck didn't say anything, and Gene couldn't truly detect any facial expression on him. Gene was breathing deeply and it was hard for him to go on, but he knew he must.

"I've not only seen how you are when I take you in my arms, I've felt it. You were screaming out for me to take you, to love you like you've never been loved before, and I was too blind to see and too deaf to hear."

"Please don't go on," Buck cautioned him. "I've got something to tell you."

"Let me finish," Gene said. "Don't you know how hard this is for me? After years and years of denial I am finally opening up to the one man I've always loved. It's you, Buck. It's always been you. From the first day I met you at the university, I wanted you. I just couldn't bring myself to admit that I wanted another man. My marriage to Susan. Everything was to deny to myself that I loved you. But I did love you. I loved you then and I love you now. The only difference between then and now is that I'm prepared to act on it. I'm prepared to be the kind of lover you want."

Buck seemed to want to say something, and Gene knew it must be as difficult for him to declare his love as it was for Gene to confess his passion.

"Let's view this morning as a celebration," Gene said. "You've won me, good buddy. The battle is over. I fought and resisted my love for you for years. Now I'm here. I belong to you. We belong together."

Gene waited for a long, tense moment. At this revelation he felt Buck would rush to his arms. They'd probably do it right in the sands. But something strange was going on with Buck. He wasn't responding to the revelation the way Gene had expected. Gene wanted to give him the benefit of the doubt. It was probably more than Buck could handle. What if you'd just learned that the one man you'd wanted above all others had just surrendered to you?

Gene decided to ease back a bit and make it easier for Buck. "I know what I just told you is going to take a little time to think about. It's all so sudden. First, my not returning your calls. How stupid of me. But please understand I was hurt. I was just being a coward. I couldn't face you, but I'm facing you now and declaring myself."

"Gene..." Buck's voice trailed off. "You don't have to go on," he finally managed to say.

"But you don't understand. For the first time in my life with another human being, I've found my voice, and I'm not afraid to use that voice to declare my love."

"I love you too. I always will."

"Good. We both have some baggage to get rid of in our lives. I'll need some time to set some matters straight, and I know you will too. I'm tempted to rush into your arms right now and crush you to the ground. Rape you right here and now. That's how strong my need is for you. But I'm sure you're tainted with the smell of Robert on you. I want you clean and fresh. You've got money, you've got power. We can get out of Okeechobee. Go anywhere. Start a new life together, and I want to begin that sooner than later. We've both waited long enough."

"Hey, let's slow down. This is..."

Gene interrupted him. He didn't want Buck to finish what he was saying. There would be time for that later. They would have the rest of their lives together. Gene rose up from the stone wall he was sitting on and approached Buck. He reached for him, crushing his body into his. He encased Buck's neck and pulled his face to his. His lips descended on Buck's and he gave him what for Gene was the kiss of a lifetime. It was a kiss filled with commitment, love, and hope for the future. At first he was a bit surprised that Buck held back, not surrendering himself completely to the kiss. But Gene's magic was still strong. In moments he had Buck responding and even gasping for breath. The kiss had obviously overpowered Buck. That was all the proof that Gene needed that the attraction was there, stronger and more powerful than ever.

Gene broke away. "Will you be in Okeechobee ten days from now?"

"I fully expect to be."

"At six o'clock Saturday night—that's ten days from now—I'm going to be playing tennis on those old courts."

"I know them well."

"I want you to meet me there. That will give you time to clear up some complicated relationships in your life. I've got a few to work out myself. I want you to come there for me. Bring your fancy limousine. I like riding in limousines. You come there for me. Don't plan any business from Saturday night on. We're going to go away together— somewhere, anywhere, it doesn't matter—and we're going to get to know each other like no two men have ever known each other before. You got that?"

"I know the date and I know the place, but life's very different now. We're no longer in the university. We've grown up. We're playing adult games."

"You got that right. You and I are going to start living our lives like two adults for the first time ever. No more games. We're going to stop calling our relationship a friendship. We're not friends. We're lovers. We're going to be the hottest pair of lovers the state of Florida has ever seen."

"Gene..." there was a hesitancy in Buck's voice again and for a deep moment it troubled Gene. But he decided to ignore it.

"It will be morning soon," Gene said. "You go back into that household and do what you've got to do, and I'll return to Barry's compound. When you and I get together again it'll be with a very different agenda. Let's start living for ourselves again and not for anybody else."

The moon seemed to shine brighter than ever, and it captured Buck's face as if lit by a spotlight. He realized that Buck was crying, and Gene knew they were tears not of despair, but of joy. Buck had just been granted what for him must have been his long cherished wish. Gene had offered himself back to Buck. Why wouldn't he cry? He was probably overcome. Gene kissed him tenderly on the lips and embraced him for one final time. "Until we meet on those tennis courts, know that I love you and you belong to me. Take care."

Without saying another word, Gene headed down the lonely stretch of deserted beach. The first streak of dawn's light cracked the night sky. It was going to be a new dawn for him in more ways than one. One thing troubled him: he'd gotten almost no reaction from Buck. He'd been strangely passive. But that was okay. Gene just knew he'd heard and accepted what he'd told him.

He sucked in the cool morning air. For the first time ever, his whole rotten life was turning around. The dark, shadowy part of his brain was sinking even deeper into its murky recesses. A new, brighter side of him was emerging, and he dared to believe he was about to embark upon a life of happiness, a prospect that had always eluded him until this morning.

Chapter Ten

It was like an airborne yacht. The moment Buck stepped aboard the customized Boeing 707 jetliner, his eyes drank in the splendor, with all the trappings of a deluxe hotel suite. Later, he would try to figure out how Rose traveled in a style befitting a super-rich Bahreini oil sheik. Now he was just glad he'd agreed to go with Rose and Shelley first to Abilene, then to Durant.

Upon entering the plane, Rose clutched his hand warmly, then excused herself, claiming she had to place an urgent call from the communications center up front. Buck looked for Shelley, but he had gone to his own private quarters.

In the lounge, a white-robed attendant fastened Buck into a bronze and ebony throne, resting on carved lion's paws, right before the plane was cleared for take-off.

Once airborne, he had time to take in the sumptuousness of the decor, which vaguely suggested the tomb of King Tutankhamen. Across from him stood a cedarwood chest carved with hieroglyphs. Golden sun disks formed window shades.

For a carrier of one of America's leading evangelists, the plane was incongruously filled with pagan symbols, with many kinds of animals—such as a lioness, representing ancient gods as decorative themes. The cow Hathor formed the endpiece of a couch, with its lyre-shaped horns holding another sun disk.

Separating the lounge from the dining area was a varnished black jackal with silver claws. When the caution lights went off, he unfastened his seat belt and headed for the rear of the cabin. The attendant directed him to a suite he was to share with Rose. At first he thought she'd be more discreet, but apparently in front of her staff she had no need to conceal a sexual relationship.

He hesitated at the door, not ready to go in. "Actually, I have some private business to discuss with Shelley. Would you show me to his suite instead?"

"Of course," the attendant said, rather coldly. He led Buck down the corridor and knocked on another door.

Within seconds, Shelley, clad only in a rose-colored robe, opened the door. "Come on in, Mr. Brooke," he said, "I've been expecting you."

Once inside, Shelley quickly locked the door, opened his robe, and pressed his nude body against Buck. "I've missed you. An hour away from you is like living in hell."

Buck grabbed the boy pressing him even closer as he kissed and licked his face before inserting his tongue for Shelley to suck which the boy always did expertly. Buck's hands wandered freely over Shelley's smooth body, settling on his buttocks which he squeezed gently and fondled, wanting to bury his face there when Shelley had finished loving it. Buck pulled back slightly. In his eagerness, Shelley was seemingly draining Buck's breath. "I love you, golden boy. I really love you."

Shelley planted lightning kisses on Buck's lips and eyelids. "Love is hardly the word I feel for you. I adore you. Worship you. I want to spend the rest of my life locked in your arms."

At a rap on the door, Buck sighed. He wanted just what Shelley wanted—to be locked away with each other forever. But, regrettably, he feared that wouldn't be the case. Shelley retreated to the bathroom and Buck opened the door.

The same attendant was there looking rather stern. "Ms. Phillips is ready to receive you now."

"I'll be there soon," Buck said, shutting and locking the door. He trailed Shelley into the bathroom where the boy stood in front of a large closet, surprising on a plane, selecting his wardrobe for the day.

"The God mother is demanding an audience," Shelley said. She'll probably want to get fucked."

"What am I going to do?" Buck asked, coming up to Shelley and taking him in his arms. "Before you, I used to be able to get it up for almost anybody. Now that I have you, I want you to have exclusive rights."

"I really believe that, and it gives me the will to live," Shelley said, kissing Buck gently. "But duty calls. Don't worry. I'll slip into the suite and make it easier for you at the final climax."

"You'll assist?" Buck said, astonished, although why anything about this mother and son astonished him now he didn't know.

"I'll take care of it. Trust me." He kissed Buck again. "You've got millions waiting for you in the desert. Let's don't fuck that up. You've also got a lot of surprises waiting for you in Abilene. I could tell you now, but I want you to hear it first hand."

"What does that mean?"

"By the time the Abilene experience is over, you'll know a whole lot more how Sister Rose sings for her supper."

"I don't think I want to know."

"We're in this together." He kissed Buck once more. "You'd better go. No need to keep God waiting."

The attendant showed him into Rose's suite. She was nowhere to be seen. Unlike the Egyptian motif up front, the suite had obviously been customized with Rose in mind. The symbol of the rose was everywhere, even in the design of the canopy over the queen-size bed. Sculpted roses cut through the deep-pile, opera-red carpeting.

The attendant left to be replaced by a young Japanese girl in a kimono. "Her highness will be detained briefly," she said. "In the meantime she wants you to try out her luxurious new bath. It's very special."

"I'm sure I could use one," he said, not unduly surprised that she'd referred to Rose by a royal title. "I had to fly from Miami this morning on Sister Rose's old jet and then hop aboard this plane. I didn't even have time to go home to change clothes."

"Please," the young woman said, holding out her hand and pointing in the direction of the bathroom. At first Buck suspected the young woman was going to assist him with the bath ritual, but such wasn't the case because she turned and left.

In the private bathroom, with its sunken tub in pink marble, he pulled off all his clothes after the attendant had left. The way he figured it, this might be his only chance to take an airborne bubble bath. He smelled the contents of an alabaster vase, inlaid with floral garlands. Picking it up, he poured some of the rose cologne into the water. While he was doing it, he might as well go rose all the way.

As he turned on the solid gold faucets to run his bath water, he compared his trail-blazing across America to that of Daniel Boone.

Reclining in the marble tub, he raised the shade of a large-scaled window. As the sun blinded him, he tried to give a command performance to any spaceship that might be passing by. In the background someone had piped in classical music. He splashed water over his chest and stomach, then oiled his firm flesh. With his eyes dreamily half-closed, he took in the spectacle of the brilliant sky. Sinking deeply into the water, letting it cover his entire body except for his head, he lost himself in this haven of peace and beauty.

Then, suddenly, he became aware of an intoxicating smell, foreign to the cologne and bath oils. Rose's body. Surreptitiously she'd entered the bathroom. He looked up at her. Clad in a see-through, rose-colored robe, she stood staring down lovingly at him.

"Some pad!" he said, deliberately making the comment ridiculous.

"I'm glad you like it," she said, seating herself at her vanity and taking a quick check of her makeup. She adjusted the scarf around her bandaged throat.

The tempo of the music seemed to quicken. "Might I ask how you acquired this flying carpet? Talk about fantasies from Arabian Nights!"

She smiled enigmatically. "No, you might not." As if to erase some of the wonder on his face, she added, "It's not really mine. On lease."

"From whom?" He sat up in the tub. "Saudi Arabia? I've heard planes like this exist. I never thought I'd be taking a bath on one."

She eyed him in her most tantalizing way. "If I didn't have this slight problem with my throat, I'd join you." She knelt beside the tub, taking his wet hand and placing it on her breast. Holding him there, she looked out the window. "I love it up here. Sometimes I never want to land."

Gently he squeezed her breast. "Do you think heaven is like this?"

"I hope so. If it is, I can't wait to get there."

The feel of her breast had a decided effect on his crotch. He released her and stood up in the tub. She reached over and handed him a rose-colored towel.

As he dried himself, he asked, "Surely, you're not trying to convert the Arabs to Christianity?"

She frowned for a moment, her loving mood broken. A cynical mask came over her. "At this stage of the game, I can't question the source of my contributions."

After he'd toweled himself dry, he slipped into the robe she held out for him. He joined her in her bedroom where, to his surprise, an Arab wearing a fringed turban and an elaborately knotted sash had opened a bottle of champagne. When the attendant left, he turned to her, "He's just one of the permanent staff," she said. "Eight of them work as servants on the plane. As I said, the plane's not really mine."

"It's about time I started expressing some gratitude," Buck said.

She raised an eyebrow provocatively. "I'd rather you show me instead of tell me how grateful you are."

He smiled wickedly at her, thinking that without really needing to he'd become a whore. "The ring—it's beautiful. I'll treasure it always. The de Koonings—they are to die for. But the private plane—that was a bit much." He shouted his pleasure like a cowboy at roundup. "I LOVE IT!"

"You're welcome. I was tired of the old thing. I wanted something new and different. Like this plane. As for that de Kooning, honey, you can have him. He's not my idea of a painter at all. I'm surprised people buy crap like that."

"It's an acquired taste," he said. He turned to pour champagne in tulip-shaped glasses decorated with a red rose motif. "Wait until I tell the temperance society about drinking champagne with Rose Phillips."

She took the glass from him, lovingly caressing his fingers as she did. "Champagne always tastes better when I'm airborne."

"You're not only closer to Jesus up here, but you can get high too."

She laughed off his remark and headed for the swan bed, her chiffon gown sweeping in a wave behind her. She slowly removed her gown and in a low, sensual voice called out to him.

The bath had given him renewed vigor and the sight of her body, in spite of his own predictions, aroused passion in him. He felt no love for her at all, although his cock was sending him a different message as it began a gradual rise. He'd never admit it to her, but he was more intrigued with the idea of an airborne fuck than he was in actually making love to her. He wished it were Shelley—and not Rose—in that bed.

"I hear you've got a big surprise waiting for me in Abilene," he said, climbing on top of her and lowering his body gently into hers.

"Let's not talk now," she said, reaching for him, tasting his soft, sweet lips. She fondled beneath him, teasing his most sensitive spots. Careful to avoid touching her throat, his hand moved with increasing agitation across her full, proud breasts, along her narrow waist and flat stomach and, finally, grazing the auburn patch itself. His stroking seemed to make her purr.

Lost in his own private world, he entered her gently at first. Her muscles seemed to clamp around him, and the grip sent thrills up his spine. This wasn't going to be bad after all. Suddenly, he started moaning uncontrollably and pounded into her. He knew that lovely pink tongue well. Shelley had slipped into the suite and had parted his buttocks, before attacking his most private possession. The sensations were driving Buck crazy with lust. He shoved himself even harder into Rose. Her face told him she had prematurely entered heaven. She dug her nails into his back and nibbled on his ear.

"Oh, God, oh, God," she kept repeating. "Nothing was ever as good as this."

For Buck, it was as if his sensations had shifted from penetrating Rose to enjoying Shelley's tongue lashings. He spread his legs even wider giving the boy more access to his target. Buck suspected that the most private and exclusive bordello in the east couldn't produce sensations like this in a man.

Time drifted by. Buck lost count of how many times. Sometimes they'd stop and drink some more champagne. Once he noted a freshly chilled bottle, and wondered how the Arab attendant had managed to enter the room without attracting his notice.

Sometimes he'd switch positions, penetrating Shelley, which was his favorite sensation. When that happened, Rose would take up her duty at Shelley's station. She was equally skilled at assaulting his rosebud. His balls, too, had never received such attentive care. These two really adored balls, obviously viewing them as God's gift to all the beautiful women and golden boys on the earth.

Once, they fell asleep. He didn't know for how long. Rose was the first to wake up. Her mouth was licking and kissing his belly before plunging down. Amazingly she could swallow every inch of him. When he was fully erect again, she positioned herself under him for one final assault. This one she wanted from the rear. She surrendered herself to him on her knees. As he entered her, Shelley woke up and slid across her back, inserting his cock into Buck's suctioning mouth.

As the plane landed on Kansas soil, its bumpy movement provided the right rhythm for a pile-driving action he needed for one final climax.

Rose, he thought, had returned to Abilene in a style her long dead parents could never have imagined.

*****

As they'd agreed, Buck remained aboard the jet after its landing in Abilene. No reporters were allowed on board, as Rose didn't want the press to see the luxurious, Arab-financed appointments inside. "It wouldn't look right," she'd told Buck.

Frankly, Buck was glad to remain behind, not wanting TV cameras recording his getting off this plane with Rose and Shelley, both of whom he'd just fucked. Who among his friends back in Okeechobee— especially Hazel—would understand that?

In the midst of the comforts of the front cabin lounge, he sipped champagne, appreciating his position set up to view Rose's press conference on a large television screen encased in a carved sandalwood cabinet.

Before leaving the phone, she'd told him she wanted to appear on camera having "beauty and fire." The state legislature had just adopted a resolution praising Rose's efforts "to restore decency to America." She was to be fêted at Rose Phillips Day, declared in Abilene for its favorite home-grown daughter. She was also to open a headquarters here of the Rose Phillips Charismatic Association.

Before Rose got off the plane, the female Japanese attendant had approached her. "Miss Phillips, I hear you're the leader of the charismatics. You know, I don't even know what that is."

"You will soon," Rose had predicted. "The entire world will know us. It is the name some give to our faith. I have my own brand," she quickly added. "Not all charismatics follow me...yet!"

"I'm sure they will," the attendant had said. "You're so beautiful."

"We're a minority movement in evangelical Christianity," she'd told the attendant within easy earshot of Buck. In fact, she'd looked at Buck and secretly winked, indicating her words were but a joke. "We're also the most vigorous force in American religion today. I predict we'll be bigger and more important than the Catholic Church. We'll draw our legions not just from the Protestants, but from Catholics as well."

In spite of the hypocrisy, she'd appeared jubilant before the flight attendant. Buck silently noted how effective she was, a true actress with a role.

"We're born again Christians," she'd told the attendant. "We witness to our faith. We speak in tongues as a prayer language. We believe in prophecy and divine healing."

"Yeah, yeah," Shelley had said. He'd dressed in a rose-colored suit with a pink tie. Buck had hated the suit but loved the boy. Shelley had presented her with an editorial he'd found contained in a mail bag that had been flown up from Okeechobee. Like a speed reader, she'd devoured the article, then tossed it on the floor in rage. "The fucking News," she'd shouted at Buck. "That rag dares attack me, those bastards. We'll take care of them."

Buck had hoped she'd forgotten his own editorial attacks on her movement.

After both Shelley and Rose had wet-kissed him good-bye, Buck had reached down and picked up the editorial.

It stated:

The trouble with Sister Rose's particular brand of charismatic Christianity is that it has had a tendency to produce a cult revolving around this strong-willed personality. From a position of power, Rose Phillips, who calls herself a doctor of theology (where did she get her doctorate?), is prepared to lead her wide-eyed converts. But lead them where? Down a backward, narrow path, we fear. Perhaps into the politics of the far right, we more than fear. Instead of trying to wipe out bigotry, Rose Phillips may even want to exploit it—that is, if it's true that anti-Zionist hate literature has been traced to her headquarters.

Our severest condemnation of Sister Rose is that she is the most heavily financed evangelist in America today, although the source of her great fortune has, to date, remained a mystery. Sister Rose has never satisfactorily explained to her critics if she had to sell her soul to the devil to obtain the fat bankroll she appears to have. We feel her moral crusade is a misnomer. Sister Rose had better clean up her own morals before condemning those of others.

The words were harsh, the criticism so pointed, Buck secretly vowed to keep this editorial writer on staff when he acquired the News, if he ever did.

He leaned back in his soft, well-padded chair. The TV cameras had just zoomed in on Rose. Shelley could hardly be seen in the background.

Incandescent, intense, she shimmered in the blazing spotlights in a white suit with a rose-colored scarf discreetly covering her bandaged neck. She carried a bouquet of roses presented to her by a cute little girl in a white, frilly lace dress.

All very virginal, Buck thought, amused. To him, the roadshow of Rose and Shelley made a very good act, a bit cynical and hypocritical, perhaps, but fantastic show business.

*****

The moment had arrived—a time of confrontation, dreaded but inevitable. It had to happen some place. Why not in her hometown of Abilene?

Waiting behind temporary barricades thrown up at the airport, her supporters had been trusting, believing. Rose could tell it in their faces. As the vile editorial attacking her had stated, these people were ready to follow her anywhere. She had only to offer them leadership.

The elderly had been there, of course, and she'd expected them— those harsh, lined faces who'd survived. What was far more gratifying to her had been the eager faces of the young people turning out to greet her, including many married couples in their twenties who thrust their children at her, wanting her to touch their offspring. She suspected that these parents believed that her own hands, coming to rest on their babies, would guarantee them a bright future.

There had been some roving youths, skeptics, no doubt financed, in her opinion, by left-wing agitators. They'd paraded in the background with placards she didn't bother to read. Their homemade signs and banners, with their crude lettering and even cruder slogans, didn't faze her. Only a great mass uprising of protest would intimidate her at this point.

Stepping off the plane, she'd had her face stung by the hot, dry air. In the presence of those who disliked her at the airport, she'd realized her own magnetism, her tone of quiet command.

In spite of the police at the cordon who had tried to redirect her, she'd approached some of the demonstrators on the fringe, noticing how the energy of their shouts and vulgarities died to a whimper as she turned the full force of her presence on them. Flushed with her victory, her head held high, she smiled grimly.

Striding through the crowds assembled on either side of the aisle stretching through the airport, she made her way to a podium set up for her in the parking lot. She smiled at the hushed crowd whose edges were dotted with members of the press corps, who had flown in from New York, Los Angeles, and cities in between.

Her opening remarks at the press conference were predictable and necessary. She knew she had to praise Abilene, even though she loathed it. She amused the crowd by telling them her daddy, Flip Phillips, had gotten her a job on the Cracklin' Jim Gospel Hour when she was just a teenager, and how she'd started to attract attention for the first time witnessing to her special power.

She talked about her ideals for the Christian state of Kansas, and led the crowd in an emotional public prayer. Finally, she raised her throaty voice to the far reaches of the asphalt-covered parking lot and said, in a tone cracking with emotion, "And to all of you well-wishers in my campaign to bring a moral revolution to our playgrounds, to our schools, and to the very institutions that have made America great, I say, God bless you."

The roar of the crowd had drowned out any further comment as Rose gracefully bowed her head in silent prayer. Privately her thoughts went back to the years before she'd ever left home, to the time of a motherless girlhood in an anonymous clapboard house she'd shared with Flip and Hazel.

Things had gone well until Flip, a driller in the oil fields, had been trapped in a collapse of a derrick. He'd had both legs smashed, and an explosion had ignited a raging fire. Hot tar had splattered his face, burning his eyes. The accident had left him crippled and blinded for life. He'd become a basket case, and Hazel had to go out and work as a waitress in a diner to support the family.

Rose was supposed to stay home and look after Flip. She'd done just that until her fourteenth birthday. One night when Hazel had come in from work, she'd found Flip seeped in his own waste and a goodbye note from Rose, wishing them "all God's blessing."

That was Rose's last goodbye to Abilene, and her fondest memory of the town had been hitching a ride in a pickup truck to get out of it, as she'd headed for Chicago.

Now she'd returned to the scene of so many bitter memories. But she'd returned as a grand lady attracting everybody's attention, and that made her feel good.

She paused in front of the microphones, then signaled that she was ready to accept questions. The first ones had been easy, mainly restatements of familiar themes already sounded in Okeechobee. Calder Martin had prepared her to face much more hostile examinations than this, and she knew the difficult questions were heading her way. She smiled at the mayor and local dignitaries who'd gathered to welcome her and present her with the key to the city.

"Are you going to export your revolution into every state?" The question came from a woman reporter who obviously dressed and talked with Barbara Walters as a role model. The sound of her voice carried a stinging, biting criticism.

A flashbulb shot off close to Rose, making her jump. She always feared some fanatic with a gun might be lurking out there. "I'm not afraid to call it a revolution," she said, regaining control of herself. "A moral revolution. Yes, we're going to export it, as you say. Not only into every state, but around the world."

Cameras banged against bodies in the background and one electrician yelled, "Push me, you son of a bitch and I'll..." His voice carried across the crowd.

The other reporters laughed, and so did Rose. Even as she did, she noticed the national press fidgeting impatiently.

"Is everyone going to hell who doesn't subscribe to your moral views?" one CBS reporter asked.

Pads ready, the press members seemed ready to jot down her answer. She paused. "Yes, as a matter of fact." She smiled at the CBS reporter. "You didn't expect me to admit that, did you?"

"What about Jews?" came a probing question from the back.

"I believe as I believe," Rose said calmly. "Jews who don't accept Jesus Christ as their personal Savior are going to hell. We consider such Jews as lost souls. Before you scream anti-Semitism, let me tell you that I'm opening up charismatic centers around the nation. There, we will help Jews willing to accept Christ. Far from persecuting or condemning the Jew, we are prepared to save him!"

A murmur arose from the audience. A wild-eyed woman near the rear of the crowd made her way down front, pushing and shoving through several editors and technicians. A public relations man signaled to Rose to ignore her waving, outstretched hand. But Rose stood firm, her voice and eyes cold. "Yes."

"What about Zionists?" the woman asked, her voice overriding all challengers. Heads turned in her direction. "Hate sheets, believed to be financed by your association, have attacked Zionists."

Every head now swiveled toward Rose. Her hand went to her bandaged throat, concealed by a scarf. She felt a parching dryness there. "I hope I'm not violating some gentleman's agreement in answering." A lone, nervous chuckle behind her greeted that pronouncement, then silence.

She remembered to keep her voice reasonable in tone, as she prepared to make inflammatory remarks. "Zionists can no longer have a honeymoon with the American public, and there are hopeful signs that this cozy arrangement is over. Israel itself must stand up and be judged by American public opinion, the way we judge all nations, including Russia and Cuba."

Her expression turned grim as she gripped the lectern with both hands. "Few senators are willing to speak out against Israel because they know the big, powerful Jewish lobby is prepared to destroy their political careers. The intimidation of our lawmakers, the threats by the Jewish lobby, has got to stop!"

She detected a triumphant smile on her woman questioner's face. It was as if she'd personally trapped her on the record. "Because they've suffered, Jews feel they have to be singled out for preferential treatment for eternity. What about the blacks? They've suffered, too, but this country has certainly leveled plenty of criticism on them."

Her face appeared eager for the spotlight. For a moment, she seemed infatuated by the sound of her own voice. "Anti-Semitism belongs to the past. Jewish power in this country destroyed it long ago." She turned away from her woman questioner and feared for a moment she hadn't made her point emphatically enough. "In the case of Israel, the oppressed has now become the oppressor, invading and destroying the homeland of others." A deafening silence fell. Even the cameramen shut up. "I find an equation between Zionism and Nazism." Her face became more serious and earnest. The mayor and other dignitaries were clearly shocked.

Live television cameras seemed to block every aisle. A few hands went up. Gaining confidence, she paused to take a sip of water. Additional television lights were turned on, "Have the Jews so quickly forgotten their own suffering? Is Israel now trying to make others suffer as much as her people did? Israel today uses Hitler's old weapons— arrest, torture, murder, and bombing of civilian populations, the forced separation of families."

She imagined how she'd look on TV news that night. "In our country, Jewish Defense League members engage in terroristic practices, while our leaders remain silent, afraid to speak out against them. I dare say, if the JDL were black, we'd have the FBI rounding them up in the middle of the night."

Great excitement seemed to build in the press section. She heard noises, movement again. Still, she went on, "I am not against Jews. I'm against many of the policies of Israel and, as an American, cherish my right to state my views publicly. As for the Jews themselves, great numbers have already joined our charismatic movement and soon I expect to have thousands more worshipping with us, renouncing their own religion."

Suddenly, there was a crash. The hushed crowd radiated tension. A reporter pushed aside two TV cameramen, knocking over their equipment. Grabbing a hand camera from a woman photographer, he broke from a security guard and dashed toward the front. Only feet from Rose's face, he hurled the camera. A sound, not quite like a woman's scream, escaped from her damaged throat. She ducked but it was too late. The impact was instant, brutal. It blinded here. She felt a gash in her cheek and instinctively her fingers went there, only to withdraw at the feel of blood. "Oh, God," she said out loud, praying silently she hadn't been disfigured. Distorted, her vision came back, and the massive spotlights became so many burning suns, glaring with ferocity, suffocating her with unbearable heat. Hands everywhere seemed to reach out for her. Dazed, she stumbled and fainted.

*****

From Rose's own communications center aboard the plane, Buck reached the injured evangelist in her hospital bedroom. Over the phone, she assured him she was all right. "Just a bit shaken, a very minor cut on my cheek. It wouldn't be discreet to have you come to the hospital. I'm spending the night here. We'll fly out tomorrow. Shelley will be back on the plane by six o'clock. You guys can have supper aboard the plane. I've ordered the best steaks in Kansas to be sent aboard. The bedrooms on the plane are far more comfortable than anything you'll find in Abilene. They still sleep on straw in Abilene."

"Glad you're okay," he said. "That was some press conference, some homecoming."

"What did you think of it?"

"Very entertaining," he said without too much emotion in his voice. "At least I've learned more about your agenda. Whoever chose you to become a spokesperson for Arab interests in this country couldn't have made a better choice."

"I'll take that as a compliment."

"You're very skilled," he said. "America's leading evangelist. What better spokesperson for Arab interests? You won't have to worry one bit about losing any of your supporters. I don't think your born again Christians like Jews anyway. If anything, you might have increased your support. I know little of these matters. I don't dislike Jews. Never have. Never will. And I don't dislike Arabs either. You've got yourself a very tolerant man."

"I know that." She sighed. "I don't dislike Jews. Even Zionists. As for Zionists or Israel I couldn't care less. I couldn't give a fuck about any Arab country either. What you know about me and what the world doesn't, is I play a role. Give me a script and I'll read it. If Israel had approached me, I would have agreed to become a spokesperson for their interests. It doesn't matter to me."

Surveying the luxury of the plane, he said, "I don't think Israel could afford you. It takes a country with a lot of oil wells pumping and pumping away to afford you, my dear."

"I have expensive tastes," she said. "Even in boy friends. A gallery of de Koonings yesterday, a to-die-for ring, and a private jet. What will I do tomorrow to top that?"

"You don't have to do anything. I'm not someone whose favors you can buy."

"Bullshit! You can be bought just as much as I can. We all play the same sinful games. The only difference between people is how we choose to deceive the world."

"I suppose you're right. I'm amazed at my own reaction. I think for the first time in my life I realize how unpolitical I really am. I was political in the university, always trying to champion the right causes. But old Buck Brooke beat something out of me by sabotaging every idea, every editorial I wrote. I'm finally admitting to myself that I don't want to take up any cause but my own. I want to devote the rest of my days to the pursuit of the good life." He paused. "Are you shocked?"

"Hell, no, I understand you completely, and I guess that's why I love you so. I loathe people who take up causes except one."

"What's that?"

"The pursuit of money and power. That's something I'm really into. It turns me on."

"Since we're being so candid, I have one confession to make."

"Spill the beans, as we say in Abilene."

"I'm so excited about picking up those checks in Palm Springs I can hardly wait. I've never seen money like that."

"Palm Springs will be only the beginning. Before you and I call it quits, I bet we'll end up owning a small country somewhere."

"Let's go for it. Everybody in Okeechobee always thought I was rich. But I'm not rich. You and Shelley have given me more than anybody else. Of course, my parents left me the house and a lot of other things. But that wasn't rich. I was comfortable. I could pay the grocery bill and hire a maid but I wasn't rich. I want to find out what it's like to be really rich and live rich. I mean, fly around the world on my own plane. Do what I want. That's a freedom I've never known, and I'm anxious to taste that freedom."

"You'll get everything you want by sticking with me, baby. I'm your meal ticket to the world."

"I don't like it put just that way, but what the hell? How can I complain?"

"You can't. You've got me. The world's most beautiful woman. And you've got Shelley, the world's most beautiful boy."

"You are two gorgeous people. Luminous, really. Both of you."

"I'm desperately in love with you, and I know that Shelley has fallen in love for the first time. I've seen him fucked before, but when you penetrated him I'd never seen such bliss on anyone's face. I could tell: you're the man of his dreams. I love to see him loving you. It gives me a cozy feeling. All in the family, so to speak."

"You guys gave me quite a time on that plane before we landed in Abilene. Tales from Arabian Nights, shit like that. I thought I'd seen a thing or two before, but you guys are incredible."

"There will be plenty more nights like that," she said. "Of course, I can't promise always to be faithful. If you're around, I'm with you. No question about that. But if we're in different cities, and an attractive waiter arrives with caviar, well." She hesitated. "You understand."

"Perfectly."

"I've got to go," she said, a slight fear to her voice. "Someone's just come in. Love you madly." She hung up abruptly.

After putting down the phone, Buck returned to the wide-screen television set, watching the immediate reaction to Rose's anti-Zionist stand.

The reporter who'd attacked Rose with the camera had been arrested, but not officially charged, according to news reports. He was identified as Gianni Roth, an "Italian Jew," who worked for the Kansas City Star.

"I fear her remarks are a threat to the very existence of the Jewish people," Roth told NBC.

Rose's staff aboard the plane had stopped their duties to listen to the news.

"We see her attempt to make us the object of charismatic evangelism dangerous in the extreme," Roth went on. "A black day in Jewish-Christian relationships in this country. Her comments about Israel and Zionists, I consider offensive and vulgar." A steely determination crossed his bearded face. "We'll not sit idly by while she launches this campaign to obliterate us. We learned our lessons well in Nazi Germany."

Buck walked to the back of the plane. He felt Roth was overstating the case a bit. He didn't think Rose was quite the menace portrayed. She was a menace all right, but not that powerful. At least that was his assessment at the moment. He was ready to change his mind at any time.

He felt vaguely uncomfortable being aboard this plane and wanted to get out and explore Abilene. Perhaps a quiet motel on the outskirts of town would suit him better. While waiting for Shelley, he was going to call Robert at some point in the afternoon and assure him of his undying love. He felt guilty being on this plane and away from Robert. He loved Robert and wished he could slip off with his friend and spend the rest of the fading day with him. He had cut himself into two pieces, one wanting to be with Robert, the other with Shelley. As for Rose, he didn't much care whether he saw her again or not. She was important to him because of Shelley and for no other reason.

Only when he decided to take another bath to cleanse himself of that sexual marathon aura he'd experienced with Rose and Shelley, and only when he was completely submerged in that tub, did he think of Gene. How quickly Gene had faded from his agenda. He'd found Gene's invitation to meet on that tennis court startling and, of course, he never for a moment seriously entertained the possibility of keeping that rendezvous. Did he love Gene? He knew he did but the more immediate point was that he couldn't be with Gene. It was a fatal attraction. It would lead to destruction. He knew that and was surprised that Gene didn't also know that. He could see only disaster in pursuing a relationship with Gene. It was over before it had begun, although in his heart he'd always love Gene. Their love just wasn't meant to be.

And while he was still in his bath, another thought occurred to him. He didn't want to be Rose's media director. His heart wasn't in it at all. So why was he doing it? He knew the reason for that. He feared for Shelley's safety in the future. Rose was placing Shelley in harm's way, and Buck vowed to himself that he was going to be here, ready, willing, and able to rescue Shelley at any point his life became endangered. He loved him and wanted to protect him. Shelley had all the beauty and money in the world, but he didn't have a good man to look after him. Buck raised himself up in the bath and reached for the shower nozzle. Shelley had that man now.

*****

In the neighboring town of Seminole, Gene sat alone at the bar, waiting for Pamela and Barry to join him for dinner. He'd driven them to this joint twenty-five miles out of town because Barry didn't want to remain in Okeechobee when reporters were converging around his home, trying to get his reaction to Sister Rose's speech in Abilene. Barry had spent most of the late afternoon in strategy sessions with his campaign advisers, seeking a way to handle the controversial position of Rose's support.

Barry had given only a brief statement when cornered by TV reporters. As Gene sat at the bar downing a drink, he saw the first clip of Barry meeting the press.

"Are you going to repudiate the Rose Phillips endorsement of your candidacy?" came the first predictable question from a TV reporter.

Giving a fast answer out of the slit-thin corners of his mouth, Barry, as if carefully rehearsed, said, "Not at all. Sister Rose has made it clear she isn't an anti-Semite. She's exercising her rights as an American citizen to criticize the military policies of a foreign power. Even members of the Jewish community are doing that these days. Does anyone dare suggest we take away Sister Rose's right to speak her mind in a free society?"

"But what about her wanting to make Christians out of Jews?" bellowed a woman reporter from the News.

Barry, clearly irritated with the question, replied, "Need I mention many Christians who have converted to Judaism? Elizabeth Taylor. Sammy Davis, Jr. The limited number of Hebrew Christians in this country is no threat to Judaism."

The ride over to Seminole had been tense. Gene could no longer tolerate the company of Pamela and Barry. He was sorry now he'd approached them about being a security guard. It was obviously a mistake. On the drive to the tavern, Pamela had groped Gene twice. He was used to being groped, but in this early evening encounter he'd had enough. "Listen, bitch" he'd told her, "do that one more time and I'm going to belt you."

In anger, Pamela had slid over closer to her side of the window. She turned to Barry in the rear seat. "Is he saving it all for you? You boys must have had a hell of a good time down in Key Biscayne."

Barry's face paled and his voice had a weary resignation. "What can I do?" he'd asked Gene in despair. "I've never been able to keep Pamela's hands from roaming over anybody she'd got the hots for. She specializes in state troopers. I think the fact that you're a cop turns her on."

"Was a cop," Gene said, as he momentarily closed his eyes, opening them in time to see the approach of a large truck in the next lane.

"At least I'm a normal woman," Pamela had said defensively. Gene had suspected she'd been drinking heavily in the afternoon. "I'm not some pervert like you," she said, turning to Gene with a bitterness in her face. With even more bitterness, she'd looked disdainfully at Barry in the rear. "Or some child molester." The rest of the ride was in silence.

As the bourbon warmed his stomach, Gene realized painfully that he was not only drinking too much, but indulging in despondency—a mood he drew upon with more and more frequency, alarmingly so. Spread out on the bar was a newspaper with a picture of Barry, Pamela, and their two daughters which had appeared in the latest edition of the News. They were the embodiment of the American dream. But it was just the gloss of the photograph—nothing real about it, an image to project onto an unsuspecting public, a deception that had obviously fooled Sister Rose herself. It made Gene wonder if anything were real any more.

Barry tapped his shoulder and ushered him over to a booth on the other side of the room. The tavern could seat seventy-five but there were only about twenty diners tonight.

Pamela had gone to the women's room, as Barry and Gene sat at the table in silence, averting each other's eyes. At the smell of perfume, he knew Pamela was back.

"When you become mayor," she said to Barry, "I want you to have the health department close this place down. The sanitary conditions are just awful."

"I'm afraid my jurisdiction won't extend this far," Barry said, studying the menu.

At the approach of a waitress, Barry quickly lost his frown, flashing his award-winning candidate's smile. She didn't seem to recognize him. She was more interested in appraising Gene.

Over filet mignon, the table remained silent until Gene asked Barry, "When is Sister Rose coming back?"

"I hope she stays away forever," Barry answered.

Gene was puzzled. "She's supporting your candidacy—over her own sister."

"Cut the shit," Barry said with impatient disgust, slamming down his fork. "My candidacy—what a joke! Rose is the real candidate. A smart cop like you should have figured everything out by now. We're nothing but puppets."

Gene's mind was like a whirlpool. He understood nothing of the world, it seemed. His brain just didn't seem to work like anybody else's.

Pamela took her drink and held it tentatively in front of her mouth. She took a long swallow, then glared at Barry. "Thanks to my husband, Rose has got us where she wants us. When that bitch calls, Barry comes running. Oh, do they spend some lovely evenings together." With increased loathing and fury, she turned to Barry. "What do you and Rose do, sweetheart? I hear she gives a great rim job!"

At Pamela's provocative question, Gene's slow, seething fury of the evening reached a boiling point. Pamela's sexual aggression with him he'd been able to handle, although just barely. But the vile, vulgar attack on Sister Rose could not be forgiven. It was wrong for him to let it go by. By doing that, it was like acquiescing to the truth of the slander. With a life of its own, Gene's palm opened wide, his fingers arched rigidly. In a flash, he reached over and slapped Pamela's garishly painted red mouth.

She jerked back in astonishment. After the initial shock, tears welled in her eyes. Several patrons of the restaurant turned and stared. Their waitress rushed over. "Is everything okay?"

With a wave of her hand, Pamela dismissed the waitress. That same hand went now to cover her face. Just sitting there, Barry looked on helplessly, first at Pamela, then at Gene. He seemed more embarrassed for himself than he was at anything that had happened to his wife.

"You're going to let him get away with that?" Pamela asked in astonishment.

"I have no choice," Barry said in a whispered tone.

"You son of a bitch!" Pamela shouted, raising her voice so loud everybody in the restaurant heard her. She picked up her glass of liquor and tossed it, ice cubes and all, in Gene's face. "I'm leaving tonight," she said to Barry. "Clearing out. The next time you hear from me, you'll regret it." She ran across the sawdust-littered floor, nearly stumbling until a waiter caught her, holding her arm, offering her support. The heel of her shoe was broken.

Barry called for the check, but Gene didn't move, not bothering to wipe his splashed face with a napkin. He felt numb somehow. A blackness rose to fill his brain. Yet in that darkness was something radiant, a blinding white light that cast a luminosity over the restaurant unlike any he'd known before.

"Is she gone?" Gene asked in a faint voice.

"Yes," Barry said with contempt. "And you and I are going to get up and walk very quietly out of this place—with smiles on our faces. Like it never happened."

"It did happen. I'll never forget what she said."

*****

Even from her hospital bed, even with all that she had going on in her life, Rose had managed to secure the best steaks in Kansas for Buck and Shelley. At least Buck thought they were.

Shelley had a different opinion. "You're the only beef I want to eat tonight."

"Go on," Buck urged. "Eat the food. You'll need it for energy after what I'm going to put you through tonight. It'll take four times to satisfy me."

In his shorts and T-shirt, Shelley held a piece of meat provocatively in the air, licked his rosy lips, then seductively bit into the meat.

"God, you even know how to make taking a bite of food sensual," Buck said. "You know I'm in love with you, and I've been so busy fucking you that I suddenly realized while sitting on this plane today that I don't know you at all. I don't know anything about you. Where you came from. Anything."

Shelley sighed and reached to take a sip from a tulip-shaped glass of red wine. "I don't know who my parents were. I was found abandoned at the age of six months. It's like a Dickens novel. Of course, I never read a Dickens novel so don't hold me to this. But at the age of six weeks I was found on someone's doorstep. No one ever found out who left me there. I was placed in an orphanage for six years. One day our beloved Sister Rose was in an adoption mood. For reasons known only to herself. She's never married, you know. At least that's what she says. Frankly, I think there are a few discarded husbands along the way, especially one very persistent one back in Chicago. She paid money to shut him up. Anyway, Rose paraded through the orphanage looking for a child. She ignored all the ethnic and black babies and settled for the most adorable, blond-haired, blue-eyed bambino in the ward. Namely this gorgeous piece of flesh that belongs today exclusively to you."

Buck reached over and kissed Shelley on the lips. "Thank God she did. I can't imagine living without you. What I would have missed out on."

You've got me, babe, and I mean forever. You won't be able to discard me very easily. I always decided when I get my claws in the right dude, I wasn't going to let go."

"I doubt that. I'll get older. You'll grow even more beautiful. When I start to get my first gray hairs around the temple and add a slight tire around my waist, you'll leave me at home and pursue some hotter, younger stud."

Shelley reached for his hand and squeezed it. "You know that's not true. When you're eighty-five, I'll be right there in bed with you loving and licking. In my vision, you'll remain always as you are today. The world's perfect male specimen. You are indeed the sexiest man alive. I can't believe you're mine. It's been a long road to my horizon."

"For me, too. A lot of detours. Even a present life that's gotta be straightened out sooner than later."

"You mean Robert?"

"Of course, I mean Robert," Buck said, slightly irritated. The whole subject made him nervous.

"God damn, don't worry about that. I'm not worried about it. How many times do I have to tell you that Robert will leave you? I have this vision thing. You've got to learn to trust my vision."

"Robert doesn't seem to want to let go, unless he might fall in love with someone new. I've hired a real hot driver. His name is Casey. Maybe while he's hauling Robert around Okeechobee on shopping binges, Robert might fall for him."

"Maybe," Shelley said enigmatically. "I've got another vision thing to share with you. It's about Barry."

"That son of a bitch. I should have belted him one."

"Don't be rash. We've got to make up with Barry and be friendly with him. After a couple of decades roll by, he's going to become president of the United States."

"Like hell. With his sexual baggage? I just can't see him up there with George Washington and Thomas Jefferson."

"But could you see him up there with Warren Harding?"

"Probably a few notches below Harding."

"Actually Barry might make a very effective president," Shelley predicted. "Just because you have a lot of dark secrets in your closet doesn't mean you can't be a good president. If Barry makes it to the White House, and I know he will, I will have at least fucked with him before he got elected president. Our darling Rose actually got to fuck with a president while he was in office."

"That I can believe," Buck said, reaching for his glass of wine as he finished off his steak, even the baked potato and stalk of broccoli. "Let me guess. Don't tell me. LBJ?"

"You're absolutely right.

"I knew it couldn't be Nixon," Buck said. "I don't think he fucks Pat. Maybe twice in his life, or were those births arranged artificially?"

"Artificially."

Later, in the living room aboard the plane, Shelley was eager to hear the news. He came and sat beside Buck on the sofa, as the female Japanese attendant served them champagne in rose-colored glasses. He held Shelley's hand, ignoring the presence of the attendant, just assuming she'd seen a lot more aboard this plane than some innocent hand-holding.

"Before we go to our bedroom and fuck like jackrabbits, I want you to let me in on what's going on with Rose and her operation. It's about time I got involved in some deep dark secrets here. Like who's behind all this?"

"You'll meet the leader in Palm Springs. He'll explain everything."

"You're not going to tell me now so I can be prepared."

"It's not that I'm holding back a lot. Actually I haven't been let in on everything that's going on around here. Calder knows everything. Even Rose herself—at least I suspect—doesn't know all that she's got herself involved in."

"I paid good money to that maid who used to work for Rose. For information. She claims that she heard Calder talking on the phone. It seems he may cause you harm, and I'm afraid. I don't want anything to happen to you. I'm going to protect you. That's the real reason I'm here."

"Calder's been talking that bullshit for years. Okay, I've been in a few jams. Had a few close calls. But Calder has always gotten me out of them. That's what he gets paid for. Until I met you, I've had a reckless spirit. Doing whatever I wanted to do if it felt good."

"That's the point! Calder fears that if some of your activities are exposed, it will bring the whole God damn Rose Phillips organization tumbling into the dust."

"Exactly. Her devout Christians are very homophobic. They couldn't tolerate such accusations against me. Her support would vanish. Even worse, it could lead to an investigation and exposé of Rose. What if the devout learned that Rose Phillips is a first-rate whore and not the mother of God?"

"I see Calder's concern. That would certainly threaten his own meal ticket."

"It would threaten everybody's meal ticket. But don't you worry. The damage control that used to be so important isn't needed any longer. Both Rose and I have settled down with you. Having you aboard as media director will justify your presence. Both Rose and I have got this one figured out. I'll be faithful to you from this day on. No man but you will ever get at my rosebud again. I can't promise that Rose will be faithful. She is a true whore. She loves and desires you but when she isn't with you, who knows about that slut?"

"She more or less suggested to me that she wouldn't necessarily opt to resist temptation if it happened to come her way." Buck rested his feet on an Egyptian stool with two Sphinx-like faces at each end. He pulled Shelley to him and kissed him hard on the lips. Then he licked the boy's tender mouth. "It's this God damn Calder. He's a scumbag. I think he'll try to do us harm, especially with me aboard."

"Calder's threatened me for years. At one point he even announced to Rose that he was going to have me kidnapped and brainwashed. He claimed that when I returned from the brainwashing clinic, that I would be a saint for the rest of my life. Can you imagine shit like that?"

"With Calder, I can imagine anything. I've suddenly made myself number one on his hit list. If he already knows of my involvement with you, I may be in for it. I realize accepting all this money that I'm about to comes at a grave personal price—and we're not talking about the political fallout. God, how in the fuck can I ever look Hazel in the eye again?"

"That's a problem. You'll find out in Durant. She's coming to the funeral."

"Oh, shit."

"Oh, shit, is right. But you've got to face Hazel. We've both got to face Calder. He can't be eliminated. Right now he and Rose are locked into a big power struggle. Calder is ruthless. He'll stop at nothing. Calder and Rose hate each other but they're forced to work together. He's trying to sabotage Rose. She's trying to cut his throat. Our workplace, my darling, is a very tense environment. You might as well know this."

"It sounds like hell. My role, as I've said, is to protect you. Of course, with Calder I'll have to be constantly looking over my shoulder to see if I'm being stalked. I was stalked in Miami at the Key Biscayne villa. It was Julius Forster. Someone at my villa spotted him. You know, he's the Nazi creep who tried to blow up the Examiner, or at least threatened to."

"I've heard of him. He was stalking you? The man is psychotic. Rose told me that. She knows a psycho when she sees one. Once I was summoned to Calder's headquarters. I'd gotten into another one of my little messes, and Calder was bailing me out. Paying off the parties, so to speak. When I came into Calder's building, I saw this creep Forster leaving. I recognized his picture from the papers. I can't actually prove that Forster was in the building meeting with Calder—there are other offices, of course. But it was mighty suspicious. I'm sure Calder has need of a Nazi psycho every now and then. God, I hope this lunatic isn't on our trail."

"I hope so too. This Calder asshole plays rough. If he's working against us, maybe we can sabotage him. Let's turn this into war. I mean a secret war. Keep it cool on the surface with Calder while fucking him behind his back."

"How do you go about that?"

"It appears to me I have a golden opportunity in Palm Springs. Perhaps when I meet this mysterious boss, who's turning over millions to me, I might seriously damage Calder's standing. At least plant enough doubt in bossman's mind that Calder is potentially the most dangerous man in his organization."

"That's entirely possible. Up to now I've always tolerated Calder. I never viewed him as harmless. But I didn't pull dirty tricks on him either."

"Let me begin then. If asshole wants us eliminated, we might have the pleasure of wiping him out first."

"If only we could." Shelley sighed. "I think I don't want to watch the news after all. I mean Rose will lead off the news tonight. Do I really need to hear it? I was there. I saw it happen. What am I going to learn from some news report? Besides, I've seen five already this afternoon." He looked up with a tenderness and a beguiling smile at Buck.

"I love you, boy," Buck said, feeling the smooth skin of Shelley's exposed shoulders.

"I know in a few minutes you're going to take me in there and do all the rough stuff. We'll exchange a lot of body fluids. There will be plenty of licking, sucking, and plunging. I want that very much—in fact, I can't live without it. But there's something I want even more than that."

"If I can give it to you, I will." He reached for Shelley, pulling him even closer to kiss him, as his hands reached to fondle the boy's buttocks.

"After all that is over, and the plane is silent, and everything has died down for the night, the thing I most want is for you to take me in your arms and hold me close so I can hear your heart beating."

Buck looked into Shelley's deep blue eyes. He was crying. Buck leaned over to kiss away the tears. "I'm here for you, babe. For always."

*****

Wandering alone down the deserted highway, Pamela was in tears. She didn't expect Barry and certainly not Gene to follow her. Barry was accustomed to her running away. Since she always had credit cards on her, he didn't have to worry. She always found a taxi and a motel, but tonight was different. The tavern they'd selected was in a remote location. There were no other buildings for miles around. As she stumbled alone in the darkness, she didn't know how far she was from the town of Seminole. It could be miles and the mosquitoes were getting to her.

Just as she was tempted to swallow her pride and turn back to the tavern, a flashing dome light appearing out of nowhere frightened her. A squad car from the town of Seminole pulled up beside her, shining a light on her. She blinked in the harsh glare.

"You in some kind of trouble, lady?" one of the policemen asked.

"Big trouble," she said, moving closer to the car. "I had a fight with my husband and ran from that restaurant back up the road. But I guess I'm lost."

"Get in," the other policeman said. "We'll take you back into town."

On the way into Seminole, Pamela relaxed. Most people hated policemen. She always liked and trusted them. The men introduced themselves as Bryan and Jeff. She gave her name only as Pam.

"So what did you guys fight about?" Bryan asked.

She decided to be provocative. "Over his acquiring a new boy friend and bringing him to our house. I told him it took a real man to satisfy a woman like me, and he wasn't man enough." She eyed both men who remained stonily silent although each kept glancing back to check her out. She smoothed her hair and reached into her purse to adjust her make-up. "The trouble today is that many men are becoming gay. It's getting harder and harder to find a real man in this world."

"Bryan here and I are real men," Jeff said. "At least I am. Sometimes I wonder about Bryan."

"Fuck you," Bryan said to him. "If a woman has a chance at me and a chance at you, she'll always go with me."

"Bullshit!" Jeff said. He glanced over his shoulder at Pamela. "If you had to choose between the two of us, which one would it be?"

"I couldn't be satisfied with just one of you," she said demurely. "I'd have to have both of you."

"You sound like one hot lady," Bryan said.

"I am." She smiled back at him. "Think you're man enough to handle it?"

"Honey, forget all about that fag husband of yours," Bryan said. "Tonight you're going to get fucked by a REAL man."

"I can't wait," Pamela said. "I like it rough. Don't hold back."

"Fuck, lady, you've got me so hot I practically can't keep the car on the road," Jeff said. "We know this little motel up the road. They owe us a few favors. Always let us check in for an hour or two free."

"Sounds great," Pamela said. "I hope you guys can go more than one round."

"After one round, we're just getting started," Bryan said immodestly.

The next three hours had passed so quickly for her on such familiar terrain. This hadn't been the first motel she'd visited with state troopers. She could no longer count the nights she'd spent in their company. Bryan and Jeff had not exaggerated their abilities between the sheets, as most men often did with her. They were real men, and hard-driving ones at that.

Bryan had been the first to crawl on top of her, presenting a long, thick prick at her mouth. "My prick too big for you, huh?"

Before opening her mouth wide, she'd said, "I never met a prick that was too big for me." He'd shoved it down her throat, causing her to struggle to adjust to the enormous penetration. Within five minutes he'd pulled out and had rearranged her body so that she could give lip service to his friend Jeff.

Jeff's prick had been almost equally long but much thinner and easier for her to swallow without breaking her jaw. She'd spread her legs and braced herself for a rough penetration from Bryan. She'd relaxed as much as possible but when the attack came, there had been enough pain to cause her to cry out. He'd apparently taken her cry for one of passion. The wide-spread head of his prick had plunged deeply into her, and, without giving her a moment to get used to it, he'd begun a wild ride. The pain long faded, an indescribable sensation of almost unendurable, sensual joy had surged through her body. She'd cried out in an ecstasy of passion. This is what she'd wanted from a husband and had never found. As Bryan had pounded away at her, she'd eagerly pushed forward onto Jeff until her nose was pressed against his pubic hairs. She had felt the pulsations swelling with him as she'd sucked voraciously. Bryan's groin had slammed more and more forcefully against her belly, and by that time she'd been moaning. Jeff had gone beyond her wriggling tongue and the roof of her mouth to reach her throat. Guttural, broken, muttered syllables had come from both men, and they had mingled with her own gasps. As if carefully rehearsed, all three had reached climax within moments of each other. As she had tasted the sweetness of Jeff, she'd enjoyed the incredibly powerful staccato bursts of hot, juice Bryan was shooting into her. She relaxed, knowing she was always protected in such matters. Her doctor had long ago seen to that. Actually, it had been Barry who insisted on it.

As Pamela rolled over in bed, she knew it was time to make decisions. She was no fool. As the days and weeks had gone by, she'd become increasingly convinced that somebody somewhere was planning an accident for her. She hadn't been drunk or bullshitting when she'd informed Susan Howard of this.

Increasingly, she feared Calder Martin. She was convinced that as much as he despised her, Barry wouldn't hurt her but Calder might destroy her. Barry was all for some sort of settlement and had even held out the possibility of their continuing to be married, although only in the public eye. More and more she feared this was unacceptable to Calder. Liver lips always referred to her as "loose lips."

Calder had always predicted that Pamela's addiction to alcohol and cops would lead to Barry's fall. Sooner or later Calder had warned both Barry and herself, she would get all of them into big trouble. Pamela had charged that Barry's relationships were far more dangerous than hers, and this was a major point hardly lost on Calder. But for better or worse he had money on Barry and was forced to stick with him. To Calder, Pamela was just a nuisance, and a dangerous one at that.

At this point a sudden thought occurred to her. Her meeting with Susan had been a desperate request to investigate the "accident" that might have caused her death. This early morning she came upon a plan that would prevent her death, keep that accident from ever happening. She'd fly to Miami and from there go to the Pier House in Key West. She'd make plans to hold a press conference. After that press conference, they wouldn't dare kill her. She wouldn't tell everything she knew about Barry and Calder, but she'd tell just enough to destroy them. She'd destroy them before they could get around to eliminating her. The image of her daughters flashed before her. But she couldn't think about them or what her actions would do to them. She was more intent on saving herself at this point. Besides, being a mother was hardly her thing. Both daughters disliked her intensely, always proclaiming their love for Barry instead.

She'd get Jeff and Bryan to take her to the airport outside Okeechobee. They were obviously off-duty at this point and owed her a favor.

Realizing they were taking an extra long time in the bathroom, she got out of bed and stumbled nude to check on them. Upon entering the door, she spotted them in the shower with the curtains pulled back. Obviously Jeff had become so turned on watching Bryan's penetration of her that he'd demanded that Bryan do the same for him.

She shut the door gently, and suspected that neither man had seen her. "Faggots," she said, sitting down before the mirror to apply enough make-up to face an early morning flight to Miami. "The whole world is going queer."

*****

The next morning Buck was anxiously awaiting Rose aboard her jet which was still parked on the tarmac at the Abilene airport. After a marathon session last night, Shelley was getting ready, knowing he'd have to face the cameras once they arrived in Dallas. Even though Buck felt relatively secure in the safety of the plane, he sensed a nasty mood at the airport. Attendants who'd left the plane had reported to him that about six-hundred dissenters had gathered at the airport to protest against Sister Rose when she arrived to board her plane for the flight to Dallas. Police barricades were holding them back.

Stopping off briefly to greet the pilot in the cockpit, Buck peered out the window. One truck seemed to be racing toward the plane with a crudely written placard proclaiming the legend, ISRAEL NOW AND FOREVER.

Airport police in a truck with a dome light flashing overtook the vehicle. The driver, it turned out, was a skinny young woman. She was taken by the security police to their van. Another officer removed the placard and got behind the wheel of her truck and drove it to another part of the airport.

The door to the plane was open and Buck stood briefly on the landing to get some fresh air. As he did, he heard a man's voice booming over a loudspeaker somewhere. "Rose Phillips is dangerous. A menace. She's dangerous because of the bigots she attracts. The Nazi Party. The KKK. Her campaign is not just against Jews. She's launching a right-wing offensive against minorities. She's got to be stopped!" The voice suddenly went dead, as if someone had pulled the plug on the speaker.

In the rear of the vessel, he was seated alone at a table waiting for breakfast. The Japanese woman attendant appeared with a morning mimosa for him, which he gladly accepted as he was feeling dry. He also felt he didn't belong aboard this plane and wanted to escape as soon as possible.

Shelley joined him at breakfast, giving him several quick kisses on the mouth. "God, I love you. You're fantastic."

"I love you too, cute stuff. Now join me in a mimosa as we get ready to welcome your mom."

"You should see the boxes of telegrams brought aboard," Shelley said.

"I hope they've been checked for bombs," Buck said apprehensively.

"They have." He smiled at Buck. "Would you believe it? The telegrams are running three to one in favor of Rose."

"Naturally, the Jews aren't pleased," he said sarcastically.

Shelley smiled sardonically. "I think Rose tested the water before she plunged in. Those charismatics who follow her don't like Jews or Arabs. They don't like any group other than those that follow their own vision. Rose knew what she was doing."

"Not our Rose," Buck said mockingly. "I certainly hope she knows what she's doing. She's inviting big trouble."

"She's getting well paid for it."

Buck finished the last of the mimosa and signaled the attendant for another one. "One should always be paid well for sticking one's fingers into a hornet's nest. The sting is something awful. They fight back."

"I know that and I dread what's coming."

"It's your vision thing again, right?"

"You're getting to know me." He leaned over and kissed Buck again. "Believe it or not, you and I are going to come through all this. A scar here, a laceration there, but the point is: we're going to come through. I'm not sure about Rose. My vision is failing me. It's all blurry and confused."

"I'm confused too." He reached over and gripped Shelley's wrist, almost pulling him closer to him on the banquette. "This media director thing. We've got to talk. Now that I know a little more about Rose's agenda, I think I've got to pull out. I'm hanging around to look after you, not to become some Arab propagandist."

"You may not sign the contract?"

"That's my own vision in the clear light of dawn. I just can't. I don't have the stomach for it. I'll return the private plane."

"You'll do nothing of the sort. I want that plane for us anyway. That's why I persuaded Rose to turn it over to you." Shelley ran a smooth hand along Buck's cheek. "If you ever leave me—or us—I'll kill myself, and I mean that."

"I'm never leaving you. I promise that."

"Then play along. Be here for me. After all this shit blows over, after Rose has paid her dues, things will get normal again."

Buck laughed. It was a bitter laugh. "Things will never be normal around this joint," he said, casting a glance at the luxurious trappings of the plane.

Fifteen minutes later, Rose, followed by two aides in rose-colored uniforms, came aboard. She rushed back to greet Buck and Shelley, kissing them both on the lips. She eagerly accepted the mimosa offered. In a trim white business suit, except for a rose-colored scarf, she appeared radiant, her eyes flashing. A small bandage was on her right cheek where she'd been hit by a camera. But it was a minor flaw. It did not diminish her beauty. She smiled triumphantly at Buck as if expecting congratulations.

"Thank you for those hot damn steaks last night," was all that Buck could manage to say. "Were they ever delectable."

She settled into the banquette, holding up a tulip-shaped glass. "You thought Abilene was fireworks. Wait until Dallas. There's more to come to this show."

"From what Shelley has told me, you were wise not to bring the Reagans into this. They would be denouncing your support this morning."

"Yes," she said demurely. "I'm sure Ron and Miss Nancy want no part of my politics now. But from a TV clip I saw, Barry is not denouncing me."

"He can't afford to break loose," Shelley said. "You've got him by the balls."

"Actually, Calder has done secret surveys," Rose said. "Barry has no support among Jewish voters in Okeechobee. All the vote is going to my dear sister, Hazel."

"I understand we're going to see Hazel in Durant," Buck said.

"Regrettably. I've heard the fat cow is showing up. She's not coming to pay her respects to Aunt Martha but to embarrass me."

"It's going to be awkward as hell—me running into Hazel," Buck said. He glanced apprehensively around the plane again. "I don't know how I'm going to explain my present..." He hesitated. "My present situation."

"Tell the bitch anything," Rose said, downing the rest of her mimosa and calling for another one. "Hazel doesn't matter. She's not important to our plans."

"And just what are our plans, mommie dearest?" Shelley asked.

She glared at him, then softened her features as she turned to Buck. "When we get to Dallas, Shelley and I will get off the plane first. He and I will meet the press, and then travel, just the two of us, in a limousine to Durant. This is done to protect you. I don't want you to have to face or be a part of what I'm going to have to face. My staff has arranged for a private limousine that will drive you, about an hour after my departure from the airport, to Durant. When you get there, the most discreet thing would be for you to check into a hotel, but only as a means of throwing off those goddamn nosy bloodhounds who make up most of the Phillips clan. Shelley and I will spend the night at a private mansion in Durant. We have a way of slipping you into the place later, so that any nocturnal games we play won't be detected by the press."

"That's good," Buck said. "I wasn't too happy at the idea of emerging from that plane arm in arm with you and Shelley. I've got my reasons."

"I'm sure you do, and we want you to be comfortable," Rose said. She turned to Shelley. "Don't we?"

Shelley smiled at Buck. "We want this living doll to be very comfortable."

The Japanese attendant came into their space and told Rose that an urgent message was waiting for her at the communications center. She slammed down her glass, gave Buck a departing kiss, and headed up front. "The general has got to return to her command post."

"I'll miss you on that ride to Durant," Shelley said, after Rose had left. "But we've prepared a suite for you at the mansion. I'll welcome you there tonight."

"When's the funeral?"

"At seven o'clock in the morning," he said. "Rose wanted an early funeral. We've got to get on that plane in Dallas and fly to Palm Springs."

"I can't wait. If I come away with all those millions, how will I know in the future that you're not pursuing me but my money?"

Shelley leaned over and pulled Buck's face close to his, inserting his tongue in Buck's mouth. "I have ways to convince you."

*****

After their good-byes and kisses, and after taking Shelley into his private bedroom for a particularly intimate farewell, Buck remained aboard the plane. He was to wait one hour, then leave with the maintenance crew. He'd honor that commitment to meet that night in the private mansion in Durant.

When the time came, he was glad to be back on the ground again. He liked the feel of earth under his feet. Told by one of Rose's staff there would be a thirty-minute delay for the limousine, he retreated to a bar in the airport. It was here he chose to relax and take in Rose's press conference in Dallas.

In front of TV cameras, she waved cartoons which had appeared in U.S. magazines. "Talk about prejudice!" she said in a strident voice. "Look at these racial slurs." She presented samples of cartoons to members of the press. "Oil-rich sheiks are drawn with swarthy physiognomies. Fat, double-chinned men, with lusty eyes and billowy robes, carry daggers with eyebrow curves. This is the type of propaganda that recalls how *Der Sturmer* used to depict Jews."

He winced and ordered another drink.

"Right when we need the friendship of the Arabs more than ever," she said, "the American public is being brainwashed! Would the Jew stand idly by as *Time* depicted him with lubricity and Shylockery? No way!"

To his astonishment, he noticed supporters carrying ROSE FOR PRESIDENT signs, parading up and down the airport corridors. Surely, occupying the White House wasn't Rose's ultimate aim?

"I seriously question the loyalty of the American Jew who takes money out of this country to finance military adventures whereby Israel invades the homelands of others," Rose told TVland.

No longer hesitant, uncertain, as she'd been at moments in Kansas, she was apparently pleased at the reception and seemed in full control of her campaign.

At a tap on his shoulder, he whirled around, taking his eyes off the television screen and focusing on what looked like a shadowy version of Rose. It took him a moment in the bright glare to realize it was Hazel.

"You're headed for the funeral?" he asked, hoping she didn't know he'd flown in with Rose.

"Sure thing," she said with a weary sigh. "I'm the black sheep of the family, but Martha was my great aunt, too. I loved her." With a quick look at the screen, she said, "Martha would turn over in her casket if she could hear Rose's remarks."

"Are you surprised to run into me in Dallas?" Buck asked.

"Hell, yes, I am, but I was too polite to ask."

He smiled and affectionately patted her arm. "I never knew the day you were too embarrassed to ask any question."

"So why are you here?"

"I've lost the Examiner. Forces close to Rose have taken it over. I don't know much about it. My grandfather arranged the deal before flying off to a clinic in Switzerland."

"Holy Shit!" she said. "I'd heard rumors. The Examiner was my one big hope in the mayor's race."

"You'll have to get along without it. I'm sure the new publisher will support Barry."

"Fuck!" She angrily summoned the bartender and ordered a drink for herself. "Naturally, Rose is behind this."

As Buck sipped his drink, he decided to go for a limited hang-out with Hazel. "I didn't count on a funeral. Actually, I'm supposed to meet with some of her staff tonight. The deal is being closed. In California I'm supposed to pick up a check for the Brooke share of stock. But I'm already out. I got the boot."

"I'm so very sorry. I thought you'd make a great publisher once you were freed of your old man censoring everything you did."

"I may get my chance yet." He smiled enigmatically.

"What does that mean?"

"Once I pick up the money, I've ordered Uncle Milty to make a serious bid to take over the News. I'm just switching from one paper to another."

"Hot damn!" she said. "We'll have some newspaper support in Okeechobee after all. Right now the News is a little lukewarm about me. They're not exactly for Barry, but in their words they find me a little strident."

"You're not strident at all," he said reassuringly. "A strong and forceful woman who stands up and fights for what she believes. But hardly strident." He sighed. "At least you know why I'm in Dallas heading for Durant. It wasn't part of my plan but losing the Examiner wasn't my idea either."

"You're far from through." She downed her drink and ordered another one. "I'm a woman who could always hold her liquor. I'll be the best mayor Okeechobee ever had, and you'll be the town's hottest publisher."

"You don't understand. I'm not going to be the publisher of the News."

She looked astonished. "If not you, who?"

"My new wife."

Her look of astonishment grew stronger. "Wife? This comes as a bit of surprise. Maybe I've been hearing all the wrong rumors—God knows there are enough of those—but I always thought..." She hesitated.

"You mean Robert?"

"I don't want to be offensive. Well, yes Robert. It's none of my business but I always thought you and Robert had a special thing."

"We do. A great friendship. People always misinterpret these things. Can you keep a secret?"

"Of course, I can."

"It'll be announced soon. My marriage that is. I married Susan."

She smiled and kissed him on the cheek. "You could find no better gal. I'm so happy for the two of you."

"If I get the News, I'm installing Susan as publisher."

"She would be great in a job like that." She belted down more liquor. "But what about you? What would you do?"

"I'm still working on that. But it won't be publisher."

One of Rose's staff appeared before him and told him that his limousine was ready. He was asked to move fast, as a large crowd of hostile demonstrators had formed north of the airport. So far, the Dallas police had held them back behind barricades.

He crushed out his cigarette and looked into Hazel's slightly bleary eyes. He wondered if it were true that she was good at holding her liquor. "Do you know the way to Durant?" he asked.

"Hell, yes, I do!"

"Come along." He turned to the attendant. "I won't be needing that limousine after all."

Although the attendant protested vehemently, Buck took Hazel by the arm and guided her out of the airport bar.

He sat with Hazel in the lounge of the rental agency, waiting for their car to be brought up. On a television set in the lounge, he caught a glimpse of Rose's hasty departure from the airport. She and Shelley were seated in the back seat of a Zaftig Stutz Blackhawk IV. A TV news reporter informed viewers that this custom-designed limousine was a type particularly popular with the sheiks of Saudi Arabia.

*****

Traveling on the open road with Hazel was a remarkably different experience from flying across the country on Rose's magic carpet. Instead of champagne, Hazel had brought along a six-pack of Budweiser for Buck.

Ten miles outside Dallas, the air-conditioning system broke down. "Where can we rent another car?" he asked.

She urged him to go on. "You know me. I can stand the heat."

The beer quickly turned hot, but they continued to drink it. He pulled off his jacket and now even his trousers seemed to cling to his body. Despite her bravado, Hazel suffered. The temperature had slipped into the nineties.

Perspiring heavily, she finally said, "Listen, I'm not trying to put the make on you, but why don't you take your pants off? If you can stand the sight of me in a bra, I'm sure I can live with you in jockey shorts."

"Good idea." He braked the car along the side of the road and slipped out of his trousers. He ducked behind the car to take a fast leak. When he got back inside, he had to help her out of her sweat-soaked pink blouse that looked two sizes too small for her.

Along the way they passed some phony cowboys working for a construction gang and, in the distance, scattered clapboard houses, turned a rosy pink from the dust.

She remembered a truck stop ahead. "It's called Dirty Edna's, and the cook there serves rattlesnake meat. You've got to sample it at least once in your life."

At the truck stop, he parked near a washing hose. He slipped into his pants and went with her inside, throwing open the screen door with a Dr. Pepper sign just as she finished hooking the top fastening on her still wet blouse.

Over a formica bar hung a picture of Lyndon Johnson, a melancholy smile on his face. They found a booth as a waitress with a dirty dishcloth came over and wiped the chipped table for them. Hazel ordered rattlesnake meat, fried potatoes and lots of cold beer for them.

After tasting snake, he compared the flavor to chicken."Why not snake?" he asked. "I've eaten everything from chocolate-coated ants to caterpillars."

She didn't like hers. "We can't ever go back, can we? Everything used to taste better. Maybe it's because our palates were young."

He smiled, sensing the humor in the situation. "I feel I've been wandering around the Garden of Eden with the Phillips sisters. Rose, as Eve, offered me the shiny red apple. You've got one up on her. You serve the fucking snake itself!"

She chuckled, downing more beer. "That's a good one. At least it breaks the ice between us. I know about Rose and you."

"I think that aide at the airport made it pretty obvious," he said, cutting off another bite-size piece of snake.

"Oh, I knew before Dallas. It's the talk of Okeechobee." A frightened look of apprehension came across her face. "I don't know how Susan fits into this picture. I assume she doesn't know. But surely a newshound like her mother, Ingrid, will find out and tell her."

"I'm one mixed-up crazy dude."

"You're a real attractive guy, and from the way you fill out those jockey shorts, I can see why everybody is after you. You must be having fun, but I also feel somebody's going to get hurt here. Maybe you."

"I try to act grown up. Playing big ball with the big boys. But sometimes I forget I'm still a kid. The guy running against you, Barry, is just a kid too. I feel our whole class at the university never took time to grow up. We rushed into adulthood thinking we could handle it. But I wonder. Tomorrow night I'm going from an out-of-work publisher making forty-five thou a year to a multi-millionaire. But am I ready for it?"

Ever the earth mother, she reached for his hand and rubbed it gently. "None of us is ever ready for the roles forced on us. By the time we figure life out, we're dead."

"I mean, a few months ago, I wasn't even certain about my own nature if you know what I mean."

"I know," she said, tackling that rattlesnake again. "I also know that regardless of what you say, Robert loves you very much. He's devoted his entire life to you."

"I know he has, and I'll always be good to him. Protect him. Give as much as I can to him."

"I know you'll do right by him but you've got to think of Susan now. She's your wife. Your real love has to go to her now."

Resentment flared in him. He felt provocative, a bit mean. "Don't tell me where my real love is supposed to go. I guess I God damn can decide that for myself."

"I didn't mean to piss you off."

"In case you're really interested, my real love is going to Shelley Phillips. He's what I love and want."

With rattlesnake still dangling on her fork, Hazel laid the meat to rest on her plate, along with the fries with far too much catsup. She looked at him in utter amazement, then her face softened before she broke into hysterical laughter. "You and Shelley—that will be the day. When and if that coupling ever occurs, I will be miraculously transformed into Marilyn Monroe."

He smiled, trying to indicate with his face and mannerism that it was all a big joke. "At least I'm not so touchy any more. Let's get back on that road. And you'd better not take off that blouse again. I'm hot already. I don't need to become hot and bothered."

She laughed with him and took his hand after he'd paid the bill and walked with him to the overheated car.

Back on the road again, the shadows of afternoon lengthened. As seen through his alcoholic gaze, the road was like a faint blur of white sand.

As they headed for Oklahoma's Red River Valley, Hazel became confidential. She decided to tell him the reason for her feud with Rose. But it was strictly *off the record,* she cautioned him more than once.

*****

By the time she was twenty-one, Rose had had some success as an evangelist in the West, but she was far from becoming a household word in America. A rally in Atlanta in the fall of 1961 changed all that. Signs proclaiming SALVATION IS COMING had plastered the town, as the advance work had been good. "Big miracles" had been promised. Hazel had driven up from Florida, hoping for a long-delayed reunion with her sister, whom she hadn't seen since Abilene.

"I remember that night so well," Hazel told Buck. "Instead of preaching, Rose attacked godless Communism. She got the congregation's blood boiling. To the sound of a booming organ and the blare of trumpeters, she'd gone into the rally to lay hands, as she'd called it, on the sick, the lame and the diseased.

Hazel admitted to Buck that every version of what happened next differed. "A man pulled a gun and pointed it directly at Rose. She'd stood paralyzed. Before the would-be assassin could fire, the policeman beside Rose raised his gun and shot the guy three times in the chest. Everything was confusion after that. Screams. Lots of screams, that's all I remember."

Buck knew how painful it must be for Hazel to relate such a story.

"I didn't get to meet up with Rose that time," Hazel said. "Her goons wouldn't let me see her. Of course, she got on every front page in the country. An unknown evangelist no more."

"But I don't understand," Buck said. "Why would that be the cause of a feud between you?"

"That came later," Hazel said, bleary-eyed, as she sipped more hot beer. "Back in Florida I got a note. It said, 'Instead of Sister Rose, I'd call her Sister Killer.'"

"What did that mean?"

"The letter claimed the whole thing was staged," Hazel said. "The guy—his name was Stephen White—was set up. He was programmed to kill Rose. Only two days before the Atlanta rally, he'd been released from an asylum."

"I can't believe Rose would deliberately take a human life."

"Neither could a lot of other people, and even to this day I'm not sure. But Rose's involvement looked mighty suspicious."

As Hazel told the story, the former mental patient, Stephen, had been released in the custody of a man presumably his father. Although two psychiatrists at the hospital had protested against Stephen's release, calling it "premature" and labelling the inmate as "potentially dangerous," the head of the institute had overruled them and granted the request.

Following his release, Stephen had registered at a downtown hotel in Atlanta. Well dressed and carrying expensive luggage, he'd demanded and received the finest suite in the hotel.

After Stephen had been shot by the policeman, a search of the suite had disclosed a batch of Marxist literature, including books, pamphlets and newspapers. Hazel's investigation learned that the suite had actually been paid for by a Mr. Paul Winston of Savannah. A check in Savannah had revealed that Paul Winston did exist, unlike Stephen's mysterious father. In fact, he was the son of the Rev. Hadley Winston, one of the deacons who'd appeared on the platform that night in Atlanta with Rose. A staunch segregationist and rabid right-wing fanatic, the Rev. Winston had been one of Rose's principal supporters in Georgia. He had not only invited Rose to his city, but had planned and publicized the rally. After the slaying, the policeman had resigned from the force and had left Atlanta.

When Hazel, on the basis of what she'd learned, had pressed for an investigation into the case, she'd received mysterious phone calls late at night, warning her she was "treading on dangerous ground."

"I followed her to one of her rallies one time," Hazel admitted. "You know, just to talk to her about Stephen. I tried to detain her as she left the platform. 'I've got to know the truth,' I whispered in her ear. 'You've got to tell me!' I remember Rose glaring at me with fury. She jerked away from me and ran backstage. That's the last time I ever laid eyes on her."

Buck put his arm around Hazel to reassure her and, hopefully, to encourage her to tell him more.

"What can I tell you now?" Hazel said. "I can't say for sure that Rose conspired with Preacher Winston to kill Stephen White. The police never proved that. Not that they tried too hard. Yet I know, deep down I know, that Rose somehow was involved in that murder. If she was capable of that back then, she's capable of far worse now."

*****

It was ten o'clock by the time they reached Durant. Still shocked at Hazel's story, Buck obtained two single rooms for them at the Holiday Inn on Main Street. In her room, Hazel collapsed on her bed as he brought in her luggage. Her revelation, the hot beer and the drive had proved too much for her. She was fast asleep so soon he had to remove her shoes and loosen her tight blouse. He gently closed the door on her snores.

Back in his own room, he pulled off all his clothes and lay on the spread. He reached for the phone beside his bed and called Robert.

"I knew it was you," Robert said in Okeechobee.

Buck hadn't even said a word. "It must be my heavy breathing."

"That Rose thing. I've been watching it on TV. I'm really worried for you. I had Patrick and Uncle Milty over tonight. I told Milty how afraid I was for you. Even though he's a Jew, he's not taking Sister Rose very seriously. At times I think all he sees is the money."

"Baby doll," Buck said in a soft, seductive voice. "I didn't call to talk politics or even money tonight. I called to tell you I love you and can't live another minute without you. I want to be with you right now. Hold you in my arms and never let you go."

"Is this relationship turning physical?" Robert asked mockingly with a slight giggle in his voice.

"This relationship should have turned physical a long time ago," Buck said. "There I was walking along campus, minding my own business, thinking what pussy I was going to fuck that night. Along you came in a pair of white shorts at least two sizes too small for you, encasing a bubble butt created by Michelangelo. I should have hauled you off right there. Why in the fuck did I wait so long?"

"You didn't know what you wanted back then."

"Bullshit, I didn't. Who am I kidding? The first time I feasted my eyes on you I knew what I wanted."

"Imagine how I felt walking along." He paused. "In shorts that were a perfect fit and not too small at all. Along comes the man of my dreams. Some Viking God, and he's eying me like some hungry kid eager to eat into a candy bar. I thought I had you right away. I didn't know at the time what a long, rocky road it would be, and how much competition I would have to get rid of before I could claim my prize."

"At least we were heading in the right direction: to the shower room."

"That was amazing. Only ten minutes after meeting you, I was standing in the shower next to you, even though there were thirty other showers empty. When I saw you completely nude for the first time, I was hopelessly in love by then. You were—and still are today—my ultimate wet dream fantasy. When that jock strap came off, I don't think I could take my eyes off it until you finally showered and got dressed."

"That's when I invited you for a beer."

"I remember it well. That beer—actually several beers—lasted all night with me ending up crashing at your place."

"Well, you didn't seem to want to go home."

"In fact, I'd found my home. You know so well: nothing happened that night even though we both knew we wanted it desperately. In fact, I spent that night and every other night at your house. You told me you liked girls."

"I thought I did at the time," Buck said. "It took me a long time to come around to it. To get totally involved."

"Even so, those nights with you as rough trade were wonderful. It's just so much better now that you're loving back."

"I'll do it always." Buck glanced at his watch. "I got an urgent meeting tonight with some advisers for Rose. By the way, I'm at the Holiday Inn in Durant with Hazel. She's in the next room."

"Give her my love," he said. "Tell her I'm sorry her Aunt Martha passed on."

"I will."

"But save most of my love for you."

"You'd better mean that," Buck said.

"I do." There was a slight pause as Buck said nothing. "There's something on your mind," Robert said. "What are you thinking about?"

"About that time you first saw me nude in the shower. There was something we never spoke of but let's admit it now."

"Let me say it: it's easier if I say it. The more I looked at you, the more intensely I took in that amazing equipment God has bestowed on you..."

Buck interrupted him. "The harder I became."

"You had to finish that shower quickly and rush to get dressed, because you knew that in minutes I'd be on my knees in front of you, devouring you. We both wanted it right then and there. I should have moved in on you quicker. What a fool I was to wait."

"If I recall, you didn't wait very long."

"At home you always found some excuse to be in a state of undress every chance you got. The first thing in the door and that business suit of yours was coming off."

"You always wanted to see what the suit was hiding, so I said, 'What the hell!'"

"There's just one thing I've got to ask. All those nights I sucked and licked you, sometimes bringing you to three explosions in one evening, and I ended up jacking off."

"Yeah, what about it?"

"If one of those nights when I had you really hot, and I had presented my dick for you to suck, what would you have done back then?"

"The truth?"

"The whole truth," Robert said.

"I would have sucked every inch of it and licked the balls and everything else."

"I was a fool not to have realized that then. A God damn fool."

"When it came, it was worth the wait. I could drink some of that juice right now. After my little cocktail, I'd throw you on the bed and plunge as far down as the Titanic."

"Get home soon. You've got me hard. I've got that damn magazine with the pictures Leroy took of you. When you get home, that magazine will be smeared."

"I'm flattered. Sleep well, my pet. Daddy's coming back a rich man and with presents for his little blond baby with blue eyes and the rosy lips and the gorgeous skin and the most beautiful belly—ideal for licking—and the world's most beautiful penis and the most delicious balls God ever put on a man."

"Stop, stop," Robert said, gasping for breath.

"You've already cummed?"

"You got that right. But it's not like the real thing."

"Real thing will be home soon. I love you, my darling husband. I will treasure you always."

"I love you too, big guy."

Putting down the phone, Buck rushed to the shower. After the hot, dusty drive through arid wasteland, he wanted to smell fresh and clean before rushing off to join Rose and Shelley at their temporary mansion.

He hoped Rose would be preoccupied with her family tonight. He wanted Shelley just for himself.

After dressing and going out into the night air, he noticed that it was a particularly beautiful moonlit evening. He found himself driving among the old mansions and magnolia trees in a residential section of Durant.

He felt dreadfully, desperately alone until he remembered the boy waiting to take him in his arms, to love him, to chase away the demons. At least for the night.

*****

Gene stood nude on Leroy's terrace overlooking the city. He stared vacantly at the city lights. Lost and alone, he didn't want to be here. He really wanted to be with Jill and Sandy tonight in the other condo.

Leroy's tongue had been insatiable, wanting to taste every inch of his body. There had been nothing left undiscovered before he'd finally had his fill and had fallen to sleep. But sleep hadn't come to Gene. His demons were marching tonight.

He wondered where Buck was and what he was doing. He needed to sit down and really talk things over with his old buddy. Rich and powerful, Buck might help him. He knew his days were limited as Barry's security guard. He had to come up with something better, and he couldn't see himself running off with Leroy to California. That wouldn't work out. After a few months, he'd be discarded for some younger, more cooperative trick. After all, there were a lot of men in California with great bodies and big dicks. He was certain Leroy wouldn't waste time finding the meat he liked to devour. Gene wanted to do something to help Jill and Sandy. He feared if anything happened to them, they might be forced back onto the street. They weren't educated and trained for any job. If only he could accumulate enough money to send them back to school. Both had been drop-outs, and he feared each of them faced a bleak future if something wasn't done now. But what? He was all out of answers in the early morning air.

Suddenly, cold hands were reaching from behind, fondling his chest and pinching his nipples before dropping below to feel and squeeze. "It's still there," he said to Leroy.

"And such an ample load," Leroy said, releasing him. "I woke up and reached for you wanting to taste you again. But you were gone. I was afraid you'd left the apartment."

"As you can see I'm still here," Gene said rather non-committally, wishing Leroy would go back to bed.

"Come back into the living room," Leroy said. "We don't have anything on. Do you want some juice?"

"I'm fine," Gene said. He went into the bathroom, with all those nude pictures of himself plastered about, and grabbed a towel, covering part of his body.

Emerging from the kitchen with a juice in hand, Leroy preferred to remain nude. "Gotten modest all of a sudden?"

"I figured you've had enough for one night."

"I'll never get enough of a stud like you."

"Enough for the sex. I've got other things on my mind."

"Like running off to California with me?"

"That and other things."

"What other things?" Leroy demanded to know.

"What's to happen to Jill and Sandy if I go with you? They've got nothing. No money. No jobs. They're only allowed in that condo because of you."

"You're not their daddy. Why worry?"

"I'm enjoying playing daddy to them. It's important to me. You've got your fantasies about me. I've got my fantasies about them. Sandy even ran into my burning house to save me, thinking I was trapped inside. I owe them something. If there is something I could do to get them started in life, I want to do it. Don't you understand?"

"Of course, I understand," Leroy said a little impatiently. "Okay, if it's important to you I could come up with something. It wouldn't be much but it would be a start. A friend of mine, a real queen, runs a hotel training school. When some young boys—or female hookers for that matter—are getting a little too long in the tooth, they've gone to his school. Some of them—the smart ones—go on to bigger things. A handful of them become hotel managers over the years. Sandy's a smart boy but he has no training. He could get it there. I don't know about this Jill or what she's like."

"Would it cost a lot of money?"

"I could get Perry—that's the manager of the school—to train them for practically nothing. He'd do it as a favor to me. That girl owes me plenty. Frankly, I don't give a damn about Jill and Sandy but I'd do this for you." He glanced at the towel covering Gene's midriff. "One small thing I could do to pay you back for the big thing you do for me."

"Please do something tomorrow. You promise?"

"If you'll come back to bed with me right now, I'll promise anything."

"You'd been good to me and I know you'll keep your word."

"If they're interested I could have them enrolled this week."

"That's great! Will they be surprised in the morning. It's about time all of us had some good news."

Still nude but aroused, Leroy got up from the sofa and headed over to Gene, reaching and removing the towel. He reached for Gene's balls and seemed to weigh them in his hand. "Now that you're my husband, I want to share some shit with you tomorrow. Maybe it'll convince you that we both should get out of town."

"What about now?" Gene said getting up and following Leroy into his bedroom.

"Not now," Leroy said, somewhat petulantly. "I don't want to mess up my mind with it now. I've got other plans. Tomorrow will be fine. Every day I remain in Okeechobee, I grow more nervous."

*****

In her borrowed mansion in Durant, Rose was throwing a black tie event for family, friends, and "admirers." Not being informed of this, Buck arrived in a white T-shirt and blue jeans. There was no live band—only Anita Bryant records blasting over a loudspeaker. In the main foyer, Buck felt lost in a sea of polyester. The curling irons had been busy, and entire vats of mousse had been used. A few wet slippery palms shaking hands made his own hands feel clammy. Every person he met glanced at his inappropriate dress but made no comment other than, "Welcome to the party."

Even though it was getting late, little girls with cascades of chiffon and ribbons apparently had been allowed to stay up late. To Buck, this hardly looked like a wake—more a wedding reception but then he'd never been to Oklahoma before.

One liver-spotted hand reached for him, taking him by the arm. A gaunt woman in her 80s wearing a red wig stood before him. "I'm Rose's Aunt Bice, and I bet I'm the only one at the party who knows who you are. Love your outfit."

"I wasn't told," he said defensively.

"Fancy dress is only for the middle class," she said, leading him into the garden. "Multi-millionaires can show up at a ball in their ten-day old fishing clothes, smelling like rotten shark, and they'll be perfectly welcome. Here in Oklahoma we love people with money, and we don't give a damn what they wear. Just so long as they leave some of that money behind before they depart."

"Aunt Bice, you are a woman after my heart."

She giggled and rubbed up against him. "If only I was seventy or a hundred years younger. One night with me back then and you'd be the straightest man in America."

He looked at her and arched a brow. "What makes you think I'm not?"

"Shelley tells me everything," she said smiling, rubbing her hand gently across Buck's cheek. "I'm the only confidante he has in the world. What men do—especially those five husbands I was married to—never surprises me."

"He's told you everything? I'm flabbergasted."

"Don't be. I'm so happy for him. It's time he settled down with one man. That that man happens to be the sexiest man alive—yes, I read magazines—and also a multi-millionaire isn't bad. Did I also mention the handsomest man I've ever feasted my eyes on, and I've seen some living dolls in my day."

"This is a bit amazing," he said, looking away from her into the party which he could see in full bloom through the open windows. A sudden wind blew through the garden. He wondered where Rose was.

"He also confided in me that there are many horses that wouldn't come off well when compared to you. That lucky, lucky boy."

He glanced at her in complete bewilderment. "He told you that?"

"He tells me everything. One of my husbands had seven and a half inches. He won the prize. One of the bastards I married didn't even measure up to four and a half."

"I'm so sorry they disappointed you," he said, feeling more than embarrassed.

"Don't cry for me," she said, brushing her hand across his cheek again. "I found plenty of cowboys on the side. The only thing I got from my rotten husbands with their tiny dicks was money."

"Maybe that was enough." He glanced apprehensively around the garden. "Why did you take me here?" He noted that several clusters of people, completely intoxicated, were heading for their cars.

"Rose is completely tied up tonight," Aunt Bice said. "She told me to take care of you and that she'd see you in the morning. She didn't think it appropriate that you two be photographed together. She's told people you're here as a journalist, covering her trip. After all, she's big news in Okeechobee where I hear you own a newspaper."

"Owned is the better word."

"Whatever." She waved the night air with mauve gloves. "I've arranged for you to share a suite with Shelley at the back of the house on the fourth floor. It's very, very private. No one will disturb you there and you can pound it to that boy all night. No one will hear. From the looks of you, he'll probably be screaming with joy."

"Aunt Bice, you amaze me. In the state of Oklahoma, land of Anita Bryant, I had no idea I'd meet such permissiveness."

"Oh, darling, we're not all Oakies here," she said. "Anita doesn't speak for all of us. Someone must have spiked that pussy's orange juice. Hell, I love gay men more than the boring straight assholes I encounter here. I'm known as the fag hag of Durant."

"I see," he said, slightly flustered.

"Gay men and I have one thing in common and one thing we always love to talk about."

"Pray tell, what's that?"

"Big dicks."

For him, this conversation was getting out of hand. He rested his hand gently on her arm and kissed both sides of her cheek. "Thanks for setting me up tonight with my boy."

"Do you love him? I mean, not just for the sex which I know must be terrific. But do you really care about him as a person?"

"I really do. I've never really loved anyone before. This is all very new to me. I'm really mixed up. Having all this media glare blasting at us from every direction only complicates matters."

She kissed his cheek, then ran her hand gently across it. "Forgive me for rubbing your cheek so much tonight. But I feel the stubble of a beard and I find that very exciting."

"Feel free."

"If only I was younger."

"You said that. But it wouldn't matter anyway. My heart belongs only to Shelley. I'm in love."

"I'm so happy for you."

Thunderous applause came from the main parlor. Apparently, Rose was going to sing. As her not bad voice drifted out, he listened briefly to her words, "From this valley they say you are leaving..."

"She knows how to pick her material," he said to Aunt Bice. He looked apprehensively around the garden. "Where's my boy?" he asked.

"He said he'll meet us out here in private. Any minute now. He's one beautiful boy. In the old days we used to say, 'He's too pretty to be a boy.' I never subscribed to that. The more beautiful men are, as in your case, the more I like it. Every time I go into a restaurant and a waiter asks me how I like my coffee, I always tell 'em, 'White and sweet, just like I like my men.'"

He laughed but the sound got lodged in his throat at the sudden appearance of Shelley who rushed into his arms and kissed him on the lips in front of Aunt Bice who only giggled and turned away.

"Step back and let me have a look," Buck said, "I've never seen you dressed up before."

Like a model, Shelley stepped back in the garden. The bottom button of his dinner jacket had lazily plopped open. Everything about him seemed perfection itself. High-waisted, his black trousers only accented his long, slender legs and promising crotch. Buck planned to spend a good part of what was left of the evening licking and kissing those thighs. He'd never gotten enough of them. He didn't think if he lived to be a hundred, he'd get enough of those thighs. He pulled Shelley to him and kissed him hard on the mouth, reaching inside his dinner jacket and running his fingers up his back.

Aunt Bice giggled again. "Before the funeral in the morning, I want you boys to come over for one of my famous Durant country breakfasts. You will probably expend a lot of energy tonight and will need proper fortification before going back to Dallas."

"Thanks, we'll be there," Buck said, looking at Shelley for agreement.

"I'll call you first thing in the morning," Shelley promised, kissing her on both cheeks.

Buck followed the example, kissing her on both cheeks before turning his attention to Shelley. He noticed that his black bow tie was crooked and was tempted for a moment to adjust it. Then he decided he didn't want to change a thing about Shelley.

Before fluttering away into the night, Aunt Bice turned to Buck and took his hand. "Shelley is gonna be pissed at me for blabbing, but I have to tell you something."

"Don't you dare," Shelley cautioned her.

"Hell with that. He'll find out sooner than later, and he's got to know. It's for his own best interest."

"Okay, go ahead," Shelley said, sounding defeated. "He's got to know."

"What is it?" Buck said, growing alarmed.

"Shelley lied to you about his age," she said. Buck looked to Shelley for confirmation. "You mean, he's not eighteen?"

"No," she said. "He's sixteen going on forty."

Buck felt a deep thud hit his heart. "Jail bait!"

"I'm sorry I lied but I thought you wouldn't go to bed with me if you thought I was sixteen."

"Good night, Aunt Bice," Buck said. "Shelley and I will talk about this privately. See you at breakfast."

"Good night, my darling boys." She waved her mauve gloves in the night air, again disappearing behind a gardenia bush. "Young love, young love," she called out to no one in particular, perhaps recalling a distant memory.

Buck turned to Shelley. He looked playful and mischievous, not remorseful at all. "You're not going to spank me, are you? For being bad. For lying."

"That's exactly what I'm going to do. I'm going to spank you—real hard—then I'm going to fuck that sixteen-year-old ass of yours like it's never been fucked before."

Shelley melted into his body. "I love you."

"I love you too. It's too late for me to stop now. Fuck, even if you were twelve, I've hopelessly fallen for you and I don't plan to sit around and wait for you to become legal."

Shelley gave him several light feathery kisses on the lips which sent erotic chills up Buck's spine. "Look at the bright side," Shelley said.

"What bright side?" Buck asked.

"Men reach their sexual peak at nineteen. That means you've got three more years to enjoy me before I peak. Then when I turn nineteen, you're going to get it, big boy."

*****

At last he was alone with Shelley. He'd waited too long since the plane. No sooner was the door shut than Buck was nibbling and licking Shelley's neck, concentrating specifically on his adam's apple which he found delectable. He gently bit the boy's chin before moving on to bathe his ears. When he'd had his fill, he inserted his tongue into the boy's mouth, an action that produced a raging hard-on in his jeans which were far too tight.

Fortunately, Shelley's slender fingers were working hard to free the long, thick tube of flesh. The boy's breathing was growing increasingly ragged. Just touching Shelley sent electric thrills through Buck's body. He could tell he gave those same thrills to Shelley, who appeared breathless, as he completely surrendered his body to Buck.

Removing his tongue from the boy's mouth, Buck resumed the licking of an earlobe which tasted very sweet to him. Buck reached inside Shelley's jacket and felt hard, firm, but not overly developed muscles. His hand traveled down to the boy's flat, hard stomach. "I want to spend decades polishing that stomach with my tongue."

"Oooo," was all the boy could say. He appeared completely mesmerized by Buck. "God, you're big." he said, massaging Buck's cock.

"I'll be gentle," he whispered in Shelley's ear. He slipped the dinner jacket from Shelley's shoulders.

Soon their clothes were dropped casually on the floor. Buck unsnapped Shelley's suspenders, massaging his arms and shoulders. When he had Shelley's chest bare, he polished that sculpted chest with his tongue, settling finally for his nipples, sucking each one into his mouth before biting down gently. Shelley was moaning.

Recovering, he ripped Buck's T-shirt off, his fingers traveling to Buck's navel before unzipping his jeans. At last Buck was freed. But he wanted to be completely nude and wanted Shelley completely nude too. Very slowly and gently they removed their pants and shoes. When he took off Shelley's socks, he nibbled and sucked his toes which made the boy squirm.

On the bed Shelley lunged for Buck's cock. Buck tousled Shelley's hair, encouraging him to gorge deeper. He always found it amazing how Shelley could open up and swallow him. It was exquisite torture for Buck, and he didn't think he could stand this fiendish sucking much longer. He had other plans for the boy. Grabbing Shelley's hair in his fist, he pulled him off his cock which was about to explode. He threw Shelley's legs up in the air. They settled finally on his firm, broad shoulders.

With Shelley's arms and legs thrashing, Buck descended on him, tasting his inner thighs before sucking each ball into his mouth for a good, long feed. He then descended and swallowed every inch of Shelley's cock, biting at the boy's pubic hair. Shelley screamed but it was a scream of joy. Reluctantly pulling himself away, Buck had another target, as his tongue traveled on its short journey to the puckered rosebud where it descended to attack and devour. Shelley's writhing little butt was at times hard to hold onto but Buck never let up. He had no intention of allowing this luscious body to go until he had his appetite completely satisfied. He was breathing hard as he sucked tender, young flesh.

Rearing up, he placed himself at the secret doorway to Shelley's body and slowly entered as the boy screamed, digging his nails into Buck's back. When he'd fully entered the tight cavity, he fell on Shelley, feeding the boy his tongue. At the first pumping of his guts, Shelley exploded. Buck reached between their bodies, grabbing some of the precious juice which he returned to his lips to taste and savor before Shelley licked him clean. His tongue was down the boy's throat, as wild sensations raged through his body. He was going to make this last.

It was going to be a long and joyous ride, and he had every intention of fucking a second orgasm out of the boy before he exploded deep within him. He felt in total control and possession of Shelley. Fortunately, he'd left the light on so he could every now and then raise up from Shelley's devouring mouth and look deeply into his beautiful, clear blue eyes. There was such trust, love, and devotion here that Buck pumped harder, moving to give the boy what Buck hoped was the greatest pleasure he'd ever known.

Shelley's face now tasted of sweat, but it was sweet and Buck kept every inch of that face licked clean. When Shelley's second explosion came, it seemed more violent than the first. Shelley moaned and gently encased Buck's balls with his delicate fingers. That did it. Buck could no longer hold back. He erupted inside Shelley, shaking with pleasure as he pumped the boy a few more times, wanting him to have the final juice. He seemed to rock Shelley back and forth in a gentle, exotic rhythm. He raised up and looked deeply into Shelley's eyes again. His primal hunger had been gratified and now a tender, loving side of him asserted itself. He was reluctant to withdraw from the boy. He kissed him instead, lovely, deep kisses that were more like caresses. He could afford to be gentle now, to love and give of himself.

"You are fabulous," Shelley whispered in his ear, his hands massaging Buck's back until he reached his buttocks.

"I've found my dreamboy."

"I want you to go to sleep in my arms," Shelley said. "But I've not had enough of you yet."

"Wha...you want me to fuck you again?" The very suggestion caused him to harden deep inside the boy.

"That would be wonderful too but I want something else."

"Anything is yours."

"Just lie back on the bed. With my lips and pretty little sixteen-year-old tongue, I want to bathe every inch of your body, leaving no crevice unexplored."

Buck gently withdrew from the boy and fell over on his back. As Shelley's lips and tongue moved to his inner thighs, Buck reached and hugged the pillow in ecstasy. "I've died and gone to heaven."

*****

By the time Shelley and Buck came downstairs the following morning, a member of the household told them that Rose had been called away for an urgent meeting and wouldn't be able to talk to either of them until after the funeral. Her entire party—minus Buck and Shelley—was slated to return to Dallas where everyone would link up for the flight to Palm Springs.

In the garage, Shelley directed Buck to the Zaftig Stutz Blackhawk IV limousine. "It's a gift," he said, beaming.

"A gift from whom?" Buck asked, admiring the vehicle, the same one he'd seen on television.

"You don't understand," Shelley said. "It's yours. Rose and I are presenting it to you. After we drive it to Dallas, it's going to be flown to Okeechobee. For your personal use."

"This is fabulous, but overwhelming," Buck said. "I don't know what to say."

"Say nothing—just hop in the back seat with me and we'll be driven to Aunt Bice's house for breakfast. After all that energy expended last night, I'm hungry."

Buck noticed a dark, shadowy figure behind the wheel of the limousine, waiting for them to get in. As they came to the rear of the car, the tall, gaunt driver, who looked Indian, got up and opened the door for them. Shelley piled in first. Buck followed but not without taking stock of Shelley's shapely buttocks that he had come to know so well.

"This car is just incredible," Buck said, feeling the maroon leather upholstery. "I'm so grateful but I don't think I can accept. I've already accepted the jet."

"Take it and don't worry about it," Shelley said nonchalantly. "After all, Rose and I didn't actually pay for it. Besides, we're getting one slightly bigger. Rose didn't like this one that much. She wants more special features and also wants the limo ingrained with the rose motif. Not that she's conceited or anything."

"Nothing like that." Shelley and most definitely Rose continued to amaze Buck. He didn't have a clue as to what they were about. As for Rose, he felt she reinvented herself every day. So how could he possibly keep up?

Over cheese grits and country-fried ham, Aunt Bice in her decaying mansion enthralled Buck and Shelley with stories of her heyday as a femme fatale in Durant. "If a man was rich, I married him," she said, "regardless of what he looked like. I figured if I accumulated enough money, I could buy all the pretty men I wanted."

"And you've had your share of beauties," Shelley said. He leaned over and rubbed delicate fingers along Buck's arm. "But none as beautiful as what I've nabbed. The sexiest man in America."

"You've got that right," Aunt Bice said. "I had a wet dream about Buck last night."

"Cut the shit," Shelley said. "You don't have wet dreams any more." He turned to Buck. "Do women have wet dreams?"

Buck put down his fork. The ham tasted too salty anyway. "What women have or don't have is becoming less important to me by the day." He reached over and ran his fingers delicately across Shelley's smooth cheek. "I've got other things on my mind."

"I can just imagine what that is," Aunt Bice said, digging into her grits with a gusto, but only after peppering them generously. "We've got to hurry up with this breakfast or we'll be late for the funeral."

"The funeral," Buck said. "I'd temporarily forgotten all about it. These last few hours could make a man forget he was attending a wake."

"I can explain that," Aunt Bice said. "The Phillips family views death as a celebration. No drab mourning. The passage into a more glorious life."

Since Buck didn't want to pursue that, he made noises about finishing his coffee, thanking his hostess for breakfast, and excusing himself for one quick visit to the bathroom before departing in his newly acquired Zaftig Stutz Blackhawk IV. Unlike last night, he was appropriately dressed in a black suit and white shirt, as was Shelley. He didn't even know Shelley owned a black suit until now.

The new limousine made it to the First Baptist Church of Durant on time. On the grassy lawn, Buck met the Phillips clan who'd gathered to bury their reigning matriarch. Not only relatives, but family friends and the idle curious who'd assembled here.

The great aunt to both Rose and Hazel, Martha had died at the age of one hundred and one. Born in western Oklahoma, she'd lived longer than all three of the younger men she'd married and buried. Right after World War I, she'd run for governor of the state of Oklahoma and had almost won. Buck sensed how important a role model Martha must have been for both Rose and Hazel, encouraging them to seek political power. At least the determined pioneer's longevity must give Rose hope for a long life.

For some reason, Hazel didn't mingle with her relatives, although she came over and kissed Buck demurely on the cheek. Shelley turned from the sight of her, not saying a word. Rose had taught him well.

Hazel's picture hat appeared too wide and her sloppy dress of flowery prints seemed ill-chosen in the somberly dressed crowd. She seemed to be viewed with suspicion by most of the relatives who wanted no part of her. Their loyalty was firmly behind Rose. One uncle had frankly admitted to Buck, "Hazel has just plain sold out." When Buck had pressed him for an explanation, the old man had turned his back to Buck and walked off.

Along with the rest of the congregation, Buck filed past the casket where Martha rested in state. To the right of the casket he noticed a massive bouquet of white roses, a gift obviously from Sister Rose herself. In her ornate, pink-satin coffin, Martha in spite of an overlay of garish makeup, revealed in death a stoic and puritanical face, with amazingly well-preserved skin for a woman who'd seen more than a century of life.

Back on the church lawn, Buck lost himself in the crowd that had gathered to watch the arrival of Rose. Shelley had deliberately distanced himself from Buck for appearance's sake and mingled and talked openly and with great charm and style among the Phillips clan.

"We're mighty proud of that boy," Aunt Bice said. "When he grows up, he'll be more famous than Billy Graham."

Before Buck could wrap his mind around such a thought, a white limousine pulled up at the entrance of the church. An Oklahoma state highway patrolman rushed to open the door. Slowly, Rose—dressed entirely in white, including a thin white veil—emerged. She was held up by the arms of two of her bodyguards. Behind her creamy veil, she appeared grief stricken, although Buck couldn't make out her features too clearly. As she was directed toward the steps of the church, her legs seemed to buckle until the strong-armed men braced her up. All of this action, pretense or otherwise, was captured by news photographers.

Once inside the church, Rose was seated on a wooden bench down front as the funeral services began. Buck was separated from Shelley by six members of the Phillips clan. Aunt Bice had chosen to sit next to Buck, holding his hand. Buck searched for Hazel's face in the crowd but she must have been assigned a rear bench. She certainly wasn't in the pews reserved for the Phillips family. Actually, Buck himself felt awkward sitting here.

At the finish of the sermon and the sound of a piano, he knew that Rose was going to sing. She was famous for singing at funerals, her voice having laid to rest many well-known statesmen. Before her appreciative audience, she'd recovered from her earlier grief.

"Oh, sweet Jesus!" she cried out when she'd assumed her familiar command of the pulpit. "Aunt Martha is with the Lord." Sounds of "Amen" greeted her, giving her the encouragement to go on. "Aunt Martha isn't here today to help me carry on my crusade, but her spirit is with me, guiding me every step of the way. Her voice soothed the congregation with "Peace in the Valley," an ironic selection. Her soft, melodious sound drifted through the raised church windows, across the graveyard and into the woods beyond.

At the gravesite, she stationed herself near the pastor. Buck stood at a discreet distance away. Hazel appeared, standing directly opposite Rose, the recently dug grave between them. It was the first time the two sisters had encountered each other since their split in the early sixties.

At first, Rose seemed unaware of her. Then Rose's white veil swirled in the breeze, revealing the disdain, the contempt on her face. A blazing anger seemed to come from Rose. The coffin was lowered into the grave to the sounds of a chorus singing "Nearer My God to Thee." The wind carried the pastor's words, "Ashes to ashes and dust to dust." Hazel dabbed at her eyes with her handkerchief.

Rose's face remained immobile, as if frozen in marble. No longer concerned with the burial, she seemed to view Hazel's presence here as an act of defiance, an intrusion upon her intimate terrain.

Then, at the approach of a news photographer, Rose's face underwent an amazing transformation, losing its stone-faced look and becoming a study in human tragedy.

As earth was thrown on Aunt Martha's coffin, the photographer managed to capture a moment for release to the wire services. The picture that would make tomorrow's front pages was of Rose's collapse at the gravesite.

*****

After the burial of Aunt Martha, Rose sent word to Buck to meet her in the pastor's private office in a wing attached to the clapboard-framed white church.

On his way to it, he ran into Hazel, her dress soaked, her makeup running. "I cried when I saw Aunt Martha lowered into her grave. Funny thing, all I could remember was the time she made Rose and me strip bareass and switched our fannies red."

The image was hard for him to visualize. "How are you getting back to Florida?"

"I'll fly but first I'm taking three days off to stay in Durant." She looked wistfully at Martha's grave. "There are a lot of memories for me here—most of them bad. But I need a little time to reflect before going back to face that mayor's race which could get ugly."

"Where will you stay?"

"Believe it or not, Aunt Bice agreed to let me stay with her. She always treated Rose and me fairly and equally—not like the rest of the family."

Buck shuddered to think that Aunt Bice would tell Hazel the real truth about Shelley and him, but then decided she wouldn't do that. He kissed her perspiring, flabby cheek and headed in rapid strides to the preacher's office. He looked over his shoulder. "See you in Okeechobee. We'll be older, wiser then."

Alone in the office with him, Rose had recovered from her collapse at the gravesite, a photographic remembrance now on its way to the developing lab where it, in turn, would be transmitted over the wire services.

"I saw you out the window," she said, using for the first time her harshest voice on him. "Kissing Hazel. Such a cozy scene."

He nodded as he unbuttoned his collar, loosened his tie, and took off his jacket. "If I kiss one sister, I guess it's only fitting and proper to kiss the other." He walked over to her, leaned down and kissed her on the cheek, as he had Hazel. She took his face in her hands holding it firmly as she planted a long, wet, lingering kiss on his lips, with short tongue lashings against his teeth. The kiss seemed to make her less stiff as her face relaxed.

"I apologize for neglecting you so much." She smiled sardonically. "I'm sure Shelley kept you amused."

"Shelley always keeps me amused. So did Aunt Bice. I like her a lot."

"Aunt Bice was always a whore, but I like her too. She's been nice to Shelley whereas a lot of the Phillips clan has had a hard time accepting Shelley. The boy is not their idea of what a clean, God-fearing American youth should look like, act like, and talk like."

"Aunt Bice told me he was only sixteen years old."

"If that. He might be fifteen."

"Fifteen for God's sake. Fifteen fucking years old."

"We're not sure of his age. He was an abandoned child." We could only guess at his age. Certainly he's no more than sixteen."

"That scares me."

"Don't worry about it," she said. "No harm will come of it. You are hardly corrupting Shelley. Do you want to hear what I once caught him doing at the age of nine—or even younger?"

"I think I'll take a raincheck on that one. Just dealing with the fact he might be fifteen is enough for me for one day." He tilted his head back, arching his chin. "Let's worry about Shelley's age some other time. Right now I'm more concerned about you. Something's going on. I know you won't or can't tell me everything, but you seem very busy, conducting a lot of negotiations."

"It's Calder. He and I are involved in a big power struggle. I'm trying to break free of him. He's trying to become my super boss. He wants to totally dominate me. To be frank, you are my secret weapon. You're the face I want to put on my future. Calder belongs to some dark, murky past. Intimidation, blackmail, dirty tricks, beatings, and I suspect even deaths, although I don't want to be informed of that."

"You think time has run out on tactics like that?"

"I certainly do. When I signed on, I didn't want to be a party to such things. It's not my style. There is just so far I can be pushed. I've not quite the demon my enemies think I am."

"I'm glad to hear that, because I don't want to be involved in any of Calder's shit. I can't stand him or his methods."

"I hooked up with him because I was desperate. But I've long outgrown him." She reached over and kissed Buck gently on the lips. "You're the type of man I need for the eighties—not asshole Calder."

Quite out of breath in the stuffy room, he stared at her without saying anything at first. He looked absently about the cramped room.

When he turned to face her again, he noticed how moist her eyes were, as if on the verge of tears. "Am I in some sort of danger?"

"Perhaps," she said enigmatically. "As far as Calder is concerned, I think all of us are in some sort of danger. I think he's losing his power in our organization. We'll know a lot more when we get to Palm Springs. I'm rising and Calder is falling. He doesn't take defeat easily."

"I've got to ask this. It's about Shelley and you've got to tell me. What threat is Calder to Shelley?"

"An enormous threat."

"How so?"

"He wants us to dump Shelley now that he's getting older. Drum him out completely—that is, let him make no more personal appearances. Shelley's sweet, cherubic look has come to an end. He's growing up. He can't be a little boy forever. Already he's leading a totally adult life. You know that better than anyone."

"Okay, so Shelley's retired. I'm sure he doesn't want to be a preacher anyway. In those God damn rose-colored suits. He hates that. That's not our Shelley."

"It's more than that. Ever since he was a child, Shelley's been a naughty boy. Far more sophisticated than any boy his age I've ever known. He's been rebellious and has gotten in endless trouble."

"What kind of trouble?"

"Men mostly. Drugs too, but he's off drugs now. That's why I've virtually thrown his ass to you to fuck. At least with you it would be discreet. With the others, it wasn't always so discreet. There have been many witnesses. Calder's paid them off. I've assured Calder that Shelley's recklessness is a thing of the past, but Calder doesn't believe me. Another scandal has developed—a major one."

"Will you let me in on it?"

"There are pictures."

"What pictures are you talking about?"

"Pictures of Shelley and Barry secretly taken by some faggot photographer in Okeechobee. Leroy Fitzgerald."

"I know him. We went to the university together."

"Fitzgerald was hired to take pictures of Barry. Calder ordered them secretly. Calder needed blackmail evidence to hold over Barry's head until the end of his days, especially if Barry goes on to high political office. Fitzgerald was supposed to turn over all the negatives and prints to Calder. He didn't. Now he's demanding big money. It seems Fitzgerald has fallen in a big way for some stud in Okeechobee. He wants to live the grand life, and his demands are outrageous. But if

Calder doesn't give in to them, Fitzgerald will release everything. It'll be the end of Barry's career in politics. Since Shelley's involved, it might be the end of my charismatic organization. The fallout will be enormous."

"Oh, shit!"

"Oh, shit, is right." She reached for his arm, her fingers tightening in her desperation. "Would you believe that is only one problem facing me? I've got a thousand others, and most of them are equally horrible if not more horrible."

Stunned at this news and not knowing how to react, he turned to the window. It overlooked the graveyard. The gravediggers shoveled the final scoops of earth onto Aunt Martha's coffin. Two teen-age boys made off with Rose's gift of white, long-stemmed roses.

"Please, get Shelley on that plane in Dallas," she said coming up behind him. "Keep the little fucker out of trouble."

"Is that what my job is going to be? A baby-sitter for Shelley? The world's most expensive baby-sitter, I might add considering what I'll get paid."

"Call it what you like. Shelley must stay out of trouble from this day forth. The thing with Barry is not resolved. Calder's method for dealing with this Fitzgerald is not my method. I want no part of it. But there's no way in hell those pictures can surface. It'll be the end of us."

Brows lifted, he swung around to look at her. Her face glittered—her eyes, her teeth radiant. Then her lips turned into a grimace. "The future of my organization is in jeopardy. My whole life is in jeopardy. Also, I've signed up for some dirty duties I don't really have the heart for."

"You mean, this Arab thing?"

"Exactly. I'm not into crap like that. I'm controversial enough. I don't need more controversy."

"Then why for God's sake did you involve yourself this way?"

"It was greed. Sheer greed. You don't know how poor poor can be. You were always rich. You don't know what it means to sell your own body for money."

"I'm sure I don't," he said, wondering if that was not, in fact, what he was doing with her. A sudden chill went over him. He feared for Shelley. As he now suspected, Rose did not have enough power to protect Shelley if Calder planned to cause him harm. Shelley was Rose's soft underbelly.

"Tonight I'm going to introduce you to a very important man," she said. "He controls everything. I want you to do everything you can to destroy Calder in this man's eyes. Would you promise me that?"

"Of course, I will. Calder has made himself my enemy number one." He balled his fists. "If he so much as lays a hand on Shelley, I'll kill him."

"The trouble with killing Calder is he might kill you first."

"He wouldn't dare."

"There is nothing so vile as Calder Martin."

Closing his eyes, he ran his fingers over his forehead. A major headache was coming on. Day by day he was entrapping himself in something he didn't know anything about. Nothing had been explained to him, not really, not satisfactorily.

He started to say something, but was interrupted by the appearance of the pastor who stood awkwardly in the doorway, his white hat in one hand, a white Bible engraved with a red rose in the other. "Excuse me, Sister Rose," he said, casting a suspicious eye at Buck.

"I was just leaving," Buck said.

"You can stay," Rose ordered.

"It's rather personal," the pastor said, but went on anyway. "It's about our church. We're nearly bankrupt and I haven't been paid in two months. Contributions are down to nothing. With all your money, I was hoping you could see your way clear to a big contribution so we can continue to do God's work."

"We'll talk about it," she said, rather curtly to him.

He turned to her and said, "I'm so very sorry about Aunt Martha's death. I would like to have known her."

"Thanks," she said. Then addressing Buck, and pretending a formality she didn't feel, she said, "Now you write something nice about us. Don't you go making us look like some redneck Oakies always bleeding the faithful for money."

"I won't," he said with a wave good-bye. He gave the pastor with his beet-red complexion a nod in departing.

In the graveled parking lot, he walked toward his newly acquired limousine, knowing Shelley would be waiting in the back seat. He looked around briefly for Aunt Bice but realized she must have departed with Hazel.

The rest of the Phillips clan was breaking up. Amid final, bittersweet waving and empty promises to get together, they drove off in opposite directions.

Chapter Eleven

She wasn't in love, but was having a marvelous time. Don Bossdum had liberated her sexually as no man ever had. After last night she was convinced that when he went to bed with a woman, he did not merely seduce her, he devoured her. Susan had never been so fulfilled sexually in her life. Hustler or not, Don was the man to put his shoes under her bed any night.

In the pool at the condo, she loved swimming as many laps as she could. She wanted to keep in tiptop shape for her loving man. Maybe money had to be exchanged, but she didn't care. It wasn't her money any way. How could Sister Rose and Shelley have kicked him out? Of course, she understood, if given the choice, you'd go for Buck. He was beautiful, richly endowed, and had all the money in Florida, or soon would. Don was a mere hustler but worth every penny.

It was hard to admit this truth to herself, but she loved being in charge of a relationship for the first time in her life. With other men, especially Gene and Buck, she had been at their beck and call. Would they or would they not ask her out? Often they wouldn't. With Don it was completely different. She made the plans for the evening, she decided when she wanted to go home, she picked the restaurant—after all, she was paying for the meal—and, yes, she even decided when it was time to mount her or do whatever.

With Don the actual penetration was the culmination of a long series of sexual foreplay that included the most divine tongue probes a woman could ever expect to receive from a man. He obviously was no virgin. This was an experienced man she was getting, no little schoolboy out on his first date. Don seemed to love women so—he virtually worshipped her, or at least pretended to—that it was hard for her to imagine his being with a man. But she had overheard that conversation with Shelley.

Maybe Shelley was his only time with a boy, but she doubted that. She suspected there had been many men in Don's life even though his basic attraction was to women. Of that, she was certain. If she could conjure up such a possibility, she felt that when Don was with men he was rough trade. The men serviced him. When Don was with women—and on this she could judge by experience—he did the servicing, at least until she made him stop so she could make love to his divine and beautifully sculpted body.

During her marriage to Gene and with all her subsequent boy friends, it never occurred to her that she'd ever part a man's buttocks and go on a tongue probe. But with Don she not only had done that, but had enjoyed the taste and sensation of it. At first she was turned on by the excitement she was causing in him, having him moaning and groaning and totally under her power. After a few minutes when she'd found she was still at the target, she realized she was enjoying it. A new sexual frontier for her. From now on, Don was going to get this sort of sexual assault from her. She knew she'd meet no resistance from him. If anything, it had turned him on so much she felt it would become part of their vast sexual repertoire with each other.

Gasping at her final lap, she pulled herself from the pool and reached for a towel. It was eleven o'clock, and she had a luncheon meeting at the home of Uncle Milty, who was going to work out the financial terms of her marriage to Buck. She needed her own money, a budget every thirty days she could depend on. She wanted a complete and total agreement as to what she could expect from Buck. He certainly could afford it. She also had made it clear to Uncle Milty that she was bringing over Don. She wanted a check for him every week. The money he was going to get from Shelley could go into the bank. After all, Don would be old and gray one day and he needed to show some savings for all his work as a hustler when he'd been such a powerful stud. It was only right that he stash some money away today to take care of himself in his old age.

Uncle Milty had assured her that before the luncheon meeting, he would be in touch with Buck. He said he didn't think Buck would object to her arrangement with Don at all. "After all," Uncle Milty had said, "when he married you, he didn't expect you to go to a nunnery. Buck's pretty involved right now. Personally, I think he'll welcome the arrangement."

"You mean take the heat off him?" she'd asked. "Make him feel less guilty?"

"I wouldn't put it that way," Uncle Milty had said. "You know why the marriage had to be this way. I appreciate your cooperation. So does Buck. We're prepared to meet any reasonable demand of yours. Don Bossdum is only a minor consideration."

"There's nothing minor about Don."

"So I have heard," Uncle Milty had told her. "His reputation has preceded him. You are one lucky girl. Gene. Buck. Now Don Bossdum. Don't you ever go to bed with a man with a small dick?"

"You bet your sweet ass I have," she'd said, shocked at how provocative she was becoming. "In fact, with the three exceptions you've named, nearly all the men I've gone to bed with had small dicks."

"That's my affliction too," Uncle Milty had confided. "But Patrick doesn't seem to mind."

"Good. See you at noon." She'd hung up. Toweling herself at the pool, she was amazed at her conversation. She'd never discussed dick sizes with a woman before, much less a man. Of course, Uncle Milty was a notorious queen in Okeechobee, so she guessed it was all right to talk about penis dimensions with a queen. She'd been told that's about all they talked about anyway.

Placing a towel around her wet head, she looked up at the condo tower where Don was still sleeping. He slept very late every morning so he'd be rested for afternoon and night games. She loved the life here. Buck had not stashed her in some dump. The pad was plush with every luxury. She could even call down for a lobster and caviar dinner with champagne if she wanted. She could be driven in a limousine wherever she wanted to go, always with Don tagging along. She didn't trust him out of her sight.

As if breaking through a cloud, the sun seemed to shine even brighter to her, momentarily blinding her. A dreadful thought crossed her mind. Was she but a high-class whore who was so well paid she could afford her own hustler? Her mouth tightened into a grimace. There was a rougher, cruder side of herself asserting itself. Before, she didn't know this side of her existed. She'd have to talk to Ingrid about that. At some point Ingrid would have to know about Don Bossdum. She was certain Ingrid had met Don before so introductions wouldn't be necessary. In fact, she wanted to meet with both Jim and Ingrid. For some reason, it was important to tell them what their daughter had become. She didn't necessarily want their approval. She just wanted them to know.

*****

Only toying with a pink grapefruit, Leroy smiled demurely at Gene as they sat on his terrace having breakfast. For Gene it had been a long night, and he wanted to get back to his own condo to be with Jill and Sandy before he drove over to the Collins house later in the day. If

Barry was going to be away for the day, he might even invite the kids for a swim in the would-be mayor's pool.

"Things are going very good for us," Leroy said as if holding back vital news. "When we fly out of this hell hole for California, we're going to have so much money with us the plane will have a hard time getting airborne."

"What fantasy is this?"

Leroy's face collapsed in disappointment. He obviously didn't like the way Gene was receiving the news. "I'm not bullshitting. This gal has come up with a way to make the big bucks I've always lusted for. Big dicks and big bucks, my two favorite things. I've got two little pricks, Calder Martin and Barry Collins, by the balls, and I'm squeezing hard."

"Better watch it," Gene cautioned, "or you'll get your own balls cut off, especially if you fuck with Calder Martin."

"I can ruin their carefully laid plans tomorrow," Leroy said, a menacing edge creeping into his voice. "I've got evidence that could destroy Barry Collins. He'll get nowhere—certainly not to the White House one day—if I come forth with my evidence. I have pictures of Shelley Phillips and Barry that would put an end to the would-be mayor's career tomorrow. Not to mention what it would do for Sister Rose's charismatic movement. Of course, she's got the Arab money now so she may not need those born-again shitheads."

Gene slammed down his coffee. The heat of the morning was already getting to him. To Gene the evidence against Shelley was quickly mounting.

"Do you want me to get up right now and go in there in the living room and open the safe?"

"I've already seen pictures of Barry. I know what that slimebag does—only too well do I know. But you're mistaken about Sister Rose's son." Actually, he didn't think Leroy was mistaken at all.

"Mistaken? Like hell. Shelley Phillips—other than myself—is the biggest whore in the state of Florida. Of course, Pamela would have to come in there somewhere. If you don't believe it, I could arrange a date for you and Shelley. I'm sure he'd like to get fucked by that dick of yours. He likes really big ones."

Gene swallowed hard. Somehow he had to figure out a way to reach Sister Rose and inform her of this cancer growing on her ministry. Shelley had obviously lied to her and deceived her. Everything she fought for could now be ruined in a scandal involving her own son.

Leroy kept on talking but at first Gene wasn't really listening. This revelation had sent his mind reeling elsewhere.

"Five million dollars."

When Leroy said that, Gene reverted to listening again. "What's that again?" he asked.

"I'm demanding five-million dollars from Calder's boys, or else I'll go public with what I know. They'll have to give in. They're worth millions. They can easily come up with the money. For all I care, they can split it."

"What do you mean?"

"Sister Rose, when she learns the news, might cough up two and a half million, with Barry's backers putting up the rest. That way, it will be less painful for them."

"You would blackmail Sister Rose?"

"Don't put it that way," Leroy said coyly. "Blackmail sounds like such a dirty word."

Tightening his robe around him, Gene rose from the terrace. He'd heard enough.

"Where are you going?" Leroy called after him.

"I've got some business to take care of this morning. I'm going to shower and get out of here today."

Leroy trailed him into the bathroom where Gene removed his robe and stepped under the shower as if that would wash away a lingering sense of dirt and contamination he felt was clinging to his body like some ink he couldn't wash off with mere soap.

"Don't you see?" Leroy said, yelling at him in the shower. "I've got a million and a half right now. On that we could live reasonably well in California. But with that extra five million, we could live like kings or queens, whatever,"

Ending his shower abruptly, Gene reached for a towel and resisted Leroy's attempts to dry him. "I'll do it myself," Gene said, drying his wet body and wrapping the towel around his waist, heading for the bedroom to get dressed.

Leroy trailed him and sat on the bed, seemingly mesmerized as Gene put on his jockey shorts and slipped on a white T-shirt and a pair of tight-fitting jeans. "Let me warn you about something," Gene said. "You fuck with Calder and you'll have an accident. You wouldn't be the first person Calder has wiped out. What about that former friend of yours who died suspiciously? Don't you think that could happen to you, you silly little fart?"

"I've already protected myself. If something happens to me, the evidence goes public. I've made arrangements through my lawyers. Calder Martin wouldn't dare harm me. If he does, he's finished. So is

Barry. And probably Sister Rose, although that pussy is probably tougher than either of the others put together."

Shaking uncontrollably, Gene grabbed Leroy's arm, digging his nails in. "Don't you dare harm her."

"You're hurting me," Leroy said petulantly, pulling away. "What in the fuck do you care about Sister Rose?"

"I believe in her. I respect her."

The sound of Leroy's bitter laughter followed him as Gene headed for the door. "Don't tell me you're one of those born-again Christians?"

Gene stopped and looked back. "I'm not. But I've got my beliefs. I believe there's a God. I believe Sister Rose is an honest, decent woman who's trying to make a lot of wrong things right in this world."

"Yeah, right," Leroy said sarcastically.

An overwhelming anger came across Gene. He wanted to punch Leroy in the mouth but got a grip on himself. "This has all been a little much for me. I need some air to breathe. Okay, guy?"

"Rush out of here if you must but it you want to share in my millions, you'd better get your beautiful ass back here sooner than later. I'll be back at three. I'm going out myself this morning. A little meeting I'm having with Calder. I think he's coming around to my way of thinking."

"I can't get back here by three," Gene said, hoping to shake free of Leroy. "I've got other plans."

Leroy arched an eyebrow. "What say at three o'clock I do something for you? Like tell you who set you up for that latest arrest. Show you some hard, concrete evidence."

At the door Gene paused. "You could find that out?"

"Indeed, I can. What I could never understand is why anyone would want to harm you. I'm sure you're nothing to the powers in this town. But somebody out there wants you out of Okeechobee. You're an embarrassment to somebody. This someone is big and powerful, and I think I know who it is."

"What possible harm could I be to someone big and powerful? It doesn't make sense. It didn't make sense the day I was arrested, and it makes very little sense now."

"Just you be here at three o'clock. I'll know a lot more then and I'll share it with you."

Without saying another word, Gene turned and went out the door, shutting it loudly and heading for the elevator bank. He had to tell Jill and Sandy about Leroy's offer to arrange for them to go to the hotel school. That was very important to him. Getting on the elevator, he found himself shaking.

Leroy's revelations had shocked and appalled him. A dangerous drama was being played out, and Gene feared the consequences. It seemed he was always reacting to other people's devastating revelations. Would he ever have any power over them or would he always be their victim? When would the day come that others would react to devastation from him?

*****

Before leaving the church grounds, Buck looked once more at the white limousine that was to take Rose to Dallas to meet them at the airport. Although the windows were darkly tinted, he suspected some men in dark suits (why do they always wear dark suits?) were waiting in the back of that limousine to talk to Rose as her chauffeur drove the limousine to Dallas and her private jet. If only he could listen in on that conversation! But he knew that not even Shelley had been completely informed of what was going on.

"I'm glad that Rose let me ride to Dallas with you and didn't hog you for herself," Shelley said, kissing him on the mouth as the Durant church faded in the background.

"I'm glad too," Buck said. "I treasure moments alone with you. There aren't enough of them."

"There was last night," the boy said. "It was last night that convinced me of what I want for the rest of my life."

"What's that—you seem to have everything."

"Going to bed with you and waking up with you. It was the most exciting night of my life. To feel that you were completely mine. When I fell asleep in your arms, I felt I'd found my mate for life. With your arms around me, I felt safe. When you're gone, I don't feel safe at all."

"That's just what I want to talk to you about. Just how safe are you? How safe are we?"

"I guess Rose told you about some of our troubles."

"I know that Leroy Fitzgerald has pictures of you and Barry."

"That should hardly come as a surprise to you. You witnessed Barry and me first hand. That cunt Leroy was supposed to take compromising pictures of Barry with other young boys—not with me. He doublecrossed me, the fuck! Calder didn't know I went to that Lolito house. Rose didn't either. They sure know now."

"Why did you take such a chance?"

"Before I met you, I needed some outlet. I only entertained very special clients selected by Leroy. I mean the real hot ones. I wasn't one of the boy whores out there selling it in the arena. As you should know by now, taking it up the ass is my reason to live. I'm a sex addict. I've got to have it. All that whoring is behind me now. I've got you. You're the man I was always looking for and never thought I'd find."

"My God," he said, slightly exasperated. "You talk like a forty year old who's been searching all his life. Hell, you're only fifteen."

"Sixteen," Shelley corrected him.

"Too young. At times I feel you're more sexually experienced than I am."

"Perhaps I am. As you get to know me better, I'll teach you more and more, including some tricks I picked up in Japan. You'll really enjoy it."

"I'm sure I will. I enjoy any form of contact with you. Hell, you've got a body sculpted by David and a face painted by Botticelli. Who wouldn't want you?"

"Many men have wanted me and had me." He cuddled closer in the rear seat to Buck, placing his hand on Buck's thigh. Buck's reaction was to grab Shelley and deep kiss him, inserting his tongue for the boy to suck. For some reason, he couldn't get enough of that. He only wished he'd brought Casey along to drive for him. He didn't like all these strange chauffeurs being privy to some of his most private moments, but found Shelley so irresistible he couldn't wait until they were alone. Buck unbuttoned Shelley's shirt so he could glide his hands inside to feel the boy's perfect chest and to finger and caress his nipples. As he did, he tongued inside each of Shelley's ears before licking his neck. "I'm hopelessly in love," he whispered to the boy.

Shelley's eyes were closed, and he was moaning softly. "Having your lips and hands on me is heaven. This is the real heaven—not the one Rose hopelessly holds out for her followers."

"I want to run away somewhere with you after I get that money," Buck said. "Just you and me. No Rose."

"No Robert?" Shelley asked provocatively, sitting up in the car and confronting Buck.

Buck swallowed hard. "You tell me. You seem to know the answers to everything. What can I do about Robert? I'm all confused."

"Don't worry about it. It'll work itself out."

"I think he's completely hung up on me. He'll never leave me, and if I leave him I'll break his heart. At times I really believe he might kill himself. I know that sounds conceited, but I really believe it."

"We've already seen the spectacle of Sister Rose trying to do herself in over you."

"I've been thinking about that. I don't think Rose tried to commit suicide over me. It was more complicated than that. I think Rose stared at the future—the future she made for herself—and decided she couldn't go through with it. She wanted out."

"You're probably right."

"I used to think she was made of steel," Buck said. "I don't feel that way now. She's vulnerable like the rest of us. I think she's gotten herself into a deep trap and sees no way out. In her heart, she knows I love you—not her. But we're not killing Rose. She's killing herself day by day. We don't know what to do about Rose. Even Rose doesn't know what to do about herself. We certainly don't know what to do about Robert."

"There's no decision to be made now. When we get back to Okeechobee, some solution, something will happen. I just feel it. There's a way out of this, believe me. It's just not apparent right now."

"I wish I could believe you. I just don't see how it's going to work. It bothers the hell out of me day and night. That's why I wish I could just take all that money I'm going to get and run away with you. We don't need any more money. Fuck my inheritance."

"We're not going to fuck your inheritance. I'm not going to let you give anything up for me. I didn't come into your life to make you poorer. Stick with me, kid. Tonight or tomorrow morning you're going to be a very rich man. But tomorrow night and the nights to follow you're going to be even richer. It's not my intention to marry a poor man."

"I can't marry you, at least not now. I'm already married."

"So you are. A bigamist in fact. Married to both Robert and Susan, with me, the hot mistress on the side, the one who truly has captured your heart."

"How you talk for a fifteen-year-old."

"Sixteen! How many times do I have to correct you?" He looked into Buck's eyes and took his hand and placed it on his heart. "I'm going to stop lying to you. I lie to Rose. I've never told Calder the truth. I lie to everybody. I lie to congregations whenever I deliver a sermon. I lie to interviewers. But for the first time I'm going to start telling somebody— and that means you and only you—the truth. I might as well begin by admitting my age."

"You aren't sixteen? Fuck! Your age keeps changing every minute. Just how old are you? I should ask that before I'm hauled off to jail."

"I'm not sixteen. But I'm going on fifteen."

"Going on!" Buck shouted. He sighed in desperation and sank back into the thick, enveloping upholstery of the luxurious limousine, which now belonged to him. He closed his eyes as the barren landscape of Oklahoma faded from view.

*****

A distraught Barry sat beside the edge of his pool. He seemed on the verge of tears. Gene could offer little comfort.

"Calder Martin's pulled the plug," Barry said. "They're going to see me through this mayor's race because believe it or not I'm ahead in the polls. Even with Rose's dubious support. Of course, anybody could beat that cow Hazel. But after this race Calder is going to recommend to the big boys that I be dumped. Just like that. They'll find a new guy. Bright faced. Young. Eager to please. Married to a faithful wife he met in college when he was eighteen. Never fucked around. Two adorable daughters. Just like mine."

"How can you fight back?" Gene asked. "There must be a way."

"I don't know. Calder seems to have a fifteen-foot steel chamber around him. He can destroy people. But he himself seems well insulated against a counter-attack."

"Nobody is that well insulated. We're all vulnerable—not just me. I have no power. But even the president of the United States is vulnerable."

"Oh, yeah. Name just one way I can strike back at Calder. Just one thing I can do to get him."

"That's a tall order."

"You'll think about it, right?" Barry asked sarcastically.

"I'll do more than that. I can't do it today or even tomorrow, but there must be a way of stopping him. There has to be."

"When you figure it out, let me know." Barry got up from the pool area and headed toward his office, seeming to dismiss Gene.

Gene watched him go, vowing to assert himself one day—sooner than later—so that he could not be so easily dismissed. Right now he didn't know how. His life was all confused. But he'd figure it out. Some way. Some how. Some day.

From a far and distant corner of the house, he heard Barry yelling into the phone. He seemed enraged. At one point he shouted the name "Calder," so Gene knew who Barry was fighting with.

The telephone by the pool rang. At first Gene was tempted to answer it but had been warned by Barry not to pick up the phone in his household. But the phone wouldn't stop ringing. It must have rung twenty times. He decided to answer it, pretending, if asked, that he was just the pool maintenance man.

With trepidation, he picked up the receiver. "It's Pamela," came an angry voice on the other end.

"Where are you?" Gene asked.

"Where I am at the moment is none of your damn business. Wouldn't Barry and Calder Martin just love to know where I am? They'd come after me—that's for sure. Is Barry there?"

"He's on the phone right now with Calder."

"How cozy. I don't even want to speak to Barry again. I've talked to my attorney. My demands are going to be delivered today by messenger. He should be arriving there any minute. Make sure you go to the door. If the demands in my letter aren't met, tell Miss Barry and that creep Calder I'm going to go public. A press conference. If they don't meet my demands, tell both assholes they're history."

Before he could say another word, she slammed down the phone.

Gene pulled off all his clothes and jumped into the refreshing waters of the pool. A plan was emerging. Even before he'd finished the first lap, he decided not to tell Barry about that phone call. He just needed to figure out a way to receive that package from the messenger without letting Barry know what was happening. Before he had fully thought out how he could do this, Barry came back onto the patio.

"Calder has really fucked me now."

Gene swam to the edge of the pool and raised himself up several feet from the water. "What now?"

"Leroy Fitzgerald—you remember that creep we went to college with?—that fucker is blackmailing me. He's got pictures of Shelley Phillips and me going at it. That asshole Leroy is demanding five million dollars."

"Are the pictures real?" Gene asked, pretending not to know as much as he did.

"They're real all right. Before I lost my support with Calder's boys, I thought they might put up the money. But there's no deal now. The latest is, Calder wants me to go to Sister Rose. She's got money to burn.

Since her own son is involved, and exposure would seriously damage her following, Calder believes she might easily succumb to blackmail."

"You would go to Sister Rose with this?"

"Hell, yes, I would—and why not? Right now she's got more going than any of us. She's the most vulnerable. Also the most heavily bankrolled. She might go for it. If not, I don't know what I can do."

"Do you have money?"

"Hell, no—maybe a million dollars, maybe a lot less. That's why I need the big boys behind me. You don't get anywhere in American politics without a big bankroll behind you. That's how I got mixed up with Calder in the first place. The money thing. I thought Calder knew everything about everybody. But he didn't know all the sexual baggage I carried with me. He does now. He knows everything. I think he's got details on encounters I had that even I have forgotten."

Gene rose up from the pool, noting the admiring glances Barry was devoting to his genitalia. Even with all his present troubles, Barry couldn't resist a good view of male genitalia. Slowly and deliberately Gene dried himself in front of Barry. "I hope you don't mind," Gene said, "but I'm expecting a messenger soon with a package for me."

"Fuck!" Barry said, not taking his eyes off Gene's penis which was beginning to rise. "I don't want your packages sent to my address."

"It's from Jim Howard. Papers about my case which as you know has been dropped. But there are still some papers for me."

"Okay, if you've already had them sent here. But don't do it again."

The doorbell rang, and there was no one in the house to answer it but Gene and Barry. Gene pulled Barry to him and kissed him hard on the lips. Almost by instinct, Barry's hands traveled to Gene's lengthening prick.

"You're all hot and sweaty," Gene said, breaking away. "Go to the shower and I'll meet you in there. Sometimes it's fun to do it in the shower." Gene reached for a robe and walked toward the front door, noting that Barry seemed very eager to meet him in the bathroom.

At the door Gene accepted the package but didn't have any money to tip the young man. He forged Barry's name to the slip and shut the door quickly. He noted the package was from a local law firm with five names, all Jewish. The firm sounded impressive.

Without even bothering to open it, he took the package and headed for the rock garden behind the pool. Lifting the largest rock he could find, he slipped the package underneath, then lowered the rock over its contents.

Tossing his robe on the tiles of the pool patio, he went at once for the shower room where he knew Barry was waiting.

*****

The brunch at Uncle Milty's had gone perfectly without any obvious tension or animosity being displayed on either side. Patrick was a great cook, impressing them with his egg soufflé Bernardine, coeurs d'artichauts Pompadour, everything climaxed by jellied bananas en Chartreuse.

"After tasting a meal like this," Uncle Milty said to Susan, "you know why I married Patrick."

Patrick smiled, his eyes focused not on Uncle Milty, but on Don Bossdum whom he seemed to be devouring.

A black maid came into the patio to remove the dishes. "Patrick does all the fancy cooking, but I'm left to clean up the mess."

"You're a very good chef," Susan said to Patrick, "and I thank you."

"I used to watch you play football," Patrick said to Don. "You were terrific—nobody better. No wonder they made you captain of the team."

"Thanks," Don said, seemingly not embarrassed by Patrick's obvious devotion.

"I must say," Uncle Milty said, "Don here lives up to the classic image of what a football captain should look like but so rarely does. You look like you stayed in terrific shape after leaving school."

"I don't want an inch of fat to accumulate on me," Don said. "I work out all the time—pumping iron." He turned to Susan and smiled mischievously, taking her hand. "That's when I'm not pumping other things."

"Now, now," Susan cautioned. "Let's not get too graphic here."

"You are one lucky lady," Patrick said to Susan. "I believe in reincarnation, and when I come back I want to be a girl and look just like you."

"I'm flattered," she said, finishing the rest of her coffee.

"If you come back looking like Susan here," Don said, "I'll be after you day and night."

Patrick only sighed.

"Gentlemen," Susan said in her most businesslike voice, "Uncle Milty and I have some matters to go over. We'll need a little privacy."

"Yeah," the attorney said, looking at Patrick. "Why don't you take Don out by the pool? Do you like to swim, Don?"

"I love to swim." He turned to Susan again. "It's my second favorite best thing. But I didn't bring a suit."

"Don't worry," Patrick said. "We have extra trunks in the shower room." He eyed Don provocatively. "That is, if we can find something that would fit you."

Uncle Milty dismissed the young men, and he seemed eager to hear Susan's demands, although he looked a little apprehensive.

When Don and Patrick headed off through the gardens, Susan turned to him. "Don't worry. I'm not a blackmailer here to demand every last penny. I just want to establish terms by which I can live comfortably." She paused. "With Don."

"That's one hot number," Uncle Milty said, glancing across the patio as the men disappeared into the fenced-off pool area. "He sure likes to reveal himself in those jeans. They couldn't get much tighter. Doesn't leave much for the imagination, does it?"

"Modesty is not a virtue of Don's."

Uncle Milty leaned over the table. "You're the only person I've ever met who's been to bed with Gene, Buck, and Don. We girls in Okeechobee have heard all the rumors and have ventured guesses but it's all gossip. No one knows first hand. Only you can answer the big question. Who wins the prize? The biggest and best."

"I've never taken exact measurements," she said, "but I'd venture to guess it's a dead heat. They all tie for first place."

"Just what I thought, but I had to know for sure."

"Gene, Buck, and Don are three incredible specimens," Susan said, "but, of course, we're here to discuss other matters today."

"Buck and I don't plan to bicker about money with you. I've got a call in to him in Dallas, and I'd like to discuss and agree on terms with you before getting back to him. That okay with you?"

"It's fine," she said, settling back, feeling vaguely uncomfortable with all this. In her heart she felt Buck didn't owe her anything.

"Let's get this Don thing over with first," Uncle Milty said. "Do you think he'd be happy with a check for seven hundred and fifty a week—that's more than he could probably make if he got—God forbid—a real job."

"I'm sure he'd be delighted. That would be spending money for him since I'm picking up the tab on everything else."

"Fine. That's agreed. Believe me, Buck will have no objections. That brings up spending money for you."

"I hope you can get more for me than for Don."

"How would two hundred and fifty thousand a year strike you?"

"I'm stunned. That's very generous. I'll be frank. That's more than I expected, a hell of a lot more."

"Buck wants to be very generous with you. After all, it is you who is helping him save his inheritance."

"He could have gotten almost anybody to do that."

"Nevertheless you came through for us when we were in a tight spot. Of course, there will be fringe benefits. You'll have charge accounts at all the major stores here and in New York. I hope you'll be reasonable in your purchases. I hate to ask this but any purchase made for more than ten thousand dollars will have to be cleared with me. I've left instructions in the stores. I hope you don't mind."

"I'm a responsible person. I'll only purchase what I need or think I need."

"Buck actually wants you to be well dressed—in fact, he'd like you to be the best dressed woman in Florida, so we're prepared to spend a bit here. Your house, transportation, restaurant bills, whatever, will be absorbed by our corporation."

"Again, all this is incredibly generous. After struggling along for years on that meager salary the Examiner paid me, I feel I've found the pot of gold at the end of the rainbow."

Uncle Milty looked at her with a smirk on his face. "Believe me, you have. If only I were a gorgeous gal like you, I'd have gone after Buck myself."

"I'm sure you would have, but I think Robert beat you there."

"You may be lucky to get your big-dicked football player. I'm lucky to have a cute kid like Patrick around, an old piece of Jewish blubber like me. But that Robert. Talk about luck. Robert's got Buck Brooke III, the sexiest man alive! I can only dream about stuff like that."

"I guess Robert is lucky to have Buck—that is, if he really does."

"Exactly what does that mean?"

"Oh, nothing." She'd been fishing but hadn't reeled anything in. Apparently, Uncle Milty didn't know about Buck and Shelley.

"There's one very important thing we haven't discussed," Uncle Milty said.

"You've covered a lot of bases."

"It appears that I can purchase the News at a fire sale price," he said. "Buck insists that you be named publisher. How would a salary of one hundred and fifty thousand a year sit with you, plus stock options and fringe benefits?"

"That would go down as smoothly as one of Patrick's soufflés. I can't wait to tell my parents. You don't mind, do you?"

"Not at all. We're going public with a lot of things. Old Buck wants to speak to our Buck. He's not been taking his calls to Switzerland but the old fart has rallied a bit. He spoke to me and wants Buck to call him. Maybe even fly to Switzerland. He wants a big public announcement of your marriage. Splashed all over the front page. Big news. Florida's richest and loveliest couple. You game for that?"

"Of course, the marriage was always meant to go public. The image thing, you know. You produce the groom and I'll show up looking lovely. Wearing something chic. Understated but chic."

"Perfect. I'll tell Buck what the old man wants. We'll pull this one off."

Susan chuckled.

"What's so funny?"

"Don't you realize? I'm getting more money posing as Buck's wife than I'm getting as publisher of the News."

"Tell me something I don't know. That's life. That's how the cookie crumbles."

"Not an original expression but I'll go for it. I adore all your terms, but I'll tell Don only about his check. I'll leave out the other money you're giving me. We don't want to make Don too greedy, do we?"

"I agree. I let Patrick know I have three million dollars. Privately, and just between you and me, I've got a cool ten million, with more on the way if all my deals with your husband come through. Buck is going to make me a very rich old queen."

"I'm sure he'll do the same for me. He may not give us his glorious golden body—that he reserves for others—but he sure can't be called stingy."

"Incidentally, he's been given a jet plane all his own. You and Don can use it to fly to the Caribbean or wherever when it's not otherwise in use."

"That's wonderful. One of those fringe benefits?"

"There will be others," Uncle Milty said enigmatically.

"Since Buck is giving me all this, it makes me wonder what he's bestowing on Robert."

"Robert asks nothing and wants nothing."

"That's not exactly true," she said defensively. "He wants more than any of us. He wants the big prize itself: Buck."

"That's one way of looking at it."

"If I had Buck for richer or poorer, I'd feel like one very happy woman. I'd go for him if he were back at the Examiner making forty-five thousand a year."

"I'd go for him if he were a street hustler without a penny." Uncle Milty heaved his hefty body from his chair. "Alas, it was not meant to be. I've got to try to reach Buck before he flies to California. Why don't you join the boys at the pool? I'll be gone all afternoon and the house is yours."

"That's generous. But I've got to do some shopping. I want just the right outfit for the photographers who are going to take pictures of me and my gorgeous new husband."

"Good idea." He reached over and kissed her on the cheek. "Welcome to our little happy family."

"Glad to be a part of it." She touched his arm and smiled affectionately at him. "Anything you can do to acquire the News would be wonderful. I'd like to feel that I'm actually in a position to earn money for Buck without taking so much. If I can turn the News around, raise circulation and boost advertising revenue, then I won't feel like some gold-digging whore."

"I understand," was all Uncle Milty said, turning to go to his office.

At the pool only Don was in view, and what a view. He was sprawled on his back completely naked on a chaise longue, his cock half hard and wet. She observed it closely. It wasn't wet from the water but from saliva. She looked around for Patrick but saw no sign of him. He could easily have heard her coming down the long brick path, especially since she'd had to open that creaky door to enter.

"I see you didn't find a bathing suit," she said to Don.

"The only suit I need in private places like this is my own birthday suit."

"It looks like someone was wetting you down," she said, eying his penis.

"No, I just took a little dip."

"Amazing isn't it that only your dick got wet."

"Cut the shit," he said getting up and flashing anger which he quickly masked. "I'm lying here taking a nude sunbath and the first thing I know this mouth is devouring me. I was asleep for Christ's sake. I told him to get the fuck out of here and let me alone. That's all. That's all that happened."

"Okay, we'll drop it. But in the future when you need a blow job, you've got my mouth, okay?"

"Agreed," he said, heading for the shower room. "Let's drop it. Every time fags see my dick they've got to taste it. It's always been that way ever since I was fourteen. I think half the fucking football team wanted to go down on me. I'll spend the rest of my life fighting off fags." He disappeared into the shower room.

She stood at the bar, lighting a cigarette and pouring herself some whisky straight. She sighed, taking in the beauty of the day and the patio. "Welcome to life with Don Bossdum," she said out loud but to herself. She downed the whisky. This little encounter, she feared, was but a preview of things to come.

*****

Learning that Rose would be delayed another four hours before reaching the plane in Dallas, Buck decided he didn't want to go aboard. Without asking Shelley, he checked them into a deluxe hotel suite two miles away. He wanted to go for a swim, freshen up from the long drive, and make some private calls, preferably when Shelley had gone to the pool. His first call would be to Robert, his next to Uncle Milty.

Deep into his conversation with Robert, his friend told him with great enthusiasm that he had a "surprise" waiting for him back in Okeechobee. "Believe it or not, I've decided to do something with my life. Take a stand. I think your grandfather was right. I'll soon be thirty and I should be making something out of my life—other than standing around with a fluffy towel waiting to dry your big balls."

On the other end of the phone, Buck paused. He didn't know what to say. All of a sudden he felt threatened. Secretly he liked the way Robert was totally dependent on him. This assertion of independence was strangely upsetting. Was he losing control over Robert? He wanted to be in charge. He hated the expression, but he did want to be "the man in the family," having his friend under his total control, even though he knew how wrong that was and how backward the attitude in the seventies.

"That's great," Buck managed to say with as much enthusiasm as he could muster. "You're not going to let me in on this surprise? You're going to leave me out here in the forlorn and barren west guessing as to what you're up to?"

"It wouldn't be a surprise if I let you in on it now. Besides, I've got to work out the final arrangements so everything will be neatly tied up with a red ribbon by the time you fly back to your loving man."

"Have it your way," Buck said a bit impatiently.

"I have one confession to make."

"You've fallen in love with Patrick?"

"Not that. Something worse. But while on the subject of Patrick, I have some gossip, and it's not pleasant."

"Spill it."

"Patrick is having an affair with your new driver, Casey. He's told me everything."

"I know that already," Buck said.

"How could you? You've been away."

"When I left our honeymoon bed in Key Biscayne to go walk along the beach, I spotted them together. I quickly figured out what was happening. God damn it, I hope Uncle Milty doesn't find out."

"I pray he won't. I begged Patrick to be discreet but you know that whore. He's my best friend but I wouldn't trust him for a minute. Not even with you."

"You don't have to worry about Patrick and me. I like him a lot, and I know he's your best friend. But he's not my kind of guy. I love Uncle Milty. My first and foremost loyalty is to old Milty."

"I understand that. I like Uncle Milty too but Patrick's my real friend. Deep down I think Uncle Milty has always resented me. Personally I think he's in love with you. I know you'd never be physically attracted to him in a million years but that doesn't mean his heart doesn't yearn for you. Once I went into his private library which, as you know, is even off-limits to Patrick. I shouldn't have but the door was slightly ajar and Uncle Milty and Patrick were having a gay old time in the pool. There were at least eighteen pictures of you lining his study. In one you looked about fourteen. All of them were pictures of you without your shirt and in swimming trunks, one in a bikini that left little for the imagination."

"It's a harmless crush—forget it," Buck said, barely concealing the anger in his voice. Instead of a loving call to a friend, he was getting pissed off by Robert. He glanced out the hotel window to see Shelley alone in the pool. Right this minute he wanted to join Shelley in that pool and not deal with what was waiting for him back in Okeechobee. "You said you had a confession to make. What is it? I know it's not about Patrick and Casey. I already knew that."

"It's our engagement ring. I figured with a wedding band on my finger, I didn't need an engagement ring. I sold it. It brought a fortune."

"You what?"

"I got a lot of money for it. You know I'm not much for jewelry. I took the money I got for the ring and I'm going to turn it into something really worthwhile. Turn my life around. I needed the money from that ring more than I needed the ring itself."

"I can't have you selling that ring. If you need money, I'm going to have all the money in the world beginning tomorrow. I'll buy you anything you want. You don't have to sell jewelry I gave you, God damn it."

"I'm sorry..." He hesitated as his voice became jerky. "I didn't know you'd react that way. I know you don't care for jewelry. I thought you'd understand."

"I understand only one thing. I'm speaking to Uncle Milty in a few minutes. I'm telling him to call you. I want to know who you sold that ring to. I want it back. Buy it back. At any cost." Buck felt his body shaking. He didn't know why he was so angry.

"If you want me to have the ring back and wear it, I will."

"It's too late for that now. I just want the fucking ring back. It's important to me."

"Do you want to wear it yourself?"

"I may only lock it up in a safety deposit box. I don't want to talk about it any more." He glanced apprehensively at his watch. "I'll call you just as soon as I know when I'm flying back. It's probably the most important day of my life."

"And I had to go and do something stupid with the ring. I am so sorry."

"We'll handle it. I've got to go now."

"Buck..." Robert seemed to want to say something but didn't know how to form the words. "You seem so distant somehow. I feel I've betrayed you in some deep way."

"Everybody betrays everybody. We're fine. I'm just very nervous— that's all. A lot is riding on tonight, and I don't want to distract myself too much."

"I love you," Robert said. "I truly love you."

"I love you too, kid." Even to himself, Buck's voice sounded non-committal. "Unless I get bit by a rattlesnake in the desert, I'll keep you posted on what's happening out here." He looked longingly at Shelley in the pool.

"I'll keep the home fires burning."

"When I get back, I'll bring the fire. You wait and see, sweet cheeks." He put down the phone. He'd found the call vaguely disturbing and unsatisfactory. He was angry at himself for giving Robert that ring. He knew with all he had going on in the world right now a ring, regardless of how valuable, was the last thought that should be troubling him. But he could think of nothing else. "Fuck it!" he said to the emptiness of the hotel room. "I'll get the god damn ring back, and I'll wear it to the day I die. I'll be buried with that ring on my finger, and I hate rings!"

With a steely determination, he placed his second call of the day, this time to Uncle Milty.

*****

In Marathon, the Florida Keys landscape looked as bleak and barren as her life. The dreary motel with its bad mattress offered no solace for Pamela either. Was she doing the right thing? Should she have run away? She didn't know the answers to these questions or any others.

After flying to Miami from the Okeechobee airport, she'd rented a car and driven to Marathon. She was heading for Key West for no other reason than it was the most remote point she could drive in the United States. She wanted to be far removed from Okeechobee when Susan interviewed her on film. She had determined that a private interview with Susan was far better than a brutal press conference.

Her fear was that if she faced an array of cameras and microphones she would become paralyzed and couldn't speak. She hated public appearances. Beauty pageants terrified her. Short on talent, she could smile and that was about it. Barry did all the public speaking in the family.

Her daughters were very articulate but they were phony. When the cameras were turned on them, they appeared like clones of Tricia Nixon. They weren't like that at all in private life. They were, in fact, worldly wise beyond their years and had had several boy friends. She'd warned them about sex but was certain her advice fell on deaf ears. After all, they were completely familiar with her own sexual history.

If anything, they were following in her well-fucked footsteps. She'd had her first boy friend when she was fourteen. A rising young politician like Barry, her lover had been thirty-three and she'd gone "all the way" on the first date. She'd loved sex and found that she could never be satisfied with one man when there were so many out there waiting to satisfy her. She never knew why she'd married Barry in the first place. She'd never loved him. She'd wanted Gene or Buck but they'd seemed taken with each other more than with her. Besides, Susan was moving in on Gene, and Robert seemed to have acquired a permanent lock on Buck's heart.

Actually the one man she'd loved more than all others was Don Bossdum. That was her kind of guy. Don didn't have the emotional hangups of Buck and Gene. When on their first date she'd greedily taken the pleasure of slipping off the bikini briefs from his well-muscled body, he'd told her, "What you see is what you get."

That promise had been true. Over the next few months she couldn't get enough of Don. He'd devoured her from all angles, as she'd fallen deeply and more deeply in love with him. Of all the men she'd known in her life, none had satisfied her like Don. He was not only an athlete on the playing fields, but an athlete in bed. She'd never known that sex with a man could be so good. It had never been before and, alas, it would never be again.

With no warning, Don had abruptly departed. He'd broken her heart, refusing to return her calls or see her. Weeks later she'd learned that he was rumored to be involved with Sister Rose. Pamela had known then she couldn't compete with that evangelist. Don wanted a sports car. He wanted fancy clothes, the good life. Pamela had never had any money and could offer Don none of those things. Even though she was a much older woman, Rose could offer him the world. And that's what she'd done. Apparently. But even that affair had come to an end.

The last Pamela had heard of Don he was living in Miami where he'd married into a prestigious and obviously wealthy Cuban family. Don wanted the wealth—that was for certain. She could provide men not with money but with sex.

For years that had seemed to be enough. But increasingly as she studied her appearance in the mirror lately, she realized the bloom was definitely off the flower. She was no longer the fresh virginal beauty queen she once was.

She'd been shocked at meeting Susan after a long time. Unlike Pamela, Susan looked as beautiful and radiant as she'd appeared in her university days. Time had marched on for Pamela, and she resented Susan's retaining her virginal glow when she'd lost hers. Of course, she figured Susan didn't spend her nights pursuing state troopers and alcohol.

In spite of her unfortunate marriage to Gene, Susan seemed to have recovered. Pamela had heard rumors that Susan was getting increasingly serious about Buck Brooke. If those rumors were true, Pamela realized that in some way Susan must have edged Robert out the door, although how she accomplished that Pamela didn't know. Robert appeared to be a lover not easily discarded.

She used to hate Robert but she didn't any more. At one time she blamed Robert for ruining her marriage but now she knew differently. Robert hadn't ruined her marriage. Barry Collins had ruined her marriage.

She was certain Buck didn't know the truth about Robert. They myth was that Robert lived only for Buck and hadn't looked at another man in his entire life. That was the stuff of fantasy, a sexual lie no doubt perpetuated by Robert himself. Pamela knew differently. Buck had gone to a different high school and hadn't met Robert until their university years together.

But Barry and Robert had gone to the same high school, and apparently their affair had begun in the tenth grade. After various break-offs, it had resumed after Buck had gone off to service. She suspected that Robert had portrayed himself as the lonely wife waiting by the barracks gate for the return of his military man.

Such was not the case. Robert and Barry had been carrying on a hot and torrid affair ever since Buck had gone into the service. This was not rumor. She knew this for a fact. One March day she'd come back unexpectedly from a shopping trip to Miami and had caught Barry and Robert in bed together. Fortunately, the girls were visiting relatives which they so often did, no doubt to escape from the tension of the Collins household. Barry had been fucking Robert. Until that day, she didn't know Barry was gay.

That was only the beginning. After Robert had hurriedly left their house, Barry had confided a lot more. He was not only gay but liked them young, the sweet, blond virginal-looking type like Robert. Although Robert must have been twenty-four at the time she'd discovered them in bed, he still looked fifteen.

More revelations and discoveries were on the way. Robert had soon tired of Barry, especially after Buck's return. Buck was obviously far more interesting in bed than Barry. But there had been no letting up for Barry. Among other encounters, he'd begun an affair with Shelley Phillips. Pamela had immediately understood the attraction. The blond, blue-eyed beautiful version of Robert, who was himself about the handsomest man in the state of Florida.

When she'd learned of Barry's affair with Shelley, Pamela had decided to extract a certain revenge. She'd called Sister Rose who had agreed to meet with her privately. Pamela was determined to put an end to her husband's involvement with Shelley. But the meeting over tea at Paradise Shores had not gone at all the way Pamela had planned. She'd hardly met Sister Rose before and most of her images of her were gleaned from television. Sister Rose, she'd painfully learned, wasn't some Bible Belt fanatic but a world weary sophisticated woman.

After listening attentively to Pamela's revelations, the evangelist had risen gracefully as if dismissing her. "I've known for a long time that Barry is carrying on with my son. I think they're a cute couple, don't you? You're married to one handsome man. Barry also has a great deal of charm. And there is no more beautiful boy breathing air in this world than Shelley Phillips."

"What do you mean cute couple? I can't believe you've known about this and allowed it to continue."

"Listen, bitch," Sister Rose had said, turning on her with a certain fury. "Yes, I know god damn well that Barry is fucking my son. Shelley loves to take it up the ass. Not only that, but I've fucked with Barry too. I've known men with better endowments, but after a few drinks I throw him a mercy fuck every now and then. He's so good looking it compensates for his lack of a dick."

"God damn you," Pamela had shouted at her. "You're not only fucking my husband, but you stole Don Bossdum from me."

"Now there's a man with a dick," she'd said. "I miss that football-playing stud. He knew how to throw a woman a fuck and reach places where no man has gone before. Don't you agree?"

"I agree that you're not the person you present yourself as at all. You're nothing but a slut."

"Oh, darling, don't feed me your shit. Barry has told me that you've fucked half the state troopers in the state of Florida."

Enraged, Pamela had run from the room, upsetting Rose's silver tea service. All she'd remembered from that dreadful afternoon was Rose calling after her, "Get a life!"

She'd followed Rose's advice. She'd gotten a life all right. If Barry could have his little blond boys, she'd have her big men. With her looks and beauty queen figure, getting men had been relatively easy. Barry had promised her fame and fortune. For years she'd believed him, and it appeared he was launched. Winning the mayor's race would be only the first step along a brilliant political career. But now she realized in her heart that she'd been dumped. Because of her many indiscretions and her drinking problem, she knew that Calder viewed her as a menace. Anything Calder viewed as a menace he got rid of somehow. Calder was out to get her. She just knew that, but couldn't prove it.

She hated to threaten them, because threatening Calder Martin was a dangerous undertaking. But she had to act quickly. She wanted money. She truly suspected Barry and Calder would give in to her demands and settle a huge amount of money on her. With that money, she could start a new life. Every hour or so she called her attorneys to see if Calder or Barry had responded to her demands. So far, nothing. This bothered her immensely, as she'd suspected they'd cave in at once after she'd threatened to go public with her revelations about Barry. It would ruin him. It would ruin all of Calder Martin's plans for Barry, plans that one day envisioned the White House itself as a possibility for her husband.

Surely, she thought, they were figuring out how to raise the money. She wanted a lot, enough to see her through her old age where she planned to live in style, taking as many men as she wanted, even if, as she got older, she had to buy them the way Sister Rose had purchased Don Bossdum. She'd use Sister Rose as her role model and purchase men on the auction block just like the evangelist.

She felt incredibly vulnerable right now. Calder's men could come for her at any time if they discovered where she was hiding. They could arrange an "accident." Perhaps a drunk driving accident. She'd been arrested for drunk driving four times in her life already, although Biff had managed to keep the news out of the papers and records of her arrest, or so she'd been told, had disappeared from police files.

She felt time was running out. She'd have to pressure Susan at once to fly to Key West for a filmed interview, which Pamela would release only if Calder and Barry didn't give in to her demands. She just knew a smart reporter like Susan could set that one up. While doing that, she'd threaten Barry one more time. She didn't dare call Calder and threaten him personally. She wasn't that much of a steel magnolia. She was even afraid to contact Barry personally, fearing she might falter and not deliver her demands. Perhaps she could call Gene and make her threat to him. She knew she could easily convince Gene of her threat. But first she had to get Susan's cooperation. From the motel phone by her bedside, she desperately dialed Susan's number in Okeechobee.

*****

"Susan's changing, even since the marriage which was only yesterday," Uncle Milty was telling Buck in this phone conversation which had already stretched out for more than thirty minutes. Buck looked at the pool area, as he spoke to his attorney, watching as Shelley leaped from the pool and grabbed a terry-cloth robe to dry himself before lying down on a pink chaise longue.

"In what way?" Buck asked, not really knowing if he wanted to hear the truth.

"She's got herself a stud hustler to take care of her lonely nights," Uncle Milty said, seeming to relish the gossip.

Buck paused. "I guess I should view that as good news. Have you met the creep?"

"He isn't exactly a creep, and you went to college with him."

Suddenly for the first time into the conversation, Buck was truly interested. "Who in the fuck?"

"Don Bossdum."

At first Buck didn't say anything. Years ago he'd even had fantasies about Don himself. Once or twice—maybe more—when he'd been jacking off and trying to think about girls, images of Don kept intruding into his brain waves. He'd seen Don more than once in the locker room at the university gym. Other than Gene, Don was the only man on campus who truly measured up to Buck. "She's got herself a real man this time," Buck finally managed to say, "unlike those other goons she's dated. I mean Don looks like he knows how to take care of a woman."

"I know," Uncle Milty said, practically drooling over the phone. "He showed up here in a tight pair of jeans. Tucked away in that basket was meat for the poor."

"I don't really want to talk about it." The picture of Don and Susan together disturbed him greatly, for reasons that weren't even clear to himself.

"You're going to be paying for it—and by the inch."

"What does that mean?"

"Susan wants you to write Don Bossdum a check for seven hundred and fifty a week. I agreed to that. I hope that was okay."

"Whatever she wants," Buck said. "I'd say I was getting off cheap. It looks as if Don has taken Susan off my hands, so I won't have to worry about how she spends her nights."

"No you won't. Now you can be with Robert all you want, with no guilt."

The mention of guilt stabbed at his chest. For one moment he wanted to tell Uncle Milty about Shelley. All his life he'd told Uncle Milty everything. Uncle Milty had always been his family's attorney and had watched Buck grow into manhood. He'd always confided everything, but today he couldn't bring himself to tell his attorney about Shelley. It was too much. Such a confession would not come from him. It wasn't just because of Uncle Milty's close ties with Robert who, after all, was more Patrick's friend. It was something else.

He felt if Uncle Milty learned of his involvement with Shelley, his attorney would lose respect for him. In his deepest heart, he was ashamed of his involvement with Shelley. It wasn't just because of the boy's age. It was more than that. He didn't want Uncle Milty to know he was betraying Robert with someone else, especially in view of the fact that his attorney was himself being betrayed by Patrick. In a way, Buck blamed himself for hiring Casey in the first place. His chauffeur was just too sexy and good looking for most gay men to resist.

"There is something I didn't tell you about Don," Uncle Milty said. "Something he said to me privately before leaving my house. Susan was already heading to the car, and God knows where Patrick was."

"Spill it."

"He said, 'Now that Buck is my sugar daddy, I'd really like to get together with him...privately, that is.' Then he groped that big basket of his. He said he'd changed a lot since the university and didn't have the same hangups any more—that he was a liberated man. 'I'm a part of the family now,' he said to me. 'You tell my good buddy Buck that any time he wants to see me, any time of the day or night, all he has to do is call and I'll come for him.'"

"He didn't actually say 'come for him,' now did he?"

"He did indeed. That's not all. He said, 'Susan will have to wait or take up knitting—I mean Buck is calling the shots around here. He comes first.'"

"What a flattering offer. I once asked Don to go out with me for a few cold ones, but he turned me down flat. I wasn't exactly planning to put the make on him. I just liked him—that was all. It was harmless. But he glowered at me and told me he was 'into girls.'"

"He's yours any time you want him. But, of course, you've got Robert now."

"Indeed, I do."

"You've also got another wife, and I've already told you about that photo shoot old Buck wants. He wants to see his grandson splashed all over the frontpages with his loving wife—read that Susan—at his side.

As soon as you get back to Okeechobee, we've got to move ahead with this. After all, we don't know how much longer old Buck is going to last."

Buck was anxious to get off the phone. Long before the talk had veered to Don Bossdum, Uncle Milty and he had concluded their business, with lots of instructions about what Buck was to do in Palm Springs. Through the window Buck noted how lonely and forlorn Shelley looked by the pool.

"I know you've got to go," Uncle Milty said. "But I've got to share one more tidbit of gossip with you."

"What's that?"

"There's a rumor going around town about you. I think it was spread by some limo driver. The word is, you and Shelley Phillips are an item." Uncle Milty burst into laughter. "Isn't that a fucking joke? When you get rich and powerful anything will be spread about you. You and Shelley Phillips! My God, the kid can't be more than twelve. That's about as funny as another report I heard that you're banging that Jew-hating bitch Rose herself. I could just see you plowing into that overripe cunt. These rumor mongers don't know Buck Brooke like I know Buck Brooke. With Robert's tight little rosebud available to you day and night, I'm sure you need some twelve-year-old boyass and the whore of Babylon. You and Shelley Phillips? What a joke."

"What a joke," Buck said in a low voice. "Gotta go, Uncle Milty. Wish your boy good luck tonight. Maybe I'll fly back home with the bacon."

Uncle Milty didn't seem to hear him. Still amused at the rumor about Shelley and Buck, he repeated himself. "What a joke."

As he said that, Buck looked at Shelley by the pool, and decided right then and there he couldn't talk one more minute on the phone. "Love you, Uncle Milty." He hung up and headed immediately for that chaise longue on which Shelley was sunning his already golden body.

*****

After Barry had kissed Gene good-bye, thanking him for the fuck in the shower, he headed out for some private meeting which Gene couldn't attend. Actually, Gene didn't want to attend any of Barry's meetings and welcomed the time alone by the pool before going over to meet Leroy at his condo.

He'd already talked earlier to Jill and Sandy. Both had agreed to set up appointments about enrolling in the hotel school. "I've been catering to people all my life," Sandy had told him. "Why not at a hotel? Maybe one day I'll become president of Hilton."

"I know you will," Gene had said proudly, hoping the boy would go far.

Jill had gotten on the phone. "We love you, Gene," she'd said. "Thanks for the pretty new clothes. I can't wait to model them for you. But you're always so busy."

"Yeah," Gene had said. "A lot of people have their claws in me." He promised to meet with them either before or after his visit with Leroy.

Alone at last, he removed his towel and flopped down on a chaise longue, enjoying the hot midday sun burning into his flesh. He didn't know where he was going. He felt forces other than himself were determining the direction of his life without his consent. He couldn't let this go on. He had to find a way to strike back but no solution became apparent to him. He was determined to find a way.

Leroy, he hoped, would provide him with a lot more information. He believed his friend knew a lot he wasn't telling. After all, Leroy had worked—or still did—for Calder Martin. Fearing Leroy's demand for five million was excessive, he planned to talk him out of it. If not that, he definitely wanted to accompany Barry to that meeting with Sister Rose.

Somehow he felt he could be of help and support to her. In return, he knew she'd be grateful and might even offer to give him the guidance he needed. Maybe she'd provide the answer for him, whatever it was. A lot of spiritual people in the past had helped lost souls. She might show him the way.

Everybody surrounding her, even her own son, seemed like a scumbag, but somehow she'd retained her purity and a certain innocence, in spite of all the vileness threatening to envelop her. One way or another, he was determined to have a meeting with her. Barry seemed his best chance to do that, even though Barry usually didn't take him to any private meetings. But somehow Gene just knew Barry would make an exception in this case. If necessary, Gene would force the issue and make Barry agree.

At the sound of laughter, Gene quickly covered his nudity with a towel. The voices of young girls were heard across the patio. He looked up to see Barry's daughters, both dressed in white. They'd obviously returned early from their trip. Barry wasn't expecting them until tomorrow. Gene knew at once who they were. He'd seen them at rallies and on television. On camera, they had a fresh-faced innocence and were always caught gazing admiringly at their father.

"Hi," one of them said. "I'm Julie."

"You must be dad's new bodyguard," the other girl said. "We know you: You're Gene Robinson. You're famous." She raised a provocative eyebrow. "If for all the wrong reasons." She didn't look as innocent in person as she did on camera.

"Barry's out right now," he said, feeling awkward in their presence. Both girls, even though they were only twelve and fourteen, seemed to be undressing him.

"Where's that bitch Pamela?" Julie asked. "Oh, by the way, this is Barbara. She's the oldest."

"Pamela's gone off. We don't know where."

"Probably out drunk somewhere getting fucked by eight state troopers, the lucky cow," Barbara said. "Even though she's a beat-up bag, yesterday's beauty queen, she gets more dick than I do."

"You're only fourteen," he said.

"Fourteen is plenty old enough to fuck," Barbara said, heading for the bar to get herself a beer.

"I bet Barry gets more dick than Pamela does," Julie said. "Our father, or so I'm told, is a better cocksucker than all the women in this household."

"You shouldn't talk about your father like that," he said.

"We don't on TV," Julie said. "In private we say what we want."

"The reason we returned from our relatives early is because they bored us to death," Barbara said. "I wasn't able to get fucked during the entire time I was away." She handed Julie a beer which she gladly accepted. Gene declined the can offered him.

He felt he was smothering in the presence of these girls and was seeking an avenue of escape. Even with the towel over him, he'd never felt so nude. The girls stared frequently and without embarrassment at his crotch.

"Other than Buck Brooke III, you're rumored to have the biggest dick in Okeechobee," Julie said. "If you won't tell us, I'm sure Barry will give us exact measurements. Surely my dad has had you by now."

"No way," he said. "I'm sure your father doesn't go in for that sort of thing."

"Bullshit!" Julie said. "He's even made it with some of my boyfriends."

Barbara looked with a sneer at Julie. "Her current boyfriend is very, very good looking. I mean we're talking drop dead good looking. But his dick is only five inches long."

"He eats a mean pussy," Julie said. "That's why I stay with him. If I want to get fucked with a big dick, your boy friend seems always available."

"You god damn slut! You keep your hands off Bryan."

Julie turned her attention to Gene. "We hear you like to flash in front of little girls. Why not give us a show?" She sat down on the chaise longue next to him. "That looks like tent city under that towel."

He'd had enough. Securing the towel around himself, he headed for the shower room and his clothes. He wanted out of this house.

"Flasher!" he heard Barbara call after him. "Flash a little for me."

It was only later heading back to the condo to see Jill and Sandy that he realized how unreal reality was. Julie and Barbara were the sparkling little sweethearts of the city but he knew now they were sluts. Jill and Sandy, although having worked in prostitution, were decent human beings. It was ironic how the world got people and images confused.

The whole Collins family made him feel unclean. He really wanted no part of them, and wondered how much longer he'd hang on to them. His days in Okeechobee were obviously numbered. It was no place for him any more. Everybody, including or especially Leroy, made him feel unclean.

There was only one friend who really cared for him, and that was Buck Brooke III. Of course, there was Sandy. There was Jill. But they were new friends. More like his children. Buck could be his chance for a new life. A daring thought occurred to him. When he met with Sister Rose—not on the first meeting, but later, when he got to know her—he might tell her of his love for Buck, hoping to get her blessing of the union. She might even agree to marry them in private. He knew that she campaigned against filth in this world, but love wasn't filth. What he felt for Buck was pure love, and he knew that Sister Rose would see it that way and bestow her approval.

She might be shocked at first when she learned the news, but he knew in time she'd come to understand and appreciate the love that both men had for each other. After all, it wasn't dirty love like that thing between Barry and her son. It was purer than that.

Buck gave him a reason to live, and he knew now that his friend must be straightening out and arranging his life so that he could come to Gene free of baggage and commitment.

As he pulled into the parking lot, he noticed TV cameras outside the entrance to his condo. Jerking his car in reverse, he headed out of the lot. There was no way he wanted to be photographed going into that building. He'd have to slip undetected into his condo to determine what news inside was worthy of getting on television news.

*****

In the pool with Shelley, he was free at last. The way he felt right now, he never wanted to return to Okeechobee and face what was waiting for him there. If anything, it seemed like a honeymoon with Shelley, however brief. Shelley was eager to see him, making Buck wish he were in a private pool with the boy. But this was a hotel and anybody could appear on the patio at any minute. Fortunately, they had the pool to themselves, at least temporarily. In the far corner of the pool area, a bartender waited to serve drinks to potential customers who never materialized.

"I hope you got your business taken care of," Shelley said, reaching under water to fondle the package encased in Buck's white bikini.

"Some really interesting things came out of my call to my attorney. I call him Uncle Milty. My grandfather wants a photo shoot of Susan and me as we announce our happy marriage to the world."

"How thrilling!" Shelley said sarcastically. "I can't wait."

"That's not all. Susan's not a problem any more. She's found herself a stud hustler."

"Someone she met in a singles bar, no doubt."

"A grade above that. Don Bossdum. A great football player—or at least he was. I'm sure you've heard of him."

Shelley backed away from Buck and pushed himself out of the pool, heading for a rack of thick towels nearby.

Surprised at this sudden departure, Buck got out of the pool too, standing beside Shelley as both of them toweled themselves dry. "What is it you want to tell me?"

"I'm embarrassed to tell you of another threat, but I promised myself I wouldn't lie to you. I know Don Bossdum—only too well. So does Rose. He was my lover. He was also Rose's lover. I never loved him, though."

"My, God," Buck said, "it looks like I'm Don's replacement."

"Don't put it that way. There's more. Don's threatening to make trouble for me. He wants money. One-hundred thousand dollars."

"That's cheaper than what Leroy wants for those pictures of Barry and you."

"A lot cheaper and I'm going to pay it. It's petty cash to me anyway. I'm glad he's got Susan to support him. Takes the heat off me. But as soon as I get back to Okeechobee, I'm delivering him the money."

"Let me do it."

"Why?"

"It'll be a chance to talk to my old college pal."

"You're going to threaten him?"

"More subtle than that. After all, he's now on my payroll. I just want to make it very clear to Don that the little bundle of cash is it. That's it. There will be no more. I've got to convince him that his best interests in the future will be in keeping Susan satisfied and the milk train continuing to make deliveries. I'll want him to understand the little one-hundred thousand dollars is a gift from you, but a final gift."

"You'd do that for me?"

"Of course, I would. I'd do anything to help you. I love you, fucker. Besides, considering my new arrangement with Don, I think it's wise for me to clear the air with him."

"Did you and Don ever make it?"

"Never," Buck said.

"Did you think about it?"

"Once or twice but nothing ever came of it."

"He's good. But I've traded him in for a better model." Shelley reached over and gently touched Buck's arm. "More than that, I'm in love."

A faraway look came into Shelley's eyes. Buck had never seen that look before. The boy was with him but seemed removed all of a sudden. "Is something wrong?"

Shelley smiled but it was only a pretend smile. He appeared crestfallen, defeated, and afraid.

Buck put his arm around him to reassure him everything was going to be okay. "I'm here for you. I want you not only to know that, but to believe it. Feel it."

"I know you are, but that's not what is making me sad."

"Then what is it?"

"I fear I'm not going to be here for you."

"I don't understand that. You say you love me. Rose approves. Later tonight we're going to have all the money in the world. If you're worried about exposure to the world because of these sex scandals, don't be. If you're exposed, we'll go away. God knows we can flee to any part of the world we want."

"It's more than that. You know I have this vision thing. Up to now it told me that we'd always be together. But in the past day, my vision thing has grown cloudy. That's why I so desperately clung to you last night."

"What is your new vision thing telling you?" Buck asked, growing alarmed as if for the first time he believed in Shelley's visions.

"I'm not sure. As I said, it's cloudy. But this strong feeling is coming over me that I'm going away somewhere. Far, far away."

"You mean to another country, another continent?"

He looked up at Buck and kissed him tenderly on the lips. "Beyond that. To another world." As tears welled in his eyes, he turned quickly and headed back to their suite.

Buck remained alone on the patio. Even though the day had been hot, a wind blew in, bringing a sudden chill. He shivered and wrapped the towel tighter around him but it brought no comfort. The wind blew again and it was even colder. He sucked air into his lungs, finding it harder to breathe. All of a sudden he felt that something had gone from his life, and he wanted it back. He headed at once for the suite, hoping to reclaim what he'd lost.

*****

Through the back entrance, Gene managed to slip into Leroy's apartment without being detected. "What in hell's all this fuss about?" Gene asked an obviously frightened Leroy, who had just gotten off the phone with someone as Gene entered his condo living room.

"The shit's hit the fan," Leroy said, still in his robe. "Calder's playing hard ball."

"Why are those fucking TV cameramen outside the building?" Gene demanded to know.

"Someone has tipped off the press that you're living here with Jill, the same girl you exposed yourself to years ago. I guess the tonight news in Okeechobee thought that was a human interest story."

"Fuck that! Where's Jill and Sandy?"

"I called the apartment. Jill is holed up there. She's afraid to go out the door. The cameramen are right outside the apartment. Sandy was away somewhere. I don't even know if he's aware of all of this crap going on."

"It's too risky for me to try to get to Jill now unless I want to be filmed going into that apartment. Let me try to get her on the phone."

"The reporters have got the phone number down there. She's not taking any more calls. I've tried three times. I think she's got the phone off the hook."

"Why is all this going on?"

Leroy went over to the bar and poured himself a drink. "Want one?"

"Hell no, not at a time like this."

"Liquor was invented for times like this."

"I need to keep my wits about me."

"And I need to calm my nerves. I knew when I demanded money from Calder, he'd play dirty tricks like this. That's what he does."

"But exactly how is Jill tied in with this? How are we involved?

"Calder knows everything going on in this town. He probably knows we're having an affair. Striking back at you might be a way to get back at me."

"Somebody out there was striking back at me long before I got involved with you. My arrest. It was all a trap."

"I'm going to level with you: tell you what I know. Calder Martin was behind that arrest. Guess who his lieutenant is? Your precious chief, Biff. Biff's on Calder's payroll. He carries out his orders. That son of a bitch was behind your arrest."

"God damn him!"

"I don't know how much you know about your former boss. I know plenty. He claims he's the biggest cocksman in Okeechobee. Actually he's impotent. I used to slip him in to the Lolito house. He'd sneak into one of the rooms where he could spy on the action. He never joined in. He even disguises himself a bit and frequents the Vulcan Baths. Always to watch what the guys are doing. That's how he gets off. That is, if he gets off."

"That asshole hypocrite. And he ridiculed me as the flasher. Why have they got it in for me? What have I done to them?"

"It's more than that. It's easy to see why they've got it in for me. But I don't completely understand how you fit into this picture. Yesterday I got a hunch. I think I know a little more."

"For God's sake, tell me. I'm going out of my skin."

"Somehow Buck Brooke is in on this, although I would never have thought that of him."

"I can't believe that. I mean, Buck's my oldest, best buddy. He'd never do anything to hurt me."

"Think again." Leroy walked over to his wall cabinet and pulled out a photograph, handing it to Gene.

Gene studied the photograph carefully. It was a picture of Buck in his jogging outfit getting into a limousine.

"I'm sure you recognize that limousine. It's seen enough around Okeechobee these days. As you know, he's getting in the car with Calder Martin."

"Buck detests Calder. I can't believe he'd be riding around in a limo with that bastard."

"Believe it."

"How did you get this picture?"

"A friend of mine was in the park snapping some pictures. You know how the handsome hunks like to go there and take off their shirts. He spotted Buck and took his picture. It was just by chance he got the picture of Buck getting into that car. He thought he was just photographing some handsome blonde stud. Until the pictures were developed, he didn't know that was Buck Brooke."

"I see," Gene said, understanding nothing.

"Also, I know for a fact that Buck has had at least one meeting in Biff's officer. A gay police officer I know keeps me informed about what's going on around there."

"But couldn't that have been about that bomb threat to the Examiner building?"

"It could have been, but then again there may not have been a bomb threat at all. Maybe the bomb threat was just a cover-up so Buck could confer with your chief."

"I still can't believe Buck would try to cause me all this trouble."

"Okay, try this on for size. Buck has hired your dear Clara and Maria. They're living at his private house, and you can check that out for yourself if you don't believe me."

"They're living at his house?" Gene felt himself trembling.

"The question is, why would Buck want to drive you out of town? What do you know about Buck—the sexiest man alive—that would make him want to kick your ass out of this cesspool?"

Gene didn't answer but stared vacantly at Leroy. Finally, he said, "Maybe I know the reason."

"Do you know some scandal about him, something you could blackmail him with?"

"Maybe."

"That stud is going to have a lot of money. I hear he's making millions off the sale of the Examiner. And that old fart of a grandfather of his is about to die, or so I hear. Buck is going to be one of the richest and most powerful men in Florida. If you've got something on him, I think he'd like to see you get out of his way."

Gene walked over to the sofa and sat down. "I hope you don't mind but I've got to stay here awhile. I want to see the six o'clock news. I don't think I can leave the building until then. When it gets dark, I'll slip out. I've got things to do. When they are no longer staking out my apartment, I'll get back in and see how Jill and Sandy are doing."

Leroy poured himself another drink. "So far I've heard no word from Calder and Barry about coughing up the money. But I expect to hear from them soon."

There was an ominous look on Gene's face as he looked over at Leroy. "Maybe we've already heard from them."

*****

At the airport, Shelley went aboard the plane. Buck kissed him good-bye and promised to join him soon after making a call to his grandfather in Switzerland.

When the connection was made, the voice of old Buck I sounded weak, feeble, not his usual booming personality. "I'm glad you called, son," he said. "I've missed you."

"I love you, guy. I always will. I want to know how you're holding up."

"I've seen better days. For a long time I didn't want you to come and see me like this. Like I am now. But I've changed my mind. I want you to fly over. But not before your wedding is announced. When you come to the hospital, I want you to bring pictures of your wedding with you."

"I will. I'll have some other news too. But you've got to keep it a secret."

"Oh, my God. I'm going to get my final wish!"

"You've got it! You didn't have to force me into a marriage with Susan. I was already in love with her, and you could tell that she's in love with me. We were carrying on like crazy before the marriage. But in secret. She's pregnant. Little Buck Brooke IV is in the oven."

There was a long pause on the other end of the line. Then Buck realized his grandfather was sobbing. "That's the greatest gift you can give a dying man."

"You'll live to see him grow up. You'll be real proud of him. Maybe you weren't always proud of me but you'll be proud of your great-grandson."

"I know I will. You've given me a reason to live, or at least something good to think about until I die. Something to take my mind off this fucking hospital. I hate the Swiss. But for some perverted reason I've always turned to their doctors when I need some major medical."

"I'm meeting tonight to conclude the sale of the Examiner," Buck said. "In Palm Springs. Then I'll fly back to Susan and we'll proudly announce our wedding. Since the baby won't be able to hide himself for long enough, we'll claim we were married months ago."

"Good idea," the old man said. "We don't want scandal attached to the Brooke name, now do we?"

"Never that."

His grandfather started to cough, the hacking growing violent.

In a few moments, another voice came on the phone. "This is Dr. Euler speaking. I'm terribly sorry but your grandfather can't talk any more. We've been alerted to your upcoming visit. I'll talk to you more then about his condition. What we've found." He abruptly hung up the phone.

Buck headed for the airplane. At the top of the ramp, the Japanese attendant told him that Shelley had gone to his cabin to rest and that Buck was to join him there.

Buck said he'd like for Shelley to rest a bit and that he preferred some champagne at the moment. He felt his whole body trembling. He was glad he'd lied to old Buck. It was taking a chance. There was a possibility that he might indeed live. Maybe he might rally at the last minute. He was a tough old goat. He might even fly home to await the delivery of his imaginary grandson. Sipping the champagne, a bitter look came across Buck's face. He'd deal with that dilemma when it came—and not a moment before.

Suddenly, he was told that Rose had arrived at the airport and was coming aboard the plane. He decided to wait for her.

She appeared suddenly in an elegantly tailored rose-colored suit with a red scarf around her neck. Behind dark sunglasses she looked like the screen legend, Arlene Dahl, at the peak of her auburn-haired beauty, with the shapely frame and legs of Marlene Dietrich at her prime. There was no doubt about it: Rose Phillips could have become a bigtime movie star if she hadn't gone into evangelism.

He moved swifty toward her, giving her a long, lingering kiss on the lips. "I've missed you."

She backed away slightly and gave him an amused smile. "I'm sure the boy kept you amused."

He whispered in her ear, "Boys are fun for a little diversion, but it takes a woman to satisfy a real man like me." His tongue gently grazed her ear.

"I know," she said smugly, apparently really believing him.

He found that lying to old Buck had come easily. It was no harder to lie to Rose.

"I'd like to join you for some of that champagne," she said. "I had a rough ride from Dallas with some of my... What shall I call them? Advisers?"

"The show's getting hot."

"Hot and bitter. I've learned there is going to be a big parade down Fifth Avenue attacking me and my positions. Large blow-ups of my gorgeous puss will be carried along the avenue beside equally large blowups of Hitler. Isn't that charming?"

"What every girl from Abilene dreams about."

"Don't make fun. This is a dreadful nightmare to me."

"I know it is. It's just so shocking and horrible I don't know how to respond. But you must have known what you were getting yourself in for when you signed on to do these dirty deeds."

She eyed him affectionately, patting the well-cushioned seat next to hers. "Believe it or not, I didn't. It is more difficult than I'd imagined. I'm in far deeper than I want to be. I want to be loved. Not hated." She reached over and kissed him on the mouth.

"We all do, I suppose. But we need to make money too."

"Exactly. Being loved and making money don't always go hand in hand."

"I'm a little nervous about tonight. Losing the Examiner and all. One thing I can't figure. If I'm going to become your media director, why are you taking the Examiner away?"

"It's not really being taken away. It's going to become a house organ for my movement. I figured you didn't want any part of that. Having the Examiner run editorials lauding my various positions is a lot better than printing some stinking little tabloid sheets to give away to rednecks in parking lots."

"I suppose. The paper was never mine. It always belonged to old Buck. He never trusted me enough to make it mine. Most of the stuff I wrote for it was killed or so grossly edited it didn't read like my copy anyway."

"There will be so many more papers, so many more triumphs, the loss of the Examiner won't matter. A mere pin prick—nothing more."

He swallowed the last of the champagne in his glass. It wasn't going down well. He was more upset over the loss of the Examiner than he pretended to be with her.

She noticed the look on his face. "Go on. Ask why Buck Number One is selling out. It's a secret I can share with you now that you're one of the family."

"You forced the sale." His voice trailed off.

"I've forced him to do many things." She downed the liquid in her glass and ordered another one from the Japanese attendant. "Fuck that! I'm telling you the truth. I've blackmailed him for years."

His breathing on the plane grew more difficult. He both wanted to hear her story and shut it out at the same time.

"I had to get my start somewhere. As a teenager, I was picked up by an oldtime evangelist, Billy Lloyd. Maybe you've heard of him. He used to be big. As big as I am today. But he lost it all. There were those who said I got him drunk and drugged at a big rally. A media event. At the last minute, I had to go on in his place. Guess who was sitting out there in the audience that night?" She paused just long enough to look into Buck's startled face. "Your granddad. He liked me a lot. He issued orders to his editor to 'puff' me."

A long silence came between them. A fly landed on Buck's nose, but he didn't bother to shoo it away.

"Yes, I had an affair with the founder of your clan." Her words stabbed at his heart. "Nothing memorable, I can assure you. When it comes to love-making, you've got him beat by yards."

He didn't want her to go on, but felt paralyzed to stop her.

A glee came over her face as she warmed to her tale. "It lasted a few months until he got tired of me. Meanwhile, I was getting a lot of publicity in the Brooke papers. There were more of them then, remember?"

He said nothing, remaining still.

"I knew he liked pretty young things. I started recruiting some for him. Pimping, I think they call it."

The blood drained from his face. As much as he now knew about Rose, it was still hard for him to reconcile the private woman with the public image.

"I met a little twelve year old. Name of Darlene. One weekend I joined old Buck and Darlene on a cruise off Catalina. If I recall, I was accompanied by a Mexican stud. We sailed down to Baja. Darlene wasn't into some of old Buck's demands. But he forced her. I could hear them fighting at night." She arched her neck and went on. "I guess the old goat got carried away."

"I don't know exactly what happened," she said. "No one living except old Buck knows exactly. Darlene was smothered to death one night. Maybe old Buck choked her in anger, I don't know. The Mexican believed that Darlene bit off half of Buck's dick when he tried to force her to go down on him. All we remember were the screams coming from old Buck's cabin. Not from Darlene, but the old man himself. One of the crew members was a male nurse. He was in Buck's cabin for most of the night. All we heard was Buck's moans. We never heard that poor girl utter another sound until she was found dead the next morning."

He sucked in more of the hot air and waited. The more he looked into her famous face, the less he wanted to conjure up what happened.

"One of the crew threw her overboard. Her body was probably eaten by sharks. Her mama—what a bloodsucker she was—was paid off very well indeed, so I heard. Actually, she was probably glad to get rid of her little whore."

Buck looked out the airplane window, the sun's brilliant reflection momentarily blinding him.

"Of course, that little boat ride didn't even rate a line in my *Hallelujah!* As I told you, you can't put everything in your autobiography. Actually, old Buck paid me to keep it out. Initially, four-hundred thousand dollars, which was a lot more money back then. With that money, I opened my first evangelical center in Tulsa."

Buck swallowed hard, almost praying she wouldn't go on. He couldn't stand any more.

"That was not the end of my demands. He couldn't buy me off so easily."

He was suddenly fractured. He believed her now. He had, in fact, believed her from the beginning. Accepting was another matter. A shock wave swept over him. The pain was too vast for his brain to focus on any one area. It was a nebulous hurt that streaked across his body and, after a reckless journey through this system, came to lodge permanently in his chest, clogging it, forming a dull ache. It was inescapable pain.

She had forced him into pure chaos. He felt lost, stranded in some state of semi-darkness. She sat before him, radiantly beautiful, exuding energy and warmth. As he stared at her face more intensely, desperately searching for clues, her beauty had become like some corrosive acid, causing disintegrations.

In his mind, he wanted to shout at her, "I'll never work for you, bitch." But he remained silent. Her words had moved into his system like a colliding planet.

"Buck was always talking about what guts he had," she said. "Always so proud of his balls. But, you see, balls are very vulnerable, sweetheart. And if you've ever seen guts strewn all over a street, they are nothing to be proud of either."

"It's not a pretty story," he said. "Ingrid Howard is working on a biography of old Buck. I don't think we need to rush to tell her this tidbit."

"I've always believed in leaving things out of biographies." She got up and moved with the grace of a dancer toward her cabin. "I'm sorry I had to tell you, but I felt it important. Tonight you'll know even more about me and tomorrow even more than that. As I said, there's a lot about me that didn't make it into my autobiography."

"A lot," he said softly, almost to himself. When he looked up again, she had just disappeared, as if flying off into space like a bird of prey.

In her wake, she'd left him in fragments. He stood up, slightly dizzy either from the champagne or her revelations. Stunned, he didn't know where to go. He felt he had to weld the fragments of himself back together again. He stood looking first at her cabin door, the more luxurious of the accommodations, and then at Shelley's airborne boudoir. He headed for Shelley's cabin.

The boy was asleep in the bed. He snuggled up against him and buried his face in Shelley's neck. He started to cry. Shelley reached out and cuddled him. One of the reasons Buck loved the boy was that he had the good taste not to ask why he was sobbing.

*****

Even as she sat in Gene's condo talking to Jill, Susan couldn't believe her good fortune in getting the interview. As the news that Gene was living with Jill came on television, Susan hadn't believed the slant given by reporters. She was also determined to become a working woman again, even if she'd been fired from the Examiner. She wanted an interview with Jill, and she was confident that the Okeechobee News would publish it. The way she figured it, appearing at the News and offering them an exclusive interview might be a good and proper introduction to a newspaper she wanted to direct in the near future if Buck came through with his plan to buy up the majority stock.

Obtaining Gene's address and phone number had been too easy. It was in Jim's possession, and he freely handed it over to her when she explained what she intended to do. Jim had both the address and phone number because he'd planned to represent Gene if the second indecent exposure charge came to court. Jim had warned her that she'd still have to gain entrance to the condo, and he doubted seriously if Jill, the beleaguered girl, would agree to the interview.

As she noticed the polite, rather sensitive young woman preparing tea for them, Susan knew that the only reason Jill had agreed to see her was because she'd once been married to Gene. That gave her a unique perspective on the story, at least according to what Susan had told Jill when she'd spoken to her on the house phone from the lobby of the condo.

As Jill approached with the tea, Susan knew in her heart she hadn't deceived the girl. Up to now reports had given a completely sexual overtone to the story, suggesting that Gene had exposed himself to the little girl and had later tracked her down and forced her into becoming his sex slave. Skirting the laws of libel, the initial TV reports hadn't exactly come right out and said that, but the suggestion was all too clear.

"What they are saying is wrong," Jill said. "Gene is the kindest, gentlest man I've ever known. I'm not his lover. What the TV people don't know is that I live here with my boyfriend, Sandy. Gene is like a daddy to us, a daddy that neither of us really had. There is no sex between us. This is no love nest, at least where Gene is concerned. If it's a love nest, it's between Sandy and me—and that's our private business."

"I didn't know about this Sandy."

"You know now. Gene didn't seek me out, kidnap me, and bring me back here. I was out on the street. He's giving Sandy and me a home we never had. Just now he's trying to get us enrolled in a hotel-training school so we can earn a decent living. Sandy and I don't have the best education in the world. A lot of what we know we picked up on the street."

"You seem to have perfect manners," Susan said. "The way you pour tea would meet the approval of Queen Elizabeth. You speak very well."

"Thank you," she said, sipping her tea. "I'm not some cheap whore, although I've done a lot of things to survive, things I'm not proud of."

"You are a very charming and gracious young lady, and I'm proud to know you. I'm also proud of Gene for befriending you the way he has and in spite of the god damn TV news."

"He's a good man. I've known many good men in my life, even though I'm young. Not all of them were abusive. One man took me in for two years. He was much older than me. If I learned how to pour tea and speak properly, it was from him. He taught me a lot. But then he had a heart attack and died, and I was turned out into the streets again with nothing. His family arrived from Ohio, and I was out the door within the hour. They wouldn't even let me take the clothes my friend had bought for me."

"I'm sorry."

Jill burst into tears. "Now somebody is trying to ruin Gene. Threatening our lives together. Making it ugly."

"I think I can write a story that puts this whole thing in a different light."

"I hope you can. I've read other stories about Gene and me, a long time ago. They were all wrong. It's true: he did expose himself to me. And, according to those old reports, and I know you've read them all too, that one act is said to have ruined my life. A lot of people even believe that it drove me onto the streets to be a prostitute. But nothing could be farther from the truth."

"Exactly what do you mean?"

"I wasn't some sweet innocent girl, even though I know that's how I appeared to Gene that day. I was pretty grown up about some things. My own mama was the whore. I'd seen many men before. Naked men getting it on with my mama. She didn't view Gene's exposing himself to me as any big thing. Other people did, though. They were pressing that we take action against Gene. My mama completely opposed that. I don't even know where she is these days. She headed for California and left me behind. We lost touch. It's not that I've had any permanent address where somebody could write me. That is, until now, and I feel even my living here is threatened."

"Do you know why Gene exposed himself to you that day? I've always wondered. Do you have any insight?"

"I've thought about it a lot. I don't know the answer. He's never told me. He's said he's sorry a million times. But he didn't have to apologize even one time. He might have thought he was exposing himself to Shirley Temple, but he wasn't. Hell, for ten dollars I would have jumped into the car and given him a blow-job on the spot. But believe it or not there was something spiritual about his revealing himself to me."

"I don't quite follow that."

"It was the look in his eyes. He was on the verge of tears. It was like he was saying, 'Look, I'm a man. Here's proof.' The only way he could prove his manhood was through his cock. I know this doesn't make much sense. But I've always felt that something happened that day, or shortly before, that made him feel he'd lost his manhood. He was just trying to get it back. To my horror, because I love him dearly, he took a crude approach. Even an illegal approach. But it wasn't to harm me or retard my growth. It had something to do with something going on deep inside him. He was a sad, pathetic person that day. Instead of being horrified, I felt sorry for him. He was reaching out to me for something. But I was too young to respond back then."

"Of course, you were. I'm sorry the whole thing happened. What you've just told me indicates far more compassion and understanding than I brought to the situation. I feel I had some responsibility in driving Gene to that desperate act. I didn't understand him at all. I married an image. The university athlete. With Gene, I never got beyond the image to see the man underneath. I was too young. Too concerned with myself. I never listened to his desperate plea for help. I gave him nothing. I only attacked him. I regret that very much right now. In fact, one of the reasons I'm here is to try to make right a lot of wrongs in the past. I hope you believe me and don't think I'm some shithead reporter trying to win your confidence—only to expose you later in the paper. That happens all the time."

Jill reached for Susan's hand. "I trust you. If you're lying, you will be the one to lose from our getting together—not me. I know the truth. Maybe it doesn't really matter what the public thinks."

Susan turned her head at the sound of a key in the lock. Very quickly she got up, fearing an intruder.

From the dark shadows of the hallway, a body appeared before her. It was Gene.

*****

In Palm Springs, it was already late in the evening when Buck arrived at the address given him by a member of Rose's staff. Although his invitation was valid from the moment his plane landed, he preferred to delay his arrival at the mansion for several hours so that he could collect his thoughts. Turning down the chauffeur-driven limousine that was waiting to meet his plane, he had rented a car and driven out into the desert, hoping a long monotonous drive through a drab landscape would clarify some ideas. It hadn't. He'd arrived at the mansion more confused than ever, and completely uncertain about the direction of his life.

Upon leaving the plane, Rose had ordered Shelley to come with her. Buck was not told where they were going, although both of them promised to meet him later at the mansion. He had gathered that they were directed by someone to attend a meeting in a mysterious location on the far side of the resort. He wasn't certain but he assumed that Calder Martin had flown in for the meeting which appeared to be a showdown of sorts. Rose had a piercing anxiety on her face, and Buck had never seen such nervous energy in Shelley before. He wanted to comfort the boy, but couldn't as he didn't really know what the problem was.

At the gateway to the mansion, a security guard telephoned the main house to receive permission for Buck's vehicle to be allowed up the winding, palm-lined driveway that led to a pair of golden doors. He wasn't certain but he suspected the doors weren't painted but were actually inlaid with the precious metal itself. In low relief on the golden doors was a replica of prehistoric cave painting, portraying a realistic bull attacked by men with bows and arrows.

As he braked his car, the golden doors were thrown open by two servants in turbans, each clad in a flowing white disdasha. Their long, lean bodies approached his car. As one of them opened the door, Buck observed their narrow faces and light skins, causing him to believe they were Berbers. Rose's "Arab connection" appeared stronger the more he saw of her private life.

He was ushered into a dimly lit hallway where the smell of incense was powerful. He was informed that Sister Rose would join him shortly. Obviously she had concluded her confrontational meeting and had arrived at the mansion before he did. He didn't know where Shelley was.

As he stood near painted columns under a vaulted ceiling, he gave his order for a Scotch. Looking about, he noticed that the split-level room was filled with copies of Roman statuary, including a Head of Zeus and a Smiling Venus.

He was shown to a large patio with an Italian fountain topped by a statue of the Three Graces standing on a pedestal over a cascade of water. Branching off from the patio was a series of rooms. He strolled into one, finding it to be a private walled garden. Its walls were painted mauve, with a wide pink border around the base. The garden had been planted with large plastic bushes, holding an abundance of amazingly realistic flowers he was forced to fondle before deciding they were fakes. An illusion of ever-bearing flowery shrubbery was created, the magic garden of some child's fantasy. The roof tiles were painted a pink and orange in a checkerboard style, evoking pop art.

He left the garden, following an entry hallway to another room. Here the floor and four walls were covered with a scarlet-colored carpet, and a white silk canopy studded with gold fleurs-de-lis hung from the ceiling. The nude statues were painted, as in classical days, with meticulous realism, including careful shading of the skin tones of the genitalia. The fountain showered pink water. Around it were placed white patent leather pillow mattresses.

He walked alongside a small pond in which gardenias floated and brilliantly colored carp swam by. At the far end of the wall stood a black marble fireplace, over which hung a portrait of a man who appeared to be in his early forties.

Buck moved closer for an inspection. The subject of the portrait was obviously an Arab, though one attired in western dress. His face appeared vaguely familiar. An article in *Esquire* flashed through his mind. The Arab was strikingly handsome, his eyes intense and purple in their luminosity, so large and powerful they dominated his finely chiseled face.

He turned abruptly at the approach of a male servant. "Who's the painting of?"

The servant didn't understand. "Who is it?" Buck asked him again before he realized that the servant found it inconceivable that he didn't know the name of, presumably, the host. "I'm a friend of Sister Rose's. I've never had the pleasure of meeting the gentleman in the painting."

"That's Mr. Pharaon," the servant answered politely in a clipped British accent.

"Pharaon who?"

"Mr. Ahmad Pharaon." The servant gave him his drink, bowed, and walked off.

The name was not unknown to Buck, even though he couldn't immediately identify it. It sounded like so many other names buzzing in his head.

Ahmad Pharaon, Ahmad Pharaon, Ahmad Pharaon, he kept repeating to himself. Settling back on a sofa he was certain was upholstered in the skin of some endangered species, he recalled who Ahmad Pharaon was. After all, his own newspaper—read that former newspaper—had once carried a story on Pharaon.

Robert and Buck three years ago had flown for a quickie two-day vacation to Paradise Island. While wandering around, they had spotted what the locals called "The House of Mystery" before they'd reached the Cloister at the Ocean Club. Their guide had told them that this was the most luxurious and opulent private mansion in all The Bahamas. The mansion was supposed to be owned by a mysterious sheik who'd created a bit of Arabian Nights fantasy on Paradise Island. Ever since it was first built, the mansion had been the subject of such local speculation. The estate was surrounded by a wall, with a total of sixteen towering lampposts lighting the night. A statue of Neptune along with four security guards protected the only gate leading into the grounds.

At the Ocean Club a banker friend of his grandfather's had encountered Buck in the bar. The banker had told Buck that he'd heard that the house belonged to Ahmad Pharaon, who was widely known in the Arab world and probably had a long file in FBI and CIA headquarters here in America.

The reason the Examiner had run a piece on him, however, was that he was rumored to have purchased a sixty-two room mansion twenty-five miles from Okeechobee, a palatial dwelling far larger than Rose's Paradise Shores. The mansion had originally been built by a tobacco heiress who had died mysteriously. Her estate had put the house on the market, and it was sold almost immediately, the name of the buyer a mystery.

Pharaon was the oil-rich relative of Libya's former ambassador to the United Nations. He was known for living in extraordinary luxury around the world and was famous for his riotous extravagances. Publicly he was the head of an Arab multinational conglomerate that was founded on traffic in guns, but now backed everything from California banks to films. Privately, he was rumored to be a fund-raiser for international terrorists, with powerful connections in Iran and Algeria as well as his native Libya.

There remained little doubt in Buck's mind. Pharaon, he was convinced, was the major source of Rose's seemingly unlimited capital.

What did remain was for him to find out why such a Moslem would offer financial backing to one of the world's leading fundamentalist Christians.

The sound of angry voices coming from a salon across the patio momentarily distracted him.

*****

"God damn you, Rose, let me alone!"

Whirling around, she screamed, "Shut up, you little faggot! I've had about all of you I can take." Words came from her injured throat as if her voicebox were constricted. She closed her eyes and everything mercifully went blank.

At times she really believed she hated Shelley so much she could kill him. Each day she regretted a little more her having adopted him. She found him threatening, fearing that at any time a quirk in his nature could sabotage her carefully laid plans.

He stood before a fireplace, facing her defiantly. Even though it was his own actions, and those of Barry Collins, he somehow seemed to blame her for his misfortune. The meeting with the power brokers had gone badly. Shelley was out. He'd been ordered to go into seclusion. He was to make no more public appearances. It was deemed best that he go away for a long time, some place where he'd wouldn't get into trouble. She'd been ordered to pay off the blackmailer with her own funds. There was no bail-out help for her.

She breathed in deeply, the pungent odor of the brandy—the smell lingered on her own breath—assailing her nostrils. "You are being sent away—and that's that," she said as calmly as she could. "Calder Martin has arranged it. That asshole Martin won the round today. You've thoroughly disgraced me. I've indulged you. But the stupidity of your going to that boy whorehouse was far too much to be tolerated. Even if you're a total idiot and didn't know better, Barry should have known better. Any man with that lack of judgment shouldn't be groomed to become president of the United States. And he won't. You're not only out yourself, but Barry is finished too. They'll stick with him until this god damn mayor's race is over. After all, they don't want Hazel in power. After that, they're dumping him."

"I won't go away. That's kidnapping. I'll go to the police. I'll tell everything. I'll report everything. I'll call a press conference."

"You do that. You just threaten that. If Calder heard what you just said, he might even have you put to sleep."

"He wouldn't dare. I'm too famous. Too many people would ask too many questions."

"You'd be surprised what Calder can get away with. What he has always gotten away with."

"Nothing about a scumbag like Calder Martin would surprise me. Fuck Calder. I'm more concerned about you. You didn't stand up for me one time today. You let the jackals tear at my flesh, and you didn't defend me."

"I can't defend you. Your stupidity is without defense. I'm buying off your blackmailer, I guess. Isn't that enough? When I get back to Okeechobee, after my little trip to the Middle East for that god damn propaganda film, I'm meeting with Barry. I just know he's going to ask me to put up all the money to bail you out of this one."

"Big fucking deal. You can afford it."

"That's not the point. The point is, I don't intend to be placed in another position where I have to give in to a blackmailer. The arrangement we had with Bossdum was perfect."

"Really? That's what you think. I haven't told you this but Bossdum is demanding one-hundred thousand dollars."

"That's chicken feed. For God's sake, give it to him."

"I plan to."

"That's a hell of a lot cheaper than what Fitzgerald is demanding."

"I said I would. But the one-hundred thousand is hush money for you too. Bossdum fucked you just as much as he fucked me."

"I have an idea. You're to make no payments to him at all. It's too risky with all this shit spinning around us. I'll give Buck the money. Let him meet with Bossdum for the pay-off. I'm sure they know each other. They went to college together."

"Buck has already agreed to do that. Your other performance today, especially in not defending me, stank worse than shit."

"You don't understand. Here is my last big chance. I'm going to be bigger than ever. Make incredible money but at great peril to myself. I could get killed by some crazed assassin with an agenda. Do you think for one minute that I would give up the biggest chance I've ever had in my life because you're running out of control? Cruising around trying to get a big dick shoved up your overstretched ass."

"Things are different. I've settled down. I've got Buck now. That's all I've ever wanted. We can keep him. Shower him with money and presents. There's enough meat there to satisfy both of us."

"I agree but you don't seem to get it. Buck has arrived too late to save you. You are history. They're continuing with me. I've been discreet, shown some judgment. You've been nothing but a whore."

"You are a whore too, bitch. Cunt would be a better word for a cow like you."

"Call me any name you want. I might be a whore but I've never been exposed yet. No one ever photographed me getting fucked in a bordello."

"But I thought I was safe there. After all, it operates with Biff's approval. Biff himself even goes there to spy on the action. That is, when he's not at the Vulcan Baths."

"That doesn't surprise me. All sheriffs are corrupt, at least all sheriffs I've known. Calder ran that whorehouse for blackmail purposes. You knew that."

"I knew that. But I didn't believe Fitzgerald would blackmail me."

"Learn now, although it may be too late, anybody in God's fucking world can blackmail you, and probably will."

"I'm only fourteen years old. How am I supposed to know how you dirty adults play your rotten games?"

"You've learned more today than you've ever learned about adult games. You want to rush into adulthood before your time. Welcome to the adult world. I hope you're enjoying it." She held her hand to her head. An ache was coming on.

"I hate everything you're doing with this Arab connection. I know why you're doing it, bitch. Money and power. You'd come out against motherhood if someone paid you enough. You're the slut of religion."

Irritated and enraged beyond control, she crossed the floor to him and, almost before he knew what had happened, she slapped him so hard the noise resounded through the room.

He rushed to the mantle of the fireplace, his fingers tightening around a piece of Egyptian statuary. He seemed ready to lunge blindly at her, attacking her with the figure. She moved back, sensing the danger.

After a silent, suspenseful moment, he dropped the statue, sending it crashing to the hearth. It had been stolen from a museum in Cairo and was a rare art work handed down from antiquity. It could not be replaced. There was nothing else like it left in the world. She searched his face for some sign of remorse. There was none. He didn't even look down to see how the pieces shattered on the floor.

The way the boy stared at her made her uncomfortably aware and self-conscious of her looks. By the very intensity of his glare he made her feel old, ugly, and misshapen, hardly the kind of mood she wanted to be in when she dined with Buck.

"Okay, *sister,*" he said, mocking the word. "I owe you one for that slap."

She felt near tears, and his threat only served to step up their tempo. He was elusive, tantalizing, as she stood white-lipped and tense, waiting to see what he was going to do next. Like a doe facing the bullet of the hunter, she remained frozen with glazed eyes, wanting to flee, knowing it was too late.

"You really believe that Pharaon is turned on by you?"

She didn't answer.

"He told me you were too old for him. Too flabby. He fucked you, he claimed, for political reasons."

The sudden shock of those words made her tremble.

He pointed at her with a swift hand movement, as if dismissing her. She knew he was about to confirm her worst suspicion.

"Now, take me. He finds my sweet little ass—so rosy pink, so tight—just delectable." He spoke with obvious glee. "You know Arabs, baby. They like them young, it doesn't matter which sex."

She burst into tears. He'd succeeded in making her feel ugly and frightened. Shoulders shaking, she turned from the sight of him. If she tried, she could blot out his words, the way she'd erased so many other episodes in her mind.

"Don't think about it," she said to herself under her breath. "Wipe it out of your mind."

After an agonizing moment, she turned to face him again, and in that short time she'd regained her composure. His smug look faded when he confronted the harshness in the lines of her face. He'd had his little moment of triumph and, as a street-smart boy, he knew it was her turn now."

She moved toward him, as in a blood-rite initiation. "You useless piece of shit!" she said, the ferocity of her own voice disturbing even her. A sharp, icy wind seemed to whip her, crackling and swirling underfoot as she came closer.

Her face and demeanor had gone through a terrifying metamorphosis in the last minute. Alarm swept over his petulant face. Right before him, staring deeply into his eyes, she said, "I'll fix you, you little bastard."

He turned from the sight of her and ran in the direction of his bedroom.

After he was gone, she checked her appearance in a Moroccan mirror, trying to soften the harsh features. To do that, she had to erase from her mind completely what had just taken place.

From somewhere deep within, a clear radiance seemed to emerge, making her eyes look translucent, shimmering like emeralds. She smiled at her ability to summon this hidden resource, and then held up her finely carved lips to inspect. Her mouth had seduced Buck in his own bedroom on his private cay and had brought him inordinate pleasure.

It could still do that again. Shelley was a liar. She was at the peak of her beauty and desirability. She knew, of course, that Pharaon was involved with her son, but Shelley was only a toy for him. When he wanted mature love, he turned to her. It was the same with Buck. Shelley was but a mere convenience to Buck. A means of getting his rocks off with a cute trick. For adult pleasures, she was available to him. His love-making was genuine. She could tell. As she'd gazed upon him, she'd known Buck was mesmerized by her.

Before meeting with Buck, she checked her appearance one final time. In spite of Shelley's blast, the woman staring back at her in the mirror was camera ready. The lighting in the room was flattering but it was more than that. She knew she'd never looked lovelier. Beauty, power, money. What man could resist her? She breathed in deeply, knowing these few moments alone with herself had restored her confidence. At last she was ready to face the challenges that still lay ahead in the evening. She'd deal with Shelley later.

*****

The artificial palm tree appeared sinister-looking as the wind blew through its fake fronds. Buck sat in the garden under this golden tree with scarlet and purple fruit. Nesting in its fronds were lifelike replicas of fantastic birds of paradise. Somehow the setting seemed appropriate for what was about to happen.

The hysterical conversation he'd just heard hadn't surprised him. In some way, it had been predictable, at least confirming the image of Shelley as that of a boy dangerously sophisticated beyond his years. Rose and Shelley struck him as two persons possessed—moving unrelentingly toward their self-destruction. Or had each selected the other to deliver the *coup de grâce*?

Interrupting his thoughts, Rose emerged from behind an Oriental drapery. It was a theatrical entrance against a dramatic scenic backdrop. Even though she'd been cruelly attacked by her son, she still exuded self-confidence. She appeared like a woman who'd just emerged from the bed of a lover. He knew what a false appearance that was, a bravado that revealed her talent as a performer.

She had the grace to serve dinner without bringing up the unpleasant business. The *cous-cous* was perfectly prepared, the best he'd ever tasted, though he had no appetite. He rested his hands on an elegant teakwood table, watching her face lit by electric candelabra. He smelled the fresh roses and Spanish lilies and admired the Swedish crystal and silver service that she informed him had once belonged to the Hapsburgs. He did manage in the meantime to drink a bottle of Dom Perignon. She only sipped at her champagne, knowing she had to keep a clear head. On the other hand, he needed a tranquilizer.

By the time the Arab coffee was served, he could no longer stand the suspense. He looked over at her and asked pointedly, "Are you buying up oil wells in Libya with your Christian donations?"

"No." Her fingers delicately traced a pattern along her tulip-shaped glass. "I have more interesting acquisitions in mind."

"Such as?"

She got up and walked over to his chair. "If you make the *right* decision, my people will buy back the chain of papers your grandfather lost." In amazement, he looked up at her. Her offer, so blatant and bold, made without hesitation and preliminaries. He met her stare, finding it fierce—almost blindingly so. For the first time to him, she appeared grotesque. "If you go with me, I'll make you the biggest newspaper publisher in America."

He slowly got up, his head reeling. A disturbing insight into his own ambition flashed. He tried to retain his cool detachment, but on a much deeper level he was far from peaceful. In this make-believe garden, he moved unsteadily. Everything was so confectionery.

What amazed him more than anything was that she had reached inside him and discovered his deepest, darkest ambition. God damn it, he did want to become the biggest newspaper publisher in America. Night after night, he used to dream of controlling not just the Examiner, but all the papers in the chain old Buck had tossed away.

The voice from behind him was imperious, the presence commanding. "Buck." The next mention of his name was turned into the most sensual of caresses. "*Buck.*"

It was an intoxicating aroma she gave off, and the smell didn't come from her expensive perfume either. It was from raw power. She wanted that, he knew, far more than the money. In that wish, his desire matched hers. She was willing to pay a higher price than he was, and both of them had totally different ideas as to what to do with that power.

Or was that true? What principles did he have to compromise if he gave in to her?

Her offer was tempting, the most tempting ever.

He felt like the young Trojan, Paris, in the old legend. Hera offered earthly power; Athena, wisdom, and Aphrodite, love. At the moment the thrill of power made him lean toward Hera's promise. For one brief flash, he told himself that perhaps for a small investment of himself ventured, the rewards would far outweigh the compromises.

He was still in that undecided state when he turned to face her again. For a moment she looked like Isadora Duncan among the columns of the Acropolis. But something was lacking in that image. She didn't possess Isadora's child-heart.

He confronted a cold statue, a woman of daring, a flamboyant actress who, faced with fading beauty, now seemed intent on following savage whims and wanton destructiveness. Her impulses couldn't be clearly defined. He wanted order, and she preferred anarchy. Even as he stood there now, he knew the Arab's fantasy house was but a background for impending violence.

Without losing eye contact, he slowly took out a cigarette and lit it. Only a foot from her face, he aggressively blew out the smoke. She stared at the cigarette, her face comprehending the arrogance of his lighting it as he did. Perplexed at first, she gave way to a sorrowful understanding. It was his way of telling her that he wanted to be an equal partner, not some rent boy summoned to her boudoir at her convenience. She stared back at him as if each were on a battlefield. This was no longer about sex, and certainly not about love. It was about power and money. Shelley had been right. But was Rose to be blamed exclusively? Couldn't the same charge be leveled against him?

From out of nowhere he thought of Hazel and his ride with her on the road to Oklahoma. How disappointed she would be in him. What had he really stood for anyway? A few vague liberal agendas and that was about it. He'd never really done anything to help anybody else. He'd lived a selfish life. Could there be redemption for him? He didn't see that happening. Each minute in this courtyard with her was moving him deeper and deeper into a web. He couldn't pull back now, and he knew it.

The more she stared into his face, the more she'd begun to realize that he was caving in, perhaps in the same way she'd caved in years ago. He sucked the cigarette smoke deeper into his lungs. "You have thoroughly corrupted me."

"Darling, I realized how corrupt you were the first moment I met you. It was, in fact, the very element of attraction that compelled me to bond with you. I looked into your face and I saw a male version of myself."

"What is happening to me? Don't I stand for anything?"

"I've asked myself that same question a thousand times. The answer eluded me for a long time. Then it became compellingly clear. I stand for Rose Phillips. I've always stood for her. No one else did. You were born with a silver spoon in your mouth. It didn't matter whether you failed or not in life. You had a cushion waiting for you. From the moment you were born it was always certain that your grandfather would make you the richest man in Florida. One day."

"He threatened to disinherit me if I didn't marry Susan and...how shall I put this? Settle down."

"Bullshit! That old bastard had no intention of disinheriting you. He would never let the Brooke money flow anywhere but within his own blood line. He doesn't really care whether you fuck Robert or anybody else. The old goat has no morals. He wanted you married for one reason and one reason only. He told me this so I'm not making it up as I go along. He wants a Buck Brooke IV. Give the bastard a great-grandson and your duty is finished to him. Pass along the Brooke millions to another boy in the next millennium. For God's sake, make it a boy. Your grandfather's only interest in little girls is to molest them."

"That's blunt. A little more blunt than I care for."

"We're beyond subtleties at this point. Sometime tonight Pharaon will be here. I've got to monopolize his time for the first few hours. But when we wake up in the morning, he'll want to meet with you. He's got some gold bars—a lot of them—to pass on to you. I know these initial gold bars will be just the start of many more to come. You may be losing the Examiner but you sure as hell are getting paid back for your loss."

"I know that. The price of the sale grossly exaggerated."

"All the more for you to enjoy."

"You mentioned that you have to be with Pharaon first. Where do you want me to go? Disappear?"

"Yes, until in the morning. Don't go up to Shelley's room tonight. He and I have some very important arrangements to work out. I'll tell you more about Miss Shelley's new status around here later."

She obviously didn't know that he'd overheard her fight with her son. Surprisingly, she had mentioned Pharaon and had never offered an explanation of her connection to him. She'd just assumed that he knew who Pharaon was and that the Arab was the man bankrolling her. He found it amazing, though, that she let him piece together the puzzle for himself. Or was it a puzzle? A fool entering the house could figure out Pharaon was her connection. In some respects, he was glad she offered no explanation about her link with Pharaon. It wasn't that he didn't want to know. He just didn't want to hear it from Rose. He much preferred to learn about Pharaon from Shelley and had to admit he was jealous, although he knew how foolish it was to be jealous of anybody's past.

"I've arranged for you to spend the night at Frank Sinatra's villa. Everything is there. The champagne. Whatever you want. Except there will be no women. No little boys. You've had enough of that for the moment. You need your beauty rest before meeting Pharaon. I want you to look like prime grade A meat."

"I'll show up movie star handsome and in tight pants."

"Great! I want you to dazzle him because the build-up I've given you has been tremendous."

"It sounds like a chorus girl getting ready for an audition."

"There's some of that in all this. After all, look what he's paying you."

"But you're making it sexually suggestive. Surely Pharaon doesn't go that route except with little boys."

"Surely not." She smiled enigmatically at him before turning and walking from the courtyard, heading for an adjoining parlor. "Let's have a brandy and a long, lingering kiss before you disappear into the night."

He followed her trail, noting the beauty of her body and how gracefully it moved across the patio. He wondered only briefly about Shelley, but thought he was all right, at least for the night. What was going to happen to their future remained a looming question. Thoughts of Robert, Susan, and Gene flashed through his mind, but only briefly. None of them seemed to belong here in this exotic setting, and the more he lingered here, the more he wondered if indeed he too were not completely out of his depth.

*****

Susan looked at Gene for a long, hard moment. The years had gone by but they had been kind to him. If anything, he appeared handsomer and more virile than he was the night she'd married him. That lost little boy quality that had attracted her to him was gone. It'd been replaced by a more strong-jawed man. There was a turbulence about him that was deeply disturbing to her. It spoke of potential violence. His desperation was all too evident.

His very stance challenged her. "You had to slip your way in here to interview Jill, didn't you? Was it really necessary to humiliate me this way? Can't you let the rest of the world do that for you?"

"It's cool, Gene," Jill said in a loving, caressing way, getting up to walk over to him to comfort him and kiss him on the cheek.

"Jill's right," Susan said. "I'm here as a friend. Someone out there is trying to crucify you. I'm on your team in this one. I'm hoping to get your side across."

He turned from the sight of her. "Isn't that what all news reporters tell their victims?"

"I know it sounds like a come-on, but I really mean what I say. I'm not going to betray you. I promise with all the honor in my body. If you ever loved me or believed in me at one time, I promise you on that old trust."

"I don't know, Susan," he said, taking a cup of tea from Jill. "I come in here seeing you talking to Jill. You can understand if I don't rush to embrace the idea."

"Of course, I understand," Susan said. "Why should you trust any one? After all that's happened to you. After all the betrayals. But what I don't understand is why these betrayals are going on."

Jill kissed Gene on the cheek again and excused herself. "You two guys had better be alone for this one. I'll be in my bedroom if you need me."

Susan watched her go, almost regretting it. In some part of her body, she was apprehensive about being alone with Gene.

When she'd gone, Gene drank from his tea, then slammed the cup into the saucer. "A lot of people are out to get me."

"But who? It doesn't make sense to me."

"Your new husband has betrayed me."

She was startled, not knowing how Gene had learned of her marriage. "Buck...?" Her voice grew hesitant. "I can't believe that."

"He wants me out of the way."

"But why? You were always his friend."

"I can't spell it out to you. It's too painful. Too private."

"Oh, I see."

"You don't see at all. Buck set me up with that girl and her mother. He was behind it. I happened to know he met with Calder Martin. He deliberately had Calder destroy me. The chief—that asshole Biff—was in on it too."

She sat up rigidly on the sofa. "I can't believe that. Buck would never do anything like that. It's not in his nature."

"Oh, yeah. What if I told you that Maria and Clara are living in Buck's house right now?"

"Surely not."

"I'm going to check it out tonight for myself. But I already know it's true."

"If it's true, there must be some explanation. Buck would never do anything to harm you."

"How well do you know the man you married?"

Her throat tightened. "I don't know him all that well. I mean there's a whole side of him I don't know."

"You don't know who he's in love with. It's not you, and I'm sure you know that."

"You mean Robert, of course."

"No," he said. "I don't mean Robert. He's in love with somebody else."

She swallowed hard. She didn't like the way this encounter was going. Not wanting Gene to go on, she tried to bring the subject back to Jill. But it appeared a useless gesture. He was determined to confront her with what she didn't want to hear.

"Buck's in love with me. He always has been."

She sank back into the sofa. Her long-time suspicion had just been confirmed. First Buck had admitted this. Now Gene.

"I made a woman out of him. He can't live with that. The sexiest man alive is nothing but a woman. The big macho stud of Okeechobee is only happy when he's lying on his back taking it like a woman."

There was a long awkward silence in the room. She didn't know what to say. When she did speak, her voice was broken, the words hard to utter. "You know me well enough to know I don't think in images as crude as that. You may have discovered some need in Buck that wasn't being satisfied. That doesn't detract from his being a big macho stud. He can be that too. He can also be tender and loving. Even big macho studs can be sensitive and have other needs and roles to play."

"How politically correct. I'll stick with my point of view. It appears that your new husband can't stand up to a real man. He picks faggy little boys so he can play the big man. He can't deal with his true nature."

"He will in time. He must be given time. He's as young as we are. We play like we're adults. But you know the truth. None of us has matured yet. Give us all some years. I don't know who I am yet. In the last few days I've discovered a side of myself I didn't know existed."

"Have you gone dyke?"

"No, I haven't. But if I did, I wouldn't be ashamed of it. Surely even you must be discovering yourself. We're all doing that. Please don't judge Buck or condemn him until you know more about the truth."

"I'll find out that truth in my own way. In the meantime, I think you'd better leave. My condo's a little small. I'm sure Buck has arranged larger living quarters for you."

"He has indeed."

"Did you marry him for his money or for some other reason?"

She reached for her tea because her throat had grown dry. The tea had turned cold. When she looked up into his face, he seemed to be demanding total honesty. She felt she could no longer lie to him. If she lied to him, he might not believe her motives in interviewing Jill. "I married him so he could save his inheritance. Old Buck threatened to cut him off if he didn't marry me. He didn't have much of a choice. Marry me or else."

"So you entered this marriage with your eyes wide open."

"Completely. I knew exactly what I was getting into. Buck doesn't love me. He never did."

"I know he doesn't love you. The son of a bitch has loved only one person in his whole life, and he's too much of a coward to admit that. He was planning to run away with me. But now I know he just tricked me into thinking that. He's too afraid to have a real relationship with a real man. He's settled for something else. I'm more than he could handle. Instead of letting me go and hiding his real feelings, he thinks he has to destroy me."

All of a sudden Jill burst from her bedroom. "A call came in. It's from police headquarters. Sandy's been arrested!"

*****

Seated on a divan in the desert night, Rose wore a melancholy face in the glow of candlelight. In a sudden move, she petulantly flung herself on the luxuriously upholstered silk sofa, hugging a satin pillow, whose motif looked like it could have belonged to Cleopatra. "It was a cold, cruel act—your making love to me, getting me to feel again. Until you came along, my heart had died. Now I feel weak and vulnerable."

"That's hardly what happened," Buck said defensively. "If I walked out that door today, I feel I would not be missed. That I would be immediately replaced."

She still wanted to speak of love, even though he felt that even she didn't believe her own words. It was a romantic party game, nothing more. "Right at this moment, I'm facing the greatest challenge of my career. I need all my energy and concentration. But I spend my time day-dreaming about you instead." She leaned forward slightly and tentatively reached for his hand.

He took it and caressed it, holding it to his lips for a gentle kiss.

"Without you in my life, I'd be helpless to stand up against the onslaught I have to face."

"The moment you popped out of the womb you were no longer helpless," he said. To soften his words, he added, "That's because I believe you're a strong and powerful woman who can stand up against anything. Certainly Calder Martin."

The windows in the room were closed, and the heat of the desert afternoon had settled. Although cool outside, the night air seemed not to have entered this room. No one had turned on the air conditioner. He got up and faced an empty fireplace, his back to her. He turned again to look at her.

She defiantly stood up too, and somehow in the movement of her body, in her command of it, she admitted the truth of what he'd just said.

She smiled vaguely, not necessarily at him. More at the irony of the world itself. "You were born with great male beauty. I was born with great beauty too. Both of us have used our beauty as a weapon to charm the world. But when it's gone, when the sun comes out and reveals the devastation of the years, one must reinvent oneself. Find another weapon to use."

"That is hardly your problem right now. I doubt if you've ever looked greater than you do now."

"That may be true." She staggered toward the bar to get herself another brandy. It was only then he realized she was drunk and getting more morbid by the minute. "In your case the loss of beauty won't matter," she said. "Women, or whatever, will still be attracted to you, regardless of how burnt out and old you become. For every man, there's somebody out there salivating. But for a woman...for me, it's different. We have a shorter time to dance on the stage."

"I'm not the only man you're capable of attracting. There will be many others, I'm sure."

"You don't understand," she said defensively, moving closer to him with her drink. "How much longer can I hold out?"

Until she'd raised that question, he'd never considered it. She did appear to be a woman working on a very tight time schedule. She was also perfectly aware of what time it was in her own life.

"Right now I can create an illusionary fire of beauty," she said. She paused momentarily, her overstated self-assessment giving way to fear. "Even at my age. But what of the next few years?"

It was a rhetorical question, he felt, not really calling for an answer.

"With you, I had begun to feel love when I thought all such feeling in me had been killed off," she said, echoing a previous sentiment. She paused for a long time as if hoping the silence between them would somehow bring them into a closer alliance. "When you say there will be many other men, was that but a subtle signal that you'll leave me?"

"Not at all. I'm just suggesting that other men will throw themselves at your feet." He smiled flirtatiously. "I'll have a lot of competition."

"You're a real man. But I can just imagine what other men I'll meet. Boys at beach cabanas. Boys in hotel lobbies. In bars where one is not known. Through discreet introductions at parties. Maybe at gatherings of my church. At fifty I'll probably be using a call service."

He felt a sense of shock at that prediction. It was something an actress like Tallulah Bankhead might have said.

He wanted her to stop this talk. But she persisted. "I'll call them 'my darling' or 'dear heart' because I won't think it important to remember their names."

Suddenly, she lunged toward him, pressing her body against him as tightly as she could, as if trying to arouse some passion that had been lost. She appeared on the verge of tears. "Oh, Buck, if all those young men emerge in my future, all their faces will become one great blur. They'll all mesh into...you!"

He grabbed her and kissed her, inserting his tongue into her brandy-smelling mouth. He was too close to collecting his millions for him to fail her now. He'd rather have Shelley sucking on his tongue but in lieu of that the mother would have to do. She was moaning, clutching him, and apparently he was doing a good job at love-making. But it was only mechanical love-making, and he was amazed that she'd interpreted it as genuine passion which he didn't feel at all.

A male Arab servant entered the room. She broke away quickly.

"Mr. Pharaon called," he announced. "He's arrived at the airport and will be here soon."

On unsteady legs, she headed for the bar again to refill her glass. She motioned for the servant to open the glass doors leading to the garishly lit patio with its bizarre nude statuary. The statues seemed like real people. He followed her, noting that the lights of the patio, combined with the flickering candles of the salon, made grotesque patterns on her face. Momentarily, she looked demented, then he realized it was her nervousness and fear in meeting Pharaon. Obviously, this wasn't going to be a happy meeting.

"I must go to Sinatra's," he said. "Too bad. You and I might have had one hot evening."

She didn't seem to hear him, appearing lost in her own drunken world. Running one hand across her cheek, she seemed to want to assure herself of her own smooth beauty. She raised her hand to her mouth as if to muffle a sound coming from her damaged throat.

"I'll tell you what age is," she said in a forlorn voice, not quite her own. "Age is climbing a tree. At first its branches are firm and covered with greenery. The higher you climb from the roots, the weaker the branches become. Eventually the leaves decay, turn colors and fall off. Still you must climb higher and higher. The branches grow brittle and break off under your weight. Soon you see the top of the tree and you know it's the end. You're compelled to reach for it. You know you can't stay where you are forever. The clothes you used to drape yourself in have grown ragged by the time you reach the top. They barely conceal your skeletal nudity. At the top, once there, you're assaulted by the coldest, bitterest wind that ever blew across the glacial desert."

He swallowed hard, and, for the first time this evening, knew exactly what she was really talking about. She wasn't lamenting the loss of her beauty. Echoing Shelley's fears, she was sensing her own upcoming doom.

He approached her to tell her good night. But he was cautious. She seemed on the verge of igniting and exploding before his eyes. He'd never seen her like this. Her eyes glistened with tears. She held up her right hand, her fingers arched, but it had no function to perform. Every muscle in her face seemed knotted.

"Life has placed me in a position of trust," she said. "Millions of my devoted turn to me for guidance. For whatever reason, I inspire them.

Give them the faith that I don't have myself." She winced and passed a nervous hand across her forehead. "But I'm not going to help those souls. I will only bring out the worst in them in the months ahead. If I'm a hate-monger, I'm a whorish one. I could even respect a real hate-monger, but I'm not one. My hate isn't real. I'm paid to hate."

He kissed her on the cheek and said good night, but she didn't seem to hear him or note his passing. She was completely enraptured by her own alcohol-induced world. He could only imagine what would come out of her meeting with Pharaon. He himself had to face Pharaon in the morning.

In the foyer of the mansion, the servant handed him neatly typed directions for reaching Sinatra's house. He looked longingly up the stairwell, wishing he could go and find Shelley's bedroom. As if sensing his impulse, the servant stood in front of the stairwell, not really blocking his way but certainly suggesting that he could do so at any moment Buck made that necessary.

Instead he turned and headed out the door to face a sleepless night. As an attendant brought his car around, Buck looked back once more at the gates of the mansion, wondering what secrets this house would hold tonight.

Chapter Twelve

Buck left the Pharaon estate, heading for Sinatra's mansion. He didn't know what awaited him there, and at this point he didn't much care. Celebrities never impressed him, and because of his newspaper work he'd met his share of them. If he'd been star-struck, he would not have turned down that invitation to meet Ronald Reagan and Nancy Davis. After all, the man might become president of the United States, although he seriously doubted that.

Without bothering to read the directions, he found himself driving aimlessly, wanting to get away from Palm Springs and escape to the desert on a road to nowhere. He welcomed the incredible blackness of night that only the desert could provide.

Instead of thinking about what might be going on in the Pharaon mansion, his thoughts were on his grandfather. He recalled playing Monopoly with the old man. It was his favorite game. His grandfather liked to play it with him because he never tired of trying to destroy his grandson's spirit. With gallows courage, young Buck would buy a tiny green house for his practically worthless Baltic Avenue property, even though his paper money had been almost wiped out and the old man sat holding clusters of red hotels and prime real estate.

That was the way young Buck was. Unlike his grandfather, he loved the challenge more than the power. When he first heard he was losing the Examiner, he was goaded to strike back. He even dreamed of starting up his own newspaper, even if he attracted only ten thousand readers. He'd raise the money somehow. But that was not to be. Everything seemed to look optimistic. It would all be given to him. He wouldn't have to struggle as he might have if he'd launched himself on his own without excessive money being handed to him by Pharaon and without his grandfather's fortune. It seemed to him, that he'd taken the easy road. By doing so, he felt less a man. He still couldn't get over the image of himself as the world's highest paid whore.

Suddenly, from the back seat, he heard a movement and then a head popped up. It was Shelley. Buck jammed his foot on the brakes. "What the hell!"

"Keep on going," Shelley said in a commanding tone. "The farther I get from that stinking rose garden, the better. And don't you love Pharaon's decorating taste?"

Buck slumped over the wheel in astonishment, then turned to look back at Shelley. "Christ, man, I'd better take you right back to big mama. I think she wants to talk to you tonight. The next thing I know she'll have me up on a kidnapping charge."

Shelley crawled over the seat and anchored into a front position with Buck, reaching for one of his cigarettes in a package on the dashboard. "Give me a break, love. Let me go away for the night with you. I need to get away from that pussy just as much as you do."

"I doubt that."

Shelley's face brightened. "I've got some hot news for you. You're a reporter, aren't you?"

"I used to be. I always thought I was. Lately I've begun to wonder." Buck steered the car into the desert, not really following directions to Sinatra's house, not at this point. Forever the reporter, he was lured with the promise of hot news. He knew Shelley wouldn't make such a remark casually.

The hard white eyes of an onrushing car—the lone sight visible for miles around—roared passed them, then was seemingly swallowed up by the desert. The only sound was of his rented car rolling across the empty mesa to the mountains in the distance.

Shelley turned, smiled at him, then stuck his unfinished cigarette between Buck's lips, lighting another for himself. "We might as well kill this night together, honey."

Buck rubbed sweat from his eyes. Just what was Shelley up to? "Okay, what are you planning to do?"

"They think they can just dismiss me because of a little transgression here and there—nothing serious. A boy's attempt to have some harmless fun. They've got another thought coming."

"You might be taking this too lightly. I think Leroy has every intention of carrying through with his threat. I know Leroy. My advice is to pay him off and get rid of the fucker. He could mean big trouble. It would ruin Barry. I certainly don't want you to be exposed. I love you, and I want to protect you."

"That's cute. But I've got to have my revenge on both Rose and Calder. They want to send me into exile. I'm a moral leper. Not fit to walk in their golden path. They are the moral lepers—and that's the exact message I plan to bring to the world. Rose is not going to be a threat to anybody when I finish with her. I've had it with that bitch. And when I tell what I know about Calder Martin he might end up in jail."

Buck was tempted to stop the car and shake some sense into Shelley's blond head. "Listen to me and listen good. You do that and you're dead. You're playing deadly adult games now. With killers. Don't ask me how but I just know they could get rid of you, and make it look all so accidental. If you defy them, they'll probably kill you."

"It will be a disaster for them. Not for me. I'll defy them. I'll get back at him. I've got plenty of money and access to it. Pharaon has given me lots of petrol dollars for services rendered, along with the world's most expensive gifts. I've got a few million held in trust for me until I turn twenty-one. Rose can't touch my money."

"If you fuck with Rose and Calder, much less Pharaon, you'll never get to be twenty-one."

"I'm not afraid of them. They should be afraid of me." Buck was stunned. In the dim light, he studied Shelley's face as best he could, finding it contemptuous, defiant, a clear menace to Rose.

"Let's face it," Shelley said, seemingly writing the script he was going to play as he went along. "Rose will peak in a few years. Become an old hag. I want to be a fucking actor. A God damn movie star. I don't want to be branded a Jew-hating fag for the rest of my life. That would destroy my chances for a movie career. By standing up and denouncing them, I will have saved myself politically. The press will call me a hero. I'll be the champion of the liberals. Standing up on my own golden little feet and denouncing bigotry and hatred. Shit, they'll give me the fucking Nobel Peace Prize."

Buck winced at this unadorned ambition, yet found it compelling, somehow, as he had once before. At least Shelley's blatant honesty was a more attractive alternative than Rose's hypocrisy.

"Just between us teddy bears," Shelley said, "I'm not interested in advancing the cause of Jews or anyone. Shelley Phillips—that's the cause I'm turned on by."

The speedometer registered seventy-five, eighty, eighty-five, then ninety. Buck's eyes felt swollen and the road ahead was blurred. He knew his driving was dangerous, yet somehow he needed speed as his own kind of exorcism.

Shelley kept right on talking, seemingly oblivious to how fast they were driving. "I've got to tell the little people out there I don't believe in what Rose is doing. That they're being used. She's exploiting them, mocking their beliefs, making them look like asses. She's going to get up on her soap box and lead them into causes they might not even have the stomach for." He stabbed out his cigarette. "She's good at her work. I've seen her take really loving, warm people and, after her brainwashing, turn their heads around. Make racists and bigots of them. She can make them feel that's what Jesus wants."

When Shelley ran out of words, a long stillness settled over the car. They were locked together in this vehicle as the nighttime desert seemed to engulf them. Surprisingly the drive together had not brought them closer. Each had different goals to accomplish. Shelley had a real hatred of Rose, and Buck had only a disdain.

At this point Rose was important to Buck's survival. He didn't believe for a minute their relationship would last more than a few months. But in some way he felt he needed her. Shelley's real threat to destroy her terrified him. He didn't believe he could convince Shelley to withdraw his plan. He felt a determination there that he never knew existed in the boy. He also realized he didn't know him at all. A sense of loss came over him. He could easily drift apart from Shelley, their momentary alliance broken.

He now had no intention of returning to the resort and finding Sinatra's house. It was a luxury and courtesy from Rose he didn't need. At first he'd been tempted to steer Shelley to some desert motel, there to spend a troubled night with him. But he suspected it would end in an argument, with him devoting the night to a vain attempt to get Shelley to turn from his stated goal. Shelley also had more on his mind tonight than getting into Buck's pants—that was obvious.

As if sensing the same thing Buck felt, and after riding for longer than either of them intended, Shelley reached for Buck's arm. "You'd better take me back to the lion's den, handsome. If I'm going to pull off my little stunt, I don't want to arouse their suspicions. I don't want them to wake up in the morning and find me gone."

Buck readily agreed. He actually needed this night alone himself to think where he was headed. He slammed on the brakes again, turned the car around in the middle of the road and headed back to the center of Palm Springs.

"Would you make a final promise to me?" Buck asked.

"Anything you want other than if it's not asking me to change my mind."

"Can we at least talk about it tomorrow? Privately. Just the two of us."

"It's a deal," Shelley said. "We're a team. I know what I'm about to do will hit you too. It's only fair that in the morning you give me your spin on things."

"I have to talk about it. If you're going to go through with this, then I'm pulling out after I meet with Pharaon. I'll pick up my money for the sale of the Examiner—after all, I'm entitled to that—then I'm out of there. Instead of becoming some media director, I'll need to spend the rest of my days covering your ass. Don't be so proud and arrogant to think you can do this alone. I love you and I'll have to stand by you. But I'm telling you not to do it. You've written a script about how you think this is going to play out. But I think that crew will bring in other scriptwriters. They'll get you. Maybe me too since I'm going with you."

The boy didn't say anything for a long moment, as if mulling something over. "Let me out several blocks from Pharaon's place. I know how to slip back in undetected. One block up ahead will be fine."

As Shelley started to get out of the car, Buck reached for him, pulling him close and kissing him long and hard. For the first time ever, Shelley appeared unresponsive, as if something else was distracting him. "Kid, take care," Buck said. "You're not only playing with a hot wire, you may be sizzling in some electric chair."

"I know what chances I'm taking," Shelley said, more defiant than ever. "But I'm going to give the old finger to Rose. A last good-bye." He held up his finger in the universal sign language of contempt. Buck heard only the slamming of the car door and, in moments, Shelley's white shirt and trousers were no longer visible. An odd apprehension came over him. He felt he'd seen Shelley for the last time. But then he dismissed such a thought.

Buck sat for a long while behind the wheel. Now more than ever, his earlier suspicion had been confirmed. Shelley and Rose were locked in a vendetta. One would finish the other off. Buck was shocked at the sheer determination of the boy in taking on Rose and her cohorts.

"The kid has balls after all," he muttered to himself. But he could take no pride in that. It would be so easy to cut off Shelley's balls, to destroy him. He felt helpless to intervene. What could he do? The battle between Rose and Shelley, supervised by Calder Martin, had been raging long before he entered the picture. He didn't even know what rules, if any, they played by.

All he knew at this point was that his return to the Pharaon mansion in the morning would be filled with surprises. He could not even imagine how his arrival there would go or what would happen to him once he entered those golden gates. Sighing deeply, he stepped on the gas pedal and headed for the loneliness of a desert motel room although he doubted if sleep would come.

*****

Elegantly dressed, his hauteur unaffected by the dismal surroundings of Biff's police station, Jim Howard had come through for Susan again. Sandy was out on bail. He'd been arrested and charged with prostitution.

When Jim and Sandy came out of the police station, Susan was waiting for them near where they'd parked above the elevated highway. She'd lit a cigarette and was watching the moon shining on the water. In spite of all the trouble swirling around her head, the moonlit Florida landscape at night was reason enough to live here.

Until an hour ago, she'd never heard of Sandy, but nevertheless had found herself begging for Jim's intervention. As the boy approached her and she could make out his features, she was struck by how handsome and charming he appeared, not the type she'd immediately associate with street prostitution or hustling. He almost resembled a choir boy.

"I know who you are," he said, coming up to her. "You were married to Gene."

"I plead guilty," she said, extending her hand. "I'm Susan." She looked at Jim, thanking him with her eyes for his rescue.

"I'm Sandy." He shook her hand firmly and proudly. "I'm sorry we had to meet like this. I've seen your picture in the paper many times. You're very beautiful."

"Thank you."

"Let's get in the car," Jim said, obviously angered by something that had happened in the police station.

The boy got into the back seat as Susan joined Jim up front. "I hope you understand all this," Sandy said. "I was going into the drug store to buy some things, and suddenly this squad car pulled up and forced me inside. They took me to the police station where I was interrogated by the police chief, that stinkhole Biff. They said I was hustling."

Jim sighed and turned to Susan. "I think the boy is telling the truth. The only trouble is, he's been arrested for solicitation twice before. It's on his record."

"I was guilty then," Sandy said. "I'm not guilty now. Gene is a good man. He took Jill and me off the streets. We've been clean ever since."

Susan tried to weigh all this information but her mind blurred. "How did you meet Gene?"

"He picked me up one day on the square."

"For sex?" she asked provocatively.

"That's what I thought at first. But he didn't want that. God knows I would have been willing. He's very handsome. But I don't have to tell you that. You were married to him."

"Exactly what did he want?" She was forever the inquiring reporter.

"He wanted information about this Lolito ring. Do you know about that?"

"Not as much as I should."

"He didn't come on to me. I came on to him. But he resisted. He just wanted information. I think he also felt sorry for me—and for Jill too. He came to like us. He provided a place for us."

"I was curious," Jim interjected. "Why are you bandaged?" Did someone beat you up. It might help my case."

"I was burned when Gene's house was set afire. The firemen wouldn't go in to save Gene. I thought he was trapped in his back bedroom. I broke away from the firemen and rushed in to save Gene myself. But thank God he wasn't there that night."

"You must love him very much," she said.

"I do."

"But I thought you were in love with Jill," Susan said.

"I am," Sandy said. "There are all kinds of love. I"m sure a smart city reporter like you knows that."

"If I don't already, I'm beginning to learn."

"Before we take you back to your condo, could you stop by my house?" Jim asked. "I want to ask you some questions. I think my wife Ingrid will want to interview you too."

"I know of her. She's a columnist. Very liberal—not like Barry Collins."

"You're right," Jim said. "My wife doesn't hold Barry in too high a regard."

"What do you think, Dad?" Susan asked.

"I think something's going on here," Jim said, "and I'd like to get to the bottom of it. I think someone's got it in for Gene. First, his own arrest. Now the thing with Jill and the TV cameras. Someone had to be behind that. Now Sandy's arrest without any provocation. I really believe he was going into that drug store on business."

"I was," Sandy protested his innocence from the back seat.

"I'll call Gene when I get home and tell him where you are," Susan said, craning her neck to talk to Sandy.

"When you're through talking to me, would you take me back to Gene's?" Sandy asked. "I want to be with him tonight...and with Jill."

Susan noted he mentioned Jill's name somewhat as an afterthought. It was at this point that she decided she didn't need to know all the details of Sandy's relationship with Gene. It was their private business, and perhaps she'd interfered enough.

Later in the evening while Ingrid and Jim talked to Sandy over sandwiches and colas in their patio, Susan went and dialed Gene.

He answered the phone at once, eager for all the details. When she'd fully informed him of everything that had happened to Sandy that day, he sighed, "I feel a rope is tightening around my throat, and I don't know why."

"I think someone's got it in for you, and I don't know who. I still refuse to believe it's Buck. I know that he's still very loyal to you."

"I hope you're right, but I still think someone's setting me up for something. I have this instinct. I always did."

"I'm not sure I understand."

"I don't understand it either," he said. "But I sure plan to find out."

"When Don Bossdum gets here, we'll drive Sandy back home to you. We'll bring him in through the rear entrance. Do you want to see me?"

"I just want to be alone with Sandy and Jill tonight. I've heard that news broadcast about Jill and me. It was shit!"

"I knew it would be." She started to ring off, but there was something in his voice that made her stay on the line. "Gene...is there something I can do?"

"You've helped us out plenty tonight, and I'm grateful."

"But there's something else, isn't there? Something you want to ask. I wasn't there for you when we were married. Maybe I could be here for you now."

"There is something," he said. "Something I don't have any right to ask."

"Go ahead. Don't be afraid to say what's on your mind."

He hesitated. "If something were to happen to me, would you help out Sandy and Jill?" Even before she could formulate a response, he put down the phone.

*****

After seeing that Jill was all right and learning that Sandy would be delayed at the house of Susan's parents, Gene wrote Sandy a note that he'd be back later. He asked Sandy to wait up for him so that they could talk over his arrest. Before the night ended, Gene had another mission: He was going to slip into Buck's compound and see if he could spot any sign that Maria and Clara were living on the estate.

On the way to Buck's home, he neared Barry's residence. On an impulse, he decided to stop by there. In theory, if he had a real job and not a fake one, he was supposed to be guarding the house along with Barry at night. He thought he'd at least report for duty, then disappear later.

Gene let himself in through the secret garden gate leading into the compound. He crossed by the rock where he'd hid Pamela's document, wondering if she'd made another attempt to get in touch with Barry's attorneys again. It had been some time since her document arrived, and Pamela had been strangely quiet. Gene suspected she'd flown to Miami and was perhaps hiding out in Key Biscayne or else a remote place in the Florida Keys. He doubted if she'd left the state, at least not until her demands were met. Secretly, he hoped Barry would be exposed by Pamela and that Rose would denounce her affiliation with him. Something had to be done to contain Sister Rose's son too. He realized that both Barry and Shelley could destroy her career.

As was his custom, Barry was talking on the phone. His daughters were nowhere to be seen, probably out on one of their endless dates. Barry's soft, cajoling voice could clearly be heard through the open window. He seemed to be pleading with someone on the phone. He had a soothing, loving tone which meant he wasn't talking to Calder Martin.

"I'm lonely tonight, and I want to see you," Barry said to someone on the phone. There was a long pause. "I know you love him, but does he love you? Robert, you and I have always been close, and I need a friend tonight. Let me come over. Let's talk. I'm coming unglued. I need an old friend to talk things over with."

Gene gathered that this Robert was resisting giving in to Barry's request. The name of Robert stuck in his brain. Could this be Robert Dante? Buck's longtime companion. Surely Barry wasn't an old friend of Robert's.

Barry's voice grew harsher. "Let me come over. I'm in deep trouble. But in some way you're involved in this too. What's going on now might change your life too. You've got to hear me out. No one will know I'm meeting with you. Buck won't be back for a day or so, right?"

Gene swallowed hard. The person on the other end of the wire could only be Robert Dante.

"That's more like it," Barry said into the phone. "I'll be right over. You've got to hear this new shit." He put down the phone.

An idea came into Gene's brain. He didn't want Barry to know he'd entered the compound. Quickly he concealed himself behind the bushes.

After making the call, Barry emerged from his office and walked over to the pool. He reached into his pocket and pulled out a cigarette. He lit it and smoked only a few draws before tossing the lit cigarette into the pool. He headed for the garage.

Gene would wait for ten minutes, then follow his trail. He knew where Barry was going. To Buck's mansion. That sprawling house had always been forbidden territory to Gene. It was Robert's domain. Nobody crossed the threshold until Robert approved, and that man had never approved of Gene or his association with Buck.

Invited or not, Gene was heading there now.

In the dark shadows of Buck's garden, Gene concealed himself behind a hedge, as he watched Clara bring drinks to Barry and Robert, who had been waiting in Buck's gazebo at the far end of the lawn. Maria sat on the steps to Buck's pillared back veranda, eating what looked like a popsicle. When Clara's face came under close scrutiny from a garden light, Gene recognized her at once, although he was completely screened from her view. She stumbled over a rock in the garden and nearly spilled the tray of drinks. She muttered something in Spanish that sounded like a curse.

Even with the evidence before him, Gene still had a hard time reconciling what his eyes told him about Buck's actions. He now knew that he'd been seriously betrayed by his friend. He'd forgiven Buck for deserting him years ago in his time of need in spite of their close bond and friendship, but he could not forgive this. Clara had allowed herself to become involved in a plot to destroy him, not only for money but because he'd spurned her sexual advances. She obviously had it in for him, and no doubt was only too willing to do the bidding of others. Calder Martin and that stinking Biff had found a willing participant in Clara. As much as he hated Clara, he hated Maria as well. Here she sat smugly sucking on that popsicle on Buck's veranda. She was a female Lolita. He didn't doubt for a moment with this early training that she'd grow up to become a puta, just like her filthy mother.

When Clara returned to the veranda after having delivered the drinks to Robert and Barry, she went inside Buck's large glass doors, apparently heading for the kitchen. Maria got up off the porch and trailed her mother inside.

Silently moving along the cover of the hedges, Gene positioned himself about five feet from the gazebo where Robert and Barry sat drinking. He could hear every word of their conversation.

"You know I told you never to come here again," Robert was saying. "This is Buck's house."

"But all during the time he was in the service, you didn't object to my being upstairs with you. Buck wasn't fucking you. You had to get it from somebody, and if I recall you're a natural bottom."

"I don't want to talk about it. My relationship with Buck has changed. He's no longer using me. He's become my lover in all ways. It wasn't like it was before when I had to turn to you."

"But I thought you loved me. You certainly told me you loved me night after night."

"That was back then. This is now. I'm going to build the rest of my life with Buck. We've made a commitment to each other. Deep vows. I'm not going to be the one who breaks those vows."

"What about him?" Barry asked.

"What do you mean?"

"What if Buck breaks the vows?"

"I don't believe he'd do that. Not now anyway. In the past, yes. But not now."

"You are so very, very gullible. He's betraying you right this minute."

"With whom?" Robert asked, a growing alarm in his voice.

"Shelley Phillips."

"I can't believe that." There was such uncertainty in Robert's voice that Gene thought Robert believed Barry at once.

"It's true. I'm not making this up. Buck's fallen in love with Shelley Phillips. Before Buck came along, the boy belonged to me, or as much as that little whore can belong to anybody. After Buck fucked Shelley, the kid obviously didn't want to get pricked with my needle dick any more."

"I can't believe this." The alarm that had first appeared in Robert's voice had grown into an almost choking sound. He gasped for breath, as if about to cry.

"There's a lot going on here. Our dear friend—that scumbag Leroy Fitzgerald—secretly photographed Shelley and me. He's threatening to destroy my career and release the pictures if I don't come up with five-million dollars."

"That's ridiculous. Five million. He doesn't want much, does he?"

"Leroy's threatening Calder Martin. That's like a suicide mission."

"This is all too much for me. Leroy's got proof of you and Shelley. There's no proof about Buck and Shelley, is there?"

"Not that I know of. I've been an eyewitness but I don't actually have a photograph. I was having this thing with Shelley at Leroy's bordello. Buck rushed into the room like a maniac and confronted me.

He kicked me out and took Shelley away. You just have my word for that. There was a time when my word meant something to you. I know I lie every day. I'm a politician. But I'm telling you the truth now."

"Why do you want me to know this? You've not just hurt me. You've ruined my God damn life."

Barry's voice grew consoling. "I'm not here to do that—and you know it. I wanted to warn you before you got deeper and deeper into all this shit. Everything could blow up in everybody's face, particularly mine. You don't have a political career to save. If it's revealed that you're gay, who cares? Everybody knows you're gay. With me, it's fatal, considering my redneck right-wing supporters."

"I believe you. I think Buck is having an affair. Sometimes when he's come to me, I've had the feeling for a long time that he's just risen from a hotbed with somebody else. I mean he performs all right but I get the impression that he's just dumped a load before coming to me. I don't mean to sound vulgar."

"I know you don't. Perhaps I shouldn't have told you. But in some strange and twisted way, I felt I owed it to you. For old time's sake."

"This is not news I wanted to hear. Buck has hired a very attractive chauffeur. For a time I've even suspected Buck was making it with this guy, too. His name is Casey."

"Maybe. I think Buck is just like me. We're both whoremongers. I don't think he's capable of being loyal to just one person. This Shelley is just a kid. Kids grow up. Shelley will be interested in Buck for a few months, then he'll toss him aside. You've got to decide if you want to wait around for Buck to get over this stupid infatuation with a teenage boy, or if you want to get on with your own life."

"I don't know what to do at this point."

"I'm not really coming clean about why I'm here," Barry said.

"I thought it was more than just to tell me this horrible news about Buck. I'm not breaking down now, but the moment you're out of here you'll hear my bellowing up and down the street. I know this sounds stupid and melodramatic. But what you've just told me is breaking my heart. What else do you have to throw at me tonight?"

"I'm really here because I want to make you an offer."

"What type of offer?" Robert asked.

"I've got to clean up my act. No more scandals. If I get through this one, I've got to become squeaky clean. I want you to leave Buck and come back with me. As my political assistant. Run the show for me. Buck himself told me once that you're the most organized person he's ever known in his life."

"I don't know."

Gene couldn't clearly see but apparently Barry had taken Robert in his arms and was kissing him.

"If you come with me," Barry said, "it will be just like the old times. We had good times back then, and we'll have good times in the future. But very discreet times. You can always be with me on the political trail. As my assistant, it's the perfect cover. I'll be faithful to you. If I get out of this mess, I've learned my lesson."

Robert seemed to be standing up and walking away. "You know I can't give you an answer right now. I'll think about it. I really will. When Buck gets back, I may learn he no longer wants me in his life. In spite of our vows. But I can't make any decision until I face him."

"I understand that." Barry seemed to be getting up too. "But will you promise to call me every day? Just talk to me to learn what I know, what's going on."

"I promise."

Barry seemed to have walked over to Robert who appeared to want to break away. "Not now," Robert said. "If there's going to be anything between us in the future, it will have to wait. I've been given enough to think about tonight."

"Okay, kid, here's looking at you. But my offer is genuine. I want you back. I want you out of this mess. It'll be a disaster for you if you stay on with Buck."

"We'll see," Robert said in a forlorn voice. "If what you say is true, and I have no doubt it is, I may be kicked out on my ass."

"You'll have another place to go."

"Thanks, Barry. But you'll understand if I want to be alone tonight."

"I understand," Barry said. "Just a kiss. A good night kiss. Okay? For old time's sake."

Barry must have held Robert for a long time. When he broke away, there were no other words exchanged between them.

A firebomb had gone off inside Gene, and he didn't know if he could contain certain impulses. He couldn't control his impulses the day when he'd exposed himself to Jill, and he feared he couldn't get a grip on himself now. He knew what he was about to do was wrong, but he found himself moving unrelentingly toward his target.

*****

The sobering cold of the night air sent an added chill through Shelley's body as he used a secret key to open a tiny gate at the far end of Pharaon's estate. His mind turned over the events of the past few hours. As he moved stealthily across the garden, he rehearsed his upcoming press conference.

At the patio doors leading into the living room, he stopped, breathing deeply all the fresh air he could pull into his seared lungs. He began to feel better, the more he breathed. Soon he'd be asleep from sheer exhaustion. He had to look his best for tomorrow. There would be many photographers and certainly plenty of TV cameramen with their cruel lenses. Unfortunately, he had a big pimple on his chin which he'd have to conceal artfully with makeup.

Later in his bedroom, he stripped and crawled into bed, watching reflections the moonlight made in Pharaon's garden. In spite of the impending excitement, his willpower was strong enough to lull his brain to sleep.

Soon he drifted off, and he didn't know how long he slept. Maybe it was a dream. He woke up at the feel of something heavy on his chest. Opening his bleary eyes, he met the stern, foreboding stare of a Berber as a light in his room went on. One of Pharaon's bodyguards stood over him. Shelley tried to get up, but the firm, broad hand of the Berber pinned him down.

"Look what we've got here, Rose," came the familiar, chilling voice of Calder Martin.

Rose remained motionless and quiet beside Calder. Staring at her, Shelley had a thought—that she was just as much a prisoner as he was.

In his hand, Calder dangled a tape recorder. He flipped it on. Soon the sound of Buck's familiar voice surged through Shelley's consciousness. The words, so recent—it was as if Buck were in the room talking to them now. "My God," Shelley said, struggling to free himself from the Berber.

"God won't help you now," Rose warned.

To Shelley's horror, he now knew that Buck's rented car had been bugged. Calder and Rose had heard everything he and Buck said. Worse, they knew Shelley's plan.

As Buck's voice still sounded on the tape recorder, Shelley, in a sudden move, slipped from the Berber's hold and darted starkly naked toward the patio door leading to his terrace. Momentarily taken aback, the Berber rushed after Shelley, grabbing the boy's arm, twisting it behind his back, totally restraining him. He cried out in pain.

Just then, on a signal from Calder, a second Berber entered the room. He headed toward Shelley with a needle. The first Berber still held him with one hand and with the other, repeatedly slapped him, very hard and very fast, making him dazed, ready to receive the needle.

Nearly blinded from the slapping, he was half conscious, too weak to resist the needle that was shot in his arm.

Rose stood over him. At least he thought it was Rose. His eyes took in only the white of the gown and, of all the things he could be thinking about right now, he remembered that Rose always liked to wear white. "You're not going to meet the press," he heard her say. "But to our place in St. Moritz. I think the time has come for you to be born again!"

At these words, a tortured scream escaped from his throat. He knew what that meant. Rose had taken everything from him but the freedom of his mind. Now he'd lose that. He kicked the Berber holding the needle and spat in the face of the bodyguard restraining him.

Calder towered over him. In one swift kick, Calder plowed his foot into Shelley's groin. The pain was unbearable. It lasted only a second before Shelley descended into blackness.

"Listen, you little fag!" he'd heard Calder say before Shelley had drifted off. The voice sounded as if it were bouncing off the walls of a tunnel. "You've caused enough trouble."

Although he had resisted it, Shelley now welcomed the memory of the needle point bursting his skin. A welling surged inside him, and he began to drift into oblivion.

It didn't matter where they sent him. What difference did it make now?

*****

After Don had left the Howard home to drive Sandy back to Gene's condo, Susan settled in with a drink to enjoy a few moments alone with Jim and Ingrid.

"I believe the boy," Ingrid said. "I don't think he was hustling. I don't know what is going on with this Biff creature. I've always detested the man. Lately I've been writing about national affairs. But I think I'd better focus on our local police department in my next few columns."

"I think you're right," Susan said. "I've told you all I know about that Lolito ring. I think it's operated with Biff's approval."

"I think Biff is just a puppet," Jim said. "Calder Martin is pulling the strings."

"Let's turn the heat up," Ingrid said.

"I'd like to see you do that," Susan said. "I'll be a stringer for you now that I don't have my job any more at the Examiner."

"Don't worry about that stupid, low-paying job," Jim said. "If our boy Buck comes through for my little girl, you'll be the publisher of the News. Not just girl reporter, the God damn publisher."

"Right now that sounds like only a dream, but I think it can happen," Susan said. "My God, when he flies back to Okeechobee, he'll have millions."

"With a lot more on the way," Ingrid said. "I hear old Buck is fading fast. Are you still interested in doing that biography on him? I've turned up some real hot stuff, and I've only begun."

"I've been thinking about that," Susan said, "and I feel I should bow out. I would need my husband's cooperation and approval, and there's no way in hell Buck would want his grandfather exposed. We're going to be living in grand style on old Buck's money. For me to expose him is wrong."

"It's not wrong—it's journalism," Ingrid protested.

"I can't do it," Susan said, pouring herself another drink at the bar. She felt she needed the extra fortification of alcohol to get through the evening. "It would be betraying my husband."

Ingrid was obviously displeased at her decision, although Jim by his silence conceded Susan was making the right move. "It seems to me," Ingrid said, "that Buck started betraying you the very day he married you."

"Where's the betrayal?" Susan asked. "I entered the marriage with my eyes completely wide open. He hasn't betrayed me. What's he done to wrong me? He's provided me a lifestyle I couldn't support on my own. He's securing one of the most important newspapers for me in the state, and letting me direct its editorial operation." She swallowed her drink, its contents burning her throat as it went down. It was hard for her to say what she was about to. "Not only that, and that's plenty, he's even agreed to support my new lover."

There was a long silence in the patio lit by colored spots. It gave everything, both the plants and people, an unnatural glow. All evening she knew there would be talk of Don Bossdum. Now was the time— before he returned.

"Don's not going to get that job, after all?" Jim asked. "He's going to sponge off you?"

"Exactly," Susan said defiantly. "We haven't updated ourselves on Don's life lately. He's changed a lot since he used to play such great football at the university. Don has become a highly paid male hustler. He's been involved with not only Rose but Shelley. In fact, he's demanding one-hundred thousand dollars from Shelley to keep quiet about their relationship. I'm sure Rose will put up the money. God knows she can afford it."

"Is this the type of man you should be involved with?" Ingrid asked. "I'd always wanted something better for you."

"A rich and handsome husband?" Susan asked. "One who might one day own Central Florida? It seems I've already got that."

Jim looked over at his wife. "I understand why Susan is with Don. Her marriage to Buck put her in this position. I was the one who started this whole Don Bossdum thing in the first place. I gave her Don's phone number. The way I see it, it's a perfect solution. You have an imitation of Buck—they do look alike—on the side while in front of the cameras you're married to Buck. Your marriage gives him the perfect cover to do what he wants."

"Please understand me," Ingrid said. "Jim might be right. I'm not opposed to your arrangement. It's not what I wanted for you, but what the hell. It's what you've got."

"It appears to me that I've got a hell of a lot," Susan said. "My career was going nowhere. All of a sudden I might become one of the powerful women in this state."

"Certainly one of the richest," Jim said. "That husband of yours is going to spend the rest of his life having his ass hauled around in a stretch limo with a long cigar in his mouth and Florida's most beautiful boy by his side."

Susan had a cynical sneer on her face as she looked carefully at both parents. "He's already got the stretch limo and Florida's most beautiful boy."

"You mean Robert?" Ingrid asked. "That is one beautiful man. If he were straight, I'd go for that myself."

"I don't mean that," Susan said. "Buck is carrying on a hot and torrid affair with Shelley Phillips."

"That's ridiculous," Jim said. "Shelley Phillips must be all of two years old. I never thought of Buck as a child molester."

"Think of it!" Susan said with a certain bitterness in her voice. "He's in love with Shelley."

Again, a long silence fell over the patio. As a newspaper columnist, Ingrid had heard almost every story, and as a criminal attorney Jim had witnessed first hand some of life's more sordid chapters. But it was obvious to Susan that this news was a bit hard for both of them to take.

It was Ingrid who broke the silence. "I must say I'm appalled. The commitment to Robert I can handle. But sexual involvement with a child—that's disgusting! It's also illegal, and Buck knows that so very well. I am so very disappointed in him. I'm not going to protest. I'm not going to do anything about it, but I will always deplore it."

"I'm worried about the fallout from such a thing," Jim said, looking more and more like an attorney prepared to defend Buck in a case. "If Rose Phillips finds out about this, there may be hell to pay."

"Let's be completely realistic about Sister Rose," Susan said, her words stabbing the night air. "I have no doubt at all that Rose not only knows of the relationship but approves of it. Even encourages it."

"You're going a bit far here," Ingrid cautioned. "I believe Rose is capable of anything. But this is a bit much."

"Not at all," Susan said. "Not for Miss Rose and Miss Shelley. With Buck they are repeating a sexual threesome they pursued with Don. It's just a repeat performance for them—nothing new, part of their pattern."

"This is one story I don't think you'll splash on the front page of the News when you take over as publisher," Jim said.

"You've got that right," Susan said. "This is one story I want kept within the walls of this garden."

"I'm a newshound," Ingrid said, "but you're blood. I will always protect my daughter even if she gets involved with the president of the United States."

"You mean Barry Collins?" Susan said. "No way. Barry's been involved with everybody but not with me. Not that one."

"If Barry doesn't drop his association with Sister Rose, Calder Martin, and the Arabs at once," Jim said, "I don't think he'll ever see the Oval Office."

"Who knows?" Susan said enigmatically. "Maybe one day."

"I agree with Jim," Ingrid said. "Pamela's disappeared. There are ugly rumors. Pamela's like a Martha Mitchell. She may bring the world crumbling in on Barry and Calder Martin. I don't think they even know where she is. Barry's camp keeps insisting that Pamela is ill and can't make public appearances. I think they're lying. They don't know where Pamela is."

"You're right about that, mother," Susan said a bit triumphantly. As a fellow reporter, she was always a bit competitive with her mother. She appeared mysterious.

"Come out with it," Ingrid said. "What do you know?"

"Would you be surprised if I let you in on something?" Susan said. "I'm not going to fill you in on all the details. But Pamela has contacted me. She's asked me—and I've agreed—to tape an interview in which she blows the lid off this town. There's a downside. I can't release it unless she gives me permission. If Barry and Calder cave in to her demands, I can never release it. But if they don't, the tape is aired. The career of Barry Collins will be terminated the moment my interview with Pamela goes on the air."

"I've got to caution you," Jim said. "After all you're my daughter. My only child. Don't fuck with Calder. Barry—at least right now—is small fry. But Calder could strike back at you in some way. You're playing a dangerous game here."

"I know all about the dangers," Susan said defensively. "After all, I've been a reporter in this town myself. But it would be terrific on the day I became publisher of the News to release this story. Circulation would rise overnight."

"Don't get too carried away," Ingrid said. "You may be day-dreaming about breaking that story. I suspect Calder and Barry will give in. I'm sure Pamela has the shit on them. They can buy her off, probably a lot more cheaply than you think. After all, Pamela has always sold out cheaply. Most state troopers she's screwed didn't even have to pick up her drink tab."

"Don't sell her short," Susan warned.

"I think you'll get your interview," Jim said, "and we'd love to see a private copy of it. But I think Ingrid's right. It sounds like a story that will never break."

"You shouldn't have accepted such conditions," Ingrid said.

"Why not?" Susan asked. "It's a chance I've got to take. Even if I don't get to break the story, and it's suppressed forever, at least I'll take over as publisher of the News knowing a hell of a lot more than most newspaperpeople in this town." She looked at Ingrid, hoping her bold statement wouldn't be interpreted as being too competitive.

Before either of them could speak again, Susan heard the sound of Don's car pulling into the driveway. "That's Don," she said, almost welcoming his presence as she wanted to end this conversation which had gone far enough. "Before he gets here, I want to invite both of you to attend a photo shoot when Buck flies back into town. Buck and his millions, I should say. We're going public with our marriage. After all, going public was what the damn thing was all about. I want you standing in the background behind the happily married couple. Beam just right. You've been to weddings before. Say something like, 'this is the happiest day of our lives.' Shit like that. The lovers like Don and Robert can appear way in the background, looking like waiters perhaps."

"Will Shelley be there to give the groom away?" Ingrid asked pointedly.

"Shelley will not be there," Susan said. "That I can almost guarantee. Neither will Gene."

Jim rose from his chair and put his arms around Susan. "We're here for you, regardless of what happens."

"That's true," Ingrid said. "We may not always approve of your behavior, but we are your parents and will always be with you."

Don came across the patio, heading immediately to Susan to hug and kiss her. "Last night I got a little drunk and did something stupid," Don said.

"What's that, boy," Jim asked.

Don looked down at Susan and kissed her on the nose. "I'm in love. I asked Susan to marry me."

"She's already married," Ingrid said.

Don looked down at Susan again and smiled. "How lucky for us she is. Not just married but married to Buck Brooke III. With all the millions he's bringing back from California, I'd marry the dude myself if he asked me."

A silence came over the patio again.

*****

It was three o'clock in the morning, and Gene sat alone in a roadside tavern. He was in the very rear of the bar, and no one came here to bother him. The bar was so dimly lit he felt the power had gone out. A man and two women occupied a table up front. They were having some sort of argument about who owned a trailer in the Cactus Grove Trailer Camp. But Gene couldn't have cared less. He had other things on his mind.

Even now he couldn't believe what had happened in the past two hours. It had not been planned. If you'd told him at midnight where he'd be at 3am, he would not have believed it. Even as he sat here, mulling over what had just happened, he still couldn't believe it. It must have been a dream. Maybe a nightmare.

He'd raped Robert.

After Barry had left the garden, Gene had emerged from behind the bushes to attack Robert. He'd already removed all of his clothing so his garments wouldn't get in the way. Panic had come over Robert. As he'd started to scream, Gene's fingers tightened around the young man's throat. "You scream and you're dead," Gene had said. "I can kill a man in an instant. I've been trained. It's your choice. Do what I say or die."

"Don't kill me," Robert had pleaded. "I'll do anything you say."

"That's more like it," Gene had told him, as he ripped off Robert's shirt and tore open his fly. His shorts had fallen on the ground. Gene had pulled down Robert's jockey underwear. Roughly he'd thrown Robert onto the garden sofa covered with weather-proof cushions. It had made a nice bed for his purposes.

"I want to look at you as I penetrate you," Gene had told Robert. Gene was already hard.

In the lights of the night garden, he had clearly seen Robert's face, although his own face had remained in shadow. The young man had trembled. He'd been terrified but had offered no resistance. He'd looked like a completely helpless victim, which he was.

Gene had taken his hand and held it over Robert's mouth even though the young man at first had made no attempt to scream. Gene had known what would eventually happen. Considering the sheer size of Gene's cock, Robert would not have been able to keep from screaming.

With his hand muffling Robert's mouth, Gene had guided himself to his target. He'd slapped Robert's ass, first one cheek, then the other. Robert's legs had been up in the air, resting on Gene's broad shoulders. But he hadn't opened for Gene. With a sudden move, Gene had grabbed Robert's balls, squeezing them as hard as he could. The target had suddenly opened. With a sudden plunge, he'd completely penetrated Robert. Robert had cried out in pain. Gene had removed his hand from Robert's mouth and had descended upon Robert, biting and sucking his lips and blowing his hot breath inside Robert's mouth. Robert had grabbed him and tried to push him away but Gene had shoved and pushed even harder.

He had also felt the intense pain wracking Robert's body. He'd replaced his hand over Robert's mouth, as his teeth and lips had descended on Robert's ears and neck. He was biting Robert and biting hard. The young man had continued to resist him, pushing and shoving him away. But Gene had him completely pinned down.

No longer able to hold back, Robert's tears had descended. Ignoring them, Gene had continued to pump Robert furiously, knowing he was following a trail already blazed by his old buddy, Buck. Gene's weight had crushed against Robert who had moaned softly.

Very soon Gene had heard a different moan coming from Robert. He'd no longer pushed Gene away but his fingers had traced caressing patterns across Gene's back. Gene had felt the wiry muscles of Robert's legs stiffen as his stomach had tightened. With a high, whining whimper, Robert had shot a stream of pungent semen across Gene's chest and had grabbed the back of Gene's head, forcing his mouth onto Gene's. Robert had virtually begged Gene to penetrate him with his tongue. Gene's tongue had entered Robert's mouth. There it had been eagerly sucked, the most powerful sucking it had ever received. Robert had no longer pushed him again, but had wrapped his arms around Gene as if demanding a deeper penetration.

Suddenly Gene had let out a muffled cry as he'd emptied himself into Robert. Gene had collapsed onto Robert. He had lain very still, gasping for breath before rolling off his victim. Within moments, Robert had moved his position and had virtually fallen on Gene's stomach, where his tongue had cleaned off his own semen. He had licked inside Gene's navel before descending to his testicles where he'd licked and sucked, giving them a bath. His head had moved upward to clean and lick Gene's penis. He'd been tender and gentle, almost arousing Gene to another bout of passion.

When he'd completely cleaned Gene, Robert's lips had moved up his chest, gently kissing his nipples. At Gene's neck, Robert had licked the sweat from him before pressing his mouth onto Gene's. Gene had inserted his tongue into Robert's mouth and that tongue had been expertly sucked again.

Robert had seemed grateful to him and had resented his going. "Stay with me," Robert had pleaded. "I want you. No man has ever taken me like that before."

As Gene had tried to slip into his jeans Robert had fallen before him, licking his thighs and fondling his testicles. "There's so much more I can do for you," Robert had said. "Please don't go."

Gene had pushed him away and gotten dressed. Robert had walked toward him, hoping for one final embrace. But Gene had moved quickly from the garden and had disappeared, eventually driving endlessly until he found this all-night bar.

On an impulse he stood up, paid his tab, and got into his car.

He knew exactly where he was going.

In less than thirty minutes he was on the veranda of Buck's mansion ringing the doorbell, wondering if he'd awaken Clara and Maria. If he encountered them, he didn't know what he was going to do.

But it was Robert—clad in a robe—who opened the door. Seeing it was Gene, he reached out and took his arm, guiding him inside, as he shut the door. Gene reached for Robert and pulled him into an embrace, inserting his tongue in Robert's mouth. Robert opened his robe and pressed his nude body against Gene's clothed one. With one hand, Gene massaged Robert's velvety smooth back. With the other he caressed the cheeks of Robert's ass, gently, ever so gently, inserting his index finger. Robert moaned in Gene's arms, as if giving himself up completely.

Robert moved from Gene's lips, planting little flickering kisses and licks on Gene's neck before bathing his ear. Into that ear, he whispered, "You can take me upstairs and do anything to me you've ever wanted to do. There will be no limits to what you can do. No limits."

*****

Back at the Pharaon mansion, Buck was ushered into the large central patio. He'd asked an Arab servant where Mrs. Phillips and her son were, but the subject had been quickly dismissed. "They're not available," the man had said. "Mr. Pharaon will have news."

Buck must have waited thirty or forty minutes, and he was growing impatient. Finally, the same servant arrived with a pot of coffee for him and a selection of juices. "If there's anything else, press this buzzer over there." He motioned to the bar. "We have everything. Caviar. Anything you want."

"I want to speak to Mr. Pharaon," Buck said firmly.

"He's in an emergency meeting. He sends his apologies and will be here shortly."

As Buck paced the patio, he began to feel the exotic vegetation was cannibalistic and might swoop down to devour him at any minute. There was some movement in the far corner of the patio, and then a man emerged. It was Pharaon. Buck recognized him immediately from his portrait. Most portraits flatter. Pharaon's portrait was but a shadow version of himself.

In real life, Pharaon was an exotic beauty from some Arabian Nights fantasy. Dressed entirely in white, he was as slender as anyone could wish. He was wearing what was most definitely the world's most expensive and most exquisitely tailored silk suit, with a violet shirt and a mauve tie. He wore the suit with the careless confidence of a man born to wear the world's most expensive clothing. From the tips of his manicured nails to his perfectly groomed hair, from his discreet but paralyzingly priced jewelry to his violet-colored eyes, he exuded sex appeal. Even though he must be over forty, his olive skin had the bloom of youth. His thin cheeks appeared as if made up, but Buck knew that was his natural tone. Even his pinkish red lips looked painted with discretion but they were real. He did not owe his beauty to art or discipline. The facility of his carriage and the grace of his gestures immediately attracted Buck to him, as Pharaon reached to shake his hand.

Then he surprised Buck by taking his hand and placing its inner palm against his lips. He gently kissed Buck's hand, then pressed the palm even closer to his lips. His tongue darted out to lick Buck's palm. Before releasing Buck's hand, he swallowed two of Buck's fingers.

"God, you taste good," Pharaon said. "If we were not civilized the way we are today, I would kidnap you and make you the favorite in my harem."

"What an introduction!" Buck said. "I assume this is not your greeting for everybody."

"It's my greeting for you," Pharaon said. "I've never met anyone quite like you. You are the world's most beautiful man. No, I'd better take that back. I am the world's most beautiful man. You are the world's sexiest man."

"How can I hate you and view you as a dreaded terrorist and international murderer if you come on like that. And with such perception." Buck raised an eyebrow to let Pharaon know he was only joking.

"I heard you were a Marine. I always liked big, handsome U.S. Marines with blue eyes and blond hair, except when they invade my country."

"I thought you liked little boys like Shelley."

"As playthings. Sex with Shelley would be like a tiny diversion. Not my true agenda. Back home I go for the little boys. It's part of my legend. My real desire is for a U.S. Marine like you. At home I am always the top. But when I go abroad, I become my true self: a bottom."

Buck sat down opposite Pharaon. Like the Arab, he too had worn a suit for this meeting. "Have you seen Rose and Shelley this morning?"

"I saw them last night. Rose and Calder left this morning to fly to the Middle East. Rose left you a note. Calder said you could go fuck yourself—that Calder. Shelley had to go to Europe. He too left you a note. I guess that leaves you and me alone together. Except for thirty-eight servants but they're discreet."

"You know why I'm here," Buck said.

"Indeed I do." He pressed a buzzer. An unfamiliar servant emerged with a leather case. In front of Pharaon he reached in and removed two checks. Pharaon glanced at them only briefly before signaling the servant to hand them to Buck. After doing that, the servant quietly left.

Buck studied first one check, then the other.

"One is for your stock interest in the Examiner," Pharaon said. "The other for your grandfather's. Are they satisfactory?"

"I don't want to sound like a country boy, but this is the most money I've ever seen in my entire life."

"Of course, if you prefer I could take the checks back and deposit gold bars in some bank account in Geneva."

"The checks will do fine," Buck said. "In this country we have something known as the IRS."

"A deplorable institution," Pharaon said.

"Thank you," Buck said. "I never thought losing the Examiner would cause such pain but these checks have helped ease it somewhat."

"You should pay me back," Pharaon said. "And cause me pain."

Buck smiled at him enigmatically. The point was all too obvious. "A tempting offer."

"Are you also going to become my media director?" Pharaon asked. Now it was his time to raise an eyebrow. "Rose highly recommends you."

"That we need to talk about."

"I have planned to spend the rest of the day talking about nothing else—except, perhaps, your raw magnetism and male beauty. I've never seen a man quite so appealing in my entire life."

"That's very flattering."

"The media director's job will give you incredible power. Not to mention the money."

"Before we venture one step forward, I must tell you I have no stomach for advancing Arab causes in this country, attacking Jews, or exploiting Born Again Christians, whoever they are."

"Neither do I. As the afternoon progresses, we will see that I have another agenda. I wouldn't be so stupid as to involve you in shit like that. I need a person to represent me in this country. With television stations. Radio stations. Especially in Hollywood. I plan to bankroll American films. I would never insult your intelligence or abilities by using you for this propaganda garbage. I have Rose for that crap. For my dirty deeds, I have Calder Martin. He's a scumbag. I know Rose told you to undermine Calder with me. Hold your breath. I know more about Calder than you ever will. Regrettably, he also knows too much about me. I can't get rid of him. The propaganda thing with Rose will not be part of your job description. I want us to move into the media elite in this country. I'm an Arab and I can't do it. But you're a blond American hunk. You can go where I'm not accepted, and I want to use you to advance my interests. Believe me, in this case, I'm interested in making money—not making war or propaganda."

"Strangely, I believe you."

"Then let's spend the day talking about it. Tell me all the reasons you're wrong for the job, and I'll tell you all the reasons you're right for it."

"The day is yours."

"The day is ours." Pharaon got up and walked over and sat down with Buck. "I want you to go for a swim with me in my private pool. It will not be necessary to put on a swimming suit. I understand from Rose you have nothing to be ashamed of. We'll talk and we'll talk. We'll make love and we'll talk some more. I will be your woman. You can use me the way a man uses a woman. Think of me as your love slave." He bent over and pressed his lips hard against Buck's. Buck returned the kiss, his mind blurring. He was about to enter a world for which he was unprepared.

"Your taste is of the Gods," Pharaon said. "I want to taste every inch of your body. But I don't offer you just my body. I offer you the world or at least that part of the world I can give you. Those checks over there. They are just the beginning."

"That's a mighty impressive beginning."

"There is so much more to come." He took Buck's hand. "Let's go for that swim so I can see your nude body in action. Later I have the most trained masseurs in the world." He reached for Buck's hand again, putting it to his mouth and licking it. "But only you can give me the ultimate massage."

*****

Buck awoke in the most luxurious bedroom he'd ever known or heard about. As his eyes slowly took in the wonder of the place, he imagined it was what Cleopatra's bedroom might have looked like. It seemed appropriate for the queen of the Nile—no one else. He wasn't quite sure where he was until he remembered he was in Palm Springs. He was in Ahmad's bedroom. He'd spent the most sensual day of his young life. Regardless of what experiences awaited him in the future, he felt nothing could compare to the day just gone by.

He ran his fingers across the satin sheets feeling for Ahmad but no one was in bed with him. He picked up rose petals, however. Someone—no doubt Ahmad—had covered his bed with rose petals. Picking up a handful of petals, he dropped them one by one across his face. It was then he became aware of a large ring on his finger. It was studded with precious gems, and it looked as if it'd cost the annual budget of the United States. He was amazed how people gave him jewelry, and he'd never worn gems before. The more he studied the ring, the more determined he was to wear it. He suspected that ring was very valuable indeed, no doubt once owned by Alexander the Great or some such towering historical figure. One day if he ever lost his male charms, he knew he could always peddle the jewelry recently bestowed on him.

In the place where the body of Ahmad had so recently rested, he picked up a piece of gold paper with mauve-colored ink. He read the words slowly: "All my life I've searched for the one perfect man, knowing that such a divine creature must exist somewhere on the face of the earth. Today I have found him. You are descended from the Gods. I have tasted every part of your body. I have known the most passionate kisses from you and the deepest penetration. You have transported me to a heaven I thought I'd never experience on the face of this earth. I'm a little black and blue, and your teeth marks are on me. You've branded me and made me yours. Your passion for me was so great you had to bite my flesh, even drawing blood, to relieve the exquisite torture I was putting you through. YOU ARE MY HUSBAND. From this day forth, everything I have is yours. A silly contract between us is meaningless now. I possess one of the fabled fortunes of all time. It is yours now to share with me. In spite of all my pretense, I am not a man after all. Today you made me a woman. When I am alone with you in the future, I will dress and act like the woman I have discovered in myself. I have left your bed only to prepare myself for you when you awake. When you have rested, please come to the boudoir upstairs. I will be there ready and waiting for you. When you come to me, we will speak of our glorious future. It is all right to continue with your boy-toy in the harem. Shelley is but a mere plaything for you to amuse yourself with while I am away, as I must often be. But I am the chief wife. When I am around, you will have need of no others. Your semen fills my body. I want you to think of my body as a willing receptacle of your nectar in the future. It will always be there for you willing to give you pleasure I know you've never known before with anyone else—man or woman. I have fallen in love with the world's most spectacular man. Your darling wife, Ahmad."

Buck rolled over in bed. "Oh, fuck," he said out loud. And he thought he'd had a complicated life before. What was the point in returning to Okeechobee now? It looked like school days down there. This afternoon he'd entered the adult world, and what fun it was.

He would soon rise from this bed and head for his bath. Immersed deep in that bath, he would remember in precious detail each thing Ahmad had so recently done to his body. He'd never known such pleasure or experienced such orgasms.

There was a gentle knock on the door. Thinking it was Ahmad, he called out, "Come on in."

A male Arab servant appeared with two notes which he handed to Buck on a gold platter. "Thank you." Without saying a word, the servant turned and left.

He picked up the first note and opened it. It was from Rose. "I will be out of phone contact for about three days. Don't ask me where I am. God, have I gotten myself in a mess with this shit. As soon as I finish this project, I'll fly back to Okeechobee and your loving arms. I am so sorry I wasn't here to say good-bye to you, but I am sure Ahmad will entertain you royally. Love, Rose."

He picked up the second note. It was from Shelley. "Buck, it was just great. Just great!!! While it lasted. But all good things come to an end. The end has come for us. Remember, I'm just a kid, and kids change their minds from day to day. One day they want to grow up to be a cowboy. The next day a fireman. One day I want to be the lover of Buck Brooke III. The next day I have another agenda and some other man. I'm sure you'll understand. To tell you the truth, you have begun to bore me. I bet we don't even have the same taste in music. Please don't try to contact me. It's over between us. I'm sure you'll find someone your own age. Why not go back to Robert? He seems ever faithful and always willing to welcome an errant husband back home. Don't forget to drop off that money to Don Bossdum. Rose had it gift wrapped—a cashier's check. He deserves it. Gotta go now. Love and kisses, Shelley."

Buck crushed the note in his hand. How utterly silly and naive Shelley was if he thought he was going to get rid of him so easily.

*****

Dust covered the American-built jeeps until their colors were completely obscured. Mounted on a swivel-head tripod at the rear of each jeep, machine guns faced the vastness of the desert, waiting for some unknown enemy to appear on the horizon.

Under the scorching sun, Rose stood as the finishing touches were applied by an Arab girl who wore a tight blouse and skirt. Instead of concentrating on Rose, she smiled invitingly at one of the cameramen. Rose sighed to herself in lament at how modesty had seemed to disappear from Arab women these days. Taking the brush from the girl's hand, she said, "God damn it, I'll do it myself."

Throughout the long hot hours, the relentless director had kept her and the crew working until her narration was "just perfect." She hadn't seen the film yet and, frankly, was grateful that her appearance in it had been limited to some introductory remarks. When she told the director of how she suffered in the heat, he reminded her of what she'd been paid. She shut up.

Surrounded by men in white robes and *keffiyeh*, she feared that in this inferno her makeup would run and distort her appearance on camera. To solve this problem, the director ordered two air-cooling machines to be blown on her for the next take. In her white Grecian gown, she imagined what she would look like on screen, her dress gently rippling in the winds. The air-cooling machines solved a lot of problems, including hot tempers.

The cooling breezes reminded her of last night when she'd slipped nude into the sparkling waters of the Red Sea. As she'd slowly cooled her overheated body, she'd seemed to wash away memories of Buck, Palm Springs, even Shelley. Of all the thoughts troubling her mind, the one she wanted to obliterate was the memory of Shelley. How could things have gone so wrong, gotten so out of control?

Later in the evening, as he'd prepared herself to face the desert heat in the morning, she'd been all too aware she didn't write the script any more. At dawn, she'd left the camp in a jeep. That bastard Calder had remained near the water, sitting under an air-conditioned Quonset hut on the beach in the company of two young girls.

Before the cameras again, she stood in front of a bleak-looking boulder, symbolizing the barren land. The glare from the mid-afternoon sun was so intense it created prismatic colors that reflected against her face. She hoped such brilliant light would remove any imperfections a cruel camera lens might pick up.

She sighed as she looked out at a "valley of the moon" landscape, in a setting of pink sands and distant black mountains.

A young man, Abdul, who'd been assigned to her as a bodyguard, had been unusually attentive all day. She'd welcomed the comfort of his presence. "After the shooting," he said, "you must come and see my town. It's a rose-colored city—just like your name." Abdul's dark, lusty eyes bored into her, thrilling her with their savagery. "My city is half as old as time."

"I feel as old as your city," she said, wanting to be contradicted.

"You're not old—you're young. A very beautiful lady."

She smiled at him, wondering if she should invite him inside her tent tonight. Shelley had been very wrong about her. She could still attract young men, without having to pay.

Sucking in the dry air, she rehearsed her dialogue—words familiar to her. "The Arab point of view is seldom heard in America. Evangelicals, in particular, avoid the subject. But the strong Zionist bloc in the United States should not affect Christian movements. We must keep our minds free to form our own opinion in a rapidly changing world."

The screeching whine of a helicopter passing directly over her head interrupted the filming, forcing the director to call "Cut!" It turned out to be Calder.

"Fuck you, Calder!" she yelled at him. "We almost had a perfect take."

In fifteen minutes, filming resumed. Only her words in the desert were heard: "Menachem Begin was once voted one of the most admired men in America. Yet this is the butcher who committed a stormtrooper-like atrocity on April 8, 1948, when he led bloodthirsty, revenging soldiers upon the small Arab village of Deier Yassin, near Jerusalem. On that infamous day, Begin and his hoodlums massacred 250 men, women and children. Menachem Begin, the less than perfect candidate for the Nobel Peace Prize!"

Calder smiled at her as if he were reviewing an honor guard marching for his inspection. These were his words anyway. This piece of information he had written surprised her. To her, Begin didn't look like a stormtrooper—more like a shopkeeper or the owner of a delicatessen.

"European Jews illegally confiscated and occupied Arab homes, even villages, where families had lived for centuries," she went on in a brave hope this was the final take. "There were no repatriations, no compensations for Arab losses. Fearing another Begin-led massacre, entire villages fled. The American Indian knows such atrocities well. The Jews who fled Hitler's Europe did so only to inflict the brutality they'd known there onto an innocent people in Palestine. A terrible irony of history!"

Calder's presence was no longer visible. All she saw was a blur of white and orange, as she continued speaking in front of camera. "As a Christian woman, I am here in this Palestinian-held territory hoping to do my part to make right a grievous wrong. I want to bring righteousness, justice and mercy to this land of suffering, homeless people."

A shiver traveled the length of her body as she realized the repercussions she'd have to face back home for making such a propaganda film. In her cold fury, she silently cursed Calder for taking her into such a scheme. The bear's claw was at her throat, not his—yet he'd collected half the fee. Suddenly, her voice chocked in that familiar strangulation.

The director seemed pleased and didn't stop the camera. It appeared as genuine concern for the Palestine people.

She gasped for breath. Her throat was parched. "For too long, Christians have avoided getting involved in this conflict. Yet it is a conflict close to our hearts. It is our Holy Land. Ground that Christ walked upon. Just as I have sympathy for the Jews after the terrible Nazi Holocaust, so I have sympathy for the Palestinians upon whom the Jews have inflicted such suffering."

"Cut!" the director yelled. "It's perfect. That's it for today."

"That's it—for good!" she said. "Let me out of this hell-hole." As she stumbled toward her tent, she felt the strong arm of Abdul around her waist. In the desert heat, he sweated heavily. Far from offending, the smell strangely attracted her. It was the smell of youth, of vigor, of freshness. She held close to him, until they'd escaped into the darkness of her tent.

She shuddered as she turned to him. That tidal wave inside her had collapsed. His skin was smooth and soft to her touch. His eyes held out such promise it filled her with a delirious kind of joy. "Don't ever leave me," came her desperate whisper in his ear.

*****

In a favorite Palm Springs haunt of Sinatra's Rat Pack, Buck noted the eyes of interest cast at his table. He and Ahmad did make a stunning couple—he, the handsome blond hunk looking like a recruiting poster for the U.S. Marines, and Ahmad, his date, appearing as a beautifully gowned young lady of elegance and refinement, perhaps some oil-rich princess from a Middle East kingdom.

Ahmad possessed great beauty as a male, but as a woman was a stunning delight, with some of the flair and grace of Audrey Hepburn at her finest moments. He played the role so well that Buck felt even the sharpest eye couldn't detect that Ahmad was a man. Every trace of his manhood had been artfully concealed. Perhaps Ahmad knew his own heart better than anyone. The role of a woman was one he was destined to play with ultimate perfection.

His makeup and hair were perfect—nothing overdone but with just the right amount of allure to be sexy and beautiful at the same time. Ahmad's perfect features, including a sensual mouth, were highlighted as never before with the discreet use of makeup including pale mauve-colored lips.

As Buck studied that mouth intensely, he knew all to well what pleasure it could provide for a man. In the presence of Ahmad the woman, he felt he'd become straight again. In spite of the world power held by this man—and Buck could only imagine that—Ahmad made him feel like a male protector. If anything, Ahmad made him more manly than he already was. When he was with Ahmad, his balls felt bigger than they were.

"You're staring," Ahmad said, smiling gently to soften the accusation. "But, of course, that's what it's all about. I didn't dress up to have you look at another woman. How can I complain that you haven't taken your eyes off me all night? I hope you approve."

"Do I ever!" Buck said, reaching for Ahmad's hand. He took it caressingly and held it to his lips for a soothing kiss. "Even now I can't believe what's happened."

"You mean my transformation into a woman."

"That too. But what I'm really thinking about is what you did to me all afternoon. I'm not exactly a virgin but I've never had sex like that in my life. I didn't even know it existed."

"I learned it in school."

"You're joking."

"I actually did go to a school for sex. It's in Egypt. I decided early when I was a teenager that if I wanted to attract men, I'd have to learn to please them. At this school you learn techniques passed down by the ancients."

"Did you ever learn your lesson well. I can't wait for a repeat performance."

"There will be many more nights to come. After all, you are my husband. The husband I've waited for all my life and never found. You are definitely marriage material."

"Aren't we going a bit fast here? After all, I never proposed. I certainly didn't agree to become your husband."

"But you're not turning it down, are you?"

Buck smiled and took a sip from his drink. "I am wearing the ring. I guess that answers the question for me." As the waiter approached, he brushed him away. He wasn't ready to order yet. If Ahmad were hungry for anything, it wasn't for food. "I have not turned you down, and I don't plan to either. You hold out such adventure for me I can't wait to see the surprises of the future."

"Are you sure you're not marrying me for my money?"

"I never thought about it. I guess you're not poor. I mean, this ring is fabulous."

"I don't even know how much money I have—an endless supply. As my husband, you will not want for anything. I can't always be with you but I'll see that you're always provided for."

"I'm not sure what that means."

"For openers, I'm going to give you a certain code and a certain address. With this code, you can tap into all the money you want, should you—for example—decide to buy the Empire State Building. The address is very secret. Actually, it's a post office box. You're to send all your bills there. A luxurious ocean-going yacht, whatever you want to buy. If I have overlooked something and didn't buy it for you already, then you're free to purchase it yourself."

"That's overwhelming. I've never heard of an offer like that."

"Few people in the world can make offers like that. They can't afford it. I can."

"I can't believe you'd do this. You just met me and you're providing for me."

"There will be so much more. What's the point in my acquiring all this money if I can't enjoy spending some of it? Take our new home. It's the largest and most splendid mansion in America. The one you wrote about in your paper."

"It is yours? We thought so."

"No, darling, it's ours. Whenever I can fly into Okeechobee, it will be ours. I've already left instructions that the place is yours to do with as you like whether I'm there or not."

"I've always wanted to see that mansion. I hear there's no place like it in Florida."

"Correction. There's no place like it anywhere in the world. The estate is called Desire. I designed it myself as a love nest for my husband, long before I knew I'd find you."

"As soon as I get back to Florida, I'll go there. I can't wait to see it. Will you accompany me through the gates?"

"How I wish I could. But I've got to leave early in the morning. I'll be out of touch for a few days but we'll schedule a rendezvous somewhere. Marriages like ours are the ways things will be in the future. One will actually have to schedule an appointment to be with one's husband. In the meantime, I'll see that you're heavily guarded so no enemy can get to you. I've assigned thirty bodyguards to you."

"Am I that precious?"

"To me you are divine. Thirty isn't all that much. Since they'll be working eight-hour shifts, and we'll need a spare or two for holidays and weekends, sickness leave, and days off."

"It'll be like I'm the president of the United States guarded by the Secret Service."

"Who knows? You might be president one day. It appears unlikely that Barry Collins will ever make it to the White House. We're grooming many people. Barry was but one of many. You've got to get to them before they're thirty. Being president takes some grooming and a lot of long-range planning, not to mention a hideous amount of money. I fear Barry and Shelley weren't too discreet."

Suddenly, the mention of Shelley brought back the painful reality of that note. He reached into his breast pocket and retrieved Shelley's note, giving it to Ahmad to read.

Ahmad studied it carefully. "It could be genuine. It could also be a fake. Calder's hot on Shelley's ass with this latest scandal, and he's putting major pressure on Rose."

Don't you think I could see the boy? I have to know if this is Shelley speaking, or something he was forced to do."

"I don't know where Shelley is. I never interfere in battles between Calder and Rose. I always let them fight it out between themselves and then I talk to the winner. You Americans and your agendas are impossible to figure out anyway."

"I'm really demanding to see him."

"So you shall. I'll force them to arrange it if nothing else. But it will take a few days. I'll be incommunicado for a while. But as soon as I've emerged into the world, believe me I will look into this matter."

"Are you jealous? I mean of Shelley and me?"

"Please, don't make me out to be a silly fool. You know how I feel about young boys. I've told you so already. Mere playthings. A young boy should never interfere in the mature relationship of a man and woman like you and me."

"You are the single most intriguing person I've ever met in my entire life."

"And so it shall be. You'll never meet another Ahmad. Life doesn't bestow blessings twice like this. So you'd better enjoy me while I'm here."

Buck slid closer to Ahmad. "You know what I want and want now."

"We're in a restaurant," Ahmad said demurely. "You men. So demanding."

The waiter appeared to take their food order. "I'm not too hungry," Buck said.

"Eat a steak," Ahmad ordered. "You'll need all your energy before we take our separate planes in the morning. He turned to the waiter. "I'll have a light green salad—hold the dressing—and my husband will have a T-bone, rare, with a baked potato and some broccoli."

"That sounds just great," Buck said after the waiter had left. "How did you know that's one of my favorite meals?"

"It was in your file."

"What God damn file are you talking about?"

"The file I read on you."

"You have a file on me? I find that hard to believe."

"We've been keeping one on you for years. Waiting for you to grow up."

"That's ridiculous."

"Okay. Test me. I know where you were on the night of April 14, 1964."

"I don't know that. The date means nothing to me."

"Pick any date, and I'll give you a complete dossier. I know everything you've ever done in your life. Well, almost."

"I find that amazing."

"Call it obsession. I've been dreaming and thinking about you for a long time. Now you're mine. I've taken possession of what I've always wanted and dreamed about. You are my fantasy."

"Don't build me up too much. I'm only a man. It's only skin."

"Don't be so modest. I've searched the world, and you're the only man who qualified."

"I hope I live up to your promise. Actually, I don't know what to say. It's all been too much."

Ahmad raised his glass. "Let's toast to our marriage."

"To our marriage," Buck said raising his glass. It wasn't the drink—he hadn't had that much—but the world suddenly seemed to spin out of control.

He just knew he'd wake up tomorrow in some bleak motel room and all this would be but a dream.

*****

Although he shook all over, he wasn't really cold in the night's wind. Like white foam, a huge wave rose above Gene's boat, a double-ended yawl with a black hull. His blood froze, and for a moment he was filled with fear. The wave seemed to seize the boat, making it rise. It crashed and shuddered to a halt until it lurched free. Hands locked to the wheel, he slumped over. God had saved him from being hurled into the watery grave.

Earlier that day he'd driven to Fort Lauderdale, where he kept his boat in a rundown marina. It had been his only luxury in life, and he'd lovingly cared for the vessel. Now it had become more important to him than ever. The boat was part of his plan.

His breathing grew more relaxed. The boat was still under him, still plowing over the water. It hadn't overturned.

His eyes stung from the burning salt as the water slapped his face. A splintering flash of lightning cut across the sky, followed by an explosion of thunder. He should have listened to radio reports before impulsively taking the boat out, as a brief respite from his troubles. Either that, or he should have returned to port earlier, at the first sign of bad weather. Getting caught in a storm was the last stupid mistake he'd make.

Rose would soon return to Paradise Shores and when she did he'd drive with Barry to meet her. Barry hadn't wanted to take him along, but he'd demanded it. He tried to blot out the visions of expectation that drifted through his mind. She might not like him. He must not hope too much. Up to now, the disappointments had been bitter, more than he could handle.

Though alone, he was comforted by the feeling that Rose was already at his side. The boat continued its wild gyrations and he took grim pleasure in this, knowing he had to protect not only himself, but her. As the sea fell on him unrelentingly, he took little notice of it. Not even the turbulent waters could alter him from his course.

It would be so easy to give in, abandoning the endless struggle and humiliation, allowing the sea to claim him. Perhaps that would come later. Not now when there was so much to do.

His sodden coat provided some protection from the wind, but he wasn't cold any more. She was beside him, and she gave off warmth.

Another wave ran in and hit his boat, causing the bowsprit to rise menacingly in the white-capped sea. It pointed at the heavens and, in one flash, he imagined his ascending there. Then it fell with a crash, plowing back into the rain-lashed waters.

Like a dipper, the boat scooped up gallons of the churning sea. Flood waters hurtled along the deck. He hadn't closed the hatch cover, another mistake.

His eyes still stung from the salt and his whole body ached from the strain of staring into the bslack frenzy. The shore line approached. He'd have to hold out a little longer. His nerves knotted tighter at the prospect of reaching the marina.

It had been wrong to take his boat out into these pitching, tossing waters, but he knew he could handle trouble. More difficult jobs awaited him. Bringing the boat back was a kind of triumph for him, letting him know that his nerves were steady enough to do the job ahead.

The lurching of the boat had made him sick at his stomach. As he got closer to shore, he noted how the full-throated roar of the wind had become just a faint cry. The boat rose and fell the way it had earlier in the evening, like an out-of-control elevator, madly going up and down.

Safely ashore, he took a taxi to a cheap apartment he'd rented in Fort Lauderdale under an assumed name. Inside the dank rooms, the smell was musty. He didn't bother to turn on the lights. He'd never turned on the lights. Stripping, he toweled himself dry. The only sound in his bedroom was the hum of a ceiling fan and an occasional snore from the old man who lived next door. Sounds traveled easily through the thin walls. He'd slip in and out of the apartment. After the trauma with that little Cuban girl and her mother, he vowed never to let his new neighbors see him.

Under the bed he kept a rifle, a new revolver, and an M-16 which he checked carefully. The M-16 had been shipped back from Vietnam, piece by piece, by a soldier Gene had known. He'd bought it from him.

For some reason not clear to him, he'd had the vision to remove the weapons and store them in a locker at the Greyhound bus station. He'd visited the weapons frequently, not only to see that the locker fee was paid up, but to check on them. It seemed a miracle to him that he'd had the foresight to remove the weapons because they would have been destroyed in the fire that swept across his home. It was as if God intended for him to keep these weapons and had given him the forewarning to remove them from his house for safekeeping.

He lay in silence, waiting, too excited to rest. He'd spent so much of his life waiting and had never resigned himself to it. If anything, this constant waiting grew more irritating by the hour. In visions of propulsive action that flashed through his mind deep into the early hours of the morning, the unjust were about to be punished.

He fell asleep with exhaustion but woke to the voice of the old man next door. It was morning. The man chased two gray alley cats from the garbage can.

He knew Sandy and Jill might be worried about him, not knowing where he was. No doubt they'd think he had spent the entire night at the home of Barry Collins. They were never to know of this secret place. This little world belonged to him and no one else.

Returning to his womb-like room had safely cradled Gene. He felt sealed like a royal mummy for the long voyage ahead.

He would be mentally wrapped, bandaged from the outside world. Only she could take off the wrappings and see what was inside.

*****

Buck had been looking forward to the flight back to Okeechobee as a means of mulling over everything Ahmad had promised him and asked him to do. Right now it was more than he could digest. It had all happened too fast.

Arriving at the airport, Buck was informed that Ahmad had routed Buck's newly acquired private jet to Palm Springs to pick him up. Buck felt foolish boarding the plane with a flank of security guards of various nationalities. It was as if overnight he'd become a potentate. Before mounting the stairs to the plane, he looked once more at the ring Ahmad had given him. In some way that ring seemed to symbolize he'd become Ahmad's property. Judging from the number of security guards, Ahmad wanted to see that his property was well protected.

The chief security guard, a handsome, blond-haired Norwegian, Lars Hensen, had gone aboard first to check out the plane. As Buck came aboard, Lars said to him, "Your companion is in the main suite. He's asking for you."

"My God, he's come back to me. You mean the one with the blond curls?"

"That's the one," Lars said. "He's waiting for you."

"Then the note was a cruel joke."

"I don't know about any note, sir."

Ignoring him, Buck fast-stepped his way to the back of the plane. He opened the door and entered the darkened suite, shutting the door behind him and locking it. In the dim light he saw Shelley's blond curly head lying on a pillow.

"You didn't leave me after all," Buck said. "I knew your note was a lie. I love you, Shelley. I always will."

The figure rose from the bed and turned on the bedside lamp. Slowly he removed his blond curly wig. Robert's own blond hair emerged from under the wig.

Buck stared into Robert's face, not believing he'd been aboard the plane. So much for Ahmad's security. Turning his back at the sight of Robert, he went over to the bar to pour himself a drink.

"I love you, Shelley," Robert said, mocking his words. "You promised to love me, and you've betrayed me."

Still not looking at him, Buck belted down a strong dose of alcohol. "You're right. I've betrayed you if you want to call it that."

"What else can I call it? All my life I've been faithful to you. I've never looked at another man. And look how you rewarded that trust."

"I know," Buck said, turning to look at him carefully for the first time. Even as he took in his features, he couldn't understand how he'd ever loved Robert, much less married him. As he stared at his old longtime friend, all feeling of love seemed to have vanished. He wasn't staring into the sophisticated face of Ahmad who'd understand sexual indiscretions with the wisdom of the ages. If anything, Robert appeared to have become a shrill of a nagging wife.

"Don't you have anything else to say to me?" Robert asked. "Just, 'I know.'"

"I know little of the human heart," Buck said as his plane became airborne. "I didn't mean to fall in love with Shelley. He's just a child. But I did fall in love with him. A lot of good it did me. He's left me."

"That's the first good news I've heard all day." He sat up in bed, revealing his golden chest which had brought such pleasure to Buck in the past. "Look, I've got the ring back. Just like you wanted." He gazed at Buck's hand. "I see you've acquired another ring. You've even got your own personal security guard now."

"Not just one," Buck said. "If you get out of bed and check out the plane, you'll find thirty security guards."

"This new job of yours has made you a very important man."

"I guess. At least a heavily guarded one." His voice had grown impatient. "All right. You've caught me. I've cheated on you. I've fallen for another guy. What do you want from me? I'm prepared to give you virtually anything you demand."

"I'm demanding nothing except your return and complete commitment to me."

"That's more than I can deliver." Buck downed the rest of his drink and figured he'd need at least a few more before this luxurious plane landed on Florida soil. "I'll give you all the money in the world. Anything you want. The only thing I can't or won't promise is myself."

"But you just said the little brat left you. We can still put this behind us."

"We can't. I married you too soon. Hell, I only came out of the closet yesterday, or so it seems to me. Just a few months ago before I started sucking cock, I thought of myself as straight. Straight maybe with a gay streak. Now my life is changing by the minute. The mistake I made was in thinking I could settle down with one person. I'm on the dawn of my life. The whole world is opening for me. I'm going to be living mainly in Beverly Hills in the future. I'm going to become a big piece of shit in Hollywood, the land of shits. Wherever I look, doors are opening for me. I'm not ready to settle down to a little domestic life in Okeechobee. I don't even know who I am."

"Suddenly, you've found your voice if only to use it to destroy my dreams."

"I don't want to destroy your dreams. I don't want to hurt you in any way. But I'm taking my life back. It's my life. No one owns me."

"It seems to me you've become nothing but a hustler. Some sort of grand courtesan, the greatest male version the world has ever known. You've suddenly got a private plane. You've got security guards. You're going to be installed in some mansion in Beverly Hills with movie stars clamoring for you to finance their projects, if I read what you said correctly. It looks to me if you're really in someone's debt. I was kind calling it grand courtesan. Back where I come from, we call a whore a whore."

Buck was tempted to take his drink and throw it in Robert's face. It wasn't that what Robert said was a lie. It was the crude truth of his accusation. But he was hardly going to allow Robert's taunt to derail his train. That was going ahead. He didn't want to be with Robert for the rest of the flight back home. He wanted to retreat to the other suite, there to dream about carrying out Ahmad's plans for their Hollywood debut. That was the most overriding ambition in his life right now.

"I've done you wrong," Buck said. "I'm sorry. I'll buy you off. I'm sure Uncle Milty can reach some sort of settlement. We're not talking small fish here. It can range in the millions. You've been a loyal friend. I'll fix you up for the rest of your life. Give you anything. You'll find a man worthy of you. I'm a two-timing bastard. I'm not worthy of your trust and devotion. Double-crossing you is the last thing I wanted to do. I can't help myself."

"It's not too late to turn back." Robert slowly removed the sheet from his nude body. "You can come over here now and reclaim this body. It's yours."

Buck closed his eyes. He didn't really want to take in the sight of Robert's body. He wanted out of this suite and even off the plane. He not only didn't want to share a life with Robert, he didn't even want to share this plane with him.

"I don't feel well," Buck said. "I've got to go to my own cabin."

"This is your cabin," Robert protested.

"I'll go somewhere else," Buck said. He put down the drink, turned and walked quickly to the door. He shut it behind him, emerging into the relative freedom of the public area of the plane. At the plane's bar, he confronted Lars. Buck might as well see that this security force earn its money. "I've had a fight with my companion," he told Lars. "I don't want to see him for the rest of the flight. I'll be in the other suite, and I don't want to be disturbed until we get to Florida. If he makes a scene, confine him to his cabin. Is that clear?"

"Your wish is my command, sir." He moved closer to Buck, brushing up against him. "I'm aboard to take care of all your needs, sir. Any that you might have."

Buck looked into eyes as blue as a Nordic lake. "That won't be necessary. At least for now."

"I understand," Lars said, "but I'm always available to you."

"Just keep Robert out of my cabin and let me have my time alone."

"It is done." Lars turned and left.

Buck headed for his cabin, knowing that in the last five minutes, and in that scene just played out with Robert, he'd changed his entire life.

He faced an uncertain future.

Chapter Thirteen

It was not the homecoming Buck envisioned. Casey was waiting at the airport in a limousine. He shook Buck's hand and treated him rather formally. "Welcome back, sir," he said until Robert had turned around. Then Casey winked at Buck. After ushering them into the back seat, he drove to Buck's mansion.

Sitting near the window, Robert remained sullen on the way home. He didn't say a word. Once in the house, he headed for his own private suite which he'd never used before. "I have a headache and don't want to be disturbed," he told Buck before heading up the stairs.

Buck put through a call to police headquarters and demanded to speak to the chief at once.

Biff immediately came on the phone. "Rich boy," the chief said as a greeting. "I hear you brought millions back from California."

"News travels fast."

"Are you calling to make a contribution to the police fund—you can afford it."

"Later perhaps. Before I left Florida, I didn't have time to report an incident to you. It's about Julius Forster."

"Here we go again."

"There's something new. He was spotted staking out my villa in Key Biscayne."

"Who spotted him?" Biff demanded to know.

"One of my staff."

"Could you bring the staff member into my office for questioning?" Biff asked.

"Not right now—he's not in town. But I thought you should know about this. Forster is stalking me. I think he's dangerous."

"If you can't produce an eyewitness, I can't help you," Biff said. "To my knowledge, he's committed no crime. Let's leave it at that. Besides, my jurisdiction doesn't extend to Key Biscayne." He slammed down the phone.

Rebuffed, Buck hung up and called Rose's Paradise Shores. Her butler came onto the phone. "Mr. Brooke, we were expecting a call from you. Sister Rose is flying back to Okeechobee. She doesn't want you to come here but plans to meet with you privately. It's very urgent. Please give me a number where we can reach you at all times."

Buck gave him the number but before hanging up, he asked, "Has there been any news from Shelley?"

"Not a word," the butler said. "I'm sure he's doing just fine out in California saving souls from the devil with his mother."

"I'm sure. Bye." Buck put down the receiver and stared vacantly at the room. Clara came in and asked him if he wanted something to eat. He declined, resenting her presence in his household. He was furious at Robert for hiring her in the first place, considering what she'd done to Gene.

"Will you guys be eating in tonight?" she asked.

"Not tonight," he said. "That will be all." He wanted her out of his presence. As she turned to leave, he called back to her. "Stay out of the pool area. I want to go for a nude swim."

"Don't worry about me," she said. "I've seen you American men nude before."

"I'm sure you have," Buck said, "but I didn't want to offend Maria and have her calling the police to have me arrested for indecent exposure."

Clara only glared at him before turning her back to him and stalking toward the kitchen. Regardless of what Robert thought, Buck was going to fire her the moment he got back from Switzerland.

Pouring himself a drink, he dialed Susan.

She picked up the phone right away. "My errant husband returns from the battlefields. How did it go?"

"I brought back all the gold in California. Winter's coming. How many furs do you want?"

"I've already found something to keep me warm."

"I've heard. Don Bossdum. Not bad. All America. What a catch. All the girls were after him in college."

"You mean the ones not stalking you and Gene?"

"Yeah, those." He hesitated a moment. "I'm calling about our wedding pictures. The announcements to the press. Stuff like that. I'm flying to Switzerland soon to see the old man. Could we get this done tomorrow morning around noon?"

"Sure. I'm certain you have a full schedule. Let me set it up. I'll arrange everything. The photographer, everything."

"Susan..." Again, he hesitated for a long time. "Would you call Leroy Fitzgerald and ask him to be the photographer? He's not only a great photographer, he can film it too. He'll need a crew."

"I thought you hated Fitzgerald."

"I don't exactly hate him—not after he took those terrific pictures of me as the sexiest man alive. After he did that, I like him a lot better."

She paused, as if she didn't believe Buck was being completely truthful with her. "If Leroy's the man you want, I'll get him if he's available. I might like to talk to him myself about doing a little film for me."

"What are you up to?"

"I want you to know, really I do. Pamela's in Key West. She wants me to put her on film in an interview. She plans—at least on film—to spill the beans. She's making demands of Calder and Barry. I can only release the interview if Barry doesn't cave in to her demands. Do I have your permission to go through with this?"

"You do indeed, and you know you don't need my permission. Tell you what: I'll arrange to have you and Don flown to Key West on my private jet. Leroy—and you can trust me on this one—is hardly a friend of Calder's. In fact, a secret interview with Pamela on tape might be just the final weapon he needs in his little negotiations going on with Calder now. Anything you can do to fuck over Calder will make me love you only more. I have little desire to harm Barry in any way. Barry is his own worst enemy. But I want to destroy Calder. Please slant your interview so that Pamela exposes Calder more than Barry. I'll love you if you can do this for me."

She laughed but it had a hollow ring. "Conditional love. Don't worry. I'll set everything up. Could you come to the condo around ten thirty in the morning? I should be back from the beauty parlor then. I want to look absolutely gorgeous when I'm photographed announcing my marriage to Florida's handsomest and richest man—not to mention the sexiest stud alive."

"I'm sure that honor should go to football-playing Don."

"Don, I fear, isn't quite as handsome as you."

"Flattery will get you everywhere."

"I doubt that," she said with just a ring of sarcasm in her voice.

"See you in the morning, love." He hung up and headed for his balcony overlooking his gardens and fountains. As wonderful as they looked to him, he was daydreaming about what the gardens and fountains at Desire looked like. Just as soon as he could slip away, he planned to have Casey drive him there. After all, in some strange new way Desire had become his new home.

He'd never take Robert there, however. The image of Robert was everywhere in this house. Even though everything had been acquired and decorated by his mother, it was Robert's presence that now filled the house, obliterating his mother. He didn't need this place any more. Perhaps he'd deed it to Robert. In some ways, Buck had outgrown it. He was anxious to begin life at Desire. It must be fabulous. Like a palace. Besides, if he wanted a place to live in Okeechobee, he could move into his grandfather's even larger mansion. Buck feared the old man would never return to the baronial splendor he'd left behind in Florida before flying to Switzerland.

"I'm not homeless," he said out loud, mainly to the breezes.

He turned when he heard the rattle of a battered old car coming up his driveway. Who could that be?

Getting out of the car, a fat Hazel could be seen waddling toward the main door. She must have returned early from Oklahoma, and she looked furious. At first he was tempted to ring for Casey and have him tell Hazel he wasn't home. But he knew Hazel would only be back tomorrow.

As he made his way across the veranda, he'd forgotten how his life had changed. From the porch he spotted five of Lars's men surrounding Hazel. Lars had told him he was going to block off all access to the property but hadn't had time to do that yet, as they'd just arrived. Hazel started struggling with the men and kicked one of them. Before they could overpower her, Buck called out to one of the guards. "It's okay," he shouted. "She's a friend of mine. Bring her into the garden."

"Thank God you're here," Hazel had shouted at him, before following the men into the garden.

Lars appeared out of nowhere. "I'm sorry but I was just assigning guard duty. I haven't secured the property yet."

"It's okay," Buck said. "An old friend."

"All of us are installed in the mansion next door."

"How in the hell did you arrange that? You've just got in town."

"Ahmad knows how to get things done from afar."

"That house is even bigger than this one. I've always envied it."

"It's yours."

"What do you mean?"

"Before he left America, Ahmad acquired it for you. After all, my security force needs a place in which to operate. We need bedrooms, stuff like that."

"What happened to the Markums? They've devoted their lives to restoring and furnishing that place with priceless antiques and paintings. That super rich bitch Pat Markum is a collector from hell. She always put us to shame."

"They left with only their clothing. Everything is still intact. Their furnishings, paintings, everything. It's yours now."

"I can't believe it. She was devoted to her possessions."

"What can I say? Ahmad made them an offer they couldn't refuse providing they'd evacuate the house within six hours. We're still packing up their things."

"Ahmad really knows how to get things done."

Lars looked at Buck enigmatically, a smile breaking across his handsome Nordic face. "You wouldn't really want to know."

"So I've acquired a new home."

"Please come over tonight or as soon as you can and take a grand tour." He moved closer to Buck. "I'll be your tour guide, or whatever."

"It's a deal. But the property I really want to see is Desire."

"The limo is waiting to take you there any time you say. I'll accompany you. I know the place well. All its secrets. And there are many secrets within that house. I'll show them all to you."

"I feel like some sugar-addicted young boy who's wandered into a candy shop."

"You have. By the way, your Blackhawk will arrive at the airport tomorrow. Flown in by cargo plane."

"Life is too good. I'll catch you later."

He sucked in the fresh air and headed for his garden patio where he could hear Hazel shouting at one of his security guards. She'd already gotten into an argument.

*****

In his garden patio Buck summoned Clara to bring Hazel a drink. In a flower-print dress, she was sweating profusely. She appeared in a fighting mood. "Sorry I didn't call first," she said. "Since when did you hire these goons to protect you, and why are all of them so handsome?"

"It's a long story," he said, motioning for her to have a seat.

She plopped down in an empty chair to catch her breath. When she'd recovered her wind, she said, "First off, we old bags on South Beach have gotten our eviction notices."

"God damn. I'm sorry to hear that."

"There's more. For the second blast, the Nazis and KKK are going to march through South Beach tomorrow morning. They've even got a parade permit. We in the Anti-Defamation League are trying to get an injunction to stop it. But it may be too late."

Like newsreel footage, visions of the upcoming event ran through Buck's head. "It could turn into a riot!"

"Swastikas on South Beach," Hazel said, near tears. "The people are mostly Jews, some thirty-five thousand of them. Some are survivors of concentration camps. They'll have heart attacks if they see Nazis parading on American streets. They won't understand. The old ones will think another holocaust has come."

"I'm sure Biff will be of no help."

"None whatsoever. He won't even return my phone calls."

"I know you're not mayor yet but here's a grand opportunity for you to show some leadership."

"Like how?"

"Give a speech. Have a before-parade rally. Print pamphlets. I'll pick up the tab for everything. Urge those old people to stay inside their homes and close the curtains. Pretend it's not happening. Don't go out to confront them. Let them have their silly parade and then the whole thing will be over."

"That's not my style. I believe in confrontational politics."

"I know you do, and I also know people could get killed. Do it my way!"

Hazel looked at him long and hard. The brilliant light of the day revealed wrinkles in her face he hadn't noticed before. The candidate appeared tired, spent, bereft of energy—not a campaigner capable of leading the oncoming fight. "I can't follow your advice. We can't stand by and see our rights trampled on. No one over there wants to be led like a docile cow to the slaughter. We're going to stand up and fight."

"I'm sure you know best," he said. "It was only a suggestion. I can't do anything about the parade but I might be able to do something about all those people being uprooted with nowhere to go."

"What, pray tell?"

"I've got to do some investigation. If I pull off my scheme, I might be able to provide a lot of housing."

"I don't know how in hell you plan to do that."

"You'll know soon enough."

"I've got to go. There's much work to be done."

He gently touched her arm, as he looked into her face, a mask of helpless despair. "I'm curious about something. Why did you come to me with this news? You know I'm not the publisher of the Examiner any more. I'm just a private citizen."

"You're fooling nobody, honey. Even without the Examiner, you may have more power in this town than anyone. I think you have power you don't even know about."

"Let's put that to a test," he said, getting up to kiss her on the cheek. "I have no jurisdiction over parades. Let's see how good I am on housing."

"If anyone can help us, you can."

"Thanks for having trust in me," he said, taking her arm as he guided her toward her battered car. She got in and started her car but the motor died. He went to his garage and returned with a set of keys. "Here, take my car. It's pretty fancy, but I won't have need of it again. I no longer drive myself around."

"You mean it?" she asked, her face lighting up.

"Sure, it's yours. I'll have the title transferred over to you. If you're going to be mayor of Okeechobee, you might as well drive around in a respectable looking vehicle. You look like Ma Kettle in that fucking death trap you're driving."

"Thanks," she said, kissing him on the cheek. "Thanks a whole lot. I see it as a campaign contribution."

"As you like." He hesitated. "I gather you've forgiven me for some of my latest..." He paused. "Affiliations."

Getting behind the wheel of his shiny new car, she turned for a final good-bye. "You won't be the first man I've ever had to forgive, and you won't be the last." She roared off down his driveway. She called back to him in her booming voice, "Eat my dust."

*****

As soon as Hazel had disappeared from view, he raced across the lawn to the Markum estate, as evening shadows fell. His mother had a long ago feud with Mrs. Markum—they'd once been friends—and he'd never set foot on the neighboring estate since he was thirteen. Feeling like an intruder, he appeared on the veranda of the Gothic-style manor. At any minute he expected Mrs. Markum to appear and chase him off her property. But if Lars was telling the truth, it was all his, a gift from Ahmad.

As he approached the door, it was thrown open by Lars himself. "Welcome, lord of the manor. We've got it all ready for your inspection."

"Thanks," was all he could manage to say. Standing in the foyer, he was overcome by the grandeur of the mansion. Since he'd last seen it,

Mrs. Markum had looted more of the showcases of Europe. It was a house filled with objets d'art from all over the world.

"I have an inventory from the appraiser if you'd like to know what all the art work and antiques are," Lars said.

"Later," Buck said. "I just want to take everything in."

"Many of her paintings are minor, although worthy of display in a museum," Lars said. "However, she sold us eight world-class masterpieces. Munch. El Greco."

"Don't go on," Buck said. "I can't believe it. I want to wander about on my own, then look at every item individually. I think I've died and gone to heaven."

"You have," Lars said. "Ahmad is an incredibly generous man. Wait until you see Desire. Perhaps later tonight."

"I can't wait. But first Mrs. Markum's treasure trove."

Long after he'd finished his own tour and then a closer inspection with Lars explaining what each item was, Buck settled into a sofa on the veranda in the rear overlooking the garden. When he used to come here with his mother, he was more interested in the tennis courts and swimming pool, both bigger than his own, although not as large as the swimming pool and courts at old Buck's estate, and certainly not as grand as the tennis courts and pool at Paradise Shores.

"I'm impressed," Buck told Lars who poured him a Scotch. "I can't believe this is all mine. A bit conservative and traditional, but fabulous."

"That little table in the tiny foyer off the hallway is worth $175,000 alone," Lars said. "Where did she get all the money?"

"Before he retired, her husband was in steel, but she had her own money. She was an heiress. Her father once owned huge real estate in North Miami Beach which he sold off. They could afford anything they wanted, and they were world class shoppers."

Lars looked around him. "Obviously."

"My dear friend Hazel brought up a question today about the guards," Buck said, sipping his drink. "I've met every man on the security guard. Beginning with the beauty before me, Mr. Norway, every guy on your force is incredibly handsome. I know that was no accident."

"Ahmad is sophisticated about sexual matters," Lars said. "He wants loyalty from you. He doesn't demand that you be faithful. He will be gone for periods of time, and he doesn't want you to be lonely. Each of my men is available to you at any time of the day or night."

"That Ahmad thinks of everything. He's incredibly generous."

"Actually he's not. He's rather frugal."

"I find that hard to believe."

"You are his husband," Lars said. "The first husband he's ever felt worthy of himself. You can have the world if you want it. There's nothing he wouldn't do for you...or give you."

"This is incredible. He hardly knows me."

"Quite the contrary. He told me you were descended directly from the gods. In fact, he said he knows every inch of you."

"That he does."

"As I said you can pick and choose among my men as you wish." He leaned over and looked Buck directly in the eye. "How I wish you'd start with me. Not only start with me, but give it all to me. Don't bother with the rest. I'm the best. I could satisfy you in every way."

"That's a very tempting offer. You are very handsome."

"If you think I'm good-looking with my clothes on, wait until you see what I look like with my clothes off."

"A future pleasure of mine, I know," Buck said. Abruptly changing the subject, he asked "When will I see Ahmad again?"

"We never know. He will just suddenly appear out of nowhere without warning. I'm almost certain you will see him within six days. He's never gone more than a week or so at a time. He spends all his time in airplanes—his own."

"I can't wait to see him again," Buck said, smiling. "I owe him so much." He reached over and took Lars's hand, squeezing it gently. "And a gift of you too."

"Any time of the day or night, I'm here for you. If you want me to be a husband to you in Ahmad's absence, I'll be the greatest husband in the world. But if you want me to be a wife, I can be that too, although I don't like that so much. I'd rather be the man."

"You look very manly. An incredible catch."

"Thank you, sir."

"Call me Buck."

"I like that name. Rhymes with..."

Buck interrupted him. "Oh, my God, I'm due to call my attorney, Uncle Milty. He's just getting out of court. Hell, do we have a lot to talk over! I want some of your men to go and pick him up. He'll think he's being kidnapped by handsome studs and he'll love it. He'll think you're bringing him to my house, but I want you to usher him into here. Tell him Mrs. Markum is filing a multi-million dollar lawsuit against me, and she's demanding to see him at once. That will attract his attention. Usher him into the library. I'll be there waiting."

"Fine, I like playing games." He got up as Buck did. In an impulsive move, Lars reached over and kissed Buck's mouth, licking his lips with his tongue. "I'd like to play games with you."

"Later," Buck promised. It was an empty promise, but not that empty.

*****

Since Uncle Milty would not be free until nine o'clock that evening, Buck returned to his own home. He still couldn't bring himself to think the Markum home was his. He felt like an invader there. As he came into his living room to pour himself a drink, Robert was sitting on the sofa, enjoying a drink himself. "Decided to come down from your room and make an appearance?" Buck asked with just a slight edge of sarcasm.

"I promised you a surprise when you came back here," Robert said, not looking at him.

"I thought I already had my surprise when I got on the plane," Buck said. "The blond wig..."

Robert interrupted him, "That's not the surprise I had in mind. I told Clara we wouldn't be eating in tonight. I want to take you to the Blue Moon."

"That dump! Why the Blue Moon?"

"I'm sure it doesn't compare to the grand palaces you've been dining in, but there's a motive to my madness."

"If you wish. I'll get ready." Buck turned and headed upstairs where he took a shower. When he came out, there was no Robert waiting to dry him off.

Along with three security guards and Casey, they drove to the Blue Moon in a decaying part of Okeechobee. When Robert and the guards went in to secure two tables, Buck remained behind with Casey.

"Welcome home, boss," Casey said. "I've missed you. There's no one around. How about leaning over and giving me a wet one?"

"Glad to oblige." He kissed Casey long and hard, sucking his tongue a bit.

"It looks like Robert is sulking and holding out on you," Casey said. "Can I see you later tonight? After all, I've got to do something to earn this fantastic salary you're paying me. With money like I'm getting, I'll be driving my own Porsche soon. We can slip off together later. I really need you."

"Maybe that's what I need, too, you good-looking mother-fucker." He kissed him again and headed inside the Blue Moon where Robert sat at a table alone, one security guard occupying a bar stool, the other two at an adjoining table. The handsome guards blended in perfectly, looking like university students in their tight-fitting jeans and T-shirts.

The tavern was dark and commodious, and in the back was a pool table at which young men played a hard-driving but not very accurate game. Music from the jukebox blared. After reading the grease-smeared menu encased in plastic, Buck ordered a hamburger, French fries, and a beer. After the blue-jeaned waiter left, Buck told Robert. "If I get the News, and if you want me to hire you as food editor, forget it!"

Robert's face was smug, enigmatic. "I have my reasons for taking you to this joint. I might be spending a lot of time here."

"You going for a waiter's job?"

"It's the only place along the south river where you can drop in for a beer."

"You might like to come here. I think this is my last visit."

A tension within Robert surfaced. His hand, with his engagement ring and wedding band, shook as he lifted his beer to his mouth. "With the loss of the Examiner, there went my job too."

"Don't worry about it," Buck said. "I can get you any job you want—at a salary from heaven. We're talking higher math here."

"That's very impressive. You've certainly come up in the world. Now that you've come into all this money and power, I'm surprised that Shelley dumped you."

"I guess my dick wasn't big enough."

"I doubt that! Surely it was some other reason."

"I'd rather not talk about it." The waiter arrived with the beers. When his hamburger was served shortly afterward, Buck slumped over his plate. He no longer had an appetite.

Robert's cloudy green eyes fixed heavily on him. Putting his beer down with a thump, Robert said, "You're young, just getting started in life. The loss of the Examiner is hardly the end for you. You no longer have the forty-five thousand annual salary. You've got millions instead and a job that seems to pay you like some Arab sheik with a whole country of oil wells pumping and pumping away."

"I work now for Ahmad Pharaon."

"Did you hit pay dirt, Pharaon—so you've completely sold out just like Sister Rose? The university liberal has become today's anti-Semitic propagandist."

"Fuck that!"

"It's the truth, isn't it?"

"Why defend myself? What do you want to hear me say? That I'm an international whore. A male slut from hell. Not only that but a child molester. Is that what you want to hear?"

"At least you can admit it. I can't believe how you betrayed me. After our marriage, I thought you'd be faithful. Even as you were marrying me, you were probably thinking of this eight-year-old. I find it disgusting."

Even though he didn't want food, Buck bit aggressively into his hamburger. He wanted out of here and away from nagging Robert. He lifted his face from his plate and stared into Robert's eyes, finding them tough and hard. Buck felt all his nerves tighten. He swallowed hard. This confrontational style with Robert was something new to him. He hated it.

"Forget your fucking hamburger," Robert said. "I'll show you my surprise."

Outside on the dimly lit street, trailed by the security guards, Buck headed for the rear of the limousine. Robert got up front with Casey directing him where to go. The guards followed in their own car.

Robert instructed Casey to park on a deserted street. He then led Buck through a parking lot and around the corner to a large red-brick building which, in the moonlight, resembled an abandoned riverfront warehouse. On the front, Buck read the letters, Rose Phillips Charismatic Association.

Remembering all the hate literature he'd discovered here, along with the axes, Buck picked up a stone from the forecourt and tossed it at the old building. "It's not a very classy joint."

"It will be. I'll make it that." He cast a snide smile at Buck, as he seemed to steam with an idea. "This is the printing plant of a new paper I'm starting up all on my own. Okeechobee's first gay and lesbian newspaper."

The revelation finally descended. Buck stood there, staring first at Robert, then at the building. "That's what you want?"

Robert's eyes filled with a steely determination. "I know it's modest by your standards. You'll probably be directing Paramount or 20th Century Fox one day. But this is what I want. That's why I peddled the ring. I needed more money for the down payment on the mortgage, but

Uncle Milty lent it to me instead and I got the ring back. I've poured my life's savings into this building. Ever since you broke the story about the axes, it's been secretly on the market. Rose doesn't want it any more. She'll have the Examiner as her house organ."

Buck was amazed. "To start a paper, you'll need equipment, a staff, advertising, a big budget."

"I'll start slow and work up to it."

"You don't have to. I'll have Uncle Milty acquire the building for you outright tomorrow morning and deliver the deed to you. If this is what you want, I'll give you a blank check. Charge all the expenses to me. Instead of a local newspaper, why not an international glossy gay magazine? You'll have unlimited funds to back it. Hire the best people. Do it big! Don't just think locally. A national magazine fighting for the rights of gays and lesbians. I can get you circulated across America."

"I never thought of something that ambitious."

Buck looked again at the moonlit building from which the hate literature had spewed, and was glad that Robert wanted to transform it into something with an entirely different message.

"You could be the publisher if you wanted to," Robert said.

"Thanks, but I have other fish to fry, mainly on the West Coast."

"I'm sure you do," Robert said turning away. "And other lovers to love."

"I didn't say that."

"You might as well. It's not exactly hard for me to figure out who your new lover is. Dumped by Shelley, you've wasted no time becoming Pharaon's boy. And let's face it: that's what you are. The most expensive kept boy on earth."

"That's right, Robert. I'm no good. No redeeming value. And I'm the private and heavily guarded property of a man who is five times as rich as the queen of England."

"I hope you'll be very happy together."

"Thanks. Right now I'm not much good to you as a lover. I'll sponsor any project you want, shower you with money, but that's it. I'm heading elsewhere tonight. I'm going to give you my house. It's yours if you want it."

"You think you can kick me out? It won't be that easy."

"I'm not kicking you out. I'm the one who's leaving. You can also have use of the island retreat. You can also use my plane to fly anywhere you want."

"In other words, you've decided to make me another Susan stashed away somewhere. That's what you do with your wives."

"She's doing fine. She's got Don Bossdum now."

"Don Bossdum? What a surprise. But I couldn't think of a better physical replacement for you." Robert looked angry and defiant. For the first time in his life, Buck saw hatred in Robert's face. "Don't expect me to wait around for you like a dutiful wife. I've had plenty of offers myself."

"I'm sure you have. You're a very attractive man."

"I'll never let you go. Until death do us part. I'll cling to you until the final hours of my life. I've got my claws in you, and I'll never retract them. I'm no pushover like Susan. I'm around for the long haul. Go and have your stupid adventures. But you'll never get rid of me. I'm wearing my wedding band, and the engagement ring, and I'll never take them off. I'll be buried with them on my fingers."

At first Buck didn't know how to respond. This was a side of Robert he'd never known. Obviously it had always been part of his personality but he'd never seen it before. He stood looking at Robert for the longest, most awkward and embarrassing moment of his life. "Where has love gone?"

"You destroyed it but I won't let you destroy me in the process. I demand to be in your life. I've earned my place here." He stared at Buck with an in-your-face look. When he spoke, he was so close he peppered Buck's face with his saliva. "You'll have to kill me to get rid of me. Is that clear?"

Buck backed away. This was going dangerously too far. He had to soften it. He smiled at Robert and took his hand in a loving way, like you'd hold an old friend if you wanted to comfort him. "Come on, amigo, I'll buy you a beer."

*****

"What in hell's going on here?" Uncle Milty was shouting in the foyer. "How dare the bitch threaten to sue my client. Show me to her."

One of Buck's security guards ushered his attorney into the grand and former living room of the Markums. "Buck," Uncle Milty shouted. "You're back, you fucker." He rushed over and planted a wet kiss on Buck's mouth.

"I had you brought here as a little joke," Buck said. "Mrs. Markum isn't suing me."

"I thought you couldn't stand the cow. What are you doing hanging out in her house?"

"It's my house now and everything in it," Buck said. "It was a gift from my new boss."

"I can't believe Rose would give you this—she's very generous, but there are limits."

"My new boss is Ahmad Pharaon."

Uncle Milty seated himself onto a luxurious sofa covered in antique silk. He accepted a drink from one of the security guards. "So, let me piece all this together. I thought you were rushing to spend all your Examiner millions pretty fast with this incredible security force."

"I'm spending nothing," Buck said provocatively. "Ahmad takes care of everything. I've become his boy."

"On the day you pick up millions, you become somebody's boy. An Arab at that. There's an irony here somewhere."

"Uncle Milty, it's going to be a long night. There is much to tell you. I hope you've dropped all your other clients. Send them over to Jim Howard. As soon as I fly to see my grandfather, you and I are going to Beverly Hills. To live in Ahmad's mansion, of course. We've got to launch him into the film community. He wants to be a major player on the west coast, and that's what we've got to set up for him. I desperately need your help. You know everybody important there."

"Honey, when you arrive in Hollywood and you're willing to spend money, you don't have to do anything. Just sit back and wait for the phone to ring."

"Let's take a stroll through the Markum garden," Buck said, getting up. "Correction: the Brooke garden. We've got a lot of plans to go over. Since I got back from Palm Springs, my world's a different place. You're my right-hand man. You've got to know what's going on."

It was shortly before midnight before a lull came in the conversation. Everything was too much. Buck thought it best to wait until tomorrow to tell Uncle Milty about his scheme to acquire the failed real-estate development of Sun City. If they could pull off that scheme, that would shut Hazel up.

Over midnight champagne and caviar, served by one of the security guards, Uncle Milty eyed him carefully. "Why didn't you invite Robert over? Is he okay? Patrick and I expected to see a lot more of him while you were away—in fact, we thought he'd be over at our place every night. But except for once he was never in when we called and hardly returned our messages."

"You might as well know: Robert and I may be finished. At least as lovers."

"I can't believe that. You guys are too close. Has he found out about Ahmad?"

"He's gotten a little bit of that picture. But he's also found out about Shelley Phillips and me."

Uncle Milty looked dumbfounded. "What about Shelley Phillips and you?"

"I may be Ahmad's boy but I've fallen for Shelley in a big way."

"Shelley must be all of six years old. A golden-haired cherub. There are laws about things like that. If Sister Rose finds out, I might have to hustle you out of the country."

"Rose knows all about Shelley and me. We've had some three-ways. You have to know this shit. You're my attorney."

"Let me have some more of that champagne. I'm not hearing right tonight. I think I need a hearing aid."

"You've heard right. I'm in love with Shelley. Ahmad knows about it. He and Shelley had this thing at one time. It's okay with Ahmad. It doesn't threaten our relationship. The problem is, Shelley's left me. At least I think he's left me. He left a note. But he could have been forced to write that note. He's in a lot of trouble. Leroy Fitzgerald has blackmail pictures of Shelley with Barry Collins. Leroy wants five-million dollars."

Uncle Milty sucked in the night air. "And I once thought I knew everything about you. It's good that I'm coming to work for you full time. It will take four or five of me just to handle a little bit of these affairs."

"You've obviously got to hire more staff. Get the best. We're going to be involved in a lot."

"We're already involved in a lot."

"I know," Buck said. "This thing with Robert. I can't believe how my feelings have changed toward him."

"He's always been a loyal, faithful friend to you. He told Patrick that all the time you were away in the service, he didn't have anything with anybody. I don't know if he's ever had sex with anybody but you. He's devoted."

"I don't want devotion. There's an unattractive side to Robert. I'll tell you more tomorrow. It's amazing how you can live with somebody for years and not really know him. I don't think Robert is the man I thought he was. He's different somehow. I don't want him to make trouble for me—and he might. He knows a lot, and I'm very vulnerable. If Robert calls you and makes demands, I think we should take him seriously, and not just about that gay mag. Of course, I'll put up the money for that. I don't want to end up in the courts getting slapped with a palimony suit. That's an embarrassment I don't want ever."

"I can't believe in just a few days the situation has deteriorated to such a point. To a point that you'd even suspect that Robert might file a lawsuit against you."

"It has come to that. From this day on, I don't trust Robert. There's more going on there than meets the eye."

"Is he scheming about money? Has he too strayed from the path?"

"It's just a feeling I have, and I have no evidence. But I feel he's got a lover on the side."

"Bring more champagne," Uncle Milty called to the security guard near the stairs. "I'm with you, baby," he said, turning to Buck. "I love Robert but you're my main man. I think I know who this new lover is."

"Spill it."

"Casey."

Buck sighed. "I wouldn't be surprised. Casey is a whore. I did leave him here to drive Robert around town. Casey's one good-looking and sexy stud. So's Robert. Perhaps the combination produced some fireworks."

"He wasn't with Casey all the time. That I know for a fact."

Buck stared at Uncle Milty. Had he found out about Patrick and Casey?

"Since you're confessing all this marital infidelity, I have a confession of my own to make. One day when Patrick was away, Casey drove over to my office. He raped me. He really did. I tried to fight him off, but he overpowered me. You know I've always been faithful to Patrick ever since the day we first met. Before the rape was over, Casey had me vowing eternal love and begging for more. He's that good. I mean I love it with Patrick and all. We're very cuddly and gentle with each other. But with Casey it was raw, animal sex."

"That Casey. He gets around."

"So Casey and I are carrying on hot and heavy." He sipped his drink. "I didn't want to tell you this."

"I'm glad you did. I need to know what's going on around here."

"Patrick must never find out."

"I understand. I'm sure he'd be devastated in more ways than one." Buck was deliberately enigmatic.

"It's getting late, and I've got to go," Uncle Milty said. "Patrick is waiting for me. Also, Susan called. I'll be there tomorrow for those wedding pictures. I really have got to get them off to old Buck soon. The hospital fears he's dying."

"Make arrangements for me to fly to Geneva," Buck said. "I need to be at his side."

"It appears to me you need to be at the bedside of a lot of people. Wish it was my bed you put your slippers under at night."

"Uncle Milty, haven't you gotten over that crush?"

"I'll never get over my obsession about you."

"Glad to know I'm loved." Buck got up. "There are more surprises. I just saw Lars come onto the veranda. He's taking me to my new home."

"I thought this was your new home."

"It's a cottage. I'm going to Desire."

"Oh, my God, Pharaon's estate. I've heard rumors. It's supposed to be splendid. I'd forgotten for a second he owned it. No one was ever really sure."

"He not only owns it, but he's offered it as a place of residence for his number one boy. I've never seen it. I'm dying to get over there tonight. Casey's going to drive me over. I'll be in the back seat with Lars."

"I'd like to get in the back seat with him too. Or some other place."

An idea occurred to Buck. "I brought you a present. All the way from California."

"I love presents. Where is it?"

"Go upstairs to the master bedroom. I'll have it delivered. It's truly spectacular. The present will be up in a minute."

Uncle Milty kissed him wetly on the mouth again. "Okay, I'll go up there and wait for my present. I'll thank you in the morning. I bet it's jewelry. I love jewelry." Uncle Milty, a little drunk, tottered back toward the Markum mansion.

Encountering Lars in the garden, Buck whispered to him. "Get three of your best hung guards. Send them to the bedroom upstairs. Uncle Milty will be waiting. Tell them to ignore Milty's protests. He likes it rough. A rape's okay. Yes, he'd like a rape."

"Your wish is my command."

"And, Lars."

Lars stopped and looked back at him.

"Make sure your men are uncut."

"I should volunteer myself then," Lars said, smiling seductively. "After all, I'm Norwegian."

"Not you, Lars," Buck said. "You and I have a rendezvous at Desire tonight."

"What an appropriate name."

*****

Crossing through the gardens with Lars, heading back to the Brooke house, Buck stopped near the gazebo. Lars too came to a halt, watching as Robert walked across the back veranda and headed for the driveway that led to the end of the property near a back street, Carroll Place. At first Buck thought he was going to the garage. It seemed unlikely Robert was going for a walk. It was so unlike him.

After he'd passed them, Lars turned to Buck. "We know all about where he's going if you're interested."

"I want to know."

"First, I don't want you to think we're interfering in your private life. But we're checking everything that remotely involves you in case of a threat to your security. Your phone is tapped. Robert is meeting Gene Robinson. A little ironic I would say. Your wife's first husband."

"Surely you're wrong." Buck felt his own heart beating wildly.

"They agreed on the rendezvous late this afternoon," Lars said. "He's walking three blocks from your house. Robinson is waiting in a car for him on a side street."

"But Robert hates Gene—always has."

"I don't need to tell a smart man like you the thin line between hatred and passion," Lars said. "We could tell from the conversation, this hot and torrid affair has been going on for a few days at least. Do you want to hear the tapes?"

"I can't," Buck said. "I'd go out of my mind. I can't believe this is happening. They've been my two best friends." He paused, still alarmed at how fast his heart was beating. "I find this amazing."

"Do you want us to follow them?" Lars asked. "We could. Report back to you with everything. We're very good at this."

"Don't. Let them have their privacy. Robert can do whatever he wants with his life." Buck headed toward his house. "I want to pick up some things and then we can go. I'm headed for Desire. I want out of here."

On the porch Casey was waiting for him. "I'm really excited about taking you to this place. I hear it's spectacular."

"We'll see for ourselves. How's it hanging, man?"

"Where you're concerned, it's always ready, willing, and able."

"Go gently into the good night with Patrick and Uncle Milty," Buck cautioned.

"You've found out about that? That I'm two-timing you. If you say so, I'll give them up tomorrow."

"They've been together a long time. I'd hate to see you break them up."

"I'm just filling in between engagements waiting for a signal to come to your bed," Casey said. "You're the big game I'm after. Uncle Milty and Patrick are mercy fucks."

"C'mon and help me pack." Buck headed upstairs as Casey trailed behind. He felt his world spinning out of control.

In the back seat of the limousine, driven by Casey, Buck relaxed more, particularly when Lars poured him a Scotch from the limousine bar. "That revelation about Robert. Robert and Gene—it's all been a bit much."

"I don't understand all the details here," Lars said, as he began a gentle massage of Buck's shoulders. "But I bet I could make you forget both of them."

"I bet you could," Buck said, leaning into them, trying to blot out the vision of Robert and Gene together. As the outskirts of Okeechobee faded behind them, and Casey hit the open road, Buck turned himself over to Lars's skilled hands. He felt like the limousine was a giant womb and he was safe and protected here.

"Lie back and imagine it's a bed," Lars said. "I'll take off your shoes and socks and massage your feet. I use my mouth in the massage. It's very nice."

"I'm sure," Buck said, settling back.

"Ahmad loves it. He really likes his toes sucked for hours but only by blonds."

"How nice," Buck said, shutting his eyes and enjoying the feel of Lars's lips and tongue on his feet. Somewhere on the road to Desire, Buck fell asleep. He woke up as they reached the gate of Desire. Lars was still sucking his toes. It was such a pleasant sensation he didn't want it to end.

Lars seemingly felt the same way, appearing reluctant to let go. He sat up, licking his lips. "I'm about to show you your new home."

"Thanks," Buck said. "That was fabulous." He pulled Lars to him and inserted his tongue in the guard's mouth. Breaking away, he said, "I really liked that."

"It's only the beginning, my love," he said. "There is so much pleasure I will give you. I've been highly trained."

No sooner had Lars pulled away, but Casey was in the back seat descending on him, kissing and tonguing him with great passion and skill. Coming up for air, Casey said, "I've not been highly trained at all. I do just what comes naturally."

"And you do it very well," Buck said, getting out of the car. "Now get the hell out and let's see this mansion."

*****

In many ways, it was like the mansion in Palm Springs, with the same fountains and painted nude statuary, only a much more gargantuan version. It was so opulent it had its own kind of beauty. It was not really a home but some giant museum, although there were pockets of comfort everywhere. It looked like no one had ever lived here or could ever live here. It was made to be visited, not lived in.

Wherever the eye peered, there was splendor, art and antiques from all over the world. The gigantic pool, the largest he'd ever seen, was surrounded by Carrara marble replicas of antiquity's most famous statuary. Alabaster globe lamps created the illusion of moonlight. Marble colonnades stretched down to the sea.

In the center of the garden was a large domed movie theater. In one part of the garden a Chinese Teahouse had been erected with a tiny railroad constructed to ferry footmen bearing tea from the main house. The gardens captured his heart. He felt he could live in them forever. They were dotted with gingerbread gazebos and fountains lit at night to color the water displays. The bronze statuary competed with the marble nudes, and there was an amazing variety of shrubs and trees, and seemingly endless sunken courtyards.

The kitchen looked like it could serve one thousand guests with no problem. The wine cellar seemed to stretch across the state. Each bedroom was decorated differently but all in luxurious taste, with the finest of silks.

In the center of one gigantic enclosed courtyard was a 23-karat gold coronation coach seemingly having no purpose in being here and no place to ride. One part of the mansion was modeled after the Petit Trianon at Versailles. It contained the most ornate gilt-encrusted ballroom Buck had ever seen.

The main dining room was dominated by a marble fireplace outlined in opalescent Tiffany brick tiles. The bronze chairs at the fifty-foot-long table looked too heavy to be lifted. The paneling was mahogany. But, Lars assured him, the ceiling was pure gold.

Back in the main foyer Buck was struck by the multicolored marbles used throughout, the arched double loggia, and the mosaic ceilings. The music room, Lars said, had been constructed in Austria and shipped here for reassembly. The billiard room was in gray-green marble, yellow alabaster, and mahogany.

"Even in the Gilded Age, robber barons didn't live this well," Buck said. "I'm sure. I don't want to see any more. I've had enough for one night, and it's getting late. I think I could live here a year and always discover something new."

"Ahmad always claims the place is smaller than it is," Lars said. "I think he says there are sixty-two rooms, something like that. Don't hold me to it. Actually, I counted them one day. There are one-hundred and ten rooms."

"My God!" was all Buck could say. "It's a fantasy house. Don't I have a bedroom here?"

"You have one specially prepared for you, and your bath is waiting. I will strip down and assist you."

"I'd like that very much," Buck said, kissing him on the mouth. "Let's go."

Buck didn't have to bathe himself in the marble tub—so large they could swim around in it. Lars, with his perfectly sculpted body, lathered and soaped Buck as he massaged him.

"Lars, soaping me has risen you to full glory, and now I know what the pride of Norway is."

"It is all yours," Lars said. "You can use me in any way you want."

Buck grabbed him and kissed him hard.

"After this bath is over, I'd like to bathe you with my tongue," Lars said.

"What a wonderful treat I have in store for me," Buck said, grabbing Lars again and kissing him real hard, inserting his tongue. "I need a distraction tonight."

An hour later when Lars had tasted every single inch of his body, Buck signaled him to get into a sixty-nine position for the finale. Lars willingly obliged. Buck sucked voraciously until he felt a finger inserting itself into him. At first he thought it was Lars. Then another finger entered him, and finally a third. With a free hand, he reached to feel another body in bed with him. When he reached below and fingered a long, thick prick with a cock ring, he knew it was Casey.

"I've waited long enough for my chance," Casey whispered into his ear before biting it. "I'm not going to wait any more. You've denied me mine long enough."

Buck screamed as Casey entered him savagely but Lars immediately crammed himself into Buck's mouth, silencing his groans.

Hours later as the three men lay in a tangled mess, an Arab servant entered the room with the morning's mint tea. "Mr. Brooke," he announced, not looking directly at the men in bed. "We were instructed to remind you about the appointment for your wedding pictures to be taken in Okeechobee."

"Thank you," Buck said as formally as he could, considering the circumstances.

After the servant had gone, Casey got out of bed and stumbled over to inspect the tea. "Who do you have to fuck around here to get some real coffee?" He headed toward the bathroom.

Lars planted gentle kisses on Buck's face, throat, and chest.

Buck's first morning at Desire had begun. He knew it would not be the last.

*****

Robert had the world's gentlest hands, as they caressed Gene's body as Gene pounded into him. Slowly and lovingly Robert's fingers traced the contours of Gene's back goading him on. One had traveled even lower, cupping the heavy globes hanging between Gene's legs. Robert gently squeezed them, spurring Gene to more intense action. Robert was chewing on Gene's left nipple, pulling with his teeth at the little tufts of hair there. Ending that action, Robert licked Gene's chest. Kissing his chin, Robert moved his lips to Gene's left ear. "You're all man," he said between gasps. "I've never known a man like you before. You're the best."

Robert might as well have finished his statement. "Better than Buck." That's obviously what he meant, and Gene knew that. These were the words he wanted to hear.

Even though Gene was only in the middle of his attack on Robert, he suddenly buckled his body as Gene's balls bounced against his ass. He bellowed and blew a thick shot of jizz up over Gene's torso and onto the motel bed where they bounced.

Gene pumped him harder, knowing he was reaching all the right targets. Robert was completely mesmerized, completely under Gene's spell. "Don't stop," Robert whispered in his ear. "I've never felt anything this good."

"Jesus," Gene cried out. His body shook as he poured what seemed like liquid fire into Robert. He wrapped his arms around Robert and pulled him close to his chest, covering the top of his head with passionate kisses. He cradled Robert against his heaving chest before collapsing on him. "I could stay inside you for the rest of the night," he whispered into Robert's ear.

Robert's mouth blindly sought Gene's. Their tongues dueled, and Gene felt a pleasurable jolt he'd never known before. Robert had awakened a side of Gene he never knew existed. Robert brought an intensity to love-making he'd never captured with Buck. Gene thought Buck was his peak experience. But that was no longer true.

As he lay against Robert, he relived every blissful moment. His whole body tingled just remembering how Robert had traced the planes and angles of his frame with his delicate fingers. Those fingers had reached for his balls to caress them, making Gene shudder and groan softly as his aching prick jerked up, extending itself to its full length.

He'd pulled Robert to him, forcing his mouth open with his tongue. Robert had responded eagerly, wrapping his legs around Gene's hips. Gene had known what Robert wanted. As Gene lay on the bed licking and tasting Robert, he liked the sweet and musky flavor. The smell of him sent sparks of pleasure racing through Gene's trembling frame, and he knew it wouldn't be long before he attacked Robert again, not really having had his fill.

He stroked Robert's velvety skin, rubbing his hands over every inch of him he could reach from his position. Robert's mouth was open in ecstasy, surrendering to Gene completely. Gene nuzzled Robert's neck, licking away the young man's sweat.

"Come in me again," Robert pleaded. "I can't get enough of you. You're fabulous."

Robert descended suddenly, mouthing Gene's right nipple, latching onto the swollen knot where he began to chew, galvanizing Gene into action again as if an electric current had surged through his body. Gene began plunging again—in and out, filling Robert as he suspected he'd never been filled before, not even by Buck.

"Don't ever leave me," Robert said when he broke free of Gene's chest and began nibbling at his ear. "Please stay with me."

"I'll never leave you," Gene said, pounding harder. "I can't live without you. You're what I've waited for all my life."

A half hour later, Gene took delight in soaping Robert's smooth skin, as Robert lathered his own muscular body.

Over an early morning breakfast in the motel coffee shop, Gene leaned over and asked Robert, "Why did Buck hire Clara and Maria after what they'd done to me?"

Robert's face looked startled for a minute as if caught unaware, then a grim look appeared. "He did it to humiliate you. I don't know why but Buck wants you destroyed. If he finds out I've fallen for you, then it will be really bad."

"I think you're right. He's turned on me. He hates me. I can only imagine the reasons." He reached for Robert's hand which was willingly extended. "There's not much future for me in this town. I've got to get out."

"I'll help you but I need a few weeks. Buck has betrayed me too, and I want revenge. It's payback time. At first I was going to hang on to him making every day of his life miserable. After falling in love with you, I have another plan. I'm going to take him for every cent I can get out of the bastard. He's going to pay and pay some more. He's become Ahmad Pharaon's boy now. He's got more money than he'll ever burn."

"Ahmad Pharaon?" The words seemed to stab at Gene's heart. "God damn that Buck. What a slimy whore!"

"As if the involvement with Shelley Phillips wasn't enough," Robert said. "Now Pharaon. I never realized what a scheming little bitch Buck is. The world's sexiest man has used his body, his cock, and his male charm to advance himself to incredible heights. Pharaon now hires a security force of thirty men to protect his little boy."

"I can't believe this," Gene said. "Pharaon owns that incredible mansion about twenty-five miles from here."

"That's where Buck is right now, I'm sure. Probably pumping it to Pharaon even as we speak."

"God, I hate his ass." A stab of jealousy shot through Gene which he tried to suppress.

"Will you go away with me?" Robert asked, squeezing Gene's hand all the harder.

"You don't have to ask. I'm your man."

"I knew from the moment I smelled you in the garden," Robert said. "You were there to rape me. It was as if I'd spent an entire life waiting for the man on the white horse to dismount and take me. When you penetrated me, I felt I'd already fallen in love. Buck is too gentle. You knew that secretly I had to have it real rough. You gave me what I'd been seeking all my life and had never found. I thought I'd spend the rest of my life with Buck, never needing another man. Then you came along. Yesterday or the day before I loved Buck with all my heart."

"I loved him too," Gene blurted out, shocked at his own confession.

"I think I've known that too. I think he probably does still love you but won't admit it. With Shelley and Pharaon he gets to play the big stud. You probably showed him up for the queer he really is. He couldn't handle that."

"I've thought that too. Otherwise, I couldn't believe how he could turn on me." Gene glanced at his watch. "I've got to get you back to town. I don't want to leave you. Ever. But we've both got business to handle."

"We may have to spend our days apart right now," Robert said. "But if it all goes according to our plan, we'll be together all our days and nights."

"I want that. In fact, right this minute I want to take you back into that motel room. I can't get enough of you."

"I certainly can't get enough of you. You're the man of my dreams. Such a handsome man. And only the Gods could have created that weapon you've got."

"Buck's got one too."

"You know how to use yours—Buck doesn't."

Gene liked hearing that. Buck might have all the money and power in the world, but Gene knew now he was a better man than his former friend. Robert was the best source to judge. It was ironic. Buck had married his former wife, and now he was going to run away with Buck's former "wife." It was with deep satisfaction that Gene imagined the shock that would race through Buck when he learned of this news.

All Gene's life he had wanted to take something away from Buck and now his chance was at hand. Buck had been given everything by life and Gene nothing. But as Gene rose from the table, motioning for Robert to follow him, Gene knew that the time had come for him to reach out and take what he wanted even if it belonged to somebody else. Looking into Robert's loving eyes, he'd never known such trust and devotion. Robert belonged to him. He'd taken him from Buck. The day was his.

*****

On the elevator to Susan's condo, Buck carried a cashier's check for one-hundred thousand dollars to pay off Don Bossdum, compliments of Shelley and Rose. At some point he'd slip the money to Don when Susan was distracted elsewhere. Considering the five-million dollars Leroy was demanding, Don's request seemed modest. At the door to Susan's condo, Buck rang the bell.

In moments the door was hesitantly opened but only a crack. "That you, Buck?" Don asked, peering out. "Come on in."

Inside the apartment, Don smiled as he greeted Buck. "Forgive me, I just got out of the shower and haven't had a chance to put on my bikini briefs."

"Great to see you again, Don," Buck said with all the enthusiasm he could muster. "I just didn't expect to see so much of you."

"What you see is what you get," Don said, walking over to the serving bar to pour Buck some coffee.

"I once invited you for a beer," Buck said. "You turned me down but I guess I can accept a drink from you even if it's only coffee."

"I can explain that," Don said apologetically, handing Buck his coffee black. He just seemed to know Buck didn't take cream or sugar. "I was fucked up in the head back then. I wasn't sure where I was going. I know a lot more about myself now. Why don't you extend the invite for a beer tonight? See what I'd say now."

Ignoring him and looking around the condo, Buck asked, "Where's Susan?"

"She's still at the beauty parlor. She called just a little while ago. She'll be here any minute now."

Don sat across from Buck, raising one bare leg and putting it on the sofa, giving Buck an even clearer view of the ample load suspended between his legs.

"Before Susan gets here, I have to tell you that Rose gave me the one-hundred thousand dollars you wanted. It's a cashier's check. Made out to you for the right amount. It looks like you and I have changed partners. You've got my wife now, and I've switched to Shelley. At least until recently. He's written me a Dear John letter."

"Shelley—that whore—was always good at French leave," Don said, getting up and taking the check from Buck. As he studied it, his equipment dangled only inches from Buck's face. Eventually he returned to his seat but made no attempt to get dressed. "I'm sorry you found out about this. Please don't let Susan know."

"She'll not hear it from me."

"Thanks. I'll owe you one, buddy. You name the time and place."

"Thanks, but no thanks. I've got a full agenda right now. The offer's tempting."

"You think it's big now. Wait till you see it fully hard and in action. You'll think you've died and gone to heaven."

"I'm sure. But right now you're plenty busy keeping Susan amused."

"Let's face facts: you've got the power and money around here. If you call for me, your needs come first. I'm out of here in a minute and off to satisfy you." He reached down and uncapped his dick, revealing a large vermilion head. "You haven't been fucked until you've been fucked by this." From his position on the sofa, he waved his penis at Buck.

"I'm sure you're right but it'll have to wait."

At the sound of a key in the door, Don bolted for the bathroom to get dressed.

When Susan came into the apartment, Buck got up to welcome her, kissing her on the mouth.

"Welcome back from California," she said. "We've kept the home fires burning."

"You look really nice," he said, admiring her tasteful hair-do. "But it's gilding on the lily. You're a natural beauty. You don't need fancy hair-dos."

"You're too kind." She danced around in front of him playfully. "Is this the right outfit?"

"It's something Jackie might have worn for an appearance with JFK."

"I guess that's a compliment." She looked around the apartment. "Where's Don?"

"He's getting dressed to come with us." He noted a look of suspicion on her face. "I just got here."

"I see."

When Don came out fully dressed in a blue suit, he rushed to Susan, kissed her on the mouth, then picked her up off the floor and whirled her around. "You look terrific."

"She always looks terrific," Buck said, as Don put her down. "I want to introduce you as the dude who was my best man at the wedding. You know, former U.S. marine marrying beauty queen. All America football hero as best man. It's best to give America images it can deal with instead of the truth, don't you agree?"

"We do indeed," Susan said.

"Hey, I'd like that," Don said. "I like having my picture taken."

"Leroy Fitzgerald's the photographer," Buck said.

"I remember him well from college," Don said. "He was always hanging around the locker room waiting to snap my picture when I took off my jock strap. What the hell! I always said if you've got it, flaunt it."

No one said anything at first. "We'd better go," Buck said, glancing at his watch, "or else we'll be late."

In the garage Casey was waiting for them. Buck introduced them to his chauffeur before inviting them to ride in the rear compartment with him. Susan selected to sit on the right side, and Don eagerly chose the middle seat.

"This car's only temporary," Buck said, somewhat apologetically. "I have a new one being flown in from California. Wait till you see it."

Susan looked around admiringly, then focused on the handsome driver. "You've really come up in the world." It was just a statement, with no detectable bitterness in her voice.

"I'll say," Don said. "This is the way to go. Only moments ago, I was unemployed without a dime. Now I'm leading the good life."

"Just goes to show you how far you can go with talent in this world," Buck said before giving Casey directions as to how to reach the old Buck estate. "I want the pictures taken in old Buck's garden. Same place as the wedding. I'm flying to his bedside soon. I think he'd like that."

"Give him my love," she said. "Tell him we miss him." Her voice had a hollow ring.

On the rest of the ride there, Buck felt Don pressing his leg against him but appeared not to notice.

Once at the estate, Susan excused herself to go inside to check her hair and dress.

Getting out of the car, Don whispered to Buck, "This tux Susan bought for me is a little tight. It's showing too much basket. I'm wearing regular underwear and I should have worn a jock strap instead. I want your wedding pictures to look really tasteful."

Buck waved good-bye to Casey, and linked his arm with Don's. "I think we can fix you up with one of my jockstraps." He paused and looked at Don. "Only problem is, are you man enough to fill out one of my jockstraps?"

"Just for that," Don said, reaching over and licking his neck. "You're going to get it shoved all the way up that bubble butt of yours, and with no lubrication."

Buck kissed him on the mouth. "I can't wait."

Battered and bruised by Don, Buck arrived looking disheveled for his wedding pictures. Leroy called him aside for some quick adjustments. "I want to talk to you privately later," Buck said to the photographer. "I'll meet you in the library after the shoot."

Leroy looked apprehensive about the confrontation but reluctantly committed himself to it.

In spite of the commando tactics at the poolhouse, Don appeared looking perfectly groomed.

Buck kissed both Jim and Ingrid on the cheeks, and took his place beside Susan. Don stood by their side, presumably as Buck's best man. Uncle Milty was out of the shoot. He'd whispered to Buck, "You don't need a fat faggot with varicose veins ruining the picture."

Within fifteen minutes it was all over. Leroy wanted one final shot of the bride and groom walking hand and hand down toward the summer gazebo that sloped to the water. On the way there, Buck offered Susan his plane to fly her to a honeymoon in the Caribbean. He said he'd soon be flying on that same plane to Switzerland to see old Buck.

"Actually Don and I are going to spend our honeymoon in Key West," Susan said. "I want to have Leroy film that interview with Pamela I told you about. I hope you don't mind if we let Leroy fly on your plane with us."

"I don't mind," he said, "but be careful around that one. He's involved in a lot of deep shit you don't know about." He stopped and looked deeply into her eyes. "You're playing with fire with the Pamela thing—you know that?"

"I know it but I want to take my chances."

"Be very, very careful. Calder Martin is a more dangerous man than I ever realized."

"I'm not afraid of him."

"You should be—believe me, I know."

Stepping onto the gazebo, Buck waved at his friends and well wishers as Leroy photographed a long distance shot of them, presumably before they embarked on their honeymoon at an undisclosed location.

"There's so much that must be happening in your life," she said. "Can you give me a quick bulletin before fleeing?"

"A lot of changes," he said, looking off at the water in the distance. "Robert and I are through."

"Does that mean I'm going to get you back? We can kick Don out."

"Not exactly. There's someone else."

"I've heard rumors." She smiled enigmatically.

"I've become Ahmad Pharaon's boy."

"Pharaon? You're filled with surprises. Pharaon? Forget the millions you picked up for the Examiner. You certainly won't be worrying where your next meal comes from, will you?"

"Not at all."

"I guess that explains the big ring on your finger, and all these security guards pretending to be your friends, blending in with the wedding guests."

"It does indeed. As soon as you get back from Key West and I return from Europe, I'll invite you and Don over to my new home. From now on, I'll be living at Desire."

"You mean that mansion everybody's been talking about?"

"That's the one. It's spectacular."

"You are one fast worker. This is all hard to believe. What's going to happen to Robert?"

"I think he's fallen in love with Gene."

She sighed and looked off at the water herself. "This is a bit much to take. Robert and Gene? I'm shocked. But I should learn not to shock so easily."

"I would never have thought it. But it's true."

"Oh, God, I'll need that plane flight to Key West to think about all this. Robert and Gene. You and Pharaon."

"Don Bossdum and you. Who would have thought that?"

"Actually it wasn't you and Pharaon I'd heard rumors about. It was you and Shelley Phillips."

He looked at her sternly, as if insulted. "Fuck that! He's only a kid. I'm not a child molester so let's put that rumor to rest."

"If you say so."

"Let's join our friends," he said, eager to change the subject. "I've got to go off with Uncle Milty. Something about a real-estate development. I think we're also in a position to acquire the News. By the time I get back from Europe, I might offer you the publisher's post."

"That would be my fondest hope, other than seeing more of you."

"I'm pretty tied up." He smiled. "Let's get back to our friends...or whatever."

Uncle Milty had arranged a cake as if this were their actual wedding day. In many ways it was like a real wedding and not merely the mock of some photo shoot.

Before telling Susan good-bye, Buck called her aside on the far end of the veranda. "Don't take condoms with you to Key West."

"And why not?" Susan demanded to know.

"If old Buck lives, I might have to come up with a little Buck Brooke IV. Don looks enough like me. I've already told old Buck it's in the oven."

"I'll think about it," she said. "After all, it's my body. Of course, I see the need. You're definitely going to need an heir to pass along all that money too. Who knows? You might end up with Pharaon's money one day."

"There's no bank big enough."

"In some perverse way I'm proud of you," she said.

At that point Leroy came onto the veranda. "We've got to go to Key West," Leroy said, looking at Susan but speaking to Buck.

"I won't be long," Buck said, taking his arm and guiding him into the house. "Excuse us, Susan."

In the library Buck confronted Leroy. "I know all about those photographs of Shelley and Barry. I have no liking for Barry at all, but I feel very protective of Shelley. I think you're making a big mistake."

"Listen, you've made your millions," Leroy said petulantly. "Why can't I have a chance? This may be the only chance I'll ever have in my life. Do you think for one moment I'm going to let you talk me out of this?"

"Probably not." He stood menacingly close to Leroy. I'm giving you a warning. You fuck with Calder and you're the one who'll get fucked. The dildo will be made of steel, and he'll heat it first in an oven before plunging it into your ass. Think about that. A fourteen-inch hot steel dildo going up your ass."

"Okay, I'm afraid, but it's a chance I'm going to take. Case closed." Leroy headed for the door.

"Do you want me to wear a white suit or a black suit to your funeral?"

A smirk appeared on Leroy's face. "You're not the only person in town who knows how to make millions." Opening the door, he turned and left.

No sooner was he gone than Don came into the room. "I came for my good-bye kiss." He walked toward Buck. "You're one hot piece of ass. You could make me give up girls for life."

"That's not going to happen—at least not now. Stay with Susan and do your duty."

"I'd rather be with you, guy." He pulled Buck to him, kissing him long and hard and inserting his tongue. "I've got to have you again and again. There's never been anything like that for me."

"You're fabulous—that's all I can say at this point."

Don pulled him close again and inserted his tongue.

Just as Buck was sucking it voraciously, Susan came into the library without knocking. "Sorry," she said, turning to exit quickly. "I didn't mean to intrude."

"It's okay," Buck said, breaking away. "It's just what guys do when they're alone together."

"Believe me, I'm learning more about what guys do when they're alone together than any woman in this town."

"It's okay, honey," Don said, walking over and kissing her on the mouth. "With Buck, it's okay. It's all in the family. The three of us are family now."

"He's got a point," Buck said, looking at Susan for affirmation.

She turned to Don. "It's okay with Buck. But don't let me catch you with anybody else—male or female."

"I'm faithful to you," Don said. He kissed her on the mouth again, then reached over and kissed Buck on the lips too. "And my new found friend here."

"Have a great honeymoon," Buck said, kissing Susan on the mouth, then Don. "The plane will be waiting for you guys at the airport."

Lars appeared suddenly at the door. He smiled knowingly at Buck. "Casey has the car waiting. I've thanked all the guests for you so you can make a fast exit. Uncle Milty's already in the car."

Without looking back at Don and Susan, Buck headed through the house toward the rear where he could see the limousine. The Blackhawk had arrived.

*****

Without explaining to Uncle Milty what his plan was, Buck asked to be driven to Sun City, a failed real-estate development opening onto the water forty miles from Okeechobee. Lars got in the front seat with Casey, and Uncle Milty crawled into the back seat with Buck so they could talk privately. Buck might share a bed with Lars and Casey, but he didn't want them to be privy to his innermost secrets.

"You made one handsome groom," Uncle Milty said. "Oh, that you were marrying me."

"Come off it," Buck said. "You're already married, and happily so."

"Yeah," Uncle Milty said. "I owe you one for that surprise. My ass is still sore. I don't know how Lars picked them but those security guards—each and every one of them—all are supermen. I haven't been worked over like that in my whole life."

"I thought you'd enjoy it."

"Enjoy it," Uncle Milty said. "I'm in love with all three and will soon be back for a repeat session." He looked at Casey's neck driving the car in front of the sealed-off rear. "That is, when I'm not otherwise involved with Casey there."

"You are one busy man, true blue to Patrick."

"That once was true but something's come over me in the last few days. I've become a wanton whore. Helps me understand you better."

"You call it being a whore. I call my experimentations a search for identity. Sounds better that way. I married Robert prematurely. Settling down wasn't for me."

"Robert called me before I came over for the photo shoot. I've wanted to talk privately about that call ever since I hung up. This is the first chance I've had."

"What's up?"

"That phone call wasn't from the Robert I have known and loved. He's someone different. Demanding, aggressive, willing to burn all bridges to get his way."

"What does he want?"

"A cool five million. Or else..." Uncle Milty paused as if he didn't want to reveal the next confidence to Buck. "Or else he's threatening a palimony suit that would cause you embarrassment for the rest of your life."

"The fuck!" Buck said. "The ultimate betrayal. I never thought Robert capable of that. But do we really know Robert? Faithful, loving Robert. Now wanting to sue me. That's hard to take."

"Let me handle this. I think I can get him way down. I mean way down. As long as he was your companion, I was supportive of him. But when he turns, I'll turn too. He'll see a side of me he never saw before. I'm my best when in the trenches."

"I know where he got the idea of five million. That's the exact figure Leroy is demanding from Calder and Barry. Robert is a mere copycat."

"Copycats have claws. Do I have your permission to bring in the mad dogs?"

"Not at all," Buck said, sighing and sinking back into the luxurious upholstery of the Blackhawk. "I'll be willing to go along with it. I can afford it. He's been a loyal, trusting friend up until now. He deserves something. I don't know how people come up with a dollar amount in cases like this, but he obviously has." Buck reached over for Uncle Milty's hand and squeezed it. "If anything, I'm relieved. Robert was smothering me to death. I didn't know how I was going to live the life I've already set up for myself with Robert hawkeying my every move. He's just solved that problem for me."

"Five-million dollars is a lot of money."

"I don't want him to have it all at once. We'll sign contracts. Pay him so much a year. I mean, I trust Robert to look after his money. It's his new lover I don't trust. In fact, I think it's because of his new lover that Robert is making these demands. Suddenly he needs money."

"What in hell are you talking about? New lover?"

"Gene Robinson."

"Now I've heard everything. The most unlikely coupling on the globe."

"I have conclusive proof. All couplings are a bit bizarre. Shelley and me. What about that? How's this one grab you: Pharaon and me?"

"You've made your point."

Buck smiled and reached over and kissed his attorney on the nose. "What about Uncle Milty and Buck Brooke IV? That, I'm sure, will be the next big romance."

"I can dream on." Uncle Milty turned serious. "Let me handle this. I've got to draw up a strong contract, play this carefully. You're going to Europe. Why not offer Robert your island place for a while?"

"That's fine with me. I don't plan to go there. Don't you want him living at my house?"

"Not until my staff has removed all documents from there. You've got a lot of potentially embarrassing stuff at that house. I feel Robert has become one of your enemies. I don't want him looking for documents."

"Then try to get him out of the house and over on the island. I store nothing there. It's always in the direct path of every hurricane that seems to hit Okeechobee."

"As soon as I return to town, I'll handle this. Damage control we call it."

Buck sat up in his seat again, looking at the road ahead. "Get used to it. I bet there will be plenty of damage control in the future. We've got enough of it now."

"It always happens," Uncle Milty said. "Once you get money, lawsuits come out of the woodwork. But I would never have thought that of Robert. Robert and Gene. What a pair! They deserve each other."

When Casey reached Sun City, Uncle Milty and Buck went for a walk on a nearby hill overlooking the development. It looked ghostly. The developers had gone belly up, and the project had been abandoned before it was half finished. Gaping condos without windows greeted them at every turn.

"Don't tell me you want to take over this project?" Uncle Milty asked.

"You've got it. For openers I'll move in all those poor souls losing their homes on the beach. You know, in Hazel's neighborhood. If this project is completed, they'll live a hell of a lot better here than they ever did in the decaying slums of the beach."

"You can't afford it although you could pick up Sun City for a song. Still, you'd have to have the money to develop it and see it through. That's why the other fuckers abandoned it. It's going to cost a lot more than they ever figured."

"I think I can afford it."

"Not with what you got from the sale of the Examiner, especially if you acquire the News."

"Pharaon has promised me all the money I'll ever need," Buck said. "Let's find out right at the beginning if that was but an idle promise. Work out all the details. Find out what it'll cost to buy the land. How much it will cost to finish this project. Maybe Pharaon will go for it, especially if he thinks it's a long cherished dream of his boy."

"If that's what you want, I'll do it. It sounds wild."

"If I can pull this one off, at least Hazel will respect me a lot more. I won't appear to be a total kisser of Arab butt, although I suspect I'll be doing a lot of that. Rose chases out the Jews. I find homes for them. Isn't that a butt-grabber?"

"That and more."

Buck took Uncle Milty's arm and turned him around to look inland. "As you know, old Buck owns a lot of that worthless land over there. If Sun City proves hot, that land will become extremely valuable. Who knows? We might actually create a new Florida city from all this shit. A model city at that."

"It's a dare. But everything depends on Pharaon and your influence with him. If he goes for it, it'll probably work. And that land of old Buck's. That will become dream real estate one day. I hope I'll live to see it."

"You'll live forever—if for no other reason than to look after your boy here."

Uncle Milty hugged Buck close.

"You've got a lot on your platter before I get back from Europe," Buck said. "Don't forget. We'll soon be descending on California."

"When I get to my office, I'm calling Jim Howard and giving him all my other clients, even the drag queens. Think he can handle it?"

"I know he can." He turned and looked Uncle Milty squarely in the eye. "Do you think we can handle all the shit thrown at us?"

"Hell, yes," Uncle Milty said. "We're a team. When are you going to invite Patrick and me over to Desire for a hot dog—kosher, of course?"

"Any day now." Buck walked over to the edge of the hill and looked at the abandoned project. He closed his eyes and looked again. In the glaringly bright light of the Florida sun, a city had miraculously emerged before his eyes.

*****

On the flight to Key West, Leroy spent most of his time trying to get Don to agree to pose nude for a Playgirl centerfold. "They couldn't get me in a centerfold," Don had protested. "They'd have to extend it with a third page."

"That could be a problem," Leroy admitted. "They once turned down one of my submissions because the model's penis was too big."

Retreating from Leroy, Don joined Susan in the back of the plane. "This is something else," he said. "Riding on Buck's private jet." He leaned over and kissed her lightly on the lips. "Thanks for introducing me to the fast lane."

"Don't pretend this is the first time you've ever sampled the good life."

"Nothing like this ever before."

"So what is it?" she demanded to know.

"What's what?"

"You know perfectly well what I'm talking about. What's this new thing between you and Buck? At least I'm assuming it's new."

"I've told you once before. He's attracted to me. I told you about that time he put the make on me at the university. He's king now. What am I supposed to do? Get kicked out on my ass because I turned down the boss man?"

She looked out the window into the brilliant glare. "Mama told me there would be days like this."

"Let's get one thing straight. I'm loyal to you. I'm with you. But you don't own my body. I'm not married to you. I'm not cheating on you with another woman. All Buck wants is for me to hold him and kiss him—nothing more. He's lonely."

"I doubt that."

"If Buck turns to me from time to time for a little comfort in the storm, what's wrong with that? Go on and tell me. What's wrong? Name one thing."

"There's no harm done," she said, sighing as she was giving in. Her attempts to control men and their desires had been an utter failure. "In some part of my body, I can understand it. I mean, who wouldn't go for the man if the choice were between a male and a female? Since I'd go for the man, I guess I can understand why another man might too. Let's face it: I'm not turned on by women. I don't understand the sexual allure of women."

"Since we've come together, I've always been there for you, haven't I?"

"You've been incredibly there. I'm very grateful."

"You've tasted my kisses. You know how good they are. What selfish streak in you demands exclusivity to those kisses? Don't you realize if they thrill you they could offer just as great a thrill to Buck? The way I look at it, I don't see that we are in a position to deny Buck anything. He certainly hasn't denied us anything, has he?"

"He's been incredibly generous."

"Now you're talking," Don said. "Now you're coming around. If I kiss Buck from time to time, my lips are still going to be in working order for you. They are not going to disappear under his assault. I'm with you all the time, and I express my gratitude to you in a million ways. I bet Buck will have almost no time for me in the future. A stolen moment here and there. If during those stolen moments, I can bring him some pleasure, then I say I owe it to him."

"Let's drop the subject," she said, growing impatient. "I don't really want to talk about it. If you absolutely insist on being with another man, I guess I'd rather you be with Buck than someone else. Certainly not Patrick."

"Patrick—that was nothing. Guys come on to me all the time. I didn't tell you why I got up abruptly and came to join you back here. Leroy got carried away. He groped me. Let's face it. I've got a big basket. Have you ever known a gay guy yet who could resist a big basket—especially when it's attached to a good-looking football hero like me with blond hair and blue eyes?"

"I can't say I have. You're one hell of a sexy man."

"Fine," he said. "It's good to hear you admit that. If Buck isn't immune to my charms, then he's not to be blamed. He's just like me: he turns people on—both men and women."

"That he does." She leaned over to kiss Don, not wanting to wreck the delicate balance of their relationship. "That's why I married him."

"The jet's about to land," Don said, staring out the window. "Before we meet Pamela, I have a confession to make. That night I had a reason for not wanting to meet Pamela in the Rusty Pelican. We parted under bad circumstances. She was still in love with me when I left her. I heard she took it really hard. I think she'll still be carrying a torch for me. She's probably never gotten over me."

"Wouldn't it be easier to give me a list of people who were not your lovers?"

"There haven't been that many. You've experienced my love-making. You should be grateful that I came to your bed with all that experience under my belt. Everybody taught me something. It's made me a better man for you." He leaned over and kissed her long and hard.

Suddenly, she was aware of Leroy snapping her picture in the arms of Don. "Stop that! Damn you. I hired you to take wedding pictures of Buck and me. Don't you dare print pictures of Don and me. You do and I'll personally cut off your little balls."

Leroy looked miffed. "How did you know I had little balls?"

"I could just tell," she said, tightening her belt for the landing.

*****

"The wedding pictures will be great," Leroy said, sipping coffee in the airport lounge as they waited for the luggage to be unloaded from Buck's jet. "Thanks for inviting me here for the job. I just love Key West."

"So do I," Susan said.

"Has Buck hired Don as your bodyguard?" Leroy asked. "I see he has quite a few, all good looking. Each one definitely centerfold material."

"That's right," she said non-committally, "He's a bodyguard."

"I might be needing one myself," Leroy said.

"What does that mean?" she asked.

"Oh, nothing. I've got some news for you if you promise not to tell."

"Even though I'm a reporter, I can keep a secret."

"In a few weeks I may be on my own honeymoon."

"Who's the lucky guy?"

"Gene Robinson."

She put down her coffee. "I've heard a lot of revelations, but this is a bit much. You and Gene? I find that hard to believe."

"I became obsessed with him long before you married him. Ever since that day I took a frontal nude of him in the locker room."

"Does Gene return your feelings?"

"He doesn't let me kiss him. But he lets me do nearly everything else."

"That's more than he did for me." She stared at him long and hard. "Are you certain Gene has made a commitment to you? I mean, that he's not involved with someone else?"

"When I pull off this deal I'm making, Gene and I are going to California. Lead the good life. I hope you're not jealous."

"I'm not. Gene and I parted a long time ago. He's free to lead his life as he chooses."

"He's one hell of a man. I don't know how you ever let him go."

"I've gone on to bigger and better things."

"Better perhaps," he said, raising an eyebrow. "Hardly bigger. I should know."

Not fully wanting to pursue this conversation, she excused herself and headed for the women's room to do some emergency repair. The class of '71 was continuing its game of musical love chairs. Before the story ended, or so it seemed to her, everybody in the class would have had everybody else. As she came to the door to the women's room, she could hear Don speaking on an open phone around the corner.

"I've got to see you, dude, just as soon as we fly back from Key West. I think I'm in love. You're fantastic. I've never known anything like it. I'm crazy about you, and can't wait until you're in my arms again. Hot damn! I'm gonna work you over."

Not wanting to hear the end of his call—it was obviously to Buck—she went inside the women's room where she checked her makeup. She appeared stunning, at the peak of her beauty. But she wondered if this was self-delusion. All the guys were turning to each other. She must not look as good as she thought she did.

Buck's security forces had arranged a limousine to pick them up and take them to the Pier House. The vehicle was pink. Even the driver was clad in pink instead of the usual black or elephant gray.

Upon their arrival, Susan checked into a suite with Don, Leroy occupying another suite a few doors down. Susan agreed to call Leroy when she'd made the arrangements with Pamela for the interview. She dialed Pamela's room, a number she'd been given before. Pamela was registered at the hotel under the name of Barbara Bennett. Pamela's hesitant, guarded voice came on the phone. "Yes."

"It's me, Susan. I'm here at the Pier House. I want to see you real soon. I've flow in Leroy Fitzgerald. He's agreed to film our interview."

"I hope I'm doing the right thing," Pamela said. "I'm afraid."

"Let me come down and talk it over with you before the interview."

"Okay, come on down. Maybe we'd better talk privately first. I get nervous in front of the camera."

After putting down the phone, she turned to see Don trying to cram himself into a very tight-fitting white bikini. "I'll be down by the pool if you need me," he said. "Might as well get in some R&R. After all, this is our honeymoon."

Thoughts of his call to Buck entered her head but she tried to blot that out. "I'm meeting with Pamela. I'll call Leroy later for the filming."

"Do you plan to tell Pamela I'm with you now?"

"I'm sure she's confined to her room. She doesn't really need to know you're here and that you and I are an item. If she's still in love with you, I don't see how her finding out about us would help."

"Then I'll make myself scarce. I don't want to see her again. What would we say to each other? Go over old times? Discuss how our relationship failed?"

"It's pointless in meeting with old flames unless a reconciliation is planned—and I doubt that is the case."

"You guessed right. I've got a full platter." He went over and kissed her, looking practically nude in that bikini.

"Between Buck and me, I'd say you have yourself fully booked. Both of us are insatiable. I'm sure we'll exhaust you."

He paused at the door, looking as if he might respond but chose not to. "Come down by the pool when you're through with Pamela. I'll be waiting."

"I'm not so sure. This is Key West and you are wearing that bikini. Someone is sure to take notice."

"I'll pay them no attention. My heart belongs just to you."

After he'd gone, she checked her makeup and outfit one final time. She was only too aware she'd be filmed and that this film might be broadcast one day. She wanted to look her best, not only for the cameras but when interviewing her old rival, Pamela. It seemed they'd competed for everything except Barry Collins. Now she was placed in an awkward position of shacking up with Pamela's former boyfriend. She dreaded the interview but was determined to see it through. After the mirror told her no emergency repairs were needed, she headed for Pamela's suite, not at all certain what she'd find there.

At the door to Pamela's suite, Susan knocked and called out her name in case Pamela was afraid to open the door. "It's Susan," she called. "Is that you, Barbara?"

Pamela opened the door. A drink in hand, she stood on unsteady legs. "Wait till you hear what I've got to say on camera."

*****

Word reached Buck at Desire that Rose had slipped back into town unannounced. Apparently, she was determined in the future to avoid widely publicized airport arrivals. "One sick nut with a gun, and I'm a frontpage obit," she'd once told him.

Buck ordered Lars to arrange a private meeting at once, or as soon as possible, even though he knew Rose must be tired from flying around the world doing who knows what. Lars got back to him at once. Rose had agreed to the meeting but it was not to be at Paradise Shores. It had to be completely secretive. He was puzzled as to why Paradise Shores had been ruled off-limits. Obviously there was a lot going on in the life of Sister Rose that he wasn't privy to. Rose had agreed to a rendezvous off the coast of Okeechobee. She was to be aboard her yacht. Buck was to take his own smaller yacht out to see and meet her offshore. His yacht was to pull up alongside her own, at which time he was to come aboard.

He accepted those terms, although they left him mystified. He still didn't know why he couldn't meet her at Paradise Shores because that place seemed to have enough security. Rose certainly didn't want to be seen with him, and in a way he felt relieved. Getting photographed sneaking into Paradise Shores might not be in his best interests either.

Casey drove Lars and Buck back to Buck's home in Okeechobee where he was to board his yacht within an hour. When he got there, he found a note from Robert.

"Dear Buck,

With Uncle Milty's permission, I am going to temporarily stay on your island. Please note that I said *your* island and not our island as I used to. Your offer of your home in town was very generous but I must decline. I plan to leave Okeechobee and all its memories of you. I feel you have betrayed me on a very serious level, and I don't find it in my heart to forgive you. I'm sure Uncle Milty has told you of my financial demands. I am taking you at your word—that you are going to be very generous. I have devoted a considerable amount of my life to you, and I expect to be fully compensated. If you were still making forty-five thousand dollars a year, I would not make such demands on you. But you now have millions, and I fully expect more millions are in your future. Although my demands may be excessive, or appear that way, they are but a small amount taken from your bag of gold. I hope you will not resist giving in to my requests. I feel I have earned the money I'm asking. Please do not contact me on the island or come here to see me. I will use old Buck's yacht to get to the island. I hope you don't mind. Uncle Milty said it was okay. You have even destroyed my friendship with Patrick. Now that I am threatening to expose you in a palimony law suit, he doesn't want to have anything else to do with me. His obvious loyalty is to you because of your connection with Uncle Milty. Patrick knows which side of his bread is buttered. Also, you have conveniently provided him with a handsome new lover—your driver, Casey, who even came on strong with me. It is also clear to me who your own newly acquired lover is: Lars. I confronted him with my suspicion of your affair. He did not admit it. Nor did he deny it. At this point it doesn't matter. I've wasted no time giving my heart to another person in the wake of your betrayal. I am truly in love with this person. I used to think I was in love with you. But I didn't know what true love was. I know that now. I view my involvement with you as a sick schoolgirl crush, and I want to wipe it from my mind. Please give me the money as soon as possible so I can leave Florida and your betrayals behind me. Robert."

After reading the note, Buck crumpled it in his hand. He turned to Lars. "Did Robert confront you about an affair between the two of us?"

"Yes, he did. I said nothing. He accused me of being in love with you. He claimed he could see it written all over my face."

"What did you say?" Buck demanded to know.

"I said nothing, but I didn't deny it."

"Why not?"

"Because Robert sensed the truth. I am in love with you."

Buck stood looking into Lars's Nordic blue eyes for a long moment. "C'mon, dude, a roll in the hay—nothing more. Even with a third party involved. Just some guys having fun. After all, it's the seventies."

Lars's lip quivered. "That's what it might have been to you. It was something more to me. Holding you and loving you and depositing my seed in you..."

Buck interrupted. "Depositing your seed? What kind of talk is this?"

"Forgive me. English is not my first language. I may sound awkward. Too formal. Whatever. But what I'm trying to tell you is I love you."

Buck stared at him for a long moment, not really wanting to believe or even hear Lars's words. "You really feel that way?"

"I do. I know I don't have much of a chance. I know what the competition is. I know how many other people have staked you out. But I also know there is something I can give you that nobody else can. I'm a good man. I'm a loving man. I have vowed to lay down my life for you at any moment someone threatens you. In the course of a lifetime, I will probably save your life on at least three occasions—no doubt. Although such devotion and such loyalty, even my love, are new to you, can't you accept them as my tribute to you for being the special man you are?"

"You've embarrassed me. I don't know what to say. I'm not often at a loss for words or even embarrassed. But the way you're looking at me. It's so honest. You sound so sincere. I'm more than flattered. I believe you. You're one hell of a guy. I bet you've never been turned down by anyone, man or woman."

"I haven't," Lars said.

"I thought so."

"I think you're not going to turn me down either. But I'm talking conditional love."

"What kind of conditions?" Buck asked, dreading the answer.

"I just ask that you take the first step toward me. If you'll walk only one step, I'll walk the other steps until we meet and I take you in my arms to press my lips against yours."

"You're a very romantic guy. I've known a few beauties in my life, and you rank up there with the best of them. Don't tempt me like that. You know I'm gay and what gay man is going to say no to some Viking God. C'mon, guy."

When Lars spoke again, his voice was harsh and commanding. "God damn it. Take the fucking step. You know you want to. But I warn you. Once you take that step, there is no turning back. Part of your heart will belong to me forever."

Buck looked deeply into Lars's face. It was a sculpted piece of male beauty with a strong jaw. His lips were perfectly formed—not too full but not thin either. A lock of his straight blond hair fell over his forehead, making him look amazingly alluring. He was Buck's age, Buck's height, and an equal of Buck in every way. It was like staring at a Nordic version of himself. Except for Ahmad, Buck was showing a strong attraction to blonds. Lars was the ultimate blond of them all. But it was Lars's eyes that enraptured Buck. They were the purest he'd ever seen. There was some compelling element in those eyes that seemed to draw you inside his body. The time in bed with Casey and Lars was as if Casey weren't even there. The communication, the sex, and, yes, the love, was strictly between Lars and Buck.

"I'm waiting," Lars said.

Looking into his eyes once more, Buck didn't make just one step. He moved quickly into Lars's arms, seeking his mouth. Lars rewarded Buck with his tongue. When Buck broke free finally and moved to kiss and plunge his tongue into Lars's ear, he whispered softly, "I'm yours."

*****

At the pier, the door to his limousine was opened by Casey, who leaned in and gave Buck a kiss before letting him out into the twilight night. Beside his own rather small yacht was a sailing ship of impressive size.

Lars took his hand and guided him not to his own yacht but to the ship nearby. "Ahmad has a present for you."

Buck looked at the ship in astonishment. "You mean this is mine?" he asked in utter astonishment.

"Ahmad has just had it completely redone."

Buck stood looking in awe at the sleek ship.

"It's called Mandalay," Lars said. "Before that it was called Mein Kampf. It used to be one of the most famous and luxurious ships in the world. When it was built by the arms baron, Alfred Krupp, it was the only armor-plated sailing vessel in the world. Its armaments influenced the outcome of the Franco-Prussian War of 1870. Hitler once came aboard to award the Iron Cross to one of its U-boat commanders. The United States seized it as war booty in 1945, and it was eventually sold to George Vanderbilt as a private yacht. After he reconfigured part of its hull, it became the fastest two-masted sailing vessel off the California coast. It once managed an almost frightening 22 knots under full sail. Ahmad has had it completely redone. It's in mint condition. He so hopes you'll like it. Come aboard."

Feeling like a schoolboy with his first car, Buck, trailed by Casey, came aboard. Lars introduced Buck to the captain and the rest of the crew.

After greeting them, Buck went to look over the railing, as the captain started the vessel, heading for a rendezvous with Sister Rose. "I've got to see Ahmad," Buck said privately to Lars. "He just steps into my life, gives me the world, and then disappears."

"Don't worry. Ahmad will be back with you soon. He's so anxious to see you. But I have to tell you. He's afraid you don't really love him. He hopes to shower you with extravagant gifts so you'll never lose interest in him, especially now that he's getting a bit older."

"He doesn't have to do all this." Buck surveyed the ship and all its splendor. "But I'm glad he does. First, letting me turn Desire into my home. Now Mandalay."

Ahmad has other yachts, but he wanted you to have this one in your own name. It's so very special—even historic. He knows you're a real sailor, and he thought you'd appreciate it."

"Appreciate it! I love it! You tell Ahmad to get his ass back to me real soon if he really wants it fucked. Before meeting up with Sister Rose, let's go on a tour. I'm dying to see everything."

Later, when Mandalay had anchored next to Rose's ocean-going yacht, Buck with Lars and two security guards crossed a hastily assembled drawbridge connecting the two vessels. He really wanted their rendezvous to take place aboard his new toy, Mandalay, but Rose had wanted to see him aboard her own yacht.

"She's in her suite," the captain of her yacht said. "She wants you to come there."

Turning from Lars, Buck said, "I'm not sure how long this will take."

"However long," Lars said. "I'll be here."

Buck kissed him gently on the lips and headed below. An attendant in a rose jacket showed him to the door to Rose's cabin. The attendant knocked lightly, then opened the door, inviting Buck in.

With a slight trepidation, Buck entered the sumptuous suite, all decorated in various shades of rose. Emerging from her bathroom, Rose rushed to him and threw her arms around him. He held her tightly, kissing her long and hard before inserting his tongue.

"God, I've missed you," she said. "I don't think I could go another day without being in your arms."

He broke away from her and looked around her cabin. "I think I need a drink. There are so many questions to ask."

She quickly called the attendant and ordered drinks sent down. "You may wonder why all the secrecy," she said. "Meeting at sea like this and everything."

"I was wondering," he said, turning around to face her, as she kissed him several times on the lips. "More than curious."

"Ahmad ordered it. He doesn't want you seen at Paradise Shores and doesn't want you to appear with me at all during the next few weeks. A lot of shit is about to happen, and he doesn't want you connected with it. I know all about what he wants you to accomplish for him in Hollywood. He wants you to arrive there looking clean as a hound's tooth and not involved in any of the political shit I have contracted for." She stood back, looking at him with a steely eyed appraisal. "You're not going to become my media director after all. That meeting with Ahmad must have gone very successfully. Instead of becoming my media director, you're going to be his media director."

"He told you that?"

"That and other things." At a discreet knock on the door, Rose went and opened it, ushering the attendant in with the drinks.

After he had left, Buck took a hefty swig of his drink before turning to Rose again. "We must talk. I am absolutely demanding to know what's happened to Shelley. I've had a lot of time to think this over. I don't think he wrote that note to me. He might have actually written it in his own handwriting, but he was forced to do that. I want to see him. Regardless of where he is in the world, I want to see him. I think Ahmad will agree to this."

She sighed and sat down on a luxurious sofa covered in rose-colored Thai silk. "I've already spoken to Ahmad about this. Whether Calder and I think it wise or not, Ahmad demands that you be allowed to see Shelley."

"Thank God. What's the problem with my seeing Shelley? Has something happened to him? Have Calder's goons beaten him up?"

He noticed tears welling in her eyes. "It's all very complicated. Shelley had to be detained. Perhaps forcibly. I was hoping you'd take the note at face value and not follow up with this. We used to be able to handle domestic disputes like this without Ahmad. Now you've involved him."

"God damn it, we're talking about your son. My lover. I have certain rights. I actually have to hear it from Shelley's own mouth that he doesn't want to see me again."

"I understand," she said, downing her drink rather fast. "But the Shelley you're going to meet isn't the Shelley you knew. He's changed."

"Calder has done something to him?"

"Okay, I'll admit it. It's no secret to you: Shelley was planning to denounce us. Destroy our work. All our carefully laid plans. Only an idiot would stand by and let that happen. Calder had to intervene. As much as I hated sending Shelley away, I knew it was in my own best interests."

"Where is Shelley?"

"He's in my chalet outside St. Moritz."

"How convenient," he said. "I'm flying to Switzerland to see old Buck. He's dying. I'll be in the same country, and I want you to set up a meeting with Shelley."

"I'll arrange it through Lars," she said, "but I must warn you. Calder has had him brainwashed. He won't be the same."

"Shelley is a young and determined young man with a strong will. I can't believe in just this short amount of time he'd give in to Calder's brainwashers."

"Calder knows these men in Switzerland. They are very effective."

"Just set it up, Rose. I'm not going to give up my demand!"

"Consider it done," she said, disguising a certain hostility in her voice. She obviously didn't want his rendezvous with Shelley to take place.

Another knock on the door, and Lars entered. "You've got an urgent message," he said to Buck, ignoring Rose. "Your grandfather's had a heart attack in Geneva. His doctors want you to come at once."

"I've got to go," Buck said, putting down his drink and turning to Rose."

"He's in a coma," Lars said. "They think he may never come out of it."

"I'll join you in a minute," Buck said. Lars turned and left.

When she looked up at Buck, she appeared lost, needing his company and dreading his leaving. "I was so hoping you could be with me tonight. I don't think I ever needed to be with you as much as I need to be with you tonight."

"I can't stay. The old man is very important to me."

"But he's dying. I'm alive. We're alive. You belong here with me."

He looked imploringly into her eyes. "I just can't stay."

She got up from the sofa and called the attendant to bring her another drink. "I think I'll hire a personal bodyguard just like the one Ahmad arranged for you." She looked at him, raising an eyebrow. "Of course, I don't expect mine to be as handsome as yours. But who knows?"

"I'll call you frequently," he said. "I've heard rumors about some march. A controversial dedication. Hazel's spreading a lot of shit, and it sounds like big trouble for you."

"It will be," she said, as if hopelessly assigned to the task. "I've got to face what I must. So sorry you won't be here. Even if you were, Ahmad wouldn't let you appear by my side. He fears the contamination. Did you think this would ever happen to me? That I would sell out to the point where merely appearing by my side could contaminate another person?"

"I can only imagine the dreadful games you're playing."

"You're playing the same dreadful games, and I resent you. I must say that even if I anger you."

"I don't really know what you mean."

"It's plain and simple. You're getting—or at least will get—far greater rewards than me, but you're not out there on the front line taking the heat like I am. I'll be the victim of hatemongers—even a potential assassin. You'll go to Hollywood and start spending Ahmad's millions and will be the toast of the town. It doesn't seem fair somehow."

"Maybe it's not and you've got a point. But then I wouldn't sign on for your particular duties. I wouldn't have the heart for it."

"I don't have the heart for it either."

"Then why do you do it? You've already got plenty of money."

"I'm doing it for the same reason you are. Surely your darling Uncle Milty has cashed Ahmad's checks for the sale of the Examiner. Isn't that all the money you'll ever need? But, like me, you're seeking even more money and power as Ahmad's boy. I'll say this: If you want money, you've hooked up with the right sugar daddy. Ahmad has millions he hasn't even counted yet. I know at least in part how he got much of that money but somehow I don't think I'll get around to telling you. I'm sure the subject will never come up between the two of you."

"Does it matter? It doesn't matter to me."

"To me either, just as long as some of that loot is coming my way."

"My time is up," he said, glancing nervously at his watch.

"Let's have our embrace here away from prying eyes," she said.

He took her in his arms, kissing her long and hard, wishing it could be any number of other people he was kissing. She clung to him, clawing into his back. He'd never seen her this desperate before. Finally, he broke away. "I won't be gone long. Your loving man will be back to you," he said with no particular conviction.

"Oh, God," she called out. "I may never see you again. I just feel it."

Back on the Mandalay, he stood on deck, surveying the calm sea. As he looked back at her yacht, he saw her standing on her own deck, her white gown billowing in the wind. She looked like a ghostly figure, not real somehow.

Was it really true? Was this the last time he'd ever see her? He shuddered in the wind before going below.

Chapter Fourteen

Once again in the comfort of Paradise Shores, Rose settled back in her favorite armchair covered in a silk upholstery of red roses. Looking across at a nervous Barry, she could never imagine why she'd ever been attracted to him. Of course, he was extraordinarily handsome and had a great body, except for his penis. It was just too small, hardly enough to satisfy a woman who had known Don Bossdum and Buck Brooke III.

If he didn't have to take off his clothes and perform, he might be the kind of guy you could look at. He was pretty enough to be a fashion model. It seemed that women he met on the campaign trail were awed by his male beauty. In fact, she'd rank him as the handsomest man she'd ever seen go into politics. John Kennedy wasn't handsome. Barry Collins was handsome. With the passing months, he'd drifted away from her bed, and she was hardly anxious to invite him back ever again. On their last encounter, if she recalled, he was unable to get an erection. Apparently, Barry had been more successful getting an erection for Shelley than for her.

At first she'd never known of Barry's interest in young boys. She once said that Barry Collins was probably the only certifiably straight man in Okeechobee. How wrong she'd been on that call.

Although he'd not been her most ardent lover, he'd always been persistent and convincing, at least back in the days when he courted her support. She realized belatedly that he'd been no more than a hustler, perhaps regarding making love to her as a distasteful duty. He obviously liked his bodies much younger. She shuddered to think what sexual images were going through his mind as he'd made love to her.

As he rambled on about the mayoral campaign, she didn't listen. She knew and he knew what the real purpose of this meeting was. It was about those photographs and her coming up with five million to pay off the blackmailer, Leroy Fitzgerald. She studied his pretty face instead. There had been almost no changes—perhaps a small line she'd never known before. He was incredibly photogenic. If any man could win an election on looks alone, it was Barry Collins, particularly when his opponent was ugly, fat Hazel.

Sitting here studying him closely, she realized she'd definitely picked the wrong man to run for mayor against her sister. This man was weak and indecisive, and his wife, Pamela, was definitely a bomb waiting to explode. Yet she knew she was locked into Barry and had to ride out the campaign with him to the bitter finish. Once, she'd dreamed of his going on to the governor's mansion and maybe the White House one day. But after the mayoral race she knew for sure he was going no further than Okeechobee. Calder and she had already determined that.

Now that Barry no longer ate his meals with her, he looked slimmer. One characteristic had drawn her to him—the man's intensity. It made everything he said take on an importance it rarely had. That feature had helped a great deal when he had to issue bland statements to the press.

She took in his blue eyes, flecked with white. That strong jaw and brow that had once looked so reliable to her had turned out to be a misleading mask.

Finally, she decided to interrupt him. "Cut the shit! I don't care about what TV ads you plan to run. I'm only interested in one thing. The five-million dollars needed to pay off this cocksucking blackmailer. I love how you and Calder have just determined that I am to come up with all the money."

"I just don't have it. You know I'm not a rich man."

"I know what you've got." She looked at his crotch. "Or don't have."

"Okay, so I'm not Buck Brooke III with his endowment...and millions."

"Nor will you ever be. I don't know why Shelley ever took up with you. He usually likes studs."

"He thought I was very handsome, and was able to overlook other things. Please stop this. You're humiliating me. It's humiliating enough to have to come here and beg you for money."

"You call five-million dollars money. That's not money. That's a fortune!"

"I know it is but as I see it we don't have much choice. I will be ruined if Leroy goes public with those pictures. But the backlash on you will be tremendous. The whole world will know that your darling Shelley isn't the innocent cherub you've made him out to be. When you arrive majestically in your pulpit, they'll boo you off the stage. They don't give a fuck about your licking Arab ass. Your Born Again Christians hate Jews too. That won't harm you at all. The only thing that drives those fuckers ballistic is homosexuality. That they can't accept."

"Shut your cocksucking mouth, faggot. You don't have to tell me what the damage will be. Damage caused by your own lunacy."

"I made a mistake and I'm sorry. Isn't it Christian to forgive?"

"Since when does Christianity have anything to do with all this shit we're facing." She rang a glass bell resting on an end table, summoning a woman servant to bring her a strong drink. She didn't bother to even offer Barry one. When the servant had gone, she turned to Barry, her face in deep distress. "I may have to buy myself out of this trap you've set for me. I've not made up my mind yet. I'll give you my decision very soon."

"Please say yes. It's for both our sakes."

"If I do it, it will be to save my own beautiful skin. It will have nothing to do with you. I couldn't care less if Calder threw you to the sharks tomorrow which he probably will." When her drink arrived, Rose took a hefty swallow. She looked at Barry intently, seeing that she was making him squirm. She liked that. "How's Pamela?"

A pained look came over his face. She was all too aware of the rumors that Pamela had deserted the campaign and disappeared. He didn't seem to have an answer. Finally, he tried to change the subject. "You don't like Pamela, do you? I want an honest opinion. Do you think it better if I get a divorce and marry some woman the public would find more acceptable?"

"Calder will have to decide that," she answered. "I was misled by Pamela. She's right pretty, a little overweight. Her clothes are too frilly. Like an aging woman trying to recapture her university days. That we could deal with. We could always hire a stylist for the bitch. It's her tongue that bothers me. The only thing that would stop it is to cut it out!"

"You're joking, of course." He laughed nervously as if not fully realizing the rules by which Calder and she played.

His question was met with stone silence. She could tell he looked at her as he'd never done before, perhaps realizing for the first time how deeply committed he was to people he didn't really know. She'd experienced the same trapped feeling, more so than he ever had. Trying to read his thoughts, she said, "I once told my congregation never to sell their souls to the devil. I wish I'd taken my own advice. I bet you do, too."

He got up and walked the floor, circling her chair in a taut, nervous way. "Look, this whole fucking thing is about to blow up in my face. Instead of becoming mayor, I could be ruined forever. Even if I pull this one off, there's no guarantee for my future. A one-term mayor of

Okeechobee. What kind of fucking shit is that on a resumé? Where's all the talk these days of running me for higher office? I bet those guys I met in Key Biscayne won't ever speak to me again or return my phone calls."

Brushing aside these concerns, she stood up and confronted him. "Exactly where is Pamela? I don't buy this bullshit about her being sick."

"She's visiting some relatives out of state."

"If you're going into politics, you've got to lie better than that. You're coming here begging me for five-million dollars to save your ass. I'm entitled to an answer to my one question."

"Okay, God damn it, I don't know where the bitch is. She ran off."

"I think what you're trying to tell me is that any day you'll be getting Pamela's demands for millions."

"That won't happen, I can assure you."

"Listen, faggot, and listen good. You bring Pamela here. I want to grill the cunt. I want to put her in the hot seat. I'm not going to pay off Fitzgerald, then suddenly be confronted with demands for more millions from Pamela. This is a bottomless sea. How many more do you have who'll appear out of the woodwork demanding more millions? I've got to know. Before I deal with this Fitzgerald thing, you've got to bring Pamela to me for an intensive interrogation."

"But I can't."

"You're lying. I think you could track her down."

"You're being unreasonable."

"Fuck that! You're asking me to put up five-million dollars. All I'm asking is for an interview with your wife. I don't consider that demand unreasonable."

"I'll see what I can do," he muttered under his breath. He turned on her with anger. "I'm not taking part in any dedication on the beach, and I'm not marching in any of your parades. I'd like to put some distance between us right now. Your coming out against the Jews like that sure caught me off guard. My campaign headquarters has been bombarded with hostile calls. A lot of people want me to denounce your support. Attacking the Jews! Have you lost your mind?"

"I do what I get paid to do. You don't have to attend anything as far as I'm concerned. But I can't let my enemies think they've driven me underground. It's not only my enemies I'm worried about. It's my so-called friends. We've just learned the Nazis and the KKK are going to march in my support. Right into the heart of the Jewish ghetto. That's a class act the media will adore."

"Then call the God damn thing off!"

"No! Calder and I knew from the beginning a campaign like ours would attract the lunatics. We're going to try to ignore them and concentrate on our own business."

"I hope you know what you're doing. I think shit will blow in your face."

"If there's an explosion coming, you've contributed to it."

"Your son played an equal role."

"Let's put the blame on a fourteen-year-old. Get me Pamela and get her as soon as possible. Fitzgerald will not wait forever. He's not the first blackmailer I've dealt with in my day." She reached for her drink, downing the rest of it in one gulp. "Now get out!"

He lingered behind, hesitant. Through slightly compressed lips, he said, "I've got a strange request. I've hired this bodyguard. He's out on the patio now, and he's dying to meet you. The guy worships you. Perhaps your most loyal fan. He used to be a policeman until he got arrested for exposing himself to a little girl. He's Gene Robinson."

"I've heard of him."

"There's a screw loose somewhere. But he wants to be your bodyguard for the parade and the dedication in case somebody tries to harm you. Frankly, if you're going through with this shit, you'd better have him there. I wouldn't trust idiot Biff's bumbling police to cover my ass."

A smirk came across her face. "Maybe you're right. I could always give Mr. Robinson an autographed white Bible." She walked over to the window and parted the drapery slightly. From where she stood, she could clearly see Gene. "My God, he's a beauty."

"And hung like a horse too."

"Does he like women or have you cocksuckers got him fully booked?"

"He's straight. He was once married to Susan Howard, your darling Buck's wife."

"How intriguing," she said. She looked back to the patio and at Gene. The policeman's very presence was magnetically male. He didn't just walk the patio, he stalked it. She thought he had tremendous animal magnetism and male flash. "Why don't you go home without him? I'll go and introduce myself to your young stallion."

Emerging from the darkness of the house into the colored lights of the patio, Rose's face was alive—so alive it seemed on fire. For one flashing moment, Gene feared such intensity would shatter both of them. He'd lived in illusions, and now wanted reality. He'd seen her at the temple and had marched close to her in the parade, but the image in front of him was not the woman he'd viewed then, but the vision he'd conjured up in his dreams. A real experience with her would free him from his fantasies. Drowned in her beauty, he reached to take the hand she extended. Her handshake was more like a caress.

"Mr. Robinson, welcome to Paradise Shores."

He was so filled with admiration he hesitated an awkward moment before speaking. "It's the most beautiful place in the world." He'd wanted to say she was the most beautiful woman in the world. He'd touched her hand, yet she still seemed untouchable, unapproachable, unavailable in any way. She was not a vision to be sullied by man.

She walked ahead, leading him toward a gazebo. Down a flower-lined path, she retreated into a dark pocket of the garden. Here she stood for a moment, waiting for him to catch up. She glanced apprehensively at the foliage on the other side of the gazebo and reached for his hand. His large hand enclosed her delicate one. He hoped his palm wasn't sweaty.

"Lately, I've been afraid to walk in my own garden. There have been so many phone threats on my life."

"You need a bodyguard," he said, his pace matching hers.

She came to a stop just long enough to look deeply into his eyes. "I know."

In the gazebo, she offered him a cola which he took with trembling unsureness. She sat facing him, a curious questioning look in her expression. She leaned forward, her eyes lighting up with discovery. "I think I've seen you somewhere before."

He shuddered at the revelation she was about to make, fearing she'd viewed his face on the television screen at the time of his arrest.

"You marched with me in my parade! Right alongside me."

He breathed easier. "That's right. I didn't think you'd remember. I didn't want to bring it up."

She leaned back and smiled. "I think both of us looked terrific, don't you?"

He took in her sly smile, her disarming dimple, her auburn hair piled high and carelessly on her head. "You certainly did, Miss Phillips."

"Rose." It seemed like a command. "We don't have to be formal. Not if you're going to protect me tomorrow from the loonies."

"Barry has already asked..."

"Yes, and I accepted." She spoke with tenderness and softness, as they sat sipping their drinks. She wasn't at all the forceful woman who stood in the pulpit, preaching to her congregation. She was warm, loving, giving—a person you could open up to.

After their first hour together, he'd begun to relax in her presence. She was infinitely desirable, but beyond the reach of man. Her earrings shimmered in the night light of the patio, and he found himself drawn closer to her. Her eyes, her mouth, her hair—everything about her fascinated him. He could easily lose himself in a woman like this.

Her voice had become a whisper as she invited him back to the house. "It's getting damp," she said. He took off his jacket and gave it to her, and she smiled her appreciation of the gesture. Her hand fondled his as he draped the jacket across her shoulders, covering her thin gown.

On their walk back from the garden, she slipped her fingers into his and, at that signal, he locked hands with her, perhaps a little more tightly than he'd meant. He didn't want to hurt her.

In the living room, she confided, "Most men I've known have resented my strength. They believe a woman should be delicate, tender, you know—not strong. What do you think?"

He was startled by the bluntness of the question. "I think you have everything. You are strong, yet a woman, too, a gentle person. You make your points without having to shout. Unlike..." he stopped himself.

"My sister, Hazel, you meant to say."

"I'm sorry."

"Don't be. We have no love for each other."

"I can't believe a vulgar woman like that is your sister."

"Sometimes I find it hard to believe, too."

Over dinner, he didn't bother to ask where Barry had gone. He didn't care. He just wanted to be alone with her. He couldn't believe that on the important night before the dedication of her new center she was spending all her time with him.

Although a lamp lit their table, he didn't need its light. The glow coming from her was enough. The more she talked, the huskier her voice became, her eyes feverish as they turned a cloudy violet. He didn't know where this evening would end. Right now he couldn't imagine it ever ending, at least not in his memory.

Finally, she got up and reached again for his hand. "I'd better get my beauty sleep if I'm going to face those TV cameras tomorrow." She led him toward the living room. "Why don't you spend the night in my guest room? I'd feel a lot safer with you in the house. It's okay with Barry."

"I don't have to report to Barry," he said defensively. "I'm free to do what I want."

"I'm glad to hear that."

As she stood before the door to her guest room wishing him a good night, he seemed enveloped in her warmth. He didn't want her to leave, but didn't know how to ask her to stay. Suddenly, she kissed his lips and, before the tingling sensation of it had traveled his body, she was gone, as if retreating into his fantasy.

Later, as he tossed and turned in bed, he still couldn't believe he'd actually met her, that she'd kissed him and made him feel like the center of her world. She'd asked him to protect her, just as she had in his imagination. However, he feared a cruel trick. Maybe this was just one of his many dreams about her, having no reality at all. Perhaps in the morning when he woke up she'd be gone. Or, worse, he'd discover she'd never existed at all, that the evening had never happened. He couldn't be sure of anything any more.

*****

In the Blackhawk limousine being driven by Casey to the airport, Buck asked Lars to turn on the radio. To his astonishment, he learned that Rose's dedication ceremony was already under way. It had been announced for ten o'clock that morning, but had started at eight-thirty. Buck suspected that this was done deliberately by Calder. Perhaps Rose hoped to get through the dedication before ugly crowds formed to protest against her, or some of her lunatic supporters showed up. The last thing she wanted was to have newsreel cameras capture her making a speech with swastikas in the background. As in her candlelight parade, she also wanted to retreat to safety before any violence broke out.

Over the radio came the sound of Rose's melodious voice. "Not only will I dedicate the greatest religious center, spiritual retreat and hospital in the entire southland, but I plan to establish one of America's greatest universities. Like a phoenix rising from the ashes of urban blight, we will have an open university where free thought is allowed. Not a university where Zionist die-hards control the curriculum."

Buck greeted that news with amazement. No one knew that Rose planned anything more than a new charismatic center. Now he realized why she needed so much land for building. There was more. He signaled Casey to turn up the volume.

"In one building we will have a research institute called the Middle East Center," came Rose's voice. "The door to thought and information has been closed long enough in America. In our Arab studies center, we will open that door, shedding light on the people who figure so importantly in our destiny today. Nobody questions Hebrew studies at the big American universities. Why is it then that a study of the history and culture of the Arab nations is called propaganda?"

He sighed, almost in exasperation. Regardless of how thoroughly he knew Rose, the evangelist managed to surprise him.

"We must explore both sides of the conflict in the Middle East," Rose claimed. "The charismatics in my own foundation are not afraid of the truth. Why should other Americans be?"

As her voice went off the radio and her all-woman chorus began to sing, "Onward, Christian Soldiers," he signaled Casey to turn off the radio. He'd heard enough.

Later as Casey opened the car door for him, light rain fell on his face. "Maybe it'll cool tempers a bit," Buck said to Casey.

Casey didn't seem to give a damn about Rose or her parade. She hadn't won him over. He looked very disappointed, as he spotted Lars attending to the loading of Buck's luggage on his own private plane, so recently flown by Rose and Shelley.

Buck sensed Casey's discomfort. "Next time I'll take you with me. I promise."

"Thanks for saying that, boss man," he said. "I am beginning to resent Lars. He has all the fun. He's with you all the time and all I get to do is drive you around."

"There's more to come," Buck said flirtatiously, bending over and kissing him on the lips. "While I'm gone, take a vacation. Drive to Desire and live it up. I'll have Lars clear it for you. You'll have a great time there."

"You mean that?"

"Of course, I do."

"But it won't be the same without you."

"I'm sure you'll find some amusement there. The staff is very good looking, and you still have that cock ring, don't you?"

"It's my special treasure."

He kissed Casey good-bye. "I'll be back soon."

Lars came up and gave Casey a kiss too. "The plane is secure," he said to Buck. "We're heading for Geneva." He paused. "A message has come in from Rose. She gave us instructions about how to set up a meeting with Shelley. But she left an ominous warning. She's asking you to reconsider and not go to St. Moritz."

"Hell with her!" Buck said. "I'm on my way now."

He kissed Casey good-bye for one final time and headed along with Lars and five security guards toward the plane.

As his jet became airborne, he was glad to be leaving Okeechobee behind. He thanked the gods he hadn't accepted the media director's job with Rose. Hollywood on the arm of Ahmad was more his scene. Rose quickly faded from his thoughts as he concentrated on what awaited him in Switzerland. He fully expected a death bed scene with his grandfather. That would be followed with a meeting with Shelley. Rose had made him extremely apprehensive about that meeting. What had Calder's goons done to Shelley?

Lars handed him an urgent communication. It was from a major studio. Based on his appearance in the magazine naming him sexiest man alive, a director had tentatively offered him the starring role in an upcoming major motion picture. He was to play a young attorney fresh out of law school who found himself in the employment of a demonic Southern law firm. With all politeness and deference, he was kindly requested to fly to Hollywood at his earliest possible convenience to test for the role. "I'm not worried if you can act or not," the director, Joel Rubuchon, wrote. "With your male beauty, the camera will love you as it did Marilyn. You were born to face the camera. I can't wait to film your nude scenes. I will find the actor in you. You will be the biggest sensation the screen has ever known."

He placed the offer on an adjoining table and turned and looked out his plane into the vastness of space. He was relieved to be high in the clouds and off the earth for a few hours. Lars was removing his shoes and socks to suck his toes and massage his feet.

All of a sudden he missed Ahmad. Where in the hell was Ahmad? Ahmad was the man who made all things possible.

An assistant to the pilot came into the rear, handing Buck two communications. The attendant, who was ever so discreet, did not look down, paying no notice of Lars sucking Buck's toes.

The first message was from Don. "Hey, guy. Fly back to my loving arms real soon. I may be pumping Susan in your absence, but you know who I really want to give my midnight kisses to. I never thought it'd happen to tough old me, but I've fallen in love. I don't go more than five minutes of any day—much less night—without remembering and thrilling to the taste of you. You are sensational. Okay, so you've turned me into a faggot. I always told myself I would turn queer if I ever met a man with a dick as big as mine. I've met that dude now. I'll spend the rest of my life regretting that I turned down your offer of that beer when we were in the university. If I'd gone with you that night, I might have had you all these years all to myself. What a stupid fool I was. Get back to me for the loving of your life. In the meantime, it's off to Susan's bed. Sigh. Your loving man, Don."

The second communication was from Uncle Milty. Ahmad had granted the financing for Sun City, all the money needed. The project was on.

"There's more," Uncle Milty wrote. "The News is now yours. I've been unable to reach Susan this morning to tell her she's the publisher. I didn't have to spend a cent of your Examiner millions. Ahmad's firm has provided financing for the whole thing. Your Examiner millions are still intact."

Buck leaned back into the soft upholstery of the plane. "There must be a downside to all this," he said to no one in particular. Lars seemed so enraptured with his toes that he didn't seem to hear Buck say anything.

Tomorrow, Buck decided, would be time enough to encounter the downside. Right now he felt like king of the world.

*****

Don had gone back to bed in their condo after having to send someone an urgent message. What urgent message did he have to convey to someone? She'd suspected it was a note to Buck but she couldn't concern herself with matters like that this morning.

After a disappointing interview with Pamela, she'd cut short their honeymoon and flown back on Buck's jet to Okeechobee. The plane had only an hour to be worked over before it was flying Buck to Geneva. She had been tempted to wait on the plane until Buck boarded it for his flight to Geneva, but an early morning meeting with Buck, and especially with Don along, seemed not the most desirable thing to be doing. She also had felt Buck didn't want to encounter Don and her this early in the morning. He obviously had another agenda. At some point she was certain that Ahmad would suddenly and mysteriously reappear in Buck's life.

Uncle Milty had told her that the sale of the News was practically a done deal. On an impulse Susan had wanted to take over as publisher with some first-hand knowledge of the story that would surely be dominating local headlines for several days to come: Rose's appearance on South Beach. Susan wanted to see that march up front and not learn about it from some reporter. Don cared not one bit for politics. She decided to tell him she had an appointment with Uncle Milty. He might object to her going to the march out of fear she might get injured. After sending his urgent message, he'd gone back to bed and fallen asleep at once. She headed out the door to the site of the demonstrations, wanting to arrive early.

She learned that militant right-wing groups planned to march down Washington Boulevard into what was often called the Jewish ghetto, to an old bandstand which hadn't been used in twenty-five years.

On the fringe of the area, she passed through a mob of milling, beer-swigging young white men, many of whom wore T-shirts, proclaiming BE A MAN, JOIN THE KLAN. Some of them had stockpiled bricks, coke bottles and firecrackers, and other brandished baseball bats.

The wail of sirens announced the arrival of dozens of policemen in the area, including Biff himself. Susan made her way through the surging crowds. She turned and headed as rapidly as possible to the bandstand, trusting that this would be the center of the storm.

Near the bandstand, the sidewalk had quickly filled up with onlookers, mainly elderly Jewish women who'd come out of their seedy retirement hotels and decaying apartment houses. They appeared bewildered and confused. Several of the women appealed to stonily silent policemen to call off the parade.

"People could get hurt," one woman told Susan.

"Including you," she said firmly. "Now get back to your room."
She led the woman over to the doorway of her apartment house, and for
some reason she obeyed and went inside.

Over a loudspeaker came Biff's booming voice.

"Ladies and gentlemen," he said, "in ten minutes a parade will
march down this boulevard for a ceremony at the bandstand. I,
personally, am against the parade. But its leaders possess valid city
permits. The people in this parade, with certain of their banners and
insignias, might disturb some of you of different political and religious
beliefs. I cannot urge you strongly enough to stay in your own homes.
Keep the peace. Allow these people to have their march. Don't attack.
Don't throw things. It'll be over soon. Then we can all go home and
forget it." Loud boos greeted the end of his appeal.

Hurrying as fast as she could, Susan cut through the largely
partisan audience assembled around the bandstand, mostly men and
women from Rose's temple.

Rose had finished the dedication ceremony and the white-robed
chorus disbanded. Under heavy guard, Rose was hustled from the
bandstand to a waiting limousine.

To her surprise, Susan spotted a man at Rose's side who looked
amazingly like Gene. She got only a glimpse of him before he
disappeared inside the limousine with Rose. But it was enough to cause
a lingering suspicion.

*****

A sizable crowd had already formed about the limousine, in spite
of police efforts to hold it back. Some were from Rose's own temple,
and Gene knew they were harmless. It was the protesters from the
decaying apartment houses he feared. During the dedication, the mob
had already grown restless and had started to push and shove.

As he guided her to her limousine, he could feel Rose holding his
hand tighter and tighter until it became almost a death-grip. Although
she appeared serene on the surface, that grip told him how frightened
she really way. It made him feel all the more protective of her.

"Just head straight for the car," he cautioned her. "No matter what
happens."

Once he'd gotten her through the sharply divided crowd into the safety of the car, he could still hear angry voices filtering through the limousine's heavy glass windows. Rose was immediately on the phone in the limousine, calling Calder to summon more police protection. "God damn you, you promised me this wouldn't happen."

The voice was unfamiliar to Gene and he was surprised to hear her curse, to take the Lord's name in vain like that.

The shouts of the huge crowd had grown angry. Now he knew there would be serious trouble. Those strange women from the apartment houses who were about to be dispossessed shouted at members of the temple and raised mocking, threatening fists to Rose in the back seat of the limousine. They'd been caught off guard when Rose had launched her dedication ceremonies an hour and a half before they were scheduled, but word had traveled fast through the ghetto.

The crowd had completely surrounded the limousine until the driver couldn't move the vehicle. People continued their shouts as they pushed and shoved. It was a confused mixture. Most of them appeared to be protesters, but some were clearly celebrity chasers—as they waved pens, pencils, and autograph books, hoping Rose would lower the window and reward them with her signature.

She seemed terrified as she edged closer on the elephant-gray seat to Gene. As much as she tried not to show it in her face, he sensed how deeply fear cut into her body. She trembled.

The police threatened the crowd with nightsticks, but that didn't seem to work. Some women pounded on the limousine with their fists, spitting on its windows. Other younger people climbed on top of it, peering upside down into all the windows.

"Make them get out of the way," she shouted to policemen who couldn't hear her. "I can't stand it. I feel like a caged animal in some fucking zoo."

For a moment Gene was paralyzed, then he was goaded into action. "I can handle it!" He squeezed her hand once more to give her assurance. Like an athlete, he bolted from the car, slamming and locking the door behind him. He knocked one woman down as he opened the door to the driver's seat, shoving the chauffeur aside.

Behind the large wheel, he started to move the limousine, using its large bumper as a people-prodder. Faced with a slow-moving car, the crowd parted, as police joined the effort to clear a path. It worked. Through his rear-view mirror, he could see Rose's tense face as she perched nervously on the edge of the seat, her hand at her throat as if gasping for breath.

As the sedan turned east on Washington Boulevard, he swallowed hard. An angry mob had formed there in front of TV cameras. With her cowgirl hat, Hazel stood out in the crowd. She'd been summoned to the bandstand so early she'd grabbed her hat, but hadn't changed out of her morning robe.

"She's planned it this way!" Rose shouted through the screen. "Look at those cameras. Don't run over her. That bitch wants to be a martyr."

Backed by a phalanx of protesting tenants, Hazel stretched out her arms like a giant bird, defying the sedan to run over her.

He braked the car as his mind whirled. A dark impulse came over him, but he struggled with it. One part of his brain wanted to step on the accelerator and plunge the limousine into the blockage of women.

Siren wailing, a squad car carrying Biff pulled up near the intersection. The chief got out and grabbed a loudspeaker, shouting for the rapidly swelling crowds to stand back. On Biff's orders, two policemen tried to restrain Hazel. But her own booming voice competed with the amplified shouts of the chief.

Hazel broke free of the policemen and ran to storm the limousine. Another policeman grabbed her and they tangled, a mass of arms and legs, until the overweight woman lost her balance, falling back into the bay of the fountain that stood in the center of the square. The event was recorded by TV cameras.

Two of her campaign workers pulled the screaming warhorse out of the water. To Gene, a wet Hazel was an even more formidable presence, as she stood hatless before Biff, threatening him with hell and damnation.

Meanwhile, a mob had moved in on the limousine from the rear, surging against the car. Threatening hands balled into fists reached out to pound the car. Rose opened the window in the limousine's divider, clutching Gene's hand. The sedan shook violently. He sensed at once what was happening. About twenty protesters tried to overturn the heavy limousine.

Protected by glass for the moment, he felt the mood of the crowd. He'd seen mobs like this one before. A breath of violence rained down on them. A smell of blood was in the air.

He had to make snap decisions and he prayed he'd do the right thing. He appeared completely blocked by abandoned cars and demonstrators. Impulsively he opened the door again, slamming its heavy metal against two protesters, knocking them back. A woman tried to slap him but he bashed her face, shoving her down on the cobblestone square.

He signaled Rose to open the door. At first thinking he wanted back in, she raised the lock, only to have him yank her off her delicate perch on the edge of the seat. Realizing what he was doing, she clung to a leather strap, holding on tenaciously, refusing to be pulled into a deadly sea. He broke her grip. "No, no!" she screamed at him. "Let me go!"

He pulled her anyway. Up close and out on the square, she clawed at his face with a fury, a sharp red nail digging into his forehead.

Ripping his jacket off, he covered her head and completely blinding her vision, carried her in the direction of Biff's waiting squad car. Past the fountain where Hazel had fallen, he looked back just in time to see the limousine overturned, making a crunching thud on the sidewalk. The chauffeur was still trapped in the front seat.

Elderly bystanders from the apartment houses were shoved aside as two young men broke through a barrier of blue-helmeted policemen. Both carried containers of gasoline. One long-haired boy fell down on the cobblestones, dropping his can. A policeman delivered chopping strokes to his head. In a stupor, the boy crawled toward the fountain, protecting his skull with his bare hands.

Gene winced as the other kid tossed gasoline on the limousine. By the time two policemen reached the boy with their flailing nightsticks, he'd covered the overturned hood. The boy was grabbed, screaming and crying as the cops leaped on him.

Churning feet crushed his toes, as Gene tried to escape with Rose. The attack on the limousine had momentarily diverted the attention of the demonstrators, who seemed carried away more with the symbol than the actual target herself. Pushing hard, he crossed the tidal wave of humanity, protecting Rose as best he could. He feared cracked ribs. Globs of spit spattered his face.

Finally, he was able to shove Rose into the back seat of Biff's squad car. He gasped for breath, feeling free of the entangling mess. Just as he looked back, the limousine went up in flames, the chauffeur trying to struggle out through the window. Flames leaped to his uniform, turning him into a human torch. Gene had seen enough.

Rose screamed hysterically, sensing what was happening, although his jacket still covered her head.

Just then, he became aware of a sharp pain that pierced his leg right above the ankle. It throbbed but his concern was for her. "You okay?"

"Get me out of here!"

In the background, Biff and his men struggled to keep the crowd from the flaming limousine.

The driver of the squad car turned on the flashing dome light and siren. The people in front of them instinctively moved out of their way. A pathway was cleared. Onlookers screamed and trampled each other as they fled in all directions before the onrushing car. The wail of firetrucks rushing to the scene could be heard in the distance.

He crushed his eyes shut, hoping the stabbing pain in his leg would go away.

Crouched down on the seat beside him, Rose pressed tighter and tighter to him. Her lips near his ear, she whispered, "Don't ever leave me...please."

*****

It all started with the sound of bricks pelting the stained-glass windows of a synagogue at the opposite end of the square. The parade down Washington Boulevard was already under way.

In the vanguard marched about two hundred blue-collar workers, all of whom were said to be jobless. They'd been protesting to the city for months about their plight, but to no avail. The retiring mayor had promised them construction jobs on Rose's new charismatic center.

Following them were about thirty white-robed members of the local chapter of the Ku Klux Klan, some of whom carried large placards proclaiming JEWS BEWARE.

Goose-stepping behind them paraded about forty marchers of the American Nazi Party, dressed in khaki uniforms and supporting swastika insignias. At the sight of these arrogant marchers, a roar of loud boos rose from the sidewalk.

Coming from the opposite side of the mall was a group of about two hundred Jewish women and men, led by Hazel.

"Stand back," a policeman cautioned Susan.

"Like hell!" she said, jerking his arm away. "I'm getting a picture of this." She reached for her camera.

Biff had ordered about thirty policemen to cordon off the Jewish marchers so as to allow the coven of Nazis to pass through and into the bandshell.

And then it happened—a full-fledged riot. Susan was caught in the middle. Bottles filled with ammonia were hurled from upper windows of the decaying apartment houses. She ducked for cover, not knowing what was happening.

People ran and screamed, tearing through the trees of the park, as huge tear-gas canisters seemed to crash around them, filling the air with an acrid smell. A phalanx of police advanced, swatting at crumpled figures. Large street-cleaning trucks swept toward the crowd, spraying more tear gas.

New police reinforcement came out of the park, armed with plastic riot shields to ward off a rain of brick and bottle missiles. Metal-studded clubs flayed the air. Fist fights broke out. The cries of *Sieg Heil* pierced the dying morning.

The crowd of young men Susan had seen earlier in the park advanced against the elderly Jews on the sidewalk, tossing the bricks, coke bottles and firecrackers they'd stockpiled in the arsenal. They broke through the police lines formed to protect the spectators.

One policeman, hit in the head by a flying brick, fell to the ground as another mounted cop accidentally ran over his squirming body.

Her eyes smarting from tear gas, Susan jumped back as another squad of police charged up to the scene. Loudspeakers urged the mob to clear the streets.

Hustled and shoved, she tried to breathe through her mouth. She made her way through the surging crowd and climbed the steps of an old apartment building, stopping on the second-floor landing where a door stood open. The tiny efficiency was abandoned. She entered the ill-kept rooms that smelled of mildew, heading for a tiny open-air terrace to get a better view of the riot.

Ambulance sirens screamed and she shuddered at the wailing moan. She felt she was choking to death. Closing her eyes in agony, she became aware of a throbbing pain in her left shoulder, not having noticed it before. She must have been hit, and didn't even know it. Mucus smeared her face. She ripped open her blouse to inspect the wound. With a handkerchief, she tried to stop the blood, apparently caused by a piece of flying glass.

Down below mobs roamed the streets. Plate-glass windows were smashed. Bricks were thrown into hotel rooms. Trash cans were turned over and set on fire. Fire engines fought for space with the ambulances. Missiles were hurled through the air.

In the distance, above the roar of the clashing crowd, large white crosses were set on fire in the bandshell—the smoke rising, billowing, curling ominously against the noonday sun.

She'd stayed long enough, and now had to get back to her condo. She needed a doctor.

Leaving the building, she ran in the direction of her car. Blood soaked through her blouse. She came to a stop about a block from the riot, which had shifted to the far side of the park. Sirens still wailed, loudspeakers boomed, but there was a new sound—that of gunfire. Her eyes smarted from tear gas.

From one of the smashed store windows at the far end of Washington Boulevard, five young men dressed as U.S. marines piled out onto the street, armed with stolen clothing.

She tried to take a picture of the looters, but they fled too quickly in the other direction.

She finally managed to reach the car fifteen blocks away. Across the causeway she drove as fast as she could, the fresh sea air momentarily reviving her.

At one point, blackness swirled around her, and she careened dangerously into the other lane, narrowly missing an oncoming car. Then she came to again and was clear-headed. To the left she could see the news tower of the Examiner rising in the distance. In the old days she'd be on her way there to file a story, whether bloody or not. But that paper had been taken away from Buck. She looked on the far horizon for the building housing the Okeechobee News. But it had no tower.

For one brief moment, she thought of rushing into the News building, announcing to the staff that she was the publisher, and sitting down and banging out a story for the next edition. But that seemed like something done only in the movies. She had to make it back to the condo. There she'd demand that Don get a doctor for her, although most doctors in Okeechobee were probably busy right now.

Back in the safety of her condo, she'd have time to collapse, giving in to her nerves and the awful memories.

*****

Her tensions had come visibly to the surface. Gene had noticed the wild, jerky rhythms of her speech. He'd comforted her. He was a much stronger personality than she'd thought at first. Originally Rose had seen him as a lovesick fan. After his rescuing her in the demonstration, she'd come to look upon him as much more of a man, a person she could depend upon.

He would soon learn that her passion matched her beauty. At first he'd been reluctant, but she'd gotten him to remove his trousers. She had dismissed the maid, preferring to help him soak his foot herself. Her hands had moved gently, yet hungrily, along his perfect leg. She'd massaged the muscled calf until he'd winced in pain. She'd eased his foot into hot, salted water, and with a soapy sponge she'd washed some blood off his kneecap where he suffered a cut.

Finding a terrycloth robe for him, she'd kissed him lightly on the forehead and invited him to sleep until tonight when she'd asked him to accompany her to her temple for the showing of a special film.

In the early evening she was so eager to be with him again she wanted to tiptoe to her guest room and wake him up. The night air was warm and she'd refused to take all calls or to listen to any more disaster reports about the rioting on South Beach. She'd been interested in only one news item. Hazel had been badly bruised, but at least she hadn't been seriously injured. Rose feared Hazel would gain much mileage from today's event, especially when newsreel footage of her was flashed across the nation's TV screens. "God damn it," Rose said out loud. "The bitch always manages to make herself the victim!"

Through a picture window, she noticed the water around her yacht appeared turbulent. Waves from the bay came crashing into shore. Bathed in an eerie white light, *Rose II*, her cruiser, looked like the vessel to sail to an adventurous escape. Right this minute, instead of attending film ceremonies, she wanted to go on that craft and run away with Gene somewhere—to some romantic place, like Buck's island had been.

She'd been wrong. Too ambitious. Misled. She'd been promised glory by Calder, but all she encountered was humiliation. Her enemies were growing by the hour. She wanted love, yet found only hate.

Just then, a sliding panel of glass opened and Gene came out onto the patio. In the background, classical music played.

The sight of him, the mere presence of the man, thrilled her. Unlike Calder, who sent her into traps, Gene was her real protector. Calder used her. Gene genuinely cared.

He grew more handsome every time she gazed upon him. Here at last was the man who could make her forget about Buck. The terrycloth robe was open at the neck, revealing his smooth, full chest. She closed her eyes for a moment, experiencing the joy of having clutched his well-muscled arms. Images of the V-outline of his jockey shorts and the promising curve flashed through her mind. A solid, large mound.

She got up slowly and made her way toward him, extending her arms for an embrace. "If it weren't for you, my obit would have been broadcast on tonight's news."

He seemed genuinely embarrassed, both wanting the intimacy of her presence, yet afraid of her at the same time. It was a contradiction she didn't understand. "I wanted to help."

"You did," she said, enjoying the odor of him. He'd sweated heavily in the protest march and still hadn't showered. His breath smelled of sleep, and she found its staleness intoxicating somehow. She wanted to kiss his full lips, settling instead for his cheek and a murmured thanks of appreciation for his rescue. "Can you walk?"

"Yeah, I'll be okay. A light limp—nothing serious."

"Are you able to go with me tonight?" she asked. "If you aren't, I'm calling the whole thing off. I can't face any more mobs unless you're with me."

He leaned closer to her and, in a voice that was a whisper, promised, "I wouldn't let you go out of this house alone."

*****

The Howard family doctor had not been recruited to deal with the many injuries caused by Rose's dedication ceremony. From Coral Shores, he drove over to her condo where he treated her for what turned out to be only a flesh wound with every guarantee of healing soon.

When he woke up, Don was angry at her for having gone to the riot. "You could have been killed. Buck would be furious if he knew you'd gone. You're not even a reporter any more. You didn't need to be there."

There was an urgent message to call Uncle Milty. Before she could dial his number, a messenger arrived in a rose-colored uniform from Rose's temple. Tipping the man, she shut the door and quickly tore open the letter.

"My dear Ms. Howard,

It was with great interest that I learned you were writing a feature about

me to appear in a magazine I've never seen or read, Esquire. I have received word that you called my office for a personal interview. I consistently refuse to give interviews of this sort. I understand the magazine carries nude pictures of women. Or perhaps I'm wrong on that. Perhaps it is Playboy. Do you really think this is a suitable venue for a feature article about me? Even though I am refusing your request for an interview, I do not want to be totally inhospitable. I would like to invite you to a showing of my film at my temple tonight at eight o'clock. Incidentally, congratulations on your marriage to Buck Brooke III. He is such a splendid man I view him as the SECOND COMING. With Christ's blessing,
Sister Rose."

That was one invitation she planned to accept. She quickly dialed Uncle Milty.

The attorney came onto the phone. "I am speaking to the new publisher of the Okeechobee News. You'll take over the paper exactly six weeks from today."

She burst into tears. From the porch balcony, Don heard her crying and rushed to her rescue.

"Oh, my God," he said. "Something's happened to Buck. Give me that phone." When he learned it was a business call from Uncle Milty, he went back to his balcony where he was writing something on lined paper.

After a long talk to Uncle Milty, she joined Don on the balcony to get some sun but mainly to talk about her plans for the News. He seemed distracted and was only half-listening, if that.

As she looked over at him, she realized how impatient he was growing with her bubbly enthusiasm and ambition.

"I don't know what in the hell you want to go to work again for," he said, not disguising the irritation in his voice. "You've got all the money in the world. You're the wife of Buck Brooke III. Isn't that enough? We've got it made. If anything, all of us should devote our time to seeing that Buck is happy and pleased, not off somewhere running some newspaper."

"It's important to me. I'm no lounge lizard. I want to do something with my life. Don't you want to do something with your life other than lie in the sun and work out to keep your magnificent body in shape?"

"I think being part of Buck's extended family is all the career we need. We shouldn't hold down jobs. We should be free at all times in case he should call us and need us for something."

"I have a slightly loftier ambition than that."

He said nothing but resumed writing his message. Finally, he got up from his chaise longue. "I've got to send this urgent message to Buck from both of us. After all, he's arriving in Geneva to face a dying grandfather, and he's all alone. He's going to need all the support he can get from the folks waiting for him back home." He politely excused himself and headed inside. "Send my love, too," she called out to Don who was already heading for the door. He obviously didn't want to send his private message from within the condo.

At the persistent ringing of her phone, she reluctantly got up to answer it. It was Don.

"Guess what?"

"I'm all ears," she said.

"The world's most spectacular sports car just arrived downstairs for me. It's red. My favorite color in cars. It's the prettiest thing I ever feasted my eyes on. I can't wait to try it out. I'm going to go for a spin up the beach. I'll be back in a couple of hours."

"Did you buy it?"

"It's a gift. There was no card with it—nothing. Just a gift. Maybe from a secret admirer. It's amazing. It was only hours ago, it seems, that I mentioned to Buck I wanted a car like this one day. Now it's on our doorstep."

"I'm sure you earned it." She put down the phone and returned to the balcony.

She sighed and lay back on her own chaise longue, absorbing the sun. Her wound still hurt. She thanked God for giving her the new position on the News. Once when she was very young, she thought she could have love, money, and power. Today she knew differently. You could have sex, money, and power.

*****

"Your buddy Barry is going to be in deep shit if he doesn't give in to Pamela's demands," Leroy was telling Gene as they sat on his balcony overlooking the city. Gene had secretly left Paradise Shores for a hasty retreat to his condo before escorting Sister Rose to her temple tonight.

Even though excluded from Buck's "court," Gene felt more

privileged than ever. Only days ago he'd been totally disgraced and shunned in his own city where he used to be a tennis champion and hero. Now he felt like an insider. He was not only privy to what Leroy was doing in blackmailing Calder and Barry, he was also an insider in Barry's own home. Best of all, only hours ago, he'd moved into Sister Rose's own special world and had become her protector.

Lost in his own reverie, he wasn't really listening to Barry until he said something that caught his attention. "Pamela's in Key West. She's staying at the Pier House. Registered under the name of Barbara Bennett. Susan Howard conducted the interview and I filmed it."

"Just what revelations did Pamela make?" Gene asked. "I understand she's got the goods on Calder and Barry."

"I thought so too. But after watching my own film, I'm not so sure. She makes a lot of accusations. She even implicates Calder in the killing of my old pal, Terry Drummond. But at no point does she produce a smoking gun."

"I suspected that Barry and Calder, especially Calder, were too smart to provide any road maps to Pamela of their dirty deeds."

"After hearing all her revelations, I'm not sure Barry was actually involved in any of those dirty deeds. He comes off clean as a hound's tooth. The only thing she'd got him on is the gay thing. Of course, that's enough to destroy him. She doesn't need anything else. But it's amazing how she couldn't really nail Calder on anything. She's got plenty of suspicions, but that's about it."

"I think she was too drunk most of the time to know what was going on."

"Susan was real disappointed with the interview. She didn't think she could broadcast much of it. Libel, you know. Even though Pamela bombed, I'm not letting Calder know that. I'm using my possession of the film to tighten the noose around him. I've already informed Calder I have this film. I'm demanding full payment of my five million within forty-eight hours—or else!"

"Or else what?"

"I go public."

"I think you've put yourself at great risk here. Calder will strike back at you. Knowing you have this film will make him move a lot faster."

"Move a lot faster toward getting me that five million so we can get the hell out of here. California here we come. Before slamming down the phone on me, Calder more or less told me that Sister Rose is right on the verge of agreeing to put up the entire five million herself. That is, if she doesn't get killed in one of the God damn riots she keeps stirring up. That is one world class hatemonger. Don't you agree?"

"I don't agree at all. She's got some hidden purpose I think. I don't understand it right now. But in time she'll reveal it to us."

"I think she's on some rich Arab's payroll. That's all the hidden purpose she's got."

"I don't want to talk about it." Gene had decided that he wasn't going to let Leroy know he'd become Sister Rose's bodyguard.

Leroy reached over and put his hand on Gene's knee. Gene backed away. "Don't worry," Leroy said. "I'm not into sex. I've got too much on my mind right now. Namely five-million dollars. I'm not sure I truly understand how much buying power five million is, but I'm going to find out. You'll help me spend it, right?"

"Sure thing," Gene said vaguely, getting up and heading inside. "I want to see Sandy and Jill. I haven't seen much of them lately. I want to find out if they got enrolled in that hotel training program."

"Don't worry about me," Leroy said. "I've got plenty to do. It's still early enough in California for me to make some calls to realtors. I've got to find a house for us or perhaps a condo. Right now I can't decide on Palm Springs or Beverly Hills. Do you have a choice?"

"Palm Springs," Gene said, heading for the door. "I always liked the desert." He looked back at Leroy only once. A strange feeling of impending doom came over Gene. Eager to see Jill and Sandy, he dismissed his own fears and headed for his own condo.

Gene hugged both Jill and Sandy before sitting down on the sofa in his living room in the same place he'd surprisingly encountered Susan. Jill brought him a beer, as Sandy snuggled in his arms. "We've missed you," Sandy said. "Can't you come home tonight?"

"I'll try," Gene said non-committally. Actually he couldn't bring himself to tell this loving, trusting boy that he'd fallen in love with Robert Dante. That was also some news he'd kept from Leroy.

After escorting Rose to the temple tonight, he planned to sneak off and meet Robert on Buck's private island. Robert had left Buck's home and was now temporarily living there. Gene had paid a retired policeman to bring his boat up from Fort Lauderdale. His small boat was waiting for him at a marina in Okeechobee. Even though Sandy was cradling up to him, Gene was thinking of Robert and how eager he was to join him on that island. Buck's private retreat would be a safe haven from all the black winds blowing through Okeechobee.

Jill sat down across from Gene and Sandy. "Thanks to you," she said, "we're in hotel training. In spite of all the shit going on, we're finally trying to make something of ourselves."

"I'm so happy to hear that," Gene said.

Sandy looked up at him. "When your main concern is where you're going to find money to eat that day or will there be a roof over your head that night, you don't exactly have time for training programs."

Gene took his strong arm and pulled the boy closer to him, bending down and kissing Sandy's forehead. Jill didn't seem jealous at all. If anything, she seemed to encourage a sexual relationship between Gene and Sandy. But Gene's feelings toward Sandy weren't sexual. He felt Sandy was like a loving son he'd never had. "If something ever happens to me," Gene said, "I want both of you to promise you'll work real hard and make something out of yourselves."

"Stop all this talk about something happening to you," Jill said. "You're going to live to be a hundred."

"We don't ever want you to leave us," Sandy said. "We're family now—just the three of us. We'll always be together."

"Don't you think this is a bit unconventional?" Gene asked. "The three of us? I don't think this is a family that would win the world's approval."

"Hell!" Jill said. "We'll never get the world's approval. We can kiss that idea good-bye."

"That's right," Sandy said. "We've created our own family."

"It's really strange how the three of us came together," Gene said. "It's so bizarre."

"I liked your former wife," Jill said. "She seemed real nice. I guess I can understand why you married her."

"I'm glad you do," Gene said. "I never figured it out. I could understand why I married her. What I can't understand is why she married me. Right from the beginning, we were so wrong for each other."

"I liked her too," Sandy said. "She was real nice to me."

Gene kissed Sandy again on the forehead, then gently moved out from under his body and went over to a desk. "I'm going to finish this beer and write a letter. I know you don't want to hear again that something might happen to me. But in case it ever does—after all I'm a bodyguard—I want you to take this letter I'm about to write and give it to Susan. Keep it here in a safe place and never open it. Even if I die, never open it. Take it directly to Susan. I want it to be read only by her.

Do you promise that?"

Sandy got up from the sofa and kissed Gene's arm before heading toward the kitchen. Jill got up to join Sandy. Before she did she went over and lightly brushed her lips against Gene's. "Take care, big guy. We don't know what you're up to when you're out at night. We worry about you all the time. We always pray that you'll be safe." She headed for the kitchen.

Gene sat for a minute, listening to the sounds of Jill and Sandy in the kitchen preparing dinner. He wished that he could stay here and have dinner with them, but he had to get back to Sister Rose. He braced himself and began to write a letter to Susan that he hoped she would never read. It was hard for him to write, as his hand was shaking.

What he didn't tell Jill and Sandy, what he couldn't confide in anyone, was that dark visions increasingly were taking over his mind. He felt he was a good and loving man, and that was the side of him he wanted to encourage to come alive even more. But he knew there was a deeper and darker side fighting to come to the surface. He tried to keep that side of himself buried. But it seemed to grow stronger each day. How long he could keep it buried inside him he didn't know. It was the greatest fear of his life.

*****

Hundreds of demonstrators had gathered in front of Rose's temple. Susan was able to pass between the police barricades and into the main lobby where a press ticket awaited her. Through the glass doors of the temple's lobby, she stood in horror watching the cops fighting back, kicking and punching some members of the Jewish Defense League. Some protesters carried placards denouncing Rose. Members of her temple tried to rip these placards to pieces. At first Susan feared the surging demonstrators would break through the glass doors of the lobby. Police efforts to hold them back were successful. The glass doors withstood the stones hurled at them by youths.

She'd been assigned a luxuriously upholstered seat near the front of the temple, and was almost the last to arrive. Every chair was full. There was a hushed stillness—no shuffling of feet, no rustling of paper.

She estimated that at least two-hundred members of the press— many sent down from New York—were in the audience. She looked for Barry Collins, but didn't see him. He had wisely chosen not to attend. The rest of the audience was composed mainly of young people and lots of middle-aged women.

She experienced a cozy feeling locked away inside the auditorium, ostensibly safe from the angry mob that had formed outside. It was womb-like, the perfect forum from which Sister Rose could give voice to her own paranoid visions of the world outside—a place ruled by dark, malign forces which she tried to defeat. In listening to broadcasts of Sister Rose's sermons, Susan knew how hard it must be for some of her followers to make those distinctions between fantasy and reality. As irrational as she could often be, Sister Rose was a powerful tool of leadership, compulsively persuasive about the conspiracies against her.

The lights dimmed. Any minute Susan expected a spot to be turned on Sister Rose as she made her welcoming address. Instead, fake stars went on overhead, bathing the temple in a rosy glow. A wide screen was lowered.

When it was fully in position, the sound of Sister Rose's melodious voice was beamed over the speakers. "I have just come from Palestine," the voice claimed. "The dust of that glory road of Jesus is still on my weary feet. I have gone there hoping to find peace as I walked in the footsteps of the Lord." She paused for a long moment before going on. Her voice seemed more strained when she spoke again. "What I found instead was unbelievable suffering and injustice. I'll let tonight's film speak for itself. Thank you good people for coming. I just ask that you view what you're about to see with an open mind."

Before a large boulder in some mysterious desert, Sister Rose's face flashed on the screen in full color. The desert light seemed to illuminate her bone structure, giving her a finely chiseled look. Her deep-set eyes, her soft and sensual lips, and her free-flowing auburn hair brought an aura of enchantment to her. Susan realized at once what a fascinating screen personality Sister Rose could have been if she hadn't become an evangelist instead. Sister Rose, not Susan Howard, was the real movie star Susan Hayward, or at least a viable replacement.

Ten minutes into the film, Susan knew the audience was witnessing a powerful, convincing documentary. It was a brilliant plea for the Palestinian inhabitants and their struggles for their ancient homeland. The film had obviously been made at great cost and with the most skilled of technicians.

Just as she watched donkeys and oxen pull plows to cultivate terraced hillsides, it came. From the back of the temple, a shattering blast. A burst of flame shot through the air, cascading into the temple's auditorium.

Stunned seconds passed before she sensed what had happened. The audience, too, remained quiet for those deadening seconds. Then an eruption of sounds and movement. Screams resounded through the auditorium as panic swept through the spectators. A wild, mad dash had begun for all available exits.

Joining in this stampede, she tried to protect her injured shoulder as best she could.

People cried out. Families were divided. Angry shouts filled the air.

Once she'd escaped to the parking lot, she found the traffic hopeless. Sirens sounded all around her as emergency equipment came in from every direction.

Ambulances converged in front of the temple to haul off the injured. Fire-fighting equipment raced to the scene, along with additional police vehicles.

In the parking lot, cars were hopelessly stalled as motorists, fearing another blast, had rushed from the temple, hoping to escape in their automobiles. Traffic jammed together, nosing and wedging each other into an impossible tangle. Finally, most drivers realized they couldn't pull out of the temple's grounds. They began to abandon their cars, fleeing on foot.

Reporters, photographers, demonstrators, temple members, maintenance men—all staggered from the parking lot. Some had head wounds. Blood ran down the faces of others.

She ran ahead until she reached the top of an artificially created hill on which Sister Rose had mounted a white cross, looking out over her temple gardens, its extensions like protective arms guarding her flock.

Susan felt safe from the driven, scattering people. After being pounded and clubbed by the hysterical mob, she could breathe more easily and was grateful she hadn't been injured or blown away. The fire at the front of the temple appeared to have been brought under control. She wouldn't know how many people were injured until she heard the news broadcast later over television.

Away from the pushing and prodding of the mob, she experienced a calm. She didn't wish to be down there at the scene of the action. Sirens and shouts of the crowd rose up to the hill, but she heard it only distantly.

*****

Gene had not understood what was happening all night. To his surprise, Rose had not wanted to go into the main auditorium of the temple, and had directed him instead to the dressing rooms in the cement cellars below. There he'd met Calder Martin in wraparound sunglasses and a green paisley tie. Although Gene was introduced to Rose's campaign manager, he'd ignored his extended hand, turning to answer an urgently ringing phone.

The atmosphere was charged with tension. Rose seemed as nervous as she had been during the riot on South Beach. In front of her dressing room mirror, she wiped her brow with a tissue, as her makeup ran. "God, it's hot in here."

"Is the air conditioning broken?"

"No," she said faintly. "We had to turn it off. Its noise interfered with the sound of the film." She smiled in a cute, upturned lip fashion. "I'm used to the heat."

At that point her male hairdresser, who introduced himself to Gene as Mister Ralph, came into the room. "Christ, your hair feels perspiry," Mister Ralph told Rose, as he began to make emergency repairs to her hairstyle. She abruptly asked him to leave.

Gene knew a press conference had been called after the screening, and he didn't see why she wouldn't want to look her best.

"Ride up in the elevator with me, won't you?" she asked, her eyes pleading as she reached for his hand.

"Of course," he reassured her. At first he was reluctant to call attention to it, but he finally remarked casually, "Your lipstick's a bit smeared."

"Oh, that," she said, glancing back in the mirror. "I'll repair it on the elevator."

As they stood in front of the elevator bank, she had grown fidgety, her movements and her speech jerky. She sucked in the hot, stale air of the underground vaults and kept swallowing as if she had a lump in her throat.

Then he heard it. A loud blast. "A bomb!" he shouted, instinctively darting for cover. He grabbed her, pressing his body against hers, bracing for another blast.

For some odd reason, she no longer appeared frightened.

"We've got to get out of here!" he yelled in panic, his eyes darting for the nearest emergency exit.

"No, no, it'll be okay," she said reassuringly.

"What in hell do you mean? Another bomb might be set off!"

As the elevator doors opened, she paused in the bright neon lighting from the hall, looking back at him. She reached out for his hand, indicating he was to join her. "I'm sure the police can handle it. Come on, I'm holding that press conference."

In one of the bustling studios of the temple, where she filmed special broadcasts without an audience, two fleeing electricians collided with them. "Come here," she urged Gene, passing a crew throwing color cables over the balcony before rushing out.

A control room engineer reported to her that the blast had gone off in the front and some people had been injured. Right now, no one knew just how many.

"That's a distance of about half a mile from here," she said, showing no concern for the injured. "Show the press in."

"You're calling it off, surely!" the engineer said.

"Like hell!" her face was adamant, fiery hot, as if sparking.

"The press is running like hell," the engineer warned.

"They'll come back," she said calmly. "Let's get started." She turned to Gene, embracing him affectionately and pressing extra hard against him, not caring if she messed up her hair, makeup or gown. "You'll stay with me, won't you?"

"Right beside you." He said nothing else, but there were many questions to ask. He was perplexed and could only hope she knew what she was doing.

A press agent whispered something to her as he took a position near Gene in front of a door. The smell of salted peanuts and peppermint Life Savers on the agent's breath nauseated Gene. He was anxious to get upstairs to see what damage had been done. But Rose wanted it this way, and he'd promised to be at her side.

Suddenly, the door burst open and she rushed into the second studio as if she'd fled from the bombing.

An announcer stood in front of a TV camera, reporting the first news of the blast. Seeing her, he called out, "Sister Rose." Turning back to the camera, he said in a nervous voice, "Ladies and gentlemen, Rose Phillips is in the studio." The announcer extended a hand-held microphone in front of her. "Can you tell us what happened?" Seeing how distraught she looked, he said, "You okay?"

"I'll be fine," she said. In front of the camera, a magic came over her face. Fatigue and nervousness had been replaced with an appealing, charming personality backed up by a beguiling voice. Some other members of the press poured into the studio room.

"The reports are just now coming in about the injured," she said on camera. "At the sound of the first blast, I ran from the main auditorium down a long corridor to the underground cellars. To tell the truth, I thought it was an assassination attempt. I receive daily threats."

Gene noticed more and more members of the press rushing into the studio.

Wavering at first, her voice picked up volume. "I had refused to bow to Zionist pressure and went ahead tonight with plans to show this important film. I made a grave mistake."

"Do you blame the Jewish Defense League?" a reporter shouted.

She ignored him. "I should have know that desperate Zionists would prevent the truth about the Palestinian people and the Palestinian Liberation Organization from being heard. The film, *To Die in Palestine*, presents the heroic and determined struggle of the Palestine people."

Reporters shouted more questions to her as she continued to speak calmly into the cameras. "The Palestinians have had to fight every step of the way in their age-long struggle to free themselves from foreign domination."

Her speech seemed to have been already prepared.

Her voice faltered. "I call upon Christian America to support these people in their struggle. Don't let bomb-tossing Zionist hoodlums destroy freedom in America. Join me in my struggle to bring out the truth about the Palestinians."

Just then, the press agent stepped forward and whispered something into her ear. "Oh, God," she cried out. "No, no, no!"

"What is it?" the announcer inquired, thrusting the microphone at her tired, strained face. "At least ten members of my temple have been killed in the bombing." She buried her face in her hands and broke into hysterical sobbing. The press agent led her away from the announcer, as the camera followed. Nearly stumbling, she was directed back to the second concealed studio.

As he rushed to her side to help her, Gene was overcome with a haunting suspicion. She had known a bomb was set to explode!

*****

Her bedroom was definitely feminine, in shades of pink and white. In the center stood a heart-shaped overscaled bed with a white ruffled and skirted cover. Gene sat on a gilded Louis XV chaise longue of pink satin with white lace pillows, and Rose perched at her Italianate dressing table in painted gilt with a three-way mirror. At the push of a button, the lights could be either harshly realistic or else flattering. In front of him, she switched to the flattering version as she splashed herself with some violet water, her favorite scent. She'd quickly restored her disheveled look and appeared superbly groomed.

"My favorite musical was *Oklahoma*," she told him. "I liked what Aunt Eller tells Laurey, you gotta be hearty, and you gotta be tough. You can't deserve the sweet and tender things in life less'n you're tough. Aunt Eller's words are the code I live by. And from what I know of you, you're the same way."

He hesitated before asking. "Rose, about the bomb?"

She didn't want to hear the rest of the question. Her features appeared contorted before she relaxed again, giving him a plastic smile. "I want the laws of God and the cultural values of man to be vindicated!"

"I do, too." Even though agreeing, he felt a sickening thud in his stomach, as if someone had plowed a fist in his gut. "You said you wanted to accomplish things peacefully. Without violence. Have you changed?"

She stared harshly at her own face in the mirror before gazing up at his reflection. "I know I said that. I was wrong! All those years in the police department must have taught you you can't accomplish some things peacefully." Quickly she got up, walking over and reaching for his hand. She had a way of diverting attention when a subject became too uncontrollable for her. "Let me show you our bathroom." Her voice was jubilant, like that of a little girl sharing a longed-for Christmas gift.

As he trailed her, he was stunned at the use of the word "our."

In her dimly lit bathroom, she pointed with pride at her sunken tub, all in gold and edged by pink roses. During the day it was lit by a skylight. On glass racks rested dozens of bottles of unusual, exotic perfumes. "I think a lady should smell pretty, don't you?"

"No," he answered sharply. "Just fresh and clean. I like unscented deodorant." He left the bath, heading back to her bedroom. Such an intimate setting embarrassed him. He shouldn't have accepted when she'd invited him into her bedroom. Nervously, he glanced around the room, studying one wall of photographs revealing her in triumphant moments of her career.

When she came in, her face indicated no concern at his leaving the bath so abruptly.

"I was surprised you ever came here—all across the country," he said. "I thought you might have settled in Hollywood. Maybe you could have become a movie star."

"Not a chance," she said harshly. "The casting directors out there— I found out the hard way—are usually lesbians. Most of the directors are fags. They like to make women appear burnt out, years older than we are. Of course, I've had plenty of offers."

As she kept talking, she directed him to the moonlit terrace overlooking her garden, where the smell of night-blooming jasmine filled the air. It was a very romantic scene, but for him something was eerily wrong and he didn't know just what it was. Being with her in such a place had been his most cherished moment in all his dreams. Yet now that it actually was happening, he was deeply disturbed to be alone with her.

When the orchestra at the temple played, when her adoring congregation rose up to salute her in prayer and glory, he'd been stunned by her beauty. Her on-stage presence filled him with erotic feelings. It was like a sacramental, sensual pageant. In the temple, he could worship her from a distance. Up close to her, smelling her, he sensed the same defeats, frustrations and failures he'd known. She wished she'd become an actress instead of an evangelist.

"I could have done all the roles Doris Day did," she went on, her face tightening, confirming his suspicion. "Much better than she did, I might add. I think she tricked America with that girl next door image. From reading her memoirs, I detect a very worldly woman there. The reason I've turned down all scripts was because I insisted that my appearance on the screen would have to be witnessing for Christ."

He found that absurd. Before now, her statements had inspired him, carrying a kind of truth. The talk about Doris Day sounded petulant, reeking of a jealousy unworthy of her. He wondered if her appearances at the temple were part of an ingenious theatricality, lacking conviction. She created magic in front of a congregation—that was true—but was it really for Jesus or was it instead cheap showmanship?

She took his hand again, leading him back into her bedroom. Here the lighting—muted and indirect—reminded him of a Hollywood set, strictly Art Deco.

Over the bed, softly lit by pink spots, hung an idealized portrait of her in a long, flowing Grecian gown. In one arm she cradled a dozen white roses—her trademark. Her face turned heavenward, and the artist had captured a look of rapturous joy.

She found the most advantageous spot on her chaise longue. Reaching out, she signaled him to join her.

Reluctantly he did. He was visibly shaken. Her auburn hair was loose and flowing, her white gown opened to reveal the large cleavage of her breasts. In spite of the horror she'd gone through, she appeared calm, not affected by the injuries and death which had been caused—at least indirectly—in her name. She had no remorse, it seemed.

In spite of that, he had to admit she'd never looked more desirable. He sought her eyes, and for a moment was mesmerized by her. Those eyes—so large and inviting—clearly extended an invitation. He fought to blot out the image, picturing his golden tanned body, completely nude, contrasting with her skin, so white and pale it was as creamy as milk glass. Excited by the closeness of her, he was erect, so powerfully he could not conceal it.

Her eyes focusing on his fly, she said, "My, oh my, what do we have here?"

He sweated heavily. Instead of a grown man, he felt like a boy again, the way he'd been when an older woman had tried to seduce him when he was only fourteen years old.

In a low, soft voice she said, "Ever since that first night I saw you on the patio, I've wanted to know what it looks like. Those two little girls know more about you than I do. That doesn't seem fair."

He jerked back, not wanting to believe he'd heard her right. Gently she pulled down his zipper and his penis reared up with a heated desire. She stroked and placated it as it grew more swollen and stretched. She reached deeper into his pants, tickling him, the globes so sensitive, her fingers caused him to wriggle in pleasure. If only she hadn't said what she'd said. If only...

She moved her lips to his mouth and kissed him gently at first. The longer she kissed, the more ferocious her lips and tongue became. "My God, baby," she whispered, breaking away from his mouth to explore his ear with her tongue. One hand still held him, stroking him. "It's so fucking big! Bigger than Buck Brooke's—and that's saying a lot!"

"What...what do you mean by that? You and Buck?"

"That's right, darling," she said, amused. "He is also my lover. Talk about changing partners."

He was astonished. Drawing away from her, he got up from the chaise, trying to stuff himself back into his pants, pulling his rapidly deflating erection down his leg.

"Just a minute," she said, her voice turning angry. "We've got some unfinished business."

"No!" he shouted at her. He sucked in the air as a serene mask came over him. Regardless of what happened—what she said and did—he wouldn't lose control, the way he'd done when he'd wrestled that police woman. Avoiding her eyes, he said, "That'll have to wait till we're married."

"Till when?"

She made it difficult for him. "You know."

"No, I don't know!" The calmer he tried to be, the louder her own voice grew.

"When we're married, it'll be different."

"Married?" she cried out, her mocking, derisive laughter exploding inside his head. "I'd use you for a stud, but not for marriage. That's a joke. So that's why you're holding out? You'd like to marry me, wouldn't you? Live like a king on money I've earned the hard way. No way, *flasher*!"

Hearing that word from Biff had been painful enough. From her, it was the most humiliating, degrading moment of his life. When he looked at her, he didn't like what he saw. She was no goddess, no unattainable angel. There was nothing sacred about her, and in her own bitter frustration she no longer appeared desirable to him. With her legs vulgarly spread apart, her face distorted by her own unrequited passion, she was just another bitch in heat. More revolting to him than Susan had been. At least Susan didn't pretend.

He hated Rose so much he could kill her. That would be too easy for her. He wanted to punish her in some other way, to make her pay for having insulted and attacked him like this. He wanted her to remember this night forever.

She was a killer and she had to pay. The guilty had escaped too long. She was one of them now. He'd thought she was on his side.

"Get out of my house!"

"I'm leaving," he said, zipping up and tucking in his white shirt. He could hardly breathe in this room and the smell of her violet water made him feel ill. He turned to ask one final question.

"What about the Jews? Are you really against them?"

"I couldn't care less."

"Then why do you attack so?"

She smiled enigmatically. "I do what I get paid for. It's show business, baby. Now get out!"

He turned and looked at her once more, though he'd promised himself he wouldn't. "You'll see me again."

"I doubt that!" She headed for the bathroom, slamming the door.

In the foyer he picked up a set of keys the maid had left on a silver tray. Quickly he slipped them into the pocket of his jacket.

He'd be back.

*****

Geneva was a city of international conventions, and Buck never liked to go here. At a time like this, he liked it even less. It was a duty call, one he didn't want to make. With Lars and a security force, he checked into the Hotel des Bergues because he liked the location, at a point where the lake becomes a river. From his bedroom window he could see Rousseau Island in the middle of the water, its towering poplars pushing toward the sky. Quickly he dialed the clinic and, after a short talk with old Buck's doctor, agreed to go there in an hour.

There had been no improvement in his grandfather's condition. As he put down the phone he noticed an envelope being slipped under his door. He rushed over, fumbling with the lock, then threw open the door, even though Lars—asleep in their bedroom—had warned him never to do that. It was too late. The hall was completely empty. Very carefully he picked up the letter, thinking it might contain some sort of explosive. As he held the envelope up to the window, he could clearly see through to its contents, a lone sheet of paper folded over. He tore open the letter.

"My dear Buck,

Thank you for your rather touching concern for Shelley. You are the only person in the world—outside of his mother—who has ever shown any concern for him. After you visit old Buck, Lars will take you to my

villa. But I'm warning you again, it is a different Shelley you'll meet. He truly doesn't want to see you. If you insist on going, you will be hurt. This is my final warning. Far from pursuing Shelley, I wish you'd return to Okeechobee and my arms. I love you desperately,
Rose."

The phone rang. Waking up and still not recovered from jet lag, Lars answered it. "It's the clinic. They want you to come over right away."

"Tell them we're on our way," Buck called from the bathroom. He hurriedly slapped water on his face and brushed his teeth, thankful for this speeded-up activity. That way, he didn't have to think about Shelley any more. If he sat down to brood over Shelley, he might go crazy. If he thought about Robert and Gene, he knew he'd go crazy. He grabbed his jacket and briefcase, gave Lars a quick kiss, and headed for the door. He informed Lars to make arrangements for them to fly to St. Moritz.

*****

For Buck, going to a hospital was like the shot of a surgical needle. In the early afternoon sun, the little Swiss doctor who stood before him smelling of some strange chemical didn't offer much comfort, either.

"When your grandfather checked in, he told me, 'Do what you can for me. Each day life grows a little more precious. I want to hold on as long as possible.' I think this stroke will be fatal. He's in a coma."

"He'll never come out, right?"

"I fear so. You can go in and see him. But if you wanted to have any last words with him, it is too late."

"Can you do anything for him?"

"We might keep him alive for weeks, maybe a month or two. But we fear he'll never come to."

As Buck waited to be shown into the private room, he recalled how the old man had tried to hold onto his life with monkey gland transplants.

"Do you think that will make you any younger?" Buck III had asked.

His grandfather's face had reflected his rising impatience. "When confronted with death and decrepitude, you grab at straws!" he'd snapped bitterly.

Crossing a thick rug in the anteroom, Buck III took a seat in a Queen Anne armchair. The room was uncomfortably chilly to him, and he wished he'd worn a sweater under his thin jacket. His grandfather had always liked cold rooms. "Heat makes old men melt away fast," had been one of his favorite sayings in later years when he'd worked out of refrigerated offices.

Through venetian blinds, a ray of sunlight blinded Buck III. He moved his head slightly, recalling that the old man used to like visitors to sit in what he called the hot seat, the sun glaring into their eyes. His desk was always in semi-darkness, the better to observe his brightly lit subject. Buck III lit a cigarette and crushed it out, not knowing the clinic rules about smoking.

As he waited, he thought of the night the old man had turned the Examiner over to him. "We're all mortal, son. I'm going to make you my successor." That had been a false promise. The Examiner had not been his after all. He knew he'd never be the successor to the old man, and he didn't want to be. In the old man's dying, in his often tawdry life, Buck could find little to respect and admire.

Words from the past kept drifting through his head. "I'm not going to turn my paper over to a playboy, do you hear?" the old man had once shouted at him. "You're going to have to quit running around with every cheap little whore who comes to town, calling herself a model."

"The old codger!" Buck III said to himself. At least Buck III knew he'd never been responsible for the death of another human being, unlike the old man.

"Find a hot little vixen who can satisfy you and settle down," old Buck had told him. "I want to see a lot of little Buck Brookes wandering around Okeechobee one day." Buck III winced and was almost tempted to light another cigarette. If he ever had a son, he wouldn't name him Buck Brooke IV. The memory of the founding father didn't need to stretch any farther.

When he was at last shown into the sick room, the doctor and attending nurse left, leaving him alone with the old man. Buck III had a headache and felt shaky inside.

He had no tears for the old man's condition. A lump filled his throat. His grandfather might live for months in his present coma, but Buck III knew he was already dead.

He felt scared, really scared. He used to think of the old man as some kind of protection for him, somebody to fall back on if it became too rough. Now he knew that had been a myth. Right now he wanted to shake the old man awake. There were so many questions he wanted to ask, but he knew how hopeless that wish was.

A wave of sadness washed over him. He leaned over the old man. His eyes were closed and his mouth formed a large O as he sucked in the chilled air.

As he stood looking, Buck III felt the end of their struggles. No more fights, no more reprimands. For a moment, he was overcome with an enormous surge of loneliness. The silence that had come between them had brought him into sharp focus. Old Buck had tried to make up for the parents Buck had lost, but young Buck had never been a real son to the old man. He'd been a bitter disappointment. He'd failed him by not being a carbon copy.

Buck III stood up, taking one last look at the old man's face. "Dad," he said softly. "I won't be coming to see you any more." He slowly traced the shape of old Buck's almost skeletal head and withered cheek. His grandfather's frail hands were clasped in a tight, fierce grip. His fingernails were blue. Some tiny little noise escaped from his throat. The body was still warm, but that was about it.

Buck III turned away. He couldn't face him any more. Thinking of the old man's turbulent life, he whispered, "Peace at last."

He left the coldness and quietness of the room. He found himself walking faster toward Lars as if in the clinic his life had become suspended and now he must catch up.

*****

After a short flight into St. Moritz, Lars had Buck's luggage transferred into a rented limousine for immediate delivery to the wedding-cake style Palace Hotel. Its V-shaped gimmicks and spires— all architectural frosting—suggested a holiday mood he didn't feel. In the lobby, Cartier of Paris had staged a multi-million dollar display of rubies, sapphires, diamonds, and emeralds. Passing through the salons, amid burnished paneling and beams, Buck overheard women in long, supple silks claiming that diamonds were *declassé*.

After checking into the hotel's most lavish suite with Lars, Buck retired to the marine bar overlooking a glass swimming pool built among rocks and a waterfall. With Lars he sipped champagne as a chaser to his first beer. In an hour, at an agreed upon time, a tall, red-haired, stocky driver came to tell them they were to trail him in their limousine to Rose's estate on the outskirts of the spa.

He'd never seen St. Moritz except in February. Without heavy snows, the resort had a dullness to it he'd never imagined—not at all chic. On his last trip, the temperature was well below zero, and he'd arrived with a French model with glossy hair and perfect teeth. They'd worn technicolored ski outfits with Abominable Snowman boots in yellow and red plastic. That was long ago, a part of his life to which he no longer felt a link. Everything had changed. Today instead of a French model he was pursuing a fourteen-year-old boy.

It was already dark when the sedan reached a large stone wall where a grill gateway was automatically opened, allowing them to enter a graveled circular driveway leading to a large stone mansion. The house appeared cold and foreboding. He couldn't imagine Shelley living here. It was too fortress-like for such a flamboyant boy. It looked like such a formidable pile he could understand why Rose had been attracted to it, as it could offer her protection.

Inside, the place reminded him of a monastery. A woman in a stiff white uniform showed him into a large living room lit by antler chandeliers. Lars waited outside the room in a grand foyer. Though the day was warm, a fire burned brightly. Offered some *Kirschwasser*, Buck refused it.

Nervously he waited for Shelley. In about fifteen minutes, the boy was shown into the living room by the woman attendant. She walked out immediately, leaving Shelley alone with him.

Buck wanted to rush over and take Shelley in his arms, but he feared they were being spied upon. He looked deeply into the boy's eyes. They were cold and distant, obviously not an invitation to an embrace. Buck studied him closely. He wore a simple uniform, like a military cadet. His face was drawn and disconsolate, and he looked gaunt, dangerously thin. His once-lustrous blonde hair seemed just a shade darker. He didn't look himself at all.

At first he didn't seem to recognize Buck. After an awkward silence, he asked hesitantly, "Buck?"

"Yeah, it's me, kid."

Shelley turned from the sight of him and walked to large picture windows opening onto dark mountains. "It's a beautiful night. The skies are so clear this time of year you can see every star in heaven. It's great."

"Sure." He walked over to join Shelley looking out the window. He hadn't remembered him as being so young, at least not this vulnerable looking. The boy's back was held rigidly, and he seemed ill at ease, like a young actor caught in a stage drama unable to recall his lines. Buck asked if they could sit down. Shelley said he wanted to remain standing.

"You okay?" Buck asked, definitely feeling observing eyes from somewhere intruding on what he hoped would be a private moment. "No one's hurt you or anything?"

The boy's gaze swept around the living room. When his eyes looked into Buck's he smiled shyly. It seemed to be an appeal for sympathy and understanding. No longer cocky and arrogant, Shelley's manner was gentle, his voice soft-spoken. "I'm fine. No one's hurt me. I hurt myself the way I was. I've changed, really changed, deep down."

"In so little time?" Buck asked with great suspicion. "I find that hard to believe. How have you changed?"

"I found Jesus." His face remained calm. "All my life I've been looking for someone to love me. Now I've found him."

"Until a few days ago I thought I was that someone to love you. I also thought you loved me. If you didn't, you gave a very convincing act."

"Please," Shelley said, walking away from him. "I'm a fourteen-year-old boy. You're a grown man. You should let me grow up away from you. You should leave me alone. Let me find myself in my own time and in my own way. You shouldn't have done some of the things you did to me. I'm too young. It was taking advantage."

Buck felt his heart beating faster. He couldn't believe this was Shelley speaking. He walked over closer to the boy. In a tiny whisper, he asked, "Is it Calder? Want me to rescue you from this zoo?"

Shelley backed away, his face indicating genuine fear, as if Buck were about to harm him. Buck reached for his arm, but Shelley jerked it away. "It's not Calder," he said in a voice loud and clear enough to bounce off the walls like an echo. "I want to stay here. I want to devote my life to serving Jesus. I want you to go and let me alone. I don't want to play your dirty games."

Moving toward Shelley and at close range, Buck was overcome by an eerie feeling, as he stared deeply into the boy's eyes. This was not Shelley. The boy's clear eyes were almost completely glazed. Shelley didn't appear afraid. The trouble was, he just didn't seem to be anything. Not even a person. Buck wasn't talking to the real Shelley but some brainwashed version. Looking into Shelley's face revealed nothing. It was a pale zombie staring back at him. Shelley's once expressive face and gutsy language were but a distant memory.

"They got to you," Buck said. "I know it. Calder's done a job on you. A very good job. I want my old Shelley back."

"That Shelley left you in the Palm Springs desert." The boy's voice was firm but he averted looking into Buck's eyes. "He's gone forever. He will not come back." Some life came to his face, but it was only momentary. Someone somewhere seemed to direct Shelley and control his movements. Buck felt Shelley was reading from a script handed to him. For one fleeting moment, he almost wanted to smash the boy in the face, hoping that would wake him from this coma. He appeared in a trance, like old Buck lying in the clinic bed in Geneva.

Shelley stood rigidly in front of Buck, as if defying him. "The devil is in you. Your mind is poisoned and perverted. You tried to poison my mind and lure me into your sick perversions. But I was stronger than you. With the Lord's help, I will destroy the evil you bring to the world. I would never do anything to harm you in any way unless you try to move in on me again. Do I have to say it again? I am a fourteen-year-old. Aren't you ashamed of yourself for making me do some of the things you forced me to do? Don't you think it's sick?"

"If I recall, and I do recall, I think you enjoyed it as much as I did and begged for seconds."

"That's disgusting." He stepped back from Buck and looked at him with a hostility he'd never seen in the boy's face before. "You're disgusting. A pervert! A child molester! Have you no shame?"

After those accusations, the attendant appeared in the living room, and Shelley rushed to her arms. "The interview is over, Mr. Brooke," she said. "Won't you please leave? Your chauffeur is waiting."

"Okay, God damn it, I'll leave." He grabbed Shelley from the attendant's arm, forcing the boy to look into his face. "You're in a jail. They've got your mind. I can help."

Shelley's face seemed to crumble before Buck. He screamed out in agony, returning to the attendant's arms to bury his face in her breasts. She stroked his hair. "Please, please," he said to the attendant, "make this dirty, filthy man leave me alone. He wants to molest me."

Buck felt the strong pressure of a hand on his shoulder. It was Lars. "The car is waiting."

Buck stood for a long moment, watching Shelley disappear down a long corridor with the attendant. As he felt Lars's firm hand on his shoulder again, he turned and headed in rapid strides to the front door.

Back in the comfort of the limousine, tears welled in his eyes.

"A message has come into the Palace Hotel from Ahmad," Lars said. "He wants you to fly to Cairo at once."

*****

In his car, Gene drove out of the city heading for the sleazy marina a few miles from town. He couldn't afford to keep his boat moored in the expensive marinas in Okeechobee. In an hour he would be on Buck's private island with Robert in his arms. The air conditioning in his car gave off foul-smelling fumes. Earlier he'd passed a slow-moving vehicle, its lights a hazy yellow in the black Florida night. Otherwise he had the road to himself.

Something struck his windshield and at first he feared it was a bullet. Someone had targeted him for assassination. It was only a gigantic insect or small bird. He couldn't tell. Whatever it was left most of its guts splattered across his windshield. Fumbling for a wiper, he turned on the blades. That only made it worse, the guck blinding his vision.

Just then, he crashed. Slamming on the brakes, he swerved off the road, going into a swampy embankment. The motor died as his wheels spun in the water. Something seemed torn loose in his shoulder when he hit the wheel. He pulled himself up, opening the door and getting out. He had veered off the road after ramming a broken down refrigerator. What idiot would leave a refrigerator in the middle of the road on the darkest night? It looked like it'd fallen off a dump truck.

He looked at his car. Even if he could get it started again, he could never haul it from its hole. There were no phone around to call for help. His breath came in such ragged gasps, it sounded like sobs. He felt utterly frustrated and defeated.

He locked the dead car and headed down the highway walking to the marina. It couldn't be more than an hour's walk. As fast as he could, he headed in rapid strides toward the water, as a sharp pain shot through his shoulder.

As he glided along in the night, picking up as much speed as he could on foot, he imagined an assassin lurking behind every tree along the way.

Once he accidentally kicked a piece of coral. The sound of it hitting the pavement made him duck for cover. Picking himself up again, he moved more cautiously down the road. "Christ, I'm paranoid tonight."

A bird from the swamp swept by with a rush of sound. After that, the only music was the croaking of frogs, which sounded ominous.

*****

On Buck's island, Robert's gentle massaging of his nude shoulder made him feel better every minute. Robert truly had magical hands. When Robert had finished, Gene placed his right hand behind Robert's neck and pulled him close for a long and deep kiss.

"I'm so sorry that happened to you," Robert said, going to get one of Buck's cigars for Gene. "I'll call a tow truck first thing in the morning and get it hauled away and repaired. Better yet, in a few days, I think I'll be able to buy you a new car. I think Buck's going to meet my financial demands."

"He can afford it," Gene said, getting up and walking completely nude to the pool. Henry had retired for the night, and Robert had requested that Gene take off all his clothes while he was here. Robert had modestly retained a pair of white shorts to wear himself.

Gene liked showing off his body before an appreciative audience like Robert. He kept feasting his eyes on one part of Gene's anatomy, and Gene liked that. After that disastrous encounter with Sister Rose, Robert restored his sense of manhood.

Out by Buck's pool, Gene smoked Buck's cigar, enjoying the luxury of this island retreat. Robert had gone into the kitchen to prepare him a light supper.

Gene liked being here enjoying the good life, all the elements that had been handed to Buck on a platter, all the things that had been denied to him. Buck had seriously betrayed him and Robert too. He felt that both he and Robert deserved to be richly rewarded for the suffering Buck had caused them.

Gene had little regret at leaving Okeechobee. The place held bitter memories for him. He wanted out. With the money Buck was going to give Robert, they could go away, perhaps to the Northwest. Gene felt he'd like the wide open wonders of the Northwest. Of course, he'd have to convince Robert that was the place to run to.

He hated leaving Sandy and Jill behind. But in the long run he thought it best if they made a life for themselves. He felt that in time Sandy would outgrow his crush on Gene and develop a full and meaningful life with Jill. He'd always be there for them if they needed him but it would be pointless and unfulfilling to continue a life with just the three of them. There had to be love and passion, or else life wasn't worth living. With Robert he'd found the love and passion he'd sought with Buck. With Buck, it'd been all wrong. Both of them had spent most of their time together in denial of who they actually were and what their true desires were.

With Robert it had been completely different. Robert was open and upfront about his need for sex with Gene. Robert loved every inch of Gene's body, licking it, kissing it, massaging it. Gene had privately cringed when Leroy had done that to him. But he loved it when Robert worshipped his body. Robert's adulation of him was always followed by the same act: a deep penetration of Robert that left him screaming in ecstasy. Gene was thrilled with his sexual power over Robert. What he most loved to hear was how much better he was than Buck at love-making.

Robert came in with the tray of food which Gene devoured, as he was enormously hungry. As he ate, Robert nested at his feet, massaging his legs. "I think you're the most beautiful man I've ever known. Your body is a work of art. It's the body all men want to have and few end up with." He reached for Gene's penis. "And your cock—it's fabulous. It's so much bigger than mine that I'm ashamed."

"This is not a competition, and you're not exactly small."

Robert crawled up Gene's body, fondling and caressing his chest and biting his nipples before coming to his mouth where he tried to find out what Gene's tonsils tasted like. It was then that Gene took two fingers and began a probe of his target for the night. Robert shivered and slammed forward into Gene. It was all too clear what Robert wanted. Not only wanted but desperately needed.

Not wanting to lose body contact with him, he picked Robert up and carried him to the bedroom. Robert's eyes focused onto the thick cock standing tall and fierce as Gene prepared it to enter his newly found love. Robert's tongue nervously flicked out across his lower lip in anticipation of the assault. As Gene moved onto him, Robert lifted his legs, granting Gene complete access. Gene locked his elbows behind Robert's knees and leaned low over his face. He wanted to stare deeply into Robert's face, so he could witness every flinch or grimace Robert experienced as he faced a rough penetration. If Robert screamed that would be music to his ears.

Holding Robert's knees and shoulder in place, Gene entered him, bringing the screams from Robert he so wanted to hear. A paralytic shudder seemed to go through Robert's body before he fully opened himself to the invasion.

There was an otherworldly look in Robert's eyes as he let out a sigh of such satisfaction that Gene knew he'd never heard such emotion expressed in his life. Gene's next strokes were harder, faster, deeper. He changed position, angle, and rhythm as the need arose. As their bodies heaved together, a kind of stunned awe came over Robert's face. Robert's hands clawed at Gene's back, as Robert locked his teeth into Gene's neck. Gene knew the young man's explosion was coming fast. Robert couldn't hold back but Gene could. The feral grunts coming from Robert were but a prelude. Gene didn't plan to withdraw until he brought Robert to at least two orgasms. Sweat dripped from Gene's body onto Robert as he plowed harder and harder.

Robert screamed out again and exploded but Gene refused to let up even though at one point Robert tried to push him away. Robert couldn't stand such intense pressure. Escaping Gene at this point was impossible. Robert was completely pinned down. Gene bent low and started biting Robert's lips. When he drew blood, he licked the taste and continued to bite and suck the blood from Robert's mouth. Gene picked up his ramming speed, and he knew he was going to bring Robert to the top again. This time he was going to go with Robert. His blood tasted so good Gene couldn't hold back forever. The sweetness and smell of Robert goaded him into his best performance. He knew he was causing Robert great pain, particularly by sucking his blood and plunging into him with no mercy, but he also realized by the animal sounds coming from Robert's throat that the young man welcomed the attack. Gene went over the edge, and so did Robert. Again.

In agonized breath, Gene collapsed onto the bed. Robert locked his body against Gene's. Robert was still breathing heavily as he whispered into Gene's ear, "No man ever...no man ever."

*****

"Do you want a woman, sir?" a slender, dark-skinned boy came out from behind a potted palm in full view of the setting sun across the Nile. Buck looked not at the boy but at a member of Lars's security force who kept his hand on the gun in his breast pocket. The fading rays turned the boy's white shirt scarlet, as he fixed purple-black eyes on Buck. More suspicious than ever these days, Buck returned the stare.

Before the question, he'd watched the sun begin its descent across the Nile where a felucca—an ancient craft loaded with water skins—floated beside a barge transporting raw cotton. It was the same falling sun Iknaton had watched.

In the hot, slow breeze, Buck continued to stare at the youth as if he didn't hear the question. The boy had turned to face the sunset which made his eyes an albino-red, like the Nile itself. He faced Buck again. "I said, sir, do you want a woman?"

"I've got my own," he answered before getting up from his peacock chair, heading back to his hotel suite. Lars was already in the suite making arrangements. The boy looked disappointed. Two security guards trailed Buck through the lobby.

In just fifteen minutes, he was due to meet with his former classmate, Ismail Pasha, who'd been named after a 19th-century khedive of Egypt. All rumors, he knew, began in Cairo and, as one of Egypt's leading journalists, Ismail was likely to know more about Rose and Calder than he did. He was amazed that Ismail was aware he'd be in Cairo. Ismail had called him for the meeting. Buck found himself in a strange new world where everybody knew how to get in touch with everybody else.

Buck had heard that Ismail's contacts ranged from Palestinian terrorist groups to Soviet generals. With melancholy satisfaction, Buck smiled at the irony of traveling this far around the world to get some insight into what was happening right in his own hometown.

Ismail was late and that was predictable. When he'd gone to the university with Buck, he even showed up late for the graduation ceremonies. Finally, he did arrive, just half an hour after he was expected. Embracing his longtime friend, Buck called for room service to bring them some mint tea, then he led Ismail to the terrace of his suite. The sun had set. From across the water came a long haunting cry.

"I love this hotel," Buck said to Ismail. "I expect Sydney Greenstreet to appear at any minute, what with all the overhead fans, peacock chairs, and potted palms."

"You're just a colonial," Ismail teased him, "nostalgic for an Egypt that no longer exists."

Over tea back in the suite, the talk was filled with reminiscence, although Buck was impatient for some news of the arrival of Ahmad. At one point, Ismail showed him a picture of a pretty, plump girl he'd married. Buck did his best to offer compliments.

After tea, they smoked a ceremonial cigarette, as Ismail observed him closely. He obviously knew Buck hadn't come here to talk about old times. "Today your hometown made the front page of our little paper in Cairo."

"I know that. The bombing."

"Exactly. Naturally my paper blamed Zionist radicals. Dr. Phillips has been invited to Cairo to show her film here. We are most interested."

A brief anger flared in Buck. "Okay," he said, anxious to get some red meat. "You know that Dr. Phillips and her cohort, Calder Martin, are Arab lobbyists?"

Ismail's eyes lit up. "Don't say that like it's a dirty word. Shall we discuss Jewish lobbyists in your country?"

"Okay," Buck said, gently fearing his impatience had offended an old friend. "What in the fuck does Dr. Phillips want? What is her secret agenda?" A bug crawled across his chair and he swatted it.

The more impatient Buck became, the calmer Ismail appeared. "I think Okeechobee, our old alma mater, is their test city."

"Test?"

At first Ismail looked inscrutable. "From my information, Dr. Phillips has been assigned a major duty—to make the Arabs more heard in the corridors of power in America. An idea whose time has come, if you ask me. As you know, there is great competition for influence over U.S. policy in the Middle East." A fan stirred the dusty air. "I understand that Dr. Phillips proposes to do just that—not by bribing U.S. senators, the usual Jewish method in America—but by creating massive propaganda for the Arab cause. Exposing the rather sickening influence of Jews over American policy."

His words angered Buck, who tried not to show it. He squeezed his arms together, as if insulating himself from Ismail's opinion, the very thing he wanted to learn.

Realizing he'd offended, Ismail asked pointedly, "Won't you admit that American Jews have an extraordinary arsenal in your country? I ask you in all fairness to admit that."

"It's true, but I wouldn't call it an arsenal. That sounds warlike to me. I would say that American Jews are highly politicized, most articulate and well organized. I think they would be stupid if they weren't."

"Perhaps the Arabs have been the stupid ones. Arab Americans have never seriously challenged the Jews in your country. They've been docile for too long."

"I don't know about that. Every Arab American I've known personally aspired to be a rich Republican. That may be changing now. I don't mean to sound racist. I do know one U.S. Senator whose mother was from Lebanon, but he's never come out of the closet with that fact."

"Yes, because the Jewish lobbies in your country have so intimidated Arab Americans they are afraid. Very simply, Martin and Dr. Phillips have proposed to change that repressive climate. To bring about a new day for Arab Americans. Not surprisingly, they have discovered the soft underbelly of the Jew lies in public opinion. Right now, most Americans are for Israel and her interests. But Dr. Phillips knows that, deep down, many good Christians in America secretly resent the Jews. That Christian America just waits for the moment when it will become respectable again to attack the Jew, the way it used to be." He sighed. "Talk about nostalgia. Dr. Phillips, I am convinced, will find many converts. Hatred of Jews is in the bone marrow of many, many people."

"I think you're right. Dr. Phillips is proving that." The ceremonial smoke had not agreed with Buck. He no longer felt a close bond with Ismail. Buck wanted no part of Arab propaganda or anti-Semitism. Crushing his cigarette, he headed for the terrace, trailed by Ismail.

"Do you know, my friend, that in some synagogues in America, they talk not of their God, but of F-15's?" Ismail asked. "Why can't Dr. Phillips talk about jet fighters at her temple, too? The Jews can do it freely, but not Dr. Phillips—without press censor. Is that fair? I always thought you were a reasonable man."

"I am reasonable—or trying to be." Buck found his shoulders straightening involuntarily. "Do you support what Dr. Phillips and Calder Martin are doing?"

"They are paid propagandists—nothing else. They don't believe in our cause, but her backers plan to use Dr. Phillips's beautiful mouth to utter a lot of statements in America that haven't been said. Dr. Phillips can command a great forum. She might start to change American public opinion. It is worth it to her backers to buy that beautiful mouth, which I understand has often been put to other uses."

"I know," Buck said sharply, an airborne blow-job still vivid in his memory.

"Dr. Phillips can say things Arabs can't say," Ismail said.

"What's their next move, or do you have any idea?"

"It depends. Before the backers of Dr. Phillips committed themselves, Dr. Phillips and her friend, Mr. Martin, had to promise to deliver one American city."

"Deliver? That sounds like Okeechobee is being served up on a silver platter. You know, like John the Baptist's head brought to Salome."

"As you wish. Let me ask you a question. Are they having success? Are they delivering?"

Buck thought a minute. "I'm not abreast of the latest developments. Through blackmail and intimidation—whatever, often outright bribery—they are making inroads. Their handpicked candidate is the front-runner for mayor. You surely remember him, Barry Collins?"

Ismail smiled with a smug satisfaction. "I remember Barry very well. Even better, I remember that beautiful blonde lady he married— Pamela, I think. She was my special prize."

"All of us knew Pamela sometime during those four years—so you weren't alone in that line-up."

"Granted," he said, smiling. "But I still like to recall it."

Buck picked up the train of his thought. "Dr. Phillips is going to found a university with an Arab studies center."

"I know and I applaud that achievement."

"Of course, the Jewish Defense League has been blamed for the bombing. That's stirring up a lot of backlash against the Jews, I'm told. Long-dead feelings of anti-Semitism are aroused." Buck swallowed hard. "Yes, I would say she's having success."

Rolling his eyes, Ismail commiserated briefly. "If Calder Martin and Dr. Phillips gain control of Okeechobee, they'll take their anti-Jewish campaign nationwide. A propaganda blitz, as you call it. They'll blame the Jews for everything. Inflation. World recession. Unemployment. They'll reveal that conspiratorial Jewish lobbies pull the strings of U.S. foreign policy."

"A distant, frightening echo," Buck said. Back in his suite it was dark, so he turned on an exposed bulb overhead. In spite of the heat of the day, the room had a chill to it.

They talked more, but something was gone between them. No longer the young men they used to be, they had different points of view and the past years had formed a deep chasm between them. Both men sensed that and knew it was pointless to talk about it.

Buck was left with a gnawing feeling and some deep regret. He saw the picture more clearly, but he didn't get what he wanted from Ismail. Not that he blamed Ismail. He'd come here hoping for a blueprint from Ismail, a detailed map giving plans and specific dates of launching offenses, as in the D-Day landings. Now he knew it was far more complicated than that. Although Calder and Rose surely had a master plan—after all, they'd have to be mighty convincing to get Arab backers to turn over millions—Buck suspected they shifted strategy daily, as in a war maneuver. As Ismail had pointed out, they struck whenever they found a soft underbelly. Faced with steely resistance, they retreated.

"I must say I've not been completely honest with you," Ismail said. "I have not given you—how do you say in America?—complete disclosure."

"What do you have to disclose?"

Ismail studied him with a certain wry amusement. "You must have found it surprising that I knew how to contact you. After all, your visit to Cairo was rather sudden and hardly announced anywhere."

"I was very curious but was too polite to ask. I realize the Arab world moves in mysterious ways."

"As you know I'm a respected journalist in the Arab world. But I hardly make my living working as a journalist. I arrived at your hotel in a chauffeured car, and I own a sumptuous villa on the outskirts of town."

"I get it. You're on someone's payroll."

"Not just someone. Ahmad Pharaon's payroll."

"I see. What you're telling me is that you know all about my connection with Ahmad.'"

"I do and I want to congratulate you. You could have made no finer choice. Long before you, I used to be Ahmad's boy but I fear he tired of me. At some point Ahmad decided he didn't really like sex with Arab boys. He prefers blonds. In parting, he was incredibly generous. He'll probably be spectacularly generous with you."

"He already has been and he hardly knows me."

"Ahmad has provided well for me. He purchased the villa for me, the chauffeur, everything. He pays me such a ridiculously high salary that I am embarrassed when I go to cash his checks."

"He's a loving, tender man—not at all like his reputation—and I have a passionate interest in him. Of course, his money and power are part of the turn-on. But what would Ahmad be without money and power? That's who he is."

"I miss those tender moments I enjoyed with him. You are one lucky man."

"Thank you. Do you know if I will get to see him soon? I came all this way, and I can hardly wait. When do you think I'll get to see him?"

"My friend," Ismail said, "all you have to do is turn around and he'll be there."

"Yeah, right." In spite of saying that, Buck whirled around.

In back of him stood Ahmad who had silently entered the suite.

Chapter Fifteen

His mind in total disarray, Gene planned to pick up some possessions at Barry's and head over to Leroy's condo. This was an important morning in his life. He was not only quitting the job he'd forced Barry to agree to, but he was telling Leroy later in the day that he wasn't going to California with him and wouldn't be visiting his apartment again. Robert had assured him that they had enough money to keep Jill and Sandy installed in their present condo, and that Gene wouldn't have to depend on Leroy any more.

At the Collins house, he found only Barry. Once again his daughters were gone. Barry lay on a sofa in the living room. He was unshaven and wearing only a pair of jockey shorts. Even though it was still morning, he'd obviously been drinking. Barry just seemed to hang here, as if suspended in space, not knowing what to do, although several campaign appointments had been made for him. He didn't look like any front-runner in the mayoral race. Gene thought how weak Barry appeared compared to the fighting spirit Hazel had shown in the South Beach riot.

Gene wanted to hate—Rose, Barry, the whole filthy mess, certainly Buck Brooke—all part of the Okeechobee dirt that covered his body with slime. He had a special venom reserved for Biff, Calder, Clara, and her daughter, all conspirators against him. But presented with that forlorn look on Barry's face, with its wide and handsome cheekbones, Gene felt a tug of sympathy for his enemy. In spite of what he knew of Barry's private life, a kind of through-it-all innocence still lived in his eyes. His life was about to be ruined, the way Gene's had been. Rose had contributed mightily to Barry's destruction. Gene thought it only a matter of time before both Rose and Calder Martin completely destroyed Barry.

The moment he saw Gene, Barry got up off the sofa and came toward him. "Thank God you're back."

This welcome shocked Gene and immediately aroused suspicion. "I don't get that at all. Every time you get mad at me, you tell me to get the hell out. Unless you're horny. Then I can stay. I've got good news for you. I'm out of here."

Suddenly, Barry's eyes blazed. The stench of liquor was strong on his breath. His steady gaze unsettled Gene. "You don't have to go." The voice was inviting.

Ignoring that—or trying to—Gene headed upstairs for Barry's bedroom where he tossed some clothes in a suitcase.

Barry appeared at the door, holding a glass of liquor in one hand. "Could I ask you something?"

"I don't have time for an interview." Gene stuffed his white shirt over his jeans and two pairs of slacks, then fastened the buckle of his suitcase.

"What happened at Rose's?" Barry asked.

"None of your fucking business."

"I want to know," Barry demanded. "She seemed real taken with you. Now that I'm no longer her lover—God, what a distasteful job—I'm reduced to pimping." His face turned angry. He walked over to the window, tossing his drink, glass and all, into the patio below. The sound of its breaking against the bricks echoed back, the noise like ice cubes tumbling into a bucket. Barry headed back to the living room down below, his sudden departure leaving a rawness in the air.

Gene glanced at his luggage. He looked briefly around the room and headed down the stairs to the living room to face Barry.

Barry had found another glass to fill. He stood looking cloying and extremely shallow. Gene could never imagine him as mayor of Okeechobee, a leader of any kind, but in public he was good at putting on masks.

"You always hated me," Gene said in a most accusatory tone. "More so than any other guy at college, and even then I had a lot of enemies."

Barry poured a drink for Gene before walking over in a bold stride. Gene accepted the liquor. He needed something strong and, even though it burned his throat going down, he welcomed the stinging sensation. His guts were already on fire.

"You're right. I rejected you as loudly as I could. I let all our college friends know how filthy I thought you were. How disgusting! How abnormal! What you did to wreck the life of that little girl."

Gene was tempted to bash Barry in the mouth. But his piercing, unvarnished statements seemed to hold him in a paralyzed amazement.

"I didn't really feel such hatred against you. I felt that by attacking you I'd thrown the wolves off my own dirty scent. You exposed yourself to that little girl. I did much worse with little boys. Much worse." Barry's eyes and mouth twisted in pain. No more than two feet from Gene's face, he looked deeply into Gene's eyes. "You know, I hated you when you blackmailed your way in here. I hated you for having power over me, just as I hate Rose and Calder now for having even more power, just as I hate Pamela for all her threats. I've never been able to lead my own life, do what I want to do. Everybody is trying to control me, direct the action. With you it's been different." His voice slowed down, his face restored to some calm. "I love you now."

"What about Robert Dante?"

"How do you know about Robert?"

"On one drunken night Pamela told me," Gene said. That was a lie but he could tell from the look on Barry's face that he believed him.

"Robert's okay," Barry said nonchalantly. "In fact, I've asked him to come back to work for me."

"What about Buck?"

"In case you don't know this, Buck has found other interests. He's dumping Robert. I wouldn't mind having Robert for myself. Robert is the kind of guy who's convenient to have around. He's into body worship. As you know, I have a great physique except for my cock. But I'm real good looking and beautifully built. I guess that was enough for Robert. But for real sex, I need to turn to a guy like you."

Gene sighed. He couldn't deal with Barry any more. First, Rose. Now, Barry. It had all been too much. He had to get out.

In the hall he heard a phone ringing. After Barry answered it, his voice became very agitated. Gene went back upstairs to retrieve a belt he'd left behind. By the time he had come back into the living room, Barry had slammed down the phone.

"It was Calder. He's hot on the trail of Pamela. Rose demands a meeting with her, and we don't know where the bitch is. We tracked her to Marathon. She stayed in a motel there. She's checked out and is probably on her way to Key West if she's not there already."

"What are you going to do with her if you find her?"

"Bring her back. Have a meeting with Rose. Listen to Pamela's demands. Shut her up any way we can."

"Any way?"

"I don't mean have her killed if that's what you're getting at. Even Calder isn't that big of a fool."

"What if she goes to the press?"

"In that case, I'm fucked. But I suspected I'm already fucked with Calder's boys. Pamela has helped destroy me."

"You had something to do with your own self-destruction."

Barry looked at him with a raised eyebrow. "That too. Maybe Pamela can be pulled together. We can dry her out in a clinic or something."

"It sounds to me like you're in deep shit."

"I am," Barry said. "This is a bad time for you to be leaving. Why don't you stick around? Even if Robert Dante comes to live here, we can work out some sleeping arrangements. The three of us might become a couple, who knows?"

"No thanks," Gene said, picking up his suitcase and heading for the door.

"Come back," Barry called after him.

Gene slammed the door, racing toward his rented car and Leroy's condo.

He'd called Jill and Sandy earlier but they had already gone to school. He hated not seeing them, but he'd promised all his nights to Robert.

*****

In the quietness of the luxurious suite, Buck cradled Ahmad in his arms, planting tender kisses on his neck. "Don't leave me, guy. I can't stand it," Buck said, whispering in his ear before inserting his tongue which caused Ahmad to squirm beneath him.

"I wasn't gone for that long," Ahmad said, running his fingers through Buck's blond hair and fondling his neck before moving lower to feel the muscles of his strong back.

"It was like an eternity," Buck whispered to him. "You come into my life, you make me fall in love with you, and then you disappear."

"I have secret business I need to take care of from time to time," Ahmad said. "But I will never be away from you for more than a few days at a time."

"That's a promise I'm going to hold you to." Buck leaned forward inserting his mouth over Ahmad's. Ahmad kissed him passionately, his hands traveling lower to fondle Buck's genitals. "Don't tell me," he said, measuring Buck's penis with his delicate fingers, "that I was able to take every inch of that prime U.S. Marine dick."

"You did it and I must say it was the most satisfying fuck of my life, even better than the first one."

"And, poor me, I won't be able to walk for a month."

"You loved every minute of it and after dinner you're going to get it again."

"I can't wait." Ahmad rose unsteadily from the bed. "Let's dress for dinner. I've arranged a private dining room for us at the hotel so we won't be disturbed." He put on a robe and looked down at the nude Buck who'd deliberately removed the sheets so Ahmad could feast on his body. "I want you to do me a favor. In the closet over there you'll find the uniform you wore in the U.S. Marines. I had Lars steal it from the back of your closet in Okeechobee. I want you to wear it for dinner tonight."

"If that is what turns you on, it's great by me. It'll be fun putting it on again."

"I, on the other hand, will wear something different. It'll take me a while to get dressed. I've had the outfit flown in from Paris."

"I'll use the other bathroom and be dressed and ready when you make your appearance."

Before heading for his own dressing room, Ahmad bent over and inserted his tongue under Buck's foreskin. "Why do Arabs and Jews remove one of the most delectable parts of a man? I could spend hours making love to just that part of you."

Buck fondled his head as Ahmad brought even more tingling pleasure to him. "Knowing how much you like it, I'll insist you pay homage to it every day."

Long after he'd showered and dressed in his military outfit, which still fitted perfectly, Buck wandered through the suite waiting for Ahmad to appear. He poured himself a drink and walked to the terrace to enjoy views over the city at night. He always liked hearing the sounds of cities in the Arab world. There was a forlorn, haunting quality to these sounds. They evoked mystery and all the enchantment of Arabian Nights.

He wasn't just playing the hustler with Ahmad. He genuinely loved the man. Who wouldn't love somebody who gave you the greatest sex you'd ever known and bestowed millions of dollars upon request or else just as a spontaneous gift? The sex, the money, the power were all there. Buck was eager to leave Okeechobee behind him and move on to California, except he could never leave Desire for long. He wanted to spend as much time at Desire as he could. No matter where he'd ever live, he knew that nothing would ever compete with the splendor of Desire.

At a sudden movement, he whirled around. Ahmad had transformed himself into a grand lady in a white low-cut gown. Buck looked stunned. Ahmad might be incredibly handsome as a man but as a woman he was one of the world's most stunning beauties—perfectly made up and elegant of stature and bearing, Buck looked upon Ahmad in astonishment. He felt an instant erection growing in his marine trousers. He loved Ahmad as a man but was sexually excited by him as a stunning woman as well. Perhaps he hadn't completely abandoned his love of women.

"I want to rush to you and crush you in my arms," Buck said. "You're beautiful. But I fear I will mar perfection."

"You're very kind. But the perfection stands in front of me. My ultimate sexual fantasy. A U.S. Marine. Six feet two. Blond, blue-eyed, with a muscled body honed to perfection. A true golden boy of the American plain. Not to mention a horse cock with balls to match. You are a gay man's fantasy."

"I want to be your fantasy. Always. I also want the pleasure of escorting you to dinner."

Ahmad planted a gentle kiss on Buck's lips, not wanting to spoil his makeup. He locked his arms with Buck's as they headed for the door.

Over dinner Buck poured out his total rapture at being allowed to live at Desire. "It's a dream place," Buck said. "I'm happiest when I'm there. But I want to be there with you."

"It is the next place where we'll meet," Ahmad promised.

Buck held up his hand to make a point and became aware of the ring Ahmad had given him the first time they'd made love. "I can't thank you enough for this ring." He started to say he loved the ring but wasn't that much into jewelry when he noticed Ahmad signaling one of the waiters. The waiter arrived with a red satin box. Ahmad presented it to Buck. "Go ahead and open it."

Buck smiled at him and opened the lid of the box. Twelve of the world's most stunning rings greeted him. His eyes were dazzled by the stones.

"They are among the rarest and most beautiful stones in the world," Ahmad said. "A king's ransom. I hope you treasure them always."

Buck stammered. "I don't know what to say. Each and every one, more beautiful than the other one. Ahmad, this is too much. You're spoiling me."

"These rings are cold stones." He raised a glass of champagne to toast Buck. "I'd throw them all away for just one taste of that foreskin of yours. I'd give away a sumptuous villa for the aroma of your beautiful butt before I plunge my very skilled tongue into its depths."

"Stop it, you're turning me on, and I need to eat dinner. I'm hungry."

"That type of hunger we can deal with immediately," Ahmad said. "There will be other types of hunger to satisfy later. I've hired the three finest chefs in Egypt to prepare us a special meal tonight. I think you'll enjoy it."

"I'd enjoy a burger and fries if I were with you."

"Aren't you just saying that to flatter an old man who's fallen hopelessly in love for the first time in my entire life?"

"I just made love to you. You answer that."

"I don't think the most skilled hustler in all the world could fake love-making like that. Perhaps I'm kidding myself but I think you're in love with me. Not as much as I'm in love with you. Nobody could be that much in love. But we are in love."

"I'm in love with you. I never expected it to happen. But I'm in love with you like I've never loved anybody else before. With you, it's different. I can't wait until we are in California together. But I bet your place there isn't as grand as Desire."

"That's true. It's not Desire. But I still think you'll be amazed. There's nothing like it in California."

"I'm so sorry to have to be separated."

"I am too. But I must continue to make millions for us. How I make those millions need not concern you."

"I don't even want to know," Buck said.

"However, I have come up with a big favor you can do for me."

"I'd do anything for you."

"I've decided I would miss you less when we're away if I had a replica of you."

"What exactly do you mean?"

"Later tonight, when I have you totally nude, when I've sucked you to your fullest potential and you are rock-hard, I want this young man I know to make a plaster replica of your penis. When I don't have the real thing penetrating me, I will have the mock. Will you agree to model for the mold?"

"Your wish, my command," Buck said. "I'm not exactly shy."

"Good," Ahmad said. "Afterward, I have this photographer I know. I want him to take incredible pictures of your anatomy. Will you agree to pose anyway that I request?"

"Providing it's for your private collection, the answer is yes."

"Good, that's settled. It should be an interesting evening."

"That's the least I can do considering what you've done for me."

"I've done nothing," Ahmad said modestly as the waiter arrived with more champagne.

"Let's list a few things. The Markum estate, for openers. I love it. I've always envied the property. But that was just the hors d'oeuvres. Mandalay. Sun City. The Okeechobee News."

"The Markum property is just a trivia," Ahmad said. "I've known about Sun City for a long time. It's a great investment idea. I've wanted to move in on it for some time. When the call came through from your lawyer, it just goaded me into action. I predict that in our life times an entire city will grow up there. It'll be spectacular. I'll make you the mayor."

"And now I have the Okeechobee News."

"You lost the Examiner."

"I was amply rewarded."

"The News one day will become one of the most important papers in Florida," Ahmad said. "The Examiner will be reduced to a mere house organ for Rose. Believe me, you got the better deal."

"I know I did. Thanks to you."

After the most sumptuous dinner of his entire life was served, Buck decided to bring up the subject of Shelley. At first he didn't dare but Ahmad made him feel so secure and comfortable that he forged ahead. "I've met with Shelley in Rose's villa outside St. Moritz," Buck said.

"Oh, yes, I've been there once or twice but only in February."

"I think Shelley is being held there as a prisoner," Buck said. "He's been brainwashed. I want to get him out of there. Do you know a way?"

"My darling, man, please believe me when I tell you I have the power to abduct the president of the United States. Normally, I don't interfere in the domestic problems between Calder and Rose. But if you want him rescued, you are indeed looking at the right woman."

"You'd do that for me?"

"Of course, I would. But you must not mention a word of this to Rose and Calder. I even have a suggestion where to take him after he's kidnapped."

"I hadn't thought about that."

"Take him to Desire. I'll have him flown to Desire and slipped into the country. No one will know where he is except you, me, and Lars. I'm sure Lars didn't tell you but I have a completely closed off apartment at Desire. Locked away from the rest of the world. I never know if I'll ever have to detain someone. No one can escape from it. No sound can come from it. I'll put Shelley there. If he's been brainwashed, he can become unbrainwashed. I don't know if that's good English."

"It doesn't matter."

"I must warn you. It won't be easy cleansing his mind again. Brainwashed victims don't immediately revert to their old selves, and, even if they do, they're different somehow. I know of such things."

Do you think it'd really work?"

"Oh, please. I don't think you know the kind of woman you're dealing with. Let me show you what power really means in this world." He signaled the waiter to bring Lars in. When Lars came to the door, Ahmad quickly whispered something in his ear. Lars then disappeared. Returning to his seat, Ahmad glanced at his diamond watch. "By this time tomorrow night, Shelley will be at Desire."

"You're amazing. Just amazing."

Ahmad leaned over and kissed him lightly on the lips. "I'm more amazing than you'll ever know. Each day of your life with me will be filled with surprises. Now let's finish our dinner and return to our suite."

At three o'clock in the morning, Buck stood nude on the balcony. Ahmad was asleep. His penis had been cast. He'd been photographed in every position and every way. Even his feet and ears were photographed. He'd enjoyed modeling and showing off for Ahmad. Everything had gone perfectly until Lars had come into the room with a grim look on his face. Buck had put on his robe. Lars had wanted to talk to him privately.

In the living room, Lars had confronted Buck. "Your grandfather passed into Valhalla an hour ago. He died in his sleep. No pain. No suffering."

Buck had stumbled toward the balcony. He both loved and hated the old man. He'd burst into uncontrollable sobbing. Lars had comforted him.

As Buck stood looking at the city where night was dying and morning was on its way, he felt the presence of Ahmad behind him. Ahmad put his arms around Buck and held him closely. "I've made arrangements for you to fly to Geneva in the morning. You can claim the body and bring it back to Florida on your plane for a proper burial."

"Thanks, Ahmad. I don't know what to say. I didn't think his death would affect me this way. But I feel all torn up inside."

"He was your shelter and refuge for years even if you refused to admit that. He is gone now. You have a new protector. I will keep you from all harm."

Buck leaned back, pressing himself into Ahmad. "I need you now more than ever."

*****

When Gene entered Leroy's condo, nothing appeared in disarray. But there was, nonetheless, an ominous foreboding. The doors leading to the terrace were open so he walked outside in the hot air, feeling he might find Leroy here. The birds that nested in the gardens below were unbelievably noisy.

The time had come to say good-bye to Leroy. Gene would be a free man at last. He felt Leroy had held him in a kind of sexual bondage and had exploited him with his friends. He'd been their paid sex toy. With Robert, it would all be different.

As he went back into the living room, his stomach felt hollow. Always an instinctive person, he feared he was in some sort of deadly trap. Coming in from the blinding sun, he had to readjust his eyes to the light. Dark shadows filled the room, and he wondered why Leroy had pulled the draperies so early in the day.

Gene was not looking forward to walking out on Leroy. The thought gave him no joy. Leroy always became sulky if things didn't go his way. He wondered if the news of Gene's leaving would goad him into some violent act.

His stomach was nervous with anticipation of facing Leroy.

Instead of thinking about Leroy, he found himself remembering Dylan Thomas. The only lines from any poetry he could ever remember, other than nursery rhymes, were by Dylan Thomas: "Do not go gentle into that good night, Rage, rage against the dying of the light."

Gene turned and walked back to the balcony. For some reason, he was delaying going into the bedroom. Leroy was obviously there—no doubt asleep. But Gene didn't want to enter the room. Was the memory that bad? Was having to give in to Leroy's insatiable sexual appetite that repugnant to him?

He returned to the terrace. The yellow sun was so hot it even seemed to prevent sea breezes from providing a welcome relief. The whole place was stifling. He couldn't imagine why Leroy had turned off the air conditioning and opened the doors to the terrace on a hot day like this. In the sky, tendrils of cumulus basked in lazy turnings.

He could postpone it no longer. He headed for the bedroom. If Leroy were asleep, he'd just have to wake him up. He could stay in this apartment no longer. He was smothering here. Life with Leroy would be but a slow death.

Leroy would suck him dry and abandon him for someone else—no doubt in California. When youth was gone, he'd be out the door. He had to build a life with someone real like Robert—not a fake messiah like Sister Rose. She was wanton. The slut of religion.

Silence and emptiness greeted him when he went into the bedroom. Like Elvis, Leroy liked to pull black draperies, shutting out all traces of light when he slept. He couldn't stand the morning sun if he had a headache. Headache or not, Gene was determined to shed some light into the room.

He pulled back the draperies. There on the bed lay a dead Leroy. A wire like a telephone cord was wrapped around his neck. In death, his eyes were open, staring at Gene. His eyes were gaping wide, really pop-eyed, and accusatory. He was completely nude. There was some horrible flesh like raw guts trapped in his mouth. It was a bloody mess.

Slowly Gene's eyes traveled the length of Leroy's body. He knew before he'd even seen the sight what awaited him. Leroy had been completely castrated, his genitals stuffed into his mouth. A pool of blood the size of Brazil had formed on the white sheets on which he lay.

Gene looked back once more into Leroy's face. He could only imagine the whimpers beseeching mercy that must have come from that mouth before the garbled protests were snuffed out by his own body parts.

Gene felt dizzy. In all his years on the police force he'd never encountered such a sight. He'd read about mutilations and murder like this—that was all.

His final memory of Leroy was his right hand gripping a pillow. It was a death grip. The pain must have been unbearable. The grip was ludicrous—and horrible.

Gene looked down at the body on the bed again. Then a miracle seemed to happen. There was no body. The bed was freshly made. Leroy was gone. He was alive and away somewhere tending to the business of the day.

This illusion was only momentary. When he blinked and looked again, Leroy was very much here. He was not only here, he seemed to be staring directly at Gene, as if blaming him for his brutal murder.

The word blame stuck in his brain. It was all too clear to him. He was set up. He was going to be blamed for this murder. His fingerprints were everywhere. Massive evidence. Biff would no doubt make this a gay lovers' quarrel. Gene knew it was but a matter of time before he was arrested for murder. The cops were probably on their way here now.

He walked rapidly toward Leroy's dressing room. He looked inside. All the incriminating evidence—the pictures of Barry and Shelley, the film of Pamela's interview—was gone. Someone had taken everything.

Clutching his side to offer some protection from a pain that seemed to have materialized within the minute, he headed for the front door. He'd lived here. Traces of him were everywhere. He opened the front door with caution. No one was in the hall. In a way he was glad Jill and Sandy were out of the building. How would they respond to the news that a manhunt was on? He knew he'd be targeted as the likely suspect.

He thought of Pamela. Perhaps Leroy was tortured. He knew where Pamela was staying. Was Pamela Calder's next victim? He had to get to her before they got to her. In some vague part of his brain, he felt that Pamela might save him and herself too. She could go public. Not wait for Barry and Calder to give in to her financial demands. The time was long past for that. Only by going public could she save herself, and maybe save him too.

There was no time to tell Robert what had happened. Buck's phone on the island might be tapped. Knowing Calder, no doubt it was. Robert would have to hear the news and trust Gene. Would Robert do that? Gene would have to risk that.

Slipping out the back entrance, he headed at once for his rented car. He didn't want to take a chance at the airport in Okeechobee. Biff's officers might have staked out that airport. He would be immediately recognized. He'd drive to a neighboring town and book a seat on the first flight to Key West.

He had to get to Pamela and get to her soon. Time was running out for both of them.

*****

The plane ride had been smooth from Okeechobee to Miami, and the transfer easy from there to the Key West airport. Once on land, Gene boarded a taxi to take him to Duval Street.

In this end-of-the-line city, the taxi drove through streets crowded with revelers. Key West was filled with bars, character, and a certain mystery just as he'd found it in the days when he'd visited it with Susan. He saw two men, both drunk, leaving a bar arm in arm. In the bright lights of a street lamp, they stopped to kiss long and passionately.

Spotting a flower shop, he asked the taxi driver to let him out there. In the shop he admired some brilliantly orange Birds of Paradise and purchased a large bouquet.

"I really shouldn't tell you this," the sales clerk, a young woman in her twenties said, "but these are from South Africa."

The saleswoman seemed worried about the political correctness of purchasing flowers from South Africa. He couldn't care less.

After purchasing the flowers, he crossed the street to the Pier House where Leroy had told him Pamela was registered under the name of Barbara Bennett. He still had to manage to get her room number.

At the reception desk, he was greeted by a tall, thin man with bleached hair and an ear ring. He smiled and seemed to take an undue interest in Gene. "We're completely full," the young man said, "but I have an extra room at my apartment. It's on William Street nearby." He looked Gene over appreciatively. "It'd be free."

"Thanks," Gene said. "I might take you up on that. But first I've got to deliver these flowers to Barbara Bennett's room. Could you give me her room number?"

"Why don't you leave them with me, and I'll have a member of the staff take them up?"

"This is a little embarrassing," Gene said, leaning over the desk. He rubbed the crotch of his tight and very revealing jeans. "You see, it was more than flowers Ms. Bennett called for. I run this ad."

"Oh," the clerk said brushing back his bleached blond hair. "Do you do only women? What about men?"

"Those are my favorite." He leaned over the desk. "It's real big. We're talking big. Why don't I go to the men's room? Why don't you excuse yourself and join me there? Let me put on a show for you." He winked at the clerk. "After I finish my duties with Ms. Bennett, I'll meet you after work."

"You've got yourself a deal, big boy."

In the men's room, Gene waited for the clerk at the urinal. He was masturbating himself to a full hard-on. In minutes, the clerk had taken the urinal next to him to observe the show. Seeing that the room was empty, he reached over and played with Gene's penis, reaching inside to free his balls. "That's the biggest I've ever seen. I've got to taste it." He leaned over and took the penis in his mouth and was trying to go all the way down on it. At that point, he heard the door open. He jerked up and stood rigidly at the urinal. "I get off at ten," he whispered to Gene. "I'll meet you outside the front door."

"You've got yourself a date."

Before leaving, he turned to Gene. "Ms. Bennett is in room 201."

"Thanks." Gathering his flowers, Gene headed for Pamela's room.

He hurried through the gardens to the back stairs. On the way there he spotted a man racing down the steps. He backed away to conceal himself from view. The man rushed past him. Only when he'd gone did he recognize the man as Julius Forster. Had Calder learned that Pamela was staying at the Pier House and sent Julius Forster to take her back to the mainland? Or had the Nazi not discovered which room she was in? Was he staking out the Pier House and hoping to locate her? Gene had to get to Pamela and quick before any harm came to her.

Upstairs he walked rapidly down the corridor, hearing the sounds of a drunken party and singing. The whole damn town tonight seemed to be humming a tune. Considering his mission, he was out of step with all these festivities.

His plan was to help her escape. But first he'd have to persuade her to listen to him. He knew that if Pamela started to talk, her voice—not his—would be listened to. She was just as much of a victim as he was.

He didn't dare knock at her door. If she knew who it was, she might scream for help, alerting the party-goers next door. Instead he had to figure out a way to force her to listen to him. He was sure he'd be able to convince her he was on her side, that he wanted to help.

She was an emotional and at times, an irrational woman. Maybe he could calm her down.

His slap in the restaurant had been a big mistake. He owed her an apology. Like Barry, she'd been right about Rose. He suspected she'd run from Calder. Somehow she had come to realize how tenuous her position was. In her blackmail attempts of Barry she'd become explosive to Calder's plans.

She was known as a woman who picked up strangers in bars for casual sex in motel rooms. If she were done away with, it would be easy to blame some sex pervert she'd picked up for having murdered her. In fact, Gene wondered, she might have already come to that conclusion.

Such a death, he suspected, would not destroy Barry's chances in the election. If anything, he could play on the sympathy of voters, portraying himself as the innocent victim of a philandering wife—a man who stayed home and watched after the upbringing of his daughters while his alcoholic wife ran out for anonymous sex.

Gene could detect no light coming from her room. Knocking lightly, he muttered, "Housekeeping." Still no answer. He tried the door, finding it unlocked. If she wasn't there, he'd wait for her return, subduing her if he had to—anything to make her listen.

He knew much of what he was doing sounded reckless and everything required more careful planning. But he couldn't come up with a better idea. He'd had no time to think things out at all. He was sure that she would get the point fast.

Opening the door, he softly entered the room, feeling like a rapist. There is always a clue on entering a room. Right away he knew something was wrong. Someone had pulled back the draperies and moonlight streamed in. The room overlooked the water where the Atlantic meets the Gulf of Mexico. No woman hiding would leave draperies open. Seeing that the bed was empty and unmade, he stole across the room and pulled the draperies shut. The room was in pitch blackness.

He switched on a lamp. With an instinct sharpened by all his years on the police force, he was overcome by an eerie feeling deep in his gut. Swirling around, he spotted her.

She lay on the floor beside the bed, her legs tucked up toward her stomach. It was like the classic fetal pose. She wore bikini panties. They were still wet, indicating her death had been recent. In her struggle for life, her right breast had slipped out of a cup of a flowered bra. A white nylon rope had been looped twice around her neck. Her eyes seemed to stare at him, wide, accusatory. Her hands were bunched up near her throat as if she'd clutched the cord cutting off her air supply. He checked her body for pulse, finding her wrist had the coldness of death.

Shaken, he moved fast to turn off the light. This was a set-up and he had to get out of here at once. It already might be too late. He waited at the door. From across the hall came the sound of partying. Cracking the door slightly, he checked the corridor, finding it deserted. As he slipped out, the door from across the hall opened and two men, one supporting the other, staggered out, "This party's dull. Let's go to Tony's."

Gene could tell the eyes of the more sober man sensed something wrong. He shut the door behind him, not wanting to appear panic-stricken. As he did, a burly man came up behind the two guys. "What's going on here? That's a woman's room. A sexy blonde. Not your room. You're a fucking thief!"

Gene turned and fled down the corridor as the burly man shouted after him. It was all too convenient, convincing him he was set up. How had that burly man known he was a thief? He jumped the railing and cut through the garden before the police were summoned.

Cutting off Duval and heading down a side street, he found a taxi and asked to be driven to Stock Island, a seedy backwater adjoining Key West. Here in the garden of a broken-down trailer, he had to figure a way out of all this. A road block might be set up.

He ripped off his jacket and shirt, wearing only a T-shirt. Mussing his hair, he wished it were longer. With a pocket knife he cut off the legs to his pants, making shorts of them.

Later, on the highway, he hitched a ride in a large van with a fat, bearded driver who introduced himself as "Whale Man." Gene took a seat near his stringy-haired girlfriend. They were headed for Pompano Beach. He told them he was going to Fort Lauderdale.

Up the Keys the van rolled, passing seemingly endless bridges. To him, it was like riding with a bunch of god damn freaks, but he knew their language well, pretending to be one of them. He didn't admit it, but suggested he'd run into a problem in Key West peddling drugs. The girlfriend, Allison, offered him a smelly sleeping bag in the rear of the van and he retreated there to avoid conversation. He only pretended to sleep.

They reached Miami just as the Beatles began to pump out "Here Comes the Sun" on the tape deck. After breakfast in a greasy spoon, Whale Man headed up the coast to Fort Lauderdale. Gene was let out five blocks from his secret apartment. He had to go there and change clothes and pick up his weapons before heading back to Okeechobee in his old car which had belonged to his mother. It was parked in the garage at the apartment house, and now he could thank God he'd kept it in good running order.

By the time he reached the apartment, the first light of day streaked the sky.

He pulled off his clothes and headed for the shower, until the whining of two gray cats in the garden below caught his attention. The cats annoyed his neighbors by raiding the garbage, but looked up sorrowfully at him. He felt their hungry, accusatory look resembled the expression trapped in Pamela's dead eyes. He couldn't stand that look. In the kitchen he opened a can of sardines, wrapped them in a thin sheet of newspaper and tossed the soggy mess to the cats.

That would be his last act of kindness. Already his mind spun with plans for the day.

*****

At Desire, Lars led Buck down a long corridor to a distant wing of the property. He inserted a security code, and a steel door opened for him. Lars turned and looked at Buck with trepidation. "Do you want me to go inside with you?"

"I'll be fine." He kissed Lars on the lips.

"He's in there. He certainly didn't want to leave Switzerland. Fought like hell. There are no blunt instruments in the suite. I must inform you. The room is monitored. If you're threatened and placed in danger at any time, my men are coming in."

"He's only a kid. I can handle him."

"Your safety is very important to me."

Buck hugged Lars again and kissed him. "Thanks for always being there for me."

"I want to stay forever," Lars whispered in his ear.

Not looking back, Buck walked down the hallway and into the open-doored suite. At first he couldn't see Shelley in the darkened room. Then he detected a movement in a chair. Shelley sat in a silk-upholstered armchair gazing upon what appeared to be an outdoor scene with vegetation. The vegetation was real but the effect of the outdoors was fake. They were underground.

"Shelley," Buck said tentatively. "Is that you?"

The boy rose to face Buck. He was clad only in the briefest of bikini underwear. He looked thinner than Buck had ever seen him before. "Who do you think it is? John Wayne?"

Buck stood looking at him for a long moment. This was not the Shelley he'd known. How could he be so different and have changed so much in such a short time?

"What are you going to do with me? Why did you kidnap me?"

"I'm going to try to undo whatever has been done to you, and I must confess I don't even know how to begin."

"I know how to begin. Let me go. Get me out of this prison. I promise if you free me, I won't bring kidnapping charges."

"Forget it. It's not going to work that way. I don't even know if you're in control of your own mind."

"I'm fine. I'm a fourteen-year-old kid who wants to go back to where I was. I was safe there. I'm afraid here."

He walked closer to Shelley who backed away, an alarming fear growing in his eyes. "Don't come any closer. I'll scream."

"Go ahead and scream. What good will that do you?"

A look of hopeless despair settled over Shelley's face. Buck walked over and sat down in the chair, looking at the vegetation in the fake daylight. "I'm not going to keep you here forever. Just long enough to determine that you're operating on your own free will again."

"I am operating under my own free will, and I want you to let me out of this trap."

"I will in time. But not now."

Shelley came tantalizingly close to Buck who took in the luminous beauty of his body before meeting his eyes. "I've got something to tell you," the boy said. "It's going to blow your mind. You're going to freak out. You won't believe me at first. But you'll believe me enough to investigate what I say. When you do, you'll know I'm telling the truth, and you'll let me go."

"Perhaps so, but I want you to hear me out first. I don't understand you at all. It looked to me like you were in a prison in Switzerland. Here in Florida or in California you could have the glamorous life you've always wanted. I could get it for you. You said you wanted to be a fucking movie star. I'll have the power to get that for you. You won't be imprisoned with me. You'll be a free man. Able to do whatever you want. You'll have all the power and money you've ever wanted. What else can you ask for?"

Shelley looked completely bewildered, as if he hadn't even considered that before.

"What I'm holding out for you is what you've told me you've always wanted," Buck said. "What is there waiting for you in Switzerland?"

Tears welled in Shelley's eyes, as a pathetic look came over his face. "I don't know. I just don't know. I'm confused."

"What's this important thing you have to blow my mind with?"

Shelley hesitated as if words were forming on his lips. The muscles in his face tightened. "It was nothing."

"One minute you're going to tell me something that's going to freak me out. The next minute you clam up."

"I'm sorry. So much has happened so fast."

Buck stood up to face the boy. This time he didn't back away. "I don't want to hurt you." He reached out and rubbed Shelley's smooth cheek with his hand.

The boy was trembling.

"Why are you so afraid of me?" Buck asked.

"I'm afraid you'll hurt me. I know what you're planning to do to me. I know why you brought me here."

"I brought you here to help free your mind. I didn't bring you here to rape you. I wouldn't want you in this frame of mind. If I'm ever with you again in that special way we had—and at this point that's highly doubtful—you will have to come to me and say you want me. I will never force myself on you."

"You're not going to rape me?"

"I'm not going to hurt you ever. But I am going to bring two or three men here to talk to you. I need their professional assurances that you're okay. That nothing has happened to your mind. There may be quite a few sessions. These men are trained to work with brainwashed victims. I hope you'll cooperate."

"You don't have to bring those men here." He moved slightly closer to Buck. "Do you really mean it? You'd take me to Hollywood and everything. I could have money. Everything I've ever wanted."

"Of course. You've got that now. You're already a millionaire. You don't control your fortune yet. But it's waiting there for you when you become of legal age. In the meantime, I'll take care of you and everything you need and want." He paused and looked deeply into Shelley's eyes again. "And I'll ask nothing in return."

Buck turned and walked toward the door.

Shelley called back to him. "Don't go. I'm lonely here."

Buck came back and took Shelley in his arms and hugged him affectionately but not too tightly. He kissed him but only on the neck.

The boy was shaking all over. "I'm afraid. I don't know what to do." He started to cry. Buck attempted to break away but Shelley held on to him.

Buck took his hands and ran his fingers over Shelley's body. This seemed to put the boy at ease.

"Please pick me up and carry me over to that bed," Shelley whispered in his ear. "Let me know how I can please you."

Buck easily picked Shelley up in his arms and carried him to the bed where he gently lowered him onto the mauve sheets. Buck started to raise his body up but Shelley reached out for him, pulling him down on top of his lithe frame.

"Would you put your mouth on mine and kiss me?" Shelley asked.

Gently Buck pressed his lips against Shelley's and kissed him tenderly. But the more Shelley hugged him and the more his fingernails tightened into Buck's back, the more he seemed to want of Buck. It was then that Buck inserted his tongue in the boy's mouth. At first Shelley didn't know what to do with this sudden intrusion. Then he began to suck Buck's tongue and once he started, he didn't want to stop.

Gently Buck ran his hands down Shelley's smooth body, caressing his flesh. Shelley was moaning and clinging to Buck. Shelley took Buck's hand and guided it into his briefs, inserting Buck's fingers inside the elastic band. Buck found the boy fully erect.

Moving away from Shelley's lips, Buck kissed his neck and tongued his ears. Soft moans escaped from Shelley's throat. "Oh, please, please," Shelley said. Buck descended on his sensitive nipples, and Shelley screamed out his pleasure, taking his hand and tugging at Buck's hair. But he was pulling him closer, not pushing him away.

Buck felt Shelley's body trembling as if he were going into convulsion. One hand of Buck's never left the young boy's penis. Buck felt it was ready to explode. He had hardly removed Shelley's bikini briefs and plunged down on him when the boy exploded in his mouth. Buck sucked him voraciously. Long after the eruption ended, he kept the penis in his mouth. At one point when he'd started to withdraw, Shelley grabbed his hair and forced him to stay down on his penis. Buck began to suck voraciously again.

It seemed to go on for fifteen or maybe twenty minutes before Buck was awarded with another explosion. Eventually he pulled himself away from the boy's groin and descended on his mouth again. This time Shelley sought out his tongue to suck. He didn't seem to want to let Buck go but was forcing his body so hard against Buck's that it appeared that he wanted to escape into Buck's body itself instead of merely clinging to him.

"Please take off your shirt and jeans," Shelley whispered into his ear. "I want to see what a real man's body is like. How it looks and feels when it's aroused."

"That's enough for one day, my pet," Buck said. "I had wanted to get back into this thing gradually. There will be no more right now."

Shelley looked disappointed. "But I thought you were going to rape me. I've been preparing for it all morning."

"It's not going to happen—not today."

"Will you come back and sleep with me tonight?"

He looked into Shelley's deep blue eyes. "When the world's prettiest boy makes a request like that, what can I say but yes?"

"I can't wait for you to come back to me." He leaned over and kissed Buck gently on the lips. "I'm still a little bit afraid. You're a very big man. Will it hurt?"

"I won't hurt you. I promise. I will give you only what you ask for—nothing more."

Shelley wrapped his arms around Buck, forcing him down on his mouth again. He pulled up Buck's shirt and felt the muscles of his back before descending lower to fondle Buck's genitals. "You're so big. I want to see you. See everything."

Buck pulled away. "This is going too fast. If you want or need anything, you press this buzzer here. It will be brought to you."

Shelley sat up in bed watching him go. "There's only one thing I want, and he's leaving the room right now."

Buck turned and winked at him. "He'll be back."

*****

After leaving Shelley locked away, Buck called Susan and Don, letting them know he was back in Okeechobee. He eagerly wanted to see both of them but for very different reasons. He invited them to Desire. Instead of arriving in a limousine, Don volunteered to drive Susan over in his new sports car.

"Let's not talk on the phone," Buck said. "You know what we're going to talk about when you get here."

In the library, locked away from the rest of the house, he seated himself before a giant TV screen. Lars propped his feet up on an ottoman, and gently removed his shoes and socks. As Buck watched the news, Lars began to suck his toes as if bathing them. He did this all the time. It was great pleasure for Buck although he couldn't understand why this toe sucking going on for hours brought such joy to Lars. The only toes Buck wanted to suck were Shelley's, because they were so young and tender. The toes on other people didn't turn him on that much.

He knew what the lead story was: the death of Leroy Fitzgerald. Gene was the prime suspect, and a manhunt was on for him. Even with some overwhelming evidence being broadcast, Buck still couldn't bring himself to believe Gene had killed Leroy. Buck suspected—and he couldn't even begin to prove this—that Calder had ordered Leroy killed. The police reports broadcast over television revealed that Leroy's safe had been robbed. Buck could only imagine what was in that safe. Perhaps the interview that Leroy had filmed with Pamela and Susan, certainly the pictures of Barry Collins and Shelley, although

Leroy surely had copies placed elsewhere.

Buck couldn't help but wonder if Gene would make contact with Robert. With the police in hot pursuit of Gene, Buck could only speculate what emotions had surged through Robert. How was he handling this? He feared Robert was placing himself in harm's way. But he couldn't really bring himself to have a confrontation with Robert over Gene.

Impulsively he dialed Robert on the island. Henry picked up the phone. "Hello, Henry. Tell me please—is Robert there?" Buck asked.

"He sure is, but I'll be glad to see you again. Mr. Dante's driving me crazy. I've never seen him so nervous. He's pacing up and down all the time. He keeps asking if Mr. Robinson has called. There ain't been no calls from Mr. Robinson."

In a minute, Robert was on the phone. "What is it?" he asked sharply without a greeting.

"I just wanted you to know that Uncle Milty has made great progress in drawing up our documents. We're prepared to meet all your requests."

"Do you mean that?"

"Of course I do. I not only mean it, but in case something should ever go wrong with you in the future, a financial reversal or whatever, I will always be there for you. Don't be afraid to pick up the phone and call for help."

"My future will be just fine when I get the money you owe me," Robert said. "I won't be calling you again for handouts or for any other reason. By the way, Clara is packing up all my stuff. I'm having it removed from your house and put into storage until I'm sure of my plans."

"Are you still going to start the paper or magazine?"

"Yes, but not here. I don't know what city I plan to launch it in."

"I'd like to help you in some way if you need me."

"When we sign those documents and money is transferred, I can assure you I won't need you ever again. Could we cut this phone call short? I want to keep the line free. I'm expecting an urgent call."

Buck wanted to ask if it were from Gene but didn't dare. "Please do me a favor. You've got to come into town to sign the documents. I've booked you the presidential suite at the Roney Plaza. Uncle Milty will call you and arrange a meeting. I suggest you hire a lawyer. I know Uncle Milty has been your lawyer up until now. But obviously he must represent my interests in this settlement."

"Naturally, you've got all the money. What would Uncle Milty be if not the little Jew?"

"Please don't say that. I thought you always liked him."

"I liked Patrick. I never liked Uncle Milty. He always had a crush on you, and I was jealous of him. Always giving you wet kisses. I didn't even want you to kiss me after Uncle Milty had liplocked you. I thought he was disgusting. Now Patrick has betrayed me too. He won't even take my calls. He'll spend the rest of his life sucking up to you—no doubt on orders from Uncle Milty. Those two will use you and then use you some more. Don't trust them."

"I love them. They are my friends."

"My final advice to you is don't trust anybody. Everybody, including slutty little Susan, is after your money."

"Do you have a lawyer? I don't think you'd trust me to recommend one."

"No, but I have an idea. There's only one lawyer who's honest in this town. He's picking up all of Uncle Milty's gay clients. Why not me? Former gay client of Uncle Milty?"

"You mean Jim Howard?"

"I sure don't mean Martha Washington."

"I think that might be perfect. He's honest. He'll be fair to all parties. In fact, I'd love it if you'd use Jim Howard. He'd keep our agreement very quiet. What I'm the most interested in here is not going public with our private agreement."

"I'll call him. If he'll represent me, I'll have him contact Uncle Milty directly."

"Then you'll leave the island?"

"I'll go to the Roney Plaza when I get things settled here. But right now I have to stay by the phone. You'll know how to reach me. If you don't mind, I'll take old Buck's yacht. When those news creeps aren't broadcasting Leroy's murder, they're broadcasting the death of your grandfather. You have my sympathy."

"Thank you," Buck said.

"But don't expect me to attend the funeral." Robert abruptly hung up without a good-bye.

When Buck put down the phone, he reached down and ran his fingers through Lars's hair. Lars raised up from Buck's toes and moved over him, kissing him long and hard. "I know we don't have much time," Lars said. "But I've had an urgent hard-on for the past twenty minutes. I've got to have relief." He raised himself up and unzipped his fly, presenting himself to Buck.

Eager to devour, Buck moved his lips toward the offering.

*****

Concealed in the Collins's backyard, he'd waited patiently until his former chief, Biff, had left after grilling Barry—no doubt about Leroy's death. He wasn't certain that the chief even knew of Pamela's death. Gene needed a smoke, but he feared lighting a cigarette would lead to his detection.

He'd left his mother's old and battered car parked eight blocks from the Collins's home and had walked to his former temporary residence. It was one of those scorching Florida days when the sun shone so brightly it scorched the garden. The plants took on a serene beauty then and seemed to vibrate in the ocean breeze.

Pamela's murder, he knew, would bring on a massive manhunt, making Leroy's death dim in comparison. After all, Leroy was only a fag. Pamela was the wife of a candidate. Her murder would be the one seriously investigated.

He'd listened to the radio. The news concerned Leroy's murder and the death of Old Buck I. No mention of Pamela's death. He was convinced that he'd be blamed for Pamela's murder.

Calder had been very clever. He'd known of Gene's relationship with Leroy and had rightly assumed that Leroy had told him where Pamela was. It must have been easy for Calder to figure out that Gene would turn to Pamela in his desperation, as the one person who might bring out the truth about Leroy's death, the one person who knew enough to save Gene.

When all the police officers had filed out, including Biff, leaving no one behind, he knew Barry had not accused him in any way. If he had, Biff would have ordered police protection for the candidate in case Gene returned.

A plan was taking shape in his mind. The jackals had to be eliminated before he took on the lions. As conceived by him, his plan was pure choreography. Breathing deeply, he looked toward the dimly lit house. Through picture windows opening onto the rear garden, he could see Barry walking around the living room, pouring himself another drink. He could have shot Barry right then and easily made an escape. He wanted to tantalize him more, make him sweat it out when he confronted him, make his eyes just as wide and as accusatory as Pamela's had been.

He crossed the lawn to get nearer to the back door, concealing himself behind a hibiscus bush. He still had Barry's keys. He pressed a lever on his red-faced watch and the ruby plastic lit up 12:01, a minute past his deadline. He smiled at the slight delay, knowing he'd unwittingly given Barry one more minute of his life. Although he carried a pistol in his holster, he gripped a nylon cord in one hand. He wanted Barry to die as Pamela had, struggling and clutching the cord as he whimpered in muffled gasps for precious air. He deserved nothing better.

He inserted his key and softly entered the house. Passing quietly through the kitchen, he slipped into the living room, concealing himself behind a library shelf. From across the room he could see most of Barry's body, curled like a fetus, as if he'd passed out on the sofa, his still full drink resting on the floor behind him.

Gene had worn mirrored sunglasses. As Barry choked to death, he wanted him to see, not Gene's eyes, but his own eyes and, in witnessing the fright and panic there, to know and experience what Pamela had felt.

All day he had been haunted by billboard pictures of Barry, staring at him as he drove through the streets of Okeechobee. There Barry was projecting a false image to fool a naïve and unsuspecting public. Not only was Barry's picture on billboards, it would soon be on television news and front pages of paper, depicting him as a grief-stricken husband, winning more undeserved sympathy for him. Pamela's murder would hold nationwide interest.

Suddenly, Barry got up from the sofa. His hand reached out as if trying to clutch some object. "Gene," he said in a hesitant voice. "I know you're here. Come out of hiding."

Nothing could have surprised Gene more than that invitation. He deftly removed his pistol from his holster, wiping the sweat from his brow. The corner of the library shelf barely concealed him.

Barry had gotten up now. Gene could clearly see his face. Baggy-eyed, he was completely disheveled.

Pointing the pistol directly at Barry, Gene stepped out of the shadows.

"I knew you were coming," Barry said, "but I didn't tell Biff. I don't believe Biff even knows of Pamela's death. The maid hasn't even gone into her room. Like you, I learned about Pamela's death the hard way."

"How did you find out?"

"I was tipped off by someone on Calder's staff." With pleading eyes, he moved closer to Gene. "Believe me, I didn't know."

"Julius Forster murdered your wife."

"Oh, my God," he said, seemingly startled by the news unless he was putting on a good act. "I didn't know."

"You guys set me up like a fucking patsy!" Gene yelled in a high, hoarse voice, his face reflecting bitter anger.

"Calder set you up. Calder and your dear, beloved Rose. Pamela could have ruined me, blackmailed me, but I wouldn't have killed her." His hands thrust into his dressing robe pockets, he fixed his eyes on Gene.

He had Barry at his complete mercy, but he was in a fog. He almost believed him.

"I could have had the police stay and guard me if I'd fingered you. You know that. I didn't. I think I wanted you to come back here and kill me."

"You're crazy, man. Completely off your rocker."

Barry turned his head away as if looking for something.

"See that statement I'm working on for the papers?" He pointed to a letter resting on his secretary. "I'm resigning from the mayor's race. I've had it!"

"Are you denouncing Calder to the press?"

"No way! He'd have me killed if I did that. I'd never suck in a safe breath of air as long as I lived. Which wouldn't be long, I can assure you."

"Then what in hell are you doing?"

"As I said, I'm resigning. Calder and Rose only had power over me when I wanted power myself. Without my ambition, they can't control me. I'm ruined anyway. What does it matter now? They'll find some other candidate without my problems."

Barry reached for a box on the stand, but Gene slapped his outstretched hand, knocking over cigarettes, scattering them all over the carpet. "You are going to die!"

"I know it," Barry said. He bent down and reached for one of the cigarettes. Gene let him light it. "In the meantime, I'm going to have a smoke."

Gene pointed the pistol at Barry. The trigger almost clicked, but he didn't fire it. Barry was pushed back into a chair. It was high time he killed him. He just couldn't bring himself to do it.

"You see, Gene, I'm like you. I'm one of their victims, too. Like Pamela. As bad as she was, she didn't deserve that. Okay, they found out about me, my little hang-up. Believe me, don't you think I've paid for that?"

The weapon felt limp and clumsy in Gene's hand. He'd forgotten about the cord.

"Like you've paid," Barry went on. "That one moment, that little girl. One silly mistake, and you've paid all your life. I believe you were framed the second time. It was all part of a conspiracy against you. That god damn Leroy Fitzgerald and his brothel. Your former wife. Hardly any better than mine. Both whores. I think Buck Brooke had you framed with that little...what's her name, Maria. Her mother works for Brooke now. Brooke is only pretending to attack Rose. Actually they're on Calder's payroll. Rose owns the Examiner. Come on, man. Don't be stupid."

Gene knew now he couldn't kill Barry.

Barry watched him closely. "Out of the whole rotten mess, you are probably the only honest one. Not your fucking police chief. Everybody's on somebody's payroll. All except you."

Gene thought Barry had come to realize he wasn't going to shoot him.

"The very qualities you looked for in Rose—honor, dignity— you've had them in yourself all along. Rose was just a mirror of what you wanted to be and what you wanted to find in a woman. The Rose you wanted doesn't exist. You just imagined her. I know this sounds corny, but you are corny. For a man who can be so smart about some things, your innocence is incredible. So was mine. I thought I was smarter than you. I'm not. I got ruined, too."

The more Barry talked, the more Gene seemed to lose contact with reality. He wanted to deny everything Barry said, yet the talk seemed sharp and true.

"I'm no good," Barry said. "I don't pretend to be, at least not with you. But I'm not as rotten as Rose. And no one's as rotten as Calder. I've never killed anyone. What originally got me into this slime was making love to bodies, not killing them."

Gene consulted his wrist watch. He was wasting time. He had other rounds to make. "Are you calling the police the moment I leave?"

Barry sighed in relief, as the question confirmed he wasn't going to be killed. "No, because I think I know what you're going to do. I finally figured it out. For once, I think I've outguessed Calder. You're the only person who will get me out of this sad, sick business. Because of you, I might one day be free of them."

"You want me to do the job for you?"

"In a way, yes. You have few choices left. They're finished with me now. You're their new game. I just hope you get them before they get you."

"Biff wants me dead, doesn't he?"

"He'll never arrest you. I know his plan and I'll tell you. He's not going to bring you in. His men are going to shoot to kill. They don't want you brought in. You know too much. You could expose all of them."

"If Biff is working so closely with Calder, why doesn't the chief know Pamela is dead?"

"With Biff, Calder operates only on a need-to-know level. Biff will learn about Pamela's death soon enough. Surely in an hour or so." Biff has been the chief agent of conspiracy against you. He takes his orders directly from Calder. Right now he wants you dead. Trust me."

"Where is he now?"

"He's gone to the Vulcan Baths for his little afternoon luncheon break."

"How can he go there without being recognized?"

"Believe me, when he takes off that wig and that red mustache, he blends in completely with all the other old sex hunters at the baths. You knew that mop of hair is a wig, didn't you?"

"I didn't know that. I thought it was a bad dye job."

"It's all fake. Like Biff himself. Our defender of law and order in this town. Other than Calder, he's the biggest lawbreaker of all."

A vivacious buzz began to play in Gene's head like a medley of voices, each calling him in different directions. The bullets in his pistol seemed like capsules, and in those capsules a heady elixir danced. He turned and ran toward the kitchen, through the open door and into the backyard.

While he was free, there was much to be done.

$$*****$$

She came into the foyer of Desire looking so fresh-faced he felt embarrassed at her seeing him in his rumpled clothes, unshaven, with ruffled hair and red eyes from lack of sleep.

In contrast, Susan appeared like a wildflower in full bloom, with her long auburn hair, her prominent breasts, her ivory skin. She wore a well-tailored suit with a porcelain rose necklace on a satin cord around her neck.

Taking in her exciting presence, Buck said, "You look great. All except the rose necklace. My least favorite flower."

In a dramatic gesture, she unfastened the rose necklace and tossed it on the sofa.

"You don't have to go that far," he cautioned her.

"I don't like Sister Rose either." She kissed him firmly on the lips.

As he pulled away, he spotted Don, in blue jeans and a T-shirt, coming into the foyer. Don came over to him and kissed him long and hard, holding him in a tight embrace. When he backed away for air, he said, "Welcome home, boss man. I've missed you."

Buck put his arm around Don's waist, tightening his grip and liking the rock hard stomach he felt.

Ignoring them, Susan was taking in the splendor of the mansion. "This is fabulous. Incredible. I've never seen anything like it."

"You have certainly come up in the world," Don said, looking around. "I can't wait for the guided tour."

"Lars is going to take you on a tour," Buck said. "He'll even show you your private suite. I want you to feel free to live here. Ahmad said it'd be great."

"I'm spellbound," Susan said. "Thanks for the invitation. I'll take you up on it. How about you, Don?"

"There is no doubt. I was born to live in such a place, and now I'm here." He reached over and kissed Buck.

Lars appeared and volunteered to take them on a tour. Susan willingly accepted but Don, in spite of claiming he couldn't wait to go on the tour, actually could wait. He said he wanted to remain behind to talk over a private matter with Buck. Shrugging her shoulders, Susan left them, trailing Lars.

"I need to thank you for that sports car, my loving man," Don said when Susan had gone. "And for the invitation to live here. For everything you've done."

"You ain't seen nothing yet," Buck said. He leaned over and kissed Don hard. "You need it, don't you?"

Don took Buck's hands and placed it on his crotch. "Desperately. I've been thinking of nothing else."

"Let's go up to my quarters. We don't have much time."

In the bedroom he welcomed the penetration from Don. It was just as good as it had been with Gene. As Don plunged deep within his body, his eyes searched Buck's. "I'm in love," Don whispered. There was an electricity between them. Buck felt Don had an overwhelming capacity to love. As his thrusts grew more powerful, he leaned down to kiss Buck—deeply, hungrily. Sparks were flying in their magnetic field of love. They were visible to no one but them.

Don lifted Buck's right leg into the air to provide more room to slam into him. He pounded Buck's body into the bed, reaming and twisting until Buck realized how good it must be for Susan. No wonder she didn't want to let this former football hero go in spite of some problems here and there. Buck's hands were busy, feeling and fondling Don's muscles. He reached below to cradle and caress his balls.

Using muscles he didn't know he had, Buck clamped down on Don, causing him to moan and yell. Buck didn't care how loud Don cried out. The walls were soundproof. Ahmad had seen to that. His body slammed up against Don, as Buck tweaked Don's swollen nipples, grabbing a fistful of chest hair to hold him in better position for the final assault. Buck felt a powerful climax building inside him, and he couldn't hold back much longer.

Don's penis was so much like Buck's that it was almost as if he were getting penetrated by himself. A whimper escaped from Don's kissable mouth, and Buck knew it wouldn't be long for both of them. Don shagged him harder with every thrust. Buck's hands reached for Don's ass, pushing him in even deeper. Don suddenly locked his teeth into Buck's shoulder as Buck exploded, screaming out in the delirium of his release. Like white hot plasma, Don poured himself deep into Buck's bowels.

Buck seemed to have lost the sense of time over the next few minutes. He yelled out when Don withdrew, wanting him to stay in longer. Don's mouth was now at his groin, licking Buck clean. He was planting delicate, sensitive kisses everywhere, causing Buck to squirm.

Later in the shower each man soaped the other's body. Under the jet spray Buck moved toward Don's ear. "Ahmad wants to have a three way. I've told him all about you."

"You've come to the right man."

"Only hitch is, you've got to dress up in one of my old Marine uniforms."

"I was in the army but I'd be great impersonating a marine."

"Then it's a deal. That Ahmad is going to have one sore ass."

*****

The police chief, Biff, had not really been part of the day's choreography. But Gene changed his mind after Barry told him he'd find him at the Vulcan Baths. The law wasn't going to punish Biff. Gene would have to.

On the portable radio, as he drove in his mother's old car, he heard the news that the manhunt for him had intensified. He was wanted for questioning in connection with Pamela's murder. A maid had discovered her body at the Pier House. A radio station, beating the TV news, had broadcast the sketchy and still unconfirmed report. Gene had been identified by that burly man who'd seen him leaving her room. He had suspected all along that his discovery coming out of that room had not been coincidental. Calder had been brilliant in anticipating that Gene was going to seek Pamela out.

With all the business whirling around his head, Biff amazed Gene. Biff must be a sex addict requiring his fix at the Vulcan even though pressing business awaited him back at his office.

After checking into the baths, Gene went directly to an anonymous cubicle where he stripped down, putting on a flimsy robe. He headed for the shower room where he found battered walls, chipped paint, dishes of soap, stacks of graying towels, and a smell of disinfectant.

He ignored the stares of middle-aged men with paunchy midriffs and brushed away a wandering hand or two. After half an hour, he'd almost given up hope that Biff would ever come down to the steam room. Time was valuable—the most valuable it had ever been to him—and he feared he was wasting it.

Back upstairs, he wandered the floors for another half hour with the sex hunters. Wet tongues flicked out at him, and the sound of convulsing bodies assailed his eardrums. Still, he endured it.

As eyes riveted on him, he was king of the mountain, the superstud center stage. He let the eyes feast on his thick, muscular legs. He let them dream of the delights his body could give them.

The smell of marijuana and amyl nitrate filled the air. One old, fat man, leaning up against a peeling wall, reached out to grope him. He slammed his fist into the guy's guts. That ended that. No more hands reached out for him. No one followed him any more. He wanted it that way from now on. He had not come here looking to be serviced.

Finally, Biff emerged from one of the cubicles, heading for the shower and sauna room. At first Gene didn't recognize him. Without his red wig and mustache, he looked completely different, and almost twenty years older. He blended in perfectly with the other middle-age sex hunters at the baths.

As Biff left the floor, Gene trailed him. In the whirlpool area, no one was in sight. At the far side of the pool, two men lay in each other's arms, fondling genitals.

Gene checked the toilets. Empty. Biff could be in only one place. He'd gone into the sauna room.

Gene stripped off his gown and removed a nylon cord he'd carried in a towel. Slowly he opened the creaking door and entered the sauna. Only one body was there. It had to be Biff. The sight of his former chief's heavily perspiring nude body with its shriveled sex disgusted Gene. He thanked God they were alone. He couldn't draw this out. Anyone could walk in at any moment.

He moved toward Biff. As Gene's massive frame came into view, he could almost see Biff's eyes light up, as if his heart were pounding furiously. Biff's eyes were transfixed by Gene's enormous genitals.

Before Biff could look up in his face, Gene walked up to where Biff was sitting on the tiled wall seat. Gene's cock was only two inches from Biff's mouth. At this point Gene knew Biff wouldn't look up.

Biff's stubby fingers reached out to fondle and weigh Gene's balls. With his other hand, Biff pulled back the skin from Gene's penis and plunged down on his cock. He was an expert, taking the whole mass of flesh down his throat. Gene hardened at once. He was overcome with a sexual excitement unlike any he'd ever known before.

As Biff slurped and devoured him, his hands traveled up to Gene's nipples. For the first time Biff looked up into Gene's face. It was a look of such astonishment Gene would remember it always, even if always had become such a short time.

Biff withdrew suddenly from Gene's cock. Before either of them could say anything or make the next move, a look was exchanged between them. It was the look of the victim meeting his executioner.

That look ended quickly, as life preserving forces welled in Biff. "What the hell...you!" His accusation stabbed the steamy air. It was an accusation no jury would hear.

In one lightning move, Gene slipped the cord around Biff's bloated neck. Like a wild animal, Biff crawled about three feet toward a broken tile ledge. Gene tightened the grip on the cord, pulling him back. Biff kicked and moaned but didn't have enough air in him to let out a real scream. His left hand jerked wildly as if looking for a target, finding it in Gene's muscular leg, where his fingernails dug in, drawing blood. Still holding him by the cord, Gene jerked it tighter and tighter before smashing Biff's unprotected head against the tiles. Biff's claws gradually withdrew from their blood-sucking hold on Gene's legs.

Up close he could smell the foulness of Biff's liquor-soaked breath. The chief's eyes bulged, a desperate plea for help, a plea that had been captured in Pamela's eyes.

As Gene held his former chief in his grip, Gene knew he was already dead. Seconds before a gurgling sound had escaped from Biff's throat, the last rattle before oblivion. Gene released his grip on the cord, letting it fall on the damp tiles. Biff collapsed on the tiles in a crumpled heap. His gaping mouth formed a large O.

Gene hurried from the steam room. Now fully erect, the two men were still engaged at the other end of the pool. Upstairs, Gene took a handkerchief and tied it around his bloody leg. He quickly slipped on his clothes. He hadn't checked any valuables so, instead of returning to the front desk, he slipped out the back entrance.

No sign of life anywhere. He raced across the parking lot and headed for his next appointment. He knew he had a rendezvous with death. His upcoming victims didn't know their time had come.

On the way to the fatal encounter, he stopped at a deserted beach. He got out of the car and decided to go for a jog. He needed a few minutes between appointments. If anyone spotted him running, Gene could easily be taken for a jogger. The air smelled clean, fresh, and, though the ocean wind had a slight chill to it, he was on fire.

About a half mile up the beach, he stopped—panting, breathless, collapsing on the sands, hoping to summon energy for what lay ahead. His thoughts were on Robert. He had to reach Robert but feared he couldn't call the island. He just knew the phone was tapped. Maybe he'd take his boat there to make contact with Robert.

Pulling himself up, he brushed off sand and decided to jog back to his waiting car. He looked up at the bright sun. The day was moving rapidly along. Before the sun set, he had several rounds to make.

*****

Buck stood looking out the gigantic picture windows of Ahmad's living room, opening onto the pool down below. At the far end of the pool, he could see Don removing all his clothes for a nude swim.

"A magnificent specimen," Susan said, coming up behind Buck and putting her arms around his waist.

"I hope you don't mind," he said, somewhat embarrassed at his recent intimacy with Don.

"Mind? Why should I? Don is a world class hustler. Hustlers do what hustlers do. He's good at his work. Let's keep him around."

He turned to her and smiled, kissed her lightly on the lips. "Let's do that. He's good for morale. His replacement might be worse."

"Actually Don is more than a hustler," she said. "He has heart, feelings, sensitivity, and a kind of loyalty."

"You're right. Let's never judge him too harshly. He's probably extremely loyal to the both of us, and can be counted on for the long haul. We're the best thing that ever happened to him—and he knows that. He's shown me nothing but tender devotion."

"I bet sometimes not so tender," she said, patting his ass.

Lars appeared in the living room. "You have an urgent call from your attorney."

"Do you want me to leave the room?" Susan asked.

"No, stay," Buck said. "I don't think this call will be anything you can't overhear."

"Uncle Milty, my darling man!" Buck said. "I'm here with Susan, my faithful wife."

"You'd better be watching TV. In about three minutes there's going to be an hour's retrospective devoted to the old man. They even have newsreel pictures of you when you were a kid. This is one show you won't want to miss. It's Channel 13."

"Susan, please turn on Channel 13," he called out to her as she stood by the window, still taking in the view of Don who looked like some Greek athlete, a statue really.

"Gene seems to have gone insane," Uncle Milty said. "Killing Leroy and all."

"If indeed he did kill Leroy," Buck said.

"If not Gene, then who?"

"Calder Martin."

"You can't prove that. Of course, in Calder Martin's case, I wouldn't put it past him. After all, Fitzgerald was blackmailing him and Sister Rose. And ultimately Shelley."

"That too." Buck said, deciding not to tell Uncle Milty that he'd kidnapped Shelley and the boy was being held at Desire. There were some things you couldn't tell even a confidential lawyer.

Uncle Milty coughed slightly. "I just had to tell you of some alarming discoveries being made. My staff and I are going over old Buck's assets. He may have been forced out of top management by stockholders of all those papers he used to own. But in every case he was incredibly rewarded in a settlement. He took millions and millions of dollars and poured the money into land most realtors viewed as worthless. But what was viewed as worthless land in the fifties isn't necessarily looked upon that way today. Twenty years from now such land might be prime real estate."

"Exactly what are you getting at?"

"You may be America's greatest land baron. In the past hour we have read only some of the holdings. It appears, to cite only one example, you may own Eastern Oregon."

"That's incredible. I've never been to Oregon."

"Perhaps a visit is long overdue."

"But we've got to go to Hollywood. Ahmad, you know."

"I know and I'm working on that right now."

"But on the way there, we might stop off in Northeastern Maine. Also Indiana."

"Indiana?" Buck said in astonishment. "No one's ever heard of Indiana."

"Old Buck Brooke has heard of Indiana, and Indiana has heard of him. Not to mention Oklahoma."

"Now that's a state I've visited, although under unusual circumstances."

"Have you ever been to Northwestern Texas or Western Kansas?"

"No one in his right mind would go there."

"Perhaps you will. And let's make one final stopover. Montana. You are now the cattle queen of Montana."

"Wasn't that an old movie with Barbara Stanwyck and Ronald Reagan?"

"Who knows? Who cares? You're taking over the role now."

"I've never been to Montana either. But I've been skiing in Wyoming."

"I don't think you own anything in Wyoming. But you do own a condo in Sun Valley, Idaho. Did you know that?"

"I didn't know any of this. He told me nothing. Nothing at all. And he paid me forty-five thousand a year."

"I know, the price of a dinner for you now. I want you to watch that TV show. Another thing. I'm afraid of Gene. If you didn't have all those security guards—well hung ones at that—I'd hire plenty of them to protect you and Susan. For all I know, Gene has a grudge against you and Susan. Your lives could be in danger."

"What about Robert?"

"You know what I think? Gene is in love with Robert. It's all tied up with you in some sick way. Let's give Robert his five million. Not in installments. The whole thing."

"Why?"

"Because with all the money they could flee the country. Give them your plane. Offer to fly Robert anywhere. Don't say anything but set it up so that Gene can be slipped aboard that plane. Perhaps as one of the members of the staff. I could arrange that somehow. Don't ask me how. But when I meet with Robert, I'll make it perfectly clear without making it perfectly clear. He'll see your plane as a means of escape with Gene. They'll probably head south. South America, some place. I'll suggest all that. Let's have that meeting with Robert like now. With Gene on the run, it's best to have him out of the country. His mind could snap at any minute. He could come looking for you and Susan."

"You may be right. We could be in some sort of danger." Susan had seated herself in front of the television, but that remark caught her interest. She looked at him with grave concern. He nodded at her, hoping to assure her everything was all right.

"One more thing, and I'll talk to you real soon," Uncle Milty said. "Nancy Reagan just called. She claims she was so very sorry she couldn't meet you for dinner with Sister Rose. She and Ronald are going to be in Miami staying at a friend's villa. She wants you to fly down and have a private dinner with just the two of them."

"My, word travels fast. Did you also inform her I'm a Democrat?"

"I didn't let on. What's your answer?"

"Call her back. Tell her I'll get back to her tomorrow. I'm involved right now. I've got a funeral to plan."

"I also need to know your funeral plans at once. The press is pounding on the door for news. When are you going to make the arrangements for the funeral? Or do you want me to handle this?"

Buck looked over at Susan. "I'm going to ask Susan."

"No better choice unless you could get Jacqueline herself. Gotta run. I love you. The show's about to begin."

Buck went over to the sofa and sat down beside Susan, reaching for her hand. On the screen flashed the title of the show: AMERICA'S LAST CITIZEN KANE.

*****

The mid-afternoon was at its hottest but Gene knew that the sun would soon begin its descent. He made his way across the garden to Buck's villa. The lawn seemed to have grown used to his footsteps. No sound came from inside the house. A yellow lamp glowed by the rear door, leading to the kitchen. It was a night light but Clara, the maid, hadn't bothered to turn it off all day. It seemed somehow like a beacon, sending out a welcome to a mariner.

Deftly he removed the globe and unscrewed the bulb. He didn't have to do that, but felt compelled to. As he extinguished the light, it seemed like all breath and life had left him, too. His body trembled as he removed a knife he'd bought. With it, he cut through the screen door, unfastening the latch. Slipping onto the porch, he took out a glass cutter from his leather bag and slashed into a window pane of a door opening onto the kitchen.

Inside, the house was still. He could only imagine what life was like when Robert and Buck inhabited the house. The kitchen was like one of those houses where he used to work as a boy, taking odd jobs where he could find them, often mowing people's lawns and carrying out their garbage. "Their kitchens are all the same," he thought to himself. Butcher block counter tops, gleaming stainless steel double sinks, copper utensils hanging from overhead racks.

He just knew Clara and Maria were still in the house, but there was no sign of them. He crept upstairs to the master bedroom where he'd made love to Robert. The door to the bedroom stood wide open. In the shadowy afternoon light, the bed was perfectly made, not a wrinkle. No one slept here any more.

As he turned his head, he heard a sound coming from an adjoining bedroom which opened onto a rear garden. He concealed himself behind a door and waited.

Another sound. Someone was getting up! Whoever it was flipped on a radio. It was one of those Spanish stations which broadcast programs to the invaders who refused to learn the language of their new country. The music was mostly static.

In the hallway, the sound of approaching footsteps alerted him. As she passed him, she didn't look in Buck's room. He saw only the side of her face and the back of her head. He knew who it was. The Cuban woman's eyes had followed him for months as he'd come and gone from his house which no longer existed because of her. Seeing the back of her head, he remembered his house going up in flames. She'd been responsible for that. Clara and Maria. How he hated the sound of those two names.

In a chenille robe, Clara slowly descended the winding staircase in her loose-fitting bedroom slippers. Rubbing sleep from her eyes following her afternoon siesta, she took one step at a time. When he heard her shuffling feet on the tile floor downstairs, he, too, trailed her down the carpeted steps, one stair at a time, just as she'd done—except his reasons were different. One of his hands iron-gripped a stiletto.

She went into the kitchen, turning on a light since the blinds were drawn. At first he feared she might see the glass cut but she was too sloppily indifferent to notice a detail like that.

She headed for the utility room right off the kitchen, a liquor bottle in her hand. She turned on the light and poured herself a drink. She left the door open. From where he stood, he could see her clearly, as her back was to him.

She rubbed her back, as if she had a sharp pain, then removed her chenille robe, hanging it on a hook. On the adjoining hook she reached for her maid's uniform. Bending over to remove her bedroom slippers, she thrust her chubby ass virtually into his face. The sight was obscene.

He moved forward, shutting the door to the utility room and locking it. He was alone in the small room with her.

Completely nude, she whirled around to face this sudden invasion. Her hand reached to cover her breasts. Her face flashed an immediate recognition. Other than Biff facing his execution, Gene had never seen such terror as that reflected in the woman's eyes.

Before she could scream, he'd muffled her mouth with the big palm of his hand, holding the tip of the stiletto at her throat. From a mirrored wall, an image of the two of them—locked in a grotesque embrace—swept before his eyes. They just stood there for a few brief seconds, locked in this dance of death, swaying back and forth. Her dark eyes were wide and luminous.

"If you scream I'll kill you," he threatened her. He slowly removed his hand from her mouth. She was too choked to utter a sound. Tears ran down her face. He seized one of her large breasts, his fingernails digging in. At her first outcry, he jabbed the tip of the stiletto into her neck, drawing blood. Her startled cry became only a low, soft moan. "Señor, señor, señor."

"Did Brooke pay you to frame me?"

The woman looked as if she'd suddenly been reprieved. "Sí, sí, sí." Her terrified eyes sought his. "He forced me. He made me lie. Kill him!"

He brought his knee up sharply into the softness of her belly, as he kept the stiletto at her throat.

Her fear finally overcame her. She fell on the floor, writhing.

He towered over her, holding the stiletto. Her ugly sex was widespread, as clearly visible as a gaping wound. His face tightened. "You wanted me, didn't you? You get your wish."

He fell on her, stabbing at her sex repeatedly—he didn't know the number of times. Her squeals were like those of a pig at castration. Blood spurted from the wounds as her bellowing cry for help filled the room. As her screams died, her throat made only gurgling noises.

After the stiletto rape, he slashed again up toward her chest. The stiletto entered so fast it hit a bone, sliding from his grasp. He clutched it again, as if fondling it, then his grip tightened once more as he slashed her neck where she'd sucked in the air that gave breath to lies against him.

He'd been oblivious to the sound, but now he heard it clearly, as it grew louder and louder, like a drum beating inside his head. Someone pounded on the door. "Mama, mama, mama!"

Getting up, covered with blood, he stood before the door for a long moment before turning the lock. He needed this respite to summon his courage. "God," he said. "God." He knew what he had to do and, even this late in his choreography, he resented the part he'd been assigned.

Maria opened the door, rushing into the room. With a life all its own, the stiletto plunged right into her heart. She didn't have a chance to scream. The sight of him holding the weapon and her own blood-soaked mother on the floor had captured her in a paralytic trance. He left the stiletto in her heart. He would have no more need for the weapon.

Maria stood there for a lost moment before falling over. When she had joined her mother in the blood bath on the tiles, he held both of his hands up to his face. Empty, but bloody.

He bolted from the room, slamming the door behind him, wanting to be free of the memory. He ran up the stairs and into the master bedroom. Here he peeled the clothes from his body, clambering toward the shower. He turned on the water at full blast, fiery hot, letting its jet spray cleanse him thoroughly. It was an act of purification.

By the time he'd showered and come back into the bedroom, he had calmed down considerably. A kind of peace had come over him. Opening the door to Buck's closet, he removed a pair of slacks and a sports shirt. He slipped into them, surprised to find they were the same size. Bundling up his bloody clothes, he took them with him, planning to destroy them later.

Downstairs again, he hurried past the utility room, not looking inside. In the kitchen, he poured himself a cup of coffee, imagining Buck doing that before he left for work. By the coffee pot he noticed a pad. On it someone had scribbled the name, Señor Dante, and a telephone number.

Impulsively he dialed the number, letting it ring seven times. It was four o'clock in the afternoon. Finally, it was answered. He recognized

Robert's voice.

"Hello," Robert repeated into the phone. He seemed ready to hang up. Gene was afraid to speak to him, fearing the line was tapped. "Gene, is that you?" Robert asked hesitantly. When there was no answer, Robert hung up.

Gene slammed down the phone. The call had confirmed it for him. Robert was still on the island. He would take his boat and go to Robert's side.

Outside the lawn was still wet as if a light rain had fallen for only a minute or so. Birds nested in the trees and the sound of their chirping filled the air. It was a perfect day.

Carrying his blood-soaked clothes, he headed five blocks down the street to his mother's old car. Beside his car an old and half-dead mongrel had come to rest. Brittle-boned and mangy, it won his sympathy immediately. He was almost tempted to go back in the house and get the dog something to eat. He was reminded of the cats and the sardines he'd offered them. But he had no time for that now.

In his car again, he headed for the distant marina. With Robert he would make plans for his escape after he'd accomplished one final mission in Okeechobee.

In the late afternoon breeze, he liked the way he'd fitted into Buck's clothes. If life had been different, if he had gotten the breaks Buck had, he could fit very well into his elegant, easy life. He just knew it.

He'd felt he'd really belonged in Buck's house, but he knew such a dream was only to be dreamed. Perhaps in some far and distant land, Robert and he would also have a fine house.

It would be a beautiful place where the weather was always warm and sunny. Maybe they'd acquire some pets. Pets would be nice. Too many animals were homeless in the world. Perhaps Robert, when he came into his millions, would hire Sandy and Jill to run the house and grounds for them. Sandy and Jill wouldn't actually have to work. But they could oversee others doing the tasks for them. They'd keep the place perfect. It would be the happy home he'd never found anywhere else.

He no longer felt he was going to die. Right now he just knew he'd live forever in Robert's arms. He could enjoy the good life just like Buck. After all, Robert had assured him he was a better man than Buck.

*****

Twelve minutes into the biography of old Buck, the program was interrupted for a news bulletin. Pamela had been found murdered at the Pier House in Key West. Broadcast first as a rumor on radio, the report had been officially confirmed by the police. Gene had been spotted leaving her motel room. The manhunt for him had been intensified. Reporters were clamoring for Biff to hold a press conference but his office claimed the chief was involved in a high-level investigation and wasn't available.

Locked in seclusion with his two daughters, Barry too was unable to face the press. A spokesperson said that Barry's first obligation now was "to console and offer comfort to his grief-stricken daughters facing the loss of their mother."

As a commercial went on, Buck turned to Susan. "That's the official news. The truth must be somewhere else."

A despondent look came over her. "I can't believe this."

"I can't believe it either. Gene may be the prime suspect in Pamela's murder. But I think he's innocent."

"He'd never take a human life." She seemed on the verge of tears. "Why would he possibly want to kill Pamela?"

"It makes no sense to me. Are you going to the police? Tell them about the interview with Pamela?"

"Not on your life. I'm developing my own story for the News. I'm going to break what I know in that paper. If the police find out Don and I were at the Pier House, then we'll deal with that if it comes up."

"Are you sure about this?"

"Never surer in my life. I don't trust Biff. What a sleaze. I may not have the film of our interview, but I've got the whole thing on my tape recorder."

"What about the gay stuff with Barry?"

"I don't think we can reveal that. Not unless it becomes some sort of police record."

"I think you're right."

"But there's plenty on that tape about Calder I can use."

"Then burn his ass—that's what I want."

Wrapped in a robe, Don came into the room. "What are you guys doing sitting in front of the TV? It's too beautiful a day for that."

BLOOD MOON / 750

Susan got up and walked over to kiss him. "Welcome back. We're watching a special program on Buck's grandfather."

"Mind if I join you?" Don asked, sitting down next to Buck and giving him a gentle kiss on the lips.

"Pamela's dead," Buck announced abruptly. "Murdered. The police suspect Gene. First, Leroy. Now Pamela."

"Oh, shit! Gene murdered Pamela. I can't believe it."

Susan interrupted. "Look, Buck, there you are at the funeral of your parents."

"I can't watch it," Buck said. "Even now, it's still too painful." He got up and walked to the window overlooking the pool. Don came up behind him, holding him in his arms. "I'm here for you. Maybe we can go upstairs. Let me hold you in my arms. I know I'm rough during sex. But I can be gentle too."

"Thanks," Buck said. He turned around and kissed Don on the neck. "Thanks for being here, big guy. We need you."

Engrossed in rare newsreel footage, Susan seemed to ignore them.

Don held Buck's hand and walked him back to the sofa to witness the rest of the biography. At the end of the special, the TV announcer said that no plans have been announced for Buck I's funeral.

"We've got to go ahead with the funeral," Buck said. "And I can't go through with it." He looked over at Susan, reaching for her hand. "I've got to ask you to do it for me. If you will."

"Of course, I'll handle everything. It's the least I can do for you. After all, I'm part of this family."

"You are indeed."

Don looked at Buck as if he were left out. "I'm part of the family too."

Buck reached over and kissed him on the lips. "You are too." He glanced at Susan. "I need both of you."

Susan came over to him and put her arm around him to comfort him.

"It was the worst of lives and the best of lives," Buck said, looking at the blank TV set that Susan had switched off. "Old Buck did a lot of good in the world, and a lot of other things best left forgotten. He was a good man and an evil one."

"Like all of us," Don said.

Buck looked into Don's eyes, finding them comforting. "Maybe." He smiled. "Glad you're here." He got up. "Thanks for agreeing to arrange the funeral," he said to Susan. "His will stipulates that he wants to be cremated. He wants me to take his ashes out aboard his yacht and toss them into the sea."

"That's very dramatic—just like him," Susan said.

Mention of the yacht brought back a memory of Robert on the island. Right now Robert had control of the yacht. Buck planned to reclaim it when Robert came back to town. But before he did Buck wanted one final meeting with Robert. He excused himself from Don and Susan and headed for a library off the main living room. "I've got to make an urgent call," he said.

Locked into the privacy of the library, he dialed Robert, hoping that he hadn't left the island. Henry picked up the phone. After greeting Henry, he asked, "Has Robert left yet?"

"He's still here," Henry said. "Do you want to talk to him?"

"Put him on."

In a minute Robert came on the line. "I was just getting ready to leave. I was writing a note thanking you for the hospitality."

"I'd like to be thanked in person."

"What does that mean?"

"It means I'm coming to the island. You used to think I was a pretty hot guy before you developed other interests. I thought for old time's sake, we should say good-bye face to face. Man to man, so to speak."

"I don't see what good it will do. But if you really want to see me, I'll wait here for you. I owe you that much."

"Fine. I'm leaving now. I'll be there as soon as possible. I'm going to want a good-bye kiss, and I'm not going to settle for a peck on the cheek. If I remember, and I remember very well, you kiss fabulously. I hope you haven't lost that talent."

Robert hesitated a long moment, as if confused by this sudden flirtation. "I haven't lost anything."

"I love you," Buck said into the phone before hanging up quickly.

*****

As Robert put down the phone, a hand reached out from behind, muffling his mouth and an attempted startled scream.

"It's me, baby," Gene whispered in his ear. Satisfied that Robert knew who he was, he removed his hand.

"Gene!" Robert practically cried out his name. "I've been half out of my mind with worry."

Gene reached to hold him in a tight embrace, before giving him a long, deep kiss. "I'm back with you where I belong."

"The police..." Robert seemed hesitant, unsure.

Gene felt Robert needed to be reassured. "We've got to talk. I don't want the black guy to know I'm here. Since the police are after me, I don't want to implicate you in any way."

"I know what to do." Robert gave him a quick kiss. In minutes he returned. "It's handled."

"But he's still here," Gene protested. "I mean we're still on an island."

"He lives in a cottage at the far end of the island. He won't disturb us at all. He's very discreet."

"Let's go into the living room," Gene said.

"A better idea. Let's go into the kitchen. I bet you're starved unless you grabbed some fast food on the run."

"I didn't. I felt the fewer people who saw me, the better off I was."

In the kitchen Robert quickly prepared Gene a plate of roast beef Henry had recently cooked. Gene devoured the food eagerly. Until Robert suggested it, he didn't know he was starving. He consumed a large can of V-8 juice. Only then did he settle back in the chair.

"I know you didn't kill anybody," Robert said.

Robert's conviction was a little too weak for Gene but it was a proclamation of his innocence he wanted to hear.

"I've killed nobody," Gene said. He had no intention of telling the truth. He was determined to tell Robert only part of the truth. "As you know, Leroy lives in the same building as Jill, Sandy, and me. He got them into a hotel training school. I went to his apartment to thank him for making the arrangements. When I got there, I found the door slightly ajar. I called out to him and went in."

"Oh, my God."

"That's not all. I not only found him dead. He'd been castrated."

"I can't stand this."

"It's true. He'd been castrated and his genitals stuffed in his mouth."

"Some sick pervert."

"I had warned Leroy that Calder Martin was on his ass. Leroy was blackmailing Calder and Sister Rose for five-million dollars. Leroy had secretly photographed Barry Collins having sex with Shelley Phillips, and he was demanding top dollar."

"Do you think Barry is implicated in this at all?"

"I think he's innocent. Leroy's murder carries Martin's stamp. I panicked. I just knew Pamela was next on their list. Leroy had told me she was staying at the Pier House. I had to get to her."

"You were walking right into a trap," Robert said. His eyes focused intently on Gene, looking him over. It wasn't the look of desire but rather a strong, cold appraisal.

Gene sensed distrust in Robert's face for the first time since he'd slipped onto Buck's private island. "You don't have to ask: I know your next question. What in hell am I doing wearing Buck's clothes?"

"I was wondering."

"I went to his house and slipped inside the door. It was unlocked. I was looking for you. I figured you would either be here or still on the island."

"Did Clara see you?"

"Nobody was at home. The bitch was gone. No doubt visiting her relatives or else going on a shopping trip with all the excessive money Buck is paying her to blackmail me."

"You're probably right. Thank God she wasn't there."

"I was in a real mess, and I feared I would attract too much attention looking like a bum."

"Even unshaven and dirty, you could never look like a bum. You're too beautiful for that."

"Thanks for the kind words. I need to hear that. I went upstairs and showered and shaved. I borrowed some of Buck's clothes so I would look respectable."

"I'm glad you did." He leaned over and kissed Gene. "I'm also glad you came looking for me. It makes me love you all the more."

"When I learned you weren't at Buck's house, I came here in my boat. I've been driving around in my mother's old car. It hasn't been seen on the streets in Okeechobee in years. But it's got an up-to-date license and registration. I always renewed them. I'm surprised, though, it's still running."

"I've got a plan for your escape. I talked to Buck's attorney. Without really knowing what he was doing, he practically provided me with a blueprint on how I can get you out of here safely. But, first, I want to hear about Pamela."

"She was dead when I got there. The way I figure it, Martin knew I'd try to save Pamela. Pamela, had she gone public with what she knew, could have saved me. Someone spotted me coming from her room. I fell into Martin's trap. He outsmarted me from the very beginning."

"The son of a bitch."

"Get this. On the way to Pamela's room, I spotted Julius Forster."

"That Nazi bastard."

"He killed Pamela. When I saw him leaving the Pier House, he had just come from her room. He's the murderer. I think he works for Martin."

"This is astonishing. But it makes perfect sense." He glanced at his watch. "You can't stay here. I don't have much time. But I've got to tell you of my plan for your escape."

"Are you expecting someone?"

"You might as well know. Buck is on his way here now."

"Buck?" Gene was startled. Part of him wanted to remain on the island to confront Buck. The other part told him to flee at once. "Why is he coming here?" Gene asked suspiciously. "I thought it was all over between the two of you."

"He wants to meet with me to work out the final details of our financial agreement. After that, I'm taking old Buck's yacht and going to that meeting with Milton, the lawyer guy."

"How can we hook up?"

"I want you to meet me at the presidential suite at the Roney Plaza. I'm sure you've been there. It's on the grounds of the hotel property. You don't have to go through the lobby or anything. I've already checked. The suite has three doors. You're to come to the door numbered 1001. That door will be open. I'll be waiting inside for you."

"What happens then?"

"Buck has agreed to give me the use of his plane. At the hotel I will have picked up a uniform for you. The same one worn by Buck's crew. We'll leave the hotel and head directly for the airport. Clearance has been arranged for me. You'll be by my side. The people at the airport will think you're one of the plane's crew."

"I think that would work. But where in hell would we fly to?"

"I've got it all arranged. God damn, I'm efficient, if nothing else.

We'll fly first to Nicaragua. That's when the plane will return to Florida. But we won't stay in Nicaragua. I've booked us on a commercial flight to Chile. I know of a place to go in Patagonia."

"The end of the world."

"You've got that right. Buck and I were on a trip to the Antarctic. We stopped off in this remote town. A German baron had built a château there. Painted a ghastly mustard yellow but it's a spectacular place. Believe it or not, it's on the market for fifty-thousand dollars. With five million, we can afford a fifty-thousand dollar residence. We'll have plenty of money to live on. It would be very hard in that part of the world to spend twenty-five thousand dollars a year for expenses."

"That sounds terrific."

"There's a little inn we can stay in until I conclude the house deal."

"Let's go for it."

"But you've got to go now. Buck will be here soon. I think by seven o'clock I'll be at the Roney Plaza."

"I think you're saving my ass." Gene pulled him over and kissed him long and hard. "I've got to go."

The television set in the far corner of the living room had been left on. Robert had been listening to the news, no doubt for any new details about the manhunt for Gene. A news bulletin caught their attention. The police chief, Biff, had been found strangled to death in the parking lot behind the building housing Gene's condo.

Gene looked at the news report in astonishment and shock. "I had nothing to do with it," he shouted. What he couldn't bring himself to tell Robert was that he had strangled Biff at the Vulcan Baths. The owners of the baths had obviously arranged for the chief's body to be removed. Calder Martin no doubt had other men working for him in the police department.

Robert turned from the TV set to Gene. "Now that the chief is dead, the police will be looking for you like a mad dog."

"I know that. We've got to move fast."

Robert kissed Gene and hugged him a final time. "I'm afraid. But now's not the time to be afraid."

Gene glanced apprehensively at his watch. He had so little time to accomplish his final mission.

"Damn!" Robert said. "That's Buck's yacht pulling into the pier. Where's your boat?"

"I anchored it down by the beach."

"Hurry." Robert kissed him one final time. When he broke away, there were tears in his eyes. "Be safe. Be safe. God protect you until you're in my arms again."

Gene looked long and hard at him one final time before fleeing across the terrace by the pool and heading down the beach. He found himself shaking, as if coming unglued. Killing Clara, Maria, and Biff had been easy compared to the daunting challenge that awaited him now. But before boarding Buck's plane to freedom, the guilty had to be punished.

*****

Even now as he stood before Robert, he didn't know why he'd done it. But before disembarking from his yacht Buck had taken off his clothes and slipped on a white bikini stored on ship that Robert had bought for him four years ago. Virtually sheer, it was so revealing that Robert had never let him appear in it before anybody else. Before the crew, Buck had slipped on his robe. Once on his island and before going in to see Robert, he had taken off the robe. He might as well have been nude.

Robert looked at him in amazement, paying particular attention to the bikini. "I haven't seen you wear that in years."

"Does it bring back a memory?" Buck asked provocatively. "If I remember correctly, and I do, you never let me wear this little string for long. You were always taking it off me to expose the goodies."

"I recall that too." There was a look of longing in Robert's eyes and a tenderness to his voice that Buck hadn't heard since he'd come back from California.

Buck returned Robert's look. It was as if each man was waiting for the other to make a move. "What's holding you back, pretty boy?" Buck finally asked. "I've got a tongue that needs to be sucked—not to mention some other things. If I recall, you were the world's expert on licking and sucking Buck Brooke III where he needs to be licked and sucked. You adored me when I was poor. I taste even better now that I'm a rich mother-fucker."

A desperate cry escaped from Robert's throat as he moved swiftly toward Buck to immerse himself in the strong, outstretched arms of his friend.

Robert planted the most incredible kiss on Buck's lips. Buck's tongue probed Robert's mouth, as his broad hands explored every inch of his body he could conveniently reach. Robert's own hands were rediscovering the skin he knew so well. With his eyes closed, he knew every curve and line, especially the tender spots. Robert's hands glided, pressed, and stroked until the white bikini could no longer contain Buck. Robert slipped it off him.

Robert's tongue began methodically tracing patterns across Buck's flesh, as if preparing him for some ritual. Robert squeezed, kissed, licked, and sucked the flesh with a dedicated sense of devotion that also took on a quality of ownership.

The little moans coming from Robert, his sheer joy at tasting Buck's flesh, told Buck what he wanted to know: Robert was back with him again. He could mesmerize Robert as before. If Buck stood beside Gene, and Robert were given a choice, Buck knew in his heart that Robert would rush to his arms, deserting Gene for his greater love. Robert had had his fling. Buck had had his fling—more than one. Now it was time for each man to come home to the other.

Buck picked Robert up in his arms, easily carrying him from the living room to their bedroom. Buck removed Robert's T-shirt and shorts. Robert appeared in a half-dreamy trance. After completely stripping him, Buck threw him on the bed, preparing him for the rough sex that was to come. The moment had come to cross the final frontier with Robert.

Buck did not care to remember when he'd first realized what Robert wanted. Perhaps the knowledge had come on one of those mornings he got up early to watch the sun rise over Florida, always his favorite time of the day. Even when Buck had grown more experimental and kinky with Robert, it still hadn't been enough. Buck had held back, not letting himself give in to what was demanded of him from Robert. He couldn't bring himself to satisfy Robert that way. It wasn't in his nature. Or he didn't think it was in his nature until this very moment on their deserted island.

He lowered himself over Robert's body, looking deeply into his friend's eyes. The men had known each other too long and too intimately for words. There was an unspoken language between them. Robert's eyes seemed to defy him, goading him on, almost daring him to take the next move.

With one hand, Buck grabbed a fistful of Robert's blond hair, yanking at the roots with his tightest grip and pulling hard. With the other hand he slapped Robert across the face rather firmly. As he got into it, the slaps grew harder and harder. Robert cried out in pain and seemed to struggle to get away but Buck held him down tighter, slapping more violently. He didn't even stop when Robert's nose started to bleed. The young man's erection pressing hard and firm against Buck's belly was all the confirmation Buck needed. He stopped slapping him, tightened his grip on the hair, and spat once, twice into Robert's face, Robert moaned in ecstasy.

"I'm not going to have to tie you up," Buck said. "You'll do what I say and stay still for me, or else it'll go very bad for you." He flipped Robert's body over until he lay spread across Buck's stomach. He explored Robert's ass with his fingers, encircling the rosebud but not penetrating it with his finger. Robert seemed in a state of perpetual joy, as Buck fondled him roughly. Buck's first smack was quick, sharp, and stinging. He saw Robert's ass redden before his onslaught. With a lot of power behind it, Buck's hand came down hard and slow. Robert screamed out in pain. Buck felt the young man's erection seemingly grow even harder and thicker. Buck used even more force on Robert's ass, the slaps growing more vicious on the tender skin. He knew Robert's flesh was on fire.

He responded by arching his back and raising his ass to meet each blow. Robert screamed louder. His flesh was beaten tender and the feel of it was achingly hot. His buttocks had turned a deep scarlet.

Without preparation Buck inserted his finger deep inside Robert. Robert cried out. Buck grabbed Robert's hair, forcing his face up and slapping him hard for screaming.

Robert was reeling high from the beating. Buck inserted another finger, then another. Robert was moaning at this sudden invasion. He was breathing harder and harder. Then his explosion came, Buck felt it erupting all over his stomach.

In the throes of Robert's orgasm, Buck hauled the boy up to his face and forced open his lips, as his tongue began to explore the depths of Robert's suddenly dry mouth. Buck's fingers still probed and explored Robert's ass. He pierced as deeply and roughly as he could.

Buck turned Robert over as he quickly withdrew his fingers. He positioned his cock, then pushed hard and entered Robert as deeply and violently as he could. There was a popping sensation and a scream from Robert that brought Buck's strong, firm hand down, slapping his face repeatedly.

"You dirty little two-timing, bitch," Buck said. "This boy-pussy belongs to me, and no one will ever probe your depths but me again. You got that?"

"I love you," Robert called out. He was crying now from the slapping. "It was always you. It was never this good."

That made Buck pound all the harder. Robert seemed to open up to him as never before, drawing him deeper and deeper. The pleasure was too incredible for Buck. He had to distract himself in some way. He descended on Robert's neck and began biting him furiously. Every time he bit down, really sinking his teeth into Robert, he cried out with joy, goading Buck on. With his thrusts, he seemed to push Robert's body deeper and deeper into the bed. He felt Robert's muscles gripping and holding him as never before. Breathing hard, Buck knew he couldn't last much longer. Robert's second eruption came before his. As Robert was experiencing the final throes of another orgasm, Buck exploded inside him. Spent, he fell across Robert, deliberately grinding his body hard against him.

Robert burst into tears. "I've waited for so long for that," he whispered into Buck's ears, as he gently fondled the muscles of Buck's sweaty back.

Bathed in perspiration and come, Buck pressed his body even harder against Robert's. "You'll never leave me again. Never. I'll never let you go. It was always you, Robert."

Robert's warm, familiar arms were wrapped around Buck, and he knew he was home, somewhere safe.

After time had passed, he pulled himself off Robert's body and carried him to the shower where he bathed Robert before his friend bathed him.

Dressed and at the pier, he stood before Robert. "I'm taking old Buck's yacht back to town and leaving mine. Old Buck wanted his ashes spread at sea from his own yacht. We've got to have this for the funeral."

"I won't be needing your yacht," Robert said. "But thanks anyway. I'm staying right here until you come for me."

"I'll be back later tonight," Buck said. "I've got some things to take care of." He paused a long time, looking deeply into Robert's eyes.

"You can keep your fucking five-million dollars," Robert said. "I don't want the man's money. I want the man himself."

"I've always known that. The flings are over. I'm walking out on Ahmad. The thing with Shelley was ridiculous and stupid. Everything is over but you." Buck held him close. "What about you?"

Robert gently kissed his lips. "No man but you will ever touch me again."

"That's what I wanted to hear." He pulled Robert even closer to him. Unlike the violence of the afternoon, Buck's kiss was passionate but tender.

"Have the bed warm for me later tonight," he told Robert before a final kiss. Heading up the gangplank, he turned again as a strange feeling came over him. Not really caring what his crew thought, he walked back to Robert. He held him in his arms again, kissing his eyes, his nose, his lips, and his ears. "Pretty boy, it was always you. No one else ever quite did it for me."

"I will love you, I will worship you until the day I die," Robert whispered to him.

As he stood on the deck of old Buck's yacht, watching Robert fade into the distance, Buck dreaded meeting with Shelley. He dreaded even more the confrontation with Ahmad. But he had to do it. He'd never been comfortable with the idea of belonging to just one man. But that's what he wanted now. All the others would have to go. He didn't need Ahmad or his power and money, and he certainly didn't need to force himself on a young boy like Shelley. "I must have been mad," he said to himself, perhaps addressing the waves that crashed around him.

He looked back at his island growing smaller and smaller. It wasn't just his island. It belonged to Robert too. Buck was moving out of Desire. He'd never really moved in.

His home was with Robert now.

*****

"You didn't have to have her killed!" It was Rose's voice.

From his concealed position in the hallway, Gene could easily overhear her. Undetected, he'd slipped into Paradise Shores, using the keys he'd stolen from her after she'd kicked him out.

In her white living room, she was having an angry confrontation with Calder.

"I had no choice," Calder said with biting anger. "Pamela was about to fuck up everything. There's one thing you just can't accept. When you make a grand commitment, you've got to see it through, no matter what happens. When the heat's on, you're chicken shit!"

The next time you get ready to go off on another one of those grand commitments, you clear it with me first, liver lips." Her words lacerated the air. It was a voice Gene had heard before in the back seat of the limousine at the South Beach riot. "If there's a chance my neck is on the guillotine, ever, you let me know that. It's my neck, but it's going to be your neck if you fuck up like this again. And so soon after the Shelley thing. I'll never forgive you for that, you bastard."

"Okay, I admit. With Shelley, things got out of control. And now that boy's been kidnapped by Buck Brooke. God only knows if the Brat starts talking. If Buck finds out the truth, it could be the end of both of us. Ahmad would toss us to the sharks. He'd side with his boy, Buck. Ahmad is acting like a lovesick schoolgirl with a hard-on over that asshole, Brooke. I've never seen him like this before."

"That's because you've never experienced love, or even affection, for anybody in your whole psychotic life. And I doubt that you've even had sex with anyone, unless you like to mutilate children and jerk off over their bodies—and if someone ever tells me that about you one day, I won't be at all surprised. You don't have a clue about the kinds of feelings love and sex can arouse."

"And I don't care to find out. I see what morons it turns the rest of you into."

"I wish I could throw you out of my house."

"I've been ordered here. You don't think I'd be here if I didn't have to, do you? I can't stand the sight of you. But we may be called upon to issue a statement to the press. I don't trust what you'd say."

"You don't trust me? You idiot. You're the fuck-up—not me."

"I run this show, bitch, and don't you forget that. Deep down, you're still a backwoods preacher waving her tambourine and shaking a collection box at a Sunday night bunch of smelly niggers."

"Go to hell!"

"Besides, you won't be implicated in Pamela's murder. Your lover boy—the flasher—will take the blame if he's not killed first."

"That's what Biff thought. Now he's dead."

"But I at least had him die in the line of duty. The press didn't find out the cocksucker died at the Vulcan Baths."

"What in hell was he doing cruising cock at a time like this?"

"Don't ask me. You understand the faggot mind a hell of a lot more than I do."

"Do you think Gene went to the Vulcan Baths and strangled Biff?"

"Hell, no, even though he'll take the rap for it. It hasn't been reported in the press, and it's still under investigation, but in the past six months two men have been strangled like Biff was. It seems this sickie can only get his rocks off if he strangles somebody. And you ask me why I loathe faggots."

"How convenient for you. You murder people and have Gene take the rap. Even for the death of Leroy Fitzgerald."

"That was one trouble-maker who thought he had me by the balls. The faggot wanted a mouthful of cock. He got it on his death bed. His mouth stuffed with his own tiny dick."

"You're the most disgusting piece of shit I've ever encountered."

"Get used to it. I'm around for the long haul. You've got to put up with me whether you like it or not. I know enough on you to send you up for twenty years."

"*Touché.* I have enough evidence on you to send you to the electric chair."

"Forget it. I'll die a rich old man on some Caribbean island in a big mansion."

"Dream on! The way you've been carrying on, you and I will never live to collect Social Security. For all I know, that boy is talking to Buck Brooke right now. Telling him everything."

"It was you who allowed Brooke to get in to see him in St. Moritz. I had things under control."

"Ahmad ordered it!"

"That fucking lovesick puppy. He's going to screw everything up."

"It seems you're doing a perfect job of that all by yourself."

"Your hand-picked candidate, Miss Barry, was about to be destroyed. You selected that faggot—I didn't. I like to run real men as candidates. Men who get into scandals with women. God knows, I've covered up enough of those in my day."

"I bet you have."

"Actually, my plan was brilliant. I get rid of Pamela and Fitzgerald, and the flasher takes the rap. I'm sorry you hand-picked the flasher as your latest stud. I was shocked when I saw you with him backstage at the temple. Of course, it was too late then. My plan was ready to swing into action."

Her voice grew softer as she asked, "What if I'd been in love with him? Would that have mattered to you?"

"To begin with, the question is stupid. You could never be in love with anybody but your own mirror. But for argument's sake—no, my dear, it wouldn't have meant shit to me."

"How does Biff's murder fit into your sick plan?"

"That was a complete and total surprise. We had to rush into overtime to come up with a cover on that one. Killed in the God damn baths. Of course, management was only too glad to cover that one up. Biff was spotted by some of the sex hunters there. They didn't know it was Biff, of course. The story was that some guy had a heart attack in the steam baths. Believe me, no faggot is going to come forward with any different version. Some people spotted a body being removed. But they hardly knew the identity of that body. Without his red wig and red mustache, Biff looked like a completely different person."

"You certainly fixed it up so that Gene would take the rap again. You're a real bastard. What if Gene is captured and brought in? What if he has a spirited defense?"

"We'll deal with that as it comes up. First, Gene isn't going to be brought in alive. The police will hunt him down. The story's already written. He was armed. He fired at the police. They had to shoot him."

"You bastard! In my day, I've done things I'm not proud of. But you really taught me the lower depths."

"Your first big lie of the day. Your record is as black as mine. I know plenty about you. All except one thing. I don't rightly know the answer to it."

"What in the hell is that?"

"Do you believe in God?"

She paused a moment before answering. "I stopped believing in God a long time ago." She turned and headed for her bedroom.

"Where in hell do you think you're going?" Calder asked.

"To get some sleep. I haven't slept in days. I don't give a fuck what you're planning to do tonight. I want no part of it—or you."

"So I'm the unwanted guest. It won't be the first time. After I take a bath and have another drink or two, I'll work on that press release. Your grief-stricken response to Pamela's death. I've already helped

Barry prepare his statement for the press."

"Oh, goodie, goodie." She left the room.

His heart pounding loudly, Gene was relieved that the conversation was over. He'd heard enough. At this point, it didn't matter. It was like Calder had said. The plan was ready to swing into action. What he heard from now on would not change his mind. Even if she had told Calder she was in love with Gene, it wouldn't have mattered.

From where he stood, he could see into the living room. Empty drink glasses were stacked on the table. The room reeked of alcohol and tobacco.

Unshaven, Calder sat on the sofa, his flabby flesh hanging loosely from his structure. The way his skin fell from his frame, it looked as if it were several sizes too large for his bones. Finally, he got up and stumbled toward the guest bedroom, the same one Gene had occupied. A drunk Calder would make his job easier.

*****

He waited in the hallway before following Calder inside. From his leather bag, Gene removed a blackjack. The bedroom, the same bed he'd lain in, was empty.

From the bathroom came the sound of water running in the shower. He gripped the blackjack, as he made his way across the carpeted floor and into the bathroom where Calder had conveniently left the door wide open.

Once his feet touched the tiles, he paused only briefly before pulling back the shower curtain. In an astonished moment of recognition, Calder opened his mouth as if to yell. The scream never escaped his throat. The blackjack smashing against his skull caused him to crumple over, falling under the running water.

Quickly, Gene turned off the shower. Returning to the bedroom, he picked up his leather bag and carried it into the bath. From it he removed a gag and two nylon cords. First he gagged Calder tightly, then tied his hands over his belly with one of the cords. With the other cord, he securely tied his feet.

Placing Calder's head under the faucet, he turned on the cold water. In a few minutes Calder came to, his eyes widening at the sight of

Gene, they way they had when he'd pulled back the shower curtain. Calder struggled to raise himself, only to have Gene knock him back against the porcelain.

From his bag, he removed a straight blade razor. With a slash, he cut deep into Calder's right wrist. The man winced in pain, although Gene feared he hadn't cut deep enough. This time he cut more deliberately, slowly and accurately. Calder's eyes told him he'd hit his target this time. Blood streamed like a fountain.

Clutching his razor tighter, he just as slowly and deliberately cut the vein on the left wrist. Blood spurted out, forming pools in the bathtub as it ran down Calder's flabby belly into the patch of hair above his shriveled sex. Every time he struggled up, Gene pushed him down. Deep low moans—easily drowned out by the running water—escaped from Calder's throat.

In a haze, Calder grew weaker. Gene moved his arms about, drawing more blood. The fight was out of Calder. He no longer struggled to get up. "You'd love it, wouldn't you, if I'd gone to the electric chair?" He hardly expected an answer.

Calder only moaned. His eyes watered heavily, mucus poured from his nose, and the blood flowed in thick streams from his wrists.

Desperately he tried to draw breath through his gagged mouth. Overcome with nausea, he retched and vomited. The vomit soaked through the gag, most of it returning to his throat. His nose clogged, his mouth gagged, Calder was suffocating.

Gene's own eyes were blurred over at this point, his body rigid and cramped from bending over Calder. He wanted Calder alive and awake to see his final action. Untying the gag, he ripped it off. Calder coughed, choking and vomiting. Gene held his head under the running water.

Grabbing a fist full of Calder's hair, he held him inches from his own face. He looked deep into Calder's squinting eyes which opened and shut, shaking off the water.

Calder's eyes fully opened in time to see the blade of the razor before it slashed across his throat.

*****

The day was softer somehow. Removing Calder from it had made the world a brighter place. Still, that voice inside him demanded more. Gene slowly moved down the carpeted hall leading to Rose's bedroom. Once that room had been the vision center of his dreams. Now all that had changed.

He was in love with her, still. When he'd been alone with her in her bedroom and she'd moved close to him, he could recall the tendrils of wild hair on her white neck. Everything had been perfect, except the timing—her wanting to rush things. Then a voice had come out of her soul and her wide mouth—made for soft caress—had turned instead to mocking laughter. It was a devouring mouth, avid. The tongue in it had lashed like a whip, the voice whirling like a sand-laden simoom wind.

He could not listen to her voice, only the other voice inside him which urged him forward. He was possessed, the voice inside him confounding and confusing, not always clear in its message. A cold fire burned in his bowels.

Before her door, he gave himself a moment of silence. The servants were in the rear wing. Calder was dead. The only hearts beating in the main house belonged to Rose and him.

That feeling of crystal-clear purpose he'd had earlier had caused his blood to rise. It was like sap in the trees. Now, at her door with his leather bag, he wasn't sure any more.

With Rose, he had never been certain. She'd always aroused conflicting feelings in him—maternal, sensual, mystical.

He still longed for an innocent time that was gone and could never return. How he wished he could go back to a bright Sunday morning in her temple.

It had taken him until now to realize it, but he'd been happy then. When you had your dreams and the wonder and beauty of life were still before you, you could look up at the shining mountain capped by a blue sky. It was only when you climbed that mountain and saw the vast emptiness beyond, that innocence ended. At the top of the mountain he'd expected glory and splendor and had found instead evil and horror.

To kill a person, even a black devil like Calder, was a sin—and he could be punished for that. Soon he'd be far away from the cesspool, out of the reach of those who would kill him.

To him, the world was a sad affair without an angel in it. He'd soon move on. Once his job was done, he'd have achieved purification. Rose still had evil in her heart—vanity, cruelty. She'd have to live to atone for those sins before she'd be allowed to join him one day in heaven.

In heaven, where both of them were cleansed of their earthly deeds, she'd be his beautiful angel again. He'd kiss her hand and worship her and bring her pretty wild flowers to put in her hair. Only these wild flowers wouldn't wilt like the blue-red orchid in his shirt pocket that he had picked on Buck's private island. These flowers would grow for eternity, as their love would grow. Once freed of the desires of flesh, their love would be pure.

He clutched his leather bag, having arrived at the perfect solution on the boat back from Buck's cay. Rose had used her beauty to entice and seduce men, to lure innocent, unsuspecting persons down a trail to disaster. Her weapon, that beautiful face, had to be taken from her so that she could discover her soul.

A panic seized him. The voice had grown angry. Lost in maudlin thoughts, he was delaying, not fulfilling the mission the voice had commanded him to.

Opening the door, he stood in the silence of her bedroom. The draperies were drawn, but from the meager light that filtered in through a crack he could see her, lying in her large bed, a satin domino keeping the world in blackness. He shut the door softly, moving toward her rapidly.

*****

Perhaps it was the onrushing air, the noise of racing feet. Whatever it was, she knew she wasn't alone. Jerking up in bed, she ripped off the domino just as a weight was thrown against her legs. A man's heavy body fell on top of her. The room was in darkness, but she knew who it was.

She tried to scream but his strong fingers cut off her breath completely. Overwhelmed with one thought, she was paralyzed with fear, knowing she was going to die. Gene had selected her as his next victim!

In the struggle for her own life, thoughts of Pamela flashed through her mind. Had it been this way with Pamela, too? In panic, her mind refused to accept what was happening. "My God," she managed to say as he released his grip on her throat. "No, no, no!" It was useless to scream. Who could hear her? Calder? He was probably dead already.

He threw her face down, turning it into the pillow, muffling her sobs. He yanked her arms behind her back. Handcuffed, she kicked and fought, biting into his wrist with her sharp teeth. She drew blood but he didn't let up until the cuffs were securely fastened on her.

"My God," she repeated. How stupid of her not to realize she'd be targeted as his next victim. Calder should have hired bodyguards to surround Paradise Shores.

He tied her kicking feet with a nylon cord, then flipped her over to face him. "Gene, please...anything. Anything you want."

Grabbing one of her strong silk scarves, he gagged her. Then he lifted himself off the bed, turning on a lamp.

Nausea rose in her, flooding her throat with hot bile. If only he hadn't gagged her, she felt the persuasive power of her voice would have reached him, stopped him from whatever he was about to do to her.

His broad trembling hand reached out to touch her face. As she softly moaned, he lovingly, caressingly circled her eyes, brows, nose— his fingers slipping beneath the gag to touch her tender lips. He was like a sculptor feeling the contours of her face.

As he removed his fingers, she tried to cry out. Sobbing continually, she had only blurred vision. In fear and pain, she braced herself to face the terror of her own death.

From a leather bag he removed a glass vial with a cork stopper, putting it on her night table. She bit the gag and twisted her handcuffed hands, desperately trying to free herself.

He let her struggle until she tried to slip from her bed. Grabbing her, he forced her back into the middle of the bed, his strong hand jamming her face against a satin pillow, suffocating her, stifling her moans.

It was only then that she'd finally realized what he was going to do to her. She preferred death.

*****

He looked down on her now. Sweating and panting, she was still a beautiful sight. After he was gone, no other man would know that beauty. She would never dare show her face to anybody ever again, particularly a young man. Forever she'd wear the dark veil of mourning for him.

Her eyes were wide as those of the terrified horse he'd been forced to shoot during her protest march through the Combat Zone.

On the table beside her bed, he reached for the glass vial of sulfuric acid. Before coming to Paradise Shores, he'd broken into a university laboratory and stolen it.

He removed an eyedropper, sucking in the sulfuric acid. Drop by drop, this would be a slow, agonizing process. He only prayed that Jesus would reveal to Rose the absolute necessity of it—that in the acid rain, she'd know it for what it was. It was an act of purification—not to harm her, but to cleanse her so that she could one day join him in heaven.

For what minor pain she'd suffer on this earth, it seemed worth it to him, considering the ultimate reward—a place in heaven beside him.

As he held the eyedropper of acid over her face, he had never known such fear reflected in the eyes of another human being.

The first drop of stinging acid hit her face, sizzling and eating into her skin, disfiguring it for all time.

She was a trapped animal awaiting slaughter. Her eyes sent a clear and unmistakable signal: she'd rather he had taken a stiletto and plunged it into her heart than ruining her this way.

*****

Back on the mainland, Susan waited with Don in the back seat of a limousine. Out from behind the driver's seat, Casey leaned against the fender of the car, smoking a cigarette. She could clearly see Buck, accompanied by Lars, on the deck of the old man's yacht which he'd retrieved from his private island.

As Buck came down the gangplank, she was there to greet him with a kiss. So was Don. Buck seemed nervous and extremely agitated. She was certain that the news of the manhunt for Gene, his recent encounter with Robert, and the upcoming funeral of the old man were taking their toll.

In the back seat of the car, Buck asked to be taken to his old house.

"My grandfather personally selected the music played at the funeral of my parents. I have everything in a safe place at the house. I think we should play the same music he wanted."

"That's a great idea," Susan said. "Frankly, I didn't have a clue what to do."

Don reached for Buck's hand. "Glad to have you back," he said. "We missed you."

Buck squeezed his hand and settled back. Leaning into the upholstery, he closed his eyes.

From the front seat, the ever-protective Lars called back to him. "Did you need a drink or something?"

"I'm fine," Buck called back.

She too settled back but uncomfortably, as Don opted to be the only one needing a drink. Lars had turned on the radio with its news of the continuing manhunt for Gene. He was wanted for the murders of Pamela, Leroy, and the police chief.

As Casey pulled the limousine into the driveway of Buck's darkened home, she stiffened, feeling the coldness of her own hands.

"You guys can wait in the car if you wish," he told them, "I won't be long."

"No!" she said in a sharp voice that surprised her. "We want to go with you."

Finishing his drink, Don said, "I'd like to go inside too."

It was important for her to be with him now and she didn't understand why. She could trust him to pick up the music and probably change his clothes by himself, couldn't she? It was something else. A dread anxiety swept over her, a lingering doubt and a deeply rooted fear that had something to do with Gene. In the deepest corner of her heart, she feared that Gene might strike back at them in some way, seeking some kind of revenge.

Something about the garden was ominous, and she didn't know what it was. The moon was shining, the flowers were still growing, and every statue or chair seemed in place. Still, it seemed too perfect, too intense, too quiet—deadly quiet.

Lars and two of his security guards were checking the grounds. She saw one of the men disappear inside a garage.

Buck climbed the steps of his back veranda. He paused at the door. "The screen's been cut!"

"Don't go inside." She called to Lars.

Bounding up the steps, Lars yelled at his men. He tried the door finding it unlocked but shut. He came into the kitchen, ordering his men to check the front rooms. "I'll go upstairs."

"I think we were robbed," Buck said. "It wouldn't be the first time. Our crime rate puts us in the top ten. Next time I'm going to ask Lars to leave a security guard here full time."

"I'm frightened," she said.

He hugged her for comfort. "Clara and Maria probably went to visit relatives since there was no work for them here. Stay here," he ordered them. The stuff I'm looking for is in my study."

"Go with him," Susan said to Don.

Don kissed her lightly on the cheek. "It'll be okay."

When they had gone, she felt the coldness of her hands again.

"Anybody home?" Buck called into the living room. "Hey, anybody here?"

The phone in the corridor rang, a persistent ring, and no one was answering it. She feared it was someone urgently trying to get in touch with them with the latest bulletin.

On the way to the phone, she looked down. A pool of blood had seeped out of the utility room, running under the door. In shuddering horror, she looked at it, too frozen to call for help. She knew—somehow she knew—what was beyond that door and, for that reason, her hand rested a hesitant moment on the knob before she turned it.

The sight that greeted her caused a sudden spasm of choking. Maria lay on the floor. Susan looked at her first, avoiding the vision of her mother. Dressed in jeans and a little pink blouse, Maria seemed to have fallen asleep. Only the back of her head was visible as she faced the tiles.

Clara lay sprawled in a massive pool of blood. Her blood was everywhere—covering her body, the tiles, the washing machine nearby. Splotches of it had been splattered on a mirrored wall, as if there had been a violent struggle. Her body was nude. Her throat had been slit and the gaping wound had festered into an ugly sore. She resembled a carcass of beef, badly butchered and thrown to the side in a slaughterhouse.

Gasping for breath, Susan felt the blood drain from her own face. As if obeying a command, some unwritten rule, she tried to touch Maria's body, to feel for pulse, some sign of life. Yet her hand only hovered there. She couldn't bring herself to rest it on the girl, fearing that by touching she, too, would be contaminated with death.

She backed away until she stood in the hallway. There she realized she'd tugged at her blouse until she'd ripped the buttons from the front. She'd done that instead of screaming.

She began to sob uncontrollably, sounds forming in her throat. As she looked into Clara's eyes—so wide, so open—she screamed. Her scream grew louder and louder. She turned and faced the wall, beating her hands against it, as if that would drive the horrible vision from her memory. She pounded the wall, releasing pent-up energy that threatened her sanity.

She was only vaguely aware of Buck's presence. At her scream, he'd rushed in, moving up behind her, holding her in his arms.

Seemingly within seconds, Lars had staked out the area. Gun pointed, he entered the utility room.

Don looked as if he were going to vomit. "Did Gene do this?" No one responded to his question.

Lars ordered one of his men to call the police.

Buck turned and escorted her toward the back veranda. "Let's wait outside."

"No," Lars shouted at him. "I want all of you to go into the library. It's the most secure room on the property. Someone might still be in the garden with a gun. It's not safe out there."

Susan needed to be told what to do. No more could she think for herself. She stumbled blindly toward the library with Buck and Don. Now the phone here was ringing.

"Would you get that?" Buck asked Don. "It's probably the police. "Maybe it's Uncle Milty."

Don answered the phone. He turned to Susan. "It's for you."

"Me?" she asked, completely astonished. "I've never been in this house before. Who could be calling me here?"

"She says her name is Jill," Don said.

*****

In his boat again, the winds remained light. The sky was darkening but there were streaks of light. All around him the blue-green sea had darkened into a vast and deep black. After leaving Paradise Shores,

Gene experienced a great release of inner tension. "Why go on killing?" he asked himself. "Let it all go." Right now, he was tempted to take his boat as far into the sea as he could, there to let himself run out of fuel and drift into a slow death, a total yielding to Jesus.

He wouldn't do that. Not when a new life with Robert awaited him. But he didn't deserve that life until he completed the final mission Jesus had sent him on. It was a terrible mission, but he had to see it through, regardless of the consequences.

In thirty minutes he reached Buck's private cay where moon rays cut into the water over the reef. With permanent smiles, conchs heaved forward as he moored his boat. Earlier in the day he'd seen sulphur yellow sponges and corals, between which rainbow parrot fish glided. Such beauty didn't greet him now. The shore looked like a watery grave.

Wading through the water, he reached the white sands. He'd landed at the west side of the cay, at the farthest point from Buck's house. Armed with his rifle, he very slowly, very carefully plowed his booted feet through mangrove swamp, brushing back palmetto bushes. At a piercing call, he froze with fear. It was only the cry of a cicada. He passed a nest of red-blue orchids, a miniature pond of crystal-clear water on which lily pads floated and a banana tree that bore fruit only wild things ate.

In fifteen minutes the house had come into view. Concealed in shrubbery, he was close enough he didn't need to sight his target through his six-power scope. In shadows, he stood no more than fifty yards from the sundeck.

As he suspected, Buck had remained on the island. His yacht was anchored at the pier. Old Buck's yacht was gone. It was clear to him: Robert had taken the yacht and gone back to town to collect the money that would buy them the freedom they wanted once they were freed from the clutches of Buck.

Henry appeared on the patio, setting up a supper tray. He went away to reappear with a tall drink. Gene smiled to himself. This was one elegant supper Buck would never finish.

Gene stood at his post, waiting, trying not to think. He wasn't even sure at this point why he was supposed to kill Buck. But the voices told him to. Up to now, he'd killed merely the jackals. Buck was the lion who awaited slaughter.

About three minutes went by before Gene's target came out from the bedroom onto the deck where he saw the tray waiting for him. His body was muscled to perfection, a real man's physique, like his own. Gene's hand tightened on the trigger, but he didn't want to fire right away, letting his victim stretch his arms and extend his handsome face up to the bright moonlight. Gene couldn't make out the face, but he'd know Buck's blond hair anywhere.

A flicker of excitement swept over his body, the feeling of spying on another man in unabashed secrecy, knowing he held the power of life and death over him.

No longer mesmerized, in complete control, he fired once, twice, hitting his victim both times in the chest. The man collapsed in death, like a youth sacrificed to the gods in some ancient pagan rite.

Gene stood there for a long moment in the same spot where he'd fired the shots. He could afford to take such a chance. The weapon made him confident. Crouched, unmoving, he continued to stand there, his mind racing. It'd been so easy. He dropped the rifle. No more need for it.

He spotted Henry rushing to the patio, stooping over the slain body. "Oh, my God!" he heard Henry cry into the night air for no one to hear but Gene himself. "Jesus, Lord Almighty!"

Turning, Gene forced himself to walk—not run—back to his boat. His booted feet splashed through the mangrove swamp, and he found himself feeling carefree and light, as if the final burden Jesus had assigned him had been removed. His only duty now was to get to the Roney Plaza Hotel where Robert would take him in his arms. He knew the plane was waiting for them on the tarmac.

Elated by his success in carrying out his mission, he was overcome by an uncontrollable joy. He wanted to shout and praise the Lord. He felt delirious. The jackals were now dead. He'd slain the lion and left the lioness so badly disfigured she'd never show her face in public again but under heavy veil.

In the name of Jesus, he had brought death where it was called for. His enemies would burn forever in the fires of hell. No doubt those fires were consuming their bodies right now. They were doomed to live in hell where the fires would burn them for all eternity. They would pray for death but death wouldn't come, only the pain of eternal burning.

Before getting on his boat, he stopped and picked a wild orchid as he'd done before. It would live for such a short time in his pocket, and that made it all the more precious. If he didn't succeed in escaping on that plane with Robert, his fate would be like that of the flower. For that reason he wanted it near to his heart. He put it in his shirt pocket as he headed toward his boat and his eventual freedom.

*****

Buck was being questioned in his library by the police.

Two officers stood before Susan taking her report about the discovery of the bodies. She was extremely suspicious of the police after Jill's call. By tomorrow morning the police would have little regard for her. She planned to publish Jill's accusations in the Okeechobee News. Jill claimed that she was looking out the window of her condo and spotted three policemen placing Biff's body into a car where he was found dead. The conclusion was all too obvious: the police chief had been killed elsewhere and brought to Gene's condo to implicate him in the murder.

Susan believed in all her heart that Gene hadn't killed the police chief. She also didn't think he'd killed Pamela and Leroy. What she did believe, and she wasn't volunteering any information, was that he'd killed Clara and Maria.

The phone near her rang and she quickly picked it up, excusing herself from the police officers who chose to remain at her side while she took the call. For one impossible moment, she felt it might be Gene himself calling.

"That you, Mrs. Buck?" came a voice courtly and polite like a black servant in antebellum days.

"It's Susan, Henry."

"I've got to speak to Mr. Buck. Right away."

"Oh, God, what's happened?"

"It's Mister Robert. Someone's shot him. He's dead."

"Robert..."

Buck came into the foyer where she was speaking on the phone. He'd obviously heard her mention Robert's name. He too seemed to be expecting a call. He faced her, picking up some message in her eyes. She held the phone tentatively not knowing what to do with it, wanting to protect him from the message at the other end.

"What...what?" Buck said.

His impatient face demanded answers and she tried to deliver, but her throat was too choked for her to speak at first. "Robert," she finally blurted out. No more words would come out. None were needed. She could tell by the look on his face. He knew. She'd never seen such anguish on a human face.

"Robert," he said, in a soft and gentle voice, all panic and hysteria gone. After the initial shock on his face, he appeared calm, pathetically accepting the news. Then his whole face seemed to collapse. "He's dead, isn't he?"

She didn't need to answer.

*****

On the ground of the Roney Plaza, where security was so lax it almost didn't exist, Gene tried the door of the suite. It was locked. Robert promised it would be open, and he'd be waiting there for him. How could he have forgotten? Gene feared he'd been trapped in legal difficulties with Buck's lawyer and hadn't been able to get over here yet. Gene decided to conceal himself on the grounds and wait for Robert's arrival.

Nearly an hour had gone by and still no Robert. It was getting late, and the suite remained in total darkness. He was anxious to hear the news. He knew Henry had called the police. He anticipated that the news of Buck's shooting would soon be on television news, with all its lurid speculation.

Gene feared he'd made a terrible mistake. Uncle Milty may have learned of Buck's murder and was withholding Robert's money. Maybe Robert himself was being held for questioning in connection with Buck's murder. His dread was that he'd placed Robert in jeopardy. He shouldn't have killed Buck, and even now couldn't figure out why he did. There was no joy in killing Buck. It'd been a dreadful nightmare.

He wanted him back and alive.

Desperate for some news, he slipped around to the back of the suite which opened onto a vine-covered stone wall. There was no one in sight. At the French doors leading into the courtyard of the suite, he cracked a glass pane and turned the door knob inside.

Inside the darkened suite he walked slowly across the living room, spotting a TV set. He quickly turned on the set to watch the local news roundup. A picture of Robert's handsome face stared back at him. Only then did he realize what was being reported. He didn't need to hear the bulletin. He already knew what the announcer would say.

He'd killed Robert instead of Buck!

Robert's connection with Buck was being flashed across the screen. Robert was being identified as Buck's longtime secretary. Pictures of Buck's recent marriage to Susan now dominated the wide screen. A lump formed in Gene's throat, choking him. He didn't want to see any pictures or hear any more. As he moved to switch off the set, something the announcer said held him spellbound. Shortly before his shooting, Robert Dante—or so it appeared—had been brutally raped.

In stunned disbelief, Gene tried to absorb the bulletin. It made no sense. How could Robert have been brutally raped? Gene knew he was meeting with Buck. But he found it unbelievable that Buck had raped Robert. Why would Buck do that? What could have been his motive?

The world was spinning out of control. After turning off the television set, Gene collapsed on the floor. All the tears he'd ever shed before were nothing until now. This was the real cry of his life. It started deep within his guts and traveled upward through his throat where the sound nearly choked him.

He wanted Robert back. A grandfather clock ticked away in the center of the room. Sobbing, he wanted to go over to that clock and turn back the hands of time. If only he could start the day over again. If only this day hadn't begun in the first place.

Robert was his chance for freedom. His one last hope to have a life, and he'd destroyed that.

The two tasks that remained were dismal indeed. But he had to summon a steely reserve, pick himself up, walk out of this suite, and do what he must before fleeing Okeechobee.

The voice that had told him what to do, the same voice that had deserted him for the past two hours, now returned inside his head. It was speaking to him again, directing him. He felt so relieved. He didn't have to think of killing Robert. The voice told him to erase that memory. He had other tasks to perform and he'd need to give his full attention to the deadly game that lay ahead.

*****

In the darkened living room of his parents' house, where he'd lived so long with Robert, Buck sat quietly with Susan and Don. He stared vacantly into space, trying to forget the sight of the dead bodies the police had removed. Consumed with grief, he listened to soft music Don played. Susan offered him a drink which he accepted. Robert's death had placed a different focus on everything. He no longer saw life as the adventure it was at the beginning of the summer. He could never be that carefree again.

Only minutes before he'd spoken to Ahmad and had agreed to fly to Palm Springs to meet with him after the funerals of Robert and old Buck. Buck wanted these funerals behind him as soon as possible, and welcomed the recuperative powers the desert could bring him. Before Robert's death, he was going to tell Ahmad that he was leaving him. After Robert's death, he wasn't so sure. He felt he needed the protection from the world that Ahmad could offer him. There remained the problem of Shelley which he planned to deal with later in the evening.

Buck looked over at Susan. "You know, don't you, that that bullet was meant for me? Who would want to kill Robert? If Gene's the killer, he loved Robert and hardly wanted him dead. Robert stopped my bullet. Don't you see: I'm alive because Robert is dead!"

"Stop it!" she said. "You can't go on talking and feeling that way." She kneeled before him, taking his hand in hers and kissing it.

Don got up from a nearby chair and came and sat with Buck on the sofa, placing his strong arm around him and holding him tight. Don kissed him on the cheek. "Robert is gone, but we're here for you now."

He leaned into Don's chest for the comfort it offered him. At his feet Susan continued to kiss and massage his hand. He took comfort in the warmth they provided.

Lars came into the room and called Susan to the phone. Getting up, she kissed Buck on the forehead.

When she'd gone, Don held him closer and whispered in his ear.

Darwin Porter / 779

"I'll always be your loving man. I'm not Robert. I'll never replace him. No one ever can. But I'll spend the rest of my life loving you and helping you forget him."

Buck reached up and kissed Don. "Thanks for being here for me. I need you."

Susan came back into the room. "This is an awful time to bring it up. But Robert's funeral is in the morning. You're his sole heir. They want to know what you want to put on the stone."

Rising from the sofa and gently easing himself from Don's protective embrace, Buck stood on his unsteady feet. "Is that it?" he asked. "Has it come to this? Reduce a man's life to something you can write on a damn stone?" He took a few steps but didn't seem to know which way to turn.

At the bay window, he pulled open the draperies and looked out at the water with the city in the background. It looked so peaceful tonight even though a killer stalked it. Was it Gene? He turned to Susan. Tell them, ROBERT DANTE, 1950-1977. HE GAVE THE GREATEST GIFT OF ALL—AN UNFINISHED LIFE."

"Thanks," she said, heading for the foyer.

He felt a presence behind him, rubbing his neck. Grabbing Don's other hand, he crushed his mouth against it and held it there. Don's wide open hand covered Buck's face, protecting and shielding him. With his other free hand, Don continued to rub Buck's neck.

When Susan came back into the room, she joined Don in a three-way embrace. He put his arm around each of them. They swayed a bit as if in a dance.

"I need you guys, I really do," Buck said.

"You've got us," Susan said.

Don kissed his neck. "We love you."

Breaking gently from the embrace, Buck walked to the mantlepiece of the fireplace. He leaned both elbows on the marble. Then he turned around to face them. "We're going to dress in white. Robert hated black. We're not going to turn his death into some morbid gathering of the clan. It must be a celebration of sorts."

She went over and kissed him gently on the lips. He was thankful she didn't ask him to explain what he meant because he didn't know. He looked at her as if she were a stranger. He stood on shaky legs, gazing into her eyes. He realized, perhaps for the first time, just how powerful a woman she was. So like Ingrid.

Reaching out for her, he pulled her to him, almost suffocating her with the power of his embrace. "You won't leave me, will you?" he asked. "The old man is gone. Now poor, poor Robert." He broke into tears, that uncontrollable sobbing he'd been holding back all day. He couldn't remember having cried like this in years. He cried now and the sound of his own voice came from deep within his gut. A sickish, shrinking feeling came over him.

In Don's strong arms, he was being half carried to the sofa. Once on the sofa, Don cradled him.

An hour must have passed and he didn't even remember it. Susan and Don had not left his side. When he came to, she asked, "Will you say something at both funerals?"

"I'll think about it." He got up from the sofa again and walked to the bay window where he stared at the well-lit tower of the Examiner, feeling strangely dispossessed. When he'd worked there with Robert, he felt he'd ruled the town.

"I'm not going to plan any words," Buck said. "I'm not going to write anything down. I'm just going to get up at both funerals and say a few words. I know one thing to be true: I'll be addressing entirely different audiences. It'll be easy saying something over the old man. He's a legend. It's easy to speak of legends. They've accomplished so much. It will be harder to find words to say about Robert. What can you say about a man who did nothing else but devote his entire life to you?"

"If Robert didn't have you, his life would have been in vain," Don said.

"He lives," Buck said. "He dies. He's buried. Anonymity. But I promise you this. Every time I'm in Okeechobee, I'll bring fresh flowers to his grave if I live to be eighty."

Lars came into the room, trailed by Casey. "The car's ready," Lars said. "It's time to go."

Buck walked over to Lars and reached out his arms. As Lars pressed hard into Buck's body, Lars whispered in his ear, "You've got me. You'll always have me. I'll devote my life to you. I promise."

The dutiful servant, Casey stood at the entrance to the room, not certain if he should enter. Breaking from Lars, Buck called Casey to him. Up close he hugged and kissed Casey on the lips. "You can take off that stupid chauffeur's uniform," Buck said. "I can always find a driver. From now on, you're not some servant. You're a member of the household."

Casey hugged him and held him close. "Thanks." When Buck looked into Casey's face, he found tears welling in his eyes. "Thanks a lot," Casey said. "I needed that."

Buck held Casey's hand and reached for the hand of Lars too. Susan and Don stood before him. Buck kissed Casey on the lips. Then he kissed Don before tasting Susan's lips. His final kiss was reserved for Lars.

Buck walked a few paces across the room. "You guys are my family now. It's not a family the world would approve of. But it's our family. I want all of you to come and live at Desire. There's certainly plenty of room for everybody. Our only problem is, the damn place is so big we'll never find each other."

No one said anything. It was Buck who broke the silence. "Remember those group hugs from the sixties?"

His friends moved toward him, encircling him into a womb of comfort and love.

*****

In the section of abandoned warehouses down by the river, Buck's limousine came to a stop. As he got out, he stumbled over weeds that had pushed their way through concrete laid in the 1920s. He paused only a moment to look down the street at the bar where, long ago, Robert had taken him.

Trailed by Don, he took Susan's hand and led her across a parking lot. "There it is," he said, as Lars and Casey came to stand beside them. "Rose's old printing plant. I was buying it for Robert. He wanted to start his own newspaper." A faint smile, the first one all day, crossed his face. Then his spirit sagged. "It was not meant to be."

"It's time to go," Lars said, reaching for his arm. "They're waiting for us."

"This next stop I'll remember until the day I die," Buck said.

Don walked up and took him in his arms. "It'll be over soon," he said to Buck.

He didn't even remember the drive to the funeral parlor. Once there, he excused himself from Lars, Susan, Don, and Casey. He wanted to be alone when he viewed the body. He'd begun to feel a little sick at his stomach.

In the rear, he faced the undertaker, a balding man with excessive saliva on his lips. The man reached out and touched his arm. Instinctively Buck pulled away.

"I shouldn't say this," the undertaker said. "I hope you'll understand how it is meant. He's a work of art. A Greek god. The most beautiful man I've ever worked on. Won't you reconsider and have an open coffin funeral?

"Please!" Buck said. "I want the coffin closed as soon as I view the body. It is not to be reopened. Ever again! Do you understand?"

The ghoulish undertaker looked crestfallen. Past satin-lined coffins and urns with grape vines and goddesses, he ushered Buck into a small room that smelled of gardenias. The undertaker turned on the lights and excused himself.

Buck looked straight ahead as a terrible fright overcame him. Not more than twelve feet away lay Robert, fully dressed in a blue suit but dead on a table.

Buck's hand shook and a lump rose to gag his throat. In death, Robert had never looked more alive. His eyes closed peacefully, he had a smile of serenity.

Somehow he had to know that Robert was really dead. He moved closer to the body, as a wave of sadness swept over him. He bent down and gently kissed Robert's lips. Cold, unmoving, it was the kiss of death. He jerked back.

The makeup had deceived him. The natural looking face was a terrible lie. It wasn't Robert any more. "Such a waste," he whispered to the dark corners of the room. An incredible surge of loneliness came over him.

Wiping his tear-streaked face, he put on dark glasses. The undertaker waited at the elevator. His face told Buck he wanted to be thanked for the beautiful job he'd done. Buck said nothing as he entered the elevator.

Downstairs, he breathed more comfortably in the presence of Susan. The other men waited behind, as he entered the front office reception lounge with Susan. Presented with a choice of coffins, he made the selection as rapidly as possible, settling on an elegantly upholstered maroon-colored one. She squeezed his hand tighter.

"That's our finest choice," the undertaker said. "You have exquisite taste. Would you like to know the cost?"

"The cost doesn't matter," Buck said. "Order lots of white carnations," he instructed the undertaker. "Plenty of gardenias."

"Are you going to deliver the eulogy?" Susan asked.

"Yes, I am. I'll find something to say."

Back in the parking lot, Buck asked Don and Susan to spend the night at his home in town. "There may be some emergency in town, and I'll need you to handle it for me. Lars will see that the house is heavily guarded. You'll be safe there."

"Where are you going?" Susan asked, alarmed.

"I have an emergency of my own at Desire, and I must go there at once."

"Are you sure you don't want us to come with you?" Don asked, obviously disappointed.

"I'll see you guys early in the morning," Buck said, kissing each of them on the mouth. A second limousine was waiting to drive them back to his home. Buck got into the back seat of his Blackhawk with Casey and Lars. One of his security forces was driving.

As the limousine pulled out of the lot, Lars took Buck's hand and held it up to his lips to kiss it. "I know what you're going to do even before we get there."

Not really understanding, Casey snuggled against Buck.

Buck leaned back in the seat. "I can't put it off another minute."

*****

It took two hours of waiting, and at times he suspected Julius Forster would never show up. Gene began to fear he wasn't even in town. But shortly before midnight Forster pulled up in his driveway and got out of his car. He lived down a narrow lane behind a bigger house. It looked like a former garage that had been converted into a cottage. From his days on the police force, Gene knew where Forster lived.

Forster walked up on his darkened porch and inserted a key in his door. Moving swiftly from behind an outdoor utility closet, Gene pressed a revolver into Forster's head. "I'm lonely tonight," he whispered in Forster's ear. "Why don't you invite me inside?"

"What the fuck!" Forster said. "Get away from me."

Gene pressed the revolver deeper into Forster's skull. "I might go but I'm taking part of your brain with me as a souvenir. So how about it? Do I get invited inside or not?"

Forster was trembling and had a hard time inserting the key. The door finally opened, and they stood alone in what appeared to be his kitchen.

"Since you're not overlooked by other houses," Gene said, "I guess it's safe to turn on the light. That way you can see my face. I'm incredibly handsome. All the guys and women tell me that. You're in for a treat."

"Fuck off!" Forster said. "I'm not a faggot." He turned on the light and stared at Gene. "I know who you are. You're Gene Robinson. The pervert who worked for Biff."

"One and the same. Forgive me for not shaking your hand. But I like to keep my gun aimed at your black little Nazi heart."

"You're sick. The police are after you. You wouldn't dare kill me."

"I'm already wanted for murder. What's the murder of one more? Earn me a second or third life sentence? Or another invitation to sit for the second time in the electric chair?"

Forster was salivating heavily, the spittle running out of his mouth.

Gene looked deliberately menacing. "Get it: He's killed before and he'll kill again."

"Get out of here. Let me alone. I've done nothing. I'm always being falsely accused."

"How's this for accusations? What were you doing at the Pier House in Key West?"

"I've never been to Key West in my life."

"What if I told you I saw you leaving the Pier House?"

"I'd say you'd better have your eyes examined."

"What were you doing stalking Buck Brooke's rented villa at Key Biscayne? I was the guy who chased you away."

"You're crazy. I've never been there either."

"Did your murder of Leroy Fitzgerald only whet your taste for blood before you killed Pamela?"

"You can't connect me with those murders. You're guilty. You did it. The police are after you. They're not after me."

"You don't seem to understand. As long as I'm holding this pistol aimed at your heart, I'm both judge and jury. I'm charging you with the murder of Leroy Fitzgerald."

"He was a faggot. He deserved to die."

"Did you have to castrate him? Then stuff his cock in his mouth?"

"The way I figure it, faggots like cock. Why not give the bastard something to chew on?"

"Why not? You've got a point there. I'm sure Leroy enjoyed that final banquet." Gene raised his gun and pointed it directly at Forster as if he were ready to fire.

"Don't shoot," Forster said in panic. "I'll confess. I killed Fitzgerald. I mutilated him. I didn't mean to castrate him. Something overcame me."

"What about Pamela? You didn't mean to do that either?"

"I was ordered to kill her."

"By whom?"

"I can't tell you. I was forced to do it. They've got stuff on me. They can make me do what they want."

"You don't have to tell me who your boss is. I already know. Before I killed him, I made him confess to ordering the murders of Pamela and Leroy."

"Calder..." Forster's eyes widened, as he continued to form saliva at an excessive rate. "Calder is dead?"

"Let's go into your living room," Gene ordered, waving the gun at him. "Turn on a lamp."

Forster did as he was ordered. In the living room he switched on a lamp, the light revealing a large Nazi flag draped across the wall over the sofa.

"I collect World War II memorabilia."

"You were on the losing side. Just like you're on the losing side tonight. Calder Martin's not here to protect you any more. He begged for his life. When are you going to start begging for yours?"

"You're not going to kill me, are you? I've done nothing to you."

"Only set me up for two murders—that's all. Only created a scenario where I'd end up in the electric chair. Would you have liked that? Seeing me tried for two murders you committed?"

"I was made to do what I did. I didn't have a choice. It was all Calder. He's behind this whole thing."

"But he's dead and I have only you to romance."

"Don't kill me. I'll go to the police. I'll tell them I did it."

"Now you're talking. Now you're telling me something I want to hear. What else will you confess to the police?"

"What do you mean?"

"What about the murder of Biff?"

Forster glanced nervously around his living room as if some passage offered escape. "I didn't kill him."

"But to protect me, will you say you did?" Gene asked.

"If that's what you want. I'll do it. I'll confess. But you'll have to tell me what I should say. If I confess to killing Fitzgerald and Pamela, what's one more murder?" He giggled nervously.

"You've got a point." Gene waved the gun at him. "But I'm demanding even more. I want you to confess to killing Buck's Cuban servants. Clara and Maria. I'm sure you've read about them in the papers.

"Yeah, but I didn't kill them."

"I know you didn't. I killed them."

"Okay, I'll do it," Forster said, stepping back as if that would remove him from the range of bullets.

"One more thing," Gene said. "I want you to confess to killing Calder Martin. We'll make up some story. Say it was pay back time for Martin. He was forcing you to commit murders."

"Just watch me go. I'll nail Martin, the son of a bitch. I always detested Liver Lips."

"One final request, and then we can talk strategy here."

"I'll do anything if you won't shoot me."

"I want you to confess to the shooting of Robert Dante."

Forster's eyes told Gene he wanted a reprieve. "I'll do that too. I'll confess to everything."

Gene's fingers tightened on his revolver. "How do I know I can trust you? You might go to the police and once in their custody blame me for all the murders. You might even claim you're innocent."

"I wouldn't do that. You can trust me. I'd never turn you in."

"I need some show of good faith."

"What can I do?" Forster asked, his eyes pleading for mercy.

"I want you to call Susan Howard. I want you to confess to all the murders. Don't give her any details. You don't know the details. Just tell her who you killed. Begin with Leroy, then go on from there. Before you hang up, threaten her own life. Tell her she's next on your list. That will show me you're bargaining with me in good faith."

"I'll do it."

"I have her number," Gene said. "She's probably at her condo." Gene gave Forster her number to call.

Forster sat down at his desk and dialed the number. After a few moments, he turned to Gene, "I'm getting her answering machine."

"Hang up." Gene gave Forster the number where he'd called Robert. "She may be at this number."

Forster called and Gene could tell he'd gotten someone on the line. "I need to speak to Susan Howard." In moments, Forster muffled the phone and turned to Gene. "They want to know who's calling."

"Give your name. Susan's one smart newspaperwoman. She knows who you are. The reporter in her will take the bait. She'll speak to you, all right."

"It's Julius Forster. I demand to speak to Susan Howard." After a long pause, she apparently came onto the phone. "I'm Julius Forster."

There was another long pause, as if Susan was saying something urgent into the phone. "I've decided to give you fair warning. You're my next victim. I've already killed Fitzgerald, the Collins whore, those Cuban sluts, Robert Dante, and even the police chief himself. And after I kill you, I'm going to kill Buck Brooke."

With his gloved hand, Gene took the phone from Forster and slammed it down. "You did well. Even a little improvising. I like the part you added about Buck Brooke. That made it more authentic." In fact, you did so well..." There was a hesitation. "You fucking creep. You didn't do what I said."

"What are you talking about? I did everything you said. I even added my threat to Buck Brooke."

"You left out Calder Martin. You didn't confess to killing Calder Martin, you dumb shit!"

"I forgot. I'll call her back."

"It's too late for that."

"Can I go now? I'll go directly to the police."

"Perhaps it's better if the police came here."

"Yeah, I'll call the police and have them come over right away."

"Before we do that, I want you to write out a confession, admitting to all the murders. And this time don't leave out Calder Martin."

Forster fidgeted in the chair. "I'll do it." He reached for a pad on his desk and quickly wrote a note.

When he'd finished, Gene picked it up and scanned it. "This time you named all the victims. You didn't leave anybody out, not even

Martin."

"I've confessed. I confessed to Susan Howard. I've even given you a written confession. What more can you want from me? It's time for me to call the police. You can run. Before they get here, you will have plenty of time to escape."

"You sweet old thing you," Gene said. "We will only imagine what you might have said at police headquarters. We'll never know that."

"What are you going to do with me?"

"You've been such a cooperative victim, I'm going to offer you a choice."

"What kind of choice? What in hell are you talking about?"

"A choice of how you want to die," Gene said. "The easy way for you is for me to take this gun and blow out your brains. I'll put the gun in your hand. It will have your fingerprints on it. Not mine. I always like to wear gloves in the evening."

"You said choice. What choice?"

"The other choice is for me to strip you naked. I'll cut off parts of your dick and feed it to you slowly, making you eat every bite. That will bring back memories of Leroy. That plan calls for you to die when you've had your fill of your own flesh."

"Don't, don't! Please! I beg you!" Forster was crying. "Oh, God. Don't do it!"

"I won't. That would be too cruel even for a dumb Nazi shit like you. The first way will be easier."

Forster screamed as Gene put the gun to his head and fired. Forster fell on the floor dead. Gene placed the revolver in Forster's hand and tightened his fingers around it, firing again into Forster's head which would leave a gunpowder residue in Forster's hand, and a tantalizing mystery of two bullets.

Within minutes he was out of Forster's cottage and driving for his final stopover for the night. It would be his last visit before leaving Okeechobee forever.

*****

Back at Desire, Buck headed down the long corridor to where Shelley was kept. "We've been unable to get Sister Rose on the phone,"

Lars said, walking by his side. "Her staff said she's retired for the night and is taking no calls from anyone."

"Shit!" Buck said. "I wanted to come clean with her—tell her I have Shelley here. It's only fair that I do that."

"Do you want me to send my men over there?"

"Let her sleep. It's the middle of the night. This thing with Shelley can wait until morning."

Leaving Lars, Buck headed alone into Shelley's darkened suite. At first he saw no sign of life. The boy may have been asleep. At a sudden movement, he whirled around to confront Shelley—still clad in his briefs—emerging from the bathroom.

There was a smile on his face when he saw it was Buck. He rushed to Buck's arms and planted kisses all over his face. "Thank God you're back. I was going out of my mind."

Buck backed away. "It's because of the problem with your mind that you're here in the first place."

"My mind is okay—just fine. I'm coming to my senses."

"I hope so," Buck went over to sit before the vegetation that gave the impression of being outdoors even though they were underground. "I've come to tell you something. I deliberately left the door open. You're free to go. I had no right to bring you here. All you have to do is walk out that door. A limousine is waiting to take you to Paradise Shores."

"What if I told you I'm not going to Paradise Shores?" Shelley came over to Buck and kneeled at his feet. "My place is here with you, and that's the way it's going to be."

"You're just a kid. You've been through a lot. You don't know what you're saying."

"I know perfectly well what I'm saying."

"What about that young man I encountered in St. Moritz? You didn't want to have a God damn thing to do with me."

"That was then. This is now. I'm different."

"You're different all right." Buck said. "You seem like a completely different person from the Shelley I left in Palm Springs. I can't put my finger on it. But it's like..."

"Like what?"

"I don't want to get into graphics. But even your body is slightly different, and it's a body I know so well. I don't know how you could have changed so much in a ridiculously short amount of time."

"Does it matter?"

"I don't know. Maybe it doesn't matter. What does matter is that in the past few hours major things have happened in my life. Horrible things. I don't want to go into all the details now because they don't concern you. Things have happened to people you don't even know. Bad things."

"I'm sorry. Can I help you?"

"You cannot. Right now I need to help myself. I'm going to go away to join Ahmad at Palm Springs. I don't know when I'm coming back."

"You're leaving me?" Shelley got up and moved away from Buck.

"Let's put it this way. I've come to my senses. I had this brief obsession about you. It wasn't real. It wasn't love. Why don't you walk out that door and never come back to Desire again? Go resume whatever life you want. Grow up. I can at least let you grow up."

"You're kicking me out?"

"God damn it!" Buck said, rising from his chair. "I brought you here by force. You can bring kidnapping charges against me if you want."

"I'll never bring charges against you or harm you in any way." He moved toward Buck, coming only inches from his face. "I love you. I want to be with you. You can do what you want with me. I'm not afraid."

Buck turned his back to Shelley, staring again at the vegetation. "I'm not going to do anything to you."

"You want to send me to Paradise Shores? How do you know I'll be safe there? Are you going to let Calder Martin get at me? Do you think I'll be safe with Calder Martin? Do you think Rose will protect me?"

"I don't know." Buck stumbled and felt dizzy. "I don't know," he shouted. "I don't know anything. I feel alone in the world. I've had a great loss in my life. I've lost someone I cherished, and I didn't even know what I had until it was too late." He moved to the bed where he fell down upon it. He didn't want to break down in front of Shelley but he couldn't help himself. He started crying, and the tears wouldn't stop. He couldn't stand it any more. He wished Shelley would go and leave him alone. He couldn't cope with the boy and all his problems. He wished tomorrow's two funerals were over.

He felt hands on his back, loving and comforting him.

"Please go away," he said to Shelley. He turned over and looked into the boy's face. Shelley too was crying.

"Please understand," Buck said softly. "I was all fucked up. I should never have had a relationship with you. It was wrong. You're just a kid." He knew he was repeating himself. "You deserve to grow up and figure out who you are without grown-ups trying to mess up your mind."

"I know who I am and I know what I want." He snuggled close to Buck. "I want to be here with you. I want you to take me in your arms and hold me close to you all night. I want to hear your heart beat."

Buck forced himself to get up from the bed. "The part of my heart that's still beating, still alive, isn't beating for you."

Shelley lay on the bed, looking shocked. The words seemed like acid rain coming down on him. He jumped up from the bed and reached for a robe. "Okay, so you won't be there for me. No one in this whole fucking world's ever been there for me when I needed someone."

"If you ever need me, and this is a solemn promise, I'll come to you at any time of the day or night. All you need to do is call out for me. I don't care if it's ten years from now, I will come to you and help you."

"Do you really mean that?" Shelley asked. "Is that something I can really count on—not some fake promise?"

"I mean it."

Shelley looked at Buck one more time, then turned and passed through the open door.

When he was gone, Buck didn't want to leave the room. He would spend the night here. He fell back on the bed and cried real tears until he felt he could cry no more.

He didn't know what time it was. But he felt hands on him again.

It was Lars, awakening him. He turned over sleepily and in a groggy voice asked, "What is it?"

"It's Shelley. He's at Paradise Shores. He wants you to come over right away before he calls the police."

Buck sat up in bed and searched Lars's face. Buck's eyes opened wide as if fully coming awake. "Oh, my God!"

*****

Purple around his eyes from lack of sleep, sweat dripping from his forehead, Gene steered his boat into the open sea, staring dull-eyed at the blackness ahead. He was going to take the boat as far as it could go.

She was with him although she appeared in a coma. He'd slipped back into Paradise Shores and removed her body from her bed. Rose's face was a study in horror, but he tried not to see that—only the beauty that had been there. He loved her, and wanted her to go on the journey with him. He'd smuggled her body out of her darkened house and had carried it to his car where he'd driven to the marina. Covered in a blanket, she lay on the deck of his boat accompanying him on their final voyage.

Images of death almost obliterated the open sea before him. But he didn't want to think of that. He wanted to remember happier days when he was part of the university class of '71. Buck, Robert, Barry, Leroy, Pamela, and Susan—all of them thought then the whole future of humankind rested on their shoulders.

He took a sharp turn to the left, heading north. He couldn't be sure. Not that it mattered. The empty sea stretched before them.

A burning in him felt like a slash of sunlight cutting into a sleepy eye. His insides were hot and hollow, and his brain groggy.

Looking back at that death-dealing carnival in Okeechobee seemed like a distant dream, more fantasy than reality.

His body was filled with a drumming fever, with a delirium, and he sailed with a rhythm all his own, having nothing to do with all the other ships or boats at sea.

Perhaps to die was the easiest thing to do, far easier than living. He stood quietly, welcoming the sea breezes cooling his body and taming the fires that burned within.

He'd had none of the answers in life and had tried to find them in others, only to be horribly misled and brutalized.

He was crying but they were tears of joy. He wasn't alone for the final journey. She was with him. She'd accompany him where he was going. God would forgive both of them. With her by his side, he would be admitted to heaven so much quicker than if he'd made the journey on his own.

He was almost out of fuel. He checked the hand grenade in his pocket. Abandoning the wheel, he walked over to the deck and picked up her near lifeless body. Gently he slipped off her gown. Placing her back on the deck, he removed all his clothing. He wanted them to enter the water nude like a symbol of rebirth, appearing naked like Adam and Eve in a different world from the one they'd left behind on the mainland.

Picking her up, he planted a kiss on her lips, ignoring the grotesqueness of her face eaten away with acid. Instead of that hideous mask, he chose to remember when he'd first seen her—all bright and radiant at her temple. A golden light had shown down on her then. The same golden light returned. The moon was lighting the sky with a brilliance he'd never known before.

He lowered her body into the water and drifted into the sea with her. He let her go only momentarily when he removed the plug from the grenade. He hurled it toward his boat. Reaching for her, he watched the boat explode in flames, momentarily chasing away the darkness of the sea.

She'd drifted a few feet from him, but he quickly recaptured her body.

He would swim out into the sea with her, carrying her along until his body could go no more. Then they would enter their watery grave but would find immediate redemption and rescue by God.

The moon had seemed to follow him all through the night, lighting his way and shining a golden light upon him.

As he found himself gasping for breath, his load growing heavier, he did something he hadn't done all night. Fearing the golden lumination of the moon was waning, he looked directly at it for the first time tonight.

It was a Blood Moon.

Epilogue

1997

The sun rose over Paradise Shores. It held out the promise of a spectacular day. He'd been in California for weeks, and was glad to be back in Okeechobee. In spite of where he wandered, this was still his city, and he wanted to be here in lieu of all other places.

Buck reached out for Shelley but the bed was empty. From the bathroom he heard noises of Shelley showering. Gradually his awakening eyes took in the bedroom. It was Rose's old bedroom. Shelley had never changed the rose motif—in fact, the entire house was just as Rose left it on that night she mysteriously disappeared twenty years ago.

Slowly he got out of bed. He stood nude in front of a floor length mirror. His body had held up well over the years but he winced at the slight tire he was developing around his midriff. He'd have to work even harder at his private gym to get rid of it. In spite of the graying at the temples, his hair was still blond. He reached for his robe. Now that he was forty-seven years old, he didn't parade around nude as he had in the past.

"Good morning, love of my life."

At the sound of the voice, Buck turned around and stared at Shelley, emerging fully nude from the bathroom except for a towel draped around his neck.

"Welcome back home," he said to Shelley. "We've been away a long time."

"I like California better anyway," Shelley said, moving toward him. "When I'm back here, they always demand that I go preach at the temple."

"Buck met him halfway at the bottom of the bed, reaching for him and kissing him. As Buck ran his hands over his friend's body, he found it as velvety smooth as ever. In spite of the passage of time, Shelley's body was perfection itself. Even though he was thirty-four years old, he still looked twenty. It was amazing. Buck always called him "the timeless wonder."

After releasing Shelley, Buck headed for the bathroom. When he emerged later after showering and dressing, he spotted Shelley at his desk by the bay window overlooking the rose garden.

"Giving 'em hell today?" Buck asked, coming up behind Shelley and kissing his ear.

Shelley reached up and ran his hand through Buck's hair. "Last night was very special. God, do you know how to make a guy feel good."

"I should," Buck said, straightening up and going over to check the morning paper. "I've had twenty years of practice. After all that time, if I don't know what turns you on, I never will."

"It was just as good as the first time."

"You remember the first time?" Buck asked.

"I'll never forget it. You'd kidnapped me."

Buck glanced quickly at the headlines. There was a ring at the door. He got up from the chaise longue and went over to let in the butler with the morning coffee. He noted a long white rose on the breakfast tray. Thanking the butler, he told him that they'd be having lunch today at Desire so there was no need to prepare anything.

Pouring coffee for both Shelley and himself, Buck settled back in his chair to read the paper. He'd long ago reacquired the Examiner and he still had the News. On Sunday he published a joint edition of both papers. Suddenly, something Shelley had said struck a strident note in his brain. He looked over at the young man who was still busily writing at his desk.

"That wasn't the first time," he said to Shelley.

Distracted, Shelley didn't seem to pay him much attention. "What's that, love?"

"I said that wasn't the first time. When I kidnapped you and made love to you, it wasn't the first time. Hell, we'd had an affair. *An affair.*" Buck was raising his voice.

He'd caught Shelley's attention. He got up and walked over to Buck, planting a kiss on top of his head. "And what a glorious affair it was."

Buck grabbed Shelley's arm and forced his face down to confront his own. "That's not the only time you've said something enigmatic like that. You don't even seem to remember intimate things between us that happened when we first met."

Shelley pulled away. A look of fright came on his face. Freeing himself from Buck's grasp, he got up and looked out the bay window overlooking the rose garden. "Don't get up," he said to Buck. "Don't look at me. The time has come for me to tell you something, and I don't want to be facing you when I tell you this. Do you promise to stay where you are until I've finished?"

"Of course, I will," Buck said. "But you've got me really scared."

"You've always suspected me, ever since you kidnapped me. You even told me you found my body slightly different. Around you I'm so unguarded, so filled with love, that I've slipped up and said things. Like I did this morning. I mean, about that time at Desire being our first time."

"I know," Buck said. "You've never been the same after you came back from Switzerland. I've always loved you but it took a long time to adjust to you. It was like I was loving a different person."

"You were."

"What do you mean? You've never explained exactly what happened to you in Switzerland. What did they do to you?"

"You didn't hear me. You were loving a different person."

"You're Shelley, aren't you? How could you be a different person?"

"I'm not Shelley. Shelley left you twenty years ago. I'm Fred."

"Fred!" Buck bolted from his seat and whirled around to confront Shelley...or was it Fred?

"Shelley's dead. He was killed in Palm Springs in 1977. It was an accident. He was injected with some substance that was supposed to knock him out for hours. It knocked him out all right. It killed him."

A sound not quite like a scream escaped from Buck's throat. "My God, this is no game. You're telling me the truth."

"I can prove it. Shelley's nude body is preserved in a block of ice in Orange County in California. Rose had his body frozen in the hope that future advances in medicine might know how to bring him back to life. She wanted to give him that one chance. It was all she could do at that point. She wanted him to finish his life one day, even if it were in another century."

"Then who are you? The man I've been making love to for twenty years?"

"I'm his twin."

"I didn't know he had a twin."

"I know you didn't. Rose knew. I was her adopted son too."

Buck started to cry. He couldn't help himself.

Fred moved toward him, taking him in his arms. "Does that mean you'll stop loving me?"

Buck pulled him close, kissing his neck. "No, I'll never stop loving you. You belong to me. You always will. I've held you in my arms for twenty years loving you night after night. Somewhere along the way I must have stopped loving Shelley and started loving Fred even if I didn't know it was Fred."

"I'm glad I told you. All these years I've had to be Shelley. I took over his role. I've inherited everything. I've become Shelley. Calder Martin knew I wasn't Shelley but he's dead. Rose knew...but."

"She left us. She'll...Fred."

There was a ring at the door. Fred went to open it.

It was Lars. "Your car is waiting. You don't have much time to get to the temple. Traffic's bad this morning. Hi, Buck."

"Good morning, Lars."

"Your car is ready too," Lars said to Buck.

"I need a few minutes alone with Shelley, and then I'll be right down. I want you to go with me this morning."

"See you downstairs." Lars turned and left.

When the door closed, Buck walked over to Fred and kissed him on the lips. "I don't know if I'll ever get over the news you just told me. I'm trembling all over. But let's keep it our little secret."

"I hope when I get back around noon, we don't have to talk of it any more," Fred said.

"You're right. I don't want to talk about it. Let's pretend this conversation never happened and go on as before."

"That's what I want too," Fred said.

Buck held him close, then kissed him tenderly. "You're going to be late. What's your sermon about this morning?"

"I'm ranting against same-sex marriages."

Buck winced and blew him a kiss. "That's a subject you know a hell of a lot about."

Fred moved toward the door but hesitated. "I've always loved you since that first time. I've never been with any other man in my whole life. You were the first and you'll be the last. That's how it's going to be with us. That's a promise."

"Just go on being Shelley. It's best this way. I can't get used to a Fred."

"I am Shelley. I've assumed his role. There's no turning back now. This house. Everything. All the money. The temple. Everything Rose had. Everything Shelley had. It's all mine now. There are times late at night that I think I really am Shelley."

"And so you are. I've called you Shelley too long to call you anything else."

"Please go on calling me that and loving me." A frown crossed his brow. "And don't forget: the President is coming today."

"How could I forget a thing like that? He's got Camp David. What does he need with our humble Desire?"

"At least we'll get to see our son."

"I know," Buck said. "That's the only reason I can tolerate these presidential visits."

Fred turned and left, leaving Buck alone in the room. He would try not to think or dwell on what Fred had just told him. He'd learned over the years to blot many things out of his mind. That's how he'd come to deal with pain and loss. He planned to go on an inspection of his homes this morning, stopping off finally at the old Brooke mansion of his grandfather's.

He didn't spend much time any more at his old homes, but he still wanted to go by them whenever he could. If for no reason, the memories.

But before he did that, he had another stop to make. Lars understood and knew where Buck must go, but he always kept it a secret from Shelley. There was no Fred. It would always be Shelley. He would forever pretend that Fred was Shelley.

*****

In the back seat of the limousine, Lars put his arm around Buck as if he sensed acute distress. "You've always been here for me for years and years," Buck said, "and I'm damn grateful. Sometimes, though, I wonder what kind of life it's been for you."

"It's been a life of service devoted to the man I love," Lars said, reaching over and kissing him. "I wouldn't change a thing."

"We've been through a lot," Buck said, snuggling into the comfort of his arms.

The familiar scenery passed before him, scenes vaguely remembered when he'd biked through the neighborhood as a boy. He wanted to think of anything today but what Shelley had told him back in their bedroom at Paradise Shores. He shared most secrets with Lars, but this was one he didn't want to divulge.

"We've got to get back to the coast soon," Lars said. "The natives are getting restless. You've got projects to make decisions about. The big but fading names are calling. Are you going to get back to them?"

"Who, for example?" Buck said, sitting up.

"Costner, Madonna, Cruise."

"I'll call Cruise this afternoon when we get to Desire. Hold Madonna for next week. As for Costner, I never got the message."

"All the biggest names in Hollywood at the millennium will be into grandparents' roles," Lars said. "There are just so many grandpa and grandma roles."

"Tell me about it," Buck said. He sighed. "With my beautiful son, I don't think I'll ever be a grandfather. There will be no Buck Brooke V."

"You said you wouldn't name him Buck Brooke IV."

Buck smiled. "I know, and then I went and did it anyway."

"Are you looking forward to seeing him this afternoon?" Lars asked.

"I always look forward to seeing him. He's my son. I wish he were with us all the time. I'm only sorry he always shows up with the President. A Republican president at that, and I'm a lifelong Democrat."

"But your son loves the President, and the President is certainly crazy about him. They don't go anywhere without each other."

"I should never have let this thing develop between them in the first place," Buck said. "He was only fourteen at the time. I should have had the jerk arrested and charged with child molestation."

"Now, now," Lars cautioned him, rubbing Buck's hand. "All your son had to do was to remind you of your involvement with Shelley at that age. That ended the argument."

"I know, I know."

"Young Buck was only a child then," Lars said. "But he's certainly at the age of consent now, and he's still with the President."

"I have this feeling that it's like a time bomb waiting to go off." He squeezed Lars's hand. "My son, an intern at the White House. The President of the United States. What a story this would make."

"The President has really concealed his tracks," Lars said. "I think the American public thinks of him as a womanizer more than anything else."

"We've concealed the President's tracks," Buck corrected him. "If I recall, and I do, it's cost me a lot of money. I don't know how long I can succeed in buying people off."

"It will all come out eventually. Hopefully he'll be out of office then."

"I don't want my son hurt." Buck closed his eyes and settled back into the upholstery. He knew and he knew that Lars knew that young Buck might not even be his son. He looked like him but in some ways he looked like Don Bossdum too. He'd never wanted to have tests done. He didn't want to know who the father is. He recalled how Susan eventually got tired of being left in a cold bed and had joined Don and Buck on more occasions than he could remember. Either Buck or Don could have been the father. No one wanted to talk about it, and that's the way he wanted to keep it.

Don and Susan would be waiting for him at Desire when he arrived with his son and the President. As always, Jill and Sandy would see that everything was perfect. Regardless of where he went, Jill and Sandy were always with him, flying around the world looking after him and anticipating his wishes before he did.

Those love-birds, Casey and Patrick, would be there too. Regardless of where he went, his extended family followed him. It was a family Buck had reached out and created himself. He loved each and every one of them, and needed them in his life. Susan was no longer publisher of the News. She'd become his own media director. At times he felt she ran the show more than he did.

So many of the others had gone from his life. He missed Uncle Milty something dreadful. He was at his bedside the morning he died. Hazel was long gone too. But at least she'd become mayor of something—not Okeechobee, but his newly created Sun City. She didn't turn out to be a good mayor, but at least she got to hold the office.

Coming back to Okeechobee always brought back a memory of Gene. He wondered if Gene were still alive. He liked to think he was. But he could never be sure. Gene was never found. He'd just disappeared from the face of the world, the way Sister Rose had gone. Rose had been officially declared dead after seven years. As her sole heir, Shelley had assumed control of her empire. Before she'd flown to the Middle East twenty years ago to make that propaganda film, she'd drawn up a final will and testament, requesting that "Mr. and Mrs. Buck Brooke III" become the guardians of Shelley until he reached legal age. When Buck learned of this provision, he was shocked, but then Rose in life always managed to shock him. So it came as no surprise that she would shock him in death. He closed his eyes and relived the night she'd disappeared. Shelley had been the first to discover Calder Martin's dead body. But Buck didn't want to dwell on that this morning. The day was too beautiful, too perfect to think of the horrors of the past.

Of all the people who had passed through his life, the one he remembered almost every hour of every waking day was Ahmad. After an unpromising beginning, theirs had grown into a great love affair. He never knew how much he loved Ahmad until Uncle Milty had called him on November 8, 1984 with the news that Ahmad's private plane had mysteriously exploded over the skies of southern Morocco. There were no survivors. Buck's scream on that dreadful afternoon still echoed within his own head. It was a scream from his heart.

Two weeks later there had been another call from Uncle Milty. "I've heard from Ahmad's people," he'd told Buck. "He's left you everything." Until the day he had a fatal stroke, Uncle Milty had spent his days trying to figure out exactly what Ahmad had left him in various parts of the world. It was a fortune so vast that its total value seemed to fluctuate wildly day by day.

Ironically, inherited wealth didn't matter in the end for Buck. He'd made his own money—not as a publisher, but as a producer of films. He'd had no preparation for such a role, but as Uncle Milty had told him, "All you need is money." Buck had had his flops—some colossal—but he was known more for his successes. He'd gotten tired of watching everybody lying out by the pool, and he'd put all of them to work—Susan, Don, Casey, Patrick. Jill and Sandy didn't have to be told to go to work. Ever since Susan read to him Gene's final request to take care of Jill and Sandy, Buck had virtually adopted them. They ended up, however, taking care of him more than he took care of them. They'd become indispensable to his life. He'd even been the best man at their wedding. They never spoke of Gene.

Gene was the one subject no one brought up any more. The truth didn't matter. In spite of overwhelming evidence to the contrary, Julius Forster had been blamed for the murders of Leroy, Pamela, Biff, Clara, Maria, Calder Martin, and Robert.

One night long ago Susan and Buck had been drinking, and in a candid moment they had speculated about Gene's own involvement in some of these murders. But they'd dropped the subject that night and no mention was ever made of it again. Their official position had always been that Julius Forster was the sole killer. That position had never fully explained Rose's disappearance. Buck had always maintained that Forster had killed Sister Rose and disposed of the body before committing suicide.

At the cemetery Lars walked with him toward the grave site. Lars always stopped fifty feet away and let Buck have his private moment. Buck carried white roses and placed them on the grave. This morning was no different from countless others. He laid the flowers on the grave and looked up at Robert's tombstone. He kneeled and closed his eyes in silent prayer.

"I love you, Robert," he said to the wind. "You're gone from my life but not my heart. I loved you once, and I'll always love you." He looked at the empty graveside beside Robert's tomb, knowing that he would one day join him there. They'd sleep side by side for eternity.

Lars came up behind him and reached down for him. Buck took one final look at Robert's grave, and walked with Lars down the flower-lined path to the mausoleum of old Buck. The chauffeur carried flowers for his grave too. Buck took the flowers from the driver and placed them on his grandfather's tomb. "You started it all, sir. You founded the dynasty. In spite of all the bitterness between them, he still loved the memory of the old man. "There's a Buck Brooke IV," Buck whispered to the silent grave. "And he's winging in now on the presidential plane."

"And we can just make it to meet the President," Lars warned him. "Not to mention be there to greet your son."

At the Okeechobee airport, where crowds had gathered, Buck was escorted to the head of the reception line, taking a position in front of the newly elected mayor. After all, Buck was the official host.

The Secret Service were the first off the plane, followed by both of the President's daughters, neither of whom had improved with age. As was his duty, a chore he'd performed so many times before, Buck kissed each woman on the cheek and welcomed them home. But even as he kissed them, his attention was really focused on the ramp where his son stood in the breeze. The wind whipped his golden hair. He was a beautiful, charming boy. A young Robert. A young Shelley. Buck couldn't wait in line. He ran to the ramp and embraced his son. "I love you, guy," he whispered in his ear.

"I love you too, dad, and I've missed you something awful."

He hugged the boy again and kissed his cheek. "Don't stay away so long."

"We've been busy," his son said, squeezing his arm. "We've got an entire world to run. We are the only superpower left."

"I know that must keep you busy, and I bet you make all the more important decisions."

His son looked a bit miffed. "Don't you tease me. You'd be surprised at some of the decisions I've made. More than you think."

The Secret Service asked them to stand back behind the line. A band was playing Hail to the Chief.

Down the ramp bounded the President of the United States. Buck was amazed at how handsome and youthful he still looked. Except for a few telltale wrinkles under his eyes, time seemed to have stood still for the President.

In front of the cameras, the President ignored Buck Brooke IV as if he didn't know him. But his face lit up as he extended his hand to Buck III.

"Glad to be back in Okeechobee," the President said.

"Welcome home, Mr. President," Buck said, extending his hand in front of the cameras to greet Barry Collins.